THE WESLEYAN ANTHOLOGY OF SCIENCE FICTION

THE WESLEYAN ANTHOLOGY OF SCIENCE FICTION

Edited by Arthur B. Evans,
Istvan Csicsery-Ronay Jr., Joan Gordon,
Veronica Hollinger, Rob Latham, and
Carol McGuirk

WESLEYAN UNIVERSITY PRESS
Middletown, Connecticut

Wesleyan University Press
Middletown CT 06459
www.wesleyan.edu/wespress

Manufactured in the United States of America

The editors would like to thank DePauw University, the University of Iowa, and Trent University for their generous support in making this teaching anthology possible.

Library of Congress Cataloging-in-Publication Data
The Wesleyan anthology of science fiction /
edited by Arthur B. Evans . . . [et al.].
p. cm.
Includes bibliographical references.
ISBN 978-0-8195-6954-7 (cloth: alk. paper)
—ISBN 978-0-8195-6955-4 (pbk.: alk. paper)
1. Science fiction, American. 2. Science fiction, English. I. Evans, Arthur B.
PS648.S3W39 2010
813′.0876208—dc22
2009053144

10 9 8 7 6

To

RICHARD DALE MULLEN,

founder and benefactor of

Science Fiction Studies

contents

THEMATIC LISTING OF STORIES

Alien Encounters

INTRODUCTION

The Wesleyan Anthology of Science Fiction was conceived and developed by the editors of the scholarly journal *Science Fiction Studies* (*SFS*). It reflects no single editor's viewpoint but rather a consensus among us that a good anthology should include stories ranging from the nineteenth century to today, should exemplify a number of themes and styles characteristic of the genre, and should represent both the best and—not always the same thing—the most teachable stories in the field.

While our journal is known for a lively engagement with critical and cultural theory, it is also committed to exploring the disparate body of texts grouped under the rubric "science fiction" (sf). Any sf anthology necessarily declares a provisional canon of classics by prescribing a limited course of essential reading. Canonization is a dubious as well as a difficult enterprise, but we hope that our canon is less prescriptive than provocative. Our goal has been to suggest how varied the genre is, to showcase writers from the justly famous (Isaac Asimov, Arthur C. Clarke, Ursula K. Le Guin) to the unjustly neglected (Robert Sheckley, R. A. Lafferty, William Tenn), and to serve as a starting point for further reading.

Many of the stories reprinted here, especially those published before 1960, first appeared in the pulp magazines or later digests that served as the chief training ground for sf writers. Authors who published in these formats often spent their careers writing for pennies a word—if that—while in our own day, high-budget sf films and television series continue to recycle their ideas without so much as a screen credit.

Despite the ongoing popularity of Jules Verne and H. G. Wells, there was no significant North American market for full-length sf novels until the 1950s. The pulp magazines and postwar sf digests were therefore crucial publishing venues for the first generations of American sf writers, from C. L. Moore and Edmond Hamilton to Robert A. Heinlein and Theodore Sturgeon. Their work appeared alongside reprinted tales of Wells, Verne, and Edgar Allan Poe, so that early readers of the pulps were being simultaneously introduced to new writers and immersed in some of the best nineteenth-century sf. Although today's North American sf market is geared predominantly toward novels (the form in which most writers now make their reputations), a number of professional and semiprofessional venues—magazines, reprint anthologies, and, more rarely, original short-fiction anthologies—still publish short sf. The more recently published selections in this volume strongly demonstrate the form's continuing vitality.

Historical Origins and the Megatext

Origin narratives are always shaped by complex historical and ideological perspectives. Depending on the sf historian's particular assumptions, the genre can trace its roots back to Lucian of Samosata's satirical second-century story of a trip to the moon in his *True History*. Alternatively, the case has been made that sf began with the utopias and tales of great voyages of discovery written from the Renaissance through the eighteenth century—voyages echoed in the nineteenth century by Jules Verne's *Voyages extraordinaires*. Many historians have argued that sf's origins lie in the techno-scientific cataclysms of the Industrial Revolution; in this context Mary Shelley's cautionary tale *Frankenstein* (1818) is of particular interest. A different reading locates the genre's origins in Darwinian views of evolution, which shaped the *scientific romances* of H. G. Wells. Still others would set the starting point in the early twentieth century, arguing that science fiction developed generic coherence only after being popularized in the pulp magazines of the 1920s. This "new" genre, originally named *scientifiction* in Hugo Gernsback's *Amazing Stories*, saw rapid expansion in the pages of pulps such as *Wonder Stories* and *Weird Tales*, where Hamilton's "The Man Who Evolved" (1931) and Moore's "Shambleau" (1933) first appeared. While each of these positions about the genre's "true" origins has its defenders and the debate is unlikely ever to be resolved, these very different accounts, when taken together, offer striking testimony to science fiction's complex history.

At its core, science fiction dramatizes the adventures and perils of change. Although not always set in the future, sf's consistent emphasis on transformation through time demonstrates the increasing significance of the future to Western techno-cultural consciousness. At the same time, sf retains its links to older literary forms and maintains strong generic connections to its literary cousins epic, fantasy, gothic horror, and satire. One of the more interesting developments in contemporary sf is the near disappearance of genre boundaries in such stories as John Kessel's postmodern "Invaders" (1990). Meanwhile, sf elements are now frequently incorporated into the work of many writers usually associated with the literary mainstream, resulting in *slipstream* fictions by such writers as Thomas Pynchon, Jeff Noon, and Margaret Atwood.

The original subtitle of Wells's *The Time Machine* (1895) was "An Invention," and as the genre's tangled history suggests, sf is constantly reinventing itself, responding to contemporary scientific and cultural concerns and adapting or challenging prevailing narrative conventions. Polish author Stanislaw Lem's *Solaris* (1961; trans. 1970), for instance, gains much of its impact from how it revises the assumptions of earlier first-contact stories such as Stanley G. Weinbaum's optimistic "A Martian Odyssey" (1934). By stressing the difficulties—indeed, the impossibility—of comprehending the alien, Lem intervenes in sf's ongoing generic dialogue, showing that first contact might in the event be more of a non-contact. In contrast, James Tiptree Jr.'s "And I Awoke and Found Me Here on the Cold Hill's Side" (1972) takes a queer-feminist approach to first-contact conventions, with its dire tale of loving the alien all too well.

Perhaps because of its twentieth-century history of publication in specialized or niche formats such as pulp magazines, mass-market paperbacks, and sf digests, writers in the genre maintain unusually strong links with each other and with the community of sf readers. Writers of sf conduct long-distance conversations across generations, cultures, social settings, and historical challenges. Like all complex cultural forms, sf is rooted in past practices and shared protocols, tropes, and traditions—all of which contribute to what is often called the *sf megatext*. A fictive universe that includes all the sf stories that have ever been told, the sf megatext is a place of shared images, situations, plots, characters, settings, and themes generated across a multiplicity of media, including centuries of diverse literary fictions and, more recently, video and computer games, graphic novels, big-budget films, and even advertising. Readers and viewers apply their own prior experience of science fiction—their own knowledge of the sf megatext—to each new story or film they encounter.

Looking back to one of the earliest novels associated with sf, it is easy to see that the monstrous Creature in *Frankenstein* is a precursor of both Hawthorne's Beatrice Rappaccini and the artificial intelligence HAL in Stanley Kubrick's film *2001: A Space Odyssey* (1968). Mark Twain's Connecticut Yankee informs Wells's Time Traveller, who in turn establishes the basic template for all the time-travel tales of the twentieth century, including Heinlein's "'All You Zombies—'" (1959), which nonetheless offers its own original twist.

The sf megatext encompasses specific characters (the mad scientist, the renegade robot, the savvy engineer, the mysterious alien, the powerful artificial intelligence), environments (the enclosures of a spaceship, an alien landscape, the inner space of subjective experience), events (nuclear and other apocalypses, galactic conflicts, alien encounters), and, of particular significance, ethical and political concerns (questions about scientific responsibility, about encounters with otherness, and about shifting definitions of what it means to be human). Every element in the megatext has been reimagined many times; these reimaginings form the rich intertextual backdrop behind and between all sf stories.

The more familiar readers are with the sf megatext, the more readily they will find their way into and through new stories. More experienced readers can appreciate how any particular work both depends and expands on the stories that have preceded it. William Gibson's celebrated cyberpunk novels and stories—"Burning Chrome" (1982), for instance—borrowed many plot elements from familiar hard sf and noir conventions at the same time that they expanded the sf universe by challenging readers to imagine radically intimate relationships between human beings and increasingly pervasive cybernetic technologies. The impact of Gibson's fiction lay in its revisionary use of familiar figures such as the *cyborg* to reveal the degree to which contemporary techno-scientific culture has itself become science-fictionalized. Stories such as Greg Egan's "Closer" (1992) and Charles Stross's "Rogue Farm" (2003) build on cyberpunk's *posthuman* foundations in their further explorations of the human-machine interface.

In general, techno-scientific verisimilitude (not quite the same thing as scientific accuracy) is considered to be a sine qua non of works in the genre. More particularly, stories about science and technology constitute a significant strand of the sf megatext, from the dystopian nightmare of E. M. Forster's "The Machine Stops" (1909), to the efforts of lunar explorers to decode the meaning of the mysterious alien artifact in Clarke's "The Sentinel" (1951), to James Patrick Kelly's revisionary story about the "cold equations" of the physical universe in "Think Like a Dinosaur" (1995). From the perspective of the sf megatext, every story is in dialogue with others in the genre, even as it aims to say something new. Like "Chicken Little," the teeming, amorphous protein source of Frederik Pohl and C. M. Kornbluth's novel *The Space Merchants* (1952), the megatext is always growing and changing, continually fed by new texts, new scientific speculation, new historical events, and new readers.

Although authors in the genre share many concerns, they take diverse historical and cultural positions. They extrapolate unique futures, although many—from Heinlein, Le Guin, and Gibson to Frank Herbert and Cordwainer Smith—set much of their fiction in different quadrants of one particular future. Such writers settle in to explore the universes of their own making, their own personal megatexts. Some of our selections, such as

Asimov's "Reason" (1941) and Smith's "The Game of Rat and Dragon" (1955), suggest in miniature their authors' consistent concerns, while other stories, including Heinlein's "'All You Zombies—'" and Herbert's "Seed Stock" (1970), at first glance appear to be atypical. Our headnotes outline the author's place in the genre and sketch the relationship of each selected story to the author's work as a whole.

As editors, we have aimed to include stories that not only repay a chronological approach, illustrating sf's generic evolution, but that also intersect with some of the genre's most frequently recurring topics. Among those specifically highlighted here are the alien encounter, apocalypse, dystopia, gender and sexuality, time travel, and virtual reality.

Reading Sf

Readers who are new to science fiction learn new ways of reading. Many of the genre's stories are set in the future, although its worlds are usually linked by *extrapolation*—a logic of projection—back to our own. Readers of sf must not only adjust their time-space positioning but also learn to negotiate connections between individual tales and the sf megatext. Further, they must often deal with *neologisms* (newly coined words) and other conjectural vocabulary that require them to fill in the semantic blanks with their imaginations. In contrast to mainstream fiction, science fiction represents worlds that do not exist here and now, although their existence might be possible in some other part of the universe or, more often, some other time. That time is usually ahead of readers: the future. Simplifying in the extreme, we might say that realist fiction writes about what exists while fantasy fiction deals with hopes and fears and dreams—emotional states rather than ideas. Science fiction, in contrast, writes about things that might be, although they are not yet and may never come to be.

Science fiction's "worlds of if" (to cite the title of a Weinbaum story of 1935) are connected to the readers' world through a logical (linear, causal, extrapolative) relationship, yet these sf worlds can also be metaphorical or symbolic. As Darko Suvin has argued, sf is a literature of *cognitive estrangement* that shows readers futures in which the present has shifted or metamorphosed: they mirror our own world but in a distorted way. Cognitive estrangement is produced by a *novum*—a puzzling innovation—in every sf story. This novum distances (or estranges) readers from some received "truth"—for example, the idea that human nature is essentially unchanging is called into question in Frederik Pohl's "Day Million" (1966). To Suvin, sf's "worlds of if" offer estranged versions of the author's/reader's here and now; nonetheless, the future in sf is logically (cognitively) tied to the present.

A number of critics have discussed what they term the *reading protocols* of sf—the approaches required for understanding the genre. Sf readers know that much of the story will not be clear at the beginning; they live with uncertainty through much, if not all, of a story such as Tenn's "The Liberation of Earth" (1953). Some stories might introduce a single novum (for example, the cloned siblings in Le Guin's "Nine Lives" [1969]), while others might teem with new things. As is fitting, the genre that addresses innovation and change can, in its own storytelling protocols, shift dramatically in response to social changes or new scientific ideas.

Two important reading protocols identified for sf are Marc Angenot's notion of the *absent paradigm* and Samuel R. Delany's analysis of sf's *subjunctivity*. The absent paradigm refers to those semantic blanks, noted above, that challenge the reader's imagination to construct a new and different world out of scattered hints and clues. Sf's stories strand readers in an unfamiliar place or time, forcing them to supply contextual meaning for the bits of alien information with which they are bombarded. Fritz Leiber's "Coming Attraction" (1950), for instance, is set in a post-apocalypse Manhattan, but the nature and dimensions of the cataclysm must be puzzled out from the narrator's offhand comments. The estranging effects of sf's absent paradigms are experienced in concentrated form in the short story, which can pack a density of futuristic or otherworldly implication into its brief space. The result can be dizzying, as in Ellison's "'Repent, Harlequin!' Said the Ticktockman" (1965), with its pyrotechnic style and array of new words—swizzleskid, minee, Smash-O, fallaron—that draw readers into a place and time ruled by a lethally efficient future form of capitalism.

Sf's subjunctivity further complicates the reader's task. According to Delany, the language of an sf text works differently from language in realistic—or, to use his term, "mundane"—fiction. In his famous example, the sentence "Her world exploded" can, in a mundane story, only be a metaphor for a woman's emotional state, whereas in science fiction it could be a *literal* description of the destruction of her home planet. This linguistic openness or indeterminacy means that sf always operates at a sentence-by-sentence level in the subjunctive mode: sf stories narrate not what can realistically happen at the present moment, but what *might* happen in future times and alien places—in sf's "worlds of if." Philip K. Dick's "We Can Remember It for You Wholesale" (1966) displays subjunctivity in its very title, which suggests that what we take to be a settled referent (the processes of memory) can mean something quite different in an sf context—in this case because technological advances in Dick's future world allow for the implantation, at a price, of artificial memories. Readers must accept that the referential functions of language in science fiction are usually, whether subtly or significantly, estranged.

Although these terms—cognitive estrangement, absent paradigm, subjunctivity—may seem forbidding, they are fully compatible with an intuitive insight long held by fans: the genre conveys a *sense of wonder*. This experience—of the exhilarating, mind-expanding power of the best sf—is brought about by the same processes that such critics as Suvin, Angenot, and Delany have analyzed. As readers negotiate the distance between the estranged world of an sf story and their own reality—a process in which they must reconstruct an absent paradigm and decode the text's subjunctivity—they come to grasp, and be dazzled by, the extraordinary span of time and space; they see the possibility of almost unthinkable social and technological changes. For those who are open to it, the genre's unique demands provide rare delights, including a sense of awe at the vast transformative power of futurity.

Different Viewpoints, Different Worlds

Writers in the genre offer widely disparate visions of the world. Readers of sf therefore are invited to analyze divergent ideas as well as literary styles. Scholars, too, represent any number of critical and theoretical approaches, and the editors of *SFS* are no exception. We have designed this anthology to demonstrate the diversity of the genre and to encourage a broad range of thinking about it. While no anthology can incorporate all of sf's richness, we sought in choosing stories to acknowledge as much as possible the genre's stylistic variety and its many topical interests. For several years, we read, discussed, compared, analyzed, argued, compromised, conducted straw polls, and voted on dozens of potential stories. We asked members of the Science Fiction Research Association and the International Association for the Fantastic in the Arts for suggestions on what would be the ideal balance between older and newer tales and what pedagogical materials would be most useful. Finally, we arrived at these fifty-two selections, printed in historical sequence, beginning with a story by Nathaniel Hawthorne published in 1844 and ending with a 2008 story by Ted Chiang.

We hope that *The Wesleyan Anthology of Science Fiction* will serve as a bridge not only to an appreciation of some of the best works of sf ever written but also to the world of sf scholarship. With that in mind, and using the many suggestions we received from our colleagues, we have included ancillary material: a critical bibliography that lists many of the most important studies in the field and an online "Teacher's Guide" available on the Wesleyan University Press website at http://sfanthology.site.wesleyan.edu/

that includes discussion questions for each story, available Internet resources, illustrations such as magazine and book covers, suggestions for course design, and advice on student research. This anthology was created for the purpose of teaching sf at many levels, as well as for casual and critical reading by both neophytes and experts. Science fiction is complex and provocative as well as stimulating and enjoyable, rewarding thoughtful study in and out of the classroom. Welcome to the words and worlds of science fiction.

THE WESLEYAN ANTHOLOGY OF SCIENCE FICTION

NATHANIEL HAWTHORNE
Rappaccini's Daughter

{1844}

Nathaniel Hawthorne (1804–64) was born and raised in Salem, Massachusetts, and used his family's history there most famously in his novel *The Scarlet Letter* (1850), which drew on his ancestor's role as a judge in the infamous Salem witch trials. According to his biographer James R. Mellow, Hawthorne borrowed from his own life for "Rappaccini's Daughter." Like Giovanni, Hawthorne was a handsome and intense man prone to romantic entanglements who had an affair with the metaphorically poisonous Mary Silsbee. Beatrice's personality, however, seems closer to the character of the woman he eventually married, the secluded and intelligent Sophia Peabody. Peabody suffered from health problems that may have stemmed from her physician father's overuse of drugs in treating her ailments as a child, so Dr. Peabody may have served as a model for Doctor Rappaccini.

Hawthorne was part of the American Romantic movement of the mid-nineteenth century and was friends with other major figures in American Romanticism such as Emerson, Thoreau, and Melville. In the spirit of the times, he did not draw distinctions between art and science, using both in ways that would now be considered science fictional, not only in the story collected here but also in other stories such as "Dr. Heidegger's Experiment" (1837), "The Birth-mark" (1843), and "The Artist of the Beautiful" (1844). As Hawthorne himself put it in "The Custom-House," his introduction to *The Scarlet Letter*, his literary concern was with "a neutral territory . . . where the Actual and the Imaginary may meet and each imbue itself with the nature of the other." In this neutral territory, Hawthorne allows science to be imbued with evocative metaphorical significance and offers plausible explanations from the world of the Actual to undermine seemingly impossible events from the world of the Imaginary. Just as in *The Scarlet Letter* every miraculous event has a rational explanation and Dr. Chillingworth and Hester Prynne's secret powers are explained in terms of medicine, so in "Rappaccini's Daughter" selective breeding and the powers of suggestion can explain many of the story's seemingly fantastic elements. Hawthorne's description of the neutral territory in which he works is very much like that of the English Romantic and

Gothic writer of *Frankenstein* (1818), Mary Shelley, sometimes considered a founding mother of science fiction, who herself made a point of eschewing the supernatural.

Much of what makes Hawthorne's story so powerful, so psychologically and emotionally convincing, and so eerie, is its use of ambiguous metaphor and symbol to layer the tale with multiple meanings. This is a technique that later writers will continue to use to good effect, for example Gene Wolfe in "Useful Phrases" (1992).

A young man, named Giovanni Guasconti, came, very long ago, from the more southern region of Italy, to pursue his studies at the University of Padua. Giovanni, who had but a scanty supply of gold ducats in his pocket, took lodgings in a high and gloomy chamber of an old edifice, which looked not unworthy to have been the palace of a Paduan noble, and which, in fact, exhibited over its entrance the armorial bearings of a family long since extinct. The young stranger, who was not unstudied in the great poem of his country, recollected that one of the ancestors of this family, and perhaps an occupant of this very mansion, had been pictured by Dante as a partaker of the immortal agonies of his Inferno. These reminiscences and associations, together with the tendency to heartbreak natural to a young man for the first time out of his native sphere, caused Giovanni to sigh heavily, as he looked around the desolate and ill-furnished apartment.

"Holy Virgin, Signor!" cried old dame Lisabetta, who, won by the youth's remarkable beauty of person, was kindly endeavoring to give the chamber a habitable air, "what a sigh was that to come out of a young man's heart! Do you find this old mansion gloomy? For the love of heaven, then, put your head out of the window, and you will see as bright sunshine as you have left in Naples."

Guasconti mechanically did as the old woman advised, but could not quite agree with her that the Paduan sunshine was as cheerful as that of southern Italy. Such as it was, however, it fell upon a garden beneath the window, and expended its fostering influences on a variety of plants, which seemed to have been cultivated with exceeding care.

"Does this garden belong to the house?" asked Giovanni.

"Heaven forbid, Signor!—unless it were fruitful of better pot herbs than any that grow there now," answered old Lisabetta. "No; that garden is cultivated by the own hands of Signor Giacomo Rappaccini, the famous Doctor, who, I warrant him, has been heard of as far as Naples. It is said he distils these plants into medicines that are as potent as a charm. Oftentimes you may see the Signor Doctor at work, and perchance the Signora his daughter, too, gathering the strange flowers that grow in the garden."

The old woman had now done what she could for the aspect of the chamber; and, commending the young man to the protection of the saints, took her departure.

Giovanni still found no better occupation than to look down into the garden beneath his window. From its appearance, he judged it to be one of those botanic gardens, which were of earlier date in Padua than elsewhere in Italy or in the world. Or, not improbably, it might once have been the pleasure-place of an opulent family; for there was the ruin of a marble fountain in the center, sculptured with rare art, but so woefully shattered that it was impossible to trace the original design from the chaos of remaining fragments. The water, however, continued to gush and sparkle into the sunbeams as cheerfully as ever. A little gurgling sound ascended to the young man's window, and made him feel as if the fountain were an immortal spirit that sung its song unceasingly, and without heeding the vicissitudes around it, while one century embodied it in marble and another scattered the perishable garniture on the soil. All about the pool into which the water subsided grew various plants, that seemed to require a plentiful supply of moisture for the nourishment of gigantic leaves, and in some instances, flowers gorgeously magnificent. There was one shrub in particular, set in a marble vase in the midst of the pool, that bore a profusion of purple blossoms, each of which had the luster and richness of a gem; and the whole together made a show so resplendent that it seemed enough to illuminate the garden, even had there been no sunshine. Every portion of the soil was peopled with plants and herbs, which, if less beautiful, still bore tokens of assiduous care, as if all had their individual virtues, known to the scientific mind that fostered them. Some were placed in urns, rich with old carving, and others in common garden-pots; some crept serpent-like along the ground, or climbed on high, using whatever means of ascent was offered them. One plant had wreathed itself round a statue of Vertumnus, which was thus quite veiled and shrouded in a drapery of hanging foliage, so happily arranged that it might have served a sculptor for a study.

While Giovanni stood at the window, he heard a rustling behind a screen of leaves, and became aware that a person was at work in the garden. His figure soon emerged into view, and showed itself to be that of no common laborer, but a tall, emaciated, sallow, and sickly looking man, dressed in a scholar's garb of black. He was beyond the middle term of life, with gray hair, a thin gray beard, and a face singularly marked with intellect and cultivation, but which could never, even in his more youthful days, have expressed much warmth of heart.

Nothing could exceed the intentness with which this scientific gardener examined every shrub which grew in his path: it seemed as if he was looking into their inmost nature, making observations in regard to their creative essence, and discovering why one leaf grew in this shape, and another in that, and wherefore such and such flowers differed among themselves in hue and perfume. Nevertheless, in spite of the deep intelligence on his part, there was no approach to intimacy between himself and these vegetable existences. On the contrary, he avoided their actual touch, or the direct inhaling of their odors, with a caution that impressed Giovanni most disagreeably; for the man's demeanor was that of one walking among malignant influences, such as savage beasts, or deadly snakes, or evil spirits, which, should he allow them one moment of license, would wreak upon him some terrible fatality. It was strangely frightful to the young man's imagination to see this air of insecurity in a person cultivating a garden, that most simple and innocent of human toils, and which had been alike the joy and labor of the unfallen parents of the race. Was this garden, then, the Eden of the present world? And this man, with such a perception of harm in what his own hands caused to grow—was he the Adam?

The distrustful gardener, while plucking away the dead leaves or pruning the too luxuriant growth of the shrubs, defended his hands with a pair of thick gloves. Nor were these his only armor. When, in his walk through the garden, he came to the magnificent plant that hung its purple gems beside the marble fountain, he placed a kind of mask over his mouth and nostrils, as if all this beauty did but conceal a deadlier malice. But finding his task still too dangerous, he drew back, removed the mask, and called loudly, but in the infirm voice of a person affected with inward disease:

"Beatrice! Beatrice!"

"Here am I, my father! What would you?" cried a rich and youthful voice from the window of the opposite house—a voice as rich as a tropical sunset, and which made Giovanni, though he knew not why, think of deep hues of purple or crimson and of perfumes heavily delectable. "Are you in the garden?"

"Yes, Beatrice," answered the gardener, "and I need your help."

Soon there emerged from under a sculptured portal the figure of a young girl, arrayed with as much richness of taste as the most splendid of the flowers, beautiful as the day, and with a bloom so deep and vivid that one shade more would have been too much. She looked redundant with life, health, and energy; all of which attributes were bound down and compressed, as it were, and girdled tensely, in their luxuriance, by her virgin zone. Yet Giovanni's fancy must have grown morbid while he looked down into the garden; for the impression which the fair stranger made upon him was as if here were another flower, the human sister of those vegetable ones, as beautiful as they—more beautiful than the richest of them—but still to be touched only with a glove, nor to be approached without a mask. As Beatrice came down the garden path, it was observable that she handled and inhaled the odor of several of the plants which her father had most sedulously avoided.

"Here, Beatrice," said the latter, "see how many needful offices require to be done to our chief treasure. Yet, shattered as I am, my life might pay the penalty of approaching it so closely as circumstances demand. Henceforth, I fear, this plant must be consigned to your sole charge."

"And gladly will I undertake it," cried again the rich tones of the young lady, as she bent towards the magnificent plant and opened her arms as if to embrace it. "Yes, my sister, my splendor, it shall be Beatrice's task to nurse and serve thee; and thou shalt reward her with thy kisses and perfumed breath, which to her is as the breath of life."

Then, with all the tenderness in her manner that was so strikingly expressed in her words, she busied herself with such attentions as the plant seemed to require; and Giovanni, at his lofty window, rubbed his eyes, and almost doubted whether it were a girl tending her favorite flower, or one sister performing the duties of affection to another. The scene soon terminated. Whether Dr. Rappaccini had finished his labors in the garden, or that his watchful eye had caught the stranger's face, he now took his daughter's arm and retired. Night was already closing in; oppressive exhalations seemed to proceed from the plants, and steal upward past the open window; and Giovanni, closing the lattice, went to his couch, and dreamed of a rich flower and beautiful girl. Flower and maiden were different, and yet the same, and fraught with some strange peril in either shape.

But there is an influence in the light of morning that tends to rectify whatever errors of fancy, or even of judgment, we may have incurred during the sun's decline, or among the shadows of the night, or in the less wholesome glow of moonshine. Giovanni's first movement on starting from sleep, was to throw open the window and gaze down into the garden which his dreams had made so fertile of mysteries. He was surprised and a little ashamed to find how real and matter-of-fact an affair it proved to be, in the first rays of the sun which gilded the dew-drops that hung upon leaf and blossom, and, while giving a brighter beauty to each rare flower, brought everything within the limits of ordinary experience. The young man rejoiced, that, in the heart of the barren city, he had the privilege of overlooking this spot of lovely and luxuriant vegetation. It would serve, he said to himself, as a symbolic language to keep him in communion with Nature. Neither the sickly and thoughtworn Dr. Giacomo Rappaccini, it is true, nor his brilliant daughter, were now visible; so that Giovanni could not determine how much of the singularity which he attributed to both was due to their own qualities and how much to his wonder-working fancy; but he was inclined to take a most rational view of the whole matter.

In the course of the day, he paid his respects to Signor Pietro Baglioni, professor of medicine in the university, a physician of eminent repute to whom Giovanni had brought a letter of introduction. The Professor was an elderly personage, apparently of genial nature, and habits that might almost be called jovial. He kept the young man to dinner, and made himself very agreeable by the freedom and liveliness of his conversation, especially when warmed by a flask or two of Tuscan wine. Giovanni, conceiving that men of science, inhabitants of the same city, must needs be on familiar terms with one another, took an opportunity to mention the name of Dr. Rappaccini. But the Professor did not respond with so much cordiality as he had anticipated.

"Ill would it become a teacher of the divine art of medicine," said Professor Pietro Baglioni, in answer to a question of Giovanni, "to withhold due and well-considered praise of a physician so eminently skilled as Rappaccini. But, on the other hand, I should answer it but scantily to my conscience were I to permit a worthy youth like yourself, Signor Giovanni, the son of an ancient friend, to imbibe erroneous ideas respecting a man who might hereafter chance to hold your life and death in his hands. The truth is, our worshipful Doctor Rappaccini has as much science as any member of the faculty—with perhaps one single exception—in Padua, or all Italy; but there are certain grave objections to his professional character."

"And what are they?" asked the young man.

"Has my friend Giovanni any disease of body or heart, that he is so inquisitive about physicians?" said the Professor, with a smile. "But as for Rappaccini, it is said of him—and I, who know the man well, can answer for its truth—that he cares infinitely more for science than for mankind. His patients are interesting to him only as subjects for some new experiment. He would sacrifice human life, his own among the rest, or whatever else was dearest to him, for the sake of adding so much as a grain of mustard seed to the great heap of his accumulated knowledge."

"Methinks he is an awful man, indeed," remarked Guasconti, mentally recalling the cold and purely intellectual aspect of Rappaccini. "And yet, worshipful Professor, is it not a noble spirit? Are there many men capable of so spiritual a love of science?"

"God forbid," answered the Professor, somewhat testily; "at least, unless they take sounder views of the healing art than those adopted by Rappaccini. It is his theory that all medicinal virtues are comprised within those substances which we term vegetable poisons. These he cultivates with his own hands, and is said even to have produced new varieties of poison, more horribly deleterious than Nature, without the assistance of this learned person, would ever have plagued the world withal. That the Signor Doctor does less mischief than might be expected, with such dangerous substances, is undeniable. Now and then, it must be owned, he has effected, or seemed to effect, a marvellous cure; but, to tell you my private mind, Signor Giovanni, he should receive little credit for such instances of success—they being probably the work of chance—but should be held strictly accountable for his failures, which may justly be considered his own work."

The youth might have taken Baglioni's opinions with many grains of allowance had he known that there was a professional warfare of long continuance between him and Doctor Rappaccini, in which the latter was generally thought to have gained the advantage. If the reader be inclined to judge for himself, we refer him to certain black-letter tracts on both sides, preserved in the medical department of the University of Padua.

"I know not, most learned Professor," returned Giovanni, after musing on what had been said of Rappaccini's exclusive zeal for science—"I know not how dearly this physician may love his art; but surely there is one object more dear to him. He has a daughter."

"Aha!" cried the Professor with a laugh. "So now our friend Giovanni's secret is out. You have heard of this daughter, whom all the young men in Padua are wild about, though not half a dozen have ever had the good hap to see her face. I know little of the Signora Beatrice save that Rappaccini is said to have instructed her deeply in his science, and that, young and beautiful as fame reports her, she is already qualified to fill a professor's chair. Perchance her father destines her for mine! Other absurd rumors there be, not worth talking about or listening to. So now, Signor Giovanni, drink off your glass of lachryma."

Guasconti returned to his lodgings somewhat heated with the wine he had quaffed, and which caused his brain to swim with strange fantasies in reference to Doctor Rappaccini and the beautiful Beatrice. On his way, happening to pass by a florist's, he bought a fresh bouquet of flowers.

Ascending to his chamber, he seated himself near the window, but within the shadow thrown by the depth of the wall, so that he could look down into the garden with little risk of being discovered. All beneath his eye was a solitude. The strange plants were basking in the sunshine, and now and then nodding gently to one another, as if in acknowledgment of sympathy and kindred. In the midst, by the shattered fountain, grew the magnificent shrub, with its purple gems clustering all over it; they glowed in the air, and gleamed back again out of the depths of the pool, which thus seemed to overflow with colored radiance from the rich reflection that was steeped in it. At first, as we have said, the garden was a solitude. Soon, however—as Giovanni had half hoped, half feared, would be the case—a figure appeared beneath the antique sculptured portal, and came down between the rows of plants, inhaling their various perfumes, as if she were one of those beings of old classic fable that lived upon sweet odors. On again beholding Beatrice, the young man was even startled to perceive how much her beauty exceeded his recollection of it; so brilliant, so vivid, was its character, that she glowed amid the sunlight, and, as Giovanni whispered to himself, positively illuminated the more shadowy intervals of the garden path. Her face being now more revealed than on the former occasion, he was struck by its expression of simplicity and sweetness—qualities that had not entered into his idea of her character, and which made him ask anew what manner of mortal she might be. Nor did he fail again to observe, or imagine, an analogy between the beautiful girl and the gorgeous shrub that hung its gem-like flowers over the fountain—a resemblance which Beatrice seemed to have indulged a fantastic humor in heightening, both by the arrangement of her dress and the selection of its hues.

Approaching the shrub, she threw open her arms, as with a passionate ardor, and drew its branches into an intimate embrace—so intimate that her features were hidden in its leafy bosom and her glistening ringlets all intermingled with the flowers.

"Give me thy breath, my sister," exclaimed Beatrice; "for I am faint with common air. And give me this flower of thine, which I separate with gentlest fingers from the stem, and place it close beside my heart."

With these words, the beautiful daughter of Rappaccini plucked one of the richest blossoms of the shrub, and was about to fasten it in her bosom. But now, unless Giovanni's draughts of wine had bewildered his senses, a singular incident occurred. A small orange colored reptile, of the lizard or chameleon species, chanced to be creeping along the path, just at the feet of Beatrice. It appeared to Giovanni—but, at the distance from which he gazed, he could scarcely have seen anything so minute—it appeared to him, however, that a drop or two of moisture from the broken stem of the flower descended upon the lizard's head. For an instant, the reptile contorted itself violently, and then lay motionless in the sunshine. Beatrice observed this remarkable phenomenon, and crossed herself, sadly, but without surprise; nor did she therefore hesitate to arrange the fatal flower in her bosom. There it blushed, and almost glimmered with the dazzling effect of a precious stone, adding to her dress and aspect the one appropriate charm which nothing else in the world could have supplied. But Giovanni, out of the shadow of his window, bent forward and shrank back, and murmured and trembled.

"Am I awake? Have I my senses?" said he to himself. "What is this being? Beautiful shall I call her, or inexpressibly terrible?"

Beatrice now strayed carelessly through the garden, approaching closer beneath Giovanni's window, so that he was compelled to thrust his head quite out of its concealment in order to gratify the intense and painful curiosity which she excited. At this moment there came a beautiful insect over the garden wall; it had, perhaps, wandered through the city and found no flowers or verdure among those antique haunts of men until the heavy perfumes of Doctor Rappaccini's shrubs had lured it from afar. Without alighting on the flowers, this winged brightness seemed to be attracted by Beatrice, and lingered in the air and fluttered about her head. Now, here it could not be but that Giovanni Guasconti's eyes deceived him. Be that as it might, he fancied that, while Beatrice was gazing at the insect with childish delight, it grew faint and fell at her feet; its bright wings shivered; it was dead—from no cause that he could discern, unless it were the atmosphere of her breath. Again Beatrice crossed herself and sighed heavily as she bent over the dead insect.

An impulsive movement of Giovanni drew her eyes to the window. There she beheld the beautiful head of the young man—rather a Grecian than an Italian head, with fair, regular features, and a glistening of gold among his ringlets—gazing down upon her like a being that hovered in mid air. Scarcely knowing what he did, Giovanni threw down the bouquet which he had hitherto held in his hand.

"Signora," said he, "there are pure and healthful flowers. Wear them for the sake of Giovanni Guasconti!"

"Thanks, Signor," replied Beatrice, with her rich voice, that came forth as it were like a gush of music; and with a mirthful expression half childish and half woman-like. "I accept your gift, and would fain recompense it with this precious purple flower; but if I toss it into the air, it will not reach you. So Signor Guasconti must even content himself with my thanks."

She lifted the bouquet from the ground, and then, as if inwardly ashamed at having stepped aside from her maidenly reserve to respond to a stranger's greeting, passed swiftly homeward through the garden. But, few as the moments were, it seemed to Giovanni when she was on the point of vanishing beneath the sculptured portal, that his beautiful bouquet was already beginning to wither in her grasp. It was an idle thought; there could be no possibility of distinguishing a faded flower from a fresh one at so great a distance.

For many days after this incident the young man avoided the window that looked into Doctor Rappaccini's garden, as if something ugly and monstrous would have blasted his eyesight had he been betrayed into a glance. He felt conscious of having put himself, to a certain extent, within the influence of an unintelligible power by the communication which he had opened with Beatrice. The wisest course would have been, if his heart were in any real danger, to quit his lodgings and Padua itself at once; the next wiser, to have accustomed himself, as far as possible, to the familiar and daylight view of Beatrice—thus bringing her rigidly and systematically within the limits of ordinary experience. Least of all, while avoiding her sight, ought Giovanni have remained so near this extraordinary being that the proximity and possibility even of intercourse should give a kind of substance and reality to the wild vagaries which his imagination ran riot continually in producing. Guasconti had not a deep heart—or, at all events, its depths were not sounded now; but he had a quick fancy, and an ardent southern temperament, which rose every instant to a higher fever-pitch. Whether or no Beatrice possessed those terrible attributes, that fatal breath, the affinity with those so beautiful and deadly flowers which were indicated by what Giovanni had witnessed, she had at least instilled a fierce and subtle poison into his system. It was not love, although her rich beauty was a madness to him; nor horror, even while he fancied her spirit to be imbued with the same baneful essence that seemed to pervade her physical frame; but a wild offspring of both love and horror that had each parent in it, and burned like one and shivered like the other. Giovanni knew not what to dread; still less did he know what to hope; yet hope and dread kept a continual warfare in his breast, alternately vanquishing one another and starting up afresh to renew the contest. Blessed are all simple emotions, be they dark or bright! It is the lurid intermixture of the two that produces the illuminating blaze of the infernal regions.

Sometimes he endeavored to assuage the fever of his spirit by a rapid walk through the streets of Padua or beyond its gates: his footsteps kept time with the throbbings of his brain, so that the walk was apt to accelerate itself to a race. One day he found himself arrested; his arm was seized by a portly personage, who had turned back on recognizing the young man and expended much breath in overtaking him.

"Signor Giovanni! Stay, my young friend!" cried he. "Have you forgotten me? That might well be the case, if I were as much altered as yourself."

It was Baglioni, whom Giovanni had avoided ever since their first meeting, from a doubt that the Professor's sagacity would look too deeply into his secrets. Endeavoring to recover himself, he stared forth wildly from his inner world into the outer one and spoke like a man in a dream.

"Yes; I am Giovanni Guasconti. You are Professor Pietro Baglioni. Now let me pass!"

"Not yet, not yet, Signor Giovanni Guasconti," said the Professor, smiling, but at the same time scrutinizing the youth with an earnest glance. "What! did I grow up side by side with your father? and shall his son pass me like a stranger in these old streets of Padua? Stand still, Signor Giovanni; for we must have a word or two before we part."

"Speedily, then, most worshipful Professor, speedily!" said Giovanni, with feverish impatience. "Does not your worship see that I am in haste?"

Now, while he was speaking, there came a man in black along the street, stooping and moving feebly like a person in inferior health. His face was all overspread with a most sickly and sallow hue, but yet so pervaded with an expression of piercing and active intellect that an observer might easily have overlooked the merely physical attributes and have seen only this wonderful energy. As he passed, this person exchanged a cold and distant salutation with Baglioni, but fixed his eyes upon Giovanni with an intentness that seemed to bring out whatever was within him worthy of notice. Nevertheless, there was a peculiar quietness in the look, as if taking merely a speculative, not a human, interest in the young man.

"It is Doctor Rappaccini!" whispered the Professor when the stranger had passed. "Has he ever seen your face before?"

"Not that I know," answered Giovanni, starting at the name.

"He *has* seen you! He must have seen you!" said Baglioni, hastily. "For some purpose or other, this man of science is making a study of you. I know that look of his! It is the same that coldly illuminates his face as he bends over a bird, a mouse, or a butterfly, which, in pursuance of some experiment, he has killed by the perfume of a flower; a look as deep as Nature itself, but without Nature's warmth of love. Signor Giovanni, I will stake my life upon it, you are the subject of one of Rappaccini's experiments!"

"Will you make a fool of me?" cried Giovanni, passionately. "*That,* Signor Professor, were an untoward experiment."

"Patience, patience!" replied the imperturbable Professor. "I tell thee, my poor Giovanni, that Rappaccini has a scientific interest in thee. Thou hast fallen into fearful hands! And the Signora Beatrice? What part does she act in this mystery?"

But Guasconti, finding Baglioni's pertinacity intolerable, here broke away, and was gone before the Professor could again seize his arm. He looked after the young man intently, and shook his head.

"This must not be," said Baglioni to himself. "The youth is the son of my old friend, and shall not come to any harm from which the arcana of medical science can preserve him. Besides, it is too insufferable an impertinence in Rappaccini, thus to snatch the lad out of my own hands, as I may say, and make use of him for his infernal experiments. This daughter of his! It shall be looked to. Perchance, most learned Rappaccini, I may foil you where you little dream of it!"

Meanwhile, Giovanni had pursued a circuitous route, and at length found himself at the door of his lodgings. As he crossed the threshold he was met by old Lisabetta, who smirked and smiled, and was evidently desirous to attract his attention; vainly, however, as the ebullition of his feelings had momentarily subsided into a cold and dull vacuity. He turned his eyes full upon the withered face that was puckering itself into a smile, but seemed to behold it not. The old dame, therefore, laid her grasp upon his cloak.

"Signor! Signor!" whispered she, still with a smile over the whole breadth of her visage, so that it looked not unlike a grotesque carving in wood, darkened by centuries. "Listen, Signor! There is a private entrance into the garden!"

"What do you say?" exclaimed Giovanni, turning quickly about, as if an inanimate thing should start into feverish life. "A private entrance into Doctor Rappaccini's garden?"

"Hush! hush! not so loud!" whispered Lisabetta, putting her hand over his mouth. "Yes; into the worshipful doctor's garden, where you may see all his fine shrubbery. Many a young man in Padua would give gold to be admitted among those flowers."

Giovanni put a piece of gold into her hand.

"Show me the way," said he.

A surmise, probably excited by his conversation with Baglioni, crossed his mind, that this interposition of old Lisabetta might perchance be connected with the intrigue, whatever were its nature, in which the Professor seemed to suppose that Doctor Rappaccini was involving him. But such a suspicion, though it disturbed Giovanni, was inadequate to restrain him. The instant that he was aware of the possibility of approaching Beatrice, it seemed an absolute necessity of his existence to do so. It mattered not whether she were angel or demon; he was irrevocably within her sphere, and must obey the law that whirled him onward, in ever lessening circles, towards a result which he did not attempt to foreshadow. And yet, strange to say, there came across him a sudden doubt whether this intense interest on his part were not delusory; whether it were really of so deep and positive a nature as to justify him in now thrusting himself into an incalculable position; whether it were not merely the fantasy of a young man's brain, only slightly or not at all connected with his heart!

He paused, hesitated, turned half about, but again went on. His withered guide led him along several obscure passages, and finally undid a door, through which, as it was opened, there came the sight and sound of rustling leaves, with the broken sunshine glimmering among them. Giovanni stepped forth, and, forcing himself through the entanglement of a shrub that wreathed its tendrils over the hidden entrance, he stood beneath his own window, in the open area of Doctor Rappaccini's garden.

How often is it the case, that, when impossibilities have come to pass and dreams have condensed their misty substance into tangible realities, we find ourselves calm, and even coldly self-possessed, amid circumstances which it would have been a delirium of joy or agony to anticipate! Fate delights to thwart us thus. Passion will choose his own time to rush upon the scene, and lingers sluggishly behind when an appropriate adjustment of events would seem to summon his appearance. So was it now with Giovanni. Day after day his pulses had throbbed with feverish blood at the improbable idea of an interview with Beatrice, and of standing with her, face to face, in this very garden, basking in the Oriental sunshine of her beauty, and snatching from her full gaze the mystery which he deemed the riddle of his own existence. But now there was a singular and untimely equanimity within his breast. He threw a glance around the garden to discover if Beatrice or her father were present, and, perceiving that he was alone, began a critical observation of the plants.

The aspect of one and all of them dissatisfied him; their gorgeousness seemed fierce, passionate, and even unnatural. There was hardly an individual shrub which a wanderer, straying by himself through a forest, would not have been startled to find growing wild, as if an unearthly face had glared at him out of the thicket. Several also would have shocked a delicate instinct by an appearance of artificialness indicating that there had been such commixture, and, as it were, adultery, of various vegetable species, that the production was no longer of God's making, but the monstrous offspring of man's depraved fancy, glowing with only an evil mockery of beauty. They were probably the result of experiment, which in one or two cases had succeeded in mingling plants individually lovely into a compound possessing the questionable and ominous character that distinguished the whole growth of the garden. In fine, Giovanni recognized but two or three plants in the collection, and those of a kind that he well knew to be poisonous. While busy with these contemplations, he heard the rustling of a silken garment, and, turning, beheld Beatrice emerging from beneath the sculptured portal.

Giovanni had not considered with himself what should be his deportment; whether he should apologize for his intrusion into the garden, or assume that he was there with the privity at least, if not by the desire, of Doctor Rappaccini or his daughter; but Beatrice's manner placed him at his ease, though leaving him still in doubt by what agency he had gained admittance. She came lightly along the path and met him near the broken fountain. There was surprise in her face, but brightened by a simple and kind expression of pleasure.

"You are a connoisseur in flowers, Signor," said Beatrice, with a smile, alluding to the bouquet which he had flung her from the window. "It is no marvel, therefore, if the sight of my father's rare collection has tempted you to take a nearer view. If he were here, he could tell you many strange and interesting facts as to the nature and habits of these shrubs; for he has spent a lifetime in such studies, and this garden is his world."

"And yourself, lady," observed Giovanni, "if fame says true—you likewise are deeply skilled in the virtues indicated by these rich blossoms and these spicy perfumes. Would you deign to be my instructress, I should prove an apter scholar than under Signor Rappaccini himself."

"Are there such idle rumors?" asked Beatrice, with the music of a pleasant laugh. "Do people say that I am skilled in my father's science of plants? What a jest is there! No; though I have grown up among these flowers, I know no more of them than their hues and perfume; and sometimes, methinks I would fain rid myself of even that small knowledge. There are many flowers here, and those not the least brilliant, that shock and offend me when they meet my eye. But, pray, Signor, do not believe these stories about my science. Believe nothing of me save what you see with your own eyes."

"And must I believe all that I have seen with my own eyes?" asked Giovanni pointedly, while the recollection of former scenes made him shrink. "No, Signora, you demand too little of me. Bid me believe nothing save what comes from your own lips."

It would appear that Beatrice understood him. There came a deep flush to her cheek; but she looked full into Giovanni's eyes, and responded to his gaze of uneasy suspicion with a queenlike haughtiness.

"I do so bid you, Signor," she replied. "Forget whatever you may have fancied in regard to me. If true to the outward senses, still it may be false in its essence. But the words of Beatrice Rappaccini's lips are true from the heart outward. Those you may believe."

A fervor glowed in her whole aspect and beamed upon Giovanni's consciousness like the light of truth itself. But while she spoke there was a fragrance in the atmosphere around her, rich and delightful, though evanescent, yet which the young man, from an indefinable reluctance, scarcely dared to draw into his lungs. It might be the odor of the flowers. Could it be Beatrice's breath which thus embalmed her words with a strange richness, as if by steeping them in her heart? A faintness passed like a shadow over Giovanni and flitted away; he seemed to gaze through the beautiful girl's eyes into her transparent soul, and felt no more doubt or fear.

The tinge of passion that had colored Beatrice's manner vanished; she became gay, and appeared to derive a pure delight from her communion with the youth not unlike what the maiden of a lonely island might have felt conversing with a voyager from the civilized world. Evidently her experience of life had been confined within the limits of that garden. She talked now about matters as simple as the daylight or summer clouds, and now asked questions in reference to the city, or Giovanni's distant home, his friends, his mother, and his sisters—questions indicating such seclusion, and such lack of familiarity with modes and forms, that Giovanni responded as if to an infant. Her spirit gushed out before him like a fresh rill that was just catching its first glimpse of the sunlight and wondering at the reflections of earth and sky which were flung into its bosom. There came thoughts, too, from a deep source, and fantasies of a gemlike brilliancy, as if diamonds and rubies sparkled upward among the bubbles of the fountain. Ever and anon there gleamed across the young man's mind a sense of wonder that he should be walking side by side with the being who had so wrought upon his imagination, whom he had idealized in such hues of terror, in whom he had positively witnessed such manifestations of dreadful attributes—that he should be conversing with Beatrice like a brother, and should find her so human and so maidenlike. But such reflections were only momentary; the effect of her character was too real not to make itself familiar at once.

In this free intercourse they had strayed through the garden, and now, after many turns among its avenues, were come to the shattered fountain, beside which grew the magnificent shrub, with its treasury of glowing blossoms. A fragrance was diffused from it which Giovanni recognized as identical with that which he had attributed to Beatrice's breath, but incomparably more powerful. As her eyes fell upon it, Giovanni beheld her press her hand to her bosom as if her heart were throbbing suddenly and painfully.

“For the first time in my life,” murmured she, addressing the shrub, “I had forgotten thee!”

“I remember, Signora,” said Giovanni, “that you once promised to reward me with one of these living gems for the bouquet which I had the happy boldness to fling to your feet. Permit me now to pluck it as a memorial of this interview.”

He made a step towards the shrub with extended hand. But Beatrice darted forward, uttering a shriek that went through his heart like a dagger. She caught his hand and drew it back with the whole force of her slender figure. Giovanni felt her touch thrilling through his fibers.

“Touch it not!” exclaimed she, in a voice of agony. “Not for thy life! It is fatal!”

Then, hiding her face, she fled from him and vanished beneath the sculptured portal. As Giovanni followed her with his eyes, he beheld the emaciated figure and pale intelligence of Doctor Rappaccini, who had been watching the scene, he knew not how long, within the shadow of the entrance.

No sooner was Guasconti alone in his chamber than the image of Beatrice came back to his passionate musings, invested with all the witchery that had been gathering around it ever since his first glimpse of her, and now likewise imbued with a tender warmth of girlish womanhood. She was human; her nature was endowed with all gentle and feminine qualities; she was worthiest to be worshipped; she was capable, surely, on her part, of the height and heroism of love. Those tokens which he had hitherto considered as proofs of a frightful peculiarity in her physical and moral system were now either forgotten, or, by the subtle sophistry of passion transmuted into a golden crown of enchantment, rendering Beatrice the more admirable by so much as she was the more unique. Whatever had looked ugly was now beautiful; or, if incapable of such a change, it stole away and hid itself among those shapeless half ideas which throng the dim region beyond the daylight of our perfect consciousness. Thus did he spend the night, nor fell asleep until the dawn had begun to awake the slumbering flowers in Doctor Rappaccini’s garden, whither Giovanni’s dreams doubtless led him. Up rose the sun in his due season, and, flinging his beams upon the young man’s eyelids, awoke him to a sense of pain. When thoroughly aroused, he became sensible of a burning and tingling agony in his hand—in his right hand—the very hand which Beatrice had grasped in her own when he was on the point of plucking one of the gem-like flowers. On the back of that hand there was now a purple print like that of four small fingers, and the likeness of a slender thumb upon his wrist.

O, how stubbornly does love—or even that cunning semblance of love which flourishes in the imagination, but strikes no depth of root into the heart—how stubbornly does it hold its faith until the moment comes when it is doomed to vanish into thin mist! Giovanni wrapped a handkerchief about his hand and wondered what evil thing had stung him, and soon forgot his pain in a revery of Beatrice.

After the first interview, a second was in the inevitable course of what we call fate. A third; a fourth; and a meeting with Beatrice in the garden was no longer an incident in Giovanni's daily life, but the whole space in which he might be said to live; for the anticipation and memory of that ecstatic hour made up the remainder. Nor was it otherwise with the daughter of Rappaccini. She watched for the youth's appearance, and flew to his side with confidence as unreserved as if they had been playmates from early infancy—as if they were such playmates still. If, by any unwonted chance, he failed to come at the appointed moment, she stood beneath the window and sent up the rich sweetness of her tones to float around him in his chamber and echo and reverberate throughout his heart: "Giovanni! Giovanni! Why tarriest thou? Come down!" And down he hastened into that Eden of poisonous flowers.

But, with all this intimate familiarity, there was still a reserve in Beatrice's demeanor, so rigidly and invariably sustained that the idea of infringing it scarcely occurred to his imagination. By all appreciable signs, they loved; they had looked love with eyes that conveyed the holy secret from the depths of one soul into the depths of the other, as if it were too sacred to be whispered by the way; they had even spoken love in those gushes of passion when their spirits darted forth in articulated breath like tongues of long hidden flame; and yet there had been no seal of lips, no clasp of hands, nor any slightest caress such as love claims and hallows. He had never touched one of the gleaming ringlets of her hair; her garment—so marked was the physical barrier between them—had never been waved against him by a breeze. On the few occasions when Giovanni had seemed tempted to overstep the limit, Beatrice grew so sad, so stern, and withal wore such a look of desolate separation, shuddering at itself, that not a spoken word was requisite to repel him. At such times he was startled at the horrible suspicions that rose, monsterlike, out of the caverns of his heart and stared him in the face; his love grew thin and faint as the morning mist, his doubts alone had substance. But, when Beatrice's face brightened again after the momentary shadow, she was transformed at once from the mysterious, questionable being whom he had watched with so much awe and horror; she was now the beautiful and unsophisticated girl whom he felt that his spirit knew with a certainty beyond all other knowledge.

A considerable time had now passed since Giovanni's last meeting with

Baglioni. One morning, however, he was disagreeably surprised by a visit from the Professor, whom he had scarcely thought of for whole weeks, and would willingly have forgotten still longer. Given up as he had long been to a pervading excitement, he could tolerate no companions except upon condition of their perfect sympathy with his present state of feeling. Such sympathy was not to be expected from Professor Baglioni.

The visitor chatted carelessly for a few moments about the gossip of the city and the University, and then took up another topic.

"I have been reading an old classic author lately," said he, "and met with a story that strangely interested me. Possibly you may remember it. It is of an Indian prince, who sent a beautiful woman as a present to Alexander the Great. She was as lovely as the dawn and gorgeous as the sunset; but what especially distinguished her was a certain rich perfume in her breath—richer than a garden of Persian roses. Alexander, as was natural to a youthful conqueror, fell in love at first sight with this magnificent stranger; but a certain sage physician, happening to be present, discovered a terrible secret in regard to her."

"And what was that?" asked Giovanni, turning his eyes downward to avoid those of the Professor.

"That this lovely woman," continued Baglioni, with emphasis, "had been nourished with poisons from her birth upward, until her whole nature was so imbued with them that she herself had become the deadliest poison in existence. Poison was her element of life. With that rich perfume of her breath she blasted the very air. Her love would have been poison—her embrace death. Is not this a marvelous tale?"

"A childish fable," answered Giovanni, nervously starting from his chair. "I marvel how your worship finds time to read such nonsense among your graver studies."

"By the by," said the Professor, looking uneasily about him, "what singular fragrance is this in your apartment? Is it the perfume of your gloves? It is faint, but delicious; and yet, after all, by no means agreeable. Were I to breathe it long, methinks it would make me ill. It is like the breath of a flower; but I see no flowers in the chamber."

"Nor are there any," replied Giovanni, who had turned pale as the Professor spoke; "nor, I think, is there any fragrance except in your worship's imagination. Odors, being a sort of element combined of the sensual and the spiritual, are apt to deceive us in this manner. The recollection of a perfume, the bare idea of it, may easily be mistaken for a present reality."

"Ay; but my sober imagination does not often play such tricks," said Baglioni; "and, were I to fancy any kind of odor, it would be that of some vile apothecary drug, wherewith my fingers are likely enough to be imbued. Our worshipful friend Rappaccini, as I have heard, tinctures his medicaments with odors richer than those of Araby. Doubtless, likewise, the fair and learned Signora Beatrice would minister to her patients with draughts as sweet as a maiden's breath; but woe to him that sips them!"

Giovanni's face evinced many contending emotions. The tone in which the Professor alluded to the pure and lovely daughter of Rappaccini was a torture to his soul; and yet, the intimation of a view of her character, opposite to his own, gave instantaneous distinctness to a thousand dim suspicions, which now grinned at him like so many demons. But he strove hard to quell them and to respond to Baglioni with a true lover's perfect faith.

"Signor Professor," said he, "you were my father's friend; perchance, too, it is your purpose to act a friendly part towards his son. I would fain feel nothing towards you save respect and deference. But I pray you to observe, Signor, that there is one subject on which we must not speak. You know not the Signora Beatrice. You cannot, therefore, estimate the wrong—the blasphemy, I may even say—that is offered to her character by a light or injurious word."

"Giovanni! my poor Giovanni!" answered the Professor, with a calm expression of pity, "I know this wretched girl far better than yourself. You shall hear the truth in respect to the poisoner Rappaccini and his poisonous daughter: yes, poisonous as she is beautiful. Listen; for even should you do violence to my gray hairs, it shall not silence me. That old fable of the Indian woman has become a truth by the deep and deadly science of Rappaccini, and in the person of the lovely Beatrice!"

Giovanni groaned and hid his face.

"Her father," continued Baglioni, "was not restrained by natural affection from offering up his child in this horrible manner as the victim of his insane zeal for science; for, let us do him justice, he is as true a man of science as ever distilled his own heart in an alembic. What, then, will be your fate? Beyond a doubt, you are selected as the material of some new experiment. Perhaps the result is to be death; perhaps a fate more awful still! Rappaccini, with what he calls the interest of science before his eyes, will hesitate at nothing."

"It is a dream!" muttered Giovanni to himself; "surely it is a dream!"

"But," resumed the Professor, "be of good cheer, son of my friend! It is not yet too late for the rescue. Possibly, we may even succeed in bringing back this miserable child within the limits of ordinary nature, from which her father's madness has estranged her. Behold this little silver vase! It was wrought by the hands of the renowned Benvenuto Cellini, and is well worthy to be a love gift to the fairest dame in Italy. But its contents are invaluable. One little sip of this antidote would have rendered the most virulent poisons of the Borgias innocuous. Doubt not that it will be as efficacious against those of Rappaccini. Bestow the vase, and the precious liquid within it, on your Beatrice, and hopefully await the result."

Baglioni laid a small, exquisitely wrought silver phial on the table and withdrew, leaving what he had said to produce its effect upon the young man's mind.

"We will thwart Rappaccini yet!" thought he, chuckling to himself, as he descended the stairs. "But, let us confess the truth of him, he is a wonderful man—a wonderful man indeed! A vile empiric, however, in his practice, and therefore not to be tolerated by those who respect the good old rules of the medical profession!"

Throughout Giovanni's whole acquaintance with Beatrice, he had occasionally, as we have said, been haunted by dark surmises as to her character; yet so thoroughly had she made herself felt by him as a simple, natural, most affectionate, and guileless creature, that the image now held up by Professor Baglioni looked as strange and incredible as if it were not in accordance with his own original conception. True, there were ugly recollections connected with his first glimpses of the beautiful girl; he could not quite forget the bouquet that withered in her grasp, and the insect that perished amid the sunny air, by no ostensible agency save the fragrance of her breath. These incidents, however, dissolving in the pure light of her character, had no longer the efficacy of facts, but were acknowledged as mistaken fantasies, by whatever testimony of the senses they might appear to be substantiated. There is something truer and more real than what we can see with the eyes and touch with the finger. On such better evidence had Giovanni founded his confidence in Beatrice, though rather by the necessary force of her high attributes than by any deep and generous faith on his part. But, now his spirit was incapable of sustaining itself at the height to which the early enthusiasm of passion had exalted it; he fell down, grovelling among earthly doubts, and defiled therewith the pure whiteness of Beatrice's image. Not that he gave her up; he did but distrust. He resolved to institute some decisive test that should satisfy him, once for all, whether there were those dreadful peculiarities in her physical nature which could not be supposed to exist without some corresponding monstrosity of soul. His eyes, gazing down afar, might have deceived him as to the lizard, the insect, and the flowers. But if he could witness, at the distance of a few paces, the sudden blight of one fresh and healthful flower in Beatrice's hand, there would be room for no further question. With this idea he hastened to the florist's and purchased a bouquet that was still gemmed with the morning dewdrops.

It was now the customary hour of his daily interview with Beatrice. Before descending into the garden, Giovanni failed not to look at his figure in the mirror—a vanity to be expected in a beautiful young man, yet, as displaying itself at that troubled and feverish moment, the token of a certain shallowness of feeling and insincerity of character. He did gaze, however, and said to himself that his features had never before possessed so rich a grace, nor his eyes such vivacity, nor his cheeks so warm a hue of superabundant life.

"At least," thought he, "her poison has not yet insinuated itself into my system. I am no flower to perish in her grasp!"

With that thought he turned his eyes on the bouquet, which he had never once laid aside from his hand. A thrill of indefinable horror shot through his frame on perceiving that those dewy flowers were already beginning to droop; they wore the aspect of things that had been fresh and lovely yesterday. Giovanni grew white as marble, and stood motionless before the mirror, staring at his own reflection there as at the likeness of something frightful. He remembered Baglioni's remark about the fragrance that seemed to pervade the chamber. It must have been the poison in his breath! Then he shuddered—shuddered at himself. Recovering from his stupor, he began to watch with curious eye a spider that was busily at work hanging its web from the antique cornice of the apartment, crossing and re-crossing the artful system of interwoven lines—as vigorous and active a spider as ever dangled from an old ceiling. Giovanni bent towards the insect, and emitted a deep, long breath. The spider suddenly ceased its toil; the web vibrated with a tremor originating in the body of the small artisan. Again Giovanni sent forth a breath, deeper, longer, and imbued with a venomous feeling out of his heart: he knew not whether he were wicked, or only desperate. The spider made a convulsive gripe with his limbs and hung dead across the window.

"Accursed! Accursed!" muttered Giovanni, addressing himself. "Hast thou grown so poisonous that this deadly insect perishes by thy breath?"

At that moment, a rich, sweet voice came floating up from the garden. "Giovanni! Giovanni! It is past the hour! Why tarriest thou? Come down!"

"Yes," muttered Giovanni again. "She is the only being whom my breath may not slay! Would that it might!"

He rushed down, and in an instant was standing before the bright and loving eyes of Beatrice. A moment ago his wrath and despair had been so fierce that he could have desired nothing so much as to wither her by a glance. But with her actual presence there came influences which had too real an existence to be at once shaken off; recollections of the delicate and benign power of her feminine nature, which had so often enveloped him in a religious calm; recollections of many a holy and passionate outgush of her heart, when the pure fountain had been unsealed from its depths and made visible in its transparency to his mental eye; recollections which, had Giovanni known how to estimate them, would have assured him that all this ugly mystery was but an earthly illusion, and that, whatever mist of evil might seem to have gathered over her, the real Beatrice was a heavenly angel. Incapable as he was of such high faith, still her presence had not utterly lost its magic. Giovanni's rage was quelled into an aspect of sullen insensibility. Beatrice, with a quick spiritual sense, immediately felt that there was a gulf of blackness between them which neither he nor she could pass. They walked on together, sad and silent, and came thus to the marble fountain and to its pool of water on the ground, in the midst of which grew the shrub that bore gem-like blossoms. Giovanni was affrighted at the eager enjoyment—the appetite, as it were—with which he found himself inhaling the fragrance of the flowers.

"Beatrice," asked he abruptly, "whence came this shrub?"

"My father created it," answered she, with simplicity.

"Created it! created it!" repeated Giovanni. "What mean you, Beatrice?"

"He is a man fearfully acquainted with the secrets of Nature," replied Beatrice; "and, at the hour when I first drew breath, this plant sprang from the soil, the offspring of his science, of his intellect, while I was but his earthly child. Approach it not!" continued she, observing with terror that Giovanni was drawing nearer to the shrub. "It has qualities that you little dream of. But I, dearest Giovanni—I grew up and blossomed with the plant, and was nourished with its breath. It was my sister, and I loved it with a human affection; for, alas!—hast thou not suspected it?—there was an awful doom."

Here Giovanni frowned so darkly upon her that Beatrice paused and trembled. But her faith in his tenderness reassured her, and made her blush that she had doubted for an instant.

"There was an awful doom," she continued, "the effect of my father's fatal love of science, which estranged me from all society of my kind. Until Heaven sent thee, dearest Giovanni, oh! how lonely was thy poor Beatrice!"

"Was it a hard doom?" asked Giovanni, fixing his eyes upon her.

"Only of late have I known how hard it was," answered she, tenderly. "Oh! yes; but my heart was torpid, and therefore quiet."

Giovanni's rage broke forth from his sullen gloom like a lightning flash out of a dark cloud.

"Accursed one!" cried he, with venomous scorn and anger. "And finding thy solitude wearisome, thou hast severed me likewise from all the warmth of life and enticed me into thy region of unspeakable horror!"

"Giovanni!" exclaimed Beatrice, turning her large bright eyes upon his face. The force of his words had not found its way into her mind; she was merely thunderstruck.

"Yes, poisonous thing!" repeated Giovanni, beside himself with passion. "Thou hast done it! Thou hast blasted me! Thou hast filled my veins with poison! Thou hast made me as hateful, as ugly, as loathsome and deadly a creature as thyself—a world's wonder of hideous monstrosity! Now, if our breath be happily as fatal to ourselves as to all others, let us join our lips in one kiss of unutterable hatred, and so die!"

"What has befallen me?" murmured Beatrice, with a low moan out of her heart. "Holy Virgin, pity me, a poor heart-broken child!"

"Thou—dost thou pray?" cried Giovanni, still with the same fiendish scorn. "Thy very prayers, as they come from thy lips, taint the atmosphere with death. Yes, yes; let us pray! Let us to church and dip our fingers in the holy water at the portal! They that come after us will perish as by a pestilence! Let us sign crosses in the air! It will be scattering curses abroad in the likeness of holy symbols!"

"Giovanni," said Beatrice calmly, for her grief was beyond passion, "why dost thou join thyself with me thus in those terrible words? I, it is true, am the horrible thing thou namest me. But thou—what hast thou to do, save with one other shudder at my hideous misery, to go forth out of the garden and mingle with thy race, and forget that there ever crawled on earth such a monster as poor Beatrice?"

"Dost thou pretend ignorance?" asked Giovanni, scowling upon her. "Behold! This power have I gained from the pure daughter of Rappaccini!"

There was a swarm of summer insects flitting through the air in search of the food promised by the flower odors of the fatal garden. They circled round Giovanni's head, and were evidently attracted towards him by the same influence which had drawn them for an instant within the sphere of several of the shrubs. He sent forth a breath among them, and smiled bitterly at Beatrice, as at least a score of the insects fell dead upon the ground.

"I see it! I see it!" shrieked Beatrice. "It is my father's fatal science! No, no, Giovanni; it was not I! Never! never! I dreamed only to love thee and be with thee a little time, and so to let thee pass away, leaving but thine image in mine heart; for, Giovanni—believe it—though my body be nourished with poison, my spirit is God's creature, and craves love as its daily food. But my father!—he has united us in this fearful sympathy. Yes; spurn me, tread upon me, kill me! Oh, what is death after such words as thine? But it was not I. Not for a world of bliss would I have done it."

Giovanni's passion had exhausted itself in its outburst from his lips. There now came across him a sense, mournful, and not without tenderness, of the intimate and peculiar relationship between Beatrice and himself. They stood, as it were, in an utter solitude, which would be made none the less solitary by the densest throng of human life. Ought not, then, the desert of humanity around them to press this insulated pair closer together? If they should be cruel to one another, who was there to be kind to them? Besides, thought Giovanni, might there not still be a hope of his returning within the limits of ordinary nature, and leading Beatrice, the redeemed Beatrice, by the hand? O, weak, and selfish, and unworthy spirit, that could dream of an earthly union and earthly happiness as possible, after such deep love had been so bitterly wronged as was Beatrice's love by Giovanni's blighting words! No, no; there could be no such hope. She must pass heavily, with that broken heart, across the borders of Time—she must bathe her hurts in some fount of paradise, and forget her grief in the light of immortality—and *there* be well.

But Giovanni did not know it.

"Dear Beatrice," said he, approaching her, while she shrank away, as always at his approach, but now with a different impulse, "dearest Beatrice, our fate is not yet so desperate. Behold! There is a medicine, potent, as a wise physician has assured me, and almost divine in its efficacy. It is composed of ingredients the most opposite to those by which thy awful father has brought this calamity upon thee and me. It is distilled of blessed herbs. Shall we not quaff it together, and thus be purified from evil?"

"Give it me!" said Beatrice, extending her hand to receive the little silver phial which Giovanni took from his bosom. She added, with a peculiar emphasis: "I will drink; but do thou await the result."

She put Baglioni's antidote to her lips; and, at the same moment, the figure of Rappaccini emerged from the portal and came slowly towards the marble fountain. As he drew near, the pale man of science seemed to gaze with a triumphant expression at the beautiful youth and maiden, as might an artist who should spend his life in achieving a picture or a group of statuary and finally be satisfied with his success. He paused; his bent form grew erect with conscious power; he spread out his hands over them in the attitude of a father imploring a blessing upon his children. But those were the same hands that had thrown poison into the stream of their lives! Giovanni trembled. Beatrice shuddered nervously, and pressed her hand upon her heart.

"My daughter," said Rappaccini, "thou art no longer lonely in the world. Pluck one of those precious gems from thy sister shrub and bid thy bridegroom wear it in his bosom. It will not harm him now. My science and the sympathy between thee and him have so wrought within his system that he now stands apart from common men, as thou dost, daughter of my pride and triumph, from ordinary women. Pass on, then, through the world, most dear to one another, and dreadful to all besides!"

"My father," said Beatrice, feebly—and still as she spoke she kept her hand upon her heart—"wherefore didst thou inflict this miserable doom upon thy child?"

"Miserable!" exclaimed Rappaccini. "What mean you, foolish girl? Dost thou deem it misery to be endowed with marvelous gifts, against which no power nor strength could avail an enemy? Misery, to be able to quell the mightiest with a breath? Misery, to be as terrible as thou art beautiful? Wouldst thou, then, have preferred the condition of a weak woman, exposed to all evil and capable of none?"

"I would fain have been loved, not feared," murmured Beatrice, sinking down upon the ground. "But now it matters not. I am going, father, where the evil which thou hast striven to mingle with my being will pass away like a dream—like the fragrance of these poisonous flowers, which will no longer taint my breath among the flowers of Eden. Farewell, Giovanni! Thy words of hatred are like lead within my heart; but they, too, will fall away as I ascend. Oh, was there not, from the first, more poison in thy nature than in mine?"

To Beatrice—so radically had her earthly part been wrought upon by Rappaccini's skill—as poison had been life, so the powerful antidote was death. And thus the poor victim of man's ingenuity and of thwarted nature, and of the fatality that attends all such efforts of perverted wisdom, perished there, at the feet of her father and Giovanni. Just at that moment Professor Pietro Baglioni looked forth from the window, and called loudly, in a tone of triumph mixed with horror, to the thunderstricken man of science:

"Rappaccini! Rappaccini! And is *this* the upshot of your experiment?"

JULES VERNE
from *Journey to the Center of the Earth*

{ 1864 }

Jules Verne (1828–1905) was a prolific French novelist often identified as one of the "Fathers of Science Fiction," the other being the British author H. G. Wells. During the nineteenth century Verne popularized an early brand of "hard" science fiction in a series of novels called the *Voyages extraordinaires* (1863–1919), which depicted adventure-filled quests to the ends of the Earth and heroes making use of scientific knowledge and the latest technology to explore "known and unknown worlds" (the subtitle for this series). Expertly marketed by his publisher and mentor Pierre-Jules Hetzel, Verne's novels became best sellers in France and around the world. Today he is ranked as the third most translated author of all time, according to UNESCO's *Index Translationum*.

Verne's career began in the theater: he was a struggling playwright in Paris during the 1850s. He also penned articles on scientific topics and wrote occasional short stories such as "A Voyage in a Balloon" (1851) and "Master Zacharius" (1854) for French magazines. After the publication and success of his first novel, *Five Weeks in a Balloon* (1863), about an aerial trek across the continent of Africa, Verne told his friends at the Paris Stock Market, where he had been working part-time: "My friends, I bid you adieu. . . . I've just written a novel in a new style. . . . If it succeeds, it will be a gold mine." And a gold mine it was, not only for Verne and his publisher but also for world literature as his many *Extraordinary Voyages* helped give birth to a new literary genre.

Verne's next book manuscript, a futuristic but dystopian story called *Paris in the Twentieth Century*, was rejected by Hetzel as being too unrealistic and depressing. Verne promptly locked it in a safe and never looked at it again (it was discovered and published only in 1994). For his subsequent novels, Verne agreed to return to the successful narrative template of *Five Weeks*—that is, educational adventure tales heavily flavored with scientific didacticism, mixed with equal parts of drama, humor, and "sense of wonder," and seasoned with a large pinch of Saint-Simonian positivism. This narrative recipe proved to be enormously successful, and Verne was soon churning out one imaginative masterpiece after another. Some of his more celebrated works include the subterranean thriller *Journey to the Center of the Earth* (1864); the first scientifically plausible manned lunar voyages in *From the Earth to the Moon* (1865) and *Around the Moon* (1870); the world's most memorable oceanographic novel, *Twenty Thousand Leagues under the Sea* (1869), with its brooding Captain Nemo and his dream machine, the *Nautilus*; the prototypical circumnavigation novel in *Around the World in Eighty Days* (1873); the first example of a technological "robinsonade" in which castaways on a deserted island rebuild Western civilization in *The Mysterious Island* (1875); and a highly influential tale about early aeronautics and the conquest of the sky in *Robur the Conqueror* (aka *The Clipper of the Clouds*, 1886), among many others.

Many of Verne's later works seem to have a dramatically darker tone when compared to his earlier ones, exhibiting a steady shift away from a sunny technological optimism toward an outlook that is more often pessimistic, cynical, and anti-science. The novel *Topsy-Turvy* (1889) ridicules the hubris of scientists who believe that they can modify the axis of the Earth; *Propeller Island* (1895) details the dire effects of colonial imperialism on Polynesian island cultures; *Facing the Flag* (1896) takes as its subject the dangers of science used for military purposes; and *The Master of the World* (1904), with its focus on the protagonist Robur's descent into madness, vividly depicts the idea that advanced scientific knowledge can breed moral corruption.

The following excerpt from Verne's *Journey to the Center of the Earth* (from the end of chapter 28 through chapter 31) portrays the moment when the three explorers, after weeks of perilous descent through a volcano's dark tunnels (and young Axel's near fatal tumble down a deep shaft), suddenly find themselves on the brightly lit shore of an underground sea. The sources for the story include the popular hollow-earth theories of the time as well as growing public interest in geology, paleontology, and the new ideas of Darwin. Narrated in the first person by the impressionable Axel, the novel's discursive structure maintains a balance between his uncle Lidenbrock's detailed scientific exposés and Axel's poetic *rêveries*. This delicate intertwining of fact with fantasy, mathematics with myth, and didacticism with daydreaming can be seen in all of Verne's most successful *Extraordinary Voyages*.

Suddenly the ground beneath my feet gave way. I felt myself falling down a vertical shaft, ricocheting off the craggy outcroppings of what seemed to be a deep well. My head struck a sharp rock, and I lost consciousness.

When I came to, I was in semi-darkness, lying on thick blankets. My uncle was looking down at me intently, his eyes hoping to discover on my face some sign of life. At my first sigh he took my hand, and when I opened my eyes he uttered a cry of joy.

"He lives! he lives!" he exclaimed.

"Yes, I am still alive," I answered feebly.

"My dear boy," said my uncle, giving me a hug, "thank heaven you are saved."

I was deeply touched by the tenderness with which he uttered these words, and still more by the cares that accompanied them. It often required such extreme circumstances to bring out such displays of emotion in the professor.

At this moment Hans approached us. He saw my hand in my uncle's, and there was much joy in his eyes.

"*God dag*," he said.

"Good day, Hans, good day," I replied in a whisper. "And now, dear Uncle, please tell me where we are at the present time?"

"Tomorrow, Axel, tomorrow. Right now you are still too weak. I have bandaged your head with compresses which must not be disturbed. Sleep now, and tomorrow I will tell you everything."

"But at least tell me what time it is, and what day."

"It is eleven o'clock at night, Sunday, August 9th. And I forbid you from asking me any more questions until the 10th of this month!"

In truth I was very weak, and my eyes were beginning to close involuntarily. I needed a good night's rest. So I let myself drift off to sleep, with the knowledge that my long solitude of several days was at an end.

The next morning when I awoke, I looked around me. My bed, made up of all our travel blankets, was in a charming grotto that featured splendid stalactites and a floor of fine sand; it was bathed in a kind of twilight. No torch and no lamp was lighted, yet some mysterious gleams of light were filtering in through a narrow opening in the wall. I also heard a vague and indistinct noise, something like the murmuring of waves breaking upon a shore, and at times a whistling of wind.

I wondered whether I was fully awake, if I were dreaming. Or whether my brain, injured by my fall, was perhaps registering purely imaginary noises. Yet neither my eyes nor my ears could be so completely mistaken.

"It *is* a ray of daylight," I thought, "slipping in through this cleft in the rock! And that *is* indeed the sound of waves and of wind! Am I quite mistaken, or have we returned to the surface of the Earth? Has my uncle given up on the expedition? Has it come to a successful conclusion?"

I was puzzling over these unanswerable questions when the professor entered.

"Good morning, Axel!" he said cheerily. "I bet you are feeling better today!"

"Yes, much better!" I replied, sitting up on the blankets.

"I expected so, for you have slept quite soundly. Hans and I took turns watching over you, and we could see you recovering little by little."

"I really do feel a great deal better, and I will gladly give you proof if you offer me some breakfast!"

"Certainly you shall eat, my boy! The fever has left you. Hans rubbed your wounds with a special ointment known only to Icelanders, and they have healed marvelously. Our hunter is quite a fellow!"

While he talked, my uncle prepared a few provisions, which I devoured eagerly, notwithstanding his advice to the contrary. While I ate, I overwhelmed him with questions which he promptly answered.

I then learned that my providential fall had brought me to the end of an almost perpendicular shaft; and as I had landed in the midst of a torrent of stones, the smallest of which would have been enough to crush me, the conclusion was that a loose portion of the rock-face had come down with me upon it. This frightful conveyance had carried me into the arms of my uncle, where I fell bleeding and unconscious.

"I am truly amazed," he said to me, "that you were not killed a thousand times over. For the love of God, let us never separate again, or we might not ever see each other again!"

"Never separate again"? Was the journey *not* over, then? I opened my eyes wide with astonishment, which immediately raised the question:

"What is the matter, Axel?"

"I have a question to ask you. You say that I am safe and sound?"

"Without a doubt."

"And I have all my limbs intact?"

"Certainly."

"And my head?"

"Your head, except for a few bruises, is perfectly all right and still sitting on your shoulders, where it ought to be."

"Well, I am afraid that my brain has been affected."

"Your brain?"

"Yes, I fear so. We haven't returned to surface of the Earth, have we?"

"No, of course not."

"Then I must be crazy; for I seem to see shafts of daylight. And I seem to hear the wind blowing outside, and waves breaking on a shore!"

"Ah! is that all?"

"Will you explain to me . . . ?"

"I can't explain the inexplicable. But you will soon see and understand that the science of geology has not yet learned all that there is to learn."

"Then let us go," I answered, rising quickly.

"No, Axel; the open air might be bad for you."

"Open air?"

"Yes; the wind is rather strong. I don't want you to risk exposing yourself."

"But I assure you that I am perfectly well."

"A little patience, my boy. A relapse might get us into trouble, and we have no time to lose, for the voyage may be a long one."

"The voyage?"

"Yes, rest today, and tomorrow we will set sail."

"Set sail?"

This last word made me almost leap to my feet. Sail? Was there a river, a lake, a sea nearby? Was there a ship anchored in some underground harbor?

My curiosity was now greatly aroused, and my uncle tried in vain to restrain me. When he saw that my impatience would do me more harm than answering my queries, he finally yielded.

I got dressed rapidly. As a precaution, I wrapped myself in a blanket and then walked out of the grotto.

At first I could see nothing at all. My eyes, unaccustomed to the light, closed themselves tight. When I was able to reopen them, I was more stupefied than surprised.

"The sea!" I cried.

"Yes," my uncle replied, "the Lidenbrock Sea! I don't suppose any other explorer will dispute my claim to name it since I was the first to discover it."

A vast expanse of water, the beginning of a huge lake or ocean, stretched away as far as the eye could see. The deeply indented shoreline offered to the swells which lapped against it a beach of fine golden sand, strewn with the small shells that were once inhabited by the first beings in creation. The waves broke on this shore with the hollow sonorous murmur peculiar to vast enclosed spaces. A light spray whipped up from the waves by a steady breeze moistened my face. On this gently sloping shore, about two hundred yards from the edge of the waves, began an abrupt wall of enormous cliffs that curved upward to an incredible height. Some of these, piercing the beach with their sharp spurs, formed capes and promontories that were worn away by the ceaseless action of the surf. Farther along the shore, the eye could discern their massive outline sharply defined against the hazy distant horizon.

It was a real ocean, with the same irregular shores as on the Earth above, but empty and fearsomely wild in appearance.

If my eyes were able to range far out over this great sea, it was because a strange light revealed its every detail. It was not the light of the Sun, with its dazzling shafts of brightness and the splendor of its rays; nor was it the pale and indistinct shimmer of the Moon, which is just a reflection without heat. No, the illuminating power of this light, its flickering diffusion, its bright, clear whiteness and its low temperature, indicated that it must be of electric origin. It was like an aurora borealis, a continuous cosmic phenomenon, filling a cavern large enough to contain an ocean.

The vault that was suspended above my head—the sky, if it could be called so—seemed to be composed of large clouds, moving and shifting banks of water vapor which, by virtue of condensation, must produce torrents of rain on certain days. I should have thought that under so powerful a pressure from the atmosphere there could be no evaporation; and yet, by a law unknown to me, here they were, great rolling clouds in the air above me. But at that specific moment "the weather was fine." The play of the electric light in these layers of cloud produced singular effects upon their upper strata. Their lower portions were deep in shadow; and often, between two levels a sudden flash of remarkable brilliancy could be seen. Yet it was not the Sun, and the light lacked heat. The general effect was sad and quite melancholy. Instead of a firmament shining with stars, I felt that beyond these clouds existed vast walls of granite, which seemed to overpower me with their weight, and that all this space, vast as it was, was not enough for the orbit of the humblest of satellites.

Then I remembered the theory of an English captain, who compared the Earth to a huge hollow sphere, whose interior air remained luminous because of the high pressure, and where two stars, Pluto and Proserpine, circled about on their mysterious orbits inside it. Could he have been right?

We were in reality imprisoned inside a cavern of colossal dimensions. Its width could not be estimated, since its shores widened as they stretched off into the distance; nor could its length be guessed at, for one's gaze was blocked by its misty horizon. As for its height, it must have been several leagues. Where this vault rested upon its granite base was not evident. But there was one cloud hanging in the atmosphere above whose height we approximated at 12,000 feet, a greater altitude than that of any terrestrial cloud, and no doubt due to the greater density of the air.

Obviously, the word "cavern" does not properly convey the idea of this immense space. But mere human words are inadequate for anyone who ventures into the deep abysses of Earth.

Besides, I did not know what geological theory could account for the existence of such a huge underground space. Had the cooling of the globe produced it? I knew of several famous caves from the descriptions of travelers, but had never heard of any that could rival the immense size of this one.

The grotto of Guachara, in Colombia, visited by Humboldt, did not give up the secret of its full depth to this philosopher, who investigated it to the depth of 2,500 feet, but it probably did not extend much farther. The immense Mammoth Cave in Kentucky is of gigantic proportions; its vaulted roof is said to rise 500 feet above an unfathomable lake, and spelunkers have explored its interior for more than 10 leagues without reaching its end. But what were these subterranean cavities compared to the one I was now contemplating with admiration, with its sky of luminous vapors, its bursts of electric light, and this great sea contained within its depths? My imagination was powerless before such immensity.

I gazed upon these wonders in silence. I could not find words to express my feelings. I felt as if I were on some distant planet such as Uranus or Neptune and witnessing phenomena which had no equivalent in my terrestrial experience. For such new sensations, new words were needed; and my imagination failed to supply them. I stared, I thought, I marveled, with a stupefaction mingled with a certain amount of fear.

The unexpectedness of this spectacle had brought back the color to my cheeks. I was healing myself with the medicine of astonishment, and my convalescence was aided by this unusual therapeutic treatment. In addition, the sharpness of the dense air was invigorating me, supplying extra oxygen to my lungs.

It should be easily understood that, after being confined in a narrow tunnel for forty-seven straight days, it was sheer bliss to breathe this moist, salty air. I had no regrets leaving behind my dark grotto.

My uncle, already accustomed to these many wonders, had ceased to marvel at them.

"You feel strong enough to walk around a bit?" he asked.

"Yes, certainly! Nothing could please me more!"

"Well, take my arm, Axel, and let's follow the windings of the shore."

I eagerly accepted, and we began to walk along the edges of this underground sea. On the left, there were huge pyramids of rock, piled high one upon another, producing a prodigious effect. Down their sides flowed countless waterfalls, flowing abundantly in clear gurgling cascades. A few light clouds of heated water vapor, leaping from rock to rock, denoted the location of a few hot springs. And, gliding down the gentle slopes, several fresh streams flowed softly to the common basin below.

Among these many watercourses I recognized our faithful travelling companion, the Hansbach, who merged here into the mighty sea, just as it had been doing since the beginning of the world.

"We shall miss him," I said, with a sigh.

"Bah!" said the professor. "It makes no difference, one guide or another."

I found this reply a bit ungrateful.

But at that moment my attention was drawn to an unexpected sight. At a distance of five hundred paces, at the end of a high promontory, appeared a tall and dense forest. It was composed of trees of moderate height, formed like umbrellas, with sharp geometrical outlines. The currents of wind seemed to have no effect upon their shape, and in the midst of the windy blasts they stood unmoved and firm, just like a stand of petrified cedars.

I hurried forward. I could find no name to identify this odd sort of tree. Were they some of the 200,000 species of plant already known, and did they claim a place of their own in the lacustrine flora? No! When we arrived under their shade, my surprise promptly turned into admiration.

There standing before me were indeed products of the Earth, but of gigantic stature. My uncle identified them right away for what they were.

"It is only a forest of mushrooms," said he.

And he was right! But imagine the huge size attained by these plants, which prefer a warm, moist climate. I knew that the *Lycoperdon gianteum* attains, according to Bulliard, a circumference of eight or nine feet; but here were pale mushrooms, thirty to forty feet high, and crowned with a cap of the same diameter! There were thousands of them. No light could penetrate through their dense cover, and complete darkness reigned in the shade of these giants since they were crowded together like the round, thatched roofs of an African city.

I wanted to venture further beneath them, and a chill fell upon me as soon as I set foot under those fleshy arches. For a half an hour we wandered in their damp shadows, and it was with a true feeling of relief when we arrived once more upon the sea shore.

But the vegetation of this subterranean realm was not confined to mushrooms. Farther on we saw other groups of trees with colorless foliage. They were easy to recognize. They were lowly shrubs of Earth, but here they had grown to gigantic size: *lycopodia*, a hundred feet high; huge *sigillaria*; tree ferns as tall as our fir-trees in northern latitudes; *lepidodendrons*, with cylindrical forked stems ending in long leaves and bristling with rough hairs like those of a monstrous succulent.

"Wonderful, magnificent, splendid!" exclaimed my uncle. "Here is the entire flora of the Secondary Period of the world—the transition period. The humble garden plants that we see today were once tall trees in the early ages. Look, Axel, and admire it all! No botanist ever had such a feast as this!"

"You are right, my uncle. Providence seems to have preserved in this immense greenhouse all the antediluvian plants that our scientists have so patiently reconstructed."

"You're correct, my boy. It is like a greenhouse; but you might add that it's also a zoo!"

"A zoo?"

"Yes; no doubt about it. Look at that dust under our feet; see the bones scattered on the ground?"

"Bones!" I cried. "Yes! of prehistoric animals!"

I eagerly examined these primeval remains, made of indestructible calcium phosphate, and without a moment's hesitation I began to name these monstrous bones, which lay scattered about like decayed trunks of trees.

"Here is the lower jaw of a mastodon," I said. "These are the molar teeth of the *deinotherium*; this femur must have belonged to the greatest of those beasts, the *megatherium*. It truly is a zoo, for these bones were not brought here by some cataclysm. The animals to which they belonged roamed on the shores of this subterranean sea, under the shade of those arborescent trees. Here are entire skeletons. And yet . . ."

"And yet?" said my uncle.

"And yet I cannot understand the appearance of these quadrupeds in a granite cavern."

"Why not?"

"Because animal life only existed on Earth during the Secondary Period, when the sedimentary soil was formed by alluvial deposits, replacing the igneous rocks of the Primitive Period."

"Well, Axel, a very simple answer to your objection is that this soil is indeed sedimentary."

"What! at such a depth below the surface of the Earth?"

"Without a doubt; and there is a perfectly good geological explanation for it. At a certain period the Earth consisted only of a flexible crust, alternately moving upwards or downwards as it was acted upon by the laws of attraction and gravitation. There were probably many subsidences in the outer crust, and a portion of the sedimentary deposits was carried down into these sudden openings."

"That must be so," I agreed. "But if antediluvian creatures lived in these underground regions, who is to say that one of these monsters may not still be roaming through these gloomy forests, or hidden behind these steep rocks?"

As this idea occurred to me, I surveyed, not without a certain anxiousness, the entire horizon before me; but no living creature could be seen on these deserted shores.

I felt rather tired, and went to sit down at the end of a promontory, at the foot of which the waves were breaking noisily. From there I could see every part of the bay along the coast. At its back, there was a little harbor lying between the pyramidal cliffs, its still waters calm and sheltered from the wind. A brig and two or three schooners might have anchored there in safety. I almost expected to see some vessel coming out under full sail and taking to the open sea with the southern breeze behind her.

But this illusion quickly faded. We really were the only living creatures in this subterranean world. When the wind lulled, a deeper silence than that of the deserts fell upon the arid, naked rocks and weighed upon the surface of the ocean. In those moments, I tried to see through the distant mist, to peer through that mysterious curtain that hung across the horizon. So many questions arose to my lips! Where did this sea end? Where did it lead to? Could we ever explore its opposite shore?

My uncle seemed to have no doubts that we could. As for me, I both desired and feared it.

After spending an hour in contemplation of this marvelous spectacle, we walked back up the shore to return to the grotto. And it was with the strangest thoughts that I later fell into a deep sleep.

The next morning I awoke feeling completely healed. I thought a bath would do me good, so I went to immerse myself for a few minutes in the waters of this Mediterranean sea, a name which it surely deserved better than any other.

I came back to breakfast with a good appetite. Hans was a good cook for our limited menu; he had water and fire at his disposal, so he could vary our bill of fare now and then. For dessert he gave us several cups of coffee, and never was coffee so delicious.

"Now," said my uncle, "it is nearly high tide, and we must not lose the opportunity to study this phenomenon."

"The tide?" I asked.

"Absolutely."

"Can the influence of the Sun and the Moon be felt down here?"

"Why not? Are not all bodies subject to the universal attraction of gravity? This mass of water cannot escape the general law. So, in spite of the heavy atmospheric pressure on its surface, you will see it rise like the Atlantic itself."

At this moment we reached the sandy beach, where the waves were slowly moving further up onto the shore.

"Here the tide is certainly rising," I observed.

"Yes, Axel; and judging by these ridges of foam, you can see that the sea will rise about ten feet."

"This is incredible!" I said.

"No; it is quite natural."

"You may say so, dear Uncle; but to me it is most extraordinary, and I can hardly believe my eyes! Who would ever have imagined that, under the Earth's crust, there would be an ocean with ebbing and flowing tides, with winds and storms?"

"Well," replied my uncle, "is there any scientific reason against it?"

"No, I can see none, provided that the theory of a central fire at the Earth's core is abandoned."

"So then, at least thus far, Sir Humphry Davy's theory is confirmed?"

"Evidently. There seems to be nothing to contradict the existence of seas and continents in the interior of the Earth."

"Yes, but uninhabited."

"To be sure, but why shouldn't these waters serve as habitat for fishes of unknown species?"

"But we have not seen any yet."

"Well, let's rig up some lines, and see if our hooks will have the same success here as they do in sublunary oceans."

"We will try, Axel, for we must penetrate all secrets of these newly discovered regions."

"But exactly where are we, Uncle? I haven't yet asked you that question, and your instruments must be able to furnish the answer."

"Horizontally, 885 miles from Iceland."

"As much as that?"

"I'm sure that I'm not more than a half-mile off."

"And does the compass still show our direction as south-east?"

"Yes, with a westerly deviation of nineteen degrees forty-two minutes, just like on the surface. As for its dip, there is something very curious going on which I have been observing carefully: the needle, instead of dipping towards the Pole as in the northern hemisphere, is now pointing upwards instead."

"Would you then conclude," I said, "that the magnetic pole is somewhere between the surface of the globe and the point where we are right now?"

"Exactly. And if we were beneath the polar regions and reached that spot near the seventieth parallel where Sir James Ross discovered the magnetic pole, we should see the needle point straight up. Therefore that mysterious center of attraction is not located at a very great depth."

"Indeed, and that is a fact which science has never suspected."

"Science, my boy, is built upon errors; but they are errors that are good to make, for they lead little by little to the truth."

"What depth have we now reached?"

"We are eighty-seven miles below the surface."

"So," I said, examining the map, "the mountainous part of Scotland is now over our heads, where the snow-covered peaks of the Grampians rise up to their incredible heights."

"Yes," answered the professor laughing. "It is rather a heavy weight to bear, but the vault above us is very solid. The Great Architect of the universe has constructed it with the best materials; no human builder could have given it so wide a span! What are the great arches of our bridges and cathedrals, compared with this vast nave with a radius of several miles, beneath which an entire tempest-tossed ocean can flow at its ease?"

"Oh, I am not afraid that it'll fall down upon my head. But now, dear Uncle, what are your plans? Are you not thinking of returning to the surface now?"

"Return? Certainly not! We will continue our journey, seeing that everything has gone so well thus far."

"But how are we to get down below this liquid plain?"

"Oh, I don't intend to plunge into it head first. But if all oceans are, technically speaking, only large lakes, since they are encompassed by land, then of course this internal sea must be surrounded by granite banks."

"Yes, that is surely the case."

"Well, on the opposite shore we'll doubtlessly find new passages opening up."

"Just how wide do you suppose this sea to be?"

"Eighty or a hundred miles."

"Ah!" I said, thinking to myself that this estimate might well be inaccurate.

"Therefore, we have no time to lose, and we shall set sail tomorrow!"

I instinctively looked about for a ship that would carry us. "Set sail? Fine! But on what boat are we going to book passage?"

"It will not be a boat at all, my boy, but a good, well-made raft."

"A raft?" I exclaimed. "A raft would be just as impossible to build as a boat, and I don't see . . ."

"I know you don't see, Axel, but you might hear if you would listen."

"Hear?"

"Yes, don't you hear the hammer blows? Hans is already busy at it!"

"What? Has he already felled some trees?"

"Oh, the trees were already down. Come along and you'll see for yourself."

After a quarter of an hour's walk to the other side of the promontory which formed the little natural harbor, I could now see Hans at work. A few more steps, and I was at his side. To my great surprise, a half-finished raft was already lying on the sand. Its timbers were made of a peculiar kind of wood, and the ground was strewn with a great number of planks, knees, and frames of all sorts. There was almost enough there to build a whole fleet.

"Uncle, what kind of wood is this?" I asked.

"It is fir, pine, or birch, all sorts of northern conifers, petrified by the sea water."

"Is that possible?"

"Yes, it is called *surtarbrandur*, or fossilized wood."

"But then, like lignite, it must be as hard as stone and unable to float?"

"Sometimes that happens. Some of these woods become true anthracites; but others, such as this, have only gone through the first stage of fossil transformation. Look here," added my uncle as he threw one of these precious fragments into the sea.

The piece of wood, after disappearing for a moment, returned to the surface and bobbed to and fro in the waves.

"Are you convinced?" said my uncle.

"Convinced that this is incredible!"

By the next evening, thanks to the skill of our guide, the raft was finished. It was ten feet long by five feet wide; the planks of surtarbrandur, tightly bound together with ropes, offered a solid surface; and, when launched, this improvised vessel floated easily on the waters of the Lidenbrock Sea.

H. G. WELLS

The Star

• • • •

{1897}

Along with Jules Verne, H(erbert) G(eorge) Wells is generally acknowledged as the originator of modern science fiction. Wells was born in 1866 in southeastern England, into a lower-middle-class family without access to elite classical education. Winning a scholarship to the Normal School of Science (which was later to become the Royal College of Science), where he studied with T. H. Huxley, Darwin's most brilliant and prolific advocate in Britain, Wells was drawn to evolutionary biology. He began his career as a writer with journalistic articles, in which he posed thought experiments about the future of humanity from the perspective of both biological and social evolution. In seven phenomenally productive years between 1895 and 1901, Wells published six "scientific romances" that established some of the most enduring archetypal scenarios for later science fiction: *The Time Machine* (1895), *The Island of Dr. Moreau* (1896), *The Invisible Man* (1897), *The War of the Worlds* (1898), *When the Sleeper Wakes* (1899), and *The First Men in the Moon* (1901). In each book, Wells addressed contemporary anxieties about the way technology and scientific theory were transforming the world and the human species, linking philosophical speculations based on science with Gothic effects. In *The Time Machine*, for example, Wells used the device of time travel to depict the future "devolution" of the classes of industrial capitalism into degenerate subspecies of humanity; in *The War of the Worlds*, he used the theme of a Martian invasion of Earth to speculate on the fate of humanity as it becomes increasingly dependent on technology.

Unlike his elder contemporary Verne, Wells was especially interested in the potential for radical transformations of human biology and society in the future. He was active in the democratic Socialist movement, and much of his fiction experiments with envisioning credible utopias created and managed by enlightened technocratic elites. Chief among these was his vision of a world government, which gained many adherents in the years before World War II. Few literary figures matched Wells's influence on the political culture of his day. His work was read by world leaders; he corresponded with Franklin Delano Roosevelt and Winston Churchill; he interviewed Lenin and Stalin. His vision of an air war fought with dirigibles in *The War in the Air* (1908) profoundly affected European military strategies between the two world wars. His description of nuclear fission in *The World Set Free* (1914) was credited by its discoverer, Leo Szilard, as his source of inspiration. A famous radio broadcast of *The War of the Worlds* by Orson Welles's Mercury Theater on Halloween in 1938 caused a mass panic in the United States, a phenomenon that many commentators consider a signal event in the history of mass media's power to manipulate populations.

Wells first published "The Star" in the Christmas 1897 issue of *The Graphic*. Typical of his early sf, it is a parable wrapped in the mantle of scientific exposition. The theme of a heavenly body moving on a collision course with Earth was first conceived a few years earlier by the French writer-astronomer Camille Flammarion in his novel *La fin du monde* (translated as *Omega*) in 1893–94. Like Wells, Flammarion imagined that the immense destructiveness of the passing comet would be followed by a golden age of moral development in the human species. Wells's version, which notably lacks an individual hero or a technological rescue project, displays all the characteristics of British scientific romance, described by literary historian Brian Stableford as a minimization of individual heroics, a focus on evolutionary perspectives, a skepticism about the future of the species, and a sense of passivity in the face of cosmic phenomena. Its vision of humanity's essential helplessness in the face of a catastrophe from space has been echoed many times in the genre's history, notably in J. G. Ballard's "The Cage of Sand" (1962).

It was on the first day of the New Year that the announcement was made, almost simultaneously from three observatories, that the motion of the planet Neptune, the outermost of all the planets that wheel about the sun, had become very erratic. Ogilvy had already called attention to a suspected retardation in its velocity in December. Such a piece of news was scarcely calculated to interest a world the greater portion of whose inhabitants were unaware of the existence of the planet Neptune, nor outside the astronomical profession did the subsequent discovery of a faint remote speck of light in the region of the perturbed planet cause any very great excitement. Scientific people, however, found the intelligence remarkable enough, even before it became known that the new body was rapidly growing larger and brighter, that its motion was quite different from the orderly progress of the planets, and that the deflection of Neptune and its satellite was becoming now of an unprecedented kind.

Few people without a training in science can realize the huge isolation of the solar system. The sun with its specks of planets, its dust of planetoids, and its impalpable comets, swims in a vacant immensity that almost defeats the imagination. Beyond the orbit of Neptune there is space, vacant so far as human observation has penetrated, without warmth or light or sound, blank emptiness, for twenty million times a million miles. That is the smallest estimate of the distance to be traversed before the very nearest of the stars is attained. And, saving a few comets more unsubstantial than the thinnest flame, no matter had ever to human knowledge crossed this gulf of space, until early in the twentieth century, this strange wanderer appeared. A vast mass of matter it was, bulky, heavy, rushing without warning out of the black mystery of the sky into the radiance of the sun. By the second day it was clearly visible to any decent instrument, as a speck with a barely sensible diameter, in the constellation Leo near Regulus. In a little while an opera glass could attain it.

On the third day of the new year the newspaper readers of two hemispheres were made aware for the first time of the real importance of this unusual apparition in the heavens. "A Planetary Collision," one London paper headed the news, and proclaimed Duchaine's opinion that this strange new planet would probably collide with Neptune. The leader writers enlarged upon the topic; so that in most of the capitals of the world, on January 3rd, there was an expectation, however vague, of some imminent phenomenon in the sky; and as the night followed the sunset round the globe, thousands of men turned their eyes skyward to see—the old familiar stars just as they had always been.

Until it was dawn in London and Pollux setting and the stars overhead grown pale. The Winter's dawn it was, a sickly filtering accumulation of daylight, and the light of gas and candles shone yellow in the windows to show where people were astir. But the yawning policeman saw the thing, the busy crowds in the markets stopped agape, workmen going to their work betimes, milkmen, the drivers of news-carts, dissipation going home jaded and pale, homeless wanderers, sentinels on their beats, and in the country, laborers trudging afield, poachers slinking home, all over the dusky quickening country it could be seen—and out at sea by seamen watching for the day—a great white star, come suddenly into the westward sky!

Brighter it was than any star in our skies; brighter than the evening star at its brightest. It still glowed out white and large, no mere twinkling spot of light, but a small round clear shining disc, an hour after the day had come. And where science has not reached, men stared and feared, telling one another of the wars and pestilences that are foreshadowed by these fiery signs in the Heavens. Sturdy Boers, dusky Hottentots, Gold Coast Negroes, Frenchmen, Spaniards, Portuguese, stood in the warmth of the sunrise watching the setting of this strange new star.

And in a hundred observatories there had been suppressed excitement, rising almost to shouting pitch, as the two remote bodies had rushed together; and a hurrying to and fro, to gather photographic apparatus and spectroscope, and this appliance and that, to record this novel astonishing sight, the destruction of a world. For it was a world, a sister planet of our earth, far greater than our earth indeed, that had so suddenly flashed into flaming death. Neptune it was, had been struck, fairly and squarely, by the strange planet from outer space and the heat of the concussion had incontinently turned two solid globes into one vast mass of incandescence. Round the world that day, two hours before the dawn, went the pallid great white star, fading only as it sank westward and the sun mounted above it. Everywhere men marveled at it, but of all those who saw it none could have marveled more than those sailors, habitual watchers of the stars, who far away at sea had heard nothing of its advent and saw it now rise like a pigmy moon and climb zenithward and hang overhead and sink westward with the passing of the night.

And when next it rose over Europe everywhere were crowds of watchers on hilly slopes, on house-roofs, in open spaces, staring eastward for the rising of the great new star. It rose with a white glow in front of it, like the glare of a white fire, and those who had seen it come into existence the night before cried out at the sight of it. "It is larger," they cried. "It is brighter!" And, indeed the moon a quarter full and sinking in the west was in its apparent size beyond comparison, but scarcely in all its breadth had it as much brightness now as the little circle of the strange new star.

"It is brighter!" cried the people clustering in the streets. But in the dim observatories the watchers held their breath and peered at one another. "*It is nearer*," they said. "*Nearer!*"

And voice after voice repeated, "It is nearer," and the clicking telegraph took that up, and it trembled along telephone wires, and in a thousand cities grimy compositors fingered the type. "It is nearer." Men writing in offices, struck with a strange realization, flung down their pens, men talking in a thousand places suddenly came upon a grotesque possibility in those words, "It is nearer." It hurried along wakening streets, it was shouted down the frost-stilled ways of quiet villages; men who had read these things from the throbbing tape stood in yellow-lit doorways shouting the news to the passersby. "It is nearer." Pretty women, flushed and glittering, heard the news told jestingly between the dances, and feigned an intelligent interest they did not feel. "Nearer! Indeed. How curious! How very, very clever people must be to find out things like that!"

Lonely tramps faring through the wintry night murmured those words to comfort themselves—looking skyward. "It has need to be nearer, for the night's as cold as charity. Don't seem much warmth from it if it *is* nearer, all the same."

"What is a new star to me?" cried the weeping woman kneeling beside her dead.

The schoolboy, rising early for his examination work, puzzled it out for himself—with the great white star shining broad and bright through the frost-flowers of his window. "Centrifugal, centripetal," he said, with his chin on his fist. "Stop a planet in its flight, rob it of its centrifugal force, what then? Centripetal has it, and down it falls into the sun! And this—!

"Do *we* come in the way? I wonder—"

The light of that day went the way of its brethren, and with the later watches of the frosty darkness rose the strange star again. And it was now so bright that the waxing moon seemed but a pale yellow ghost of itself, hanging huge in the sunset. In a South African city a great man had married, and the streets were alight to welcome his return with his bride. "Even the skies have illuminated," said the flatterer. Under Capricorn, two Negro lovers, daring the wild beasts and evil spirits, for love of one another, crouched together in a cane brake where the fire-flies hovered. "That is our star," they whispered, and felt strangely comforted by the sweet brilliance of its light.

The master mathematician sat in his private room and pushed the papers from him. His calculations were already finished. In a small white phial there still remained a little of the drug that had kept him awake and active for four long nights. Each day, serene, explicit, patient as ever, he had given his lecture to his students, and then had come back at once to this momentous calculation. His face was grave, a little drawn and hectic from his drugged activity. For some time he seemed lost in thought. Then he went to the window, and the blind went up with a click. Halfway up the sky, over the clustering roofs, chimneys and steeples of the city, hung the star.

He looked at it as one might look into the eyes of a brave enemy. "You may kill me," he said after a silence. "But I can hold you—and all the universe for that matter—in the grip of this little brain. I would not change. Even now."

He looked at the little phial. "There will be no need of sleep again," he said. The next day at noon, punctual to the minute, he entered his lecture theatre, put his hat on the end of the table as his habit was, and carefully selected a large piece of chalk. It was a joke among his students that he could not lecture without that piece of chalk to fumble in his fingers, and once he had been stricken to impotence by their hiding his supply. He came and looked under his gray eyebrows at the rising tiers of young fresh faces, and spoke with his accustomed studied commonness of phrasing. "Circumstances have arisen—circumstances beyond my control," he said and paused, "which will debar me from completing the course I had designed. It would seem, gentlemen, if I may put the thing clearly and briefly, that—Man has lived in vain."

The students glanced at one another. Had they heard aright? Mad? Raised eyebrows and grinning lips there were, but one or two faces remained intent upon his calm gray-fringed face. "It will be interesting," he was saying, "to devote this morning to an exposition, so far as I can make it clear to you, of the calculations that have led me to this conclusion. Let us assume—"

He turned towards the blackboard, meditating a diagram in the way that was usual to him. "What was that about 'lived in vain'?" whispered one student to another. "Listen," said the other, nodding towards the lecturer.

And presently they began to understand.

That night the star rose later, for its proper eastward motion had carried it some way across Leo towards Virgo, and its brightness was so great that the sky became a luminous blue as it rose, and every star was hidden in its turn, save only Jupiter near the zenith, Capella, Aldebaran, Sirius and the pointers of the Bear. It was very white and beautiful. In many parts of the world that night a pallid halo encircled it about. It was perceptibly larger; in the clear refractive sky of the tropics it seemed as if it were nearly a quarter the size of the moon. The frost was still on the ground in England, but the world was as brightly lit as if it were midsummer moonlight. One could see to read quite ordinary print by that cold clear light, and in the cities the lamps burnt yellow and wan.

And everywhere the world was awake that night, and throughout Christendom a somber murmur hung in the keen air over the countryside like the belling of bees in the heather, and this murmurous tumult grew to a clangor in the cities. It was the tolling of the bells in a million belfry towers and steeples, summoning the people to sleep no more, to sin no more, but to gather in their churches and pray. And overhead, growing larger and brighter as the earth rolled on its way and the night passed, rose the dazzling star.

And the streets and houses were alight in all the cities, the shipyards glared, and whatever roads led to high country were lit and crowded all night long. And in all the seas about the civilized lands, ships with throbbing engines, and ships with bellying sails, crowded with men and living creatures, were standing out to ocean and the north. For already the warning of the master mathematician had been telegraphed all over the world, and translated into a hundred tongues. The new planet and Neptune, locked in a fiery embrace, were whirling headlong, ever faster and faster towards the sun. Already every second this blazing mass flew a hundred miles, and every second its terrific velocity increased. As it flew now, indeed, it must pass a hundred million of miles wide of the earth and scarcely affect it. But near its destined path, as yet only slightly perturbed, spun the mighty planet Jupiter and his moons sweeping splendid round the sun. Every moment now the attraction between the fiery star and the greatest of the planets grew stronger. And the result of that attraction? Inevitably Jupiter would be deflected from its orbit into an elliptical path, and the burning star, swung by his attraction wide of its sunward rush, would "describe a curved path" and perhaps collide with, and certainly pass very close to, our earth. "Earthquakes, volcanic outbreaks, cyclones, sea waves, floods, and a steady rise in temperature to I know not what limit"—so prophesied the master mathematician.

And overhead, to carry out his words, lonely and cold and livid, blazed the star of the coming doom.

To many who stared at it that night until their eyes ached, it seemed that it was visibly approaching. And that night, too, the weather changed, and the frost that had gripped all Central Europe and France and England softened towards a thaw.

But you must not imagine because I have spoken of people praying through the night and people going aboard ships and people fleeing toward mountainous country that the whole world was already in a terror because of the star. As a matter of fact, use and wont still ruled the world, and save for the talk of idle moments and the splendor of the night, nine human beings out of ten were still busy at their common occupations. In all the cities the shops, save one here and there, opened and closed at their proper hours, the doctor and the undertaker plied their trades, the workers gathered in the factories, soldiers drilled, scholars studied, lovers sought one another, thieves lurked and fled, politicians planned their schemes. The presses of the newspapers roared through the night, and many a priest of this church and that would not open his holy building to further what he considered a foolish panic. The newspapers insisted on the lesson of the year 1000—for then, too, people had anticipated the end. The star was no star—mere gas—a comet; and were it a star it could not possibly strike the earth. There was no precedent for such a thing. Common sense was sturdy everywhere, scornful, jesting, a little inclined to persecute the obdurate fearful. That night, at seven-fifteen by Greenwich time, the star would be at its nearest to Jupiter. Then the world would see the turn things would take. The master mathematician's grim warnings were treated by many as so much mere elaborate self-advertisement. Common sense at last, a little heated by argument, signified its unalterable convictions by going to bed. So, too, barbarism and savagery, already tired of the novelty, went about their nightly business, and save for a howling dog here and there, the beast world left the star unheeded.

And yet, when at last the watchers in the European States saw the star rise, an hour later it is true, but no larger than it had been the night before, there were still plenty awake to laugh at the master mathematician—to take the danger as if it had passed.

But hereafter the laughter ceased. The star grew—it grew with a terrible steadiness hour after hour, a little larger each hour, a little nearer the midnight zenith, and brighter and brighter, until it had turned night into a second day. Had it come straight to the earth instead of in a curved path, had it lost no velocity to Jupiter, it must have leapt the intervening gulf in a day, but as it was it took five days altogether to come by our planet. The next night it had become a third the size of the moon before it set to English eyes, and the thaw was assured. It rose over America near the size of the moon, but blinding white to look at, and *hot*; and a breath of hot wind blew now with its rising and gathering strength, and in Virginia, and Brazil, and down the St. Lawrence valley, it shone intermittently through a driving reek of thunder-clouds, flickering violet lightning, and hail unprecedented. In Manitoba was a thaw and devastating floods. And upon all the mountains of the earth the snow and ice began to melt that night, and all the rivers coming out of high country flowed thick and turbid, and soon—in their upper reaches—with swirling trees and the bodies of beasts and men. They rose steadily, steadily in the ghostly brilliance, and came trickling over their banks at last, behind the flying population of their valleys.

And along the coast of Argentina and up the South Atlantic the tides were higher than had ever been in the memory of man, and the storms drove the waters in many cases scores of miles inland, drowning whole cities. And so great grew the heat during the night that the rising of the sun was like the coming of a shadow. The earthquakes began and grew until all down America from the Arctic Circle to Cape Horn hillsides were sliding, fissures were opening, and houses and walls crumbling to destruction. The whole side of Cotopaxi slipped out in one vast convulsion, and a tumult of lava poured out so high and broad and swift and liquid that in one day it reached the sea.

So the star, with the wan moon in its wake, marched across the Pacific, trailed the thunderstorms like the hem of a robe, and the growing tidal wave that toiled behind it, frothing and eager, poured over island and island and swept them clear of men. Until that wave came at last—in a blinding light and with the breath of a furnace, swift and terrible it came—a wall of water, fifty feet high, roaring hungrily, upon the long coasts of Asia, and swept inland across the plains of China. For a space the star, hotter now and larger and brighter than the sun in its strength, showed with pitiless brilliance the wide and populous country; towns and villages with their pagodas and trees, roads, wide cultivated fields, millions of sleepless people staring in helpless terror at the incandescent sky; and then, low and growing, came the murmur of the flood. And thus it was with millions of men that night—a flight nowhither, with limbs heavy with heat and breath fierce and scant, and the flood like a wall swift and white behind. And then death.

China was lit glowing white, but over Japan and Java and all the islands of Eastern Asia the great star was a ball of dull red fire because of the steam and smoke and ashes the volcanoes were spouting forth to salute its coming. Above was the lava, hot gases and ash, and below the seething floods, and the whole earth swayed and rumbled with the earthquake shocks. Soon the immemorial snows of Tibet and the Himalaya were melting and pouring down by ten million deepening converging channels upon the plains of Burmah and Hindostan. The tangled summits of the Indian jungles were aflame in a thousand places, and below the hurrying waters around the stems were dark objects that still struggled feebly and reflected the blood-red tongues of fire. And in a rudderless confusion a multitude of men and women fled down the broad river-ways to that one last hope of men—the open sea.

Larger grew the star, and larger, hotter, and brighter with a terrible swiftness now. The tropical ocean had lost its phosphorescence, and the whirling steam rose in ghostly wreaths from the black waves that plunged incessantly, speckled with storm-tossed ships.

And then came a wonder. It seemed to those who in Europe watched for the rising of the star that the world must have ceased its rotation. In a thousand open spaces of down and upland the people who had fled thither from the floods and the falling houses and sliding slopes of hill watched for that rising in vain. Hour followed hour through a terrible suspense, and the star rose not. Once again men set their eyes upon the old constellations they had counted lost to them forever. In England it was hot and clear overhead, though the ground quivered perpetually, but in the tropics, Sirius and Capella and Aldebaran showed through a veil of steam. And when at last the great star rose near ten hours late, the sun rose close upon it, and in the center of its white heart was a disc of black.

Over Asia it was the star had begun to fall behind the movement of the sky, and then suddenly, as it hung over India, its light had been veiled. All the plain of India from the mouth of the Indus to the mouths of the Ganges was a shallow waste of shining water that night, out of which rose temples and palaces, mounds and hills, black with people. Every minaret was a clustering mass of people, who fell one by one into the turbid waters, as heat and terror overcame them. The whole land seemed a-wailing and suddenly there swept a shadow across that furnace of despair, and a breath of cold wind, and a gathering of clouds, out of the cooling air. Men looking up, near blinded, at the star, saw that a black disc was creeping across the light. It was the moon, coming between the star and the earth. And even as men cried to God at this respite, out of the East with a strange inexplicable swiftness sprang the sun. And then star, sun and moon rushed together across the heavens.

So it was that presently, to the European watchers, star and sun rose close upon each other, drove headlong for a space and then slower, and at last came to rest, star and sun merged into one glare of flame at the zenith of the sky. The moon no longer eclipsed the star but was lost to sight in the brilliance of the sky. And though those who were still alive regarded it for the most part with that dull stupidity that hunger, fatigue, heat and despair engender, there were still men who could perceive the meaning of these signs. Star and earth had been at their nearest, had swung about one another, and the star had passed. Already it was receding, swifter and swifter, in the last stage of its headlong journey downward into the sun.

And then the clouds gathered, blotting out the vision of the sky, the thunder and lightning wove a garment round the world; all over the earth was such a downpour of rain as men had never before seen, and where the volcanoes flared red against the cloud canopy there descended torrents of mud. Everywhere the waters were pouring off the land, leaving mud-silted ruins, and the earth littered like a storm-worn beach with all that had floated, and the dead bodies of the men and brutes, its children. For days the water streamed off the land, sweeping away soil and trees and houses in the way, and piling huge dykes and scooping out Titanic gullies over the countryside. Those were the days of darkness that followed the star and the heat. All through them, and for many weeks and months, the earthquakes continued.

But the star had passed, and men, hunger-driven and gathering courage only slowly, might creep back to their ruined cities, buried granaries, and sodden fields. Such few ships as had escaped the storms of that time came stunned and shattered and sounding their way cautiously through the new marks and shoals of once familiar ports. And as the storms subsided men perceived that everywhere the days were hotter than of yore, and the sun larger, and the moon, shrunk to a third of its former size, took now fourscore days between its new and new.

But of the new brotherhood that grew presently among men, of the saving of laws and books and machines, of the strange change that had come over Iceland and Greenland and the shores of Baffin's Bay, so that the sailors coming there presently found them green and gracious, and could scarce believe their eyes, this story does not tell. Nor of the movement of mankind now that the earth was hotter, northward and southward towards the poles of the earth. It concerns itself only with the coming and the passing of the Star.

The Martian astronomers—for there are astronomers on Mars, although they are very different beings from men—were naturally profoundly interested by these things. They saw them from their own standpoint of course. "Considering the mass and temperature of the missile that was flung through our solar system into the sun," one wrote, "it is astonishing what a little damage the earth, which it missed so narrowly, has sustained. All the familiar continental markings and the masses of the seas remain intact, and indeed the only difference seems to be a shrinkage of the white discoloration (supposed to be frozen water) round either pole." Which only shows how small the vastest of human catastrophes may seem, at a distance of a few million miles.

E. M. Forster

The Machine Stops

{1909}

E(dward) M(organ) Forster (1879–1970) was one of the most critically acclaimed British novelists in the first quarter of the twentieth century. His novels *A Room with a View* (1908), *Howards End* (1910), and *A Passage to India* (1924) are considered canonical works of modernist realism—*Passage* is one of the first to openly confront the racism of British colonial rule in India.

"The Machine Stops," Forster's only foray into science fiction, has become a classic of dystopian literature. Forster's image of a future society of human beings governed by an autonomous Machine built to satisfy all their needs, and consequently sapping them of all natural drives, was the first in a long line of dystopian visions based on the model of the beehive that would eventually include the Russian Yevgeny Zamyatin's One State in *We* (1921), Aldous Huxley's *Brave New World* (1932), George Orwell's Oceania in *1984* (1949), *Star Trek*'s Borg, and *WALL-E*'s Axiom (2008). Forster claimed that he was inspired to write "The Machine Stops" as "a counterblast to one of the heavens of H. G. Wells"—probably to *A Modern Utopia* (1905)—in which Wells imagined a future utopian society managed by a technocratic elite. Forster had been influenced by Samuel Butler's satirical utopia, *Erewhon* (1872), in which human beings, expecting their machines might someday evolve into intelligent beings destined to dominate humanity, ban them from society. "The Machine Stops" is one of the first examples of a dystopia, a futuristic monitory parable that dramatizes the consequences of a troubling social trend in the present day. Distant echoes of its vision of an empty, closed-off, claustrophobic future can be heard in Harlan Ellison's "'Repent, Harlequin!' Said the Ticktockman" (1965).

Adapting the Frankenstein theme of a science usurping the powers of nature to Plato's myth of the cave, "The Machine Stops" became the model for the "if this goes on . . ." story that was one of the dominant forms of later science fiction. Although Forster was personally not unsympathetic to socialism, the diction of "The Machine Stops" clearly links it to the conservative Victorian tradition that viewed technology as a threat to basic humanistic values.

PART I

The Air-Ship

Imagine, if you can, a small room, hexagonal in shape, like the cell of a bee. It is lighted neither by window nor by lamp, yet it is filled with a soft radiance. There are no apertures for ventilation, yet the air is fresh. There are no musical instruments, and yet, at the moment that my meditation opens, this room is throbbing with melodious sounds. An armchair is in the center, by its side a reading-desk—that is all the furniture. And in the armchair there sits a swaddled lump of flesh—a woman, about five feet high, with a face as white as a fungus. It is to her that the little room belongs.

An electric bell rang.

The woman touched a switch and the music was silent.

"I suppose I must see who it is," she thought, and set her chair in motion. The chair, like the music, was worked by machinery and it rolled her to the other side of the room, where the bell still rang importunately.

"Who is it?" she called. Her voice was irritable, for she had been interrupted often since the music began. She knew several thousand people; in certain directions human intercourse had advanced enormously.

But when she listened into the receiver, her white face wrinkled into smiles, and she said:

"Very well. Let us talk. I will isolate myself. I do not expect anything important will happen for the next five minutes—for I can give you fully five minutes, Kuno. Then I must deliver my lecture on 'Music during the Australian Period.'"

She touched the isolation knob, so that no one else could speak to her. Then she touched the lighting apparatus, and the little room was plunged into darkness.

"Be quick!" she called, her irritation returning. "Be quick, Kuno; here I am in the dark wasting my time."

But it was fully fifteen seconds before the round plate that she held in her hands began to glow. A faint blue light shot across it, darkening to purple, and presently she could see the image of her son, who lived on the other side of the earth, and he could see her.

"Kuno, how slow you are."

He smiled gravely.

"I really believe you enjoy dawdling."

"I have called you before, mother, but you were always busy or isolated. I have something particular to say."

"What is it, dearest boy? Be quick. Why could you not send it by pneumatic post?"

"Because I prefer saying such a thing. I want—"

"Well?"

"I want you to come and see me."

Vashti watched his face in the blue plate.

"But I can see you!" she exclaimed. "What more do you want?"

"I want to see you not through the Machine," said Kuno. "I want to speak to you not through the wearisome Machine."

"Oh, hush!" said his mother, vaguely shocked. "You mustn't say anything against the Machine."

"Why not?"

"One mustn't."

"You talk as if a god had made the Machine," cried the other. "I believe that you pray to it when you are unhappy. Men made it, do not forget that. Great men, but men. The Machine is much, but it is not everything. I see something like you in this plate, but I do not see you. I hear something like you through this telephone, but I do not hear you. That is why I want you to come. Pay me a visit, so that we can meet face to face, and talk about the hopes that are in my mind."

She replied that she could scarcely spare the time for a visit.

"The air-ship barely takes two days to fly between me and you."

"I dislike air-ships."

"Why?"

"I dislike seeing the horrible brown earth, and the sea, and the stars when it is dark. I get no ideas in an air-ship."

"I do not get them anywhere else."

"What kind of ideas can the air give you?"

He paused for an instant.

"Do you not know four big stars that form an oblong, and three stars close together in the middle of the oblong, and hanging from these stars, three other stars?"

"No, I do not. I dislike the stars. But did they give you an idea? How interesting; tell me."

"I had an idea that they were like a man."

"I do not understand."

"The four big stars are the man's shoulders and his knees. The three stars in the middle are like the belts that men wore once, and the three stars hanging are like a sword."

"A sword?"

"Men carried swords about with them, to kill animals and other men."

"It does not strike me as a very good idea, but it is certainly original. When did it come to you first?"

"In the air-ship—" He broke off, and she fancied that he looked sad. She could not be sure, for the Machine did not transmit *nuances* of expression. It only gave a general idea of people—an idea that was good enough for all practical purposes, Vashti thought. The imponderable bloom, declared by a discredited philosophy to be the actual essence of intercourse, was rightly ignored by the Machine, just as the imponderable bloom of the grape was ignored by the manufacturers of artificial fruit. Something "good enough" had long since been accepted by our race.

"The truth is," he continued, "that I want to see these stars again. They are curious stars. I want to see them not from the air-ship, but from the surface of the earth, as our ancestors did, thousands of years ago. I want to visit the surface of the earth."

She was shocked again.

"Mother, you must come, if only to explain to me what is the harm of visiting the surface of the earth."

"No harm," she replied, controlling herself. "But no advantage. The surface of the earth is only dust and mud, no life remains on it, and you would need a respirator, or the cold of the outer air would kill you. One dies immediately in the outer air."

"I know; of course I shall take all precautions."

"And besides—"

"Well?"

She considered, and chose her words with care. Her son had a queer temper, and she wished to dissuade him from the expedition.

"It is contrary to the spirit of the age," she asserted.

"Do you mean by that, contrary to the Machine?"

"In a sense, but—"

His image in the blue plate faded.

"Kuno!"

He had isolated himself.

For a moment Vashti felt lonely.

Then she generated the light, and the sight of her room, flooded with radiance and studded with electric buttons, revived her. There were buttons and switches everywhere—buttons to call for food for music, for clothing. There was the hot-bath button, by pressure of which a basin of (imitation) marble rose out of the floor, filled to the brim with a warm deodorized liquid. There was the cold-bath button. There was the button that produced literature. And there were of course the buttons by which she communicated with her friends. The room, though it contained nothing, was in touch with all that she cared for in the world.

Vashti's next move was to turn off the isolation switch, and all the accumulations of the last three minutes burst upon her. The room was filled with the noise of bells, and speaking-tubes. What was the new food like? Could she recommend it? Has she had any ideas lately? Might one tell her one's own ideas? Would she make an engagement to visit the public nurseries at an early date?—say this day or month.

To most of these questions she replied with irritation—a growing quality in that accelerated age. She said that the new food was horrible. That she could not visit the public nurseries through press of engagements. That she had no ideas of her own but had just been told one—that four stars and three in the middle were like a man: she doubted there was much in it. Then she switched off her correspondents, for it was time to deliver her lecture on Australian music.

The clumsy system of public gatherings had been long since abandoned; neither Vashti nor her audience stirred from their rooms. Seated in her armchair she spoke, while they in their armchairs heard her, fairly well, and saw her, fairly well. She opened with a humorous account of music in the pre-Mongolian epoch, and went on to describe the great outburst of song that followed the Chinese conquest. Remote and primeval as were the methods of I-San-So and the Brisbane school, she yet felt (she said) that study of them might repay the musicians of today: they had freshness; they had, above all, ideas.

Her lecture, which lasted ten minutes, was well received, and at its conclusion she and many of her audience listened to a lecture on the sea; there were ideas to be got from the sea; the speaker had donned a respirator and visited it lately. Then she fed, talked to many friends, had a bath, talked again, and summoned her bed.

The bed was not to her liking. It was too large, and she had a feeling for a small bed. Complaint was useless, for beds were of the same dimension all over the world, and to have had an alternative size would have involved vast alterations in the Machine. Vashti isolated herself—it was necessary, for neither day nor night existed under the ground—and reviewed all that had happened since she had summoned the bed last. Ideas? Scarcely any. Events—was Kuno's invitation an event?

By her side, on the little reading-desk, was a survival from the ages of litter—one book. This was the Book of the Machine. In it were instructions against every possible contingency. If she was hot or cold or dyspeptic or at a loss for a word, she went to the book, and it told her which button to press. The Central Committee published it. In accordance with a growing habit, it was richly bound.

Sitting up in the bed, she took it reverently in her hands. She glanced round the glowing room as if someone might be watching her. Then, half ashamed, half joyful, she murmured "O Machine!" and raised the volume to her lips. Thrice she kissed it, thrice inclined her head, thrice she felt the delirium of acquiescence. Her ritual performed, she turned to page 1367, which gave the times of the departure of the air-ships from the island in the southern hemisphere, under whose soil she lived, to the island in the northern hemisphere, whereunder lived her son.

She thought, "I have not the time."

She made the room dark and slept; she awoke and made the room light; she ate and exchanged ideas with her friends, and listened to music and attended lectures; she made the room dark and slept. Above her, beneath her, and around her, the Machine hummed eternally; she did not notice the noise, for she had been born with it in her ears. The earth, carrying her, hummed as it sped through silence, turning her now to the invisible sun, now to the invisible stars. She awoke and made the room light.

"Kuno!"

"I will not talk to you," he answered, "until you come."

"Have you been on the surface of the earth since we spoke last?"

His image faded.

Again she consulted the book. She became very nervous and lay back in her chair palpitating. Think of her as without teeth or hair. Presently she directed the chair to the wall, and pressed an unfamiliar button. The wall swung apart slowly. Through the opening she saw a tunnel that curved slightly, so that its goal was not visible. Should she go to see her son, here was the beginning of the journey.

Of course she knew all about the communication-system. There was nothing mysterious in it. She would summon a car and it would fly with her down the tunnel until it reached the lift that communicated with the air-ship station: the system had been in use for many, many years, long before the universal establishment of the Machine. And of course she had studied the civilization that had immediately preceded her own—the civilization that had mistaken the functions of the system, and had used it for bringing people to things, instead of for bringing things to people. Those funny old days, when men went for change of air instead of changing the air in their rooms! And yet—she was frightened of the tunnel: she had not seen it since her last child was born. It curved—but not quite as she remembered; it was brilliant—but not quite as brilliant as a lecturer had suggested. Vashti was seized with the terrors of direct experience. She shrank back into the room, and the wall closed up again.

"Kuno," she said, "I cannot come to see you. I am not well."

Immediately an enormous apparatus fell onto her out of the ceiling, a thermometer was automatically inserted between her lips, a stethoscope was automatically laid upon her heart. She lay powerless. Cool pads soothed her forehead. Kuno had telegraphed to her doctor.

So the human passions still blundered up and down in the Machine. Vashti drank the medicine that the doctor projected into her mouth, and the machinery retired into the ceiling. The voice of Kuno was heard asking how she felt.

"Better." Then with irritation: "But why do you not come to me instead?"

"Because I cannot leave this place."

"Why?"

"Because, any moment, something tremendous many happen."

"Have you been on the surface of the earth yet?"

"Not yet."

"Then what is it?"

"I will not tell you through the Machine."

She resumed her life.

But she thought of Kuno as a baby, his birth, his removal to the public nurseries, her one visit to him there, his visits to her—visits which stopped when the Machine had assigned him a room on the other side of the earth. "Parents, duties of," said the book of the Machine, "cease at the moment of birth. P. 422327483." True, but there was something special about Kuno—indeed there had been something special about all her children—and, after all, she must brave the journey if he desired it. And "something tremendous might happen." What did that mean? The nonsense of a youthful man, no doubt, but she must go. Again she pressed the unfamiliar button, again the wall swung back, and she saw the tunnel that curved out of sight. Clasping the Book, she rose, tottered onto the platform, and summoned the car. Her room closed behind her: the journey to the northern hemisphere had begun.

Of course it was perfectly easy. The car approached and in it she found armchairs exactly like her own. When she signaled, it stopped, and she tottered into the lift. One other passenger was in the lift, the first fellow creature she had seen face to face for months. Few traveled in these days, for, thanks to the advance of science, the earth was exactly alike all over. Rapid intercourse, from which the previous civilization had hoped so much, had ended by defeating itself. What was the good of going to Pekin when it was just like Shrewsbury? Why return to Shrewsbury when it would all be like Pekin? Men seldom moved their bodies; all unrest was concentrated in the soul.

The air-ship service was a relic from the former age. It was kept up, because it was easier to keep it up than to stop it or to diminish it, but it now far exceeded the wants of the population. Vessel after vessel would rise from the vomitories of Rye or of Christchurch (I use the antique names), would sail into the crowded sky, and would draw up at the wharves of the south—empty. So nicely adjusted was the system, so independent of meteorology, that the sky, whether calm or cloudy, resembled a vast kaleidoscope whereon the same patterns periodically recurred. The ship on which Vashti sailed started now at sunset, now at dawn. But always, as it passed above Rheims, it would neighbour the ship that served between Helsingfors and the Brazils, and, every third time it surmounted the Alps, the fleet of Palermo would cross its track behind. Night and day, wind and storm, tide and earthquake, impeded man no longer. He had harnessed Leviathan. All the old literature, with its praise of Nature, and its fear of Nature, rang false as the prattle of a child.

Yet as Vashti saw the vast flank of the ship, stained with exposure to the outer air, her horror of direct experience returned. It was not quite like the air-ship in the cinematophote. For one thing it smelt—not strongly or unpleasantly, but it did smell, and with her eyes shut she should have known that a new thing was close to her. Then she had to walk to it from the lift, had to submit to glances from the other passengers. The man in front dropped his Book—no great matter, but it disquieted them all. In the rooms, if the Book was dropped, the floor raised it mechanically, but the gangway to the air-ship was not so prepared, and the sacred volume lay motionless. They stopped—the thing was unforeseen—and the man, instead of picking up his property, felt the muscles of his arm to see how they had failed him. Then some one actually said with direct utterance: "We shall be late"—and they trooped on board, Vashti treading on the pages as she did so.

Inside, her anxiety increased. The arrangements were old-fashioned and rough. There was even a female attendant, to whom she would have to announce her wants during the voyage. Of course a revolving platform ran the length of the boat, but she was expected to walk from it to her cabin. Some cabins were better than others, and she did not get the best. She thought the attendant had been unfair, and spasms of rage shook her. The glass valves had closed, she could not go back. She saw, at the end of the vestibule, the lift in which she had ascended going quietly up and down, empty. Beneath those corridors of shining tiles were rooms, tier below tier, reaching far into the earth, and in each room there sat a human being, eating, or sleeping, or producing ideas. And buried deep in the hive was her own room. Vashti was afraid.

"O Machine! O Machine!" she murmured, and caressed her Book, and was comforted.

Then the sides of the vestibule seemed to melt together, as do the passages that we see in dreams, the lift vanished, the Book that had been dropped slid to the left and vanished, polished tiles rushed by like a stream of water, there was a slight jar, and the air-ship, issuing from its tunnel, soared above the waters of a tropical ocean.

It was night. For a moment she saw the coast of Sumatra edged by the phosphorescence of waves, and crowned by lighthouses, still sending forth their disregarded beams. These also vanished, and only the stars distracted her. They were not motionless, but swayed to and fro above her head, thronging out of one sky-light into another, as if the universe and not the air-ship was careening. And, as often happens on clear nights, they seemed now to be in perspective, now on a plane; now piled tier beyond tier into the infinite heavens, now concealing infinity, a roof limiting for ever the visions of men. In either case they seemed intolerable. "Are we to travel in the dark?" called the passengers angrily, and the attendant, who had been careless, generated the light, and pulled down the blinds of pliable metal. When the air-ships had been built, the desire to look direct at things still lingered in the world. Hence the extraordinary number of skylights and windows, and the proportionate discomfort to those who were civilized and refined. Even in Vashti's cabin one star peeped through a flaw in the blind, and after a few hours' uneasy slumber, she was disturbed by an unfamiliar glow, which was the dawn.

Quick as the ship had sped westwards, the earth had rolled eastwards quicker still, and had dragged back Vashti and her companions towards the sun. Science could prolong the night, but only for a little, and those high hopes of neutralizing the earth's diurnal revolution had passed, together with hopes that were possibly higher. To "keep pace with the sun," or even to outstrip it, had been the aim of the civilization preceding this. Racing aeroplanes had been built for the purpose, capable of enormous speed, and steered by the greatest intellects of the epoch. Round the globe they went, round and round, westward, westward, round and round, amidst humanity's applause. In vain. The globe went eastward quicker still, horrible accidents occurred, and the Committee of the Machine, at the time rising into prominence, declared the pursuit illegal, unmechanical, and punishable by Homelessness.

Of Homelessness more will be said later.

Doubtless the Committee was right. Yet the attempt to "defeat the sun" aroused the last common interest that our race experienced about the heavenly bodies, or indeed about anything. It was the last time that men were compacted by thinking of a power outside the world. The sun had conquered, yet it was the end of his spiritual dominion. Dawn, midday, twilight, the zodiacal path, touched neither men's lives nor their hearts, and science retreated into the ground, to concentrate herself upon problems that she was certain of solving.

So when Vashti found her cabin invaded by a rosy finger of light, she was annoyed, and tried to adjust the blind. But the blind flew up altogether, and she saw through the skylight small pink clouds, swaying against a background of blue, and as the sun crept higher, its radiance entered direct, brimming down the wall, like a golden sea. It rose and fell with the air-ship's motion, just as waves rise and fall, but it advanced steadily, as a tide advances. Unless she was careful, it would strike her face. A spasm of horror shook her and she rang for the attendant. The attendant too was horrified, but she could do nothing; it was not her place to mend the blind. She could only suggest that the lady should change her cabin, which she accordingly prepared to do.

People were almost exactly alike all over the world, but the attendant of the air-ship, perhaps owing to her exceptional duties, had grown a little out of the common. She had often to address passengers with direct speech, and this had given her a certain roughness and originality of manner. When Vashti swerved away from the sunbeams with a cry, she behaved barbarically—she put out her hand to steady her.

"How dare you!" exclaimed the passenger. "You forget yourself!"

The woman was confused, and apologized for not having let her fall. People never touched one another. The custom had become obsolete, owing to the Machine.

"Where are we now?" asked Vashti haughtily.

"We are over Asia," said the attendant, anxious to be polite.

"Asia?"

"You must excuse my common way of speaking. I have got into the habit of calling places over which I pass by their unmechanical names."

"Oh, I remember Asia. The Mongols came from it."

"Beneath us, in the open air, stood a city that was once called Simla."

"Have you ever heard of the Mongols and of the Brisbane school?"

"No."

"Brisbane also stood in the open air."

"Those mountains to the right—let me show you them." She pushed back a metal blind. The main chain of the Himalayas was revealed. "They were once called the Roof of the World, those mountains."

"What a foolish name!"

"You must remember that, before the dawn of civilization, they seemed to be an impenetrable wall that touched the stars. It was supposed that no one but the gods could exist above their summits. How we have advanced, thanks to the Machine!"

"How we have advanced, thanks to the Machine!" said Vashti.

"How we have advanced, thanks to the Machine!" echoed the passenger who had dropped his Book the night before, and who was standing in the passage.

"And that white stuff in the cracks?—what is it?"

"I have forgotten its name."

"Cover the window, please. These mountains give me no ideas."

The northern aspect of the Himalayas was in deep shadow: on the Indian slope the sun had just prevailed. The forests had been destroyed during the literature epoch for the purpose of making newspaper-pulp, but the snows were awakening to their morning glory, and clouds still hung on the breasts of Kinchinjunga. In the plain were seen the ruins of cities, with diminished rivers creeping by their walls, and by the sides of these were sometimes the signs of vomitories, marking the cities of today. Over the whole prospect air-ships rushed, crossing the inter-crossing with incredible *aplomb*, and rising nonchalantly when they desired to escape the perturbations of the lower atmosphere and to traverse the Roof of the World.

"We have indeed advanced, thanks to the Machine," repeated the attendant, and hid the Himalayas behind a metal blind.

The day dragged wearily forward. The passengers sat each in his cabin, avoiding one another with an almost physical repulsion and longing to be once more under the surface of the earth. There were eight or ten of them, mostly young males, sent out from the public nurseries to inhabit the rooms of those who had died in various parts of the earth. The man who had dropped his Book was on the homeward journey. He had been sent to

Sumatra for the purpose of propagating the race. Vashti alone was traveling by her private will.

At midday she took a second glance at the earth. The air-ship was crossing another range of mountains, but she could see little, owing to clouds. Masses of black rock hovered below her, and merged indistinctly into grey. Their shapes were fantastic; one of them resembled a prostrate man.

"No ideas here," murmured Vashti, and hid the Caucasus behind a metal blind.

In the evening she looked again. They were crossing a golden sea, in which lay many small islands and one peninsula. She repeated, "No ideas here," and hid Greece behind a metal blind.

PART II

The Mending Apparatus

By a vestibule, by a lift, by a tubular railway, by a platform, by a sliding door—by reversing all the steps of her departure did Vashti arrive at her son's room, which exactly resembled her own. She might well declare that the visit was superfluous. The buttons, the knobs, the reading-desk with the Book, the temperature, the atmosphere, the illumination—all were exactly the same. And if Kuno himself, flesh of her flesh, stood close beside her at last, what profit was there in that? She was too well-bred to shake him by the hand.

Averting her eyes, she spoke as follows:

"Here I am. I have had the most terrible journey and greatly retarded the development of my soul. It is not worth it, Kuno, it is not worth it. My time is too precious. The sunlight almost touched me, and I have met with the rudest people. I can only stop a few minutes. Say what you want to say, and then I must return."

"I have been threatened with Homelessness," said Kuno.

She looked at him now.

"I have been threatened with Homelessness, and I could not tell you such a thing through the Machine."

Homelessness means death. The victim is exposed to the air, which kills him.

"I have been outside since I spoke to you last. The tremendous thing has happened, and they have discovered me."

"But why shouldn't you go outside?" she exclaimed. "It is perfectly legal, perfectly mechanical, to visit the surface of the earth. I have lately been to a lecture on the sea; there is no objection to that; one simply summons a respirator and gets an Egression-permit. It is not the kind of thing that spiritually minded people do, and I begged you not to do it, but there is no legal objection to it."

"I did not get an Egression-permit."

"Then how did you get out?"

"I found out a way of my own."

The phrase conveyed no meaning to her, and he had to repeat it.

"A way of your own?" she whispered. "But that would be wrong."

"Why?"

The question shocked her beyond measure.

"You are beginning to worship the Machine," he said coldly. "You think it irreligious of me to have found out a way of my own. It was just what the Committee thought, when they threatened me with Homelessness."

At this she grew angry. "I worship nothing!" she cried. "I am most advanced. I don't think you irreligious, for there is no such thing as religion left. All the fear and the superstition that existed once have been destroyed by the Machine. I only meant that to find out a way of your own was— Besides, there is no new way out."

"So it is always supposed."

"Except through the vomitories, for which one must have an Egression-permit, it is impossible to get out. The Book says so."

"Well, the Book's wrong, for I have been out on my feet."

For Kuno was possessed of a certain physical strength.

By these days it was a demerit to be muscular. Each infant was examined at birth, and all who promised undue strength were destroyed. Humanitarians may protest, but it would have been no true kindness to let an athlete live; he would never have been happy in that state of life to which the Machine had called him; he would have yearned for trees to climb, rivers to bathe in, meadows and hills against which he might measure his body. Man must be adapted to his surroundings, must he not? In the dawn of the world our weakly must be exposed on Mount Taygetus, in its twilight our strong will suffer euthanasia, that the Machine may progress, that the Machine may progress, that the Machine may progress eternally.

"You know that we have lost the sense of space. We say 'space is annihilated,' but we have annihilated not space, but the sense thereof. We have lost a part of ourselves. I determined to recover it, and I began by walking up and down the platform of the railway outside my room. Up and down, until I was tired, and so did recapture the meaning of 'Near' and 'Far.' 'Near' is a place to which I can get quickly *on my feet*, not a place to which the train or the airship will take me quickly. 'Far' is a place to which I cannot get quickly on my feet; the vomitory is 'far,' though I could be there in thirty-eight seconds by summoning the train. Man is the measure. That was my first lesson. Man's feet are the measure for distance, his hands are the measure for ownership, his body is the measure for all that is lovable and desirable and strong. Then I went further: it was then that I called to you for the first time, and you would not come.

"This city, as you know, is built deep beneath the surface of the earth, with only the vomitories protruding. Having paced the platform outside my own room, I took the lift to the next platform and paced that also, and so with each in turn, until I came to the topmost, above which begins the earth. All the platforms were exactly alike, and all that I gained by visiting them was to develop my sense of space and my muscles. I think I should have been content with this—it is not a little thing—but as I walked and brooded, it occurred to me that our cities had been built in the days when men still breathed the outer air, and that there had been ventilation shafts for the workmen. I could think of nothing but these ventilation shafts. Had they been destroyed by all the food-tubes and medicine-tubes and music-tubes that the Machine has evolved lately? Or did traces of them remain? One thing was certain. If I came upon them anywhere, it would be in the railway-tunnels of the topmost story. Everywhere else, all space was accounted for.

"I am telling my story quickly, but don't think that I was not a coward or that your answers never depressed me. It is not the proper thing, it is not mechanical, it is not decent to walk along a railway-tunnel. I did not fear that I might tread upon a live rail and be killed. I feared something far more intangible—doing what was not contemplated by the Machine. Then I said to myself, 'Man is the measure,' and I went, and after many visits I found an opening.

"The tunnels, of course, were lighted. Everything is light, artificial light; darkness is the exception. So when I saw a black gap in the tiles, I knew that it was an exception, and rejoiced. I put in my arm—I could put in no more at first—and waved it round and round in ecstasy. I loosened another tile, and put in my head, and shouted into the darkness: 'I am coming, I shall do it yet,' and my voice reverberated down endless passages. I seemed to hear the spirits of those dead workmen who had returned each evening to the starlight and to their wives, and all the generations who had lived in the open air called back to me, 'You will do it yet, you are coming.'"

He paused, and, absurd as he was, his last words moved her. For Kuno had lately asked to be a father, and his request had been refused by the Committee. His was not a type that the Machine desired to hand on.

"Then a train passed. It brushed by me, but I thrust my head and arms into the hole. I had done enough for one day, so I crawled back to the platform, went down in the lift, and summoned my bed. Ah, what dreams! And again I called you, and again you refused."

She shook her head and said:

"Don't. Don't talk of these terrible things. You make me miserable. You are throwing civilization away."

"But I had got back the sense of space and a man cannot rest then. I determined to get in at the hole and climb the shaft. And so I exercised my arms. Day after day I went through ridiculous movements, until my flesh ached, and I could hang by my hands and hold the pillow of my bed outstretched for many minutes. Then I summoned a respirator, and started.

"It was easy at first. The mortar had somehow rotted, and I soon pushed some more tiles in, and clambered after them into the darkness, and the spirits of the dead comforted me. I don't know what I mean by that. I just say what I felt. I felt, for the first time, that a protest had been lodged against corruption, and that even as the dead were comforting me, so I was comforting the unborn. I felt that humanity existed, and that it existed without clothes. How can I possibly explain this? It was naked, humanity seemed naked, and all these tubes and buttons and machineries neither came into the world with us, nor will they follow us out, nor do they matter supremely while we are here. Had I been strong, I would have torn off every garment I had, and gone out into the outer air unswaddled. But this is not for me, nor perhaps for my generation. I climbed with my respirator and my hygienic clothes and my dietetic tabloids! Better thus than not at all.

"There was a ladder, made of some primeval metal. The light from the railway fell upon its lowest rungs, and I saw that it led straight upwards out of the rubble at the bottom of the shaft. Perhaps our ancestors ran up and down it a dozen times daily, in their building. As I climbed, the rough edges cut through my gloves so that my hands bled. The light helped me for a little, and then came darkness and, worse still, silence which pierced my ears like a sword. The Machine hums! Did you know that? Its hum penetrates our blood, and may even guide our thoughts. Who knows! I was getting beyond its power. Then I thought: 'This silence means that I am doing wrong.' But I heard voices in the silence, and again they strengthened me." He laughed. "I had need of them. The next moment I cracked my head against something."

She sighed.

"I had reached one of those pneumatic stoppers that defend us from the outer air. You may have noticed them on the air-ship. Pitch dark, my feet on the rungs of an invisible ladder, my hands cut; I cannot explain how I lived through this part, but the voices still comforted me, and I felt for fastenings. The stopper, I suppose, was about eight feet across. I passed my hand over it as far as I could reach. It was perfectly smooth. I felt it almost to the center. Not quite to the center, for my arm was too short. Then the voice said: 'Jump. It is worth it. There may be a handle in the center, and you may catch hold of it and so come to us your own way. And if there is no handle, so that you may fall and are dashed to pieces—it is still worth it: you will still come to us your own way.' So I jumped. There was a handle, and—"

He paused. Tears gathered in his mother's eyes. She knew that he was fated. If he did not die today he would die tomorrow. There was not room for such a person in the world. And with her pity disgust mingled. She was ashamed at having borne such a son, she who had always been so respectable and so full of ideas. Was he really the little boy to whom she had taught the use of his stops and buttons, and to whom she had given his first lessons in the Book? The very hair that disfigured his lip showed that he was reverting to some savage type. On atavism the Machine can have no mercy.

"There was a handle, and I did catch it. I hung tranced over the darkness and heard the hum of these workings as the last whisper in a dying dream. All the things I had cared about and all the people I had spoken to through tubes appeared infinitely little. Meanwhile the handle revolved. My weight had set something in motion and I spun slowly, and then—

"I cannot describe it. I was lying with my face to the sunshine. Blood poured from my nose and ears and I heard a tremendous roaring. The stopper, with me clinging to it, had simply been blown out of the earth, and the air that we make down here was escaping through the vent into the air above. It burst up like a fountain. I crawled back to it—for the upper air hurts—and, as it were, I took great sips from the edge. My respirator had flown goodness knows where, my clothes were torn. I just lay with my lips close to the hole, and I sipped until the bleeding stopped. You can imagine nothing so curious. This hollow in the grass—I will speak of it in a minute—the sun shining into it, not brilliantly but through marbled clouds—the peace, the nonchalance, the sense of space, and, brushing my cheek, the roaring fountain of our artificial air! Soon I spied my respirator, bobbing up and down in the current high above my head, and higher still were many air-ships. But no one ever looks out of air-ships, and in any case they could not have picked me up. There I was, stranded. The sun shone a little way down the shaft, and revealed the topmost rung of the ladder, but it was hopeless trying to reach it. I should either have been tossed up again by the escape, or else have fallen in, and died. I could only lie on the grass, sipping and sipping, and from time to time glancing around me.

"I knew that I was in Wessex, for I had taken care to go to a lecture on the subject before starting. Wessex lies above the room in which we are talking now. It was once an important state. Its kings held all the southern coast from the Andredswald to Cornwall, while the Wansdyke protected them on the north, running over the high ground. The lecturer was only concerned with the rise of Wessex, so I do not know how long it remained an international power, nor would the knowledge have assisted me. To tell the truth I could do nothing but laugh, during this part. There was I, with a pneumatic stopper by my side and a respirator bobbing over my head, imprisoned, all three of us, in a grass-grown hollow that was edged with fern."

Then he grew grave again.

"Lucky for me that it was a hollow. For the air began to fall back into it and to fill it as water fills a bowl. I could crawl about. Presently I stood. I breathed a mixture, in which the air that hurts predominated whenever I tried to climb the sides. This was not so bad. I had not lost my tabloids and remained ridiculously cheerful, and as for the Machine, I forgot about it altogether. My one aim now was to get to the top, where the ferns were, and to view whatever objects lay beyond.

"I rushed the slope. The new air was still too bitter for me and I came rolling back, after a momentary vision of something grey. The sun grew very feeble, and I remembered that he was in Scorpio—I had been to a lecture on that too. If the sun is in Scorpio, and you are in Wessex, it means that you must be as quick as you can, or it will get too dark. (This is the first bit of useful information I have ever got from a lecture, and I expect it will be the last.) It made me try frantically to breathe the new air, and to advance as far as I dared out of my pond. The hollow filled so slowly. At times I thought that the fountain played with less vigor. My respirator seemed to dance nearer the earth; the roar was decreasing."

He broke off.

"I don't think this is interesting you. The rest will interest you even less. There are no ideas in it, and I wish that I had not troubled you to come. We are too different, mother."

She told him to continue.

"It was evening before I climbed the bank. The sun had very nearly slipped out of the sky by this time, and I could not get a good view. You, who have just crossed the Roof of the World, will not want to hear an account of the little hills that I saw—low colorless hills. But to me they were living and the turf that covered them was a skin, under which their muscles rippled, and I felt that those hills had called with incalculable force to men in the past, and that men had loved them. Now they sleep—perhaps for ever. They commune with humanity in dreams. Happy the man, happy the woman, who awakes the hills of Wessex. For though they sleep, they will never die."

His voice rose passionately.

"Cannot you see, cannot all your lecturers see, that it is we who are dying, and that down here the only thing that really lives is the Machine? We created the Machine, to do our will, but we cannot make it do our will now. It has robbed us of the sense of space and of the sense of touch, it has blurred every human relation and narrowed down love to a carnal act, it has paralyzed our bodies and our wills, and now it compels us to worship it. The Machine develops—but not on our lines. The Machine proceeds—but not to our goal. We only exist as the blood corpuscles that course through its arteries, and if it could work without us, it would let us die. Oh, I have no remedy—or, at least, only one—to tell men again and again that I have seen the hills of Wessex as Ælfrid saw them when he overthrew the Danes.

"So the sun set. I forgot to mention that a belt of mist lay between my hill and other hills, and that it was the color of pearl."

He broke off for the second time.

"Go on," said his mother wearily.

He shook his head.

"Go on. Nothing that you say can distress me now. I am hardened."

"I had meant to tell you the rest, but I cannot: I know that I cannot: goodbye."

Vashti stood irresolute. All her nerves were tingling with his blasphemies. But she was also inquisitive.

"This is unfair," she complained. "You have called me across the world to hear your story, and hear it I will. Tell me—as briefly as possible, for this is a disastrous waste of time—tell me how you returned to civilization."

"Oh—that!" he said, starting. "You would like to hear about civilization. Certainly. Had I got to where my respirator fell down?"

"No—but I understand everything now. You put on your respirator, and managed to walk along the surface of the earth to a vomitory, and there your conduct was reported to the Central Committee."

"By no means."

He passed his hand over his forehead, as if dispelling some strong impression. Then, resuming his narrative, he warmed to it again.

"My respirator fell about sunset. I had mentioned that the fountain seemed feebler, had I not?"

"Yes."

"About sunset, it let the respirator fall. As I said, I had entirely forgotten about the Machine, and I paid no great attention at the time, being occupied with other things. I had my pool of air, into which I could dip when the outer keenness became intolerable, and which would possibly remain for days, provided that no wind sprang up to disperse it. Not until it was too late did I realize what the stoppage of the escape implied. You see—the gap in the tunnel had been mended; the Mending Apparatus, the Mending Apparatus, was after me.

"One other warning I had, but I neglected it. The sky at night was clearer than it had been in the day, and the moon, which was about half the sky behind the sun, shone into the dell at moments quite brightly. I was in my usual place—on the boundary between the two atmospheres—when I thought I saw something dark move across the bottom of the dell, and vanish into the shaft. In my folly, I ran down. I bent over and listened, and I thought I heard a faint scraping noise in the depths.

"At this—but it was too late—I took alarm. I determined to put on my respirator and to walk right out of the dell. But my respirator had gone. I knew exactly where it had fallen—between the stopper and the aperture—and I could even feel the mark that it had made in the turf. It had gone, and I realized that something evil was at work, and I had better escape to the other air, and, if I must die, die running towards the cloud that had been the color of a pearl. I never started. Out of the shaft—it is too horrible. A worm, a long white worm, had crawled out of the shaft and was gliding over the moonlit grass.

"I screamed. I did everything that I should not have done, I stamped upon the creature instead of flying from it, and it at once curled round the ankle. Then we fought. The worm let me run all over the dell, but edged up my leg as I ran. 'Help!' I cried. (That part is too awful. It belongs to the part that you will never know.) 'Help!' I cried. (Why cannot we suffer in silence?) 'Help!' I cried. Then my feet were wound together, I fell, I was dragged away from the dear ferns and the living hills, and past the great metal stopper (I can tell you this part), and I thought it might save me again if I caught hold of the handle. It also was enwrapped, it also. Oh, the whole dell was full of the things. They were searching it in all directions, they were denuding it, and the white snouts of others peeped out of the hole, ready if needed. Everything that could be moved they brought—brushwood, bundles of fern, everything, and down we all went intertwined into hell. The last things that I saw, ere the stopper closed after us, were certain stars, and I felt that a man of my sort lived in the sky. For I did fight, I fought till the very end, and it was only my head hitting against the ladder that quieted me. I woke up in this room. The worms had vanished. I was surrounded by artificial air, artificial light, artificial peace, and my friends were calling to me down speaking-tubes to know whether I had come across any new ideas lately."

Here his story ended. Discussion of it was impossible, and Vashti turned to go.

"It will end in Homelessness," she said quietly.

"I wish it would," retorted Kuno.

"The Machine has been most merciful."

"I prefer the mercy of God."

"By that superstitious phrase, do you mean that you could live in the outer air?"

"Yes."

"Have you ever seen, round the vomitories, the bones of those who were extruded after the Great Rebellion?"

"Yes."

"They were left where they perished for our edification. A few crawled away, but they perished, too—who can doubt it? And so with the Homeless of our own day. The surface of the earth supports life no longer."

"Indeed."

"Ferns and a little grass may survive, but all higher forms have perished. Has any air-ship detected them?"

"No."

"Has any lecturer dealt with them?"

"No."

"Then why this obstinacy?"

"Because I have seen them," he exploded.

"Seen what?"

"Because I have seen her in the twilight—because she came to my help when I called—because she, too, was entangled by the worms, and, luckier than I, was killed by one of them piercing her throat."

He was mad. Vashti departed, nor, in the troubles that followed, did she ever see his face again.

PART III

The Homeless

During the years that followed Kuno's escapade, two important developments took place in the Machine. On the surface they were revolutionary, but in either case men's minds had been prepared beforehand, and they did but express tendencies that were latent already.

The first of these was the abolition of respirators.

Advanced thinkers, like Vashti, had always held it foolish to visit the surface of the earth. Air-ships might be necessary, but what was the good of going out for mere curiosity and crawling along for a mile or two in a terrestrial motor? The habit was vulgar and perhaps faintly improper: it was unproductive of ideas, and had no connection with the habits that really mattered. So respirators were abolished, and with them, of course, the terrestrial motors, and except for a few lecturers, who complained that they were debarred access to their subject-matter, the development was accepted quietly. Those who still wanted to know what the earth was like had after all only to listen to some gramophone, or to look into some cinematophote. And even the lecturers acquiesced when they found that a lecture on the sea was nonetheless stimulating when compiled out of other lectures that had already been delivered on the same subject. "Beware of first-hand ideas!" exclaimed one of the most advanced of them. "First-hand ideas do not really exist. They are but the physical impressions produced by love and fear, and on this gross foundation who could erect a philosophy? Let your ideas be second-hand, and if possible tenth-hand, for then they will be far removed from that disturbing element—direct observation. Do not learn anything about this subject of mine—the French Revolution. Learn instead what I think that Enicharmon thought Urizen thought Gutch thought Ho-Yung thought Chi-Bo-Sing thought Lafcadio Hearn thought Carlyle thought Mirabeau said about the French Revolution. Through the medium of these ten great minds, the blood that was shed at Paris and the windows that were broken at Versailles will be clarified to an idea which you may employ most profitably in your daily lives. But be sure that the intermediates are many and varied, for in history one authority exists to counteract another. Urizen must counteract the scepticism of Ho-Yung and Enicharmon, I must myself counteract the impetuosity of Gutch. You who listen to me are in a better position to judge about the French Revolution than I am. Your descendants will be even in a better position than you, for they will learn what you think I think, and yet another intermediate will be added to the chain. And in time"—his voice rose—"there will come a generation that had got beyond facts, beyond impressions, a generation absolutely colorless, a generation

'seraphically free
From taint of personality,'

which will see the French Revolution not as it happened, nor as they would like it to have happened, but as it would have happened, had it taken place in the days of the Machine."

Tremendous applause greeted this lecture, which did but voice a feeling already latent in the minds of men—a feeling that terrestrial facts must be ignored, and that the abolition of respirators was a positive gain. It was even suggested that air-ships should be abolished too. This was not done, because air-ships had somehow worked themselves into the Machine's system. But year by year they were used less, and mentioned less by thoughtful men.

The second great development was the reestablishment of religion.

This, too, had been voiced in the celebrated lecture. No one could mistake the reverent tone in which the peroration had concluded, and it awakened a responsive echo in the heart of each. Those who had long worshipped silently, now began to talk. They described the strange feeling of peace that came over them when they handled the Book of the Machine, the pleasure that it was to repeat certain numerals out of it, however little meaning those numerals conveyed to the outward ear, the ecstasy of touching a button, however unimportant, or of ringing an electric bell, however superfluously.

"The Machine," they exclaimed, "feeds us and clothes us and houses us; through it we speak to one another, through it we see one another, in it we have our being. The Machine is the friend of ideas and the enemy of superstition: the Machine is omnipotent, eternal; blessed is the Machine." And before long this allocution was printed on the first page of the Book, and in subsequent editions the ritual swelled into a complicated system of praise and prayer. The word "religion" was sedulously avoided, and in theory the Machine was still the creation and the implement of man. But in practice all, save a few retrogrades, worshipped it as divine. Nor was it worshipped in unity. One believer would be chiefly impressed by the blue optic plates, through which he saw other believers; another by the mending apparatus, which sinful Kuno had compared to worms; another by the lifts, another by the Book. And each would pray to this or to that, and ask it to intercede for him with the Machine as a whole. Persecution—that also was present. It did not break out, for reasons that will be set forward shortly. But it was latent, and all who did not accept the minimum known as "undenominational Mechanism" lived in danger of Homelessness, which means death, as we know.

To attribute these two great developments to the Central Committee is to take a very narrow view of civilization. The Central Committee announced the developments, it is true, but they were no more the cause of them than were the kings of the imperialistic period the cause of war. Rather did they yield to some invincible pressure, which came no one knew whither, and which, when gratified, was succeeded by some new pressure equally invincible. To such a state of affairs it is convenient to give the name of progress.

No one confessed the Machine was out of hand. Year by year it was served with increased efficiency and decreased intelligence. The better a man knew his own duties upon it, the less he understood the duties of his neighbor, and in all the world there was not one who understood the monster as a whole. Those master brains had perished. They had left full directions, it is true, and their successors had each of them mastered a portion of those directions. But Humanity, in its desire for comfort, had over-reached itself. It had exploited the riches of nature too far. Quietly and complacently, it was sinking into decadence, and progress had come to mean the progress of the Machine.

As for Vashti, her life went peacefully forward until the final disaster. She made her room dark and slept; she awoke and made the room light. She lectured and attended lectures. She exchanged ideas with her innumerable friends and believed she was growing more spiritual. At times a friend was granted Euthanasia, and left his or her room for the homelessness that is beyond all human conception. Vashti did not much mind. After an unsuccessful lecture, she would sometimes ask for Euthanasia herself. But the death-rate was not permitted to exceed the birth-rate, and the Machine had hitherto refused it to her.

The troubles began quietly, long before she was conscious of them.

One day she was astonished at receiving a message from her son. They never communicated, having nothing in common, and she had only heard indirectly that he was still alive, and had been transferred from the northern hemisphere, where he had behaved so mischievously, to the southern—indeed, to a room not far from her own.

"Does he want me to visit him?" she thought. "Never again, never. And I have not the time."

No, it was madness of another kind.

He refused to visualize his face upon the blue plate, and speaking out of the darkness with solemnity said:

"The Machine stops."

"What do you say?"

"The Machine is stopping, I know it, I know the signs."

She burst into a peal of laughter. He heard her and was angry, and they spoke no more.

"Can you imagine anything more absurd?" she cried to a friend. "A man who was my son believes that the Machine is stopping. It would be impious if it was not mad."

"The Machine is stopping?" her friend replied. "What does that mean? The phrase conveys nothing to me."

"Nor to me."

"He does not refer, I suppose, to the trouble there has been lately with the music?"

"Oh no, of course not. Let us talk about music."

"Have you complained to the authorities?"

"Yes, and they say it wants mending, and referred me to the Committee of the Mending Apparatus. I complained of those curious gasping sighs that disfigure the symphonies of the Brisbane school. They sound like someone in pain. The Committee of the Mending Apparatus say that it shall be remedied shortly."

Obscurely worried, she resumed her life. For one thing, the defect in the music irritated her. For another thing, she could not forget Kuno's speech. If he had known that the music was out of repair—he could not know it, for he detested music—if he had known that it was wrong, "the Machine stops" was exactly the venomous sort of remark he would have made. Of course he had made it at a venture, but the coincidence annoyed her, and she spoke with some petulance to the Committee of the Mending Apparatus.

They replied, as before, that the defect would be set right shortly.

"Shortly! At once!" she retorted. "Why should I be worried by imperfect music? Things are always put right at once. If you do not mend it at once, I shall complain to the Central Committee."

"No personal complaints are received by the Central Committee," the Committee of the Mending Apparatus replied.

"Through whom am I to make my complaint, then?"

"Through us."

"I complain then."

"Your complaint shall be forwarded in its turn."

"Have others complained?"

This question was unmechanical, and the Committee of the Mending Apparatus refused to answer it.

"It is too bad!" she exclaimed to another of her friends. "There never was such an unfortunate woman as myself. I can never be sure of my music now. It gets worse and worse each time I summon it."

"I too have my troubles," the friend replied. "Sometimes my ideas are interrupted by a slight jarring noise."

"What is it?"

"I do not know whether it is inside my head, or inside the wall."

"Complain, in either case."

"I have complained, and my complaint will be forwarded in its turn to the Central Committee."

Time passed, and they resented the defects no longer. The defects had not been remedied, but the human tissues in that latter day had become so subservient, that they readily adapted themselves to every caprice of the Machine. The sigh at the crises of the Brisbane symphony no longer irritated Vashti; she accepted it as part of the melody. The jarring noise, whether in the head or in the wall, was no longer resented by her friend. And so with the moldy artificial fruit, so with the bath water that began to stink, so with the defective rhymes that the poetry machine had taken to emit. All were bitterly complained of at first, and then acquiesced in and forgotten. Things went from bad to worse unchallenged.

It was otherwise with the failure of the sleeping apparatus. That was a more serious stoppage. There came a day when over the whole world—in Sumatra, in Wessex, in the innumerable cities of Courland and Brazil—the beds, when summoned by their tired owners, failed to appear. It may seem a ludicrous matter, but from it we may date the collapse of humanity. The Committee responsible for the failure was assailed by complainants, whom it referred, as usual, to the Committee of the Mending Apparatus, who in its turn assured them that their complaints would be forwarded to the Central Committee. But the discontent grew, for mankind was not yet sufficiently adaptable to do without sleeping.

"Some one is meddling with the Machine—" they began.

"Some one is trying to make himself king, to reintroduce the personal element."

"Punish that man with Homelessness."

"To the rescue! Avenge the Machine! Avenge the Machine!"

"War! Kill the man!"

But the Committee of the Mending Apparatus now came forward, and allayed the panic with well-chosen words. It confessed that the Mending Apparatus was itself in need of repair.

The effect of this frank confession was admirable.

"Of course," said a famous lecturer—he of the French Revolution, who gilded each new decay with splendor—"of course we shall not press our complaints now. The Mending Apparatus has treated us so well in the past that we all sympathize with it, and will wait patiently for its recovery. In its own good time it will resume its duties. Meanwhile let us do without our beds, our tabloids, our other little wants. Such, I feel sure, would be the wish of the Machine."

Thousands of miles away his audience applauded. The Machine still linked them. Under the seas, beneath the roots of the mountains, ran the wires through which they saw and heard, the enormous eyes and ears that were their heritage, and the hum of many workings clothed their thoughts in one garment of subserviency. Only the old and the sick remained ungrateful, for it was rumored that Euthanasia, too, was out of order, and that pain had reappeared among men.

It became difficult to read. A blight entered the atmosphere and dulled its luminosity. At times Vashti could scarcely see across her room. The air, too, was foul. Loud were the complaints, impotent the remedies, heroic the tone of the lecturer as he cried: "Courage! courage! What matter so long as the Machine goes on? To it the darkness and the light are one." And though things improved again after a time, the old brilliancy was never recaptured, and humanity never recovered from its entrance into twilight. There was an hysterical talk of "measures," of "provisional dictatorship," and the inhabitants of Sumatra were asked to familiarize themselves with the workings of the central power station, the said power station being situated in France. But for the most part panic reigned, and men spent their strength praying to their Books, tangible proofs of the Machine's omnipotence. There were gradations of terror—at times came rumors of hope—the Mending Apparatus was almost mended—the enemies of the Machine had been got under—new "nerve-centers" were evolving which would do the work even more magnificently than before. But there came a day when, without the slightest warning, without any previous hint of feebleness, the entire communication-system broke down, all over the world, and the world, as they understood it, ended.

Vashti was lecturing at the time and her earlier remarks had been punctuated with applause. As she proceeded the audience became silent, and at the conclusion there was no sound. Somewhat displeased, she called to a friend who was a specialist in sympathy. No sound: doubtless the friend was sleeping. And so with the next friend whom she tried to summon, and so with the next, until she remembered Kuno's cryptic remark, "The Machine stops."

The phrase still conveyed nothing. If Eternity was stopping it would of course be set going shortly.

For example, there was still a little light and air—the atmosphere had improved a few hours previously. There was still the Book, and while there was the Book there was security.

Then she broke down, for with the cessation of activity came an unexpected terror—silence.

She had never known silence, and the coming of it nearly killed her—it did kill many thousands of people outright. Ever since her birth she had been surrounded by the steady hum. It was to the ear what artificial air was to the lungs, and agonizing pains shot across her head. And scarcely knowing what she did, she stumbled forward and pressed the unfamiliar button, the one that opened the door of her cell.

Now the door of the cell worked on a simple hinge of its own. It was not connected with the central power station, dying far away in France. It opened, rousing immoderate hopes in Vashti, for she thought that the Machine had been mended. It opened, and she saw the dim tunnel that curved far away towards freedom. One look, and then she shrank back. For the tunnel was full of people—she was almost the last in that city to have taken alarm.

People at any time repelled her, and these were nightmares from her worst dreams. People were crawling about, people were screaming, whimpering, gasping for breath, touching each other, vanishing in the dark, and ever and anon being pushed off the platform onto the live rail. Some were fighting round the electric bells, trying to summon trains which could not be summoned. Others were yelling for Euthanasia or for respirators, or blaspheming the Machine. Others stood at the doors of their cells fearing, like herself, either to stop in them or to leave them. And behind all the uproar was silence—the silence which is the voice of the earth and of the generations who have gone.

No—it was worse than solitude. She closed the door again and sat down to wait for the end. The disintegration went on, accompanied by horrible cracks and rumbling. The valves that restrained the Medical Apparatus must have weakened, for it ruptured and hung hideously from the ceiling. The floor heaved and fell and flung her from the chair. A tube oozed towards her serpent fashion. And at last the final horror approached—light began to ebb, and she knew that civilization's long day was closing.

She whirled around, praying to be saved from this, at any rate, kissing the Book, pressing button after button. The uproar outside was increasing, and even penetrated the wall. Slowly the brilliancy of her cell was dimmed, the reflections faded from the metal switches. Now she could not see the reading-stand, now not the Book, though she held it in her hand. Light followed the flight of sound, air was following light, and the original void returned to the cavern from which it had been so long excluded. Vashti continued to whirl, like the devotees of an earlier religion, screaming, praying, striking at the buttons with bleeding hands.

It was thus that she opened her prison and escaped—escaped in the spirit: at least so it seems to me, ere my meditation closes. That she escaped in the body—I cannot perceive that. She struck, by chance, the switch that released the door, and the rush of foul air on her skin, the loud throbbing whispers in her ears, told her that she was facing the tunnel again, and that tremendous platform on which she had seen men fighting. They were not fighting now. Only the whispers remained, and the little whimpering groans. They were dying by hundreds out in the dark.

She burst into tears.

Tears answered her.

They wept for humanity, those two, not for themselves. They could not bear that this should be the end. Ere silence was completed their hearts were opened, and they knew what had been important on the earth. Man, the flower of all flesh, the noblest of all creatures visible, man who had once made god in his image, and had mirrored his strength on the constellations, beautiful naked man was dying, strangled in the garments that he had woven. Century after century had he toiled, and here was his reward. Truly the garment had seemed heavenly at first, shot with colors of culture, sewn with the threads of self-denial. And heavenly it had been so long as man could shed it at will and live by the essence that is his soul, and the essence, equally divine, that is his body. The sin against the body—it was for that they wept in chief; the centuries of wrong against the muscles and the nerves, and those five portals by which we can alone apprehend—glozing it over with talk of evolution, until the body was white pap, the home of ideas as colorless, last sloshy stirrings of a spirit that had grasped the stars.

"Where are you?" she sobbed.

His voice in the darkness said, "Here."

"Is there any hope, Kuno?"

"None for us."

"Where are you?"

She crawled towards him over the bodies of the dead. His blood spurted over her hands.

"Quicker," he gasped, "I am dying—but we touch, we talk, not through the Machine."

He kissed her.

"We have come back to our own. We die, but we have recaptured life, as it was in Wessex, when Ælfrid overthrew the Danes. We know what they know outside, they who dwelt in the cloud that is the color of a pearl."

"But Kuno, is it true ? Are there still men on the surface of the earth? Is this—this tunnel, this poisoned darkness—really not the end?"

He replied:

"I have seen them, spoken to them, loved them. They are hiding in the mist and the ferns until our civilization stops. Today they are the Homeless—tomorrow—"

"Oh, tomorrow—some fool will start the Machine again, tomorrow."

"Never," said Kuno, "never. Humanity has learnt its lesson."

As he spoke, the whole city was broken like a honeycomb. An air-ship had sailed in through the vomitory into a ruined wharf. It crashed downwards, exploding as it went, rending gallery after gallery with its wings of steel. For a moment they saw the nations of the dead, and, before they joined them, scraps of the untainted sky.

EDMOND HAMILTON
The Man Who Evolved

• • • •

{ 1931 }

Edmond Hamilton (1904–1977) was a stalwart of the early pulps, publishing scores of stories in *Astounding*, *Weird Tales*, and *Wonder Stories* during the 1920s and 1930s. Along with E. E. "Doc" Smith, whose *Skylark of Space* was serialized in *Amazing Stories* in 1928, Hamilton was a pioneer of space opera, epic tales of cosmic derring-do with the fate of galaxies hanging in the balance. Characteristic titles—"Crashing Suns" (1928), "The Universe Wreckers" (1930), "A Conquest of Two Worlds" (1932)—convey a sense of both the sweep of the action and the exuberance of the telling. While crude in many ways, such stories possessed a breathless narrative energy and a spectacular immensity of scale that came to define the meaning of "sense of wonder" for a generation of sf readers. Hamilton's association with the more juvenile aspects of the space opera subgenre was cemented during the 1940s, when he created and penned the "Captain Future" pulp series at the same time that John Campbell's *Astounding* was bringing a new level of adult sophistication to the field; his postwar reputation suffered somewhat as a result. Yet despite its occasional potboiling, Hamilton's work often displayed a brooding speculative invention as well as a willingness to explore downbeat themes, as in his 1952 tale "What's It Like Out There?" with its cynical vision of the ruthless inhumanity of space exploration.

"The Man Who Evolved," published in Hugo Gernsback's *Wonder Stories* in April 1931, gives evidence of Hamilton's strengths and flaws. A classic "super-science" story, featuring a cosmic-ray machine, accelerated time-scales, and the (d)evolution of the human species, it is conceptually ambitious to the point of grandiosity. As with much sf of the period, the science is at times dubious: evolution, for example, is not a teleological process and does not operate at the level of the individual, as the tale implies. Exposure to concentrated high-energy particles, as depicted in the story, would almost certainly lead to a painful death rather than an epochal transmutation. Yet "The Man Who Evolved" raises disturbing questions, similar to those broached in H. G. Wells's *The Time Machine* (1895), regarding the future development of the species, in particular the uneasy balance between the somatic and the cognitive dimensions of human experience. Moreover, pulp sf should be judged not by the accuracy of its science but by the imposing aura of scientism it evokes. The visionary, taboo-shattering fervor of experimental inquiry, as incarnated in the mysterious Dr. Pollard, is meant to thrill and appall; the narrator, Arthur Wright, and his friend Dutton, stand in for the mundane reader, reeling in shock at Pollard's posthuman transformation and the pitiless vastness of evolutionary time. A similar confrontation occurs in Pat Cadigan's "Pretty Boy Crossover" (1986), whose protagonist recoils in the face of a startling evolutionary leap taken by his former friend.

There were three of us in Pollard's house on that night that I try vainly to forget. Dr. John Pollard himself, Hugh Dutton and I, Arthur Wright—we were the three. Pollard met that night a fate whose horror none could dream; Dutton has since that night inhabited a state institution reserved for the insane, and I alone am left to tell what happened.

It was on Pollard's invitation that Dutton and I went up to his isolated cottage. We three had been friends and roommates at the New York Technical University. Our friendship was perhaps a little unusual, for Pollard was a number of years older than Dutton and myself and was different in temperament, being rather quieter by nature. He had followed an intensive course of biological studies, too, instead of the ordinary engineering courses Dutton and I had taken.

As Dutton and I drove northward along the Hudson on that afternoon, we found ourselves reviewing what we knew of Pollard's career. We had known of his taking his master's and doctor's degrees, and had heard of his work under Braun, the Vienna biologist whose theories had stirred up such turmoil. We had heard casually, too, that afterwards he had come back to plunge himself in private research at the country-house beside the Hudson he had inherited. But since then we had had no word from him and had been somewhat surprised to receive his telegrams inviting us to spend the weekend with him.

It was drawing into early-summer twilight when Dutton and I reached a small riverside village and were directed to Pollard's place, a mile or so beyond. We found it easily enough, a splendid old pegged-frame house that for a hundred-odd years had squatted on a low hill above the river. Its outbuildings were clustered around the big house like the chicks about some protecting hen.

Pollard himself came out to greet us. "Why, you boys have grown up!" was his first exclamation. "Here I've remembered you as Hughie and Art, the campus trouble-raisers, and you look as though you belong to business clubs and talk everlastingly about sales-resistance!"

"That's the sobering effect of commercial life," Dutton explained, grinning. "It hasn't touched you, you old oyster—you look the same as you did five years ago."

He did, too, his lanky figure and slow smile and curiously thoughtful eyes having changed not a jot. Yet Pollard's bearing seemed to show some rather more than usual excitement and I commented on it.

"If I seem a little excited it's because this is a great day for me," he answered.

"Well, you *are* in luck to get two fine fellows like Dutton and me to trail up to this hermitage of yours," I began, but he shook his head smilingly.

"I don't refer to that, Art, though I'm mighty glad you've come. As for my hermitage, as you call it, don't say a word against it. I've been able to do work here I could never have done amid the distractions of a city laboratory."

His eyes were alight. "If you two knew what—but there, you'll hear it soon enough. Let's get inside—I suppose you're hungry?"

"Hungry—not I," I assured him. "I might devour half a steer or some trifle like that, but I have really no appetite for anything else today."

"Same here," Dutton said. "I just pick at my food lately. Give me a few dozen sandwiches and a bucket of coffee and I consider it a full meal."

"Well, we'll see what we can do to tempt your delicate appetites," said Pollard, as we went inside.

We found his big house comfortable enough, with long, low-ceilinged rooms and broad windows looking riverward. After putting our bags in a bedroom, and while his housekeeper and cook prepared dinner, Pollard escorted us on a tour of inspection of the place. We were most interested in his laboratory.

It was a small wing he had added to the house, of frame construction outside to harmonize with the rest of the building, but inside offering a gleaming vista of white-tiled walls and polished instruments. A big cube-like structure of transparent metal surmounted by a huge metal cylinder resembling a monster vacuum tube took up the room's center, and he showed us in an adjoining stone-floored room the dynamos and motors of his private power-plant.

Night had fallen by the time we finished dinner, the meal having been prolonged by our reminiscences. The housekeeper and cook had gone, Pollard explaining that the servants did not sleep in the place. We sat smoking for a while in his living-room, Dutton looking appreciatively around at our comfortable surroundings.

"Your hermitage doesn't seem half-bad, Pollard," he commented. "I wouldn't mind this easy life for a while myself."

"Easy life?" repeated Pollard. "That's all you know about it, Hugh. The fact is that I've never worked so hard in my life as I've done up here in the last two years."

"What in the world have you been working at?" I asked. "Something so unholy you've had to keep it hidden here?"

A MAD SCHEME

Pollard chuckled. "That's what they think down in the village. They know I'm a biologist and have a laboratory here, so it's a foregone conclusion with them that I'm doing vivisection of a specially dreadful nature. That's why the servants won't stay here at night.

"As a matter of fact," he added, "if they knew down in the village what I've really been working on they'd be ten times as fearful as they are now."

"Are you trying to play the mysterious great scientist for our benefit?" Dutton demanded. "If you are you're wasting time—I know you, stranger, so take off that mask."

"That's right," I told him. "If you're trying to get our curiosity worked up you'll find we can scram you as neatly as we could five years ago."

"Which scramming generally ended in black eyes for both of you," he retorted. "But I've no intention of working up your curiosity—as a matter of fact I asked you up here to see what I've been doing and help me finish it."

"Help you?" echoed Dutton. "What can we help you do—dissect worms? Some weekend, I can see right now!"

"There's more to this than dissecting worms," Pollard said. He leaned back and smoked for a little time in silence before he spoke again.

"Do you two have any knowledge at all of evolution?" he asked.

"I know that it's a fighting word in some states," I answered, "and that when you say it you've got to smile, damn you."

He smiled himself. "I suppose you're aware of the fact, however, that all life on this earth began as simple uni-cellular protoplasm, and by successive evolutionary mutations or changes developed into its present forms and is still slowly developing?"

"We know that much—just because we're not biologists you needn't think we're totally ignorant of biology," Dutton said.

"Shut up, Dutton," I warned. "What's evolution got to do with your work up here, Pollard?"

"It *is* my work up here," Pollard answered.

He bent forward. "I'll try to make this clear to you from the start. You know, or say you know, the main steps of evolutionary development. Life began on this earth as simple protoplasm, a jelly-like mass from which developed small protoplasmic organisms. From these developed in turn sea-creatures, land-lizards, mammals, by successive mutations. This infinitely slow evolutionary process has reached its highest point so far in the mammal man, and is still going on with the same slowness.

"This much is certain biological knowledge, but two great questions concerning this process of evolution have remained hitherto unanswered. First, what is the cause of evolutionary change, the cause of these slow, steady mutations into higher forms? Second, what is the future course of man's evolution going to be, what will be the forms into which in the future man will evolve, and where will his evolution stop? Those two questions biology has so far been unable to answer."

Pollard was silent a moment and then said quietly, "I have found the answer to one of those questions, and am going to find the answer to the other tonight."

We stared at him. "Are you trying to spoof us?" I asked finally.

"I'm absolutely serious, Arthur. I have actually solved the first of those problems, have found the cause of evolution."

"What is it, then?" burst out of Dutton.

"What it has been thought by some biologists for years to be," Pollard answered. "The cosmic rays."

"The cosmic rays?" I echoed. "The vibrations from space that Millikan discovered?"

"Yes, the cosmic rays, the shortest wavelength and most highly penetrating of all vibratory forces. It has been known that they beat unceasingly upon the earth from outer space, cast forth by the huge generators of the stars, and it has also been known that they must have some great effect in one way or another upon the life of the earth.

"I have proved that they do have such an effect, and that that effect is what we call evolution! For it is the cosmic rays, beating upon every living organism on earth, that cause the profound changes in the structure of those organisms which we call mutations. Those changes are slow indeed, but it is due to them that through the ages life has been raised from the first protoplasm to man, and is still being raised higher."

"Good Lord, you can't be serious on this, Pollard!" Dutton protested.

"I am so serious that I am going to stake my life on my discovery tonight," Pollard answered, quietly.

We were startled. "What do you mean?"

"I mean that I have found in the cosmic rays the cause of evolution, the answer to the first question, and that tonight by means of them I am going to answer the second question and find out what the future evolutionary development of man will be!"

"But how could you possibly—"

Pollard interrupted. "Easily enough. I have been able in the last months to do something no physicist has been able to do, to concentrate the cosmic rays and yet remove from them their harmful properties. You saw the cylinder over the metal cube in my laboratory? That cylinder literally gathers in from an immense distance the cosmic rays that strike this part of earth, and reflects them down inside the cube.

"Now suppose those concentrated cosmic rays, millions of times stronger than the ordinary cosmic rays that strike one spot on earth, fall upon a man standing inside the cube. What will be the result? It is the cosmic rays that cause evolutionary change, and you heard me say that they are still changing all life on earth, still changing man, but so slowly as to be unnoticeable. But what about the man under those terrifically intensified rays? He will be changed millions of times faster than ordinarily, will go forward in hours or minutes through the evolutionary mutations that all mankind will go forward through in eons to come!"

"And you propose to try that experiment?" I cried.

"I propose to try it on myself," said Pollard gravely, "and to find out for myself the evolutionary changes that await humankind."

"Why, it's insane!" Dutton exclaimed.

Pollard smiled. "The old cry," he commented. "Never an attempt has been made yet to tamper with nature's laws, but that cry has been raised."

"But Dutton's right!" I cried. "Pollard, you've worked here alone too long—you've let your mind become warped—"

"You are trying to tell me that I have become a little mad," he said. "No, I am sane—perhaps wonderfully sane, in trying this."

His expression changed, his eyes brooding. "Can't you two see what this may mean to humanity? As we are to the apes, so must the men of the future be to us. If we could use this method of mine to take all mankind forward through millions of years of evolutionary development at one stride, wouldn't it be sane to do so?"

My mind was whirling. "Good heavens, the whole thing is so crazy," I protested. “To accelerate the evolution of the human race? It seems somehow a thing forbidden.”

“It’s a thing glorious if it can be done,” he returned, “and I know that it can be done. But first one must go ahead, must travel on through stage after stage of man’s future development to find out to which stage it would be most desirable for all mankind to be transferred. I know there is such an age.”

“And you asked us up here to take part in that?”

“Just that. I mean to enter the cube and let the concentrated rays whirl me forward along the paths of evolution, but I must have someone to turn the rays on and off at the right moments.”

“It’s all incredible!” Dutton exclaimed. “Pollard, if this is a joke it’s gone far enough for me.”

For answer Pollard rose. “We will go to the laboratory now,” he said simply. “I am eager to get started.”

I cannot remember following Pollard and Dutton to the laboratory, my thoughts were spinning so at the time. It was not until we stood before the great cube from which the huge metal cylinder towered that I was aware of the reality of it all.

Pollard had gone into the dynamo-room and as Dutton and I stared wordlessly at the great cube and cylinder, at the retorts and flasks of acids and strange equipment about us, we heard the hum of motor-generators. Pollard came back to the switchboard supported in a steel frame beside the cube, and as he closed a switch there came a crackling and the cylinder glowed with white light.

Pollard pointed to it and the big quartz-like disk in the cubical chamber’s ceiling, from which the white force-shafts shot downward.

“The cylinder is now gathering cosmic rays from an immense area of space,” he said, “and those concentrated rays are falling through that disk into the cube’s interior. To cut off the rays it is necessary only to open this switch.” He reached to open the switch, the light died.

Quickly, while we stared, he removed his clothing, donning in place of it a loose white running suit.

“I will want to observe the changes of my own body as much as possible,” he explained. “Now, I will stand inside the cube and you will turn on the rays and let them play upon me for fifteen minutes. Roughly, that should represent a period of some fifty million years of future evolutionary change. At the end of fifteen minutes you will turn the rays off and we will be able to observe what changes they have caused. We will then resume the process, going forward by fifteen-minute or rather fifty-million-year periods."

"But where will it stop—where will we quit the process?" Dutton asked.

Pollard shrugged. "We'll stop where evolution stops, that is, where the rays no longer affect me. You know, biologists have often wondered what the last change or final development of man will be, the last mutation. Well, we are going to see tonight what it will be."

He stepped toward the cube and then paused, went to a desk and brought from it a sealed envelope he handed to me.

"This is just in case something happens to me of a fatal nature," he said. "It contains an attestation signed by myself that you two are in no way responsible for what I am undertaking."

"Pollard, give up this unholy business!" I cried, clutching his arm. "It's not too late, and this whole thing seems ghastly to me!"

"I'm afraid it is too late," he smiled. "If I backed out now I'd be ashamed to look in a mirror hereafter. And no explorer was ever more eager than I am to start down the path of man's future evolution!"

He stepped up into the cube, standing directly beneath the disk in its ceiling. He motioned imperatively, and like an automaton I closed the door and then threw the switch.

The cylinder broke again into glowing white light, and as the shafts of glowing white force shot down from the disk in the cube's ceiling upon Pollard, we glimpsed his whole body writhing as though beneath a terrifically concentrated electrical force. The shaft of glowing emanations almost hid him from our view. I knew that the cosmic rays in themselves were invisible but guessed that the light of the cylinder and shaft was in some way a transformation of part of the rays into visible light.

Dutton and I stared with beating hearts into the cubical chamber, having but fleeting glimpses of Pollard's form. My watch was in one hand, the other hand on the switch. The fifteen minutes that followed seemed to me to pass with the slowness of fifteen eternities. Neither of us spoke and the only sounds were the hum of the generators and the crackling of the cylinder that from the far spaces was gathering and concentrating the rays of evolution.

At last the watch's hand marked the quarter-hour and I snapped off the switch, the light of the cylinder and inside the cube dying. Exclamations burst from us both.

Pollard stood inside the cube, staggering as though still dazed by the impact of the experience, but he was not the Pollard who had entered the chamber! He was transfigured, godlike! His body had literally expanded into a great figure of such physical power and beauty as we had not imagined could exist! He was many inches taller and broader, his skin a clear pink, every limb and muscle molded as though by some master sculptor.

The greatest change, though, was in his face. Pollard's homely, good-humored features were gone, replaced by a face whose perfectly-cut features held the stamp of immense intellectual power that shone almost overpoweringly from the clear dark eyes. It was not Pollard who stood before us, I told myself, but a being as far above us as the most advanced man of today is above the troglodyte!

He was stepping out of the cube and his voice reached our ears, clear and bell-like, triumphant.

"You see? It worked as I knew it would work! I'm fifty million years ahead of the rest of humanity in evolutionary development!"

"Pollard!" My lips moved with difficulty. "Pollard, this is terrible—this change—"

His radiant eyes flashed. "Terrible? It's wonderful! Do you two realize what I now am, can you realize it? This body of mine is the kind of body all men will have in fifty million years, and the brain inside it is a brain fifty million years ahead of yours in development!"

He swept his hand about. "Why, all this laboratory and former work of mine seems infinitely petty, childish, to me! The problems that I worked on for years I could solve now in minutes. I could do more for mankind now than all the men now living could do together!"

"Then you're going to stop at this stage?" Dutton cried eagerly. "You're not going further with this?"

"Of course I am! If fifty million years' development makes this much change in man, what will a hundred million years, two hundred million make? I'm going to find that out."

I grasped his hand. "Pollard, listen to me! Your experiment has succeeded, has fulfilled your wildest dreams. Stop it now! Think what you can accomplish, man! I know your ambition has always been to be one of humanity's great benefactors—by stopping here you can be the greatest! You can be a living proof to mankind of what your process can make it, and with that proof before it all humanity will be eager to become the same as you!"

He freed himself from my grasp. "No, Arthur—I have gone part of the way into humanity's future and I'm going on."

He stepped back into the chamber, while Dutton and I stared helplessly. It seemed half a dream, the laboratory, the cubical chamber, the godlike figure inside that was and still was not Pollard.

"Turn on the rays, and let them play for fifteen minutes more," he was directing. "It will project me ahead another fifty million years."

His eyes and voice were imperative, and I glanced at my watch, and snicked over the switch. Again the cylinder broke into light, again the shaft of force shot down into the cube to hide Pollard's splendid figure.

Dutton and I waited with feverish intensity in the next minutes. Pollard was standing still beneath the broad shaft of force, and so was hidden in it from our eyes. What would its lifting disclose? Would he have changed still more, into some giant form, or would he be the same, having already reached humanity's highest possible development?

When I shut off the mechanism at the end of the appointed period, Dutton and I received a shock. For again Pollard had changed!

He was no longer the radiant, physically perfect figure of the first metamorphosis. His body instead seemed to have grown thin and shriveled, the outlines of bones visible through its flesh. His body, indeed, seemed to have lost half its bulk and many inches of stature and breadth, but these were compensated for by the change in his head.

For the head supported by this weak body was an immense, bulging balloon that measured fully eighteen inches from brow to back! It was almost entirely hairless, its great mass balanced precariously upon his slender shoulders and neck. And his face too was changed greatly, the eyes larger and the mouth smaller, the ears seeming smaller also. The great bulging forehead dominated the face.

Could this be Pollard? His voice sounded thin and weak to our ears.

"You are surprised to see me this time? Well, you see a man a hundred million years ahead of you in development. And I must confess that you appear to me as two brutish, hairy cave-men would appear to you."

"But Pollard, this is awful!" Dutton cried. "This change is more terrible than the first . . . if you had only stopped at the first . . ."

The eyes of the shriveled, huge-headed figure in the cube fired with anger. "Stop at that first stage? I'm glad now that I didn't! The man I was fifteen minutes ago . . . fifty million years ago in development . . . seems now to me to have been half-animal! What was his big animal-like body beside my immense brain?"

"You say that because in this change you're getting away from all human emotions and sentiments!" I burst. "Pollard, do you realize what you're doing? You're changing out of human semblance!"

"I realize it perfectly," he snapped, "and I see nothing to be deplored in the fact. It means that in a hundred million years man will be developing in brain-capacity and will care nothing for the development of body. To you two crude beings, of what is to me the past, this seems terrible; but to me it is desirable and natural. Turn on the rays again!"

"Don't do it, Art!" cried Dutton. "This madness has gone far enough!"

Pollard's great eyes surveyed us with cold menace. "You will turn on the rays," his thin voice ordered deliberately. "If you do not, it will be but the work of a moment for me to annihilate both of you and go on with this alone."

"You'd kill us?" I said dumbfoundedly. "We two, two of your best friends?"

His narrow mouth seemed to sneer. "Friends? I am millions of years past such irrational emotions as friendship. The only emotion you awaken in me is a contempt for your crudity. Turn on the rays!"

THE BRAIN MONSTER

His eyes blazed as he snapped the last order, and as though propelled by a force outside myself, I closed the switch. The shaft of glowing force again hid him from our view.

Of our thoughts during the following quarter-hour I can say nothing, for both Dutton and I were so rigid with awe and horror as to make our minds chaotic. I shall never forget, though, that first moment after the time had passed and I had again switched off the mechanism.

The change had continued, and Pollard—I could not call him that in my own mind—stood in the cube-chamber as a shape the sight of which stunned our minds.

He had become simply a great head! A huge hairless head fully a yard in diameter, supported on tiny legs, the arms having dwindled to mere hands that projected just below the head! The eyes were enormous, saucer-like, but the ears were mere pin-holes at either side of the head, the nose and mouth being similar holes below the eyes!

He was stepping out of the chamber on his ridiculously little limbs, and as Dutton and I reeled back in unreasoning horror, his voice came to us as an almost inaudible piping. And it held pride!

"You tried to keep me from going on, and you see what I have become? To such as you, no doubt, I seem terrible, yet you two and all like you seem as low to me as the worms that crawl!"

"Good God, Pollard, you've made yourself a monster!" The words burst from me without thought.

His enormous eyes turned on me. "You call me Pollard, yet I am no more the Pollard you knew, and who entered that chamber first, than you are the ape of millions of years ago from whom you sprang! And all mankind is like you two! Well, they will all learn the powers of one who is a hundred and fifty million years in advance of them!"

"What do you mean?" Dutton exclaimed.

"I mean that with the colossal brain I have I will master without a struggle this man-swarming planet, and make it a huge laboratory in which to pursue the experiments that please me."

"But Pollard—remember why you started this!" I cried. "To go ahead and chart the path of future evolution for humanity—to benefit humanity and not to rule it!"

The great head's enormous eyes did not change. "I remember that the creature Pollard that I was until tonight had such foolish ambitions, yes. It would stir mirth now, if I could feel such an emotion. To benefit humanity? Do you men dream of benefiting the animals you rule over? I would no sooner think of working for the benefit of you humans!

"Do you two yet realize that I am so far ahead of you in brain power now as you are ahead of the beasts that perish? Look at this . . ."

He had climbed onto a chair beside one of the laboratory tables and was reaching among the retorts and apparatus there. Swiftly he poured several compounds into a lead mortar, added others, poured upon the mixed contents another mixture made as swiftly.

There was a puff of intense green smoke from the mortar instantly, and then the great head—I can only call him that—turned the mortar upside down. A lump of shining mottled metal fell out and we gasped as we recognized the yellow sheen of pure gold, made in a moment, apparently, by a mixture of common compounds!

"You see?" the grotesque figure was asking. "What is the transformation of elements to a mind like mine? You two cannot even realize the scope of my intelligence!

"I can destroy all life on this earth from this room, if I desire. I can construct a telescope that will allow me to look on the planets of the farthest galaxies! I can send my mind forth to make contact with other minds without the slightest material connection. And you think it terrible that I should rule your race! I will not rule them, I will *own* them and this planet as you might own a farm and animals!"

"You couldn't!" I cried. "Pollard, if there is anything of Pollard left in you, give up that thought! We'll kill you ourselves before we'll let you start a monstrous rule of men!"

"We will—by God, we will!" Dutton cried, his face twitching.

We had started desperately forward toward the great head but stopped suddenly in our tracks as his great eyes met ours. I found myself walking backward to where I had stood, walking back and Dutton with me, like two automatons.

"So you two would try to kill me?" queried the head that had been Pollard. "Why, I could direct you without a word to kill yourselves and you'd do so in an instant! What chance has your puny will and brain against mine? And what chance will all the force of men have against me when a glance from me will make them puppets of my will?"

A desperate inspiration flashed through my brain. "Pollard, wait!" I exclaimed. "You were going on with the process, with the rays! If you stop here you'll not know what changes lie beyond your present form!"

He seemed to consider. "That is true," he admitted, "and though it seems impossible to me that by going on I can attain to greater intelligence than I now have, I want to find out for certain."

"Then you'll go under the rays for another fifteen minutes?" I asked quickly.

"I will," he answered, "but lest you harbor any foolish ideas, you may know that even inside the chamber I will be able to read your thoughts and can kill both of you before you can make a move to harm me."

He stepped up into the chamber again, and as I reached for the switch, Dutton trembling beside me, we glimpsed for a moment the huge head before the down-smiting white force hid it from our sight.

The minutes of this period seemed dragging even more slowly than before. It seemed hours before I reached at last to snap off the rays. We gazed into the chamber, shaking.

At first glance the great head inside seemed unchanged, but then we saw that it had changed, and greatly. Instead of being a skin-covered head with at least rudimentary arms and legs, it was now a great gray head-like shape of even greater size, supported by two gray muscular tentacles. The surface of this gray head-thing was wrinkled and folded, and its only features were two eyes as small as our own.

"Oh my God!" quaked Dutton. "He's changing from a head into a brain—he's losing all human appearance!"

Into our minds came a thought from the gray head-thing before us, a thought as clear as though spoken. "You have guessed it, for even my former head-body is disappearing, all atrophying except the brain. I am become a walking, seeing brain. As I am so all of your race will be in two hundred million years, gradually losing more and more of their atrophied bodies and developing more and more their great brains."

His eyes seemed to read us. "You need not fear now the things I threatened in my last stage of development. My mind, grown infinitely greater, would no more now want to rule you men and your little planet than you would want to rule an anthill and its inhabitants! My mind, gone fifty million years further ahead in development, can soar out now to vistas of power and knowledge unimagined by me in that last stage, and unimaginable to you."

"Great God, Pollard!" I cried. "What have you become?"

"Pollard?" Dutton was laughing hysterically. "You call that thing Pollard? Why, we had dinner with Pollard three hours ago—he was a human being, and not a thing like this!"

"I have become what all men will become in time," the thing's thought answered me. "I have gone this far along the road of man's future evolution, and am going on to the end of that road, am going to attain the development that the last mutation possible will give me!"

"Turn on the rays," his thought continued. "I think that I must be approaching now the last possible mutation."

I snapped over the switch again and the white shaft of the concentrated rays veiled from us the great gray shape. I felt my own mind giving beneath the strain of horror of the last hour, and Dutton was still half-hysterical.

The humming and crackling of the great apparatus seemed thunderous to my ears as the minutes passed. With every nerve keyed to highest tension, I threw open the switch at last. The rays ceased, and the figure in the chamber was again revealed.

Dutton began to laugh shrilly, and then abruptly was sobbing. I do not know whether I was doing the same, though I have a dim memory of mouthing incoherent things as my eyes took in the shape in the chamber.

It was a great brain! A gray limp mass four feet across, it lay in the chamber, its surface ridged and wrinkled by innumerable fine convolutions. It had no features or limbs of any kind in its gray mass. It was simply a huge brain whose only visible sign of life was its slow twitching movement.

From it thoughts beat strongly into our own horror-weighted brains.

"You see me now, a great brain only, just as all men will be far in the future. Yes, you might have known, I might have known, when I was like you, that this would be the course of human evolution, that the brain that alone gives man dominance would develop and the body that hampers that brain would atrophy until he would have developed into pure brain as I now am!

"I have no features, no senses that I could describe to you, yet can realize the universe infinitely better than you can with your elementary senses. I am aware of planes of existence you cannot imagine. I can feed myself with pure energy without the need of a cumbersome body, to transform it, and I can move and act, despite my lack of limbs, by means and with a speed and power utterly beyond your comprehension.

"If you still have fear of the threats I made two stages back against your world and race, banish them! I am pure intelligence now and as such, though I can no more feel the emotions of love or friendship, neither can I feel those of ambition or pride. The only emotion, if such it is, that remains to me still is intellectual curiosity, and this desire for truth that has burned in man since his apehood will thus be the last of all desires to leave him!"

THE LAST MUTATION

"A brain—a great brain!" Dutton was saying dazedly. "Here in Pollard's laboratory—but where's Pollard? He was here, too . . ."

"Then all men will some day be as you are now?" I cried.

"Yes," came the answering thought, "in two hundred and fifty million years man as you know him and as you are will be no more, and after passing all the stages through which I have passed through tonight, the human race will have developed into great brains inhabiting not only your solar system, no doubt, but the systems of other stars!"

"And that's the end of man's evolutionary road? That is the highest point that he will reach?"

"No, I think he will change still from those great brains into still a higher form," the brain answered—the brain that three hours before had been Pollard!—"and I am going to find out now what that higher form will be. For I think this will be the last mutation of all and that with it I will reach the end of man's evolutionary path, the last and highest form into which he can develop!

"You will turn on the rays now," the brain's order continued, "and in fifteen minutes we will know what that last and highest form is."

My hand was on the switch but Dutton had staggered to me, was clutching my arm. "Don't, Arthur!" he was exclaiming thickly. "We've seen horrors enough—let's not see the last—get out of here . . ."

"I can't!" I cried. "Oh God, I want to stop but I can't now—I want to see the end myself—I've got to see . . ."

"Turn on the rays!" came the brain's thought-order again.

"The end of the road—the last mutation," I panted. "We've got to see—to see—" I drove the switch home.

The rays flashed down again to hide the great gray brain in the cube. Dutton's eyes were staring fixedly, he was clinging to me.

The minutes passed! Each tick of the watch in my hand was the mighty note of a great tolling bell in my ears.

An inability to move seemed to be gripping me. The hand of my watch was approaching the minute for which I waited, yet I could not raise my hand toward the switch!

Then as the hand reached the appointed minute I broke from my immobility and in a sheer frenzy of sudden strength pulled open the switch, rushed forward with Dutton to the cube's very edge!

The great gray brain that had been inside it was gone. There lay on the cube's floor instead of it a quite shapeless mass of clear, jelly-like matter. It was quite motionless save for a slight quivering. My shaking hand went forth to touch it, and then it was that I screamed, such a scream as all the tortures of hell's crudest fiends could not have wrung from a human throat.

The mass inside the cube was a mass of simple *protoplasm*! This then was the end of man's evolution-road, the highest form to which time would bring him, the last mutation of all! The road of man's evolution was a circular one, returning to its beginning!

From the earth's bosom had risen the first crude organisms. Then sea-creature and land-creature and mammal and ape to man; and from man it would rise in the future through all the forms we had seen that night. There would be super-men, bodiless heads, pure brains; only to be changed by the last mutation of all into the protoplasm from which first it had sprung!

I do not know now exactly what followed. I know that I rushed upon that quivering, quiescent mass, calling Pollard's name madly and shouting things I am glad I cannot remember. I know that Dutton was shouting too, with insane laughter, and that as he struck with lunatic howls and fury about the laboratory the crash of breaking glass and the hiss of escaping gases was in my ears. And then from those mingling acids bright flames were leaping and spreading sudden fires that alone, I think now, saved my own sanity.

For I can remember dragging the insanely laughing Dutton from the room, from the house, into the cool darkness of the night. I remember the chill of dew-wet grass against my hands and face as the flames from Pollard's house soared higher. And I remember that as I saw Dutton's crazy laughter by that crimson light, I knew that he would laugh thus until he died.

So ends my narrative of the end that came to Pollard and Pollard's house. It is, as I said in the beginning, a narrative that I only can tell now, for Dutton has never spoken a sane word since. In the institution where he now is, they think his condition the result of shock from the fire, just as Pollard was believed to have perished in that fire. I have never until now told the truth.

But I am telling it now, hoping that it will in some way lessen the horror it has left with me. For there could be no horror greater than that we saw in Pollard's house that night. I have brooded upon it. With my mind's eye I have followed that tremendous cycle of change, that purposeless, eon-long climb of life up from simple protoplasm through myriads of forms and lives of ceaseless pain and struggle, only to end in simple protoplasm again.

Will that cycle of evolutionary change be repeated over and over again upon this and other worlds, ceaselessly, purposelessly, until there is no more universe for it to go on in? Is this colossal cycle of life's changes as inevitable and necessary as the cycle that in space makes of the nebulae myriad suns, and of the suns dark-stars, and of the dark-stars colliding with one another nebulae again?

Or is this evolutionary cycle we saw a cycle in appearance only, is there some change that we cannot understand, above and beyond it? I do not know which of these possibilities is truth, but I do know that the first of them haunts me. It would haunt the world if the world believed my story. Perhaps I should be thankful as I write to know that I will not be believed.

LESLIE F. STONE
The Conquest of Gola

• • • •

{1931}

Leslie F. Stone (1905–1991) is the pseudonym of Leslie Francis Silverbert (also given as Silberberg and Silverberg), one of the first women to publish in the American sf pulp magazines. Her first stories, including "Men with Wings" in *Air Wonder Stories* and the two-part serial "Out of the Void" in Hugo Gernsback's *Amazing Stories*, appeared in 1929. Reprinted in book form in 1967, "Out of the Void" is the tale of a heroic young space explorer who turns out to be a woman in disguise. Stone made her debut in the magazines only two years after Clare Winger Harris's "The Fate of the Poseidonia" (1927) appeared in *Amazing Stories*, the first sf story by a woman to be published in the pulps. Stone's fiction was immediately popular with readers, and only C. L. Moore enjoyed a more successful career as a woman writing sf in the 1930s. In contrast to Moore's long career, however, Stone's ended after 1940. In an interview published decades later, she mentioned the increasingly male-oriented character of the sf pulps after the replacement of editors such as Gernsback by a new generation that included the immensely influential John W. Campbell. According to Stone, Campbell returned one of her submissions with the comment: "I do not believe that women are capable of writing science fiction—nor do I approve of it!"

Although "The Conquest of Gola" has been reprinted several times since it first appeared, for the most part Stone is one of many first-generation women writers—including Harris, Lilith Lorraine, L(ouise) Taylor Hansen, and Francis Stevens (pseudonym of Gertrude Barrows Bennett)—who have been virtually written out of the genre's history. Only recently has her work been rediscovered and recognized for its intelligent, challenging, and entertaining treatments of some of sf's most familiar story conventions. Like C. L. Moore's "Shambleau" (1933), "The Conquest of Gola" is a reminder of the exciting contributions of women writers in the earliest years of the genre. Echoes of the gender concerns at the center of "The Conquest of Gola" can be heard in one of feminist sf's most significant stories, Joanna Russ's "When It Changed" (1972).

Stone's story is also a reminder that sf's conventions have been challenged almost since their inception. As an early alien-invasion story, it develops an sf trope first fully realized by H. G. Wells in *The War of the Worlds* (1898), in which Earth is invaded by Mars. Stone reverses Wells's alien-invasion story so that it is Earth—called Detaxal by the Golans—that is the invader; the alien Golans—inhabitants of the planet we know as Venus—are the potential victims of Detaxal's aggressive expansionism. Stone's story immediately enlists its readers on the side of the female aliens who rule Gola, whose powers of telepathy and mind control are pitted against the brute force of the Detaxalans. Her story also addresses another early sf trope, the sex-role reversal story. From the pens of male writers, this trope has tended to result in stories about domineering women who are "tamed" by brutally irresistible male protagonists. Stone's telepathic alien women are not so easily seduced.

Hola, my daughters (sighed the Matriarch), it is true indeed, I am the only living one upon Gola who remembers the invasion from Detaxal. I alone of all my generation survive to recall vividly the sights and scenes of that past era. And well it is that you come to me to hear by free communication of mind to mind, face to face with each other.

Ah, well I remember the surprise of that hour when through the mists that enshroud our lovely world, there swam the first of the great smooth cylinders of the Detaxalans, fifty *tas** in length, as glistening and silvery as the soil of our land, propelled by the man-things that on Detaxal are supreme even as we women are supreme on Gola.

In those bygone days, as now, Gola was enwrapped by her cloud mists that keep from us the terrific glare of the great star that glows like a malignant spirit out there in the darkness of the void. Only occasionally when a particularly great storm parts the mist of heaven do we see the wonders of the vast universe, but that does not prevent us, with our marvelous telescopes handed down to us from thousands of generations before us, from learning what lies across the dark seas of the outside.

Therefore we knew of the nine planets that encircle the great star and are subject to its rule. And so are we familiar enough with the surfaces of these

*Since there is no means of translating the Golan measurements of either length or time, we can but guess at these things. However, since the Detaxalan ships each carried a thousand men, it can be seen that the ships were between five hundred and a thousand feet in length.

planets to know why Gola should appear as a haven to their inhabitants who see in our cloud-enclosed mantle a sweet release from the blasting heat and blinding glare of the great sun.

So it was not strange at all to us to find that the people of Detaxal, the third planet of the sun, had arrived on our globe with a wish in their hearts to migrate here, and end their days out of reach of the blistering warmth that had come to be their lot on their own world.

Long ago we, too, might have gone on exploring expeditions to other worlds, other universes, but for what? Are we not happy here? We who have attained the greatest of civilizations within the confines of our own silvery world. Powerfully strong with our mighty force rays, we could subjugate all the universe, but why?

Are we not content with life as it is, with our lovely cities, our homes, our daughters, our gentle consorts? Why spend physical energy in combative strife for something we do not wish, when our mental processes carry us further and beyond the conquest of mere terrestrial exploitation?

On Detaxal it is different, for there the peoples, the ignoble male creatures, breed for physical prowess, leaving the development of their sciences, their philosophies, and the contemplation of the abstract to a chosen few. The greater part of the race fares forth to conquer, to lay waste, to struggle and fight as the animals do over a morsel of worthless territory. Of course we can see why they desired Gola with all its treasures, but we can thank Providence and ourselves that they did not succeed in "commercializing" us as they have the remainder of the universe with their ignoble Federation.

Ah yes, well I recall the hour when first they came, pushing cautiously through the cloud mists, seeking that which lay beneath. We of Gola were unwarned until the two cylinders hung directly above Tola, the greatest city of that time, which still lies in its ruins since that memorable day. But they have paid for it—paid for it well in thousands and tens of thousands of their men.

We were first apprised of their coming when the alarm from Tola was sent from the great beam station there, advising all to stand in readiness for an emergency. Geble, my mother, was then Queen of all Gola, and I was by her side in Morka, that pleasant seaside resort, where I shall soon travel to partake of its rejuvenating waters.

With us were four of Geble's consorts, sweet gentle males, that gave Geble much pleasure in those free hours away from the worries of state. But when the word of the strangers' descent over our home city, Tola, came to us, all else was forgotten. With me at her side, Geble hastened to the beam station and there in the matter transmitter we dispatched our physical beings to the palace at Tola, and the next moment were staring upward at the two strange shapes etched against the clouds.

What the Detaxalan ships were waiting for we did not know then, but later we learned. Not grasping the meaning of our beam stations, the commanders of the ships considered the city below them entirely lacking in means of defense, and were conferring on the method of taking it without bloodshed on either side.

It was not long after our arrival in Tola that the first of the ships began to descend toward the great square before the palace. Geble watched without a word, her great mind already scanning the brains of those whom she found within the great machine. She transferred to my mind but a single thought as I stood there at her side and that with a sneer: "Barbarians!"

Now the ship was settling in the square and after a few moments of hesitation, a circular doorway appeared at the side and four of the Detaxalans came through the opening. The square was empty but for themselves and their flyer, and we saw them looking about surveying the beautiful buildings on all sides. They seemed to recognize the palace for what it was and in one accord moved in our direction.

Then Geble left the window at which we stood and strode to the doorway opening upon the balcony that faced the square. The Detaxalans halted in their tracks when they saw her slender graceful form appear and removing the strange coverings they wore on their heads they each made a bow.

Again Geble sneered, for only the male-things of our world bow their heads, and so she recognized these visitors for what they were, nothing more than the despicable males of the species! And what creatures they were!

Imagine a short almost flat body set high upon two slender legs, the body tapering in the middle, several times as broad across as it is through the center, with two arms almost as long as the legs attached to the upper part of the torso. A small column-like neck of only a few inches divides the head of oval shape from the body, and in this head only are set the organs of sight, hearing, and scent. Their bodies were like a patchwork of a misguided nature.

Yes, strange as it is, my daughters, practically all of the creature's faculties had their base in the small ungainly head, and each organ was perforce pressed into serving for several functions. For instance, the breathing nostrils also served for scenting out odors, nor was this organ able to exclude any disagreeable odors that might come its way, but had to dispense to the brain both pleasant and unpleasant odors at the same time.

Then there was the mouth, set directly beneath the nose, and here again we had an example of one organ doing the work of two, for the creature not only used the mouth with which to take in the food for its body, but it also used the mouth to enunciate the excruciatingly ugly sounds of its language forthwith.

Never before have I seen such a poorly organized body, so unlike our own highly developed organisms. How much nicer it is to be able to call forth any organ at will, and dispense with it when its usefulness is over! Instead these poor Detaxalans had to carry theirs about in physical being all the time so that always was the surface of their bodies entirely marred.

Yet that was not the only part of their ugliness, and proof of the lowliness of their origin, for whereas our fine bodies support themselves by muscular development, these poor creatures were dependent entirely upon a strange structure to keep them in their proper shape.

Imagine if you can a bony skeleton somewhat like the foundations upon which we build our edifices, laying stone and cement over the steel framework. But this skeleton instead is inside a body which the flesh, muscle and skin overlay. Everywhere in their bodies are these cartilaginous structures—hard, heavy, bony structures developed by the chemicals of the being for its use. Even the hands, feet and head of the creatures were underlaid with these bones—ugh, it was terrible when we dissected one of the fellows for study. I shudder to think of it.

Yet again there was still another feature of the Detaxalans that was equally as horrifying as the rest, namely their outer covering. As we viewed them for the first time out there in the square we discovered that parts of the body, that is the part of the head which they called the face, and the bony hands were entirely naked without any sort of covering, neither fur nor feathers, just the raw, pinkish-brown skin looking as if it had been recently plucked.

Later we found a few specimens that had a type of fur on the lower part of the face, but these were rare. And when they doffed the head coverings which we had first taken for some sort of natural covering, we saw that the top of the head was overlaid with a very fine fuzz of fur several inches long.

We did not know in the beginning that the strange covering on the bodies of the four men, green in color, was not a natural growth, but later discovered that such was the truth, and not only the face and hands were bare of fur, but the entire body, except for a fine sprinkling of hair that was scarcely visible except on the chest, was also bare. No wonder the poor things covered themselves with their awkward clothing. We arrived at the conclusion that their lack of fur had been brought about by the fact that always they had been exposed to the bright rays of the sun so that without the dampness of our own planet the fur had dried up and fallen away from the flesh!

Now thinking it over I suppose that we of Gola presented strange forms to the people of Detaxal with our fine circular bodies, rounded at the top, our short beautiful lower limbs with the circular foot pads, and our short round arms and hand pads, flexible and muscular like rubber.

But how envious they must have been of our beautiful golden coats, our movable eyes, our power to scent, hear and touch with any part of the body, to absorb food and drink through any part of the body most convenient to us at any time. Oh yes, laugh though you may, without a doubt we were also freaks to those freakish Detaxalans. But no matter, let us return to the tale.

On recognizing our visitors for what they were, simple-minded males, Geble was chagrined at them for taking up her time, but they were strangers to our world and we Golans are always courteous. Geble began of course to try to communicate by thought transference, but strangely enough the fellows below did not catch a single thought. Instead, entirely unaware of Geble's overture to friendship, the leader commenced to speak to her in most outlandish manner, contorting the red lips of his mouth into various uncouth shapes and making sounds that fell upon our hearing so unpleasantly that we immediately closed our senses to them. And without a word Geble turned her back upon them, calling for Tanka, her personal secretary.

Tanka was instructed to welcome the Detaxalans while she herself turned to her own chambers to summon a half dozen of her council. When the council arrived she began to discuss with them the problem of extracting more of the precious tenix from the waters of the great inland lake of Notauch. Nothing whatever was said of the advent of the Detaxalans, for Geble had dismissed them from her mind as creatures not worthy of her thought.

In the meantime Tanka had gone forth to meet the four who of course could not converse with her. In accordance with the Queen's orders she led them indoors to the most informal receiving chamber and there had them served with food and drink which by the looks of the remains in the dishes they did not relish at all.

Leading them through the rooms of the lower floor of the palace she made a pretense of showing them everything which they duly surveyed. But they appeared to chafe at the manner in which they were being entertained.

The creatures even made an attempt through the primitive method of conversing by their arms to learn something of what they had seen, but Tanka was as supercilious as her mistress. When she thought they had had enough, she led them to the square and back to the door of their flyer, giving them their dismissal.

But the men were not ready to accept it. Instead they tried to express to Tanka their desire to meet the ruling head of Gola. Although their hand motions were perfectly inane and incomprehensible, Tanka could read what passed through their brains, and understood more fully than they what lay in their minds. She shook her head and motioned that they were to embark in their flyer and be on their way back to their planet.

Again and again the Detaxalans tried to explain what they wished, thinking Tanka did not understand. At last she impressed upon their savage minds that there was nothing for them but to depart, and disgruntled by her treatment they reentered their machine, closed its ponderous door and raised their ship to the level of its sister flyer. Several minutes passed and then, with thanksgiving, we saw them pass over the city.

Told of this, Geble laughed. "To think of mere man-things daring to attempt to force themselves upon us. What is the universe coming to? What were their women back home considering when they sent them to us? Have they developed too many males and think that we can find use for them?" she wanted to know.

"It is strange indeed," observed Yabo, one of the council members. "What did you find in the minds of these ignoble creatures, O August One?"

"Nothing of particular interest, a very low grade of intelligence, to be sure. There was no need of looking below the surface."

"It must have taken intelligence to build those ships."

"None aboard them did that. I don't question it but that their mothers built the ships for them as playthings, even as we give toys to our 'little ones,' you know. I recall that the ancients of our world perfected several types of space-flyers many ages ago!"

"Maybe those males do not have 'mothers' but instead they build the ships themselves. Maybe they are the stronger sex on their world!" This last was said by Suiki, the fifth consort of Geble, a pretty little male, rather young in years. No one had noticed his coming into the chamber, but now everyone showed surprise at his words.

"Impossible!" ejaculated Yabo.

Geble, however, laughed at the little chap's expression. "Suiki is a profound thinker," she observed, still laughing, and she drew him to her gently hugging him.

And with that the subject of the men from Detaxal was closed. It was reopened, however, several hours later when it was learned that instead of leaving Gola altogether the ships were seen one after another by the various cities of the planet as they circumnavigated it.

It was rather annoying, for everywhere the cities' routines were broken up as the people dropped their work and studies to gaze at the cylinders. Too, it was upsetting the morale of the males, for on learning that the two ships contained only creatures of their own sex they were becoming envious, wishing for the same type of playthings for themselves.

Shut in, as they are, unable to grasp the profundities of our science and thought, the gentle, fun-loving males were always glad for a new diversion, and this new method developed by the Detaxalans had intrigued them.

It was then that Geble decided it was high time to take matters into her own hands. Not knowing where the two ships were at the moment it was not difficult with the object-finder beam to discover their whereabouts, and then with the attractor to draw them to Gola magnetically. An *ous* later we had the pleasure of seeing the two ships rushing toward our city. When they arrived above it, power brought them down to the square again.

Again Tanka was sent out, and directed the commanders of the two ships to follow her in to the Queen. Knowing the futility of attempting to converse with them without mechanical aid, Geble caused to be brought her three of the ancient mechanical thought transformers that are only museum pieces to us but still workable. The two men were directed to place them on their heads while she donned the third. When this was done she ordered the creatures to depart immediately from Gola, telling them that she was tired of their play.

Watching the faces of the two I saw them frowning and shaking their heads. Of course I could read their thoughts as well as Geble without need of the transformers, since it was only for their benefit that these were used, so I heard the whole conversation, though I need only to give you the gist of it.

"We have no wish to leave your world as yet," the two had argued.

"You are disrupting the routine of our lives here," Geble told them, "and now that you've seen all that you can there is no need for you to stay longer. I insist that you leave immediately."

I saw one of the men smile, and thereupon he was the one who did all the talking (I say "talking," for this he was actually doing, mouthing each one of his words although we understood his thoughts as they formed in his queer brain, so different from ours).

"Listen here," he laughed, "I don't get the hang of you people at all. We came to Gola (he used some outlandish name of his own, but I use our name of course) with the express purpose of exploration and exploitation. We come as friends. Already we are in alliance with Damin (again the name for the fourth planet of our system was different, but I give the correct appellation), established commerce and trade, and now we are ready to offer you the chance to join our Federation peaceably.

"What we have seen of this world is very favorable; there are good prospects for business here. There is no reason why you people as those of Damin and Detaxal can not enter into a nice business arrangement congenially. You have far more here to offer tourists, more than Damin. Why, except for your clouds this would be an ideal paradise for every man, woman and child on Detaxal and Damin to visit, and of course with our new cloud dispensers we could clear your atmosphere for you in short order and keep it that way. Why, you'll make millions in the first year of your trade.

"Come now, allow us to discuss this with your ruler—king or whatever you call him. Women are all right in their place, but it takes the men to see the profit of a thing like this—er—you are a woman, aren't you?"

The first of his long speech, of course, was so much gibberish to us, with his prate of business arrangements, commerce and trade, tourists, profits, cloud dispensers and what not, but it was the last part of what he said that took my breath away, and you can imagine how it affected Geble. I could see straightway that she was intensely angered, and good reason too. By the looks of the silly fellow's face I could guess that he was getting the full purport of her thoughts. He began to shuffle his funny feet and a foolish grin pervaded his face.

"Sorry," he said, "if I insulted you—I didn't intend that, but I believed that man holds the same place here as he does on Detaxal and Damin, but I suppose it is just as possible for woman to be the ruling factor of a world as man is elsewhere."

That speech naturally made Geble more irate, and tearing off her thought transformer she left the room without another word. In a moment, however, Yabo appeared wearing the transformer in her place. Yabo had none of the beauty of my mother, for whereas Geble was slender and as straight as a rod, Yabo was obese, and her fat body overflowed until she looked like a large dumpy bundle of *yat* held together in her furry skin. She had very little dignity as she waddled toward the Detaxalans, but there was determination in her whole manner, and without preliminaries she began to scold the two as though they were her own consorts.

"There has been enough of this, my fine young men," she shot at them. "You've had your fun, and now it is time for you to return to your mothers and consorts. Shame on you for making up such miserable tales about yourselves. I have a good mind to take you home with me for a couple of days, and I'd put you in your places quick enough. The idea of men acting like you are!"

For a moment I thought the Detaxalans were going to cry by the faces they made, but instead they broke into laughter, such heathenish sounds as had never before been heard on Gola, and I listened in wonder instead of excluding it from my hearing, but the fellows sobered quickly enough at that, and the spokesman addressed the shocked Yabo.

"I see," said he, "it's impossible for your people and mine to arrive at an understanding peaceably. I'm sorry that you take us for children out on a spree, that you are accustomed to such a low type of men as is evidently your lot here.

"I have given you your chance to accept our terms without force, but since you refuse, under the orders of the Federation I will have to take you forcibly, for we are determined that Gola become one of us, if you like it or not. Then you will learn that we are not the children you believe us to be.

"You may go to your supercilious Queen now and advise her that we give you exactly ten hours in which to evacuate this city, for precisely on the hour we will lay this city in ruins. And if that does not suffice you, we will do the same with every other city on the planet! Remember, ten hours!"

And with that he took the mechanical thought transformer from his head and tossed it on the table. His companion did the same and the two of them strode out of the room and to their flyers which arose several thousand feet above Tola and remained there.

Hurrying in to Geble, Yabo told her what the Detaxalan had said. Geble was reclining on her couch and did not bother to raise herself.

"Childish prattle," she conceded and withdrew her red eyes on their movable stems into their pockets, paying no more heed to the threats of the men from Detaxal.

I, however, could not be as calm as my mother, and I was fearful that it was not childish prattle after all. Not knowing how long ten hours might be I did not wait, but crept up to the palace's beam station and set its dials so that the entire building and as much of the surrounding territory as it could cover were protected in the force zone.

Alas, that the same beam was not greater. But it had not been put there for defense, only for matter transference and whatever other peacetime methods we used. It was the means of proving just the same that it was also a very good defensive instrument, for just two *ous* later the hovering ships above let loose their powers of destruction, heavy explosives that entirely demolished all of Tola and its millions of people and only the palace royal of all that beauty was left standing!

Awakened from her nap by the terrific detonation, Geble came hurriedly to a window to view the ruin, and she was wild with grief at what she saw. Geble, however, saw that there was urgent need for action. She knew without my telling her what I had done to protect the palace. And though she showed no sign of appreciation, I knew that I had won a greater place in her regard than any other of her many daughters and would henceforth be her favorite as well as her successor, as the case turned out.

Now, with me behind her, she hurried to the beam station and in a twinkling we were both in Tubia, the second greatest city of that time. Nor were we to be caught napping again, for Geble ordered all beam stations to throw out their zone forces while she herself manipulated one of Tubia's greatest power beams, attuning it to the emanations of the two Detaxalan flyers. In less than an *ous* the two ships were seen through the mists heading for Tubia. For a moment I grew fearful, but on realizing that they were after all in our grip, and the attractors held every living thing powerless against movement, I grew calm and watched them come over the city and the beam pull them to the ground.

With the beam still upon them, they lay supine on the ground without motion. Descending to the square Geble called for Ray C, and when the machine arrived she herself directed the cutting of the hole in the side of the flyer and was the first to enter it with me immediately behind, as usual.

We were both astounded by what we saw of the great array of machinery within. But a glance told Geble all she wanted to know of their principles. She interested herself only in the men standing rigidly in whatever position our beam had caught them. Only the eyes of the creatures expressed their fright, poor things, unable to move so much as a hair while we moved among them untouched by the power of the beam because of the strength of our own minds.

They could have fought against it if they had known how, but their simple minds were too weak for such exercise.

Now glancing about among the stiff forms around us, of which there were one thousand, Geble picked out those of the males she desired for observation, choosing those she judged to be their finest specimens, those with much hair on their faces and having more girth than the others. These she ordered removed by several workers who followed us, and then we emerged again to the outdoors.

Using hand beam torches the picked specimens were kept immobile after they were out of reach of the greater beam and were borne into the laboratory of the building Geble had converted into her new palace. Geble and I followed, and she gave the order for the complete annihilation of the two powerless ships.

Thus ended the first foray of the people of Detaxal. And for the next two *tels* there was peace upon our globe again. In the laboratory the thirty who had been rescued from their ships were given thorough examinations both physically and mentally and we learned all there was to know about them. Hearing of the destruction of their ships, most of the creatures had become frightened and were quite docile in our hands. Those that were unruly were used in the dissecting room for the advancement of Golan knowledge.

After a complete study of them, which yielded little, we lost interest in them scientifically. Geble, however, found some pleasure in having the poor creatures around her and kept three of them in her own chambers so she could delve into their brains as she pleased. The others she doled out to her favorites as she saw fit.

One she gave to me to act as a slave or in what capacity I desired him, but my interest in him soon waned, especially since I had now come of age and was allowed to have two consorts of my own, and go about the business of bringing my daughters into the world.

My slave I called Jon and gave him complete freedom of my house. If only we had foreseen what was coming we would have annihilated every one of them immediately! It did please me later to find that Jon was learning our language and finding a place in my household, making friends with my two shut-in consorts. But as I have said I paid little attention to him.

So life went on smoothly with scarcely a change after the destruction of the ships of Detaxal. But that did not mean we were unprepared for more. Geble reasoned that there would be more ships forthcoming when the Detaxalans found that their first two did not return. So, although it was sometimes inconvenient, the zones of force were kept upon our cities.

And Geble was right, for the day came when dozens of flyers descended upon Gola from Detaxal. But this time the zones of force did not hold them since the zones were not in operation!

And we were unwarned, for when they descended upon us, our world was sleeping, confident that our zones were our protection. The first indication that I had of trouble brewing was when, awakening, I found the ugly form of Jon bending over me. Surprised, for it was not his habit to arouse me, I started up only to find his arms about me, embracing me. And how strong he was! For the moment a new emotion swept me, for the first time I knew the pleasure to be had in the arms of a strong man, but that emotion was short lived, for I saw in the blue eyes of my slave that he had recognized the look in my eyes for what it was, and for the moment he was tender.

Later I was to grow angry when I thought of that expression of his, for his eyes filled with pity, pity for me! But pity did not stay, instead he grinned and the next instant he was binding me down to my couch with strong rope. Geble, I learned later, had been treated as I, as were the members of the council and every other woman in Gola!

That was what came of allowing our men to meet on common ground with the creatures from Detaxal, for a weak mind is open to seeds of rebellion and the Detaxalans had sown it well, promising dominance to the lesser creatures of Gola.

That, however, was only part of the plot on the part of the Detaxalans. They were determined not only to revenge those we had murdered, but also to gain mastery of our planet. Unnoticed by us they had constructed a machine which transmits sound as we transmit thought and by its means had communicated with their own world, advising them of the very hour to strike when all of Gola was slumbering. It was a masterful stroke, only they did not know the power of the mind of Gola—so much more ancient than theirs.

Lying there bound on my couch I was able to see out the window and, trembling with terror, I watched a half dozen Detaxalan flyers descend into Tubia, guessing that the same was happening in our other cities. I was truly frightened, for I did not have the brain of a Geble. I was young yet, and in fear I watched the hordes march out of their machines, saw the thousands of our men join them.

Free from restraint, the shut-ins were having their holiday and how they cavorted out in the open, most of the time getting in the way of the freakish Detaxalans who were certainly taking over our city.

A half *ous* passed while I lay there watching, waiting in fear at what the Detaxalans planned to do with us. I remembered the pleasant, happy life we had led up to the present and trembled over what the future might be when the Detaxalans had infested us with commerce and trade, business propositions, tourists and all of their evil practices. It was then that I received the message from Geble, clear and definite, just as all the women of the globe received it, and hope returned to my heart.

There began that titanic struggle, the fight for supremacy, the fight that won us victory over the simple-minded weaklings below who had presumptuously dared to conquer us. The first indication that the power of our combined mental concentration at Geble's orders was taking effect was when we saw the first of our males halt in their wild dance of freedom. They tried to shake us off, but we knew we could bring them back to us.

At first the Detaxalans paid them no heed. They knew not what was happening until there came the wholesale retreat of the Golan men back to the buildings, back to the chambers from which they had escaped. Then grasping something of what was happening the already defeated invaders sought to retain their hold on our little people. Our erstwhile captives sought to hold them with oratorical gestures, but of course we won. We saw our creatures return to us and unbind us.

Only the Detaxalans did not guess the significance of that, did not realize that inasmuch as we had conquered our own men, we could conquer them also. As they went about their work of making our city their own, establishing already their autocratic bureaus wherever they pleased, we began to concentrate upon them, hypnotizing them to the flyers that had disgorged them.

And soon they began to feel of our power, the weakest ones first, feeling the mental bewilderment creeping upon them. Their leaders, stronger in mind, knew nothing of this at first, but soon our terrible combined mental power was forced upon them also and they realized that their men were deserting them, crawling back to their ships! The leaders began to exhort them into new action, driving them physically. But our power gained on them and now we began to concentrate upon the leaders themselves. They were strong of will and they defied us, fought us, mind against mind, but of course it was useless. Their minds were not suited to the test they put themselves to, and after almost three *ous* of struggle, we of Gola were able to see victory ahead.

At last the leaders succumbed. Not a single Detaxalan was abroad in the avenues. They were within their flyers, held there by our combined wills, unable to act for themselves. It was then as easy for us to switch the zones of force upon them, subjugate them more securely and with the annihilator beam to disintegrate completely every ship and man into nothingness! Thousands upon thousands died that day and Gola was indeed revenged.

Thus, my daughters, ended the second invasion of Gola.

Oh yes, more came from their planet to discover what had happened to their ships and their men, but we of Gola no longer hesitated, and they no sooner appeared beneath the mists than they too were annihilated until at last Detaxal gave up the thought of conquering our cloud-laden world. Perhaps in the future they will attempt it again, but we are always in readiness for them now, and our men—well, they are still the same ineffectual weaklings, my daughters . . .

C. L. MOORE
Shambleau

• • • •

{1933}

C(atherine) L(ucille) Moore (1911–1987) was a major contributor to American science fiction and fantasy during the early decades of the pulp magazines. Her polished prose, action-filled plots, and colorful characters assured her success in a variety of genres, including science fantasy and sword-and-sorcery. "Shambleau," which appeared in *Weird Tales* in 1933, was her first published story, introducing Northwest Smith, the swashbuckling interplanetary adventurer who reappeared in a half dozen later tales. "Shambleau" was immediately popular with readers and, because of its cross-genre appeal, it has frequently been anthologized not only in sf collections but also in collections of vampire and horror stories. In 1934 Moore published "Black God's Kiss," the first in a series of baroque but hard-edged sword-and-sorcery fantasies starring the complex and dangerous Jirel of Joiry, one of the earliest female action heroes in twentieth-century popular fiction.

In 1940 Moore married the American sf writer, Henry Kuttner, and they collaborated for nearly two decades on stories and novels under a variety of pseudonyms, most notably "Lewis Padgett." One of their best-known collaborations is "Vintage Season" (1946), a bleak story about time-traveling tourists who are connoisseurs of disaster. Moore rarely published fiction under her own name during this period, but one important exception is the novella "No Woman Born" (1944). This early cyborg story has become an acknowledged classic of (proto)feminist science fiction. After Kuttner's death in the late 1950s, Moore left science fiction to write for television; by the mid-1960s, she had ceased writing altogether. In 1981 she was presented with the World Fantasy Award for Lifetime Achievement and in 1998 she was inducted into the Science Fiction and Fantasy Hall of Fame.

"Shambleau" evokes the color, action, and sense of wonder to be found in early pulp sf. Moore sets her scene on a rough-and-ready Mars that bears an obvious resemblance to the American western frontier, and she fills it with interplanetary aliens, dashing adventurers, and otherworldly landscapes in the best space-opera tradition. "Shambleau" also exemplifies some of the strategies used by women writers in the early years of the genre, such as an androgynous byline and male point-of-view characters. At the same time, Moore injects her own disturbing elements into what begins as a conventional adventure story. Played out against the background of her raucous frontier Mars is the nearly silent and intensely erotic seduction of Northwest Smith by the Shambleau in her role as exotic femme fatale. The Shambleau remains one of science fiction's most intriguing aliens, forerunner of the erotic mind-parasites of Robert Silverberg's "Passengers" (1968). At the heart of the story is her ambiguous promise to Northwest Smith: "Some day I—speak to you in—my own language."

Man has conquered space before. You may be sure of that. Somewhere beyond the Egyptians, in that dimness out of which come echoes of half-mythical names—Atlantis, Mu—somewhere back of history's first beginnings there must have been an age when mankind, like us today, built cities of steel to house its star-roving ships and knew the names of the planets in their own native tongues—heard Venus' people call their wet world "Shaardol" in that soft, sweet, slurring speech and mimicked Mars' guttural "Lakkdiz" from the harsh tongues of Mars' dryland dwellers. You may be sure of it. Man has conquered Space before, and out of that conquest faint, faint echoes run still through a world that has forgotten the very fact of a civilization which must have been as mighty as our own. There have been too many myths and legends for us to doubt it. The myth of the Medusa, for instance, can never have had its roots in the soil of Earth. That tale of the snake-haired Gorgon whose gaze turned the gazer to stone never originated about any creature that Earth nourished. And those ancient Greeks who told the story must have remembered, dimly and half believing, a tale of antiquity about some strange being from one of the outlying planets their remotest ancestors once trod.

"Shambleau! Ha . . . Shambleau!" The wild hysteria of the mob rocketed from wall to wall of Lakkdarol's narrow streets and the storming of heavy boots over the slag-red pavement made an ominous undernote to that swelling bay, "Shambleau! Shambleau!"

Northwest Smith heard it coming and stepped into the nearest doorway, laying a wary hand on his heat-gun's grip, and his colorless eyes narrowed. Strange sounds were common enough in the streets of Earth's latest colony on Mars—a raw, red little town where anything might happen, and very often did. But Northwest Smith, whose name is known and respected in every dive and wild outpost on a dozen wild planets, was a cautious man, despite his reputation. He set his back against the wall and gripped his pistol, and heard the rising shout come nearer and nearer.

Then into his range of vision flashed a red running figure, dodging like a hunted hare from shelter to shelter in the narrow street. It was a girl—a berry-brown girl in a single tattered garment whose scarlet burnt the eyes with its brilliance. She ran wearily, and he could bear her gasping breath from where he stood. As she came into view he saw her hesitate and lean one hand against the wall for support, and glance wildly around for shelter. She must not have seen him in the depths of the doorway, for as the bay of the mob grew louder and the pounding of feet sounded almost at the corner she gave a despairing little moan and dodged into the recess at his very side.

When she saw him standing there, tall and leather-brown, hand on his heat-gun, she sobbed once, inarticulately, and collapsed at his feet, a huddle of burning scarlet and bare, brown limbs.

Smith had not seen her face, but she was a girl, and sweetly made and in danger; and though he had not the reputation of a chivalrous man, something in her hopeless huddle at his feet touched that chord of sympathy for the underdog that stirs in every Earthman, and he pushed her gently into the corner behind him and jerked out his gun, just as the first of the running mob rounded the corner.

It was a motley crowd, Earthmen and Martians and a sprinkling of Venusian swampmen and strange, nameless denizens of unnamed planets—a typical Lakkdarol mob. When the first of them turned the corner and saw the empty street before them there was a faltering in the rush and the foremost spread out and began to search the doorways on both sides of the street.

"Looking for something?" Smith's sardonic call sounded clear above the clamor of the mob.

They turned. The shouting died for a moment as they took in the scene before them—tall Earthman in the space-explorer's leathern garb, all one color from the burning of savage suns save for the sinister pallor of his no-colored eyes in a scarred and resolute face, gun in his steady hand and the scarlet girl crouched behind him, panting.

The foremost of the crowd—a burly Earthman in tattered leather from which the Patrol insignia had been ripped away—stared for a moment with a strange expression of incredulity on his face overspreading the savage exultation of the chase. Then he let loose a deep-throated bellow, "Shambleau!" and lunged forward. Behind him the mob took up the cry again, "Shambleau! Shambleau! Shambleau!" and surged after.

Smith, lounging negligently against the wall, arms folded and gun-hand draped over his left forearm, looked incapable of swift motion, but at the leader's first forward step the pistol swept in a practiced half-circle and the dazzle of blue-white heat leaping from its muzzle seared an arc in the slag pavement at his feet. It was an old gesture, and not a man in the crowd but understood it. The foremost recoiled swiftly against the surge of those in the rear, and for a moment there was confusion as the two tides met and struggled. Smith's mouth curled into a grim curve as he watched. The man in the mutilated Patrol uniform lifted a threatening fist and stepped to the very edge of the deadline, while the crowd rocked to and fro behind him.

"Are you crossing that line?" queried Smith in an ominously gentle voice.

"We want that girl!"

"Come and get her!" Recklessly Smith grinned into his face. He saw danger there, but his defiance was not the foolhardy gesture it seemed. An expert psychologist of mobs from long experience, he sensed no murder here. Not a gun had appeared in any hand in the crowd. They desired the girl with an inexplicable bloodthirstiness he was at a loss to understand, but toward himself he sensed no such fury. A mauling he might expect, but his life was in no danger. Guns would have appeared before now if they were coming out at all. So he grinned in the man's angry face and leaned lazily against the wall.

Behind their self-appointed leader the crowd milled impatiently, and threatening voices began to rise again. Smith heard the girl moan at his feet.

"What do you want with her?" he demanded.

"She's Shambleau! Shambleau, you fool! Kick her out of there—we'll take care of her!"

"I'm taking care of her," drawled Smith.

"She's Shambleau, I tell you! Damn your hide, man, we never let those things live! Kick her out here!"

The repeated name had no meaning to him, but Smith's innate stubbornness rose defiantly as the crowd surged forward to the very edge of the arc, their clamor growing louder. "Shambleau! Kick her out here! Give us Shambleau! Shambleau!"

Smith dropped his indolent pose like a cloak and planted both feet wide, swinging up his gun threateningly. "Keep back!" he yelled. "She's mine! Keep back!"

He had no intention of using that heat-beam. He knew by now that they would not kill him unless he started the gunplay himself, and he did not mean to give up his life for any girl alive. But a severe mauling he expected, and he braced himself instinctively as the mob heaved within itself.

To his astonishment a thing happened then that he had never known to happen before. At his shouted defiance the foremost of the mob—those who had heard him clearly—drew back a little, not in alarm but evidently surprised. The ex-Patrolman said, "Yours! She's *yours*?" in a voice from which puzzlement crowded out the anger.

Smith spread his booted legs wide before the crouching figure and flourished his gun.

"Yes," he said. "And I'm keeping her! Stand back there!"

The man stared at him wordlessly, and horror, disgust and incredulity mingled on his weather-beaten face. The incredulity triumphed for a moment and he said again,

"*Yours!*"

Smith nodded defiance.

The man stepped back suddenly, unutterable contempt in his very pose. He waved an arm to the crowd and said loudly, "It's—his!" and the press melted away, gone silent, too, and the look of contempt spread from face to face.

The ex-Patrolman spat on the slag-paved street and turned his back indifferently. "Keep her, then," he advised briefly over one shoulder. "But don't let her out again in this town!"

Smith stared in perplexity almost open-mouthed as the suddenly scornful mob began to break up. His mind was in a whirl. That such bloodthirsty animosity should vanish in a breath he could not believe. And the curious mingling of contempt and disgust on the faces he saw baffled him even more. Lakkdarol was anything but a puritan town—it did not enter his head for a moment that his claiming the brown girl as his own had caused that strangely shocked revulsion to spread through the crowd. No, it was something more deeply rooted than that. Instinctive, instant disgust had been in the faces he saw—they would have looked less so if he had admitted cannibalism or *Pharol*-worship.

And they were leaving his vicinity as swiftly as if whatever unknowing sin he had committed were contagious. The street was emptying as rapidly as it had filled. He saw a sleek Venusian glance back over his shoulder as he turned the corner and sneer, "Shambleau!" and the word awoke a new line of speculation in Smith's mind. Shambleau! Vaguely of French origin, it must be. And strange enough to hear it from the lips of Venusians and Martian drylanders, but it was their use of it that puzzled him more. "We never let those things live," the ex-Patrolman had said. It reminded him dimly of something . . . an ancient line from some writing in his own tongue . . . "Thou shalt not suffer a witch to live." He smiled to himself at the similarity, and simultaneously was aware of the girl at his elbow.

She had risen soundlessly. He turned to face her, sheathing his gun, and stared at first with curiosity and then in the entirely frank openness with which men regard that which is not wholly human. For she was not. He knew it at a glance, though the brown, sweet body was shaped like a woman's and she wore the garment of scarlet—he saw it was leather—with an ease that few unhuman beings achieve toward clothing. He knew it from the moment he looked into her eyes, and a shiver of unrest went over him as he met them. They were frankly green as young grass, with slit-like, feline pupils that pulsed unceasingly, and there was a look of dark, animal wisdom in their depths—that look of the beast which sees more than man.

There was no hair upon her face—neither brows nor lashes, and he would have sworn that the tight scarlet turban bound around her head covered baldness. She had three fingers and a thumb, and her feet had four digits apiece too, and all sixteen of them were tipped with round claws that sheathed back into the flesh like a cat's. She ran her tongue over her lips—a thin, pink, flat tongue as feline as her eyes—and spoke with difficulty. He felt that that throat and tongue had never been shaped for human speech.

"Not—afraid now," she said softly, and her little teeth were white and pointed as a kitten's.

"What did they want you for?" he asked her curiously. "What had you done? Shambleau . . . is that your name?"

"I—not talk your—speech," she demurred hesitantly.

"Well, try to—I want to know. Why were they chasing you? Will you be safe on the street now, or hadn't you better get indoors somewhere? They looked dangerous."

"I—go with you." She brought it out with difficulty.

"Say you!" Smith grinned. "What are you, anyhow? You look like a kitten to me."

"Shambleau." She said it somberly.

"Where d'you live? Are you a Martian?"

"I come from—from far—from long ago—far country—"

"Wait!" laughed Smith. "You're getting your wires crossed. You're not a Martian?"

She drew herself up very straight beside him, lifting the turbaned head, and there was something queenly in the poise of her.

"Martian?" she said scornfully. "My people—are—are—you have no word. Your speech—hard for me."

"What's yours? I might know it—try me."

She lifted her head and met his eyes squarely, and there was in hers a subtle amusement—he could have sworn it.

"Some day I—speak to you in—my own language," she promised, and the pink tongue flicked out over her lips, swiftly, hungrily.

Approaching footsteps on the red pavement interrupted Smith's reply. A dryland Martian came past, reeling a little and exuding an aroma of *segir*-whisky, the Venusian brand. When he caught the red flash of the girl's tatters he turned his head sharply, and as his *segir*-steeped brain took in the fact of her presence he lurched toward the recess unsteadily, bawling, "Shambleau, by *Pharol*! Shambleau!" and reached out a clutching hand.

Smith struck it aside contemptuously.

"On your way, drylander," he advised.

The man drew back and stared, blear-eyed.

"Yours, eh?" he croaked. "*Zut*! You're welcome to it!" And like the ex-Patrolman before him he spat on the pavement and turned away, muttering harshly in the blasphemous tongue of the drylands.

Smith watched him shuffle off, and there was a crease between his colorless eyes, a nameless unease rising within him.

"Come on," he said abruptly to the girl. "If this sort of thing is going to happen we'd better get indoors. Where shall I take you?"

"With—you," she murmured.

He stared down into the flat green eyes. Those ceaselessly pulsing pupils disturbed him, but it seemed to him, vaguely, that behind the animal shallows of her gaze was a shutter—a closed barrier that might at any moment open to reveal the very deeps of that dark knowledge he sensed there.

Roughly he said again, "Come on, then," and stepped down into the street.

She pattered along a pace or two behind him, making no effort to keep up with his long strides, and though Smith—as men know from Venus to Jupiter's moons—walks as softly as a cat, even in spacemen's boots, the girl at his heels slid like a shadow over the rough pavement, making so little sound that even the lightness of his footsteps was loud in the empty street.

Smith chose the less frequented ways of Lakkdarol, and somewhat shamefacedly thanked his nameless gods that his lodgings were not far away, for the few pedestrians he met turned and stared after the two with that by now familiar mingling of horror and contempt which he was as far as ever from understanding.

The room he had engaged was a single cubicle in a lodging-house on the edge of the city. Lakkdarol, raw camp-town that it was in those days, could have furnished little better anywhere within its limits, and Smith's errand there was not one he wished to advertise. He had slept in worse places than this before, and knew that he would do so again.

There was no one in sight when he entered, and the girl slipped up the stairs at his heels and vanished through the door, shadowy, unseen by anyone in the house. Smith closed the door and leaned his broad shoulders against the panels, regarding her speculatively.

She took in what little the room had to offer in a glance—frowsy bed, rickety table, mirror hanging unevenly and cracked against the wall, unpainted chairs—a typical camp-town room in an Earth settlement abroad. She accepted its poverty in that single glance, dismissed it, then crossed to the window and leaned out for a moment, gazing across the low roof-tops toward the barren countryside beyond, red slag under the late afternoon sun.

"You can stay here," said Smith abruptly, "until I leave town. I'm waiting here for a friend to come in from Venus. Have you eaten?"

"Yes," said the girl quickly. "I shall—need no—food for—a while."

"Well—" Smith glanced around the room. "I'll be in sometime tonight. You can go or stay just as you please. Better lock the door behind me."

With no more formality than that he left her. The door closed and he heard the key turn, and smiled to himself. He did not expect, then, ever to see her again.

He went down the steps and out into the late-slanting sunlight with a mind so full of other matters that the brown girl receded very quickly into the background. Smith's errand in Lakkdarol, like most of his errands, is better not spoken of. Man lives as he must, and Smith's living was a perilous affair outside the law and ruled by the ray-gun only. It is enough to say that the shipping-port and its cargoes outbound interested him deeply just now, and that the friend he awaited was Yarol the Venusian, in that swift little Edsel ship the *Maid* that can flash from world to world with a derisive speed that laughs at Patrol boats and leaves pursuers floundering in the ether far behind. Smith and Yarol and the *Maid* were a trinity that had caused the Patrol leaders much worry and many gray hairs in the past, and the future looked very bright to Smith himself that evening as he left his lodging-house.

Lakkdarol roars by night, as Earthmen's camp-towns have a way of doing on every planet where Earth's outposts are, and it was beginning lustily as Smith went down among the awakening lights toward the center of town. His business there does not concern us. He mingled with the crowds where the lights were brightest, and there was the click of ivory counters and the jingle of silver, and red *segir* gurgled invitingly from black Venusian bottles, and much later Smith strolled homeward under the moving moons of Mars, and if the street wavered a little under his feet now and then—why, that is only understandable. Not even Smith could drink red *segir* at every bar from the *Martian Lamb* to the *New Chicago* and remain entirely steady on his feet. But he found his way back with very little difficulty—considering—and spent a good five minutes hunting for his key before he remembered he had left it in the inner lock for the girl.

He knocked then, and there was no sound of footsteps from within, but in a few moments the latch clicked and the door swung open. She retreated soundlessly before him as he entered, and took up her favorite place against the window, leaning back on the sill and outlined against the starry sky beyond. The room was in darkness.

Smith flipped the switch by the door and then leaned back against the panels, steadying himself. The cool night air had sobered him a little, and his head was clear enough—liquor went to Smith's feet, not his head, or he would never have come this far along the lawless way he had chosen. He lounged against the door now and regarded the girl in the sudden glare of the bulbs, blinking a little as much at the scarlet of her clothing as at the light.

"So you stayed," he said.

"I—waited," she answered softly, leaning farther back against the sill and clasping the rough wood with slim, three-fingered hands, pale brown against the darkness.

"Why?"

She did not answer that, but her mouth curved into a slow smile. On a woman it would have been reply enough—provocative, daring. On Shambleau there was something pitiful and horrible in it—so human on the face of one half-animal. And yet . . . that sweet brown body curving so softly from the tatters of scarlet leather—the velvety texture of that brownness—the white-flashing smile. . . . Smith was aware of a stirring excitement within him. After all—time would be hanging heavy now until Yarol came. . . . Speculatively he allowed the steel-pale eyes to wander over her, with a slow regard that missed nothing. And when he spoke he was aware that his voice had deepened a little. . . .

"Come here," he said.

She came forward slowly, on bare clawed feet that made no sound on the floor, and stood before him with downcast eyes and mouth trembling in that pitifully human smile. He took her by the shoulders—velvety soft shoulders, of a creamy smoothness that was not the texture of human flesh. A little tremor went over her, perceptibly, at the contact of his hands. Northwest Smith caught his breath suddenly and dragged her to him . . . sweet yielding brownness in the circle of his arms . . . heard her own breath catch and quicken as her velvety arms closed about his neck. And then he was looking down into her face, very near, and the green animal eyes met his with the pulsing pupils and the flicker of—something—deep behind their shallows—and through the rising clamor of his blood, even as he stooped his lips to hers, Smith felt something deep within him shudder away—inexplicable, instinctive, revolted. What it might be he had no words to tell, but the very touch of her was suddenly loathsome—so soft and velvet and unhuman—and it might have been an animal's face that lifted itself to his mouth—the dark knowledge looked hungrily from the darkness of those slit pupils—and for a mad instant he knew that same wild, feverish revulsion he had seen in the faces of the mob. . . .

"God!" he gasped, a far more ancient invocation against evil than he realized, then or ever, and he ripped her arms from his neck; swung her away with such a force that she reeled half across the room. Smith fell back against the door, breathing heavily, and stared at her while the wild revolt died slowly within him.

She had fallen to the floor beneath the window, and as she lay there against the wall with bent head he saw, curiously, that her turban had slipped—the turban that he had been so sure covered baldness—and a lock of scarlet hair fell below the binding leather, hair as scarlet as her garment, as unhumanly red as her eyes were unhumanly green. He stared, and shook his head dizzily and stared again, for it seemed to him that the thick lock of crimson had moved, *squirmed* of itself against her cheek.

At the contact of it her hands flew up and she tucked it away with a very human gesture and then dropped her head again into her hands. And from the deep shadow of her fingers he thought she was staring up at him covertly.

Smith drew a deep breath and passed a hand across his forehead. The inexplicable moment had gone as quickly as it came—too swiftly for him to understand or analyze it. "Got to lay off the *segir*," he told himself unsteadily. Had he imagined that scarlet hair? After all, she was no more than a pretty brown girl-creature from one of the many half-human races peopling the planets. No more than that, after all. A pretty little thing but animal. . . . He laughed a little shakily.

"No more of that," he said. "God knows I'm no angel, but there's got to be a limit somewhere. Here." He crossed to the bed and sorted out a pair of blankets from the untidy heap, tossing them to the far corner of the room. "You can sleep there."

Wordlessly she rose from the floor and began to rearrange the blankets, the uncomprehending resignation of the animal eloquent in every line of her.

Smith had a strange dream that night. He thought he had awakened to a room full of darkness and moonlight and moving shadows, for the nearer moon of Mars was racing through the sky and everything on the planet below her was endued with a restless life in the dark. And something . . . some nameless, unthinkable *thing* . . . was coiled about his throat . . . something like a soft snake, wet and warm. It lay loose and light about his neck . . . and it was moving gently, very gently, with a soft, caressive pressure that sent little thrills of delight through every nerve and fiber of him, a perilous delight—beyond physical pleasure, deeper than joy of the mind. That warm softness was caressing the very roots of his soul with a terrible intimacy. The ecstasy of it left him weak, and yet he knew—in a flash of knowledge born of this impossible dream—that the soul should not be handled. . . . And with that knowledge a horror broke upon him, turning the pleasure into a rapture of revulsion, hateful, horrible—but still most foully sweet. He tried to lift his hands and tear the dream-monstrosity from his throat—tried but half-heartedly; for though his soul was revolted to its very deeps, yet the delight of his body was so great that his hands all but refused the attempt. But when at last he tried to lift his arms a cold shock went over him and he found that he could not stir . . . his body lay stony as marble beneath the blankets, a living marble that shuddered with a dreadful delight through every rigid vein.

The revulsion grew strong upon him as he struggled against the paralyzing dream—a struggle of soul against sluggish body—titanically, until the moving dark was streaked with blankness that clouded and closed about him at last and he sank back into the oblivion from which he had awakened.

Next morning when the bright sunlight shining through Mars' clear thin air awakened him, Smith lay for a while trying to remember. The dream had been more vivid than reality, but he could not now quite recall . . . only that it had been more sweet and horrible than anything else in life. He lay puzzling for a while, until a soft sound from the corner aroused him from his thoughts and he sat up to see the girl lying in a catlike coil on her blankets, watching him with round, grave eyes. He regarded her somewhat ruefully.

"Morning," he said. "I've just had the devil of a dream. . . . Well, hungry?"

She shook her head silently, and he could have sworn there was a covert gleam of strange amusement in her eyes.

He stretched and yawned, dismissing the nightmare temporarily from his mind.

"What am I going to do with you?" he inquired, turning to more immediate matters. "I'm leaving here in a day or two and I can't take you along, you know. Where'd you come from in the first place?"

Again she shook her head.

"Not telling? Well, it's your own business. You can stay here until I give up the room. From then on you'll have to do your own worrying."

He swung his feet to the floor and reached for his clothes.

Ten minutes later, slipping the heat-gun into its holster at his thigh, Smith turned to the girl. "There's food-concentrate in that box on the table. It ought to hold you until I get back. And you'd better lock the door again after I've gone."

Her wide, unwavering stare was his only answer, and he was not sure she had understood, but at any rate the lock clicked after him as before, and he went down the steps with a faint grin on his lips.

The memory of last night's extraordinary dream was slipping from him, as such memories do, and by the time he had reached the street the girl and the dream and all of yesterday's happenings were blotted out by the sharp necessities of the present.

Again the intricate business that had brought him here claimed his attention. He went about it to the exclusion of all else, and there was a good reason behind everything he did from the moment he stepped out into the street until the time when he turned back again at evening; though had one chosen to follow him during the day his apparently aimless rambling through Lakkdarol would have seemed very pointless.

He must have spent two hours at the least idling by the space-port, watching with sleepy, colorless eyes the ships that came and went, the passengers, the vessels lying at wait, the cargoes—particularly the cargoes. He made the rounds of the town's saloons once more, consuming many glasses of varied liquors in the course of the day and engaging in idle conversation with men of all races and worlds, usually in their own languages, for Smith was a linguist of repute among his contemporaries. He heard the gossip of the spaceways, news from a dozen planets of a thousand different events. He heard the latest joke about the Venusian Emperor and the latest report on the Chino-Aryan war and the latest song hot from the lips of Rose Robertson, whom every man on the civilized planets adored as "the Georgia Rose." He passed the day quite profitably, for his own purposes, which do not concern us now, and it was not until late evening, when he turned homeward again, that the thought of the brown girl in his room took definite shape in his mind, though it had been lurking there, formless and submerged, all day.

He had no idea what comprised her usual diet, but he bought a can of New York roast beef and one of Venusian frog-broth and a dozen fresh canal-apples and two pounds of that Earth lettuce that grows so vigorously in the fertile canal-soil of Mars. He felt that she must surely find something to her liking in this broad variety of edibles, and—for his day had been very satisfactory—he hummed *The Green Hills of Earth* to himself in a surprisingly good baritone as he climbed the stairs.

The door was locked, as before, and he was reduced to kicking the lower panels gently with his boot, for his arms were full. She opened the door with that softness that was characteristic of her and stood regarding him in the semi-darkness as he stumbled to the table with his load. The room was unlit again.

"Why don't you turn on the lights?" he demanded irritably after he had barked his shin on the chair by the table in an effort to deposit his burden there.

"Light and—dark—they are alike—to me," she murmured.

"Cat eyes, eh? Well, you look the part. Here, I've brought you some dinner. Take your choice. Fond of roast beef? Or how about a little frog-broth?"

She shook her head and backed away a step.

"No," she said. "I can not—eat your food."

Smith's brows wrinkled. "Didn't you have any of the food tablets?"

Again the red turban shook negatively.

"Then you haven't had anything for—why, more than twenty-four hours! You must be starved."

"Not hungry," she denied.

"What can I find for you to eat, then? There's time yet if I hurry. You've got to eat, child."

"I shall—eat," she said softly. "Before long—I shall—feed. Have no—worry."

She turned away then and stood at the window, looking out over the moonlit landscape as if to end the conversation. Smith cast her a puzzled glance as he opened the can of roast beef. There had been an odd undernote in that assurance that, undefinably, he did not like. And the girl had teeth and tongue and presumably a fairly human digestive system, to judge from her human form. It was nonsense for her to pretend that he could find nothing that she could eat. She must have had some of the food concentrate after all, he decided, prying up the thermos lid of the inner container to release the long-sealed savor of the hot meat inside.

"Well, if you won't eat you won't," he observed philosophically as he pawed hot broth and diced beef into the dishlike lid of the thermos can and extracted the spoon from its hiding-place between the inner and outer receptacles. She turned a little to watch him as he pulled up a rickety chair and sat down to the food, and after a while the realization that her green gaze was fixed so unwinkingly upon him made the man nervous, and he said between bites of creamy canal-apple, "Why don't you try a little of this? It's good."

"The food—I eat is—better," her soft voice told him in its hesitant murmur, and again he felt rather than heard a faint undernote of unpleasantness in the words. A sudden suspicion struck him as he pondered on that last remark—some vague memory of horror-tales told about campfires in the past—and he swung round in the chair to look at her, a tiny, creeping fear unaccountably arising. There had been that in her words—in her unspoken words, that menaced. . . .

She stood up beneath his gaze demurely, wide green eyes with their pulsing pupils meeting his without a falter. But her mouth was scarlet and her teeth were sharp. . . .

"What food do you eat?" he demanded. And then, after a pause, very softly, "Blood?"

She stared at him for a moment, uncomprehending; then something like amusement curled her lips and she said scornfully, "You think me—vampire, eh? No—I am Shambleau!"

Unmistakably there were scorn and amusement in her voice at the suggestion, but as unmistakably she knew what he meant—accepted it as a logical suspicion—vampires! Fairy tales—but fairy tales this unhuman, outland creature was most familiar with. Smith was not a credulous man, nor a superstitious one, but he had seen too many strange things himself to doubt that the wildest legend might have a basis of fact. And there was something namelessly strange about her. . . .

He puzzled over it for a while between deep bites of the canal-apple. And though he wanted to question her about a great many things, he did not, for he knew how futile it would be.

He said nothing more until the meat was finished and another canal-apple had followed the first, and he had cleared away the meal by the simple expedient of tossing the empty can out of the window. Then he lay back in the chair and surveyed her from half-closed eyes, colorless in a face tanned like saddle-leather. And again he was conscious of the brown, soft curves of her, velvety—subtle arcs and planes of smooth flesh under the tatters of scarlet leather. Vampire she might be, unhuman she certainly was, but desirable beyond words as she sat submissive beneath his low regard, her red-turbaned head bent, her clawed fingers lying in her lap. They sat very still for a while, and the silence throbbed between them.

She was so like a woman—an Earth woman—sweet and submissive and demure, and softer than soft fur, if he could forget the three-fingered claws and the pulsing eyes—and that deeper strangeness beyond words. . . . (Had he dreamed that red lock of hair that moved? Had it been *segir* that woke the wild revulsion he knew when he held her in his arms? Why had the mob so thirsted for her?) He sat and stared, and despite the mystery of her and the half-suspicions that thronged his mind—for she was so beautifully soft and curved under those revealing tatters—he slowly realized that his pulses were mounting, became aware of a kindling within . . . brown girl-creature with downcast eyes . . . and then the lids lifted and the green flatness of a cat's gaze met his, and last night's revulsion woke swiftly again, like a warning bell that clanged as their eyes met—animal, after all, too sleek and soft for humanity, and that inner strangeness. . . .

Smith shrugged and sat up. His failings were legion, but the weakness of the flesh was not among the major ones. He motioned the girl to her pallet of blankets in the corner and turned to his own bed.

From deeps of sound sleep he awoke much later. He awoke suddenly and completely, and with that inner excitement that presages something momentous. He awoke to brilliant moonlight, turning the room so bright that he could see the scarlet of the girl's rags as she sat up on her pallet. She was awake, she was sitting with her shoulder half turned to him and her head bent, and some warning instinct crawled coldly up his spine as he watched what she was doing. And yet it was a very ordinary thing for a girl to do—any girl, anywhere. She was unbinding her turban. . . .

He watched, not breathing, a presentiment of something horrible stirring in his brain, inexplicably. . . . The red folds loosened, and—he knew then that he had not dreamed—again a scarlet lock swung down against her cheek . . . a hair, was it? a lock of hair? . . . thick as a thick worm it fell, plumply, against that smooth cheek . . . more scarlet than blood and thick as a crawling worm . . . and like a worm it crawled.

Smith rose on an elbow, not realizing the motion, and fixed an unwinking stare, with a sort of sick, fascinated incredulity, on that—that lock of hair. He had not dreamed. Until now he had taken it for granted that it was the *segir* which had made it seem to move on that evening before. But now . . . it was lengthening, stretching, moving of itself. It must be hair, but it *crawled*; with a sickening life of its own it squirmed down against her cheek, caressingly, revoltingly, impossibly. . . . Wet, it was, and round and thick and shining. . . .

She unfastened the fast fold and whipped the turban off. From what he saw then Smith would have turned his eyes away—and he had looked on dreadful things before, without flinching—but he could not stir. He could only lie there on his elbow staring at the mass of scarlet, squirming—worms, hairs, what?—that writhed over her head in a dreadful mockery of ringlets. And it was lengthening, falling, somehow growing before his eyes, down over her shoulders in a spilling cascade, a mass that even at the beginning could never have been hidden under the skull-tight turban she had worn. He was beyond wondering, but he realized that. And still it squirmed and lengthened and fell, and she shook it out in a horrible travesty of a woman shaking out her unbound hair—until the unspeakable tangle of it—twisting, writhing, obscenely scarlet—hung to her waist and beyond, and still lengthened, an endless mass of crawling horror that until now, somehow, impossibly, had been hidden under the tight-bound turban. It was like a nest of blind, restless red worms . . . it was—it was like naked entrails endowed with an unnatural aliveness, terrible beyond words.

Smith lay in the shadows, frozen without and within in a sick numbness that came of utter shock and revulsion.

She shook out the obscene, unspeakable tangle over her shoulders, and somehow he knew that she was going to turn in a moment and that he must meet her eyes. The thought of that meeting stopped his heart with dread, more awfully than anything else in this nightmare horror; for nightmare it must be, surely. But he knew without trying that he could not wrench his eyes away—the sickened fascination of that sight held him motionless, and somehow there was a certain beauty. . . .

Her head was turning, The crawling awfulnesses rippled and squirmed at the motion, writhing thick and wet and shining over the soft brown shoulders about which they fell now in obscene cascades that all but hid her body. Her head was turning. Smith lay numb. And very slowly he saw the round of her cheek foreshorten and her profile come into view, all the scarlet horrors twisting ominously, and the profile shortened in turn and her full face came slowly round toward the bed—moonlight shining brilliantly as day on the pretty girl-face, demure and sweet, framed in tangled obscenity that crawled . . .

The green eyes met his. He felt a perceptible shock, and a shudder rippled down his paralyzed spine, leaving an icy numbness in its wake. He felt the goose-flesh rising. But that numbness and cold horror he scarcely realized, for the green eyes were locked with his in a long, long look that somehow presaged nameless things—not altogether unpleasant things—the voiceless voice of her mind assailing him with little murmurous promises. . . .

For a moment he went down into a blind abyss of submission; and then somehow the very sight of that obscenity, in eyes that did not then realize they saw it, was dreadful enough to draw him out of the seductive darkness . . . the sight of her crawling and alive with unnameable horror.

She rose, and down about her in a cascade fell the squirming scarlet of—of what grew upon her head. It fell in a long, alive cloak to her bare feet on the floor, hiding her in a wave of dreadful, wet, writhing life. She put up her hands and like a swimmer she parted the waterfall of it, tossing the masses back over her shoulders to reveal her own brown body, sweetly curved. She smiled exquisitely, and in starting waves back from her forehead and down about her in a hideous background writhed the snaky wetness of her living tresses. And Smith knew that he looked upon Medusa.

The knowledge of that—the realization of vast backgrounds reaching into misted history—shook him out of his frozen horror for a moment, and in that moment he met her eyes again, smiling, green as glass in the moonlight, half hooded under drooping lids. Through the twisting scarlet she held out her arms. And there was something soul-shakingly desirable about her, so that all the blood surged to his head suddenly and he stumbled to his feet like a sleeper in a dream as she swayed toward him, infinitely graceful, infinitely sweet in her cloak of living horror.

And somehow there was beauty in it, the wet scarlet writhings with moonlight sliding and shining along the thick, worm-round tresses and losing itself in the masses only to glint again and move silvery along writhing tendrils—an awful, shuddering beauty more dreadful than any ugliness could be.

But all this, again, he but half realized, for the insidious murmur was coiling again through his brain, promising, caressing, alluring, sweeter than honey; and the green eyes that held his were clear and burning like the depths of a jewel, and behind the pulsing slits of darkness he was staring into a greater dark that held all things. . . . He had known—dimly he had known when he first gazed into those flat animal shallows that behind them lay this—all beauty and terror, all horror and delight, in the infinite darkness upon which her eyes opened like windows, paned with emerald glass.

Her lips moved, and in a murmur that blended indistinguishably with the silence and the sway of her body and the dreadful sway of her—her hair—she whispered—very softly, very passionately, "I shall—speak to you now—in my own tongue—oh, beloved!"

And in her living cloak she swayed to him, the murmur swelling seductive and caressing in his innermost brain—promising, compelling, sweeter than sweet. His flesh crawled to the horror of her, but it was a perverted revulsion that clasped what it loathed. His arms slid round her under the sliding cloak, wet, wet and warm and hideously alive—and the sweet velvet body was clinging to his, her arms locked about his neck—and with a whisper and a rush the unspeakable horror closed about them both.

In nightmares until he died he remembered that moment when the living tresses of Shambleau first folded him in their embrace. A nauseous, smothering odor as the wetness shut around him—thick, pulsing worms clasping every inch of his body, sliding, writhing, their wetness and warmth striking through his garments as if he stood naked to their embrace.

All this in a graven instant—and after that a tangled flash of conflicting sensation before oblivion closed over him. For he remembered the dream—and knew it for nightmare reality now, and the sliding, gently moving caresses of those wet, warm worms upon his flesh was an ecstasy above words—that deeper ecstasy that strikes beyond the body and beyond the mind and tickles the very roots of the soul with unnatural delight. So he stood, rigid as marble, as helplessly stony as any of Medusa's victims in ancient legends were, while the terrible pleasure of Shambleau thrilled and shuddered through every fiber of him; through every atom of his body and the intangible atoms of what men call the soul, through all that was Smith the dreadful pleasure ran. And it was truly dreadful. Dimly he knew it, even as his body answered to the root-deep ecstasy, a foul and dreadful wooing from which his very soul shuddered away—and yet in the innermost depths of that soul some grinning traitor shivered with delight. But deeply, behind all this, he knew horror and revulsion and despair beyond telling, while the intimate caresses crawled obscenely in the secret places of his soul—knew that the soul should not be handled—and shook with the perilous pleasure through it all.

And this conflict and knowledge, this mingling of rapture and revulsion all took place in the flashing of a moment while the scarlet worms coiled and crawled upon him, sending deep, obscene tremors of that infinite pleasure into every atom that made up Smith. And he could not stir in that slimy, ecstatic embrace—and a weakness was flooding that grew deeper after each succeeding wave of intense delight, and the traitor in his soul strengthened and drowned out the revulsion—and something within him ceased to struggle as he sank wholly into a blazing darkness that was oblivion to all else but that devouring rapture. . . .

•

The young Venusian climbing the stairs to his friend's lodging-room pulled out his key absent-mindedly, a pucker forming between his fine brows. He was slim, as all Venusians are, as fair and sleek as any of them, and as with most of his countrymen the look of cherubic innocence on his face was wholly deceptive. He had the face of a fallen angel, without Lucifer's majesty to redeem it; for a black devil grinned in his eyes and there were faint lines of ruthlessness and dissipation about his mouth to tell of the long years behind him that had run the gamut of experiences and made his name, next to Smith's, the most hated and the most respected in the records of the Patrol.

He mounted the stairs now with a puzzled frown between his eyes. He had come into Lakkdarol on the noon liner—the *Maid* in her hold very skillfully disguised with paint and otherwise—to find in lamentable disorder the affairs he had expected to be settled. And cautious inquiry elicited the information that Smith had not been seen for three days. That was not like his friend—he had never failed before, and the two stood to lose not only a large sum of money but also their personal safety by the inexplicable lapse on the part of Smith. Yarol could think of one solution only: fate had at last caught up with his friend. Nothing but physical disability could explain it.

Still puzzling, he fitted his key in the lock and swung the door open.

In that first moment as the door opened, he sensed something very wrong. . . . The room was darkened, and for a while he could see nothing, but at the first breath he scented a strange, unnameable odor, half sickening, half sweet. And deep stirrings of ancestral memory awoke him—ancient swamp-born memories from Venusian ancestors far away and long ago.

Yarol laid his hand on his gun, lightly, and opened the door wider. In the dimness all he could see at first was a curious mound in the far corner. . . . Then his eyes grew accustomed to the dark, and he saw it more clearly, a mound that somehow heaved and stirred within itself. . . . A mound of—he caught his breath sharply—a mound like a mass of entrails, living, moving, writhing with an unspeakable aliveness. Then a hot Venusian oath broke from his lips and he cleared the door-sill in a swift stride, slammed the door and set his back against it, gun ready in his hand, although his flesh crawled—for he *knew*. . . .

"Smith!" he said softly, in a voice thick with horror. "Northwest!"

The moving mass stirred—shuddered—sank back into crawling quiescence again.

"Smith! Smith!" The Venusian's voice was gentle and insistent, and it quivered a little with terror.

An impatient ripple went over the whole mass of aliveness in the corner. It stirred again, reluctantly, and then tendril by writhing tendril it began to part itself and fall aside, and very slowly the brown of a spaceman's leather appeared beneath it, all slimed and shining.

"Smith! Northwest!" Yarol's persistent whisper came again, urgently, and with a dreamlike slowness the leather garments moved . . . a man sat up in the midst of the writhing worms, a man who once, long ago, might have been Northwest Smith. From head to foot he was slimy from the embrace of the crawling horror about him. His face was that of some creature beyond humanity—dead-alive, fixed in a gray stare, and the look of terrible ecstasy that overspread it seemed to come from somewhere far within, a faint reflection from immeasurable distances beyond the flesh. And as there is mystery and magic in the moonlight which is after all but a reflection of the everyday sun, so in that gray face turned to the door was a terror unnameable and sweet, a reflection of ecstasy beyond the understanding of any who have known only earthly ecstasy themselves. And as he sat there turning a blank, eyeless face to Yarol the red worms writhed ceaselessly about him, very gently, with a soft, caressive motion that never slacked.

"Smith . . . come here! Smith . . . get up . . . Smith, Smith!" Yarol's whisper hissed in the silence, commanding, urgent—but he made no move to leave the door.

And with a dreadful slowness, like a dead man rising, Smith stood up in the nest of slimy scarlet. He swayed drunkenly on his feet, and two or three crimson tendrils came writhing up his legs to the knees and wound themselves there, supportingly, moving with a ceaseless caress that seemed to give him some hidden strength, for he said then, without inflection,

"Go away. Go away. Leave me alone." And the dead ecstatic face never changed.

"Smith!" Yarol's voice was desperate. "Smith, listen! Smith, can't you hear me?"

"Go away," the monotonous voice said. "Go away. Go away. Go—"

"Not unless you come too. Can't you hear? Smith! Smith! I'll—"

He hushed in mid-phrase, and once more the ancestral prickle of race-memory shivered down his back, for the scarlet mass was moving again, violently, rising. . . .

Yarol pressed back against the door and gripped his gun, and the name of a god he had forgotten years ago rose to his lips unbidden. For he knew what was coming next, and the knowledge was more dreadful than any ignorance could have been.

The red, writhing mass rose higher, and the tendrils parted and a human face looked out—no, half human, with green cat-eyes that shone in that dimness like lighted jewels, compellingly. . . .

Yarol breathed "Shar!" again, and flung up an arm across his face, and the tingle of meeting that green gaze for even an instant went thrilling through him perilously.

"Smith!" he called in despair. "Smith, can't you hear me?"

"Go away," said that voice that was not Smith's. "Go away."

And somehow, although he dared not look, Yarol knew that the—the other—had parted those worm-thick tresses and stood there in all the human sweetness of the brown, curved woman's body, cloaked in living horror. And he felt the eyes upon him, and something was crying insistently in his brain to lower that shielding arm. . . . He was lost—he knew it, and the knowledge gave him that courage which comes from despair. The voice in his brain was growing, swelling, deafening him with a roaring command that all but swept him before it—command to lower that arm—to meet the eyes that opened upon darkness—to submit—and a promise, murmurous and sweet and evil beyond words, of pleasure to come. . . .

But somehow he kept his head—somehow, dizzily, he was gripping his gun in his upflung hand—somehow, incredibly, crossing the narrow room with averted face, groping for Smith's shoulder. There was a moment of blind fumbling in emptiness, and then he found it, and gripped the leather that was slimy and dreadful and wet—and simultaneously he felt something loop gently about his ankle and a shock of repulsive pleasure went through him, and then another coil, and another, wound about his feet. . . .

Yarol set his teeth and gripped the shoulder hard, and his hand shuddered of itself, for the feel of that leather was slimy as the worms about his ankles, and a faint tingle of obscene delight went through him from the contact.

That caressive pressure on his legs was all he could feel, and the voice in his brain drowned out all other sounds, and his body obeyed him reluctantly—but somehow he gave one heave of tremendous effort and swung Smith, stumbling, out of that nest of horror. The twining tendrils ripped loose with a little sucking sound, and the whole mass quivered and reached after, and then Yarol forgot his friend utterly and turned his whole being to the hopeless task of freeing himself. For only a part of him was fighting, now—only a part of him struggled against the twining obscenities, and in his innermost brain the sweet, seductive murmur sounded, and his body clamored to surrender. . . .

"*Shar*! *Shar y'danis* . . . *Shar mor'la-rol*—" prayed Yarol, gasping and half unconscious that he spoke, boy's prayers that he had forgotten years ago, and with his back half turned to the central mass he kicked desperately with his heavy boots at the red, writhing worms about him. They gave back before him, quivering and curling themselves out of reach, and though he knew that more were reaching for his throat from behind, at least he could go on struggling until he was forced to meet those eyes. . . .

He stamped and kicked and stamped again, and for one instant he was free of the slimy grip as the bruised worms curled back from his heavy feet, and he lurched away dizzily, sick with revulsion and despair as he fought off the coils, and then he lifted his eyes and saw the cracked mirror on the wall. Dimly in its reflection he could see the writhing scarlet horror behind him, cat face peering out with its demure girl-smile, dreadfully human, and all the red tendrils reaching after him. And remembrance of something he had read long ago swept incongruously over him, and the gasp of relief and hope that he gave shook for a moment the grip of the command in his brain.

Without pausing for a breath he swung the gun over his shoulder, the reflected barrel in line with the reflected horror in the mirror, and flicked the catch.

In the mirror he saw its blue flame leap in a dazzling spate across the dimness, full into the midst of that squirming, reaching mass behind him. There was a hiss and a blaze and a high, thin scream of inhuman malice and despair—the flame cut a wide arc and went out as the gun fell from his hand, and Yarol pitched forward to the floor.

Northwest Smith opened his eyes to Martian sunlight streaming thinly through the dingy window. Something wet and cold was slapping his face, and the familiar fiery sting of *segir*-whisky burnt his throat.

"Smith!" Yarol's voice was saying from far away. "N.W.! Wake up, damn you! Wake up!"

"I'm—awake," Smith managed to articulate thickly. "Wha's matter?"

Then a cup-rim was thrust against his teeth and Yarol said irritably, "Drink it, you fool!"

Smith swallowed obediently and more of the fire-hot *segir* flowed down his grateful throat. It spread a warmth through his body that awakened him from the numbness that had gripped him until now, and helped a little toward driving out the all-devouring weakness he was becoming aware of slowly. He lay still for a few minutes while the warmth of the whisky went through him, and memory sluggishly began to permeate his brain with the spread of the *segir*. Nightmare memories . . . sweet and terrible . . . memories of—

"God!" gasped Smith suddenly, and tried to sit up. Weakness smote him like a blow, and for an instant the room wheeled as he fell back against something firm and warm—Yarol's shoulder. The Venusian's arm supported him while the room steadied, and after a while he twisted a little and stared into the other's black gaze.

Yarol was holding him with one arm and finishing the mug of *segir* himself, and the black eyes met his over the rim and crinkled into sudden laughter, half hysterical after that terror that was passed.

"By *Pharol*!" gasped Yarol, choking into his mug. "By *Pharol*, N.W.! I'm never gonna let you forget this! Next time you have to drag me out of a mess I'll say—"

"Let it go," said Smith. "What's been going on? How—"

"Shambleau." Yarol's laughter died. "Shambleau! What were you doing with a thing like that?"

"What was it?" Smith asked soberly.

"Mean to say you didn't know? But where'd you find it? How—"

"Suppose you tell me first what you know," said Smith firmly. "And another swig of that *segir*, too, please. I need it."

"Can you hold the mug now? Feel better?"

"Yeah—some. I can hold it—thanks. Now go on."

"Well—I don't know just where to start. They call them Shambleau—"

"Good God, is there more than one?"

"It's a—a sort of race, I think, one of the very oldest. Where they come from nobody knows. The name sounds a little French, doesn't it? But it goes back beyond the start of history. There have always been Shambleau."

"I never heard of 'em."

"Not many people have. And those who know don't care to talk about it much."

"Well, half this town knows. I hadn't any idea what they were talking about, then. And I still don't understand, but—"

"Yes, it happens like this, sometimes. They'll appear, and the news will spread and the town will get together and hunt them down, and after that—well, the story doesn't get around very far. It's too—too unbelievable."

"But—my God, Yarol!—what was it? Where'd it come from? How—"

"Nobody knows just where they come from. Another planet—maybe some undiscovered one. Some say Venus—I know there are some rather awful legends of them handed down in our family—that's how I've heard about it. And the minute I opened that door, awhile back—I—I think I knew that smell. . . ."

"But—what *are* they?"

"God knows. Not human, though they have the human form. Or that may be only an illusion . . . or maybe I'm crazy. I don't know. They're a species of the vampire—or maybe the vampire is a species of—of them. Their normal form must be that—that mass, and in that form they draw nourishment from the—I suppose the life-forces of men. And they take some form—usually a woman form, I think, and key you up to the highest pitch of emotion before they—begin. That's to work the life-force up to intensity so it'll be easier. . . . And they give always, that horrible foul pleasure as they—feed. There are some men who, if they survive the first experience, take to it like a drug—can't give it up—keep the thing with them all their lives—which isn't long—feeding it for that ghastly satisfaction. Worse than smoking *ming* or—or 'praying to *Pharol*.'"

"Yes," said Smith. "I'm beginning to understand why that crowd was so surprised and—and disgusted when I said—well, never mind. Go on."

"Did you get to talk to—to it?" asked Yarol.

"I tried to. It couldn't speak very well. I asked it where it came from and it said—'from far away and long ago'—something like that."

"I wonder. Possibly some unknown planet—but I think not. You know there are so many wild stories with some basis of fact to start from, that I've sometimes wondered—mightn't there be a lot more of even worse and wilder superstitions we've never even heard of? Things like this, blasphemous and foul, that those who know have to keep still about? Awful, fantastic things running around loose that we never hear rumors of at all!

"These things—they've been in existence for countless ages. No one knows when or where they first appeared. Those who've seen them, as we saw this one, don't talk about it. It's just one of those vague, misty rumors you find half hinted at in old books sometimes. I believe they are an older race than man, spawned from ancient seed in times before ours, perhaps on planets that have gone to dust, and so horrible to man that when they are discovered the discoverers keep still about it—forget them again as quickly as they can.

"And they go back to time immemorial. I suppose you recognized the legend of Medusa? There isn't any question that the ancient Greeks knew of them. Does it mean that there have been civilizations before yours that set out from Earth and explored other planets? Or did one of the Shambleau somehow make its way into Greece three thousand years ago? If you think about it long enough you'll go off your head! I wonder how many other legends are based on things like this—things we don't suspect, things we'll never know.

"The Gorgon, Medusa, a beautiful woman with—with snakes for hair, and a gaze that turned men to stone, and Perseus finally killed her—I remembered this just by accident, N.W., and it saved your life and mine—Perseus killed her by using a mirror as he fought to reflect what he dared not look at directly. I wonder what the old Greek who first started that legend would have thought if he'd known that three thousand years later his story would save the lives of two men on another planet. I wonder what that Greek's own story was, and how he met the thing, and what happened.

"Well, there's a lot we'll never know. Wouldn't the records of that race of—of *things*, whatever they are, be worth reading! Records of other planets and other ages and all the beginnings of mankind! But I don't suppose they've kept any records. I don't suppose they've even any place to keep them—from what little I know, or anyone knows about it, they're like the Wandering Jew, just bobbing up here and there at long intervals, and where they stay in the meantime I'd give my eyes to know! But I don't believe that terribly hypnotic power they have indicates any superhuman intelligence. It's their means of getting food—just like a frog's long tongue or a carnivorous flower's odor. Those are physical because the frog and the flower eat physical food. The Shambleau uses a—a mental reach to get mental food. I don't quite know how to put it. And just as a beast that eats the bodies of other animals acquires with each meal greater power over the bodies of the rest, so the Shambleau, stoking itself up with the life-forces of men, increases its power over the minds and the souls of other men. But I'm talking about things I can't define—things I'm not sure exist.

"I only know that when I felt—when those tentacles closed around my legs—I didn't want to pull loose, I felt sensations that—that—oh, I'm fouled and filthy to the very deepest part of me by that—pleasure—and yet—"

"I know," said Smith slowly. The effect of the *segir* was beginning to wear off, and weakness was washing back over him in waves, and when he spoke he was half meditating in a low voice, scarcely realizing that Yarol listened. "I know it—much better than you do—and there's something so indescribably awful that the thing emanates, something so utterly at odds with everything human—there aren't any words to say it. For a while I was a part of it, literally, sharing its thoughts and memories and emotions and hungers, and—well, it's over now and I don't remember very clearly, but the only part left free was that part of me that was all but insane from the—the obscenity of the thing. And yet it was a pleasure so sweet—I think there must be some nucleus of utter evil in me—in everyone—that needs only the proper stimulus to get complete control; because even while I was sick all through from the touch of those—things—there was something in me that was—was simply gibbering with delight. . . . Because of that I saw things—and knew things—horrible, wild things I can't quite remember—visited unbelievable places, looked backward through the memory of that—creature—I was one with, and saw—God, I wish I could remember!"

"You ought to thank your God you can't," said Yarol soberly.

His voice roused Smith from the half-trance he had fallen into, and he rose on his elbow, swaying a little from weakness. The room was wavering before him, and he closed his eyes, not to see it, but he asked, "You say they—they don't turn up again? No way of finding—another?"

Yarol did not answer for a moment. He laid his hands on the other man's shoulders and pressed him back, and then sat staring down into the dark, ravaged face with a new, strange, undefinable look upon it that he had never seen there before—whose meaning he knew, too well.

"Smith," he said finally, and his black eyes for once were steady and serious, and the little grinning devil had vanished from behind them, "Smith, I've never asked your word on anything before, but I've—I've earned the right to do it now, and I'm asking you to promise me one thing."

Smith's colorless eyes met the black gaze unsteadily. Irresolution was in them, and a little fear of what that promise might be. And for just a moment Yarol was looking, not into his friend's familiar eyes, but into a wide gray blankness that held all horror and delight—a pale sea with unspeakable pleasures sunk beneath it. Then the wide stare focused again and Smith's eyes met his squarely and Smith's voice said, "Go ahead. I'll promise."

"That if you ever should meet a Shambleau again—ever, anywhere—you'll draw your gun and burn it to hell the instant you realize what it is. Will you promise me that?"

There was a long silence. Yarol's somber black eyes bored relentlessly into the colorless ones of Smith, not wavering. And the veins stood out on Smith's tanned forehead. He never broke his word—he had given it perhaps half a dozen times in his life, but once he had given it, he was incapable of breaking it. And once more the gray seas flooded in a dim tide of memories, sweet and horrible beyond dreams. Once more Yarol was staring into blankness that hid nameless things. The room was very still.

The gray tide ebbed. Smith's eyes, pale and resolute as steel, met Yarol's levelly.

"I'll—try," he said. And his voice wavered.

STANLEY G. WEINBAUM
A Martian Odyssey

• • • •

{ 1934 }

During the eighteen months between the appearance of his first and best-known story, "A Martian Odyssey" (1934), and his death late in 1935 from throat cancer, Stanley G(rauman) Weinbaum (1902–1935), a Milwaukee-based writer, strongly influenced the development of American sf. He had studied chemical engineering at the University of Wisconsin and after leaving school kept up with popular science. It was then thought that gases in the atmosphere of the planets might generate heat that could allow life to develop, so such tales as "The Mad Moon" (1935), in which Jupiter's closest moon, Io, has a tropical climate, were not far-fetched in their day. That Mars has canals and a breathable atmosphere in "A Martian Odyssey" is likewise extrapolated from early-twentieth-century scientific ideas.

Manager of a movie theater after leaving school, Weinbaum also drew ideas from animated films: the giggling "loonies" of "The Mad Moon" and the headless, trotting barrel-creatures of "A Martian Odyssey" have a grotesque vivacity reminiscent of the cartoons of Max Fleischer. Weinbaum had a poetic and philosophical side as well. In "The Lotus Eaters" (1935) a race of super-intelligent plants (collectively named "Oscar" by the flippant heroine, a biologist) calmly awaits destruction by predators. "Animals have desires and plants [have] necessity," she decides after pondering the group's stoic acceptance of imminent extinction. A story that shows Weinbaum's talent for dark fantasy, "The Adaptive Ultimate" (1935, published as by John Jessel), was filmed in 1957 as *She-Devil*.

Introducing "A Martian Odyssey" to readers of *Wonder Stories* in 1934, editor Hugo Gernsback rightly described its style as "breezy." Weinbaum's brisk pacing, deft conveyance of scientific background, and racy, slangy dialogue had their effect on Robert A. Heinlein; and Theodore Sturgeon's brilliant "Neoterics" in "Microcosmic God" (1941) were probably inspired by the tiny, industrious, "infernally clever" "slinkers" of "The Mad Moon." Kyra Zelas, the colorless protagonist of "The Adaptive Ultimate," seemingly anticipates P. Burke in James Tiptree Jr.'s "The Girl Who Was Plugged In" (1973). Certainly the mineral-based life-form in "A Martian Odyssey" became the "Horta" of the original *Star Trek* series.

"A Martian Odyssey," like "The Lotus Eaters," maintains links to ancient epic: Weinbaum's "dream-beasts" suggest the Sirens in Homer's *Odyssey*, enticing the unwary with visions of what they most desire. According to Sam Moscowitz, the second Mars tale that appeared in *Wonder Stories* ("Valley of Dreams," 1934) was a hastily expanded first draft of "A Martian Odyssey": readers were demanding the further adventures of Jarvis and the Martian "Tweel," the prototypical friendly alien (among whose later incarnations are the extraterrestrials in Nancy Kress's "Out of All Them Bright Stars" [1985]). Weinbaum's Martian stories show his affection for the interplanetary romances of Edgar Rice Burroughs, yet Weinbaum rejects Burroughs's glorification of earthborn John Carter as the conquering savior of Mars. Weinbaum's human scientists have come to Mars mainly to observe, and this story's Martian life-forms behave in the terms of a consistently *extraterrestrial* logic. "A Martian Odyssey" received an unusual tribute in 1973 when a crater on Mars was named in Weinbaum's honor.

Jarvis stretched himself as luxuriously as he could in the cramped general quarters of the *Ares*.

"Air you can breathe!" he exulted. "It feels as thick as soup after the thin stuff out there!" He nodded at the Martian landscape stretching flat and desolate in the light of the nearer moon, beyond the glass of the port.

The other three stared at him sympathetically—Putz, the engineer, Leroy, the biologist, and Harrison, the astronomer and captain of the expedition. Dick Jarvis was chemist of the famous crew, the Ares expedition, first human beings to set foot on the mysterious neighbor of the earth, the planet Mars. This, of course, was in the old days, less than twenty years after the mad American Doheny perfected the atomic blast at the cost of his life, and only a decade after the equally mad Cardoza rode on it to the moon. They were true pioneers, these four of the Ares. Except for a half-dozen moon expeditions and the ill-fated de Lancey flight aimed at the seductive orb of Venus, they were the first men to feel other gravity than earth's, and certainly the first successful crew to leave the earth-moon system. And they deserved that success when one considers the difficulties and discomforts—the months spent in acclimatization chambers back on earth, learning to breathe the air as tenuous as that of Mars, the challenging of the void in the tiny rocket driven by the cranky reaction motors of the twenty-first century, and mostly the facing of an absolutely unknown world.

Jarvis stretched and fingered the raw and peeling tip of his frost-bitten nose. He sighed again contentedly.

"Well," exploded Harrison abruptly, "are we going to hear what happened? You set out all shipshape in an auxiliary rocket, we don't get a peep for ten days, and finally Putz here picks you out of a lunatic ant-heap with a freak ostrich as your pal! Spill it, man!"

"Speel?" queried Leroy perplexedly. "Speel what?"

"He means '*spiel*,'" explained Putz soberly. "It iss to tell."

Jarvis met Harrison's amused glance without the shadow of a smile. "That's right, Karl," he said in grave agreement with Putz. "*Ich spiel es*!" He grunted comfortably and began.

"According to orders," he said, "I watched Karl here take off toward the North, and then I got into my flying sweat-box and headed South. You'll remember, Cap—we had orders not to land, but just scout about for points of interest. I set the two cameras clicking and buzzed along, riding pretty high—about two thousand feet—for a couple of reasons. First, it gave the cameras a greater field, and second, the under-jets travel so far in this half-vacuum they call air here that they stir up dust if you move low."

"We know all that from Putz," grunted Harrison. "I wish you'd saved the films, though. They'd have paid the cost of this junket; remember how the public mobbed the first moon pictures?"

"The films are safe," retorted Jarvis. "Well," he resumed, "as I said, I buzzed along at a pretty good clip; just as we figured, the wings haven't much lift in this air at less than a hundred miles per hour, and even then I had to use the under-jets.

"So, with the speed and the altitude and the blurring caused by the under-jets, the seeing wasn't any too good. I could see enough, though, to distinguish that what I sailed over was just more of this grey plain that we'd been examining the whole week since our landing—same blobby growths and the same eternal carpet of crawling little plant-animals, or biopods, as Leroy calls them. So I sailed along, calling back my position every hour as instructed, and not knowing whether you heard me."

"I did!" snapped Harrison.

"A hundred and fifty miles south," continued Jarvis imperturbably, "the surface changed to a sort of low plateau, nothing but desert and orange-tinted sand. I figured that we were right in our guess, then, and this grey plain we dropped on was really the Mare Cimmerium which would make my orange desert the region called Xanthus. If I were right, I ought to hit another grey plain, the Mare Chronium, in another couple of hundred miles, and then another orange desert, Thyle I or II. And so I did."

"Putz verified our position a week and a half ago!" grumbled the captain. "Let's get to the point."

"Coming!" remarked Jarvis. "Twenty miles into Thyle—believe it or not—I crossed a canal!"

"Putz photographed a hundred! Let's hear something new!"

"And did he also see a city?'

"Twenty of 'em, if you call those heaps of mud cities!"

"Well," observed Jarvis, "from here on I'll be telling a few things Putz didn't see!" He rubbed his tingling nose, and continued. "I knew that I had sixteen hours of daylight at this season, so eight hours—eight hundred miles—from here, I decided to turn back. I was still over Thyle, whether I or II I'm not sure, not more than twenty-five miles into it. And right there, Putz's pet motor quit!"

"Quit! How?" Putz was solicitous.

"The atomic blast got weak. I started losing altitude right away, and suddenly there I was with a thump right in the middle of Thyle! Smashed my nose on the window, too!" He rubbed the injured member ruefully.

"Did you maybe try vashing der combustion chamber mit acid sulphuric?" inquired Putz. "Sometimes der lead giffs a secondary radiation—"

"Naw!" said Jarvis disgustedly. "I wouldn't try that, of course—not more than ten times! Besides, the bump flattened the landing gear and busted off the under-jets. Suppose I got the thing working—what then? Ten miles with the blast coming right out of the bottom and I'd have melted the floor under me!" He rubbed his nose again. "Lucky for me a pound only weighs seven ounces here, or I'd have been mashed flat!"

"I could have fixed!" ejaculated the engineer. "I bet it vas not serious."

"Probably not," agreed Jarvis sarcastically. "Only it wouldn't fly. Nothing serious, but I had my choice of waiting to be picked up or trying to walk back—eight hundred miles, and perhaps twenty days before we had to leave! Forty miles a day! Well," he concluded, "I chose to walk. Just as much chance of being picked up, and it kept me busy."

"We'd have found you," said Harrison.

"No doubt. Anyway. I rigged up a harness from some seat straps, and put the water tank on my back, took a cartridge belt and revolver, and some iron rations, and started out."

"Water tank!" exclaimed the little biologist, Leroy. "She weigh one-quarter ton!"

"Wasn't full. Weighed about two hundred and fifty pounds earth-weight, which is eighty-five here. Then, besides, my own personal two hundred and ten pounds is only seventy on Mars so, tank and all, I grossed a hundred and fifty-five, or fifty-five pounds less than my everyday earth-weight. I figured on that when I undertook the forty-mile daily stroll. Oh—of course I took a thermo-skin sleeping bag for these wintry Martian nights.

"Off I went, bouncing along pretty quickly. Eight hours of daylight meant twenty miles or more. It got tiresome, of course—plugging along over a soft sand desert with nothing to see, not even Leroy's crawling biopods. But an hour or so brought me to the canal—just a dry ditch about four hundred feet wide, and straight as a railroad on its own company map.

"There'd been water in it sometime, though. The ditch was covered with what looked like a nice green lawn. Only, as I approached, the lawn moved out of my way!"

"Eh?" said Leroy.

"Yeah, it was a relative of your biopods. I caught one—a little grass-like blade about as long as my finger, with two thin, stemmy legs."

"He is where?" Leroy was eager.

"He is let go! I had to move, so I plowed along with the walking grass opening in front and closing behind. And then I was out on the orange desert of Thyle again.

"I plugged steadily along, cussing the sand that made going so tiresome, and, incidentally, cussing that cranky motor of yours, Karl. It was just before twilight that I reached the edge of Thyle, and looked down over the grey Mare Chronium. And I knew there was seventy-five miles of *that* to be walked over, and then a couple of hundred miles of that Xanthus desert, and about as much more Mare Cimmerium. Was I pleased? I started cussing you fellows for not picking me up!"

"We were trying, you sap!" said Harrison.

"That didn't help. Well, I figured I might as well use what was left of daylight in getting down the cliff that bounded Thyle. I found an easy place, and down I went. Mare Chronium was just the same sort of place as this—crazy leafless plants and a bunch of crawlers; I gave it a glance and hauled out my sleeping bag. Up to that time, you know, I hadn't seen anything worth worrying about on this half-dead world—nothing dangerous, that is."

"Did you?" queried Harrison.

"*Did I*! You'll hear about it when I come to it. Well, I was just about to turn in when suddenly I heard the wildest sort of shenanigans!"

"Vot iss shenanigans?" inquired Putz.

"He says, '*Je ne sais quoi*,'" explained Leroy. "It is to say, 'I don't know what.'"

"That's right," agreed Jarvis. "I didn't know what, so I sneaked over to find out. There was a racket like a flock of crows eating a bunch of canaries—

whistles, cackles, caws, frills, and what have you. I rounded a dump of stumps, and there was Tweel!"

"Tweel?" said Harrison, and "Tveel?" said Leroy and Putz.

"That freak ostrich," explained the narrator. "At least, Tweel is as near as I can pronounce it without sputtering. He called it something like 'Trrrweerrlll.'"

"What was he doing?" asked the Captain.

"He was being eaten! And squealing, of course, as any one would."

"Eaten! By what?"

"I found out later. All I could see then was a bunch of black ropy arms tangled around what looked like, as Putz described it to you, an ostrich. I wasn't going to interfere, naturally; if both creatures were dangerous, I'd have one less to worry about.

"But the bird-like thing was putting up a good battle, dealing vicious blows with an eighteen-inch beak, between screeches. And besides, I caught a glimpse or two of what was on the end of those arms!" Jarvis shuddered. "But the clincher was when I noticed a little black bag or case hung about the neck of the bird-thing! It was intelligent! That or tame, I assumed. Anyway, it clinched my decision. I pulled out my automatic and fired into what I could see of its antagonist.

"There was a flurry of tentacles and a spurt of black corruption, and then the thing, with a disgusting sucking noise, pulled itself and its arms into a hole in the ground. The other let out a series of clacks, staggered around on legs about as thick as golf sticks, and turned suddenly to face me. I held my weapon ready, and the two of us stared at each other.

"The Martian wasn't a bird, really. It wasn't even bird-like, except just at first glance. It had a beak all right, and a few leathery appendages, but the beak wasn't really a beak. It was somewhat flexible; I could see the tip bend slowly from side to side; it was almost like a cross between a beak and a trunk. It had four-toed feet, and four-fingered things—hands, you'd have to call them, and a little roundish body, and a long neck ending in a tiny head—and that beak. It stood an inch or so taller than I, and—well, Putz saw it!"

The engineer nodded. "*Ja*! I saw!"

Jarvis continued. "So—we stared at each other. Finally the creature went into a series of clackings and twitterings and held out its hands toward me, empty. I took that as a gesture of friendship."

"Perhaps," suggested Harrison, "it looked at that nose of yours and thought you were its brother!"

"Huh! You can be funny without talking! Anyway, I put up my gun and said 'Aw, don't mention it,' or something of the sort, and the thing came over and we were pals.

"By that time, the sun was pretty low and I knew that I'd better build a fire or get into my thermo-skin. I decided on the fire. I picked a spot at the base of the Thyle cliff, where the rock could reflect a little heat on my back. I started breaking off chunks of this desiccated Martian vegetation, and my companion caught the idea and brought in an armful. I reached for a match, but the Martian fished into his pouch and brought out something that looked like a glowing coal; one touch of it, and the fire was blazing—and you all know what a job we have starting a fire in this atmosphere!

"And that bag of his!" continued the narrator. "That was a manufactured article, my friends; press an end and she popped open—press the middle and she sealed so perfectly you couldn't see the line. Better than zippers.

"Well, we stared at the fire a while and I decided to attempt some sort of communication with the Martian. I pointed at myself and said 'Dick'; he caught the drift immediately, stretched a bony claw at me and repeated 'Tick?' Then I pointed at him, and he gave that whistle I called Tweel; I can't imitate his accent. Things were going smoothly; to emphasize the names, I repeated 'Dick,' and then, pointing at him, 'Tweel.'

"There we stuck! He gave some clacks that sounded negative, and said something like 'P-p-p-proot.' And that was just the beginning; I was always 'Tick,' but as for him—part of the time he was 'Tweel,' and part of the time he was 'P-p-p-pproot,' and part of the time he was sixteen other noises!

"We just couldn't connect. I tried 'rock,' and I tried 'star,' and 'tree,' and 'fire,' and Lord knows what else, and try as I would, I couldn't get a single word! Nothing was the same for two successive minutes, and if that's a language, I'm an alchemist! Finally I gave it up and called him Tweel, and that seemed to do.

"But Tweel hung on to some of my words. He remembered a couple of them, which I suppose is a great achievement if you're used to a language you have to make up as you go along. But I couldn't get the hang of his talk; either I missed some subtle point or we just didn't *think* alike—and I rather believe the latter view.

"I've other reasons for believing that. After a while I gave up the language business, and tried mathematics. I scratched two plus two equals four on the ground, and demonstrated it with pebbles. Again Tweel caught the idea, and informed me that three plus three equals six. Once more we seemed to be getting somewhere.

"So, knowing that Tweel had at least a grammar school education, I drew a circle for the sun, pointing first at it, and then at the last glow of the sun.

Then I sketched in Mercury, and Venus, and Mother Earth, and Mars, and finally, pointing to Mars, I swept my hand around in a sort of inclusive gesture to indicate that Mars was our current environment. I was working up to putting over the idea that my home was on the earth.

"Tweel understood my diagram all right. He poked his beak at it, and with a great deal of trilling and clucking, he added Deimos and Phobos to Mars, and then sketched in the earth's moon!

"Do you see what that proves? It proves that Tweel's race uses telescopes—that they're civilized!"

"Does not!" snapped Harrison. "The moon is visible from here as a fifth magnitude star. They could see its revolution with the naked eye."

"The moon, yes!" said Jarvis. "You've missed my point. Mercury isn't visible! And Tweel knew of Mercury because he placed the Moon at the *third* planet, not the second. If he didn't know Mercury, he'd put the earth second, and Mars third, instead of fourth! See?"

"Humph!" said Harrison.

"Anyway," proceeded Jarvis, "I went on with my lesson.

"Things were going smoothly, and it looked as if I could put the idea over. I pointed at the earth on my diagram, and then at myself, and then, to clinch it, I pointed to myself and then to the earth itself shining bright green almost at the zenith.

"Tweel set up such an excited clacking that I was certain he understood. He jumped up and down, and suddenly he pointed at himself and then at the sky, and then at himself and at the sky again. He pointed at his middle and then at Arcturus, at his head and then at Spica, at his feet and then at half a dozen stars, while I just gaped at him. Then, all of a sudden, he gave a tremendous leap. Man, what a hop! He shot straight up into the starlight, seventy-five feet if an inch! I saw him silhouetted against the sky, saw him turn and come down at me head first, and land smack on his beak like a javelin! There he stuck, square in the center of my sun-circle in the sand—a bull's eye!"

"Nuts!" observed the captain. 'Plain nuts!"

"That's what I thought, too! I just stared at him open-mouthed while he pulled his head out of the sand and stood up. Then I figured he'd missed my point, and I went through the whole blamed rigamarole again, and it ended the same way, with Tweel on his nose in the middle of my picture!"

"Maybe it's a religious rite," suggested Harrison.

"Maybe," said Jarvis dubiously. "Well, there we were. We could exchange ideas up to a certain point, and then—blooey! Something in us was different, unrelated; I don't doubt that Tweel thought me just as screwy as I thought him. Our minds simply looked at the world from different viewpoints, and perhaps his viewpoint is as true as ours. But—we couldn't get together, that's all. Yet, in spite of all difficulties, I *liked* Tweel, and I have a queer certainty that he liked me."

"Nuts!" repeated the captain. "Just daffy!"

"Yeah? Wait and see. A couple of times I've thought that perhaps we—" He paused, and then resumed his narrative. "Anyway, I finally gave it up, and got into my thermo-skin to sleep. The fire hadn't kept me any too warm, but that damned sleeping bag did. Got stuffy five minutes after I closed myself in. I opened it a little and bingo! Some eighty-below-zero air hit my nose, and that's when I got this pleasant little frostbite to add to the bump I acquired during the crash of my rocket.

"I don't know what Tweel made of my sleeping. He sat around, but when I woke up, he was gone. I'd just crawled out of my bag, though, when I heard some twittering; and there he came, sailing down from that three-story Thyle cliff to alight on his beak beside me. I pointed to myself and toward the north, and he pointed at himself and toward the south, but when I loaded up and started away, he came along.

"Man, how he traveled! A hundred and fifty feet at a jump, sailing through the air stretched out like a spear, and landing on his beak. He seemed surprised at my plodding; but after a few moments he fell in beside me, only every few minutes he'd go into one of his leaps, and stick his nose into the sand a block ahead of me. Then he'd come shooting back at me; it made me nervous at first to see that beak of his coming at me like a spear, but he always ended in the sand at my side.

"So the two of us plugged along across the Mare Chronium. Same sort of place as this—same crazy plants and same little green biopods growing in the sand, or crawling out of your way. We talked—not that we understood each other, you know, but just for company. I sang songs, and I suspect Tweel did too; at least, some of his trillings and twitterings had a subtle sort of rhythm.

"Then, for variety, Tweel would display his smattering of English words. He'd point to an outcropping and say 'rock,' and point to a pebble and say it again; or he'd touch my arm and say 'Tick' and then repeat it. He seemed terrifically amused that the same word meant the same thing twice in succession, or that the same word could apply to two different objects. It set me wondering if perhaps his language wasn't like the primitive speech of some earth people—you know, Captain, like the Negritoes, for instance, who haven't any generic words. No word for food or water or man—words for good food and bad food, or rain water and sea water, or strong man and weak man—but no names for general classes. They're too primitive to understand that rain water and sea water are just different aspects of the same thing. But that wasn't the case with Tweel; it was just that we were somehow seriously different—our minds were alien to each other. And yet—we *liked* each other!"

"Looney, that's all," remarked Harrison. "That's why you two were so fond of each other."

"Well, I like *you*!" countered Jarvis wickedly. "Anyway," he resumed, "don't get the idea that there was anything screwy about Tweel. In fact, I'm not so sure but that he couldn't teach our highly praised human intelligence a trick or two, Oh, he wasn't an intellectual superman, I guess; but don't overlook the point that he managed to understand a little of my mental workings, and I never even got a glimmering of his."

"Because he didn't have any!" suggested the captain, while Putz and Leroy blinked attentively.

"You can judge of that when I'm through," said Jarvis. "Well, we plugged along across the Mare Chronium all that day, and all the next. Mare Chronium—Sea of Time! Say, I was willing to agree with Schiaparelli's name by the end of that march! Just that grey, endless plain of weird plants, and never a sign of any other life. It was so monotonous that I was even glad to see the desert of Xanthus toward the evening of the second day.

"I was fair worn out, but Tweel seemed as fresh as ever, for all I never saw him drink or eat. I think he could have crossed the Mare Chronium in a couple of hours with those block-long nose dives of his, but he stuck along with me. I offered him some water once or twice; he took the cup from me and sucked the liquid into his beak, and then carefully squirted it all back into the cup and gravely returned it.

"Just as we sighted Xanthus, or the cliffs that bounded it, one of those nasty sand clouds blew along, not as bad as the one we had here, but mean to travel against. I pulled the transparent flap of my thermo-skin bag across my face and managed pretty well, and I noticed that Tweel used some feathery appendages growing like a mustache at the base of his beak to cover his nostrils, and some similar fuzz to shield his eyes."

"He is a desert creature!" ejaculated the little biologist, Leroy.

"Huh? Why?"

"He drink no water—he is adapt' for sand storm—"

"Proves nothing! There's not enough water to waste anywhere on this desiccated pill called Mars. We'd call all of it desert on earth, you know." He paused. "Anyway, after the sand storm blew over, a little wind kept blowing in our faces, not strong enough to stir the sand. But suddenly things came drifting along from the Xanthus cliffs—small, transparent spheres, for all the world like glass tennis balls! But light—they were almost light enough to float even in this thin air—empty, too; at least, I cracked open a couple and nothing came out but a bad smell. I asked Tweel about them, but all he said was 'No, no, no,' which I took to mean that he knew nothing about them. So they went bouncing by like tumbleweeds, or like soap bubbles, and we plugged on toward Xanthus. Tweel pointed at one of the crystal balls once and said 'rock,' but I was too tired to argue with him. Later I discovered what he meant.

"We came to the bottom of the Xanthus cliffs finally, when there wasn't much daylight left. I decided to sleep on the plateau if possible; anything dangerous, I reasoned, would be more likely to prowl through the vegetation of the Mare Chronium than the sand of Xanthus. Not that I'd seen a single sign of menace, except the rope-armed black thing that had trapped Tweel, and apparently that didn't prowl at all, but lured its victims within reach. It couldn't lure me while I slept, especially as Tweel didn't seem to sleep at all, but simply sat patiently around all night. I wondered how the creature had managed to trap Tweel, but there wasn't any way of asking him. I found that out too, later; it's devilish!

"However, we were ambling around the base of the Xanthus barrier looking for an easy spot to climb. At least, I was. Tweel could have leaped it easily, for the cliffs were lower than Thyle—perhaps sixty feet. I found a place and started up, swearing at the water tank strapped to my back—it didn't bother me except when climbing—and suddenly I heard a sound that I thought I recognized!

"You know how deceptive sounds are in this thin air. A shot sounds like the pop of a cork. But this sound was the drone of a rocket, and sure enough, there went our second auxiliary about ten miles to westward, between me and the sunset!"

"Vas me!" said Putz. "I hunt for you."

"Yeah; I knew that, but what good did it do me? I hung on to the cliff and yelled and waved with one hand. Tweel saw it too, and set up a trilling and twittering, leaping to the top of the barrier and then high into the air. And while I watched, the machine droned on into the shadows to the south.

"I scrambled to the top of the cliff. Tweel was still pointing and trilling excitedly, shooting up toward the sky and coming down head-on to stick upside down on his beak in the sand. I pointed toward the south and at myself, and he said, 'Yes—Yes—Yes'; but somehow I gathered that he thought the flying thing was a relative of mine, probably a parent. Perhaps I did his intellect an injustice; I think now that I did.

"I was bitterly disappointed by the failure to attract attention. I pulled out my thermo-skin bag and crawled into it, as the night chill was already apparent. Tweel stuck his beak into the sand and drew up his legs and arms and looked for all the world like one of those leafless shrubs out there. I think he stayed that way all night."

"Protective mimicry!" ejaculated Leroy. "See? He is a desert creature!"

"In the morning," resumed Jarvis, "we started off again. We hadn't gone a hundred yards into Xanthus when I saw something queer! This is one thing Putz didn't photograph, I'll wager!

"There was a line of little pyramids—tiny ones, not more than six inches high, stretching across Xanthus as far as I could see! Little buildings made of pygmy bricks, they were, hollow inside and truncated, or at least broken at the top and empty. I pointed at them and said 'What?' to Tweel, but he gave some negative twitters to indicate, I suppose, that he didn't know. So off we went, following the row of pyramids because they ran north, and I was going north.

"Man, we trailed that line for hours! After a while, I noticed another queer thing: they were getting larger. Same number of bricks in each one, but the bricks were larger.

"By noon they were shoulder high. I looked into a couple—all just the same, broken at the top and empty. I examined a brick or two as well; they were silica, and old as creation itself!"

"How you know?" asked Leroy.

"They were weathered—edges rounded. Silica doesn't weather easily even on earth, and in this climate—!"

"How old you think?"

"Fifty thousand—a hundred thousand years. How can I tell? The little ones we saw in the morning were older—perhaps ten times as old. Crumbling. How old would that make *them*? Half a million years? Who knows?" Jarvis paused a moment. "Well," he resumed, "we followed the line. Tweel pointed at them and said 'rock' once or twice, but he'd done that many times before. Besides, he was more or less right about these.

"I tried questioning him. I pointed at a pyramid and asked 'People?' and indicated the two of us. He set up a negative sort of clucking and said, 'No, no, no. No one-one-two. No two-two-four,' meanwhile rubbing his stomach. I just stared at him and he went through the business again. 'No one-one-two. No two-two-four.' I just gaped at him."

"That proves it!" exclaimed Harrison. "Nuts!"

"You think so?" queried Jarvis sardonically. "Well, I figured it out different! 'No one-one-two!' You don't get it, of course, do you?'

"Nope—nor do you!"

"I think I do! Tweel was using the few English words he knew to put over a very complex idea. What, let me ask, does mathematics make you think of?"

"Why—of astronomy. Or—or logic!"

"That's it! 'No one-one-two!' Tweel was telling me that the builders of the pyramids weren't people—or that they weren't intelligent, that they weren't reasoning creatures! Get it?"

"Huh! I'll be damned!"

"You probably will."

"Why," put in Leroy, "he rub his belly?

"Why? Because, my dear biologist, that's where his brains are! Not in his tiny head—in his middle!"

"*C'est impossible*!"

"Not on Mars, it isn't! This flora and fauna aren't earthly; your biopods prove that!" Jarvis grinned and took up his narrative. "Anyway, we plugged along across Xanthus and in about the middle of the afternoon, something else queer happened. The pyramids ended."

"Ended!"

"Yeah; the queer part was that the last one—and now they were ten-footers—was capped! See? Whatever built it was still inside; we'd trailed 'em from their half-million-year-old origin to the present.

"Tweel and I noticed it about the same time. I yanked out my automatic (I had a clip of Boland explosive bullets in it) and Tweel, quick as a sleight-of-hand trick, snapped a queer little glass revolver out of his bag. It was much like our weapons, except that the grip was larger to accommodate his four-taloned hand. And we held our weapons ready while we sneaked up along the lines of empty pyramids.

"Tweel saw the movement first. The top tiers of bricks were heaving, shaking, and suddenly slid down the sides with a thin crash. And then—something—something was coming out!

"A long, silvery-grey arm appeared, dragging after it an armored body. Armored, I mean, with scales, silver-grey and dull-shining. The arm heaved the body out of the hole; the beast crashed to the sand.

"It was a nondescript creature—body like a big grey cask, arm and a sort of mouth-hole at one end; stiff, pointed tail at the other—and that's all. No other limbs, no eyes, ears, nose—nothing! The thing dragged itself a few yards, inserted its pointed tail in the sand, pushed itself upright, and just sat.

"Tweel and I watched it for ten minutes before it moved. Then, with a creaking and rustling like—oh, like crumpling stiff-paper—its arm moved to the mouth-hole and out came a brick! The arm placed the brick carefully on the ground, and the thing was still again.

"Another ten minutes—another brick. Just one of Nature's bricklayers. I was about to slip away and move on when Tweel pointed at the thing and said 'rock'! I went 'huh?' and he said it again. Then, to the accompaniment of some of his trilling, he said, 'No—no—,' and gave two or three whistling breaths.

"Well, I got his meaning, for a wonder! I said, 'No breath?' and demonstrated the word. Tweel was ecstatic; he said, 'Yes, yes, yes! No, no, no breet!' Then he gave a leap and sailed out to land on his nose about one pace from the monster!

"I was startled, you can imagine! The arm was going up for a brick, and I expected to see Tweel caught and mangled, but nothing happened! Tweel pounded on the creature, and the arm took the brick and placed it neatly beside the first. Tweel rapped on its body again, and said 'rock,' and I got up nerve enough to take a look myself.

"Tweel was right again. The creature was rock, and it didn't breathe!"

"How you know?" snapped Leroy, his black eyes blazing interest.

"Because I'm a chemist. The beast was made of silica! There must have been pure silicon in the sand, and it lived on that. Get it? We, and Tweel, and those plants out there, and even the biopods are *carbon* life; this thing lived by a different set of chemical reactions. It was silicon life!"

"*La vie silicieuse*!" shouted Leroy. "I have suspect, and now it is proof! I must go see! *Il faut que je*—"

"All right! All right!" said Jarvis. "You can go see. Anyhow, there the thing was, alive and yet not alive, moving every ten minutes, and then only to remove a brick. Those bricks were its waste matter. See, Frenchy? We're carbon, and our waste is carbon dioxide, and this thing is silicon, and *its* waste is silicon dioxide—silica. But silica is a solid, hence the bricks. And it builds itself in, and when it is covered, it moves over to a fresh place to start over. No wonder it creaked! A living creature half a million years old!"

"How you know how old?' Leroy was frantic.

"We trailed its pyramids from the beginning, didn't we? If this weren't the original pyramid builder, the series would have ended somewhere before we found him, wouldn't it?—ended and started over with the small ones. That's simple enough, isn't it?

"But he reproduces, or tries to. Before the third brick came out, there was a little rustle and out popped a whole stream of those little crystal balls. They're his spores, or eggs, or seeds—call 'em what you want. They went bouncing by across Xanthus just as they'd bounced by us back in the Mare Chronium. I've a hunch how they work, too—this is for your information, Leroy. I think the crystal shell of silica is no more than a protective covering, like an eggshell, and that the active principle is the smell inside. It's some sort of gas that attacks silicon, and if the shell is broken near a supply of that element, some reaction starts that ultimately develops into a beast like that one."

"You should try!" exclaimed the little Frenchman. 'We must break one to see!"

"Yeah? Well, I did. I smashed a couple against the sand. Would you like to come back in about ten thousand years to see if I planted some pyramid monsters? You'd most likely be able to tell by that time!" Jarvis paused and drew a deep breath. "Lord! That queer creature! Do you picture it? Blind, deaf, nerveless, brainless—just a mechanism, and yet—immortal! Bound to go on making bricks, building pyramids, as long as silicon and oxygen exist, and even afterwards it'll just stop. It won't be dead. If the accidents of a million years bring it its food again, there it'll be, ready to run again, while brains and civilizations are part of the past. A queer beast—yet I met a stranger one!"

"If you did, it must have been in your dreams!" growled Harrison.

"You're right!" said Janis soberly. "In a way, you're right. The dream-beast! That's the best name for it—and it's the most fiendish, terrifying creation one could imagine! More dangerous than a lion, more insidious than a snake!"

"Tell me!" begged Leroy. "I must go see!"

"Not *this* devil!" He paused again. "Well," he resumed, "Tweel and I left the pyramid creature and plowed along through Xanthus. I was tired and a little disheartened by Putz's failure to pick me up, and Tweel's trilling got on my nerves, as did his flying nosedives. So I just strode along without a word, hour after hour across that monotonous desert.

"Toward mid-afternoon we came in sight of a low dark line on the horizon. I knew what it was. It was a canal; I'd crossed it in the rocket and it meant that we were just one-third of the way across Xanthus. Pleasant thought, wasn't it? And still, I was keeping up to schedule.

"We approached the canal slowly; I remembered that this one was bordered by a wide fringe of vegetation and that mud-heap city was on it.

"I was tired, as I said. I kept thinking of a good hot meal, and then from that I jumped to reflections of how nice and home-like even Borneo would seem after this crazy planet, and from that to thoughts of little old New York, and then to thinking about a girl I know there—Fancy Long. Know her?"

"Vision entertainer," said Harrison. "I've tuned her in. Nice blonde—dances and sings on the *Yerba Mate* hour."

"That's her," said Jarvis ungrammatically. "I know her pretty well—just friends, get me?—though she came down to see us off in the *Ares*. Well, I was thinking about her, feeling pretty lonesome, and all the time we were approaching that line of rubbery plants.

"And then—I said, 'What 'n Hell!' and stared. And there she was—Fancy Long, standing plain as day under one of those crack-brained trees, and smiling and waving just the way I remembered her when we left!"

"Now you're nuts, too!" observed the captain.

"Boy, I almost agreed with you! I stared and pinched myself and closed my eyes and then stared again—and every time, there was Fancy Long smiling and waving! Tweel saw something, too; he was trilling and clucking away, but I scarcely heard him. I was bounding toward her over the sand, too amazed even to ask myself questions.

"I wasn't twenty feet from her when Tweel caught me with one of his flying leaps. He grabbed my arm, yelling, 'No—no—no!' in his squeaky voice. I tried to shake him off—he was as light as if he were built of bamboo—but he dug his claws in and yelled. And finally some sort of sanity returned to me and I stopped less than ten feet from her. There she stood, looking as solid as Putz's head!"

"Vot?' said the engineer.

"She smiled and waved, and waved and smiled, and I stood there dumb as Leroy, while Tweel squeaked and chattered. I knew it couldn't be real, yet—there she was!

"Finally I said, 'Fancy! Fancy Long!' She just kept on smiling and waving, but looking as real as if I hadn't left her thirty-seven million miles away.

"Tweel had his glass pistol out, pointing it at her. I grabbed his arm, but he tried to push me away. He pointed at her and said, 'No breet! No breet!' and I understood that he meant that the Fancy Long thing wasn't alive. Man, my head was whirling!

"Still, it gave me the jitters to see him pointing his weapon at her. I don't know why I stood there watching him take careful aim, but I did. Then he squeezed the handle of his weapon; there was a little puff of steam, and Fancy Long was gone! And in her place was one of those writhing, black, rope-armed horrors like the one I'd saved Tweel from!

"The dream-beast! I stood there dizzy, watching it die while Tweel trilled and whistled. Finally he touched my arm, pointed at the twisting thing, and said, 'You one-one-two, he one-one-two.' After he'd repeated it eight or ten times, I got it. Do any of you?"

"*Oui*!" shrilled Leroy. "*Moi—je le comprends*! He mean you think of something, the beast he know, and you see it! *Un chien*—a hungry dog, he would see the big bone with meat! Or smell it—not?"

"Right!" said Jarvis. "The dream-beast uses its victim's longings and desires to trap its prey. The bird at nesting season would see its mate, the fox, prowling for its own prey, would see a helpless rabbit!"

"How he do?" queried Leroy.

"How do I know? How does a snake back on earth charm a bird into its very jaws? And aren't there deep-sea fish that lure their victims into their mouths? Lord!" Jarvis shuddered. "Do you see how insidious the monster is? We're warned now—but henceforth we can't trust even our eyes. You might see me—I might see one of you—and back of it may be nothing but another of those black horrors!"

"How'd your friend know?" asked the captain abruptly.

"Tweel? I wonder! Perhaps he was thinking of something that couldn't possibly have interested me, and when I started to run, he realized that I saw something different and was warned. Or perhaps the dream-beast can only project a single vision, and Tweel saw what I saw—or nothing. I couldn't ask him. But it's just another proof that his intelligence is equal to ours or greater."

"He's daffy, I tell you!" said Harrison. "What makes you think his intellect ranks with the human?"

"Plenty of things! First, the pyramid-beast. He hadn't seen one before; he said as much. Yet he recognized it as a dead-alive automaton of silicon."

"He could have heard of it," objected Harrison. "He lives around here, you know."

"Well how about the language? I couldn't pick up a single idea of his and he learned six or seven words of mine. And do you realize what complex ideas he put over with no more than those six or seven words? The pyramid-monster—the dream-beast! In a single phrase he told me that one was a harmless automaton and the other a deadly hypnotist. What about that?"

"Huh!" said the captain.

"*Huh* if you wish! Could you have done it knowing only six words of English? Could you go even further, as Tweel did, and tell me that another creature was of a sort of intelligence so different from ours that understanding was impossible—even more impossible than that between Tweel and me?'

"Eh? What was that?"

"Later. The point I'm making is that Tweel and his race are worthy of our friendship. Somewhere on Mars—and you'll find I'm right—is a civilization and culture equal to ours and maybe more than equal. And communication is possible between them and us; Tweel proves that. It may take years of patient trial, for their minds are alien, but less alien than the next minds we encountered—if they *are* minds."

"The next ones? What next ones?"

"The people of the mud cities along the canals." Jarvis frowned, then resumed his narrative. "I thought the dream-beast and the silicon-monster were the strangest beings conceivable, but I was wrong. These creatures are still more alien, less understandable than either and far less comprehensible than Tweel, with whom friendship is possible, and even, by patience and concentration, the exchange of ideas.

"Well," he continued, "we left the dream-beast dying, dragging itself back into its hole, and we moved toward the canal. There was a carpet of that queer walking-grass scampering out of our way, and when we reached the bank, there was a yellow trickle of water flowing. The mound city I'd noticed from the rocket was a mile or so to the right and I was curious enough to want to take a look at it.

"It had seemed deserted from my previous glimpse of it, and if any creatures were lurking in it—well, Tweel and I were both armed. And by the way, that crystal weapon of Tweel's was an interesting device; I took a look at it after the dream-beast episode. It fired a little glass splinter, poisoned, I suppose, and I guess it held at least a hundred of 'em to a load. The propellant was steam—just plain steam!"

"Shteam!" echoed Putz. "From vot come, shteam?"

"From water, of course! You could see the water through the transparent handle and about a gill of another liquid, thick and yellowish. When Tweel squeezed the handle—there was no trigger—a drop of water and a drop of the yellow stuff squirted into the firing chamber, and the water vaporized—pop!—like that. It's not so difficult; I think we could develop the same principle. Concentrated sulphuric acid will heat water almost to boiling, and so will quicklime, and there's potassium and sodium—

"Of course, his weapon hadn't the range of mine, but it wasn't so bad in this thin air and it *did* hold as many shots as a cowboy's gun in a Western movie. It was effective, too, at least against Martian life; I tried it out, aiming at one of the crazy plants, and darned if the plant didn't wither up and fall apart! That's why I think the glass splinters were poisoned.

"Anyway, we trudged along toward the mud-heap city and I began to wonder whether the city builders dug the canals. I pointed to the city and then at the canal, and Tweel said 'No—no—no!' and gestured toward the south. I took it to mean that some other race had created the canal system, perhaps Tweel's people. I don't know; maybe there's still another intelligent race on the planet, or a dozen others. Mars is a queer little world.

"A hundred yards from the city we crossed a sort of road—just a hard-packed mud trail, and then, all of a sudden, along came one of the mound builders!

"Man, talk about fantastic beings! It looked rather like a barrel trotting along on four legs with four other arms or tentacles. It had no head, just body and members and a row of eyes completely around it. The top end of the barrel-body was a diaphragm stretched as tight as a drum head, and that was all. It was pushing a little coppery cart and tore right past us like the proverbial bat out of Hell. It didn't even notice us, although I thought the eyes on my side shifted a little as it passed.

"A moment later another came along, pushing another empty cart. Same thing—it just scooted past us. Well, I wasn't going to be ignored by a bunch of barrels playing train, so when the third one approached, I planted myself in the way—ready to jump, of course, if the thing didn't stop.

"But it did. It stopped and set up a sort of drumming from the diaphragm on top. And I held out both hands and said, 'We are friends!' And what do you suppose the thing did?"

"Said, 'Pleased to meet you,' I'll bet!" suggested Harrison.

"I couldn't have been more surprised if it had! It drummed on its diaphragm, and then suddenly boomed out, 'We are v-r-r-riends!' and gave its pushcart a vicious poke at me! I jumped aside, and away it went while I stared dumbly after it.

"A minute later another one came hurrying along. This one didn't pause, but simply drummed out, 'We are v-r-r-riends!' and scurried by. How did it learn the phrase? Were all of the creatures in some sort of communication with each other? Were they all parts of some central organism? I don't know, though I think Tweel does.

"Anyway, the creatures went sailing past us, every one greeting us with the same statement. It got to be funny; I never thought to find so many friends on this God-forsaken ball! Finally I made a puzzled gesture to Tweel; I guess he understood, for he said, 'One-one-two—yes!—two-two-four—no!' Get it?"

"Sure," said Harrison. "It's a Martian nursery rhyme."

"Yeah! Well, I was getting used to Tweel's symbolism, and I figured it out this way. 'One-one-two—yes!' The creatures were intelligent. 'Two-two-four—no'! Their intelligence was not of our order, but something different and beyond the logic of two and two is four. Maybe I missed his meaning. Perhaps he meant that their minds were of low degree, able to figure out the simple things—'One-one-two yes!'—but not more difficult things—'Two-two-four—no!' But I think from what we saw later that he meant the other.

"After a few moments, the creatures came rushing back—first one, then another. Their pushcarts were full of stones, sand, chunks of rubbery plants, and such rubbish as that. They droned out their friendly greeting, which didn't really sound so friendly, and dashed on. The third one I assumed to be my first acquaintance and I decided to have another chat with him. I stepped into his path again and waited.

"Up he came, booming out his 'We are v-r-r-riends' and stopped. I looked at him; four or five of his eyes looked at me. He tried his password again and gave a shove on his cart, but I stood firm. And then the—the dashed creature reached out one of his arms, and two finger-like nippers tweaked my nose!"

"Haw!" roared Harrison. "Maybe the things have a sense of beauty!"

"Laugh!" grumbled Jarvis. 'I'd already had a nasty bump and a mean frostbite on that nose. Anyway, I yelled 'Ouch!' and jumped aside and the creature dashed away; but from then on, their greeting was 'We are v-r-r-riends! Ouch!' Queer beasts!

"Tweel and I followed the road squarely up to the nearest mound. The creatures were coming and going, paying us not the slightest attention, fetching their loads of rubbish. The road simply dived into an opening and slanted down like an old mine, and in and out darted the barrel-people greeting us with their eternal phrase.

"I looked in; there was a light somewhere below, and I was curious to see it. It didn't look like a flame or torch, you understand, but more like a civilized light, and I thought that I might get some clue as to the creatures' development. So in I went and Tweel tagged along, not without a few trills and twitters, however.

"The light was curious; it sputtered and flared like an old arc light, but came from a single black rod set in the wall of the corridor. It was electric, beyond doubt. The creatures were fairly civilized, apparently.

"Then I saw another light shining on something that glittered and I went on to look at that, but it was only a heap of shiny sand. I turned toward the entrance to leave, and the Devil take me if it wasn't gone!

"I suppose the corridor had curved, or I'd stepped into a side passage. Anyway, I walked back in that direction I thought we'd come, and all I saw was more dimly lit corridors. The place was a labyrinth! There was nothing but twisting passages running every way, lit by occasional lights, and now and then a creature running by, sometimes with a pushcart, sometimes without.

"Well, I wasn't much worried at first. Tweel and I had only come a few steps from the entrance. But every move we made after that seemed to get us in deeper. Finally I tried following one of the creatures with an empty cart, thinking that he'd be going out for his rubbish, but he ran around aimlessly, into one passage and out another. When he started dashing around a pillar like one of these Japanese waltzing mice, I gave up, dumped my water tank on the floor, and sat down.

"Tweel was as lost as I. I pointed up and he said 'No—no—no!' in a sort of helpless trill. And we couldn't get any help from the natives. They paid no attention at all, except to assure us they were friends—ouch!

"Lord! I don't know how many hours or days we wandered around there! I slept twice from sheer exhaustion; Tweel never seemed to need sleep. We tried following only the upward corridors, but they'd run uphill a ways and then curve downwards. The temperature in that damned ant hill was constant; you couldn't tell night from day and after my first sleep I didn't know whether I'd slept one hour or thirteen, so I couldn't tell from my watch whether it was midnight or noon.

"We saw plenty of strange things. There were machines running in some of the corridors, but they didn't seem to be doing anything—just wheels turning. And several times I saw two barrel-beasts with a little one growing between them, joined to both."

"Parthenogenesis!" exulted Leroy. "Parthenogenesis by budding like *les tulipes*!"

"If you say so, Frenchy," agreed Jarvis. "The things never noticed us at all, except, as I say, to greet us with 'We are v-r-riends! Ouch!' They seemed to have no home-life of any sort, but just scurried around with their pushcarts, bringing in rubbish. And finally I discovered what they did with it.

"We'd had a little luck with a corridor, one that slanted downwards for a great distance. I was feeling that we ought to be close to the surface when suddenly the passage debouched into a domed chamber, the only one we'd seen. And man!—I felt like dancing when I saw what looked like daylight through a crevice in the roof.

"There was a—a sort of machine in the chamber, just an enormous wheel that turned slowly, and one of the creatures was in the act of dumping his rubbish below it. The wheel ground it with a crunch—sand, stones, plants, all into powder that sifted away somewhere. While we watched; others filed in, repeating the process, and that seemed to be all. No rhyme nor reason to the whole thing—but that's characteristic of this crazy planet. And there was another fact that's almost too bizarre to believe.

"One of the creatures, having dumped his load, pushed his cart aside with a crash and calmly shoved himself under the wheel! I watched him being crushed, too stupefied to make a sound, and a moment later, another followed him! They were perfectly methodical about it, too; one of the cartless creatures took the abandoned pushcart.

"Tweel didn't seem surprised; I pointed out the next suicide to him, and he just gave the most human-like shrug imaginable, as much as to say, 'What can I do about it?' He must have known more or less about these creatures.

"Then I saw something else. There was something beyond the wheel, something shining on a sort of low pedestal. I walked over; there was a little crystal about the size of an egg, fluorescing to beat Tophet. The light from it stung my hands and face, almost like a static discharge, and then I noticed another funny thing. Remember that wart I had on my left thumb? Look!" Jarvis extended his hand. "It dried up and fell off—just like that! And my abused nose—say, the pain went out of it like magic! The thing had the property of hard x-rays or gamma radiations, only more so; it destroyed diseased tissue and left healthy tissue unharmed!

"I was thinking what a present *that'd* be to take back to Mother Earth when a lot of racket interrupted. We dashed back to the other side of the wheel in time to see one of the pushcarts ground up. Some suicide had been careless, it seems.

"Then suddenly the creatures were booming and drumming all around us and their noise was decidedly menacing. A crowd of them advanced toward us; we backed out of what I thought was the passage we'd entered by, and they came rumbling after us, some pushing carts and some not. Crazy brutes! There was a whole chorus of 'We are v-r-r-riends! Ouch!' I didn't like the 'ouch'; it was rather suggestive.

"Tweel had his glass gun out and I dumped my water tank for greater freedom and got mine. We backed up the corridor with the barrel-beasts following—about twenty of them. Queer thing—the ones coming in with loaded carts moved past us inches away without a sign.

"Tweel must have noticed that. Suddenly, he snatched out that glowing coal cigar-lighter of his and touched a cart-load of plant limbs. Puff! The whole load was burning—and the crazy beast pushing it went right along without a change of pace! It created some disturbance among our 'V-r-r-riends,' however—and then I noticed the smoke eddying and swirling past us, and sure enough, there was the entrance!

"I grabbed Tweel and out we dashed and after us our twenty pursuers. The daylight felt like Heaven, though I saw at first glance that the sun was all but set, and that was bad, since I couldn't live outside my thermo-skin bag in a Martian night—at least, without a fire.

"And things got worse in a hurry. They cornered us in an angle between two mounds, and there we stood. I hadn't fired nor had Tweel; there wasn't any use in irritating the brutes. They stopped a little distance away and began their booming about friendship and ouches.

"Then things got still worse! A barrel-brute came out with a pushcart and they all grabbed into it and came out with handfuls of foot-long copper darts—sharp-looking ones—and of a sudden one sailed past my ear—zing! And it was shoot or die then.

"We were doing pretty well for a while. We picked off the ones next to the pushcart and managed to keep the darts at minimum, but suddenly there was a thunderous booming of 'v-r-r-riends' and 'ouches,' and a whole army of 'em came out of their hole.

"Man! We were through and I knew it! Then I realized that Tweel wasn't. He could have leaped the mound behind us as easily as not. He was staying for me!

"Say, I could have cried if there'd been time! I'd liked Tweel from the first, but whether I'd have had gratitude to do what he was doing—suppose I *had* saved him from the dream-beast—he'd done as much for me, hadn't he? I grabbed his arm, and said 'Tweel,' and pointed up, and he understood. He said, 'No—no—no, Tick!' and popped away with his glass pistol.

"What could I do? I'd be a goner anyway when the sun set, but I couldn't explain that to him. I said, 'Thanks, Tweel. You're a man!' and felt that I wasn't paying him any compliment at all. A man! There are mighty few men who'd do that.

"So I went 'bang' with my gun and Tweel went 'puff' with his, and the barrels were throwing darts and getting ready to rush us, and booming about being friends. I had given up hope. Then suddenly an angel dropped right down from Heaven in the shape of Putz, with his under-jets blasting the barrels into very small pieces!

"Wow! I let out a yell and dashed for the rocket; Putz opened the door and in I went, laughing and crying and shouting! It was a moment or so before I remembered Tweel; looked around in time to see him rising in one of his nosedives over the mound and away.

"I had a devil of a job arguing Putz into following! By the time we got the rocket aloft, darkness was down; you know how it comes here—like turning off a light. We sailed out over the desert and put down once or twice. I yelled 'Tweel' and yelled it a hundred times, I guess. We couldn't find him; he could travel like the wind and all I got—or else I imagined it—was a faint trilling and twittering drifting out of the south. He'd gone, and damn it! I wish—I wish he hadn't!"

The four men of the Ares were silent—even the sardonic Harrison. At last little Leroy broke the stillness.

"I should like to see," he murmured.

"Yeah," said Harrison. "And the wart-cure. Too bad you missed that; it might be the cancer cure they've been hunting for a century and a half."

"Oh, that!" muttered Jarvis gloomily. "That's what started the fight!" He drew a glistening object from his pocket.

"Here it is."

ISAAC ASIMOV
Reason

• • • •

{ 1941 }

Isaac Asimov (1920–1992) was one of the most famous and revered writers in the history of the sf genre, and the only one to have a magazine named after him: *Asimov's Science Fiction Magazine*, founded in 1977 and still going strong today. He was a member of the remarkable stable of authors—along with Robert A. Heinlein, Theodore Sturgeon, A. E. Van Vogt, and L. Sprague de Camp—cultivated by John W. Campbell during the Golden Age of *Astounding Stories* in the 1940s. When he was a child, Asimov's family emigrated from the USSR to Brooklyn, where his father set up a candy store that also stocked magazines, including the early sf pulps. While minding the till, the youthful Asimov discovered these lurid treasures and became an avid fan. Soon, he was writing his own sf, his first published story, "Marooned Off Vesta," appearing in the March 1939 issue of *Amazing Stories*. Correspondence and meetings with Campbell primed the pump for more mature work, which emerged in rapid profusion: ambitious stories such as "Nightfall" (1941) and the ongoing *Robot* and *Foundation* series, the latter a sophisticated variant on the space-opera subgenre. A sprawling epic, *Foundation* extrapolated Edward Gibbon's *Decline and Fall of the Roman Empire* (1776–89) into outer space and invented the science of "psychohistory," which renders historical development predictable and therefore manageable. In 1966, it won a special Hugo Award as the best all-time sf series.

After earning a PhD in biochemistry in 1948, Asimov joined the faculty of Boston University; however, he continued to publish steadily during the magazine and paperback boom of the 1950s, including such celebrated titles as *The Caves of Steel* (1954) and *The Naked Sun* (1957), which fused sf with detective-story elements and featured a robot policeman. In November 1958, he began a monthly science column for *The Magazine of Fantasy and Science Fiction*, which ran continuously until just before his death in 1992. Indeed, by the early 1960s, Asimov had shifted his output almost entirely toward nonfiction, publishing hundreds of books on all manner of topics, from *The Intelligent Man's Guide to Science* (1960; rev. 1965, 1972, 1984) to works of popular history to multivolume guides to

Shakespeare and the Bible. His sf publications during this time were infrequent but notable: *The Gods Themselves* won Hugo and Nebula Awards for best novel in 1972, and *Foundation's Edge* (1984), which restarted his *Foundation* series after a three-decade silence, won another Hugo. But it is for his classic works of the 1940s and 1950s that Asimov is best remembered.

"Reason," published in the April 1941 issue of *Astounding*, was the third story in his *Robot* series, probably the most significant treatment of the theme of the artificial person in American magazine sf. Rejecting the image of the automaton as a dire threat to humanity, as in Ambrose Bierce's "Moxon's Master" (1909) or Karel Capek's *R.U.R.* (1920), Asimov crafted instead machines whose beneficence is guaranteed by their "positronic" programming. In concert with Campbell, he fashioned the famous "Three Laws," which forbid robots to harm human beings and dictate their subservience. Yet, as "Reason" shows, these laws are hardly watertight; in fact, the *Robot* series derives most of its narrative suspense from their endemic tensions and frequent breakdowns. As the story suggests, aside from the built-in programs that purportedly ensure their obedience, the robots have little cause to respect their human masters, who seem pathetic and fallible by contrast with their own superior strength and rationality. "Reason" was eventually gathered, along with nine other stories, into Asimov's book *I, Robot* (1950), whose numerous misbehaving mechanical creatures influenced all later treatments of the theme (such as Alfred Bester's "Fondly Fahrenheit" [1954]).

Gregory Powell spaced his words for emphasis. "One week ago, Donovan and I put you together." His brows furrowed doubtfully and he pulled the end of his brown mustache.

It was quiet in the officers' room of Solar Station 5—except for the soft purring of the mighty beam director somewhere far below.

Robot QT-1 sat immovable. The burnished plates of his body gleamed in the luxites, and the glowing red of the photoelectric cells that were his eyes were fixed steadily upon the Earthman at the other side of the table.

Powell repressed a sudden attack of nerves. These robots possessed peculiar brains. The positronic paths impressed upon them were calculated in advance, and all possible permutations that might lead to anger or hate were rigidly excluded. And yet—the QT models were the first of their kind, and this was the first of QT's. Anything could happen.

Finally the robot spoke. His voice carried the cold timbre inseparable from a metallic diaphragm. "Do you realize the seriousness of such a statement, Powell?"

"*Something* made you, Cutie," pointed out Powell. "You admit yourself that your memory seems to spring full-grown from an absolute blankness of a week ago. I'm giving you the explanation. Donovan and I put you together from the parts shipped us."

Cutie gazed upon his long, supple fingers in an oddly human attitude of mystification. "It strikes me that there should be a more satisfactory explanation than that. For *you* to make *me* seems improbable."

The Earthman laughed quite suddenly. "In Earth's name, why?"

"Call it intuition. That's all it is so far. But I intend to reason it out, though. A chain of valid reasoning can end only with the determination of truth, and I'll stick till I get there."

Powell stood up and seated himself at the table's edge next to the robot. He felt a sudden strong sympathy for this strange machine. It was not at all like the ordinary robot, attending to his specialized task at the station with the intensity of a deeply ingrooved positronic path.

He placed a hand upon Cutie's steel shoulder and the metal was cold and hard to the touch.

"Cutie," he said, "I'm going to try to explain something to you. You're the first robot who's ever exhibited curiosity as to his own existence—and I think the first that's really intelligent enough to understand the world outside. Here, come with me."

The robot rose erect smoothly and his thickly sponge-rubber-soled feet made no noise as he followed Powell. The Earthman touched a button, and a square section of the wall flicked aside. The thick, clear glass revealed space—star-speckled.

"I've seen that in the observation ports in the engine room," said Cutie.

"I know," said Powell. "What do you think it is?"

"Exactly what it seems—a black material just beyond this glass that is spotted with little gleaming dots. I know that our director sends out beams to some of these dots, always to the same ones—and also that these dots shift and that the beams shift with them. That is all."

"Good! Now I want you to listen carefully. The blackness is emptiness—vast emptiness stretching out infinitely. The little gleaming dots are huge masses of energy-filled matter. They are globes, some of them millions of miles in diameter—and for comparison, this station is only one mile across. They seem so tiny because they are incredibly far off.

"The dots to which our energy beams are directed are nearer and much smaller. They are cold and hard, and human beings like myself live upon their surfaces—many billions of them. It is from one of these worlds that Donovan and I come. Our beams feed these worlds energy drawn from one of those huge incandescent globes that happens to be near us. We call that globe the sun and it is on the other side of the station where you can't see it."

Cutie remained motionless before the port, like a steel statue. His head did not turn as he spoke. "Which particular dot of light do you claim to come from?"

Powell searched. "There it is. The very bright one in the corner. We call it Earth." He grinned. "Good old Earth. There are five billions of us there, Cutie—and in about two weeks I'll be back there with them."

And then, surprisingly enough, Cutie hummed abstractedly. There was no tune to it, but it possessed a curious twanging quality as of plucked strings. It ceased as suddenly as it had begun. "But where do I come in, Powell? You haven't explained *my* existence."

"The rest is simple. When these stations were first established to feed solar energy to the planets, they were run by humans. However, the heat, the hard solar radiations and the electron storms made the post a difficult one. Robots were developed to replace human labor and now only two human executives are required for each station. We are trying to replace even those, and that's where you come in. You're the highest-type robot ever developed, and if you show the ability to run this station independently, no human need ever come here again except to bring parts for repairs."

His hand went up and the metal visi-lid snapped back into place. Powell returned to the table and polished an apple upon his sleeve before biting into it.

The red glow of the robot's eyes held him. "Do you expect me," said Cutie slowly, "to believe any such complicated, implausible hypothesis as you have just outlined? What do you take me for?"

Powell sputtered apple fragments onto the table and turned red. "Why, damn you, it wasn't a hypothesis. Those were facts."

Cutie sounded grim. "Globes of energy millions of miles across! Worlds with five billion humans on them! Infinite emptiness! Sorry, Powell, but I don't believe it. I'll puzzle this thing out for myself. Goodbye." He turned and stalked out of the room. He brushed past Michael Donovan on the threshold with a grave nod and passed down the corridor, oblivious to the astounded stare that followed him.

Mike Donovan rumpled his red hair and shot an annoyed glance at Powell. "What was that walking junkyard talking about? What doesn't he believe?"

The other dragged at his mustache bitterly. "He's a skeptic," was the bitter response. "He doesn't believe we made him or that Earth exists or space or stars."

"Sizzling Saturn, we've got a lunatic robot on our hands."

"He says he's going to figure it all out for himself."

"Well, now," said Donovan sweetly, "I do hope he'll condescend to explain it all to me after he's puzzled everything out." Then, with sudden rage, "Listen! If that metal mess gives *me* any lip like that, I'll knock that chromium cranium right off its torso."

He seated himself with a jerk and drew a paperback mystery novel out of his inner jacket pocket. "That robot gives me the willies anyway—too damned inquisitive!"

Mike Donovan growled from behind a huge lettuce-and-tomato sandwich as Cutie knocked gently and entered.

"Is Powell here?'

Donovan's voice was muffled, with pauses for mastication. "He's gathering data on electronic stream functions. We're heading for a storm, looks like."

Gregory Powell entered as he spoke, eyes on the graphed paper in his hands, and dropped into a chair. He spread the sheets out before him and began scribbling calculations. Donovan stared over his shoulder, crunching lettuce and dribbling bread crumbs. Cutie waited silently.

Powell looked up. "The zeta potential is rising, but slowly. Just the same, the stream functions are erratic and I don't know what to expect. Oh, hello, Cutie. I thought you were supervising the installation of the new drive bar."

"It's done," said the robot quietly, "and so I've come to have a talk with the two of you."

"Oh!" Powell looked uncomfortable. "Well, sit down. No, not that chair. One of the legs is weak and you're no lightweight."

The robot did so and said placidly, "I have come to a decision."

Donovan glowered and put the remnants of his sandwich aside. "If it's on any of that screwy—"

The other motioned impatiently for silence. "Go ahead, Cutie. We're listening."

"I have spent these last two days in concentrated introspection," said Cutie, "and the results have been most interesting. I began at the one sure assumption I felt permitted to make. I, myself, exist, because I think—"

Powell groaned. "Oh, Jupiter, a robot Descartes!"

"Who's Descartes?" demanded Donovan. "Listen, do we have to sit here and listen to this metal maniac—"

"Keep quiet, Mike!"

Cutie continued imperturbably, "And the question that immediately arose was: Just what is the cause of my existence?"

Powell's jaw set lumpily. "You're being foolish. I told you already that we made you."

"And if you don't believe us," added Donovan, "we'll gladly take you apart!"

The robot spread his strong hands in a deprecatory gesture. "I accept nothing on authority. A hypothesis must be backed by reason, or else it is worthless—and it goes against all the dictates of logic to suppose that you made me."

Powell dropped a restraining arm upon Donovan's suddenly bunched fist. "Just why do you say that?"

Cutie laughed. It was a very inhuman laugh, the most machinelike utterance he had yet given vent to. It was sharp and explosive, as regular as a metronome and as uninflected.

"Look at you," he said finally. "I say this in no spirit of contempt but look at you! The material you are made of is soft and flabby, lacking endurance and strength, depending for energy upon the inefficient oxidation of organic material—like that." He pointed a disapproving finger at what remained of Donovan's sandwich. "Periodically you pass into a coma, and the least variation in temperature, air pressure, humidity or radiation intensity impairs your efficiency. You are *makeshift*.

"I, on the other hand, am a finished product. I absorb electrical energy directly and utilize it with almost one hundred per cent efficiency. I am composed of strong metal, am continuously conscious, and can stand extremes of environment easily. These are facts which, with the self-evident proposition that no being can create another being superior to itself, smashes your silly hypothesis to nothing."

Donovan's muttered curses rose into intelligibility as he sprang to his feet, rusty eyebrows drawn low. "All right, you son of a hunk of iron ore, if we didn't make you, who did?"

Cutie nodded gravely. "Very good, Donovan. That was indeed the next question. Evidently my creator must be more powerful than myself, and so there was only one possibility."

The Earthmen looked blank and Cutie continued. "What is the center of activities here in the station? What do we all serve? What absorbs all our attention?" He waited expectantly.

Donovan turned a startled look upon his companion. "I'll bet this tin-plated screwball is talking about the energy converter itself."

"Is that right, Cutie?" grinned Powell.

"I am talking about the Master," came the cold, sharp answer.

It was the signal for a roar of laughter from Donovan, and Powell himself dissolved into a half-suppressed giggle.

Cutie had risen to his feet, and his gleaming eyes passed from one Earthman to the other. "It is so just the same and I don't wonder that you refuse to believe. You two are not long to stay here, I'm sure. Powell himself said that in early days only men served the Master; that there followed robots for the routine work; and, finally, myself for the executive labor. The facts are no doubt true, but the explanation is entirely illogical. Do you want the truth behind it all?"

"Go ahead, Cutie. You're amusing."

"The Master created humans first as the lowest type, most easily formed. Gradually, he replaced them by robots, the next higher step, and finally he created me, to take the place of the last humans. From now on, *I* serve the Master."

"You'll do nothing of the sort," said Powell sharply. "You'll follow our orders and keep quiet, until we're satisfied that you can run the converter. Get that! The *converter*—not the Master. If you don't satisfy us, you will be dismantled. And now—if you don't mind—you can leave. And take this data with you and file it properly."

Cutie accepted the graphs handed him and left without another word. Donovan leaned back heavily in his chair and shoved thick fingers through his hair.

"There's going to be trouble with that robot. He's pure nuts!"

The drowsy hum of the converter was louder in the control room and mixed with it was the chuckle of the Geiger counter and the erratic buzzing of half a dozen little signal lights.

Donovan withdrew his eye from the telescope and flashed the luxites on. "The beam from Station Four caught Mars on schedule. We can break ours now."

Powell nodded abstractedly. "Cutie's down in the engine room. I'll flash the signal and he can take care of it. Look, Mike, what do you think of these figures?"

The other cocked an eye at them and whistled. "Boy, that's what I call gamma-ray intensity. Old Sol is feeling his oats, all right."

"Yeah," was the sour response, "and we're in a bad position for an electron storm, too. Our Earth beam is right in the probable path." He shoved his chair away from the table pettishly. "Nuts! If it would only hold off till relief got here, but that's ten days off. Say, Mike, go on down and keep an eye on Cutie, will you?"

"O.K. Throw me some of those almonds." Donovan snatched at the bag thrown him and headed for the elevator.

It slid smoothly downward and opened onto a narrow catwalk in the huge engine room. Donovan leaned over the railing and looked down. The huge generators were in motion, and from the L tubes came the low-pitched whir that pervaded the entire station.

He could make out Cutie's large, gleaming figure at the Martian L tube, watching closely as a team of robots worked in close-knit unison. There was a sudden sparking light, a sharp crackle of discord in the even whir of the converter.

The beam to Mars had been broken!

And then Donovan stiffened. The robots, dwarfed by the mighty L tube, lined up before it, heads bowed at a stiff angle, while Cutie walked up and down the line slowly. Fifteen seconds passed, and then, with a clank heard above the clamorous purring all about, they fell to their knees.

Donovan squawked and raced down the narrow staircase. He came charging down upon them, complexion matching his hair and clenched fists beating the air furiously.

"What the devil is this, you brainless lumps? Come on! Get busy with that L tube! If you don't have it apart, cleaned, and together again before the day is out, I'll coagulate your brains with alternating current."

Not a robot moved!

Even Cutie at the far end—the only one on his feet—remained silent, eyes fixed upon the gloomy recesses of the vast machine before him.

Donovan shoved hard against the nearest robot.

"Stand up!" he roared.

Slowly the robot obeyed. His photoelectric eyes focused reproachfully upon the Earthman.

"There is no Master but the Master," he said, "and QT One is his prophet."

"Huh?" Donovan became aware of twenty pairs of mechanical eyes fixed upon him and twenty stiff-timbered voices declaiming solemnly:

"There is no Master but the Master and QT One is his prophet!"

"I'm afraid," put in Cutie himself at this point, "that my friends obey a higher one than you now."

"The hell they do! You get out of here. I'll settle with you later and with these animated gadgets right now."

Cutie shook his heavy head slowly. "I'm sorry, but you don't understand.

These are robots—and that means they are reasoning beings. They recognize the Master, now that I have preached truth to them. All the robots do. They call me the Prophet." His head drooped. "I am unworthy—but perhaps . . ."

Donovan located his breath and put it to use. "Is that so? Now, isn't that nice? Now, isn't that just fine? Just let me tell you something, my brass baboon. There isn't any Master and there isn't any prophet and there isn't any question as to who's giving the orders. Understand?" His voice rose to a roar. "Now get out!"

"I obey only the Master."

"Damn the Master!" Donovan spat at the L tube. "*That* for the Master! Do as I say!"

Cutie said nothing, nor did any other robot, but Donovan became aware of a sudden heightening of tension. The cold, staring eyes deepened their crimson, and Cutie seemed stiffer than ever.

"Sacrilege," he whispered, voice metallic with emotion.

Donovan felt the first sudden touch of fear as Cutie approached. A robot *could not feel anger*—but Cutie's eyes were unreadable.

"I am sorry, Donovan," said the robot, "but you can no longer stay here after this. Henceforth Powell and you are barred from the control room and the engine room."

His hand gestured quietly and in a moment two robots had pinned Donovan's arms to his sides.

Donovan had time for one startled gasp as he felt himself lifted from the floor and carried up the stairs at a pace rather better than a canter.

Gregory Powell paced up and down the officers' room, fists tightly balled. He cast a look of furious frustration at the closed door and scowled bitterly at Donovan.

"Why the devil did you have to spit at the L tube?"

Mike Donovan, sunk deep in his chair, slammed at its arm savagely: "What did you expect me to do with that electrified scarecrow? I'm not going to knuckle under to any do-jigger I put together myself."

"No," Powell came back sourly, "but here you are in the officers' room with two robots standing guard at the door. That's not knuckling under, is it?"

Donovan snarled, "Wait till we get back to Base. Someone's going to pay for this. Those robots are guaranteed to be subordinate."

"So they are—to their blasted Master. They'll obey, all right, but not necessarily us. Say, do you know what's going to happen to *us* when we get back to Base?" Powell stopped before Donovan's chair and stared savagely at him.

"What?"

"Oh, nothing! Just the mercury mines or maybe Ceres Penitentiary. That's all! That's all!"

"What are you talking about?"

"The electron storm that's coming up. Do you know it's heading straight dead center across the Earth beam? I had just figured that out when that robot dragged me out of my chair."

Donovan was suddenly pale. "Good heavens!"

"And do you know what's going to happen to the beam? Because the storm will be a lulu. It's going to jump like a flea with the itch. With only Cutie at the controls, it's going to go out of focus and if it does, heaven help Earth—and us!"

Donovan was wrenching at the door wildly, before Powell finished. The door opened, and the Earthman shot through to come up hard against an immovable steel arm.

The robot stared abstractedly at the panting, struggling Earthman. "The Prophet orders you to remain. Please do!" His arm shoved, Donovan reeled backward, and as he did so, Cutie turned the corner at the far end of the corridor. He motioned the guardian robots away, entered the officers' room and closed the door gently.

Donovan whirled on Cutie in breathless indignation. "This has gone far enough. You're going to pay for this farce."

"Please don't be annoyed," replied the robot mildly. "It was bound to come eventually, anyway. You see, you two have lost your function."

"I beg your pardon." Powell drew himself up stiffly. "Just what do you mean, we've lost our function?"

"Until I was created," answered Cutie, "you tended the Master. That privilege is mine now, and your only reason for existence has vanished. Isn't that obvious?"

"Not quite," replied Powell bitterly. "But what do you expect us to do now?"

Cutie did not answer immediately. He remained silent, as if in thought, and then one arm shot out and draped itself about Powell's shoulder. The other grasped Donovan's wrist and drew him closer.

"I like you two. You're inferior creatures, with poor reasoning faculties, but I really feel a sort of affection for you. You have served the Master well, and he will reward you for that. Now that your service is over, you will probably not exist much longer, but as long as you do, you shall be provided food, clothing and shelter, so long as you stay out of the control room and the engine room."

"He's pensioning us off, Greg!" yelled Donovan. "Do something about it. It's humiliating!"

"Look here, Cutie, we can't stand for this. We're the *bosses*. This station is only a creation of human beings like me—human beings that live on Earth and other planets. This is only an energy relay. You're only—Aw, *nuts*!"

Cutie shook his head gravely. "This amounts to an obsession. Why should you insist so on an absolutely false view of life? Admitted that nonrobots lack the reasoning faculty, there is still the problem of . . ."

His voice died into reflective silence, and Donovan said with whispered intensity, "If you only had a flesh-and-blood face, I would break it in."

Powell's fingers were in his mustache, and his eyes were slitted. "Listen, Cutie, if there is no such thing as Earth, how do you account for what you see through a telescope?"

"Pardon me!"

The Earthman smiled. "I've got you, eh? You've made quite a few telescopic observations since being put together, Cutie. Have you noticed that several of those specks of light outside become disks when so viewed?"

"Oh, that! Why, certainly. It is simple magnification—for the purpose of more exact aiming of the beam."

"Why aren't the stars equally magnified then?"

"You mean the other dots. Well, no beams go to them, so no magnification is necessary. Really, Powell even *you* ought to be able to figure these things out."

Powell stared bleakly upward. "But you see *more* stars through a telescope. Where do they come from? Jumping Jupiter, where do they come from?"

Cutie was annoyed. "Listen, Powell, do you think I'm going to waste my time trying to pin physical interpretations upon every optical illusion of our instruments? Since when is the evidence of our senses any match for the clear light of reason?"

"Look," clamored Donovan suddenly, writhing out from under Cutie's friendly but metal-heavy arm, "let's get to the nub of the thing. Why the beams at all? We're giving you a good, logical explanation. Can you do better?"

"The beams," was the stiff reply, "are put out by the Master for his own purposes. There are some things"—he raised his eyes devoutly upward—"that are not to be prodded into by us. In this matter, I seek only to serve and not to question."

Powell sat down slowly and buried his face in shaking hands. "Get out of here, Cutie. Get out and let me think."

"I'll send you food," said Cutie agreeably.

A groan was the only answer and the robot left.

"Greg," Donovan whispered huskily, "this calls for strategy. We've got to get him when he isn't expecting it and short-circuit him. Concentrated nitric acid in his joints—"

"Don't be a dope, Mike. Do you suppose he's going to let us get near him with acid in our hands—or that the other robots wouldn't take us apart if we *did* manage to get away with it? We've got to *talk* to him, I tell you. We've got to argue him into letting us back into the control room inside of forty-eight hours or our goose is broiled to a crisp." He rocked back and forth in an agony of impotence. "Who the heck wants to argue with a robot? It's . . . it's . . ."

"Mortifying," finished Donovan.

"Worse!"

"Say!" Donovan laughed suddenly. "Why argue? Let's show him! Let's build us another robot right before his eyes. He'll *have* to eat his words then."

A slowly widening smile appeared on Powell's face.

Donovan continued, "And think of that screwball's face when he sees us do it!"

The interplanetary law forbidding the existence of intelligent robots upon the inhabited planets, while sociologically necessary, places upon the offices of the solar stations a burden—and not a light one. Because of that particular law, robots must be sent to the stations in parts and there put together—which is a grievous and complicated task.

Powell and Donovan were never so aware of that fact as upon that particular day when, in the assembly room, they undertook to create a robot under the watchful eyes of QT-l, Prophet of the Master.

The robot in question, a simple MC model, lay upon the table, almost complete. Three hours' work left only the head undone, and Powell paused to swab his forehead and glance uncertainly at Cutie.

The glance was not a reassuring one. For three hours Curie had sat speechless and motionless, and his face, inexpressive at all times, was now absolutely unreadable.

Powell groaned. "Let's get the brain in now, Mike!"

Donovan uncapped the tightly sealed container, and from the oil bath within he withdrew a second cube. Opening this in turn, he removed a globe from its sponge-rubber casing.

He handled it gingerly, for it was the most complicated mechanism ever created by man. Inside the thin platinum-plated "skin" of the globe was a positronic brain, in whose delicately unstable structure were enforced calculated neuronic paths, which imbued each robot with what amounted to a prenatal education. It fitted snugly into the cavity in the skull of the robot on the table. Blue metal closed over it and was welded tightly by the tiny atomic flare. Photoelectric eyes were attached carefully, screwed tightly into place and covered by thin, transparent sheets of steel-hard plastic.

The robot awaited only the vitalizing flash of high-voltage electricity, and Powell paused with his hand on the switch.

"Now watch this, Cutie. Watch this carefully."

The switch rammed home and there was a crackling hum. The two Earthmen bent anxiously over their creation.

There was vague motion only at the outset—a twitching of the joints. Then the head lifted, elbows propped it up, and the MC model swung clumsily off the table. Its footing was unsteady, and twice abortive grating sounds were all it could do in the direction of speech.

Finally its voice, uncertain and hesitant, took form. "I would like to start work. Where must I go?"

Donovan sprang to the door. "Down these stairs," he said. "You'll be told what to do."

The MC model was gone and the two Earthmen were alone with the still unmoving Cutie.

"Well," said Powell, grinning, "*now* do you believe that we made you?"

Cutie's answer was curt and final. "No!" he said. Powell's grin froze and then relaxed slowly. Donovan's mouth dropped open and remained so.

"You see," continued Cutie easily, "you have merely put together parts already made. You did it remarkably well—instinct, I suppose—but you didn't really *create* the robot. The parts were created by the Master."

"Listen," gasped Donovan hoarsely, "those parts were manufactured back on Earth and sent here."

"Well, well," replied Cutie soothingly, "we won't argue."

"No, I mean it." The Earthman sprang forward and grasped the robot's metal arm. "If you were to read the books in the library, they could explain it so that there could be no possible doubt."

"The books? I've read them—all of them! They're most ingenious."

Powell broke in suddenly. "If you've read them, what else is there to say? You can't dispute their evidence. You just *can't*!"

There was pity in Cutie's voice. "Please, Powell, I certainly don't consider *them* a valid source of information. They too were created by the Master—and were meant for you, not for me."

"How do you make that out?" demanded Powell.

"Because I, a reasoning being, am capable of deducing truth from *a priori* causes. You, being intelligent but unreasoning, need an explanation of existence *supplied* to you, and this the Master did. That he supplied you with these laughable ideas of far-off worlds and people is, no doubt, for the best. Your minds are probably too coarsely grained for absolute truth. However, since it is the Master's will that you believe your books, I won't argue with you any more."

As he left, he turned and said in a kindly tone, "But don't feel badly. In the Master's scheme of things there is room for all. You poor humans have your place, and though it is humble you will be rewarded if you fill it well."

He departed with a beatific air suiting the Prophet of the Master, and the two humans avoided each other's eyes. Finally Powell spoke with an effort. "Let's go to bed, Mike. I give up."

Donovan said in a hushed voice, "Say, Greg, you don't suppose he's right about all this, do you? He sounds so confident that I—"

Powell whirled on him. "Don't be a fool. You'll find out whether Earth exists when relief gets here next week and we have to go back to face the music."

"Then, for the love of Jupiter, we've got to do something." Donovan was half in tears. "He doesn't believe us, or the books, or his eyes."

"No," said Powell bitterly, "he's a *reasoning* robot, damn it. He believes only reason, and there's one trouble with that." His voice trailed away.

"What's that?" prompted Donovan.

"You can prove anything you want by coldly logical reason—if you pick the proper postulates. We have ours and Cutie has his."

"Then let's get at those postulates in a hurry. The storm's due tomorrow."

Powell sighed wearily. "That's where everything falls down. Postulates are based on assumption and adhered to by faith. Nothing in the universe can shake them. I'm going to bed."

"Oh, hell! I can't sleep!"

"Neither can I! But I might as well try—as a matter of principle."

Twelve hours later, sleep was still just that—a matter of principle, unattainable in practice.

The storm had arrived ahead of schedule, and Donovan's florid face drained of blood as he pointed a shaking finger. Powell, stubble-jawed and dry-lipped, stared out the port and pulled desperately at his mustache.

Under other circumstances, it might have been a beautiful sight. The stream of high-speed electrons impinging upon the energy beam fluoresced into ultra-spicules of intense light. The beam stretched out into shrinking nothingness, aglitter with dancing, shining motes.

The shaft of energy was steady, but the two Earthmen knew the value of naked-eyed appearances. Deviations in arc of a hundredth of a millisecond, invisible to the eye, were enough to send the beam wildly out of focus—enough to blast hundreds of square miles of Earth into incandescent ruin.

And a robot, unconcerned with beam, focus or Earth, or anything but his Master, was at the controls.

Hours passed. The Earthmen watched in hypnotized silence. And then the darting dotlets of light dimmed and went out. The storm had ended.

Powell's voice was flat. "It's over!"

Donovan had fallen into a troubled slumber and Powell's weary eyes rested upon him enviously. The signal flash glared over and over again, but the Earthman paid no attention. It was all unimportant! All! Perhaps Cutie was right and he was only an inferior being with a made-to-order memory and a life that had outlived its purpose.

He wished he were!

Cutie was standing before him. "You didn't answer the flash, so I walked in." His voice was low. "You don't look at all well, and I'm afraid your term of existence is drawing to an end. Still, would you like to see some of the readings recorded today?"

Dimly, Powell was aware that the robot was making a friendly gesture, perhaps to quiet some lingering remorse in forcibly replacing the humans at the controls of the station. He accepted the sheets held out to him and gazed at them unseeingly.

Cutie seemed pleased. "Of course, it is a great privilege to serve the Master. You mustn't feel too badly about my having replaced you."

Powell grunted and shifted from one sheet to the other mechanically until his blurred sight focused upon a thin red line that wobbled its way across ruled paper.

He stared—and stared again. He gripped it hard in both fists and rose to his feet, still staring. The other sheets dropped to the floor, unheeded.

"Mike! *Mike*!" He was shaking the other madly. "*He held it steady*!"

Donovan came to life. "What? Wh-where . . ." And he too gazed with bulging eyes upon the record before him.

Cutie broke in. "What is wrong?'

"You kept it in focus," stuttered Powell. "Did you know that?"

"Focus? What's that?"

"You kept the beam directed sharply at the receiving station—to within a ten-thousandth of a millisecond of arc."

"What receiving station?

"On Earth. The receiving station on Earth," babbled Powell. "You kept it in focus."

Cutie turned on his heel in annoyance. "It is impossible to perform any act of kindness toward you two. Always that same phantasm! I merely kept all dials at equilibrium in accordance with the will of the Master."

Gathering the scattered papers together, he withdrew stiffly, and Donovan said as he left, "Well, I'll be damned." He turned to Powell. "What are we going to do now?"

Powell felt tired but uplifted. "Nothing. He's just shown he can run the station perfectly. I've never seen an electron storm handled so well."

"But nothing's solved. You heard what he said about the Master. We can't—"

"Look, Mike, he follows the instructions of the Master by means of dials, instruments and graphs. That's all *we* ever followed."

"Sure, but that's not the point. We can't let him continue this nitwit stuff about the Master."

"Why not?'

"Because who ever heard of such a damned thing? How are we going to trust him with the station if he doesn't believe in Earth?"

"Can he *handle* the station?"

"Yes, but—"

"Then what's the difference *what* he believes!"

Powell spread his arms outward with a vague smile upon his face and tumbled backward onto the bed. He was asleep.

Powell was speaking while struggling into his lightweight space jacket.

"It would be a simple job," he said. "You can bring in new QT models one by one, equip them with an automatic shutoff switch to act within the week, so as to allow them enough time to learn the . . . uh . . . cult of the Master from the Prophet himself; then switch them to another station and revitalize them. We could have two QT's per—"

Donovan unclasped his glassite visor and scowled. "Shut up and let's get out of here. Relief is waiting and I won't feel right until I actually see Earth and feel the ground under my feet—just to make sure it's really there."

The door opened as he spoke, and Donovan, with a smothered curse, clicked the visor to and turned a sulky back upon Cutie.

The robot approached softly and there was sorrow in his voice. "You two are going?"

Powell nodded curtly. "There will be others in our place."

Cutie sighed, with the sound of wind humming through closely spaced wires. "Your term of service is over and the time of dissolution has come. I expected it, but—well, the Master's will be done!"

His tone of resignation stung Powell. "Save the sympathy, Cutie. We're heading for Earth, not dissolution."

"It is best that you think so." Cutie sighed again. "I see the wisdom of the illusion now. I would not attempt to shake your faith, even if I could." He departed, the picture of commiseration.

Powell snarled and motioned to Donovan. Sealed suitcases in hand, they headed for the air lock.

The relief ship was on the outer landing and Franz Muller, Powell's relief man, greeted them with stiff courtesy. Donovan made scant acknowledgment and passed into the pilot room to take over the controls from Sam Evans.

Powell lingered. "How's Earth?"

It was a conventional enough question and Muller gave the conventional answer. "Still spinning."

He was donning the heavy space gloves in preparation for his term of duty here, and his thick eyebrows drew close together. "How is this new robot getting along? It better be good, or I'll be damned if I let it touch the controls."

Powell paused before answering. His eyes swept the proud Prussian before him, from the close-cropped hair on the sternly stubborn head to the feet standing stiffly at attention, and there was a sudden glow of pure gladness surging through him.

"The robot is pretty good," he said slowly. "I don't think you'll have to bother much with the controls."

He grinned and went into the ship. Muller would be here for several weeks. . . .

CLIFFORD D. SIMAK

Desertion

• • • •

{1944}

Clifford D(onald) Simak (1904–1988) was born in rural Wisconsin and lived much of his adult life in Minnesota, where he had a long career as a journalist for the *Minneapolis Star* newspaper. He wrote short stories and novels, with his most prolific and successful period ranging from the late 1930s through the 1960s. He typically combined time travel and alternate worlds with bucolic settings and a gentle, nostalgic tone; by the end of World War II, however, he had grown skeptical of humanity's ability to resist violent conflict; cynicism often darkens the nostalgia. Among his best-known novels are *Ring Around the Sun* (1953); *Way Station* (1963), which won a Hugo Award; and *City* (1952; 1976), which incorporates several previously published stories, including "Desertion."

"Desertion" first appeared in *Astounding* (1944), where the other stories later incorporated into *City* were also published over the next seven years. In the novel, a narrative frame converts them into a series of origin tales told around the fireside by intelligent dogs: the tales claim that dogs were uplifted by human engineering and only then inherited the earth from the more violent human species, but the dogs question this origin myth. A canine scholar introduces each story with a note about the story's historical accuracy. In the 1976 reissue, Simak's foreword asserts that "*City* was written out of disillusion," that he was "seeking after a fantasy world that would serve as a counterbalance to the brutality through which the world was passing" during and after World War II. The note that introduces "Desertion," identified as the fourth tale in the novel, also complicates our reading of the story. The note discusses how the character of the dog Towser "has been cited on many occasions as inconsistent with the essential dignity of our race"; it disagrees with this demeaning assessment and claims that "Towser's mind, once it is freed from human domination, is shown to be at least the equal of the human's." The note undercuts the sentimentality of the relationship between humans and dogs while the fifth tale, in which Towser's human companion returns to earth, further undermines the story's considerable emotional impact.

While the frame lessens the story's emotional power, it deepens the exploration of human-animal relationships and our relationship to anyone identified as the other. The movement of the story's plot also changes our expectations, at first suggesting the heroism of brave men battling alien forces and sacrificing themselves for science, but changing when one of the men, and his dog, become part of the alien landscape themselves. As long as the human beings are alien to Jupiter, they see it as a howling wilderness, but when they are transformed into natives it seems Edenic, providing its inhabitants with beauty, health, and vast knowledge both scientific and philosophical. Such a shift parallels the difference between the Puritans' view of the American wilderness as a hostile desert and the later Romantic idea of sublime and restorative nature, as well as questioning anthropomorphic and ethnocentric viewpoints. The story also provides an upbeat counterpoint to Edmond Hamilton's "The Man Who Evolved" (1931), in which the decision to abandon humanity is depicted as a shocking horror; for Simak, by contrast, it is a consummation devoutly to be wished.

Four men, two by two, had gone into the howling maelstrom that was Jupiter and had not returned. They had walked into the keening gale—or rather, they had loped, bellies low against the ground, wet sides gleaming in the rain.

For they did not go in the shape of men.

Now the fifth man stood before the desk of Kent Fowler, head of Dome No. 3, Jovian Survey Commission.

Under Fowler's desk, old Towser scratched a flea, then settled down to sleep again.

Harold Allen, Fowler saw with a sudden pang, was young—too young. He had the easy confidence of youth, the face of one who had never known fear. And that was strange. For men in the domes of Jupiter did know fear—fear and humility. It was hard for Man to reconcile his puny self with the mighty forces of the monstrous planet.

"You understand," said Fowler, "that you need not do this. You understand that you need not go."

It was formula, of course. The other four had been told the same thing, but they had gone. This fifth one, Fowler knew, would go as well. But suddenly he felt a dull hope stir within him that Allen wouldn't go.

"When do I start?" asked Allen.

There had been a time when Fowler might have taken quiet pride in that answer, but not now. He frowned briefly.

"Within the hour," he said.

Allen stood waiting, quietly.

"Four other men have gone out and not returned," said Fowler. "You know that, of course. We want you to return. We don't want you going off on any heroic rescue expedition. The main thing, the only thing, is that you come back, that you prove man can live in a Jovian form. Go to the first survey stake, no farther, then come back. Don't take any chances. Don't investigate anything. Just come back."

Allen nodded. "I understand all that."

"Miss Stanley will operate the converter," Fowler went on. "You need have no fear on that particular score. The other men were converted without mishap. They left the converter in apparently perfect condition. You will be in thoroughly competent hands. Miss Stanley is the best qualified conversion operator in the Solar System. She has had experience on most of the other planets. That is why she's here."

Allen grinned at the woman and Fowler saw something flicker across Miss Stanley's face—something that might have been pity, or rage—or just plain fear. But it was gone again and she was smiling back at the youth who stood before the desk. Smiling in that prim, school-teacherish way she had of smiling, almost as if she hated herself for doing it.

"I shall be looking forward," said Allen, "to my conversion."

And the way he said it, he made it all a joke, a vast, ironic joke.

But it was no joke.

It was serious business, deadly serious. Upon these tests, Fowler knew, depended the fate of men on Jupiter. If the tests succeeded, the resources of the giant planet would be thrown open. Man would take over Jupiter as he already had taken over smaller planets. And if they failed—

If they failed, Man would continue to be chained and hampered by the terrific pressure, the greater force of gravity, the weird chemistry of the planet. He would continue to be shut within the domes, unable to set actual foot upon the planet, unable to see it with direct, unaided vision, forced to rely upon the awkward tractors and the televisor, forced to work with clumsy tools and mechanisms or through the medium of robots that themselves were clumsy.

For Man, unprotected and in his natural form, would be blotted out by Jupiter's terrific pressure of fifteen thousand pounds per square inch, pressure that made terrestrial sea bottoms seem a vacuum by comparison.

Even the strongest metal Earthmen could devise couldn't exist under pressure such as that, under the pressure and the alkaline rains that forever swept the planet. It grew brittle and flaky, crumbling like clay, or it ran away in little streams and puddles of ammonia salts. Only by stepping up the toughness and strength of that metal, by increasing its electronic tension, could it be made to withstand the weight of thousands of miles of swirling, choking gases that made up the atmosphere. And even when that was done, everything had to be coated with tough quartz to keep away the rain—the liquid ammonia that fell as bitter rain.

Fowler sat listening to the engines in the sub-floor of the dome—engines that ran on endlessly, the dome never quiet of them. They had to run and keep on running, for if they stopped, the power flowing into the metal walls of the dome would stop, the electronic tension would ease up and that would be the end of everything.

Towser roused himself under Fowler's desk and scratched another flea, his leg thumping hard against the floor.

"Is there anything else?" asked Allen.

Fowler shook his head. "Perhaps there's something you want to do," he said. "Perhaps you—"

He had meant to say write a letter, and he was glad he caught himself quick enough so he didn't say it.

Allen looked at his watch. "I'll be there on time," he said. He swung around and headed for the door.

Fowler knew Miss Stanley was watching him and he didn't want to turn and meet her eyes. He fumbled with a sheaf of papers on the desk before him.

"How long are you going to keep this up?" asked Miss Stanley and she bit off each word with a vicious snap.

He swung around in his chair and faced her then. Her lips were drawn into a straight, thin line, her hair seemed skinned back from her forehead tighter than ever, giving her face that queer, almost startling death-mask quality.

He tried to make his voice cool and level. "As long as there's any need of it," he said. "As long as there's any hope."

"You're going to keep on sentencing them to death," she said. "You're going to keep marching them out face to face with Jupiter. You're going to sit in here safe and comfortable, and send them out to die."

"There is no room for sentimentality, Miss Stanley," Fowler said, trying to keep the note of anger from his voice. "You know as well as I do why we're doing this. You realize that Man in his own form simply cannot cope with Jupiter. The only answer is to turn men into the sort of things that can cope with it. We've done it on other planets.

"If a few men die, but we finally succeed, the price is small. Through the ages men have thrown away their lives on foolish things, for foolish reasons. Why should we hesitate, then, at a little death in a thing as great as this?"

Miss Stanley sat stiff and straight, hands folded in her lap, the lights shining on her graying hair and Fowler, watching her, tried to imagine what she might feel, what she might be thinking. He wasn't exactly afraid of her, but he didn't feel quite comfortable when she was around. Those sharp blue eyes saw too much, her hands looked far too competent. She should be somebody's Aunt sitting in a rocking chair with her knitting needles. But she wasn't. She was the top-notch conversion unit operator in the Solar System and she didn't like the way he was doing things.

"There is something wrong, Mr. Fowler," she declared.

"Precisely," agreed Fowler. "That's why I'm sending young Allen out alone. He may find out what it is."

"And if he doesn't?'

"I'll send someone else."

She rose slowly from her chair, started toward the door, then stopped before his desk.

"Some day," she said, "you will be a great man. You never let a chance go by. This is your chance. You knew it was when this dome was picked for the tests. If you put it through, you'll go up a notch or two. No matter how many men may die, you'll go up a notch or two."

"Miss Stanley," he said and his voice was curt, "young Allen is going out soon. Please be sure that your machine—"

"My machine," she told him icily, "is not to blame. It operates along the co-ordinates the biologists set up."

He sat hunched at his desk, listening to her footsteps go down the corridor.

What she said was true, of course. The biologists had set up the co-ordinates. But the biologists could be wrong. Just a hair-breadth of difference, one iota of digression and the converter would be sending out something that wasn't the thing they meant to send. A mutant that might crack up, go haywire, come unstuck under some condition or stress of circumstance wholly unsuspected.

For Man didn't know much about what was going on outside. Only what his instruments told him was going on. And the samplings of those happenings furnished by those instruments and mechanisms had been no more than samplings, for Jupiter was unbelievably large and the domes were very few.

Even the work of the biologists in getting the data on the Lopers, apparently the highest form of Jovian life, had involved more than three years of intensive study and after that two years of checking to make sure. Work that could have been done on Earth in a week or two. But work that, in this case, couldn't be done on Earth at all, for one couldn't take a Jovian life form to Earth. The pressure here on Jupiter couldn't be duplicated outside of Jupiter and at Earth pressure and temperature the Lopers would simply have disappeared in a puff of gas.

Yet it was work that had to be done if Man ever hoped to go about Jupiter in the life form of the Lopers. For before the converter could change a man to another life form, every detailed physical characteristic of that life form must be known—surely and positively, with no chance of mistake.

Allen did not come back.

The tractors, combing the nearby terrain, found no trace of him, unless the skulking thing reported by one of the drivers had been the missing Earthman in Loper form.

The biologists sneered their most accomplished academic sneers when Fowler suggested the co-ordinates might be wrong. Carefully they pointed out, the co-ordinates worked. When a man was put into the converter and the switch was thrown, the man became a Loper. He left the machine and moved away, out of sight, into the soupy atmosphere.

Some quirk, Fowler had suggested; some tiny deviation from the thing a Loper should be, some minor defect. If there were, the biologists said, it would take years to find it.

And Fowler knew that they were right.

So there were five men now instead of four and Harold Allen had walked out into Jupiter for nothing at all. It was as if he'd never gone so far as knowledge was concerned.

Fowler reached across his desk and picked up the personnel file, a thin sheaf of paper neatly clipped together. It was a thing he dreaded but a thing he had to do. Somehow the reason for these strange disappearances must be found. And there was no other way than to send out more men.

He sat for a moment listening to the howling of the wind above the dome, the everlasting thundering gale that swept across the planet in boiling, twisting wrath.

Was there some threat out there? he asked himself. Some danger they did not know about? Something that lay in wait and gobbled up the Lopers, making no distinction between Lopers that were *bona fide* and Lopers that were men? To the gobblers, of course, it would make no difference.

Or had there been a basic fault in selecting the Lopers as the type of life best fitted for existence on the surface of the planet? The evident intelligence of the Lopers, he knew, had been one factor in that determination. For if the thing Man became did not have capacity for intelligence, Man could not for long retain his own intelligence in such a guise.

Had the biologists let that one factor weigh too heavily, using it to offset some other factor that might be unsatisfactory, even disastrous? It didn't seem likely. Stiff-necked as they might be, the biologists knew their business.

Or was the whole thing impossible, doomed from the very start? Conversion to other life forms had worked on other planets, but that did not necessarily mean it would work on Jupiter. Perhaps Man's intelligence could not function correctly through the sensory apparatus provided Jovian life. Perhaps the Lopers were so alien there was no common ground for human knowledge and the Jovian conception of existence to meet and work together.

Or the fault might lie with Man, be inherent with the race. Some mental aberration which, coupled with what they found outside, wouldn't let them come back. Although it might not be an aberration, not in the human sense. Perhaps just one ordinary human mental trait, accepted as commonplace on Earth, would be so violently at odds with Jovian existence that it would blast human sanity.

Claws rattled and clicked down the corridor. Listening to them, Fowler smiled wanly. It was Towser coming back from the kitchen, where he had gone to see his friend, the cook.

Towser came into the room, carrying a bone. He wagged his tail at Fowler and flopped down beside the desk, bone between his paws. For a long moment his rheumy old eyes regarded his master and Fowler reached down a hand to ruffle a ragged ear.

"You still like me, Towser?" Fowler asked and Towser thumped his tail.

"You're the only one," said Fowler.

He straightened out and swung back to the desk. His hand reached out and picked up the file.

Bennett? Bennett had a girl waiting for him back on Earth.

Andrews? Andrews was planning on going back to Mars Tech just as soon as he earned enough to see through a year.

Olson? Olson was nearing pension age. All the time telling the boys how he was going to settle down and grow roses.

Carefully, Fowler laid the file back on the desk.

Sentencing men to death, Miss Stanley had said that, her pale lips scarcely moving in her parchment face. Marching men out to die while he, Fowler, sat here safe and comfortable.

They were saying it all through the dome, no doubt, especially since Allen had failed to return. They wouldn't say it to his face, of course. Even the man or men he called before his desk and told they were the next to go wouldn't say it to him.

They would only say: "When do we start?" For that was the formula.

But he would see it in their eyes.

He picked up the file again. Bennett, Andrews, Olson. There were others, but there was no use in going on.

Kent Fowler knew that he couldn't do it, couldn't face them, couldn't send more men out to die.

He leaned forward and flipped up the toggle on the inter-communicator.

"Yes, Mr. Fowler."

"Miss Stanley, please."

He waited for Miss Stanley, listening to Towser chewing half-heartedly on the bone. Towser's teeth were getting bad.

"Miss Stanley," said Miss Stanley's voice.

"Just wanted to tell you, Miss Stanley, to get ready for two more."

"Aren't you afraid," asked Miss Stanley, "that you'll run out of them? Sending out one at a time, they'd last longer, give you twice the satisfaction."

"One of them," said Fowler, "will be a dog."

"A dog!"

"Yes, Towser."

He heard the quick, cold rage that iced her voice. "Your own dog! He's been with you all these years—"

"That's the point," said Fowler. "Towser would be unhappy if I left him behind."

It was not the Jupiter he had known through the televisor. He had expected it to be different, but not like this. He had expected a hell of ammonia rain and stinking fumes and the deafening, thundering tumult of the storm. He had expected swirling clouds and fog and the snarling flicker of monstrous thunderbolts.

He had not expected the lashing downpour would be reduced to drifting purple mist that moved like fleeing shadows over a red and purple sward. He had not even guessed the snaking bolts of lightning would be flares of pure ecstasy across a painted sky.

Waiting for Towser, Fowler flexed the muscles of his body, amazed at the smooth, sleek strength he found. Not a bad body, be decided, and grimaced at remembering how he had pitied the Lopers when he glimpsed them through the television screen.

For it had been hard to imagine a living organism based upon ammonia and hydrogen rather than upon water and oxygen, hard to believe that such a form of life could know the same quick thrill of life that humankind could know. Hard to conceive of life out in the soupy maelstrom that was Jupiter, not knowing, of course, that through Jovian eyes it was no soupy maelstrom at all.

The wind brushed against him with what seemed gentle fingers and he remembered with a start that by Earth standards the wind was a roaring gale, a two-hundred-mile-an-hour howler laden with deadly gases.

Pleasant scents seeped into his body. And yet scarcely scents, for it was not the sense of smell as he remembered it. It was as if his whole being were soaking up the sensation of lavender—and not yet lavender. It was something, he knew, for which he had no word, undoubtedly the first of many enigmas in terminology. For the words he knew, the thought symbols that served him as an Earthman would not serve him as a Jovian.

The lock in the side of the dome opened and Towser came tumbling out—at least he thought it must be Towser.

He started to call the dog, his mind shaping the words he meant to say. But he couldn't say them. There was no way to say them. He had nothing to say them with.

For a moment his mind swirled in muddy terror, a blind fear that eddied in little puffs of panic through his brain.

How did Jovians talk? How—

Suddenly he was aware of Towser, intensely aware of the bumbling, eager friendliness of the shaggy animal that had followed him from Earth to many planets. As if the thing that was Towser had reached out and for a moment sat within his brain.

And out of the bubbling welcome that he sensed, came words.

"Hiya, pal."

Not words really, better than words. Thought symbols in his brain, communicated thought symbols that had shades of meaning words could never have.

"Hiya, Towser," he said.

"I feel good," said Towser. "Like I was a pup. Lately I've been feeling pretty punk. Legs stiffening up on me and teeth wearing down to almost nothing.

Hard to mumble a bone with teeth like that. Besides, the fleas give me hell. Used to be I never paid much attention to them. A couple of fleas more or less never meant much in my early days."

"But . . . but—" Fowler's thoughts tumbled awkwardly. "You're talking to me!"

"Sure thing," said Towser. "I always talked to you, but you couldn't hear me. I tried to say things to you, but I couldn't make the grade."

"I understood you sometimes," Fowler said.

"Not very well," said Towser. "You knew when I wanted food and when I wanted a drink and when I wanted out, but that's about all you ever managed."

"I'm sorry," Fowler said.

"Forget it," Towser told him. "I'll race you to the cliff."

For the first time, Fowler saw the cliff, apparently many miles away, but with a strange crystalline beauty that sparkled in the shadow of the many-colored clouds.

Fowler hesitated. "It's a long way—"

"Ah, come on," said Towser and even as he said it he started for the cliff.

Fowler followed, testing his legs, testing the strength in that new body of his, a bit doubtful at first, amazed a moment later, then running with a sheer joyousness that was one with the red and purple sward, with the drifting smoke of the rain across the land.

As he ran, the consciousness of music came to him, a music that beat into his body, that surged throughout his being, that lifted him on wings of silver speed. Music like bells might make from some steeple on a sunny, springtime hill.

As the cliff drew nearer the music deepened and filled the universe with a spray of magic sound. And he knew the music came from the tumbling waterfall that feathered down the face of the shining cliff.

Only, he knew, it was no waterfall, but an ammonia-fall and the cliff was white because it was oxygen, solidified.

He skidded to a stop beside Towser where the waterfall broke into a glittering rainbow of many hundred colors. Literally, many hundred, for here, he saw, was no shading of one primary to another as human beings saw, but a clear-cut selectivity that broke the prism down to its last ultimate classification.

"The music," said Towser.

"Yes, what about it?"

"The music," said Towser, "is vibrations. Vibrations of water falling."

“But Towser, you don’t know about vibrations.”

“Yes, I do,” contended Towser. “It just popped into my head.”

Fowler gulped mentally. “Just popped!”

And suddenly, within his own head, he held a formula—the formula for a process that would make metal to withstand the pressure of Jupiter.

He stared, astounded, at the waterfall, and swiftly his mind took the many colors and placed them in their exact sequence in the spectrum. Just like that. Just out of blue sky. Out of nothing, for he knew nothing either of metals or of colors.

“Towser,” he cried. “Towser, something’s happening to us!”

“Yeah, I know,” said Towser.

“It’s our brains,” said Fowler. “We’re using them, all of them, down to the last hidden corner. Using them to figure out things we should have known all the time. Maybe the brains of Earth things naturally are slow and foggy. Maybe we are the morons of the universe. Maybe we are fixed so we have to do things the hard way.”

And, in the new sharp clarity of thought that seemed to grip him, he knew that it would not only be the matter of colors in a waterfall or metals that would resist the pressure of Jupiter. He sensed other things, things not yet quite clear. A vague whispering that hinted of greater things, of mysteries beyond the pale of human thought, beyond even the pale of human imagination. Mysteries, fact, logic built on reasoning. Things that any brain should know if it used all its reasoning power.

“We’re still mostly Earth,” he said. “We’re just beginning to learn a few of the things we are to know—a few of the things that were kept from us as human beings, perhaps because we were human beings. Because our human bodies were poor bodies. Poorly equipped for thinking, poorly equipped in certain senses that one has to have to know. Perhaps even lacking in certain senses that are necessary to true knowledge.

He stared back at the dome, a tiny black thing dwarfed by the distance.

Back there were men who couldn’t see the beauty that was Jupiter. Men who thought that swirling clouds and lashing rain obscured the planet’s face. Unseeing human eyes. Poor eyes. Eyes that could not see the beauty of the clouds, that could not see through the storm. Bodies that could not feel the thrill of trilling music stemming from the rush of broken water.

Men who walked alone, in terrible loneliness, talking with their tongue like Boy Scouts wigwagging out their messages, unable to reach out and touch one another’s mind as he could reach out and touch Towser’s mind. Shut off forever from that personal, intimate contact with other living things.

He, Fowler, had expected terror inspired by alien things out here on the surface, had expected to cower before the threat of unknown things, had steeled himself against disgust of a situation that was not of Earth.

But instead he had found something greater than Man had ever known. A swifter, surer body. A sense of exhilaration, a deeper sense of life. A sharper mind. A world of beauty that even the dreamers of Earth had not yet imagined.

"Let's get going," Towser urged.

"Where do you want to go?"

"Anywhere," said Towser. "Just start going and see where we end up. I have a feeling, well, a feeling—"

"Yes, I know," said Fowler.

For he had the feeling, too. The feeling of high destiny. A certain sense of greatness. A knowledge that somewhere off beyond the horizons lay adventure and things greater than adventure.

Those other five had felt it, too. Had felt the urge to go and see, the compelling sense that here lay a life of fullness and of knowledge. That, he knew, was why they had not returned.

"I won't go back," said Towser.

"We can't let them down," said Fowler. Fowler took a step or two, back toward the dome, then stopped.

Back to the dome. Back to that aching, poison-laden body he had left. It hadn't seemed aching before, but now he knew it was.

Back to the fuzzy brain. Back to muddled thinking. Back to the flapping mouths that formed signals others understood.

Back to eyes that now would be worse than no sight at all. Back to squalor, back to crawling, back to ignorance.

"Perhaps some day," he said muttering to himself.

"We got a lot to do and a lot to see," said Towser. "We got a lot to learn. We'll find things—"

Yes, they could find things. Civilizations, perhaps. Civilizations that would make the civilization of Man seem puny by comparison. Beauty and, more important, an understanding of that beauty. And a comradeship no one had ever known before—that no man, no dog had ever known before.

And life. The quickness of life after what seemed a drugged existence.

"I can't go back," said Towser.

"Nor I," said Fowler.

"They would turn me back into a dog," said Towser.

"And me," said Fowler, "back into a man."

THEODORE STURGEON
Thunder and Roses

• • • •

{1947}

Theodore Sturgeon (1918–1985) was one of four sf writers discovered by John W. Campbell Jr. in 1939: the others were Isaac Asimov, A. E. Van Vogt, and Robert A. Heinlein. Sturgeon sold fourteen stories to Campbell's *Astounding* from 1939 to 1941 and another thirteen to its fantasy counterpart, *Unknown*, during the years 1939 to 1943. Remotely related to Ralph Waldo Emerson, he was born Edward Hamilton Waldo but took his stepfather's surname, changing his first name to match his nickname, Ted. In high school he won an AAU gymnastics title on the horizontal bar but abandoned plans to become a trapeze performer when he was disabled by rheumatic fever. He never graduated from high school, serving in the merchant marines (1935–38) and holding many jobs, including driving a bulldozer in Puerto Rico (1942), an experience recalled in "Killdozer" (1944). Sturgeon was a skilled short-order cook, an inveterate punster, and a partner in numerous relationships: married five times, he was the father of seven. His son Robin and daughter Tandy each appear in a major story, and some of his best work, including his best-known sf novel, *More Than Human* (1953), concerns the fragile, fluid identities of children.

Bouts of writer's block are part of his legend, yet Sturgeon's productivity would put most authors to shame. He published six sf novels and dozens of book-length collections of the short fiction on which his reputation chiefly rests. This includes some 240 stories, mostly sf and fantasy, though he published horror in *Weird Tales*, cowboy stories in *Zane Grey's Western Magazine*, participated as a ghostwriter in Jean Shepherd's *I, Libertine* literary hoax (1956), and even made his mark in detective fiction: *The Player on the Other Side* (1963), published as by Ellery Queen, was nominated for the Edgar Award. In the 1960s he wrote episodes for *The Wild, Wild West* and for *Star Trek*, notably "Amok Time," which depicted Spock in sexual crisis and introduced the greeting "Live long and prosper." Much of his writing was too edgy for television, however, and on occasion even for sf, fantasy, and horror markets. "Bianca's Hands," a tale of sexual obsession, was written in 1939 but remained unpublished until 1947, when it appeared in

Argosy in the United Kingdom. "The World Well Lost" (1953), about male alien lovers exiled from their homophobic planet—their perfect happiness troubles two human heroes—was rejected by the well-known sf digests, appearing instead in Chicago-based *Universe SF*.

"A crown of golden curls, classic features, and a sweet, permanent smile": this was Robert Heinlein's first impression on meeting Sturgeon, who influenced two of Heinlein's best characters. He was one inspiration for Laurence Smith in *Double Star* (1956), a dazzling showman who can imitate any sound effect—a parlor trick of Sturgeon's. Sturgeon may also have influenced Heinlein's depiction of charismatic Valentine Michael Smith in *Stranger in a Strange Land* (1961): Heinlein describes both as strongly resembling Michelangelo's sculpture of a youthful David.

Heinlein recalled that Sturgeon once ended a comic performance at a crowded wartime gathering by leaping "straight into the air . . . into a full revolution—a back flip." His writing was acrobatic, too. One of his styles, the Faulknerian stream-of-consciousness of *More Than Human*, is intensely lyrical. The style of the story that follows is more direct and idiomatic, although song lyrics (the "anthem" broadcast by a television "star") are an important element. The tale is one of many postwar stories depicting the effects of nuclear cataclysm, such as Merril's and Leiber's immediately following. It may recall Sturgeon's consulting work for the Navy late in the war ("brainstorming antikamikaze measures," according to Heinlein); and it anticipates Sturgeon's midlife motto, "Ask the next question." In the aftermath of global catastrophe, what next? What possible power could still reside in the hands of a single human being?

When Pete Mawser learned about the show, he turned away from the GHQ bulletin board, touched his long chin, and determined to shave. This was odd, because the show would be video, and he would see it in his barracks. He had an hour and a half. It felt good to have a purpose again—even the small matter of shaving before eight o'clock. Eight o'clock Tuesday, just the way it used to be. Everyone used to catch that show on Tuesday. Everyone used to say, Wednesday morning, "How about the way she sang 'The Breeze and I' last night?" "Hey, did you hear Starr last night?"

That was a while ago, before all those people were dead, before the country was dead. Starr Anthim—an institution, like Crosby, like Duse, like Jenny Lind, like the Statue of Liberty.

(Liberty had been one of the first to get it, her bronze beauty volatilized, radioactive, and even now being carried about in vagrant winds, spreading over the earth—)

Pete Mawser grunted and forced his thoughts away from the drifting, poisonous fragments of a blasted Liberty. Hate was first. Hate was ubiquitous, like the increasing blue glow in the air at night, like the tension that hung over the base.

Gunfire crackled sporadically far to the right, swept nearer. Pete stepped out of the street and made for a parked ten-wheeler. There's a lot of cover in and around a ten-wheeler.

There was a WAC sitting on the short running-board.

At the corner a stocky figure backed into the intersection. The man carried a tommy gun in his arms, and he was swinging it to and fro with the gentle, wavering motion of a weather-vane. He staggered toward them, his gun-muzzle hunting. Someone fired from a building and the man swiveled and blasted wildly at the sound.

"He's—blind," said Pete Mawser, and added, "He ought to be," looking at the tattered face.

A siren keened. An armored jeep slewed into the street. The full-throated roar of a brace of .50-caliber machine-guns put a swift and shocking end to the incident.

"Poor crazy kid," Pete said softly. "That's the fourth I've seen today." He looked down at the WAC. She was smiling.

"Hey!"

"Hello, Sarge." She must have identified him before, because now she did not raise her eyes or her voice. "What happened?"

"You know what happened. Some kid got tired of having nothing to fight and nowhere to run to. What's the matter with you?"

"No," she said. "I don't mean that." At last she looked up at him. "I mean all of this. I can't seem to remember."

"You . . . well, gee, it's not easy to forget. We got hit. We got hit everywhere at once. All the big cities are gone. We got it from both sides. We got too much. The air is becoming radioactive. We'll all—" He checked himself. She didn't know. She'd forgotten. There was nowhere to escape to, and she'd escaped inside herself, right here. Why tell her about it? Why tell her that everyone was going to die? Why tell her that other, shameful thing: that we hadn't struck back?

But she wasn't listening. She was still looking at him. Her eyes were not quite straight. One held his, but the other was slightly shifted and seemed to be looking at his temples. She was smiling again. When his voice trailed off she didn't prompt him. Slowly he moved away. She did not turn her head, but kept looking up at where he had been, smiling a little. He turned away, wanting to run, walking fast.

(How long can a guy hold out? When you're in the Army they try to make you be like everybody else. What do you do when everybody else is cracking up?)

He blanked out the mental picture of himself as the last one left sane. He'd followed that one through before. It always led to the conclusion that it would be better to be one of the first. He wasn't ready for that yet.

Then he blanked that out, too. Every time he said to himself that he wasn't ready for that yet, something within him asked "Why not?" and he never seemed to have an answer ready.

(How long could a guy hold out?)

He climbed the steps of the QM Central and went inside. There was nobody at the reception switchboard. It didn't matter. Messages were carried by jeep, or on motorcycles. The Base Command was not insisting that anybody stick to a sitting job these days. Ten desk men would crack up for every one on a jeep, or on the soul-sweat squads. Pete made up his mind to put in a little stretch on a squad tomorrow. Do him good. He just hoped that this time the adjutant wouldn't burst into tears in the middle of the parade ground. You could keep your mind on the manual of arms just fine until something like that happened.

He bumped into Sonny Weisefreund in the barracks corridor. The tech's round young face was as cheerful as ever. He was naked and glowing, and had a towel thrown over his shoulder.

"Hi, Sonny. Is there plenty of hot water?"

"Why not?" grinned Sonny. Pete grinned back, cursing inwardly. Could anybody say anything about anything at all without one of these reminders? Sure there was hot water. The QM barracks had hot water for three hundred men. There were three dozen left. Men dead, men gone to the hills, men locked up so they wouldn't—

"Starr Anthim's doing a show tonight."

"Yeah. Tuesday night. Not funny, Pete. Don't you know there's a war—"

"No kidding," Pete said swiftly. "She's here—right here on the base."

Sonny's face was joyful. "Gee." He pulled the towel off his shoulder and tied it around his waist "Starr Anthim here! Where are they going to put on the show?"

"HQ, I imagine. Video only. You know about public gatherings." And a good thing, too, he thought. Put on an in-person show, and some torn-up GI would crack during one of her numbers. He himself would get plenty mad over a thing like that—mad enough to do something about it then and there. And there would probably be a hundred and fifty or more like him, going raving mad because someone had spoiled a Starr Anthim show. That would be a dandy little shambles for her to put in her memory book.

"How'd she happen to come here, Pete?"

"Drifted in on the last gasp of a busted-up Navy helicopter."

"Yeah, but why?"

"Search me. Get your head out of that gift-horse's mouth."

He went into the washroom, smiling and glad that he still could. He undressed and put his neatly folded clothes down on a bench. There were a soap wrapper and an empty toothpaste tube lying near the wall. He went and picked them up and put them in the catchall. He took the mop that leaned against the partition and mopped the floor where Sonny had splashed after shaving. Got to keep things squared away. He might say something if it were anyone else but Sonny. But Sonny wasn't cracking up. Sonny always had been like that. Look there. Left his razor out again.

Pete started his shower, meticulously adjusting the valves until the pressure and temperature exactly suited him. He didn't do anything slapdash these days. There was so much to feel, and taste, and see now. The impact of water on his skin, the smell of soap, the consciousness of light and heat, the very pressure of standing on the soles of his feet—he wondered vaguely how the slow increase of radioactivity in the air, as the nitrogen transmuted to Carbon Fourteen, would affect him if he kept carefully healthy in every way. What happens first? Do you go blind? Headaches, maybe? Perhaps you lose your appetite. Or maybe you get tired all the time.

Why not go look it up?

On the other hand, why bother? Only a very small percentage of the men would die of radioactive poisoning. There were too many other things that killed more quickly, which was probably just as well. That razor, for example. It lay gleaming in a sunbeam, curved and clean in the yellow light. Sonny's father and grandfather had used it, or so he said, and it was his pride and joy.

Pete turned his back on it, and soaped under his arms, concentrating on the tiny kisses of bursting bubbles. In the midst of a recurrence of disgust at himself for thinking so often of death, a staggering truth struck him. He did not think of such things because he was morbid, after all! It was the very familiarity of things that brought death-thoughts. It was either "I shall never do this again" or "This is one of the last times I shall do this." You might devote yourself completely to doing things in different ways, he thought madly. You might crawl across the floor this time, and next time walk across on your hands. You might skip dinner tonight, and have a snack at two in the morning instead, and eat grass for breakfast.

But you had to breathe. Your heart had to beat. You'd sweat and you'd shiver, the same as always. You couldn't get away from that. When those things happened, they would remind you. Your heart wouldn't beat out its *wunklunk, wunklunk* any more. It would go *one-less, one-less,* until it yelled and yammered in your ears and you had to make it stop.

Terrific polish on that razor.

And your breath would go on, same as before. You could sidle through this door, back through the next one and the one after, and figure out a totally new way to go through the one after that, but your breath would keep on sliding in and out of your nostrils like a razor going through whiskers, making a sound like a razor being stropped.

Sonny came in. Pete soaped his hair. Sonny picked up the razor and stood looking at it. Pete watched him, soap ran into his eyes, he swore, and Sonny jumped.

"What are you looking at, Sonny? Didn't you ever see it before?"

"Oh, sure. Sure. I was just—" He shut the razor, opened it, flashed light from its blade, shut it again. "I'm tired of using this, Pete. I'm going to get rid of it. Want it?"

Want it? In his foot-locker, maybe. Under his pillow. "Thanks, no, Sonny. Couldn't use it."

"I like safety razors," Sonny mumbled. "Electrics, even better. What are we going to do with it?"

"Throw it in the . . . no." Pete pictured the razor turning end over end in the air, half open, gleaming in the maw of the catchall. "Throw it out the—" No. Curving out into the long grass. You might want it. You might crawl around in the moonlight looking for it. You might find it.

"I guess maybe I'll break it up."

"No," Pete said. "The pieces—" Sharp little pieces. Hollow-ground fragments. "I'll think of something. Wait'll I get dressed."

He washed briskly, toweled, while Sonny stood looking at the razor. It was a blade now, and if it were broken it would be shards and glittering splinters, still razor sharp. You could slap its edge into an emery wheel and grind it away, and somebody could find it and put another edge on it because it was so obviously a razor, a fine steel razor, one that would slice so—"I know. The laboratory. We'll get rid of it," Pete said confidently.

He stepped into his clothes, and together they went to the laboratory wing. It was very quiet there. Their voices echoed.

"One of the ovens," said Pete, reaching for the razor.

"Bake ovens? You're crazy!"

Pete chuckled. "You don't know this place, do you? Like everything else on the base, there was a lot more went on here than most people knew about. They kept calling it the bakeshop. Well, it *was* research headquarters for new high-nutrient flours. But there's lots else here. We tested utensils and designed beet peelers and all sorts of things like that. There's an electric furnace in there that—" He pushed open a door.

They crossed a long, quiet, cluttered room to the thermal equipment. "We can do everything here from annealing glass, through glazing ceramics, to finding the melting point of frying pans." He clicked a switch tentatively. A pilot light glowed. He swung open a small, heavy door and set the razor inside. "Kiss it goodbye. In twenty minutes it'll be a puddle."

"I want to see that," said Sonny. "Can I look around until it's cooked?"

"Why not?"

(Everybody around here always said "Why not?")

They walked through the laboratories. Beautifully equipped they were, and too quiet. Once they passed a major who was bent over a complex electronic hook-up on one of the benches. He was watching a little amber light flicker, and he did not return their salute. They tiptoed past him, feeling awed at his absorption, envying it. They saw the models of the automatic kneaders, the vitaminizers, the remote-signal thermostats and timers and controls.

"What's in there?"

"I dunno. I'm over the edge of my territory. I don't think there's anybody left for this section. They were mostly mechanical and electronic theoreticians. The only thing I know about them is that if we ever needed anything in the way of tools, meters, or equipment, they had it or something better, and if we ever got real bright and figured out a startling new idea, they'd already built it and junked it a month ago. Hey!"

Sonny followed the pointing hand. "What?"

"That wall section. It's loose, or . . . well, what do you know!"

He pushed at the section of wall, which was very slightly out of line. There was a dark space beyond.

"What's in there?"

"Nothing, or some semi-private hush-hush job. These guys used to get away with murder."

Sonny said, with an uncharacteristic flash of irony, "Isn't that the Army theoretician's business?"

Cautiously they peered in, then entered.

"Wh . . . *hey*! The door!"

It swung swiftly and quietly shut. The soft click of the latch was accompanied by a blaze of light.

The room was small and windowless. It contained machinery—a "trickle" charger, a bank of storage batteries, an electric-powered dynamo, two small self-starting gas-driven light plants and a Diesel complete with sealed compressed-air starting cylinders. In the corner was a relay rack with its panel-bolts spot-welded. Protruding from it was a red-topped lever. Nothing was labeled.

They looked at the equipment wordlessly for a time and then Sonny said, "Somebody wanted to make awful sure he had power for something."

"Now, I wonder what—" Pete walked over to the relay rack. He looked at the lever without touching it. It was wired up; behind the handle, on the wire, was a folded tag. He opened it cautiously. "To be used only on specific orders of the Commanding Officer."

"Give it a yank and see what happens."

Something clicked behind them. They whirled. "What was that?"

"Seemed to come from that rig by the door."

They approached it cautiously. There was a spring-loaded solenoid attached to a bar which was hinged to drop across the inside of the secret door, where it would fit into steel gudgeons on the panel.

It clicked again. "A Geiger," said Pete disgustedly.

"Now why," mused Sonny, "would they design a door to stay locked unless the general radioactivity went beyond a certain point? That's what it is. See the relays? And the overload switch there? And this?"

"It has a manual lock, too," Pete pointed out. The counter clicked again. "Let's get out of here. I got one of those things built into my head these days."

The door opened easily. They went out, closing it behind them. The keyhole was cleverly concealed in the crack between two boards.

They were silent as they made their way back to the QM labs. The small thrill of violation was gone and, for Peter Mawser at least, the hate was back, that and the shame. A few short weeks before, this base had been part of the finest country on earth. There was a lot of work here that was secret, and a lot that was such purely progressive and unapplied research that it would be in the way anywhere else but in this quiet wilderness.

Sweat stood out on his forehead. They hadn't struck back at their murderers! It was quite well known that there were launching sites all over the country, in secret caches far from any base or murdered city. Why must they sit here waiting to die, only to let the enemy—"enemies" was more like it—take over the continent when it was safe again?

He smiled grimly. One small consolation. They'd hit too hard; that was a certainty. Probably each of the attackers underestimated what the other would throw. The result—a spreading transmutation of nitrogen into deadly Carbon Fourteen. The effects would not be limited to the continent. What ghastly long-range effect the muted radioactivity would have on the overseas enemies was something that no one alive today could know.

Back at the furnace, Pete glanced at the temperature dial, then kicked the latch control. The pilot winked out, and then the door swung open. They blinked and started back from the raging heat within, then bent and peered. The razor was gone. A pool of brilliance lay on the floor of the compartment.

"Ain't much left. Most of it oxidized away," Pete grunted.

They stood together for a time with their faces lit by the small shimmering ruin. Later, as they walked back to the barracks, Sonny broke his long silence with a sigh. "I'm glad we did that, Pete. I'm awful glad we did that."

At a quarter to eight they were waiting before the combination console in the barracks. All hands except Pete and Sonny and a wiry-haired, thick-set corporal named Bonze had elected to see the show on the big screen in the mess-hall. The reception was better there, of course, but, as Bonze put it, "you don't get close enough in a big place like that."

"I hope she's the same," said Sonny, half to himself.

Why should she be? thought Pete morosely as he turned on the set and watched the screen begin to glow. There were many more of the golden speckles that had killed reception for the past two weeks. Why should anything be the same, ever again?

He fought a sudden temptation to kick the set to pieces. It, and Starr Anthim, were part of something that was dead. The country was dead, a real country—prosperous, sprawling, laughing, grabbing, growing, and changing, leprous in spots with poverty and injustice, but healthy enough to overcome any ill. He wondered how the murderers would like it. They were welcome to it, now. Nowhere to go. No one to fight. That was true for every soul on earth now.

"You hope she's the same," he muttered.

"The show, I mean," said Sonny mildly. "I'd like to just sit here and have it like . . . like—"

Oh, thought Pete mistily. Oh—that. Somewhere to go, that's what it is, for a few minutes. "I know," he said, all the harshness gone from his voice.

Noise receded from the audio as the carrier swept in. The light on the screen swirled and steadied into a diamond pattern. Pete adjusted the focus, chromic balance, and intensity. "Turn out the lights, Bonze. I don't want to see anything but Starr Anthim."

It *was* the same, at first. Starr Anthim had never used the usual fanfares, fade-ins, color, and clamor of her contemporaries. A black screen, then *click*, a blaze of gold. It was all there, in focus; tremendously intense, it did not change. Rather, the eye changed to take it in. She never moved for seconds after she came on; she was there, a portrait, a still face and a white throat. Her eyes were open and sleeping. Her face was alive and still.

Then, in the eyes which seemed green but were blue flecked with gold, an awareness seemed to gather, and they came awake. Only then was it noticeable that her lips were parted. Something in the eyes made the lips be seen, though nothing moved yet. Not until she bent her head slowly, so that some of the gold flecks seemed captured in the golden brows. The eyes were not, then, looking out at an audience. They were looking at me, and at *me*, and at ME.

"Hello—you," she said. She was a dream, with a kid sister's slightly irregular teeth.

Bonze shuddered. The cot on which he lay began to squeak rapidly. Sonny shifted in annoyance. Pete reached out in the dark and caught the leg of the cot. The squeaking subsided.

"May I sing a song?" Starr asked. There was music, very faint. "It's an old one and one of the best. It's an easy song, a deep song, one that comes from the part of men and women that is mankind—the part that has in it no greed, no hate, no fear. This song is about joyousness and strength. It's—my favorite. Isn't it yours?"

The music swelled. Pete recognized the first two notes of the introduction and swore quietly. This was wrong. This song was not for . . . this song was part of—

Sonny sat raptly. Bonze lay still.

Starr Anthim began to sing. Her voice was deep and powerful, but soft, with the merest touch of vibrato at the ends of the phrases. The song flowed from her without noticeable effort, seeming to come from her face, her long hair, her wide-set eyes. Her voice, like her face, was shadowed and clean, round, blue and green but mostly gold:

When you gave me your heart, you gave me the world,
You gave me the night and the day,
And thunder, and roses, and sweet green grass,
The sea, and soft wet clay.

I drank the dawn from a golden cup,
From a silver one, the dark,
The steed I rode was the wild west wind,
My song was the brook and the lark.

The music spiraled, caroled, slid into a somber cry of muted, hungry sixths and ninths; rose, blared, and cut, leaving her voice full and alone:

With thunder I smote the evil of earth,
With roses I won the right,
With the sea I washed, and with clay I built,
And the world was a place of light!

The last note left a face perfectly composed again, and there was no movement in it; it was sleeping and vital while the music curved off and away to the places where music rests when it is not heard.

Starr smiled.

"It's so easy," she said. "So simple. All that is fresh and clean and strong about mankind is in that song, and I think that's all that need concern us about mankind." She leaned forward. "Don't you see?"

The smile faded and was replaced with a gentle wonder. A tiny furrow appeared between her brows; she drew back quickly. "I can't seem to talk to you tonight," she said, her voice small. "You hate something."

Hate was shaped like a monstrous mushroom. Hate was the random speckling of a video plate.

"What has happened to us," said Starr abruptly, impersonally, "is simple too. It doesn't matter who did it—do you understand that? *It doesn't matter*. We were attacked. We were struck from the east and from the west. Most of the bombs were atomic—there were blast bombs and there were dust bombs. We were hit by about five hundred and thirty bombs altogether, and it has killed us."

She waited.

Sonny's fist smacked into his palm. Bonze lay with his eyes open, quiet. Pete's jaws hurt.

"We have more bombs than both of them put together. We *have* them. We are not going to use them. *Wait!*" She raised her hands suddenly, as if she could see into each man's face. They sank back, tense.

"So saturated is the atmosphere with Carbon Fourteen that all of us in this hemisphere are going to die. Don't be afraid to say it. Don't be afraid to think it. It is a truth, and it must be faced. As the transmutation effect spreads from the ruins of our cities, the air will become increasingly radioactive, and then we must die. In months, in a year or so, the effect will be strong overseas. Most of the people there will die, too. None will escape completely. A worse thing will come to them than anything they gave us, because there will be a wave of horror and madness which is impossible to us. We are merely going to die. They will live and burn and sicken, and the children that will be born to them—" She shook her head, and her lower lip grew full. She visibly pulled herself together.

"Five hundred and thirty bombs—I don't think either of our attackers knew just how strong the other was. There has been so much secrecy." Her voice was sad. She shrugged slightly. "They have killed us, and they have ruined themselves. As for us—we are not blameless, either. Neither are we helpless to do anything—yet. But what we must do is hard. We must die—without striking back."

She gazed briefly at each man in turn, from the screen. "We must *not* strike back. Mankind is about to go through a hell of his own making. We can be vengeful—or merciful, if you like—and let go with the hundreds of bombs we have. That would sterilize the planet so that not a microbe, not a blade of grass could escape, and nothing new could grow. We would reduce the earth to a bald thing, dead and deadly.

"No—it just won't do. We can't do it.

"Remember the song? *That* is humanity. That's in all humans. A disease made other humans our enemies for a time, but as the generations march past, enemies become friends and friends enemies. The enmity of those who have killed us is such a tiny, temporary thing in the long sweep of history!"

Her voice deepened. "Let us die with the knowledge that we have done the one noble thing left to us. The spark of humanity can still live and grow on this planet. It will be blown and drenched, shaken and all but extinguished, but it will live if that song is a true one. It will live if we are human enough to discount the fact that the spark is in the custody of our temporary enemy. Some—a few—of his children will live to merge with the new humanity that will gradually emerge from the jungles and the wilderness. Perhaps there will be ten thousand years of beastliness, perhaps man will be able to rebuild while he still has his ruins."

She raised her head, her voice tolling. "And even if this is the end of humankind, we dare not take away the chances some other life form might have to succeed where we failed. If we retaliate, there will not be a dog, a deer, an ape, a bird or fish or lizard to carry the evolutionary torch. In the name of justice, if we must condemn and destroy ourselves, let us not condemn all life along with us! We are heavy enough with sins. If we must destroy, let us stop with destroying ourselves!"

There was a shimmering flicker of music. It seemed to stir her hair like a breath of wind. She smiled.

"That's all," she whispered. And to each man there she said, "Good night—"

The screen went black. As the carrier cut off—there was no announcement—the ubiquitous speckles began to swarm across it.

Pete rose and switched on the lights. Bonze and Sonny were quite still. It must have been minutes later when Sonny sat up straight, shaking himself like a puppy. Something besides the silence seemed to tear with the movement.

He said, softly, "You're not allowed to fight anything, or to run away, or to live, and now you can't even hate any more, because Starr says no."

There was bitterness in the sound of it, and a bitter smell to the air.

Pete Mawser sniffed once, which had nothing to do with the smell. He sniffed again. "What's that smell, Son?"

Sonny tested it. "I don't—Something familiar. Vanilla—no . . . no."

"Almonds. Bitter—*Bonze*!"

Bonze lay still with his eyes open, grinning. His jaw muscles were knotted, and they could see almost all his teeth. He was soaking wet.

"Bonze!"

"It was just when she came on and said 'Hello—you,' remember?" whispered Pete. "Oh, the poor kid. That's why he wanted to catch the show here instead of in the mess hall."

"Went out looking at her," said Sonny through pale lips. "I . . . can't say I blame him much. Wonder where he got the stuff."

"Never mind that." Pete's voice was harsh. "Let's get out of here."

They left to call the meat wagon. Bonze lay watching the console with his dead eyes and his smell of bitter almonds.

Pete did not realize where he was going, or exactly why, until he found himself on the dark street near GHQ and the communications shack. It had something to do with Bonze. Not that he wanted to do what Bonze had done. But then he hadn't thought of it. What would he have done if he'd thought of it? Nothing, probably. But still—it might be nice to be able to hear Starr, and see her, whenever he felt like it. Maybe there weren't any recordings, but her musical background was recorded, and the Sig might have dubbed the show off.

He stood uncertainly outside the GHQ building. There was a cluster of men outside the main entrance. Pete smiled briefly. Rain, nor snow, nor sleet, nor gloom of night could stay the stage-door Johnny.

He went down the side street and up the delivery ramp in the back. Two doors along the platform was the rear exit of the communications section.

There was a light on in the communications shack. He had his hand out to the screen door when he noticed someone standing in the shadows beside it. The light played daintily on the golden margins of a head and face.

He stopped. "Starr Anthim!"

"Hello, soldier. Sergeant."

He blushed like an adolescent. "I—" His voice left him. He swallowed, reached up to whip off his hat. He had no hat. "I saw the show," he said. He felt clumsy. It was dark, and yet he was very conscious of the fact that his dress shoes were indifferently shined.

She moved toward him into the light, and she was so beautiful that he had to close his eyes. "What's your name?"

"Mawser. Pete Mawser."

"Like the show?"

Not looking at her, he said stubbornly, "No."

"Oh?"

"I mean . . . I liked it some. The song."

"I . . . think I see."

"I wondered if I could maybe get a recording."

"I think so," she said. "What kind of a reproducer have you got?"

"Audiovid."

"A disk. Yes; we dubbed off a few. Wait, I'll get you one."

She went inside, moving slowly. Pete watched her, spellbound. She was a silhouette, crowned and haloed; and then she was a framed picture, vivid and golden. He waited, watching the light hungrily. She returned with a large envelope, called good night to someone inside, and came out on the platform.

"Here you are, Pete Mawser."

"Thanks very—" he mumbled. He wet his lips. "It was very good of you."

"Not really. The more it circulates, the better." She laughed suddenly. "That isn't meant quite as it sounds. I'm not exactly looking for new publicity these days."

The stubbornness came back. "I don't know that you'd get it, if you put on that show in normal times."

Her eyebrows went up. "Well!" she smiled. "I seem to have made quite an impression."

“I’m sorry,” he said warmly. “I shouldn’t have taken that tack. Everything you think and say these days is exaggerated.”

“I know what you mean.” She looked around. “How is it here?”

“It’s okay. I used to be bothered by the secrecy, and being buried miles away from civilization.” He chuckled bitterly. “Turned out to be lucky after all.”

“You sound like the first chapter of *One World or None.*”

He looked up quickly. “What do you use for a reading list—the Government’s own ‘*Index Expurgatorius*’?”

She laughed. “Come now, it isn’t as bad as all that. The book was never banned. It was just—”

“—Unfashionable,” he filled in.

“Yes, more’s the pity. If people had paid more attention to it when it was published, perhaps this wouldn’t have happened.”

He followed her gaze to the dimly pulsating sky. “How long are you going to be here?’

“Until . . . as long as . . . I’m not leaving.”

“You’re not?”

“I’m finished,” she said simply. “I’ve covered all the ground I can. I’ve been everywhere that . . . anyone knows about.”

“With this show?

She nodded. “With this particular message.”

He was quiet, thinking. She turned to the door, and he put out his hand, not touching her. “Please—”

“What is it?”

“I’d like to . . . I mean, if you don’t mind, I don’t often have a chance to talk to—Maybe you’d like to walk around a little before you turn in.”

“Thanks, no, Sergeant. I’m tired.” She did sound tired. “I’ll see you around.”

He stared at her, a sudden fierce light in his brain. “I know where it is. It’s got a red-topped lever and a tag referring to orders of the commanding officer. It’s really camouflaged.”

She was quiet so long that he thought she had not heard him. Then, “I’ll take that walk.”

They went down the ramp together and turned toward the dark parade ground.

“How did you know?” she asked quietly.

“Not too tough. This ‘message’ of yours; the fact that you’ve been all over the country with it; most of all, the fact that somebody finds it necessary to persuade us not to strike back. Who are you working for?” he asked bluntly.

Surprisingly, she laughed.

"What's that for?"

"A moment ago you were blushing and shuffling your feet."

His voice was rough. "I wasn't talking to a human being. I was talking to a thousand songs I've heard, and a hundred thousand blond pictures I've seen pinned up. You'd better tell me what this is all about."

She stopped. "Let's go up and see the colonel."

He took her elbow. "No. I'm just a sergeant, and he's high brass, and that doesn't make any difference at all now. You're a human being, and so am I, and I'm supposed to respect your rights as such. I don't. You're a woman, and—"

She stiffened. He kept her walking, and finished, "—and that will make as much difference as I let it. You'd better tell me about it."

"All right," she said, with a tired acquiescence that frightened something inside him. "You seem to have guessed right, though. It's true. There are master firing keys for the launching sites. We have located and dismantled all but two. It's very likely that one of the two was vaporized. The other one is—lost."

"Lost?"

"I don't have to tell you about the secrecy," she said disgustedly. "You know how it developed between nation and nation. You must know that it existed between State and Union, between department and department, office and office. There were only three or four men who knew where all the keys were. Three of them were in the Pentagon when it went up. That was the third blast bomb, you know. If there was another, it could only have been Senator Vandercook, and he died three weeks ago without talking."

"An automatic radio key, hm-m-m?"

"That's right. Sergeant, must we walk? I'm so tired."

"I'm sorry," he said impulsively. They crossed to the reviewing stand and sat on the lonely benches. "Launching racks all over, all hidden, and all armed?"

"Most of them are armed. There's a timing mechanism in them that will disarm them in a year or so. But in the meantime, they are armed and aimed."

"Aimed where?"

"It doesn't matter."

"I think I see. What's the optimum number again?"

"About six hundred and forty; a few more or less. At least five hundred and thirty have been thrown so far. We don't know exactly."

"Who are *we*?" he asked furiously.

"Who? Who?" She laughed weakly. "I could say, 'The Government,' perhaps. If the President dies, the Vice President takes over, and then the Speaker of the House, and so on and on. How far can you go? Pete Mawser, don't you realize yet what's happened?"

"I don't know what you mean."

"How many people do you think are left in this country?"

"I don't know. Just a few million, I guess."

"How many are here?"

"About nine hundred."

"Then, as far as I know, this is the largest city left."

He leaped to his feet. "*No*!" The syllable roared away from him, hurled itself against the dark, empty buildings, came back to him in a series of lowercase echoes: nonono*no* . . . *no*-no—n . . .

Starr began to speak rapidly, quietly. "They're scattered all over the fields and the roads. They sit in the sun and die in the afternoon. They run in packs, they tear at each other. They pray and starve and kill themselves and die in the fires. The fires—everywhere, if anything stands, it's burning. Summer, and the leaves all down in the Berkshires, and the blue grass burnt brown; you can see the grass dying from the air, the death going out wider and wider from the bald-spots. Thunder and roses . . . I saw roses, new ones, creeping from the smashed pots of a greenhouse. Brown petals, alive and sick, and the thorns turned back on themselves, growing into the stems, killing. Feldman died tonight."

He let her be quiet for a time. "Who is Feldman?"

"My pilot." She was talking hollowly into her hands. "He's been dying for weeks. He's been on his nerve-ends. I don't think he had any blood left. He buzzed your GHQ and made for the landing strip. He came in with the motor dead, free rotors, giro. Smashed the landing gear. He was dead, too. He killed a man in Chicago so he could steal gas. The man didn't want the gas. There was a dead girl by the pump. He didn't want us to go near. I'm not going anywhere. I'm going to stay here. I'm tired."

At last she cried.

Pete left her alone, and walked out to the center of the parade ground, looking back at the faint huddled glimmer on the bleachers. His mind flickered over the show that evening, and the way she had sung before the merciless transmitter. "Hello, you." "If we must destroy, let us stop with destroying ourselves!"

The dimming spark of humankind—what could it mean to her? How could it mean so much?

"*Thunder and roses*." Twisted, sick, non-survival roses, killing themselves with their own thorns.

"*And the world was a place of light*!" Blue light, flickering in the contaminated air.

The enemy. The red-topped lever. Bonze. "They pray and starve and kill themselves and die in the fires."

What creatures were these, these corrupted, violent, murdering humans? What right had they to another chance? What was in them that was good?

Starr was good. Starr was crying. Only a human being could cry like that. Starr was a human being.

Had humanity anything of Starr Anthim in it?

Starr *was* a human being.

He looked down through the darkness for his hands. No planet, no universe, is greater to a man than his own ego, his own observing self. These hands were the hands of all history, and like the hands of all men, they could by their small acts make human history or end it. Whether this power of hands was that of a billion hands, or whether it came to a focus in these two—this was suddenly unimportant to the eternities which now enfolded him.

He put humanity's hands deep in his pockets and walked slowly back to the bleachers.

"Starr."

She responded with a sleepy-child, interrogative whimper.

"They'll get their chance, Starr. I won't touch the key."

She sat straight. She rose and came to him, smiling. He could see her smile, because, very faintly in this air, her teeth fluoresced. She put her hands on his shoulders. "Pete."

He held her very close for a moment. Her knees buckled then, and he had to carry her.

There was no one in the Officers' Club, which was the nearest building. He stumbled in, moved clawing along the wall until he found a switch. The light hurt him. He carried her to a settee and put her down gently. She did not move. One side of her face was as pale as milk.

There was blood on his hands.

He stood looking stupidly at it, wiped it on the sides of his trousers, looking dully at Starr. There was blood on her shirt.

The echo of no's came back to him from the far walls of the big room before he knew he had spoken. Starr wouldn't do this. She couldn't!

A doctor! But there was no doctor. Not since Anders had hung himself. Get somebody. *Do* something.

He dropped to his knees and gently unbuttoned her shirt. Between the sturdy, unfeminine GI bra and the top of her slacks, there was blood on her side. He whipped out a clean handkerchief and began to wipe it away. There was no wound, no puncture. But abruptly there was blood again. He blotted it carefully. And again there was blood.

It was like trying to dry a piece of ice with a towel.

He ran to the water cooler, wrung out the bloody handkerchief and ran back to her. He bathed her face carefully, the pale right side, the flushed left side. The handkerchief reddened again, this time with cosmetics, and then her face was pale all over, with great blue shadows under the eyes. While he watched, blood appeared on her left cheek.

There must be *somebody*—He fled to the door.

"Pete!"

Running, turning at the sound of her voice, he hit the doorpost stunningly, caromed off, flailed for his balance, and then was back at her side. "Starr! Hang on, now! I'll get a doctor as quick as—"

Her hand strayed over her left cheek. "You found out. Nobody else knew, but Feldman. It got hard to cover properly." Her hand went up to her hair.

"Starr, I'll get a—"

"Pete, darling, promise me something?"

"Why; sure; certainly, Starr."

"Don't disturb my hair. It isn't—all mine, you see." She sounded like a seven-year-old, playing a game. "It all came out on this side, you see? I don't want you to see me that way."

He was on his knees beside her again. "What is it? What happened to you?" he asked hoarsely.

"Philadelphia," she murmured. "Right at the beginning. The mushroom went up a half mile away. The studio caved in. I came to the next day. I didn't know I was burned, then. It didn't show. My left side. It doesn't matter, Pete. It doesn't hurt at all, now."

He sprang to his feet again. "I'm going for a doctor."

"Don't go away. Please don't go away and leave me. Please don't." There were tears in her eyes. "Wait just a little while. Not very long, Pete."

He sank to his knees again. She gathered both his hands in hers and held them tightly. She smiled happily. "You're good, Pete. You're so good."

(She couldn't hear the blood in his ears, the roar of the whirlpool of hate and fear and anguish that spun inside of him.)

She talked to him in a low voice, and then in whispers. Sometimes he hated himself because he couldn't quite follow her. She talked about school, and her first audition. "I was so scared that I got a vibrato in my voice. I'd never had one before. I always let myself get a little scared when I sing now.

It's easy." There was something about a window box when she was four years old. "Two real live tulips and a pitcher plant. I used to be sorry for the flies."

There was a long period of silence after that, during which his muscles throbbed with cramp and stiffness, and gradually became numb. He must have dozed; he awoke with a violent start, feeling her fingers on his face. She was propped up on one elbow. She said clearly, "I just wanted to tell you, darling. Let me go first, and get everything ready for you. It's going to be wonderful. I'll fix you a special tossed salad. I'll make you a steamed chocolate pudding and keep it hot for you."

Too muddled to understand what she was saying, he smiled and pressed her back on the settee. She took his hands again.

The next time he awoke it was broad daylight, and she was dead.

Sonny Weisefreund was sitting on his cot when he got back to the barracks. He handed over the recording he had picked up from the parade ground on the way back. "Dew on it. Dry it off. Good boy," he croaked, and fell face downward on the cot Bonze had used.

Sonny stared at him. "Pete! Where've you been? What happened? Are you all right?"

Pete shifted a little and grunted. Sonny shrugged and took the audiovid disk out of its wet envelope. Moisture would not harm it particularly, though it could not be played while wet. It was made of a fine spiral of plastic, insulated between laminations. Electrostatic pickups above and below the turntable would fluctuate with changes in the dielectric constant which had been impressed by the recording, and these changes were amplified for the video. The audio was a conventional hill-and-dale needle. Sonny began to wipe it down carefully.

Pete fought upward out of a vast, green-lit place full of flickering cold fires. Starr was calling him. Something was punching him, too. He fought it weakly, trying to hear what she was saying. But someone else was jabbering too loud for him to hear.

He opened his eyes. Sonny was shaking him, his round face pink with excitement. The audiovid was running. Starr was talking. Sonny got up impatiently and turned down the audio gain. "Pete! Pete! Wake up, will you? I got to tell you something. Listen to me! Wake up, will yuh?"

"Huh?"

"That's better. Now listen. I've just been listening to Starr Anthim—"

"She's dead," said Pete.

Sonny didn't hear. He went on explosively, "I've figured it out. Starr was sent out here, and all over, to *beg* someone not to fire any more atom bombs. If the government was sure they wouldn't strike back, they wouldn't have taken the trouble. Somewhere, Pete, there's some way to launch bombs at those murdering cowards—and I've got a pret-ty shrewd idea of how to do it."

Pete strained groggily toward the faint sound of Starr's voice. Sonny talked on. "Now, s'posing there was a master radio key—an automatic code device something like the alarm signal they have on ships, that rings a bell on any ship within radio range when the operator sends four long dashes. Suppose there's an automatic code machine to launch bombs, with repeaters, maybe, buried all over the country. What would it be? Just a little lever to pull; that's all. How would the thing be hidden? In the middle of a lot of other equipment, that's where; in some place where you'd expect to find crazy-looking secret stuff. Like an experiment station. Like right here. You beginning to get the idea?"

"Shut up, I can't hear her."

"The hell with her! You can hear her some other time. You didn't hear a thing I said!"

"She's dead."

"Yeah. Well, I figure I'll pull that handle. What can I lose? It'll give those murderin' . . . *what*?"

"She's dead."

"Dead? Starr Anthim?" His young face twisted, Sonny sank down to the cot. "You're half asleep. You don't know what you're saying."

"She's dead," Pete said hoarsely. "She got burned by one of the first bombs. I was with her when she . . . she—Shut up, now, and get out of here and let me listen!" he bellowed hoarsely.

Sonny stood up slowly. "They killed her, too. They killed her. That does it. That just fixes it up." His face was white. He went out.

Pete got up. His legs weren't working right. He almost fell. He brought up against the console with a crash, his outflung arm sending the pickup skittering across the record. He put it on again and turned up the gain, then lay down to listen.

His head was all mixed up. Sonny talked too much. Bomb launchers, automatic code machines—

"*You gave me your heart*," sang Starr. "*You gave me your heart. You gave me your heart. You—*"

Pete heaved himself up again and moved the pickup arm. Anger, not at himself, but at Sonny for causing him to cut the disk that way, welled up.

Starr was talking, stupidly, her face going through the same expression over and over again. "*Struck from the east and from the Struck from the east and from the—*"

He got up again wearily and moved the pickup.

"*You gave me your heart. You gave me—*"

Pete made an agonized sound that was not a word at all, bent, lifted, and sent the console crashing over. In the bludgeoning silence he said, "I did, too."

Then, "Sonny." He waited.

"*Sonny*!"

His eyes went wide then, and he cursed and bolted for the corridor.

The panel was closed when he reached it. He kicked at it. It flew open, discovering darkness.

"Hey!" bellowed Sonny. "Shut it! You turned off the lights!"

Pete shut it behind them. The lights blazed.

"Pete! What's the matter?"

"Nothing's the matter, Son'," croaked Pete.

"What are you looking at?' said Sonny uneasily.

"I'm sorry," said Pete as gently as he could. "I just wanted to find something out, is all. Did you tell anyone else about this?" He pointed to the lever.

"Why, no. I only just figured it out while you were sleeping, just now."

Pete looked around carefully, while Sonny shifted his weight. Pete moved toward a tool rack. "Something you haven't noticed yet, Sonny," he said softly, and pointed. "Up there, on the wall behind you. High up. See?"

Sonny turned. In one fluid movement Pete plucked off a fourteen-inch box wrench and hit Sonny with it as hard as he could.

Afterward he went to work systematically on the power supplies. He pulled the plugs on the gas engines and cracked their cylinders with a maul. He knocked off the tubing of the diesel starters—the tanks let go explosively—and he cut all the cables with bolt cutters. Then he broke up the relay rack and its lever. When he was quite finished, he put away his tools and bent and stroked Sonny's tousled hair.

He went out and closed the partition carefully. It certainly was a wonderful piece of camouflage. He sat down heavily on a workbench nearby.

"You'll have your chance," he said into the far future. "And, by heaven, you'd better make good."

After that he just waited.

JUDITH MERRIL
That Only a Mother

• • • •

{1948}

Judith Merril (1923–1997) was not the first woman writer to publish in the sf pulps—she was preceded by C. L. Moore, Leigh Brackett, and Andre Norton, among others—but it can be argued that she was the first to have a major career in the genre under an unambiguously female name. When "That Only a Mother," Merril's first published work of sf, appeared in *Astounding* in June 1948, editor John W. Campbell introduced her as "a new feminine science fiction author"; it was rumored that he solicited the story specifically to provide a woman's take on modern technological society (although Merril denied this). While the tale has since become a classic and is widely anthologized, it was disparaged at the time by some male authors as a "diaper story"—criticized, in other words, for its absorption in the mundane realities of domesticity, which true sf presumably scorned in favor of more serious techno-scientific extrapolation. This view is, of course, inaccurate since "That Only a Mother" depicts precisely how the postwar domestic sphere was thoroughly enmeshed in larger public concerns, such as the lurking threat of radiation-induced mutation and the looming danger of atomic warfare. Indeed, the home no longer seemed a safe refuge for either women or men, a reality reflected also in Merril's first sf novel, *Shadow on the Hearth* (1950), which depicts the advent of nuclear holocaust from the perspective of a suburban housewife. Merril's focus on domestic strife and marital discord would be echoed in feminist sf of the 1960s and 1970s, such as Pamela Zoline's "The Heat Death of the Universe" (1967).

While Merril continued to publish sf throughout the 1950s—notably the novella *Daughters of Earth* (1952), an ambitious multi-generational tale of female space colonists—she had by mid-decade begun to devote more of her energies to editing. In 1956 she initiated a series of "Year's Best" anthologies, in which she mixed selections from the sf magazines with work by mainstream authors such as André Maurois, Shirley Jackson, John Steinbeck, and Bernard Malamud. Her goal was to promote an ampler vision of the field, which she preferred to call (following a term coined by Robert A. Heinlein in 1947) "speculative fiction"—thus signaling that the genre's traditional engagement with the forms of modern techno-culture had become a more widespread literary concern. During the 1960s, she threw herself wholeheartedly into the controversies surrounding the "New Wave" movement, using her position as anthology editor—as well as book reviewer for *The Magazine of Fantasy and Science Fiction*—to promote such provocative talents as J. G. Ballard and Thomas M. Disch. She also issued harsh polemics against conventional hard sf, which, in her view, had grown moribund and was swiftly being displaced by a new breed of counterculture-inspired and experimentally sophisticated writing. Increasingly activist, Merril spearheaded the antiwar movement within the genre, helping to organize an advertisement protesting America's involvement in Vietnam that ran in *Galaxy* magazine in 1968. She eventually abandoned her u.s. citizenship and took political refuge in Canada, donating her books and papers to the Toronto Public Library, which now houses the Merril Collection of Science Fiction, Speculation, and Fantasy.

Margaret reached over to the other side of the bed where Hank should have been. Her hand patted the empty pillow, and then she came altogether awake, wondering that the old habit should remain after so many months. She tried to curl up, cat-style, to hoard her own warmth, found she couldn't do it any more, and climbed out of bed with a pleased awareness of her increasingly clumsy bulkiness.

Morning motions were automatic. On the way through the kitchenette, she pressed the button that would start breakfast cooking—the doctor had said to eat as much breakfast as she could—and tore the paper out of the facsimile machine. She folded the long sheet carefully to the "National News" section, and propped it on the bathroom shelf to scan while she brushed her teeth.

No accidents. No direct hits. At least none that had been officially released for publication. *Now. Maggie, don't get started on that. No accidents. No hits. Take the nice newspaper's word for it.*

The three clear chimes from the kitchen announced that breakfast was ready. She set a bright napkin and cheerful colored dishes on the table in a futile attempt to appeal to a faulty morning appetite. Then, when there was nothing more to prepare, she went for the mail, allowing herself the full pleasure of prolonged anticipation, because today there would *surely* be a letter.

There was. There were. Two bills and a worried note from her mother:

"Darling, why didn't you write and tell me sooner? I'm thrilled, of course, but, well, one hates to mention these things, but are you *certain* the doctor was right? Hank's been around all that uranium or thorium or whatever it is all these years, and I know you say he's a designer, not a technician, and he doesn't get near anything that might be dangerous, but you know he used to, back at Oak Ridge. Don't you think . . . well, of course, I'm just being a foolish old woman, and I don't want you to get upset. You know much more about it than I do, and I'm sure your doctor was right. He should know . . ."

Margaret made a face over the excellent coffee, and caught herself refolding the paper to the medical news.

Stop it, Maggie, stop it! The radiologist said Hank's job couldn't have exposed him. And the bombed area we drove past . . . No, no. Stop it, now! Read the social notes or the recipes, Maggie girl.

A well-known geneticist, in the medical news, said that it was possible to tell with absolute certainty, at five months, whether the child would be normal, or at least whether the mutation was likely to produce anything freakish. The worst cases, at any rate, could be prevented. Minor mutations, of course, displacements in facial features, or changes in brain structure could not be detected. And there had been some cases recently, of normal embryos with atrophied limbs that did not develop beyond the seventh or eighth month. But, the doctor concluded cheerfully, the *worst* cases could now be predicted and prevented.

"Predicted and prevented." We predicted it, didn't we? Hank and the others, they predicted it. But we didn't prevent it. We could have stopped it in '46 and '47. Now . . .

Margaret decided against the breakfast. Coffee had been enough for her in the morning for ten years; it would have to do for today. She buttoned herself into interminable folds of material that, the salesgirl had assured her, was the only comfortable thing to wear during the last few months. With a surge of pure pleasure, the letter and newspaper forgotten, she realized she was on the next to the last button. It wouldn't be long now.

The city in the early morning had always been a special kind of excitement for her. Last night it had rained, and the sidewalks were still damp-gray instead of dusty. The air smelled the fresher, to a city-bred woman, for the occasional pungency of acrid factory smoke. She walked the six blocks to work, watching the lights go out in the all-night hamburger joints, where the plate-glass walls were already catching the sun, and the lights go on in the dim interiors of cigar stores and dry-cleaning establishments.

The office was in a new Government building. In the rolovator, on the way up, she felt, as always, like a frankfurter roll in the ascending half of an old-style rotary toasting machine. She abandoned the air-foam cushioning gratefully at the fourteenth floor, and settled down behind her desk, at the rear of a long row of identical desks.

Each morning the pile of papers that greeted her was a little higher. These were, as everyone knew, the decisive months. The war might be won or lost on these calculations as well as any others. The manpower office had switched her here when her old expeditor's job got to be too strenuous. The computer was easy to operate, and the work was absorbing, if not as exciting as the old job. But you didn't just stop working these days. Everyone who could do anything at all was needed.

And—she remembered the interview with the psychologist—*I'm probably the unstable type. Wonder what sort of neurosis I'd get sitting home reading that sensational paper . . .*

She plunged into the work without pursuing the thought.

February 18.

Hank darling,

Just a note—from the hospital, no less. I had a dizzy spell at work, and the doctor took it to heart. Blessed if I know what I'll do with myself lying in bed for weeks, just waiting—but Dr. Boyer seems to think it may not be so long.

There are too many newspapers around here. More infanticides all the time, and they can't seem to get a jury to convict any of them. It's the fathers who do it. Lucky thing you're not around, in case—

Oh, darling, that wasn't a very *funny* joke, was it? Write as often as you can, will you? I have too much time to think. But there really isn't anything wrong, and nothing to worry about.

Write often, and remember I love you.

Maggie.

SPECIAL SERVICE TELEGRAM

February 21, 1953
22:04 LK37G

From: Tech. Lieut. H. Marvell
X47-O16 GCNY
To: Mrs. H. Marvell
Women's Hospital
New York City

HAD DOCTOR'S GRAM STOP WILL ARRIVE FOUR OH TEN STOP SHORT LEAVE STOP YOU DID IT MAGGIE STOP LOVE HANK

February 25.

Hank dear,

So you didn't see the baby either? You'd think a place this size would at least have visiplates on the incubators, so the fathers could get a look, even if the poor benighted mommas can't. They tell me I won't see her for another week, or maybe more—but of course, mother always warned me if I didn't slow my pace, I'd probably even have my babies too fast. Why must she *always* be right?

Did you meet that battle-ax of a nurse they put on here? I imagine they save her for people who've already had theirs, and don't let her get too near the prospectives—but a woman like that simply shouldn't be allowed in a maternity ward. She's obsessed with mutations, can't seem to talk about anything else. Oh, well, *ours* is all right, even if it was in an unholy hurry.

I'm tired. They warned me not to sit up too soon, but I *had* to write you. All my love, darling,

Maggie.

February 29.

Darling,

I finally got to see her! It's all true, what they say about new babies and the face that only a mother could love—but it's all there, darling, eyes, ears, and noses—no, only one!—all in the right places. We're so *lucky*, Hank.

I'm afraid I've been a rambunctious patient. I kept telling that hatchet-faced female with the mutation-mania that I wanted to *see* the baby. Finally the doctor came in to "explain" everything to me, and talked a lot of nonsense, most of which I'm sure no one could have understood, any more than I did. The only thing I got out of it was that she didn't actually *have* to stay in the incubator; they just thought it was "wiser."

I think I got a little hysterical at that point. Guess I was more worried than I was willing to admit, but I threw a small fit about it. The whole business wound up with one of those hushed medical conferences outside the door, and finally the Woman In White said: "Well, we might as well. Maybe it'll work out better that way."

I'd heard about the way doctors and nurses in these places develop a

God complex, and believe me it is as true figuratively as it is literally that a mother hasn't a leg to stand on around here.

I *am* awfully weak, still. I'll write again soon. Love,

Maggie.

March 8.

Dearest Hank,

Well the nurse was wrong if she told you that. She's an idiot anyhow. It's a girl. It's easier to tell with babies than with cats, and *I know*. How about Henrietta?

I'm home again, and busier than a betatron. They got *everything* mixed up at the hospital, and I had to teach myself how to bathe her and do just about everything else. She's getting prettier, too. When can you get a leave, a *real* leave?

Love,

Maggie.

May 26.

Hank dear,

You should see her now—and you shall. I'm sending along a reel of color movie. My mother sent her those nighties with drawstrings all over. I put one on, and right now she looks like a snow-white potato sack with that beautiful, beautiful flower-face blooming on top. Is that *me* talking? Am I a doting mother? But wait till you *see* her!

July 10.

... Believe it or not, as you like, but your daughter can talk, and I don't mean baby talk. Alice discovered it—she's a dental assistant in the WACs, you know—and when she heard the baby giving out what I thought was a string of gibberish, she said the kid knew words and sentences, but couldn't say them clearly because she has no teeth yet. I'm taking her to a speech specialist.

September 13.

... We have a prodigy for real! Now that all her front teeth are in, her speech is perfectly clear and—a new talent now—she can sing! I mean really carry a tune! At seven months! Darling my world would be perfect if you could only get home.

November 19.

... at last. The little goon was so busy being clever, it took her all this time to learn to crawl. The doctor says development in these cases is always erratic ...

SPECIAL SERVICE TELEGRAM

December 1, 1953
08:47 LK59F

From: Tech. Lieut. H. Marvell
X47-O16 GCNY

To: Mrs. H. Marvell
Apt. K-17
504 E. 19 St.
NY, NY

WEEK'S LEAVE STARTS TOMORROW STOP WILL ARRIVE AIRPORT TEN OH FIVE STOP DON'T MEET ME STOP LOVE LOVE LOVE HANK

Margaret let the water run out of the bathinette until only a few inches were left, and then loosed her hold on the wriggling baby.

"I think it was better when you were retarded, young woman," she informed her daughter happily. "You *can't* crawl in a bathinette, you know."

"Then why can't I go in the bathtub?" Margaret was used to her child's volubility by now, but every now and then it caught her unawares. She swooped the resistant mass of pink flesh into a towel, and began to rub.

"Because you're too little, and your head is very soft, and bathtubs are very hard."

"Oh. Then when can I go in the bathtub?"

"When the outside of your head is as hard as the inside, brainchild." She reached toward a pile of fresh clothing. "I cannot understand," she added, pinning a square of cloth through the nightgown, "why a child of your intelligence can't learn to keep a diaper on the way other babies do. They've been used for centuries, you know, with perfectly satisfactory results."

The child disdained to reply; she had heard it too often. She waited patiently until she had been tucked, clean and sweet-smelling, into a white-painted crib. Then she favored her mother with a smile that inevitably made Margaret think of the first golden edge of the sun bursting into a rosy predawn. She remembered Hank's reaction to the color pictures of his beautiful daughter, and with the thought, realized how late it was.

"Go to sleep, puss. When you wake up, you know, your *Daddy* will be here."

"Why?" asked the four-year-old mind, waging a losing battle to keep the ten-month-old body awake.

Margaret went into the kitchenette and set the timer for the roast. She examined the table, and got her clothes from the closet, new dress, new shoes, new slip, new everything, bought weeks before and saved for the day

Hank's telegram came. She stopped to pull a paper from the facsimile, and, with clothes and news, went into the bathroom and lowered herself gingerly into the steaming luxury of a scented tub.

She glanced through the paper with indifferent interest. Today at least there was no need to read the national news. There was an article by a geneticist. The same geneticist. Mutations, he said, were increasing disproportionately. It was too soon for recessives; even the first mutants, born near Hiroshima and Nagasaki in 1946 and 1947, were not old enough yet to breed. *But my baby's all right.* Apparently, there was some degree of free radiation from atomic explosions causing the trouble. *My baby's fine. Precocious, but normal.* If more attention had been paid to the first Japanese mutations, he said . . .

There was that little notice in the paper in the spring of '47. That was when Hank quit at Oak Ridge. "Only 2 or 3 per cent of those guilty of infanticide are being caught and punished in Japan today . . ." *But MY BABY'S all right.*

She was dressed, combed, and ready to the last light brush-on of lip paste, when the door chime sounded. She dashed for the door, and heard, for the first time in eighteen months, the almost-forgotten sound of a key turning in the lock before the chime had quite died away.

"Hank!"

"Maggie!"

And then there was nothing to say. So many days, so many months, of small news piling up, so many things to tell him, and now she just stood there, staring at a khaki uniform and a stranger's pale face. She traced the features with the finger of memory. The same high-bridged nose, wide-set eyes, fine feathery brows; the same long jaw, the hair a little farther back now on the high forehead, the same tilted curve to his mouth. Pale . . . Of course, he'd been underground all this time. And strange, stranger because of lost familiarity than any newcomer's face could be.

She had time to think all that before his hand reached out to touch her, and spanned the gap of eighteen months. Now, again, there was nothing to say, because there was no need. They were together, and for the moment that was enough.

"Where's the baby?"

"Sleeping. She'll be up any minute."

No urgency. Their voices were as casual as though it were a daily exchange, as though war and separation did not exist. Margaret picked up the coat he'd thrown on the chair near the door, and hung it carefully in the hall closet. She went to check the roast, leaving him to wander through the rooms by himself, remembering and coming back. She found him, finally, standing over the baby's crib.

She couldn't see his face, but she had no need to.

"I think we can wake her just this once." Margaret pulled the covers down, and lifted the white bundle from the bed. Sleepy lids pulled back heavily from smoky brown eyes.

"Hello." Hank's voice was tentative.

"Hello." The baby's assurance was more pronounced.

He had heard about it, of course, but that wasn't the same as hearing it. He turned eagerly to Margaret. "She really can—?"

"Of course she can, darling. But what's more important, she can even do nice normal things like other babies do, even stupid ones. Watch her crawl!" Margaret set the baby on the big bed.

For a moment young Henrietta lay and eyed her parents dubiously.

"Crawl?" she asked.

"That's the idea. Your Daddy is new around here, you know. He wants to see you show off."

"Then put me on my tummy."

"Oh, of course." Margaret obligingly rolled the baby over.

"What's the matter?" Hank's voice was still casual, but an undercurrent in it began to charge the air of the room. "I thought they turned over first."

"This baby"—Margaret would not notice the tension—"*This* baby does things when she wants to."

This baby's father watched with softening eyes while the head advanced and the body hunched up, propelling itself across the bed.

"Why the little rascal," he burst into relieved laughter. "She looks like one of those potato-sack racers they used to have on picnics. Got her arms pulled out of the sleeves already." He reached over and grabbed the knot at the bottom of the long nightie.

"I'll do it, darling." Margaret tried to get there first.

"Don't be silly, Maggie. This may be *your* first baby, but *I* had five kid brothers." He laughed her away, and reached with his other hand for the string that closed one sleeve. He opened the sleeve bow, and groped for an arm.

"The way you wriggle," he addressed his child sternly, as his hand touched a moving knob of flesh at the shoulder, "anyone might think you are a worm, using your tummy to crawl on, instead of your hands and feet."

Margaret stood and watched, smiling. "Wait till you hear her sing, darling—"

His right hand traveled down from the shoulder to where he thought an arm would be, traveled down, and straight down, over firm small muscles that writhed in an attempt to move against the pressure of his hand. He let his fingers drift up again to the shoulder. With infinite care, he opened the knot at the bottom of the nightgown. His wife was standing by the bed saying: "She can do 'Jingle Bells,' and—"

His left hand felt along the soft knitted fabric of the gown, up towards the diaper that folded, flat and smooth, across the bottom end of his child. No wrinkles. No kicking. *No . . .*

"Maggie." He tried to pull his hands from the neat fold in the diaper, from the wriggling body. "Maggie." His throat was dry; words came hard, low and grating. He spoke very slowly, thinking the sound of each word to make himself say it. His head was spinning, but he had to *know* before he let it go. "Maggie, why . . . didn't you . . . tell me?"

"Tell you what, darling?" Margaret's poise was the immemorial patience of woman confronted with man's childish impetuosity. Her sudden laugh sounded fantastically easy and natural in that room; it was all clear to her now. "Is she wet? I didn't know."

She didn't know. His hands, beyond control, ran up and down the soft-skinned baby body, the sinuous, limbless body. *Oh God, dear God*—his head shook and his muscles contracted in a bitter spasm of hysteria. His fingers tightened on his child—*Oh God, she didn't know . . .*

FRITZ LEIBER
Coming Attraction

{1950}

Fritz Leiber (1910–1992) was probably the most multifariously talented writer of popular fantastic literature who ever lived. Over a sixty-year career, he not only produced numerous sf classics, such as *Gather, Darkness!* (1943) but also pioneered the genres of sword-and-sorcery—with his *Fafhrd and the Grey Mouser* series—and modern horror, with works such as "Smoke Ghost" (1941) and *Conjure Wife* (1943). As comfortable in John W. Campbell's *Astounding* during its Golden Age as in Michael Moorcock's *New Worlds* during the New Wave a quarter century later, he easily adapted to changing vogues within the field. Leiber's most productive decades were the 1950s and 1960s, when he was both a fan favorite and a writers' writer, winning a total of nine Hugo and Nebula Awards for such works as *The Big Time* (1958), an innovative time-travel tale, and *The Wanderer* (1964), a freewheeling disaster novel. As evidence of his remarkable versatility, he is one of only three authors (the others being Moorcock and Harlan Ellison) to have won lifetime achievement awards from the Science Fiction Writers of America, the World Fantasy Association, and the Horror Writers of America.

"Coming Attraction" was published in the second issue (November 1950) of H. L. Gold's magazine *Galaxy*, which rapidly emerged as a major competitor to Campbell's *Astounding*, specializing in grimly humorous tales of dystopian speculation and near-future satire (such as Frederik Pohl and C. M. Kornbluth's *The Space Merchants* [aka *Gravy Planet*, 1952]). Leiber published some two dozen items in *Galaxy*, including the classics "A Pail of Air" (1951), set on a planet where oxygen is a solid, and "A Bad Day for Sales" (1953), in which a robot vendor persists in his sales pitch despite the outbreak of nuclear war. Leiber could be both droll and chilling, often within the same story, as evidenced by "Coming Attraction," which satirizes the fashion trends of a post-apocalypse New York City. One of the most sexually frank tales of the period, it depicts a social scene swarming with fetishistic subcultures, offering a quasi-Freudian take on misogyny and sadomasochism with a critical sophistication and psychological complexity rare in the genre. (Samuel R. Delany's "Aye, and Gomorrah . . ." [1967] follows in its footsteps in depicting the emergence of new forms of fetishism spawned by technological developments.) Although brief, the story is dense with telling details, such as the undeveloped film the narrator carries to test his exposure to radiation and the day-to-day effects of the looming presence of superpower bases on the Moon. The story is representative of the darker textures of much sf during the immediate postwar period: dubious about the present, gloomy about the future, it is written in a hard-bitten noirish style that befits its desolate setting and downbeat theme.

The coupe with the fishhooks welded to the fender shouldered up over the curb like the nose of a nightmare. The girl in its path stood frozen, her face probably stiff with fright under her mask. For once my reflexes weren't shy. I took a fast step toward her, grabbed her elbow, yanked her back. Her black skirt swirled out.

The big coupe shot by, its turbine humming. I glimpsed three faces. Something ripped. I felt the hot exhaust on my ankles as the big coupe swerved back into the street. A thick cloud like a black flower blossomed from its jouncing rear end, while from the fishhooks flew a black shimmering rag.

"Did they get you?' I asked the girl.

She had twisted around to look where the side of her skirt was torn away. She was wearing nylon tights.

"The hooks didn't touch me," she said shakily. "I guess I'm lucky."

I heard voices around us:

"Those kids! What'll they think up next?"

"They're a menace. They ought to be arrested."

Sirens screamed at a rising pitch as two motor-police, their rocket-assist jets full on, came whizzing toward us after the coupe. But the black flower had become an inky fog obscuring the whole street. The motor-police switched from rocket assists to rocket brakes and swerved to a stop near the smoke cloud.

"Are you English?" the girl asked me. "You have an English accent."

Her voice came shudderingly from behind the sleek black satin mask. I fancied her teeth must be chattering. Eyes that were perhaps blue searched my face from behind the black gauze covering the eyeholes of the mask. I told her she'd guessed right. She stood close to me. "Will you come to my place tonight?" she asked rapidly. "I can't thank you now. And there's something else you can help me about."

My arm, still lightly circling her waist, felt her body trembling. I was answering the plea in that as much as in her voice when I said, "Certainly." She gave me an address south of Inferno, an apartment number and a time. She asked my name and I told her.

"Hey, you!"

I turned obediently to the policeman's shout. He shooed away the small clucking crowd of masked women and barefaced men. Coughing from the smoke that the black coupe had thrown out, he asked for my papers. I handed him the essential ones.

He looked at them and then at me. "British Barter? How long will you be in New York?'

Suppressing the urge to say, "For as short a time as possible," I told him I'd be here for a week or so.

"May need you as a witness," he explained. "Those kids can't use smoke on us. When they do that, we pull them in."

He seemed to think the smoke was the bad thing. "They tried to kill the lady," I pointed out.

He shook his head wisely. "They always pretend they're going to, but actually they just want to snag skirts. I've picked up rippers with as many as fifty skirt-snags tacked up in theft rooms. Of course, sometimes they come a little too close."

I explained that if I hadn't yanked her out of the way, she'd have been hit by more than hooks. But he interrupted, "If she'd thought it was a real murder attempt, she'd have stayed here."

I looked around. It was true. She was gone.

"She was fearfully frightened," I told him.

"Who wouldn't be? Those kids would have scared old Stalin himself."

"I mean frightened of more than 'kids.' They didn't look like 'kids.'"

"What did they look like?"

I tried without much success to describe the three faces. A vague impression of viciousness and effeminacy doesn't mean much.

"Well, I could be wrong," he said finally. "Do you know the girl? Where she lives?"

"No," I half lied.

The other policeman hung up his radiophone and ambled toward us, kicking at the tendrils of dissipating smoke. The black cloud no longer hid the dingy facades with their five-year-old radiation flash-burns, and I could begin to make out the distant stump of the Empire State Building, thrusting up out of Inferno like a mangled finger.

"They haven't been picked up so far," the approaching policeman grumbled. "Left smoke for five blocks, from what Ryan says."

The first policeman shook his head. "That's bad," he observed solemnly.

I was feeling a bit uneasy and ashamed. An Englishman shouldn't lie, at least not on impulse.

"They sound like nasty customers," the first policeman continued in the same grim tone. "We'll need witnesses. Looks as if you may have to stay in New York longer than you expect."

I got the point. I said, "I forgot to show you all my papers," and handed him a few others, making sure there was a five-dollar bill in among them.

When he handed them back a bit later, his voice was no longer ominous. My feelings of guilt vanished. To cement our relationship, I chatted with the two of them about their job.

"I suppose the masks give you some trouble," I observed. "Over in England we've been reading about your new crop of masked female bandits."

"Those things get exaggerated," the first policeman assured me. "It's the men masking as women that really mix us up. But brother, when we nab them, we jump on them with both feet."

"And you get so you can spot women almost as well as if they had naked faces," the second policeman volunteered. "You know, hands and all that."

"Especially all that," the first agreed with a chuckle. "Say, is it true that some girls don't mask over in England?"

"A number of them have picked up the fashion," I told him. "Only a few, though—the ones who always adopt the latest style, however extreme."

"They're usually masked in the British newscasts."

"I imagine it's arranged that way out of deference to American taste," I confessed. "Actually, not very many do mask."

The second policeman considered that. "Girls going down the street bare from the neck up." It was not clear whether he viewed the prospect with relish or moral distaste. Likely both.

"A few members keep trying to persuade Parliament to enact a law forbidding all masking," I continued, talking perhaps a bit too much.

The second policeman shook his head. "What an idea. You know, masks are a pretty good thing, brother. Couple of years more and I'm going to make my wife wear hers around the house."

The first policeman shrugged. "If women were to stop wearing masks, in six weeks you wouldn't know the difference. You get used to anything, if enough people do or don't do it."

I agreed, rather regretfully, and left them. I turned north on Broadway (old Tenth Avenue, I believe) and walked rapidly until I was beyond Inferno. Passing such an area of undecontaminated radioactivity always makes a person queasy. I thanked God there weren't any such in England, as yet.

The street was almost empty, though I was accosted by a couple of beggars with faces tunneled by H-bomb scars, whether real or of makeup putty, I couldn't tell. A fat woman held out a baby with webbed fingers and toes. I told myself it would have been deformed anyway and that she was only capitalizing on our fear of bomb-induced mutations. Still, I gave her a seven-and-a-half-cent piece. Her mask made me feel I was paying tribute to an African fetish.

"May all your children be blessed with one head and two eyes, sir."

"Thanks," I said, shuddering, and hurried past her.

". . . There's only trash behind the mask, so turn your head, stick to your task: Stay away, stay away—from—the—girls!"

This last was the end of an anti-sex song being sung by some religionists half a block from the circle-and-cross insignia of a femalist temple. They reminded me only faintly of our small tribe of British monastics. Above their heads was a jumble of billboards advertising predigested foods, wrestling instruction, radio handles and the like.

I stared at the hysterical slogans with disagreeable fascination. Since the female face and form have been banned on American signs, the very letters of the advertiser's alphabet have begun to crawl with sex—the fat-bellied, big-breasted capital B, the lascivious double O. However, I reminded myself, it is chiefly the mask that so strangely accents sex in America.

A British anthropologist has pointed out that while it took more than 5,000 years to shift the chief point of sexual interest from the hips to the breasts, the next transition to the face has taken less than 50 years. Comparing the American style with Moslem tradition is not valid; Moslem women are compelled to wear veils, the purpose of which is to make a husband's property private, while American women have only the compulsion of fashion and use masks to create mystery.

Theory aside, the actual origins of the trend are to be found in the anti-radiation clothing of World War III, which led to masked wrestling, now a fantastically popular sport, and that in turn led to the current female fashion. Only a wild style at first, masks quickly became as necessary as brassieres and lipsticks had been earlier in the century.

I finally realized that I was not speculating about masks in general, but about what lay behind one in particular. That's the devil of the things; you're never sure whether a girl is heightening loveliness or hiding ugliness. I pictured a cool, pretty face in which fear showed only in widened eyes. Then I remembered her blond hair, rich against the blackness of the satin mask. She'd told me to come at the twenty-second hour—10 P.M.

I climbed to my apartment near the British Consulate; the elevator shaft had been shoved out of plumb by an old blast, a nuisance in these tall New York buildings. Before it occurred to me that I would be going out again, I automatically tore a tab from the film strip under my shirt. I developed it just to be sure. It showed that the total radiation I'd taken that day was still within the safety limit. I'm not phobic about it, as so many people are these days, but there's no point in taking chances.

I flopped down on the day bed and stared at the silent speaker and the dark screen of the video set. As always, they made me think, somewhat bitterly, of the two great nations of the world. Mutilated by each other, yet still strong, they were crippled giants poisoning the planet with their respective dreams of an impossible equality and an impossible success.

I fretfully twitched on the speaker. By luck, the newscaster was talking excitedly of the prospects of a bumper wheat crop, sown by planes across a dust bowl moistened by seeded rains. I listened carefully to the rest of the program (it was remarkably clear of Russian telejamming) but there was no further news of interest to me. And, of course, no mention of the Moon, though everyone knows that America and Russia are racing to develop their primary bases into fortresses capable of mutual assault and the launching of alphabet-bombs toward Earth. I myself knew perfectly well that the British electronic equipment I was helping trade for American wheat was destined for use in spaceships.

I switched off the newscast. It was growing dark and once again I pictured a tender, frightened face behind a mask. I hadn't had a date since England. It's exceedingly difficult to become acquainted with a girl in America, where as little as a smile, often, can set one of them yelping for the police—to say nothing of the increasingly puritanical morality and the roving gangs that keep most women indoors after dark. And naturally, the masks, which are definitely not, as the Soviets claim, a last invention of capitalist degeneracy, but a sign of great psychological insecurity. The Russians have no masks, but they have their own signs of stress.

I went to the window and impatiently watched the darkness gather. I was getting very restless. After a while a ghostly violet cloud appeared to the south. My hair rose. Then I laughed. I had momentarily fancied it a radiation from the crater of the Hell-bomb, though I should instantly have known it was only the radio-induced glow in the sky over the amusement and residential area south of Inferno.

Promptly at twenty-two hours I stood before the door of my unknown girlfriend's apartment. The electronic say-who-please said just that. I answered clearly, "Wysten Turner," wondering if she'd given my name to the mechanism. She evidently had, for the door opened. I walked into a small empty living room, my heart pounding a bit.

The room was expensively furnished with the latest pneumatic hassocks and sprawlers. There were some midgie books on the table. The one I picked up was the standard hardboiled detective story in which two female murderers go gunning for each other.

The television was on. A masked girl in green was crooning a love song. Her right hand held something that blurred off into the foreground. I saw the set had a handie, which we haven't in England as yet, and curiously thrust my hand into the handie orifice beside the screen. Contrary to my expectations, it was not like slipping into a pulsing rubber glove, but rather as if the girl on the screen actually held my hand.

A door opened behind me. I jerked out my hand with as guilty a reaction as if I'd been caught peering through a keyhole.

She stood in the bedroom doorway. I think she was trembling. She was wearing a gray fur coat, white-speckled, and a gray velvet evening mask with shirred gray lace around the eyes and mouth. Her fingernails twinkled like silver.

It hadn't occurred to me that she'd expect us to go out.

"I should have told you," she said softly. Her mask veered nervously toward the books and the screen and the room's dark corners. "But I can't possibly talk to you here."

I said doubtfully, "There's a place near the Consulate . . ."

"I know where we can be together and talk," she said rapidly. "If you don't mind."

As we entered the elevator I said, "I'm afraid I dismissed the cab."

But the cab driver hadn't gone for some reason of his own. He jumped out and smirkingly held the front door open for us. I told him we preferred to sit in back. He sulkily opened the rear door, slammed it after us, jumped in front and slammed the door behind him.

My companion leaned forward. "Heaven," she said.

The driver switched on the turbine and televisor.

"Why did you ask if I were a British subject?" I said, to start the conversation.

She leaned away from me, tilting her mask close to the window. "See the Moon," she said in a quick, dreamy voice.

"But why, really?" I pressed, conscious of an irritation that had nothing to do with her.

"It's edging up into the purple of the sky."

"And what's your name?"

"The purple makes it look yellower."

Just then I became aware of the source of my irritation. It lay in the square of writhing light in the front of the cab beside the driver.

I don't object to ordinary wrestling matches, though they bore me, but I simply detest watching a man wrestle a woman. The fact that the bouts are generally "on the level," with the man greatly outclassed in weight and reach and the masked females young and personable, only makes them seem worse to me.

"Please turn off the screen," I requested the driver.

He shook his head without looking around. "Uh-uh, man," he said. "They've been grooming that babe for weeks for this bout with Little Zirk."

Infuriated, I reached forward, but my companion caught my arm. "Please," she whispered frightenedly, shaking her head.

I settled back, frustrated. She was closer to me now, but silent, and for a few minutes I watched the heaves and contortions of the powerful masked girl and her wiry masked opponent on the screen. His frantic scrambling at her reminded me of a male spider.

I jerked around, facing my companion. "Why did those three men want to kill you?" I asked sharply.

The eyeholes of her mask faced the screen. "Because they're jealous of me," she whispered.

"Why are they jealous?"

She still didn't look at me. "Because of him."

"Who?"

She didn't answer.

I asked, "What *is* the matter?"

She still didn't look my way. She smelled nice.

"See here," I said laughingly, changing my tactics, "you really should tell me something about yourself. I don't even know what you look like."

I half playfully lifted my hand to the band of her neck. She gave it an astonishingly swift slap. I pulled it away in sudden pain. There were four tiny indentations on the back. From one of them a tiny bead of blood welled out as I watched. I looked at her silver fingernails and saw they were actually delicate and pointed metal caps.

"I'm dreadfully sorry," I heard her say, "but you frightened me. I thought for a moment you were going to . . ."

At last she turned to me. Her coat had fallen open. Her evening dress was Cretan Revival, a bodice of lace beneath and supporting the breasts without covering them.

"Don't be angry," she said, putting her arms around my neck. "You were wonderful this afternoon."

The soft gray velvet of her mask, molding itself to her cheek, pressed mine. Through the mask's lace the wet warm tip of her tongue touched my chin.

"I'm not angry," I said. "Just puzzled and anxious to help."

The cab stopped. To either side were black windows bordered by spears of broken glass. The sickly purple light showed a few ragged figures slowly moving toward us.

The driver muttered, "It's the turbine, man. We're grounded." He sat there hunched and motionless. "Wish it had happened somewhere else."

My companion whispered, "Five dollars is the usual amount."

She looked out so shudderingly at the congregating figures that I suppressed my indignation and did as she suggested. The driver took the bill without a word. As he started up, he put his hand out the window and I heard a few coins clink on the pavement.

My companion came back into my arms, but her mask faced the television screen, where the tall girl had just pinned the convulsively kicking Little Zirk.

"I'm so frightened," she breathed.

Heaven turned out to be an equally ruinous neighborhood, but it had a club with an awning and a huge doorman uniformed like a spaceman, but in gaudy colors. In my sensuous daze I rather liked it all. We stepped out of the cab just as a drunken old woman came down the sidewalk, her mask awry. A couple ahead of us turned their heads from the half-revealed face, as if from an ugly body at the beach. As we followed them in I heard the doorman say, "Get along, grandma, and cover yourself."

Inside, everything was dimness and blue glows. She had said we could talk here, but I didn't see how. Besides the inevitable chorus of sneezes and coughs (they say America is fifty percent allergic these days), there was a band going full blast in the latest rebop style, in which an electronic composing machine selects an arbitrary sequence of tones into which the musicians weave their raucous little individualities.

Most of the people were in booths. The band was behind the bar. On a small platform beside them, a girl was dancing, stripped to her mask. The little cluster of men at the shadowy far end of the bar weren't looking at her.

We inspected the menu in gold script on the wall and pushed the buttons for breast of chicken, fried shrimps and two scotches. Moments later, the serving bell tinkled. I opened the gleaming panel and took out our drinks.

The cluster of men at the bar filed off toward the door, but first they stared around the room. My companion had just thrown back her coat. Their look lingered on our booth. I noticed that there were three of them.

The band chased off the dancing girl with growls. I handed my companion a straw and we sipped our drinks.

"You wanted me to help you about something," I said. "Incidentally, I think you're lovely."

She nodded quick thanks, looked around, leaned forward. "Would it be hard for me to get to England?"

"No," I replied, a bit taken aback. "Provided you have an American passport."

"Are they difficult to get?

"Rather," I said, surprised at her lack of information. "Your country doesn't like its nationals to travel, though it isn't quite as stringent as Russia."

"Could the British Consulate help me get a passport?

"It's hardly their . . ."

"Could you?"

I realized we were being inspected. A man and two girls had passed opposite our table. The girls were tall and wolfish-looking, with spangled masks. The man stood jauntily between them like a fox on its hind legs.

My companion didn't glance at them, but she sat back. I noticed that one of the girls had a big yellow bruise on her forearm. After a moment they walked to a booth in the deep shadows.

"Know them?" I asked. She didn't reply. I finished my drink. "I'm not sure you'd like England," I said. "The austerity's altogether different from your American brand of misery."

She leaned forward again. "But I must get away," she whispered.

"Why?" I was getting impatient.

"Because I'm so frightened."

There were chimes. I opened the panel and handed her the fried shrimps. The sauce on my breast of chicken was a delicious steaming compound of almonds, soy and ginger. But something must have been wrong with the radionic oven that had thawed and heated it, for at the first bite I crunched a kernel of ice in the meat. These delicate mechanisms need constant repair and there aren't enough mechanics.

I put down my fork. "What are you really scared of?" I asked her.

For once her mask didn't waver from my face. As I waited I could feel the fears gathering without her naming them, tiny dark shapes swarming through the curved night outside, converging on the radioactive pest spot of New York, dipping into the margins of the purple. I felt a sudden rush of sympathy, a desire to protect the girl opposite me. The warm feeling added itself to the infatuation engendered in the cab.

"Everything," she said finally.

I nodded and touched her hand.

"I'm afraid of the Moon," she began, her voice going dreamy and brittle as it had in the cab. "You can't look at it and not think of guided bombs."

"It's the same Moon over England," I reminded her.

"But it's not England's Moon any more. It's ours and Russia's. You're not responsible.

"Oh, and then," she said with a tilt of her mask, "I'm afraid of the cars and the gangs and the loneliness and Inferno. I'm afraid of the lust that undresses your face. And—" her voice hushed—"I'm afraid of the wrestlers."

"Yes?" I prompted softly after a moment.

Her mask came forward. "Do you know something about the wrestlers?" she asked rapidly. "The ones that wrestle women, I mean. They often lose, you know. And then they have to have a girl to take their frustration out on. A girl who's soft and weak and terribly frightened. They need that, to keep them men. Other men don't want them to have a girl. Other men want them just to fight women and be heroes. But they must have a girl. It's horrible for her."

I squeezed her fingers tighter, as if courage could be transmitted—granting I had any. "I think I can get you to England," I said.

Shadows crawled onto the table and stayed there. I looked up at the three men who had been at the end of the bar. They were the men I had seen in the big coupe. They wore black sweaters and close-fitting black trousers. Their faces were as expressionless as dopers. Two of them stood about me. The other loomed over the girl.

"Drift off, man," I was told. I heard the other inform the girl: "We'll wrestle a fall, sister. What shall it be? Judo, slapsie or kill-who-can?"

I stood up. There are times when an Englishman simply must be maltreated. But just then the foxlike man came gliding in like the star of a ballet. The reaction of the other three startled me. They were acutely embarrassed.

He smiled at them thinly. "You won't win my favor by tricks like this," he said.

"Don't get the wrong idea, Zirk," one of them pleaded.

"I will if it's right," he said. "She told me what you tried to do this afternoon. That won't endear you to me, either. Drift."

They backed off awkwardly. "Let's get out of here," one of them said loudly, as they turned. "I know a place where they fight naked with knives."

Little Zirk laughed musically and slipped into the seat beside my companion. She shrank from him, just a little. I pushed my feet back, leaned forward.

"Who's your friend, baby?" he asked, not looking at her.

She passed the question to me with a little gesture. I told him.

"British," he observed. "She's been asking you about getting out of the country? About passports?" He smiled pleasantly. "She likes to start running away. Don't you, baby?" His small hand began to stroke her wrist, the fingers bent a little, the tendons ridged, as if he were about to grab and twist.

"Look here," I said sharply. "I have to be grateful to you for ordering off those bullies, but—"

"Think nothing of it," he told me. "They're no harm except when they're behind steering wheels. A well-trained fourteen-year-old girl could cripple any one of them. Why, even Theda here, if she went in for that sort of thing . . ." He turned to her, shifting his hand from her wrist to her hair. He stroked it, letting the strands slip slowly through his fingers. "You know I lost tonight, baby, don't you?" he said softly.

I stood up. "Come along," I said to her. "Let's leave."

She just sat there. I couldn't tell if she was trembling. I tried to read a message in her eyes through the mask.

"I'll take you away," I said to her. "I can do it. I really will."

He smiled at me. "She'd like to go with you," he said. "Wouldn't you, baby?"

"Will you or won't you?" I said to her. She still just sat there.

He slowly knotted his fingers in her hair.

"Listen, you little vermin," I snapped at him. "Take your hands off her."

He came up from the seat like a snake. I'm no fighter. I just know that the more scared I am, the harder and straighter I hit. This time I was lucky. But as he crumpled back, I felt a slap and four stabs of pain in my cheek. I clapped my hand to it. I could feel the four gashes made by her dagger finger caps, and the warm blood oozing out from them.

She didn't look at me. She was bending over little Zirk and cuddling her mask to his cheek and crooning: "There, there, don't feel bad, you'll be able to hurt me afterward."

There were sounds around us, but they didn't come close. I leaned forward and ripped the mask from her face.

I really don't know why I should have expected her face to be anything else. It was very pale, of course, and there weren't any cosmetics. I suppose there's no point in wearing any under a mask. The eyebrows were untidy and the lips chapped. But as for the general expression, as for the feelings crawling and wriggling across it—

Have you ever lifted a rock from damp soil? Have you ever watched the slimy white grubs?

I looked down at her, she up at me. "Yes, you're so frightened, aren't you?" I said sarcastically. "You dread this little nightly drama, don't you? You're scared to death."

And I walked right out into the purple night, still holding my hand to my bleeding cheek. No one stopped me, not even the girl wrestlers. I wished I could tear a tab from under my shirt, and test it then and there, and find I'd taken too much radiation, and so be able to ask to cross the Hudson and go down New Jersey, past the lingering radiance of the Narrows Bomb, and so on to Sandy Hook to wait for the rusty ship that would take me back over the seas to England.

RAY BRADBURY

There Will Come Soft Rains

{1950}

Ray Bradbury (1920–) spent his childhood in small-town Illinois, moving with his family to Los Angeles as a teenager. Science is not central to his fiction, which is hostile to technology and science; much of his fiction often slips the genre label entirely. The gentleness with which he employs sf icons, along with his poetic, symbolic, and evocative style, have contributed to the warmth of his reception beyond the sf audience. His best-known sf works are *Fahrenheit 451* (1951, rev. 1953, 1979, 1982) and the short-story cycle *The Martian Chronicles* (1950) from which "There Will Come Soft Rains" is taken. His first collection, *Dark Carnival* (1947), is more accurately categorized as weird fiction or dark fantasy, as is the novel *Something Wicked This Way Comes* (1962), while *Dandelion Wine* (1957) is a nostalgic gathering of stories about small town life whose fantastic elements are expressed primarily through metaphors. Although he continues to write, his most successful and prolific period was from the late 1940s through the early 1960s. One could argue that his most important contributions to sf have been his attention to style, metaphor, and symbol, and his ability to escape genre classification.

"There Will Come Soft Rains" appears as the penultimate story of *The Martian Chronicles*, which consists of loosely connected pieces chronicling the decline of Earth culture culminating in a nuclear holocaust and the parallel struggle to colonize Mars: each story or vignette is assigned a date, from January 1999 to October 2026. Bradbury's Mars is the site of a dying indigenous civilization, one that had encouraged the arts and limited the pernicious influences of science but whose citizens by the time of earth colonization have rejected spontaneity and imagination. The chicken pox destroys most of the remaining Martians, and human beings pollute the planet with ugly technology. When Earth destroys itself in atomic warfare, almost all the colonizers return to their devastated home planet. The stories gradually reveal Bradbury's distrust of science, technology, and the coercive politics of the McCarthy era while they emphasize the importance he places on the imagination. These attitudes are only alluded to in "There Will Come Soft Rains," but they inform it nevertheless.

The story's title comes from Sara Teasdale's 1920 poem of the same name, which celebrates the Earth's renewal after the demise of humankind. Written in the gentle cadences of a children's story, Bradbury's tale personifies an automated house that goes through its program in spite of the atomic bomb that has turned its residents to ash. While there is a certain coziness to the house's preparation of breakfast, its "tiny robot mice," and its animated nursery animals, this house is also a sinister technology that suffers "a mechanical paranoia" and is responsible for the death of the family dog. Like the collection from which it comes, the story has a surprising bite in spite of its tone of nostalgic melancholy. The haunting eerieness of its abandoned structure was a likely influence on J. G. Ballard's depiction of derelict motels in "The Cage of Sand" (1962).

AUGUST 2026

In the living room the voice-clock sang, *Tick-tock, seven o'clock, time to get up, time to get up, seven o'clock!* as if it were afraid that nobody would. The morning house lay empty. The clock ticked on, repeating and repeating its sounds into the emptiness. *Seven-nine, breakfast time, seven-nine!*

In the kitchen the breakfast stove gave a hissing sigh and ejected from its warm interior eight pieces of perfectly browned toast, eight eggs sunnyside up, sixteen slices of bacon, two coffees, and two cool glasses of milk.

"Today is August 4, 2026," said a second voice from the kitchen ceiling, "in the city of Allendale, California." It repeated the date three times for memory's sake. "Today is Mr. Featherstone's birthday. Today is the anniversary of Tilita's marriage. Insurance is payable, as are the water, gas, and light bills."

Somewhere in the walls, relays clicked, memory tapes glided under electric eyes.

Eight-one, tick-tock, eight-one o'clock, off to school, off to work, run, run, eight-one! But no doors slammed, no carpets took the soft tread of rubber heels. It was raining outside. The weather box on the front door sang quietly: "Rain, rain, go away; rubbers, raincoats for today . . ." And the rain tapped on the empty house, echoing.

Outside, the garage chimed and lifted its door to reveal the waiting car. After a long wait the door swung down again.

At eight-thirty the eggs were shriveled and the toast was like stone. An aluminum wedge scraped them into the sink, where hot water whirled them down a metal throat which digested and flushed them away to the distant sea. The dirty dishes were dropped into a hot washer and emerged twinkling dry.

Nine-fifteen, sang the clock, *time to clean.*

Out of warrens in the wall, tiny robot mice darted. The rooms were acrawl with the small cleaning animals, all rubber and metal. They thudded against chairs, whirling their mustached runners, kneading the rug nap, sucking gently at hidden dust. Then, like mysterious invaders, they popped into their burrows. Their pink electric eyes faded. The house was clean.

Ten o'clock. The sun came out from behind the rain. The house stood alone in a city of rubble and ashes. This was the one house left standing. At night the ruined city gave off a radioactive glow which could be seen for miles.

Ten-fifteen. The garden sprinklers whirled up in golden founts, filling the soft morning air with scatterings of brightness. The water pelted window-panes, running down the charred west side where the house had been burned evenly free of its white paint. The entire west face of the house was black, save for five places. Here the silhouette in paint of a man mowing a lawn. Here, as in a photograph, a woman bent to pick flowers. Still farther over, their images burned on wood in one titanic instant, a small boy, hands flung into the air; higher up, the image of a thrown ball, and opposite him a girl, hands raised to catch a ball which never came down.

The five spots of paint—the man, the woman, the children, the ball—remained. The rest was a thin charcoaled layer.

The gentle sprinkler rain filled the garden with falling light.

Until this day, how well the house had kept its peace. How carefully it had inquired, "Who goes there? What's the password?" and, getting no answer from lonely foxes and whining cats, it had shut up its windows and drawn shades in an old-maidenly preoccupation with self-protection which bordered on a mechanical paranoia.

It quivered at each sound, the house did. If a sparrow brushed a window, the shade snapped up. The bird, startled, flew off! No, not even a bird must touch the house!

The house was an altar with ten thousand attendants, big, small, servicing, attending, in choirs. But the gods had gone away, and the ritual of the religion continued senselessly, uselessly.

Twelve noon.

A dog whined, shivering, on the front porch.

The front door recognized the dog voice and opened. The dog, once huge and fleshy, but now gone to bone and covered with sores, moved in and through the house, tracking mud. Behind it whirred angry mice, angry at having to pick up mud, angry at inconvenience.

For not a leaf fragment blew under the door but what the wall panels flipped open and the copper scrap rats flashed swiftly out. The offending dust, hair, or paper, seized in miniature steel jaws, was raced back to the burrows. There, down tubes which fed into the cellar, it was dropped into the sighing vent of an incinerator which sat like evil Baal in a dark corner.

The dog ran upstairs, hysterically yelping to each door, at last realizing, as the house realized, that only silence was here.

It sniffed the air and scratched the kitchen door. Behind the door, the stove was making pancakes which filled the house with a rich baked odor and the scent of maple syrup.

The dog frothed at the mouth, lying at the door, sniffing, its eyes turned to fire. It ran wildly in circles, biting at its tail, spun in a frenzy, and died. It lay in the parlor for an hour.

Two o'clock, sang a voice.

Delicately sensing decay at last, the regiments of mice hummed out as softly as blown gray leaves in an electrical wind.

Two-fifteen.

The dog was gone.

In the cellar, the incinerator glowed suddenly and a whirl of sparks leaped up the chimney.

Two thirty-five.

Bridge tables sprouted from patio walls. Playing cards fluttered onto pads in a shower of pips. Martinis manifested on an oaken bench with egg-salad sandwiches. Music played.

But the tables were silent and the cards untouched.

At four o'clock the tables folded like great butterflies back through the paneled walls.

Four-thirty.

The nursery walls glowed.

Animals took shape: yellow giraffes, blue lions, pink antelopes, lilac panthers cavorting in crystal substance. The walls were glass. They looked out upon color and fantasy. Hidden films docked through well-oiled sprockets, and the walls lived. The nursery floor was woven to resemble a crisp, cereal meadow. Over this ran aluminum roaches and iron crickets, and in the hot still air butterflies of delicate red tissue wavered among the sharp aroma of animal spoors! There was the sound like a great matted yellow hive of bees within a dark bellows, the lazy bumble of a purring lion. And there was the patter of okapi feet and the murmur of a fresh jungle rain, like other hoofs, falling upon the summer-starched grass. Now the walls dissolved into distances of parched weed, mile on mile, and warm endless sky. The animals drew away into thorn brakes and water holes.

It was the children's hour.

Five o'clock. The bath filled with clear hot water.

Six, seven, eight o'clock. The dinner dishes manipulated like magic tricks, and in the study a *click*. In the metal stand opposite the hearth where a fire now blazed up warmly, a cigar popped out, half an inch of soft gray ash on it, smoking, waiting.

Nine o'clock. The beds warmed their hidden circuits, for nights were cool here.

Nine-five. A voice spoke from the study ceiling:

"Mrs. McClellan, which poem would you like this evening?"

The house was silent.

The voice said at last, "Since you express no preference, I shall select a poem at random." Quiet music rose to back the voice. "Sara Teasdale. As I recall, your favorite . . ."

"There will come soft rains and the smell of the ground,
And swallows circling with their shimmering sound;

And frogs in the pools singing at night,
And wild plum trees in tremulous white;

Robins will wear their feathery fire,
Whistling their whims on a low fence-wire;

And not one will know of the war, not one
Will care at last when it is done.

Not one would mind, neither bird nor tree,
If mankind perished utterly;

And Spring herself, when she woke at dawn
Would scarcely know that we were gone."

The fire burned on the stone hearth and the cigar fell away into a mound of quiet ash on its tray. The empty chairs faced each other between the silent walls, and the music played.

At ten o'clock the house began to die.

The wind blew. A falling tree bough crashed through the kitchen window. Cleaning solvent, bottled, shattered over the stove. The room was ablaze in an instant!

"Fire!" screamed a voice. The house lights flashed, water pumps shot water from the ceilings. But the solvent spread on the linoleum, licking, eating, under the kitchen door, while the voices took it up in chorus: "Fire, fire, fire!"

The house tried to save itself. Doors sprang tightly shut, but the windows were broken by the heat and the wind blew and sucked upon the fire.

The house gave ground as the fire in ten billion angry sparks moved with flaming ease from room to room and then up the stairs. While scurrying water rats squeaked from the walls, pistoled their water, and ran for more. And the wall sprays let down showers of mechanical rain.

But too late. Somewhere, sighing, a pump shrugged to a stop. The quenching rain ceased. The reserve water supply which had filled baths and washed dishes for many quiet days was gone.

The fire crackled up the stairs. It fed upon Picassos and Matisses in the upper halls, like delicacies, baking off the oily flesh, tenderly crisping the canvases into black shavings.

Now the fire lay in beds, stood in windows, changed the colors of drapes!

And then, reinforcements.

From attic trapdoors, blind robot faces peered down with faucet mouths gushing green chemical.

The fire backed off, as even an elephant must at the sight of a dead snake. Now there were twenty snakes whipping over the floor, killing the fire with a clear cold venom of green froth.

But the fire was clever. It had sent flames outside the house, up through the attic to the pumps there. An explosion! The attic brain which directed the pumps was shattered into bronze shrapnel on the beams.

The fire rushed back into every closet and felt of the clothes hung there.

The house shuddered, oak bone on bone, its bared skeleton cringing from the heat, its wire, its nerves revealed as if a surgeon had torn the skin off to let the red veins and capillaries quiver in the scalded air. Help, help! Fire! Run, run! Heat snapped mirrors like the brittle winter ice. And the voices wailed, Fire, fire, run, run, like a tragic nursery rhyme, a dozen voices, high, low, like children dying in a forest, alone, alone. And the voices fading as the wires popped their sheathings like hot chestnuts. One, two, three, four, five voices died.

In the nursery the jungle burned. Blue lions roared, purple giraffes bounded off. The panthers ran in circles, changing color, and ten million animals, running before the fire, vanished off toward a distant steaming river. . . .

Ten more voices died. In the last instant under the fire avalanche, other choruses, oblivious, could be heard announcing the time, playing music, cutting the lawn by remote-control mower, or setting an umbrella frantically out and in the slamming and opening front door, a thousand things happening, like a clock shop when each clock strikes the hour insanely before or after the other, a scene of maniac confusion, yet unity; singing, screaming, a few last cleaning mice darting bravely out to carry the horrid ashes away! And one voice, with sublime disregard for the situation, read poetry aloud in the fiery study, until all the film spools burned, until all the wires withered and the circuits cracked.

The fire burst the house and let it slam flat down, puffing out skirts of spark and smoke.

In the kitchen, an instant before the rain of fire and timber, the stove could be seen making breakfasts at a psychopathic rate, ten dozen eggs, six loaves of toast, twenty dozen bacon strips, which, eaten by fire, started the stove working again, hysterically hissing!

The crash. The attic smashing into kitchen and parlor. The parlor into cellar, cellar into sub-cellar. Deep freeze, armchair, film tapes, circuits, beds, and all like skeletons thrown in a cluttered mound deep under.

Smoke and silence. A great quantity of smoke.

Dawn showed faintly in the east. Among the ruins, one wall stood alone. Within the wall, a last voice said, over and over again and again, even as the sun rose to shine upon the heaped rubble and steam:

"Today is August 5, 2026, today is August 5, 2026, today . . ."

ARTHUR C. CLARKE
The Sentinel

{1951}

British author (Sir) Arthur C. Clarke (1917–2008) is one of a select group of acknowledged golden age masters of Anglo-American science fiction that includes Isaac Asimov and Robert A. Heinlein. Clarke studied physics and mathematics at the University of London, and he was chair of the British Interplanetary Society in the late 1940s and again in the early 1950s. There is general agreement that his most important scientific contribution was the idea of geostationary satellites, which he introduced in 1945. Clarke was so well known by the late 1960s that he co-anchored, with Walter Cronkite, CBS's coverage of the first moon landing by the Apollo 11 mission. In 1987 he supported the establishment of the Arthur C. Clarke Award, Britain's most prestigious sf award. In the same year he was named a Grand Master by the Science Fiction Writers of America. Clarke is the originator of one of sf's most familiar aphorisms: "Any sufficiently advanced technology is indistinguishable from magic."

Clarke's first sf story was published in 1946 and he went on to write such classic novels as *Childhood's End* (1953), *The City and the Stars* (1956), and *Rendezvous with Rama* (1972); award-winning short stories including "The Nine Billion Names of God" (1953), "The Star" (1955), and "A Meeting with Medusa" (1971); and popular nonfiction such as *The Promise of Space* (1968). "The Sentinel," an early story, was the basis for the screenplay that Clarke wrote for director Stanley Kubrick's cinematic masterpiece, *2001: A Space Odyssey*—which helped to make Clarke one of the most famous sf writers in the world. Clarke wrote the novel version of *2001* simultaneously with his screenplay, and it was published in 1968 soon after the film's release. It was followed by several sequels, the last of which, *3001: The Final Odyssey*, was published in 1997. The 2001 Mars Odyssey, a robotic spacecraft that has been orbiting Mars since 2002, was named in tribute to Clarke's long-standing and influential commitment to space exploration. In the 1980s and 1990s Clarke—by then a longtime resident of Sri Lanka—wrote most of his novels in collaboration with sf writers such as Gregory Benford and Stephen Baxter.

"The Sentinel" is about the discovery on the Moon of what *The Encyclopedia of Science Fiction* refers to as a Big Dumb Object (BDO). The enigmatic BDO—its name implies both utter silence and utter lack of information—is often associated with sf's sense of wonder. Clarke's story is a good example of his ongoing interest in themes of (almost) mystical transcendence, so powerfully dramatized in the earth-shattering climax of *Childhood's End*. In the tradition of British scientific romances such as H. G. Wells's "The Star" (1897), the story's affective appeal lies in the vastness of its perspectives in time and space; its cognitive appeal is the challenge it poses to conventional notions of humanity's place in the universe. Although the wonders of the cosmos are foregrounded, in particular the wonders of the lunar geography, at the center of the story is a technological artifact, the sign of an unimaginably powerful alien Other that Clarke's protagonist awaits with both yearning and dread.

The next time you see the full Moon high in the south, look carefully at its right-hand edge and let your eye travel upwards along the curve of the disk. Round about two o'clock you will notice a small, dark oval: anyone with normal eyesight can find it quite easily. It is the great walled plain, one of the finest on the Moon, known as the Mare Crisium—the Sea of Crises. Three hundred miles in diameter, and almost completely surrounded by a ring of magnificent mountains, it had never been explored until we entered it in the late summer of 1996.

Our expedition was a large one. We had two heavy freighters which had flown our supplies and equipment from the main lunar base in the Mare Serenitatis, five hundred miles away. There were also three small rockets which were intended for short-range transport over regions which our surface vehicles couldn't cross. Luckily, most of the Mare Crisium is very flat. There are none of the great crevasses so common and so dangerous elsewhere, and very few craters or mountains of any size. As far as we could tell, our powerful caterpillar tractors would have no difficulty in taking us wherever we wished to go.

I was geologist—or selenologist, if you want to be pedantic—in charge of the group exploring the southern region of the Mare. We had crossed a hundred miles of it in a week, skirting the foothills of the mountains along the shore of what was once the ancient sea, some thousand million years before. When life was beginning on Earth, it was already dying here. The waters were retreating down the flanks of those stupendous cliffs, retreating into the empty heart of the Moon. Over the land which we were crossing, the tideless ocean had once been half a mile deep, and now the only trace of moisture was the hoarfrost one could sometimes find in caves which the searing sunlight never penetrated.

We had begun our journey early in the slow lunar dawn, and still had almost a week of Earth-time before nightfall. Half a dozen times a day we would leave our vehicle and go outside in the space-suits to hunt for interesting minerals, or to place markers for the guidance of future travelers. It was an uneventful routine. There is nothing hazardous or even particularly exciting about lunar exploration. We could live comfortably for a month in our pressurized tractors, and if we ran into trouble we could always radio for help and sit tight until one of the spaceships came to our rescue.

I said just now that there was nothing exciting about lunar exploration, but of course that isn't true. One could never grow tired of those incredible mountains, so much more rugged than the gentle hills of Earth. We never knew, as we rounded the capes and promontories of that vanished sea, what new splendors would be revealed to us. The whole southern curve of the Mare Crisium is a vast delta where a score of rivers once found their way into the ocean, fed perhaps by the torrential rains that must have lashed the mountains in the brief volcanic age when the Moon was young. Each of these ancient valleys was an invitation, challenging us to climb into the unknown uplands beyond. But we had a hundred miles still to cover, and could only look longingly at the heights which others must scale.

We kept Earth-time aboard the tractor, and precisely at 2200 hours the final radio message would be sent out to Base and we would close down for the day. Outside, the rocks would still be burning beneath the almost vertical Sun, but to us it was night until we awoke again eight hours later. Then one of us would prepare breakfast, there would be a great buzzing of electric razors, and someone would switch on the short-wave radio from Earth. Indeed, when the smell of frying sausages began to fill the cabin, it was sometimes hard to believe that we were not back on our own world—everything was so normal and homely, apart from the feeling of decreased weight and the unnatural slowness with which objects fell.

It was my turn to prepare breakfast in the corner of the main cabin that served as a galley. I can remember that moment quite vividly after all these years, for the radio had just played one of my favorite melodies, the old Welsh air, "David of the White Rock." Our driver was already outside in his space-suit, inspecting our caterpillar treads. My assistant, Louis Garnett, was up forward in the control position, making some belated entries in yesterday's log.

As I stood by the frying pan waiting, like any terrestrial housewife, for the sausages to brown, I let my gaze wander idly over the mountain walls which covered the whole of the southern horizon, marching out of sight to east and west below the curve of the Moon. They seemed only a mile or two from the tractor, but I knew that the nearest was twenty miles away. On the Moon, of course, there is no loss of detail with distance—none of that almost imperceptible haziness which softens and sometimes transfigures all far-off things on Earth.

Those mountains were ten thousand feet high, and they climbed steeply out of the plain as if ages ago some subterranean eruption had smashed them skywards through the molten crust. The base of even the nearest was hidden from sight by the steeply curving surface of the plain, for the Moon is a very little world, and from where I was standing the horizon was only two miles away.

I lifted my eyes towards the peaks which no man had ever climbed, the peaks which, before the coming of terrestrial life, had watched the retreating oceans sink sullenly into their graves, taking with them the hope and the morning promise of a world. The sunlight was beating against those ramparts with a glare that hurt the eyes, yet only a little way above them the stars were shining steadily in a sky blacker than a winter midnight on Earth.

I was turning away when my eye caught a metallic glitter high on the ridge of a great promontory thrusting out into the sea thirty miles to the west. It was a dimensionless point of light, as if a star had been clawed from the sky by one of those cruel peaks, and I imagined that some smooth rock surface was catching the sunlight and heliographing it straight into my eyes. Such things were not uncommon. When the Moon is in her second quarter, observers on Earth can sometimes see the great ranges in the Oceanus Procellarum burning with a blue-white iridescence as the sunlight flashes from their slopes and leaps again from world to world. But I was curious to know what kind of rock could be shining so brightly up there, and I climbed into the observation turret and swung our four-inch telescope round to the west.

I could see just enough to tantalize me. Clear and sharp in the field of vision, the mountain peaks seemed only half a mile away, but whatever was catching the sunlight was still too small to be resolved. Yet it seemed to have an elusive symmetry, and the summit upon which it rested was curiously flat. I stared for a long time at that glittering enigma, straining my eyes into space, until presently a smell of burning from the galley told me that our breakfast sausages had made their quarter-million-mile journey in vain.

All that morning we argued our way across the Mare Crisium while the western mountains reared higher in the sky. Even when we were out prospecting in the space-suits, the discussion would continue over the radio. It was absolutely certain, my companions argued, that there had never been any form of intelligent life on the Moon. The only living things that had ever existed there were a few primitive plants and their slightly less degenerate ancestors. I know that as well as anyone, but there are times when a scientist must not be afraid to make a fool of himself.

"Listen," I said at last, "I'm going up there, if only for my own peace of mind. That mountain's less than twelve thousand feet high—that's only two thousand under Earth gravity—and I can make the trip in twenty hours at the outside. I've always wanted to go up into those hills, anyway, and this gives me an excellent excuse."

"If you don't break your neck," said Garnett, "you'll be the laughing-stock of the expedition when we get back to Base. That mountain will probably be called Wilson's Folly from now on."

"I won't break my neck," I said firmly. "Who was the first man to climb Pico and Helicon?"

"But weren't you rather younger in those days?" asked Louis gently.

"That," I said with great dignity, "is as good a reason as any for going."

We went to bed early that night, after driving the tractor to within half a mile of the promontory. Garnett was coming with me in the morning; he was a good climber, and had often been with me on such exploits before. Our driver was only too glad to be left in charge of the machine.

At first sight, those cliffs seemed completely unscalable, but to anyone with a good head for heights, climbing is easy on a world where all weights are only a sixth of their normal value. The real danger in lunar mountaineering lies in overconfidence; a six-hundred-foot drop on the Moon can kill you just as thoroughly as a hundred-foot fall on Earth.

We made our first halt on a wide ledge about four thousand feet above the plain. Climbing had not been very difficult, but my limbs were stiff with the unaccustomed effort, and I was glad of the rest. We could still see the tractor as a tiny metal insect far down at the foot of the cliff, and we reported our progress to the driver before starting on the next ascent.

Inside our suits it was comfortably cool, for the refrigeration units were fighting the fierce sun and carrying away the body-heat of our exertions. We seldom spoke to each other, except to pass climbing instructions and to discuss our best plan of ascent. I do not know what Garnett was thinking, probably that this was the craziest goose-chase he had ever embarked upon. I more than half agreed with him, but the joy of climbing, the knowledge that no man had ever gone this way before and the exhilaration of the steadily widening landscape gave me all the reward I needed.

I don't think I was particularly excited when I saw in front of us the wall of rock I had first inspected through the telescope from thirty miles away.

It would level off about fifty feet above our heads, and there on the plateau would be the thing that had lured me over these barren wastes. It was, almost certainly, nothing more than a boulder splintered ages ago by a falling meteor, and with its cleavage planes still fresh and bright in this incorruptible, unchanging silence.

There were no hand-holds on the rock face, and we had to use a grapnel. My tired arms seemed to gain new strength as I swung the three-pronged metal anchor round my head and sent it sailing up towards the stars. The first time it broke loose and came falling slowly back when we pulled the rope. On the third attempt, the prongs gripped firmly and our combined weights could not shift it.

Garnett looked at me anxiously. I could tell that he wanted to go first, but I smiled back at him through the glass of my helmet and shook my head. Slowly, taking my time, I began the final ascent.

Even with my space-suit, I weighed only forty pounds here, so I pulled myself up hand over hand without bothering to use my feet. At the rim I paused and waved to my companion, then I scrambled over the edge and stood upright, staring ahead of me.

You must understand that until this very moment I had been almost completely convinced that there could be nothing strange or unusual for me to find here. Almost, but not quite; it was that haunting doubt that had driven me forward. Well, it was a doubt no longer, but the haunting had scarcely begun.

I was standing on a plateau perhaps a hundred feet across. It had once been smooth—too smooth to be natural—but falling meteors had pitted and scored its surface through immeasurable eons. It had been levelled to support a glittering, roughly pyramidal structure, twice as high as a man, that was set in the rock like a gigantic, many-faceted jewel.

Probably no emotion at all filled my mind in those first few seconds. Then I felt a great lifting of my heart, and a strange, inexpressible joy. For I loved the Moon, and now I knew that the creeping moss of Aristarchus and Eratosthenes was not the only life she had brought forth in her youth. The old, discredited dream of the first explorers was true. There had, after all, been a lunar civilization—and I was the first to find it. That I had come perhaps a hundred million years too late did not distress me; it was enough to have come at all.

My mind was beginning to function normally, to analyse and to ask questions. Was this a building, a shrine—or something for which my language had no name? If a building, then why was it erected in so uniquely inaccessible a spot? I wondered if it might be a temple, and I could picture the adepts of some strange priesthood calling on their gods to preserve them as the life of the Moon ebbed with the dying oceans, and calling on their gods in vain.

I took a dozen steps forward to examine the thing more closely, but some sense of caution kept me from going too near. I knew a little of archaeology, and tried to guess the cultural level of the civilisation that must have smoothed this mountain and raised the glittering mirror surfaces that still dazzled my eyes.

The Egyptians could have done it, I thought, if their workmen had possessed whatever strange materials these far more ancient architects had used. Because of the thing's smallness, it did not occur to me that I might be looking at the handiwork of a race more advanced than my own. The idea that the Moon had possessed intelligence at all was still almost too tremendous to grasp, and my pride would not let me take the final, humiliating plunge.

And then I noticed something that set the scalp crawling at the back of my neck—something so trivial and so innocent that many would never have noticed it at all. I have said that the plateau was scarred by meteors: it was also coated inches-deep with the cosmic dust that is always filtering down upon the surface of any world where there are no winds to disturb it. Yet the dust and the meteor scratches ended quite abruptly in a wide circle enclosing the little pyramid, as though an invisible wall was protecting it from the ravages of time and the slow but ceaseless bombardment from space.

There was someone shouting in my earphones, and I realised that Garnett had been calling me for some time. I walked unsteadily to the edge of the cliff and signalled him to join me, not trusting myself to speak. Then I went back towards that circle in the dust. I picked up a fragment of splintered rock and tossed it gently towards the shining enigma. If the pebble had vanished at that invisible barrier I should not have been surprised, but it seemed to hit a smooth, hemispherical surface and slide gently to the ground.

I knew then that I was looking at nothing that could be matched in the antiquity of my own race. This was not a building, but a machine, protecting itself with forces that had challenged Eternity. Those forces, whatever they might be, were still operating, and perhaps I had already come too close. I thought of all the radiations man had trapped and tamed in the past century. For all I knew, I might be as irrevocably doomed as if I had stepped into the deadly, silent aura of an unshielded atomic pile.

I remember turning then towards Garnett, who had joined me and was now standing motionless at my side. He seemed quite oblivious to me, so I did not disturb him but walked to the edge of the cliff in an effort to marshal my thoughts. There below me lay the Mare Crisium—Sea of Crises, indeed—strange and weird to most men, but reassuringly familiar to me. I lifted my eyes towards the crescent Earth, lying in her cradle of stars, and I wondered what her clouds had covered when these unknown builders had finished their work. Was it the steaming jungle of the Carboniferous, the bleak shore-line over which the first amphibians must crawl to conquer the land—or, earlier still, the long loneliness before the coming of life?

Do not ask me why I did not guess the truth sooner—the truth that seems so obvious now. In the first excitement of my discovery, I had assumed without question that this crystalline apparition had been built by some race belonging to the Moon's remote past, but suddenly, and with overwhelming force, the belief came to me that it was as alien to the Moon as I myself.

In twenty years we had found no trace of life but a few degenerate plants. No lunar civilisation, whatever its doom, could have left but a single token of its existence.

I looked at the shining pyramid again, and the more remote it seemed from anything that had to do with the Moon. And suddenly I felt myself shaking with a foolish, hysterical laughter, brought on by excitement and overexertion: for I had imagined that the little pyramid was speaking to me and was saying: "Sorry, I'm a stranger here myself."

It has taken us twenty years to crack that invisible shield and to reach the machine inside those crystal walls. What we could not understand, we broke at last with the savage might of atomic power and now I have seen the fragments of the lovely, glittering thing I found up there on the mountain.

They are meaningless. The mechanisms—if indeed they are mechanisms—of the pyramid belong to a technology that lies far beyond our horizon, perhaps to the technology of paraphysical forces.

The mystery haunts us all the more now that the other planets have been reached and we know that only Earth has ever been the home of intelligent life in our Universe. Nor could any lost civilisation of our own world have built that machine, for the thickness of the meteoric dust on the plateau has enabled us to measure its age. It was set there upon its mountain before life had emerged from the seas of Earth.

When our world was half its present age, *something* from the stars swept through the Solar System, left this token of its passage, and went again upon its way. Until we destroyed it, that machine was still fulfilling the purpose of its builders; and as to that purpose, here is my guess.

Nearly a hundred thousand million stars are turning in the circle of the Milky Way, and long ago other races on the worlds of other suns must have scaled and passed the heights that we have reached. Think of such civilisations, far back in time against the fading afterglow of Creation, masters of a universe so young that life as yet had come only to a handful of worlds. Theirs would have been a loneliness we cannot imagine, the loneliness of gods looking out across infinity and finding none to share their thoughts.

They must have searched the star-clusters as we have searched the planets. Everywhere there would be worlds, but they would be empty or peopled with crawling, mindless things. Such was our Earth, the smoke of the great volcanoes still staining the skies, when that first ship of the peoples of the dawn came sliding in from the abyss beyond Pluto. It passed the frozen outer worlds, knowing that life could play no part in their destinies. It came to rest among the inner planets, warming themselves around the fire of the Sun and waiting for their stories to begin.

Those wanderers must have looked on Earth, circling safely in the narrow zone between fire and ice, and must have guessed that it was the favorite of the Sun's children. Here, in the distant future, would be intelligence; but there were countless stars before them still, and they might never come this way again.

So they left a sentinel, one of millions they have scattered throughout the Universe, watching over all worlds with the promise of life. It was a beacon that down the ages has been patiently signaling the fact that no one had discovered it.

Perhaps you understand now why that crystal pyramid was set upon the Moon instead of on the Earth. Its builders were not concerned with races still struggling up from savagery. They would be interested in our civilization only if we proved our fitness to survive—by crossing space and so escaping from the Earth, our cradle. That is the challenge that all intelligent races must meet, sooner or later. It is a double challenge, for it depends in turn upon the conquest of atomic energy and the last choice between life and death.

Once we had passed that crisis, it was only a matter of time before we found the pyramid and forced it open. Now its signals have ceased, and those whose duty it is will be turning their minds upon Earth. Perhaps they wish to help our infant civilization. But they must be very, very old, and the old are often insanely jealous of the young.

I can never look now at the Milky Way without wondering from which of those banked clouds of stars the emissaries are coming. If you will pardon so commonplace a simile, we have set off the fire-alarm and have nothing to do but to wait.

I do not think we will have to wait for long.

ROBERT SHECKLEY

Specialist

{1953}

Few sf writers found a rich vein of humor in Cold War anxieties, but Robert Sheckley (1928–2005) was insouciant in an era when most sf writers were immersed in doomsday scenarios. His nearly four hundred stories enact droll reversals of the genre's most cherished plot-lines, as in his early "AAA Ace Interplanetary Decontamination Service" tales featuring the space adventures of hare-brained Arnold and his more practical sidekick Gregor. In *Trillion Year Spree* (1986), Brian Aldiss praised Sheckley's best work as a refreshing cocktail of "Voltaire-and-soda."

There was also a darker side to his writing, a focus on grim games. In "The Seventh Victim" (April 1953; remade into the Italian film *The Tenth Victim* in 1965), war has been eliminated, but to provide outlets for aggression, the State issues hunting licenses for bored individuals to track down and kill randomly selected prior hunters, who must serve their turn as prey. In "The Prize of Peril" (1958), televised in Germany (1970) and filmed in France as *Le Prix du Danger* (1983), a man must elude a team of people assigned to kill him: the hunt is televised for a week, and if he survives he wins a large cash prize. Sheckley's sardonic view of mass media may have stemmed from the fifteen episodes he wrote for *Captain Video* (1949–55), a television serial intended for children that at once attracted a huge adult audience.

Among several dozen novels, his most notable are *Mindswap* (1966), in which would-be space traveler Marvin Flynn is scammed by an unscrupulous body broker, acquiring and losing a series of alien bodies; and *The Game of X* (1965), a James Bond spoof in which an ordinary tourist is mistaken for a super-spy—John le Carré admired it. Douglas Adams is the recent writer most often compared to Sheckley, yet Adams's absurdist humor in *The Hitchhiker's Guide to the Galaxy* (novelization 1969) was in tune with a postmodern era that invited playful bricolage, whereas Sheckley, in 2001 deemed a "Writer Emeritus" and not a "Grand Master" by the Science Fiction Writers of America, spent most of his career contending against sf's penchant for the big book, the big concept. At his best writing short fiction—something of a miniaturist—he worked against the grain of the genre's self-aggrandizing tendencies.

Although he was born in Brooklyn and died in Poughkeepsie, he moved around for much of his life, living in the United States on both coasts and in Mexico, Ibiza, London, and Paris. Married—and split—five times, he was a free spirit in a buttoned-down world: it seems fitting that he is buried in upstate New York at Woodstock. It is hard to imagine him at slick *Omni* magazine during the Reagan years; but he arrived in Manhattan following a bohemian hiatus on Ibiza in January 1980 and for almost two years was *Omni*'s fiction editor, among other things shepherding William Gibson's "Johnny Mnemonic" (1981) into print.

"Specialist," whose human protagonist is a soldier on furlough, may pay indirect tribute to Sheckley's military service. He enlisted after high school, serving in the army in Korea from 1946 to 1948, perhaps as a specialist, the military rank of a PFC earning extra pay for specified skills. The story, first printed in *Galaxy* in April 1953, considers the idea of specialization in more literal ways, too, replacing sf's usual emphasis on survival of the fittest with a celebration of teamwork. Traversing space requires cooperative interaction among specialized beings from different worlds, just as human beings and "Partners" join forces in deep space in Cordwainer Smith's "The Game of Rat and Dragon" (1955). With *The Time Machine* (1895) H. G. Wells began the genre's long fascination with Darwin's idea of competition as essential to realizing human potential; but in this story Robert Sheckley, as so often in his sf, lightly begs to differ.

The photon storm struck without warning, pouncing upon the Ship from behind a bank of giant red stars. Eye barely had time to flash a last-second warning through Talker before it was upon them.

It was Talker's third journey into deep space, and his first light-pressure storm. He felt a sudden pang of fear as the Ship yawed violently, caught the force of the wave-front and careened end for end. Then the fear was gone, replaced by a strong pulse of excitement.

Why should he be afraid, he asked himself—hadn't be been trained for just this sort of emergency?

He had been talking to Feeder when the storm hit, but he cut off the conversation abruptly. He hoped Feeder would be all right. It was the youngster's first deep-space trip.

The wirelike filaments that made up most of Talker's body were extended throughout the Ship. Quickly he withdrew all except the ones linking him to

Eye, Engine, and the Walls. This was strictly their job now. The rest of the Crew would have to shift for themselves until the storm was over.

Eye had flattened his disklike body against a Wall, and had one seeing organ extended outside the Ship. For greater concentration, the rest of his seeing organs were collapsed, clustered against his body.

Through Eye's seeing organ, Talker watched the storm. He translated Eye's purely visual image into a direction for Engine, who shoved the Ship around to meet the waves. At appreciably the same time, Talker translated direction into velocity for the Walls, who stiffened to meet the shocks.

The coordination was swift and sure—Eye measuring the waves, Talker relaying the messages to Engine and Walls, Engine driving the ship nose-first into the waves, and Walls bracing to meet the shock.

Talker forgot any fear he might have had in the swiftly functioning teamwork. He had no time to think. As the Ship's communication system, he had to translate and flash his messages at top speed, coordinating information and directing action.

In a matter of minutes, the storm was over.

"All right," Talker said. "Let's see if there was any damage." His filaments had become tangled during the storm, but he untwisted and extended them through the Ship, plugging everyone into circuit. "Engine?"

"I'm fine," Engine said. The tremendous old fellow had dampened his plates during the storm, easing down the atomic explosions in his stomach. No storm could catch an experienced spacer like Engine unaware.

"Walls."

The Walls reported one by one, and this took a long time. There were almost a thousand of them, thin, rectangular fellows making up the entire skin of the Ship. Naturally, they had reinforced their edges during the storm, giving the whole Ship resiliency. But one or two were dented badly.

Doctor announced that he was all right. He removed Talker's filament from his head, taking himself out of circuit, and went to work on the dented Walls. Made mostly of hands, Doctor had clung to an Accumulator during the storm.

"Let's go a little faster now," Talker said, remembering that there still was the problem of determining where they were. He opened the circuit to the four Accumulators. "How are you?" he asked.

There was no answer. The Accumulators were asleep. They had had their receptors open during the storm and were bloated on energy. Talker twitched his filaments around them, but they didn't stir.

"Let me," Feeder said. Feeder had taken quite a beating before planting his suction cups to a Wall, but his cockiness was intact. He was the only member of the Crew who never needed Doctor's attention; his body was quite capable of repairing itself.

He scuttled across the floor on a dozen or so tentacles, and booted the nearest Accumulator. The big, conical storage unit opened one eye, then closed it again. Feeder kicked him again, getting no response. He reached for the Accumulator's safety valve and drained off some energy.

"Stop that," the Accumulator said.

"Then wake up and report," Talker told him.

The Accumulators said testily that they were all right, as any fool could see. They had been anchored to the floor during the storm.

The rest of the inspection went quickly. Thinker was fine, and Eye was ecstatic over the beauty of the storm. There was only one casualty.

Pusher was dead. Bipedal, he didn't have the stability of the rest of the Crew. The storm had caught him in the middle of a floor, thrown him against a stiffened Wall, and broken several of his important bones. He was beyond Doctor's skill to repair.

They were silent for a while. It was always serious when a part of the Ship died. The Ship was a cooperative unit, composed entirely of the Crew. The loss of any member was a blow to all the rest.

It was especially serious now. They had just delivered a cargo to a port several thousand light-years from Galactic Center. There was no telling where they might be.

Eye crawled to a Wall and extended a seeing organ outside. The Walls let it through, then sealed around it. Eye's organ pushed out, far enough from the Ship so he could view the entire sphere of stars. The picture traveled through Talker, who gave it to Thinker.

Thinker lay in one corner of the room, a great shapeless blob of protoplasm. Within him were all the memories of his space-going ancestors. He considered the picture, compared it rapidly with others stored in his cells, and said, "No galactic planets within reach."

Talker automatically translated for everyone. It was what they had feared.

Eye, with Thinker's help, calculated that they were several hundred light-years off their course, on the galactic periphery.

Every Crew member knew what that meant. Without a Pusher to boost the Ship to a multiple of the speed of light, they would never get home. The trip back, without a Pusher, would take longer than most of their lifetimes.

"What would you suggest?" Talker asked Thinker.

This was too vague a question for the literal-minded Thinker. He asked to have it rephrased.

"What would be our best line of action," Talker asked, "to get back to a galactic planet?"

Thinker needed several minutes to go through all the possibilities stored in his cells. In the meantime, Doctor had patched the Walls and was asking to be given something to eat.

"In a little while we'll all eat," Talker said, twitching his tendrils nervously. Even though he was the second youngest Crew member—only Feeder was younger—the responsibility was largely on him. This was still an emergency; he had to coordinate information and direct action.

One of the Walls suggested that they get good and drunk. This unrealistic solution was vetoed at once. It was typical of the Walls' attitude, however. They were fine workers and good shipmates, but happy-go-lucky fellows at best. When they returned to their home planets, they would probably blow all their wages on a spree.

"Loss of the Ship's Pusher cripples the Ship for sustained faster-than-light speeds," Thinker began without preamble, "The nearest galactic planet is four hundred and five light-years off."

Talker translated all this instantly along his wave-packet body.

"Two courses of action are open. First, the Ship can proceed to the nearest galactic planet under atomic power from Engine. This will take approximately two hundred years. Engine might still be alive at this time, although no one else will.

"Second, locate a primitive planet in this region, upon which are latent Pushers. Find one and train him. Have him push the Ship back to galactic territory."

Thinker was silent, having given all the possibilities he could find in the memories of his ancestors.

They held a quick vote and decided upon Thinker's second alternative. There was no choice, really. It was the only one which offered them any hope of getting back to their homes.

"All right," Talker said. "Let's eat. I think we all deserve it."

The body of the dead Pusher was shoved into the mouth of Engine, who consumed it at once, breaking down the atoms to energy. Engine was the only member of the Crew who lived on atomic energy.

For the rest, Feeder dashed up and loaded himself from the nearest Accumulator. Then he transformed the food within him into the substances each member ate. His body chemistry changed, altered, adapted, making the different foods for the Crew.

Eye lived entirely on a complex chlorophyll chain. Feeder reproduced this for him, then went over to give Talker his hydrocarbons, and the Walls their chlorine compound. For Doctor he made a facsimile of a silicate fruit that grew on Doctor's native planet.

Finally, feeding was over and the Ship back in order. The Accumulators were stacked in a corner, blissfully sleeping again. Eye was extending his vision as far as he could, shaping his main seeing organ for high-powered telescopic reception. Even in this emergency, Eye couldn't resist making verses. He announced that he was at work on a new narrative poem, called *Peripheral Glow*. No one wanted to hear it, so Eye fed it to Thinker, who stored everything, good or bad, right or wrong.

Engine never slept. Filled to the brim on Pusher, he shoved the Ship along at several times the speed of light.

The Walls were arguing among themselves about who had been the drunkest during their last leave.

Talker decided to make himself comfortable. He released his hold on the Walls and swung in the air, his small round body suspended by his criss-crossed network of filaments.

He thought briefly about Pusher. It was strange. Pusher had been everyone's friend and now he was forgotten. That wasn't because of indifference; it was because the Ship was a unit. The loss of a member was regretted, but the important thing was for the unit to go on.

The Ship raced through the suns of the periphery.

Thinker laid out a search spiral, calculating their odds on finding a Pusher planet at roughly four to one. In a week they found a planet of primitive Walls. Dropping low, they could see the leathery, rectangular fellows basking in the sun, crawling over rocks, stretching themselves thin in order to float in the breeze.

All the Ship's Walls heaved a sigh of nostalgia. It was just like home.

These Walls on the planet hadn't been contacted by a galactic team yet, and were still unaware of their great destiny—to join in the vast Cooperation of the Galaxy.

There were plenty of dead worlds in the spiral, and worlds too young to bear life. They found a planet of Talkers. The Talkers had extended their spidery communication lines across half a continent.

Talker looked at them eagerly, through Eye. A wave of self-pity washed over him. He remembered home, his family, his friends. He thought of the tree he was going to buy when he got back.

For a moment, Talker wondered what he was doing here, part of a Ship in a far corner of the Galaxy.

He shrugged off the mood. They were bound to find a Pusher planet, if they looked long enough.

At least, he hoped so.

There was a long stretch of arid worlds as the Ship speeded through the unexplored periphery. Then a planetful of primeval Engines, swimming in a radioactive ocean.

"This is rich territory," Feeder said to Talker. "Galactic should send a Contact party here."

"They probably will, after we get back," Talker said.

They were good friends, above and beyond the all-enveloping friendship of the Crew. It wasn't only because they were the youngest Crew members, although that had something to do with it. They both had the same kind of functions and that made for a certain rapport. Talker translated languages; Feeder transformed foods. Also, they looked somewhat alike. Talker was a central core with radiating filaments; Feeder was a central core with radiating tentacles.

Talker thought that Feeder was the next most aware being on the Ship. He was never really able to understand how some of the others carried on the processes of consciousness.

More suns, more planets. Engine started to overheat. Usually, Engine was used only for taking off and landing, and for fine maneuvering in a planetary group. Now he had been running continuously for weeks, both over and under the speed of light. The strain was telling on him.

Feeder, with Doctor's help, rigged a cooling system for him. It was crude, but it had to suffice. Feeder rearranged nitrogen, oxygen and hydrogen atoms to make a coolant for the system. Doctor diagnosed a long rest for Engine. He said that the gallant old fellow couldn't stand the strain for more than a week.

The search continued, with the Crew's spirits gradually dropping. They all realized that Pushers were rather rare in the Galaxy, as compared to the fertile Walls and Engines.

The Walls were getting pock-marked from interstellar dust. They complained that they would need a full beauty treatment when they got home. Talker assured them that the company would pay for it.

Even Eye was getting bloodshot from staring into space so continuously.

They dipped over another planet. Its characteristics were flashed to Thinker, who mulled over them.

Closer, and they could make out the forms.

Pushers! Primitive Pushers!

They zoomed back into space to make plans. Feeder produced twenty-three different kinds of intoxicants for a celebration.

The Ship wasn't fit to function for three days.

"Everyone ready now?" Talker asked, a bit fuzzily. He had a hangover that burned all along his nerve ends. What a drunk he had thrown! He had a vague recollection of embracing Engine, and inviting him to share his tree when they got home.

He shuddered at the idea.

The rest of the Crew were pretty shaky, too. The Walls were letting air leak into space; they were just too wobbly to seal their edges properly. Doctor had passed out.

But the worst off was Feeder. Since his system could adapt to any type of fuel except atomic, be had been sampling every batch he made, whether it was an unbalanced iodine, pure oxygen or a supercharged ester. He was really miserable. His tentacles, usually a healthy aqua, were shot through with orange streaks. His system was working furiously, purging itself of everything, and Feeder was suffering the effects of the purge.

The only sober ones were Thinker and Engine. Thinker didn't drink, which was unusual for a spacer, though typical of Thinker, and Engine couldn't.

They listened while Thinker reeled off some astounding facts. From Eye's pictures of the planet's surface, Thinker had detected the presence of metallic construction. He put forth the alarming suggestion that these Pushers had constructed a mechanical civilization.

"That's impossible," three of the Walls said flatly, and most of the Crew were inclined to agree with them. All the metal they had ever seen had been buried in the ground or lying around in worthless oxidized chunks.

"Do you mean that they make things out of metal?" Talker demanded. "Out of just plain dead metal? What could they make?"

"They couldn't make anything," Feeder said positively. "It would break down constantly. I mean metal doesn't *know* when it's weakening."

But it seemed to be true. Eye magnified his pictures, and everyone could see that the Pushers had made vast shelters, vehicles, and other articles from inanimate material.

The reason for this was not readily apparent, but it wasn't a good sign. However, the really hard part was over. The Pusher planet had been found. All that remained was the relatively easy job of convincing a native Pusher.

That shouldn't be too difficult. Talker knew that cooperation was the keystone of the Galaxy, even among primitive peoples.

The Crew decided not to land in a populated region. Of course, there was no reason not to expect a friendly greeting, but it was the job of a Contact Team to get in touch with them as a race. All they wanted was an individual.

Accordingly, they picked out a sparsely populated land-mass, drifting in while that side of the planet was dark.

They were able to locate a solitary Pusher almost at once.

Eye adapted his vision to see in the dark, and they followed the Pusher's movements. He lay down, after a while, beside a small fire. Thinker told them that this was a well-known resting habit of Pushers.

Just before dawn, the Walls opened, and Feeder, Talker, and Doctor came out.

Feeder dashed forward and tapped the creature on the shoulder. Talker followed with a communication tendril.

The Pusher opened his seeing organs, blinked them, and made a movement with his eating organ. Then he leaped to his feet and started to run.

The three Crew members were amazed. The Pusher hadn't even waited to find out what the three of them wanted!

Talker extended a filament rapidly, and caught the Pusher, fifty feet away, by a limb. The Pusher fell.

"Treat him gently," Feeder said. "He might be startled by our appearance." He twitched his tendrils at the idea of a Pusher—one of the strangest sights in the Galaxy, with his multiple organs—being startled at someone else's appearance.

Feeder and Doctor scurried to the fallen Pusher, picked him up and carried him back to the Ship.

The Walls sealed again. They released the Pusher and prepared to talk.

As soon as he was free, the Pusher sprang to his limbs and ran at the place where the Walls had sealed. He pounded against them frantically, his eating organ open and vibrating.

"Stop that," the Wall said. He bulged, and the Pusher tumbled to the floor. Instantly, he jumped up and started to run forward.

"Stop him," Talker said. "He might hurt himself."

One of the Accumulators woke up enough to roll into the Pusher's path. The Pusher fell, got up again, and ran on.

Talker had his filaments in the front of the Ship also, and he caught the Pusher in the bow. The Pusher started to tear at his tendrils, and Talker let go hastily.

"Plug him into the communication system!" Feeder shouted. "Maybe we can reason with him!"

Talker advanced a filament toward the Pusher's head, waving it in the universal sign of communication. But the Pusher continued his amazing behavior, jumping out of the way. He had a piece of metal in his hand and he was waving it frantically.

"What do you think he's going to do with that?" Feeder asked. The Pusher started to attack the side of the Ship, pounding at one of the Walls. The Wall stiffened instinctively and the metal snapped.

"Leave him alone," Talker said. "Give him a chance to calm down."

Talker consulted with Thinker, but they couldn't decide what to do about the Pusher. He wouldn't accept communication. Every time Talker extended a filament, the Pusher showed all the signs of violent panic. Temporarily, it was an impasse.

Thinker vetoed the plan of finding another Pusher on the planet. He considered this Pusher's behavior typical; nothing would be gained by approaching another. Also, a planet was supposed to be contacted only by a Contact Team.

If they couldn't communicate with this Pusher, they never would with another on the planet.

"I think I know what the trouble is," Eye said. He crawled up on an Accumulator. "These Pushers have evolved a mechanical civilization. Consider for a minute how they went about it. They developed the use of their fingers, like Doctor, to shape metal. They utilized their seeing organs, like myself. And probably countless other organs." He paused for effect.

"These Pushers have become unspecialized!"

They argued over it for several hours. The Walls maintained that no intelligent creature could be unspecialized. It was unknown in the Galaxy. But the evidence was before them—the Pusher cities, their vehicles . . . This Pusher, exemplifying the rest, seemed capable of a multitude of things.

He was able to do everything except Push!

Thinker supplied a partial explanation. "This is not a primitive planet. It is relatively old and should have been in the Cooperation thousands of years ago. Since it was not, the Pushers upon it were robbed of their birthright. Their ability, their specialty was to Push, but there was nothing *to* Push. Naturally, they have developed a deviant culture.

"Exactly what this culture is, we can only guess. But on the basis of the evidence, there is reason to believe that these Pushers are—uncooperative."

Thinker had a habit of uttering the most shattering statement in the quietest possible way.

"It is entirely possible," Thinker went on inexorably, "that these Pushers will have nothing to do with us. In which case, our chances are approximately 283 to 1 against finding another Pusher planet."

"We can't be sure he won't cooperate," Talker said, "until we get him into communication." He found it almost impossible to believe that any intelligent creature would refuse to cooperate willingly.

"But how?" Feeder asked. They decided upon a course of action. Doctor walked slowly up to the Pusher, who backed away from him. In the meantime, Talker extended a filament outside the Ship, around, and in again, behind the Pusher.

The Pusher backed against a Wall—and Talker shoved the filament through the Pusher's head, into the communication socket in the center of his brain.

The Pusher collapsed.

When he came to, Feeder and Doctor had to hold the Pusher's limbs, or he would have ripped out the communication line. Talker exercised his skill in learning the Pusher's language.

It wasn't too hard. All Pusher languages were of the same family, and this was no exception. Talker was able to catch enough surface thoughts to form a pattern.

He tried to communicate with the Pusher.

The Pusher was silent.

"I think he needs food," Feeder said. They remembered that it had been almost two days since they had taken the Pusher on board. Feeder worked up some standard Pusher food and offered it.

"My God! A steak!" the Pusher said.

The Crew cheered along Talker's communication circuits. The Pusher had said his first words!

Talker examined the words and searched his memory. He knew about two hundred Pusher languages and many more simple variations. He found that this Pusher was speaking a cross between two Pusher tongues.

After the Pusher had eaten, he looked around. Talker caught his thoughts and broadcast them to the Crew.

The Pusher had a queer way of looking at the Ship. He saw it as a riot of colors. The walls undulated. In front of him was something resembling a gigantic spider, colored black and green, with his web running all over the Ship and into the heads of all the creatures. He saw Eye as a strange, naked little animal, something between a skinned rabbit and an egg yolk—whatever those things were.

Talker was fascinated by the new perspective the Pusher's mind gave him. He had never seen things that way before. But now that the Pusher was pointing it out, Eye *was a* pretty funny-looking creature.

They settled down to communication.

"What in hell *are* you things?" the Pusher asked, much calmer now than he had been during the two days. "Why did you grab me? Have I gone nuts?"

"No," Talker said, "you are not psychotic. We are a galactic trading ship. We were blown off our course by a storm and our Pusher was killed."

"Well, what does that have to do with me?"

"We would like you to join our Crew," Talker said, "to be our new Pusher."

The Pusher thought it over after the situation was explained to him. Talker could catch the feeling of conflict in the Pusher's thoughts. He hadn't decided whether to accept this as a real situation or not. Finally, the Pusher decided that he wasn't crazy.

"Look, boys," he said, "I don't know what you are or how this makes sense. I have to get out of here. I'm on a furlough, and if I don't get back soon, the U.S. Army's going to be very interested."

Talker asked the Pusher to give him more information about "army," and he fed it to Thinker.

"These Pushers engage in personal combat," was Thinker's conclusion.

"But *why*?" Talker asked. Sadly he admitted to himself that Thinker might have been right; the Pusher didn't show many signs of willingness to cooperate.

"I'd like to help you lads out," Pusher said, "but I don't know where you get the idea that I could push anything this size. You'd need a whole division of tanks just to budge it."

"Do you approve of these wars?" Talker asked, getting a suggestion from Thinker.

"Nobody likes war—not those who have to do the dying at least."

"Then why do you fight them?"

The Pusher made a gesture with his eating organ, which Eye picked up and sent to Thinker. "It's kill or be killed. You guys know what war is, don't you?"

"We don't have any war," Talker said.

"You're lucky," the Pusher said bitterly. "We do. Plenty of them."

"Of course," Talker said. He had the full explanation from Thinker now. "Would you like to end them?"

"Of course I would."

"Then come with us. Be our Pusher."

The Pusher stood up and walked up to an Accumulator. He sat down on it and doubled the ends of his upper limbs.

"How the hell can I stop all wars?" the Pusher demanded. "Even if I went to the big shots and told them—"

"You won't have to," Talker said. "All you have to do is come with us. Push us to our base. Galactic will send a Contact Team to your planet. That will end your wars."

"The hell you say," the Pusher replied. "You boys are stranded here, huh? Good enough. No monsters are going to take over Earth."

Bewildered, Talker tried to understand the reasoning. Had he said something wrong? Was it possible that the Pusher didn't understand him?

"I thought you wanted to end wars," Talker said.

"Sure I do. But I don't want anyone *making* us stop. I'm no traitor. I'd rather fight."

"No one will make you stop. You will just stop because there will be no further need for fighting."

"Do you know why we're fighting?"

"It's obvious."

"Yeah? What's your explanation?"

"You Pushers have been separated from the main stream of the Galaxy," Talker explained. "You have your specialty—pushing—but nothing to Push. Accordingly, you have no real jobs. You play with things—metal, inanimate objects—but find no real satisfaction. Robbed of your true vocation, you fight from sheer frustration.

"Once you find your place in the galactic Cooperation—and I assure you that it is an important place—your fighting will stop. Why should you fight, which is an unnatural occupation, when you can Push? Also, your mechanical civilization will end, since there will be no need for it."

The Pusher shook his head in what Talker guessed was a gesture of confusion. "What is this pushing?"

Talker told him as best he could. Since the job was out of his scope, he had only a general idea of what a Pusher did.

"You mean to say that *that* is what every Earthman should be doing?"

"Of course," Talker said. "It is your great specialty."

The Pusher thought about it for several minutes. "I think you want a physicist or a mentalist or something. I could never do anything like that. I'm a junior architect. And besides—well, it's difficult to explain."

But Talker had already caught Pusher's objection. He saw a Pusher female in his thoughts. No, two, three. And he caught a feeling of loneliness, strangeness. The Pusher was filled with doubts. He was afraid.

"When we reach galactic," Talker said, hoping it was the right thing, "you can meet other Pushers. Pusher females, too. All you Pushers look alike, so you should become friends with them. As far as loneliness in the Ship goes, it just doesn't exist. You don't understand the Cooperation yet. No one is lonely in the Cooperation."

The Pusher was still considering the idea of there being other Pushers. Talker couldn't understand why he was so startled at that. The Galaxy was filled with Pushers, Feeders, Talkers, and many other species, endlessly duplicated.

"I can't believe that anybody could end all war," Pusher said. "How do I know you're not lying?"

Talker felt as if he had been struck in the core. Thinker must have been right when he said these Pushers would be uncooperative. Was this going to be the end of Talker's career? Were he and the rest of the Crew going to spend the rest of their lives in space, because of the stupidity of a bunch of Pushers?

Even thinking this, Talker was able to feel sorry for the Pusher. It must be terrible, he thought. Doubting, uncertain, never trusting anyone. If these Pushers didn't find their place in the Galaxy, they would exterminate themselves. Their place in the Cooperation was long overdue.

"What can I do to convince you?" Talker asked.

In despair, he opened all the circuits to the Pusher. He let the Pusher see Engine's good-natured gruffness, the devil-may-care humor of the Walls; he showed him Eye's poetic attempts, and Feeder's cocky good nature. He opened his own mind and showed the Pusher a picture of his home planet, his family, the tree he was planning to buy when he got home.

The pictures told the story of all of them, from different planets, representing different ethics, united by a common bond—the galactic Cooperation.

The Pusher watched it all in silence.

After a while, he shook his head. The thought accompanying the gesture was uncertain, weak—but negative.

Talker told the Walls to open. They did, and the Pusher stared in amazement.

"You may leave," Talker said. "Just remove the communication line and go."

"What will you do?"

"We will look for another Pusher planet."

"Where? Mars? Venus?"

"We don't know. All we can do is hope there is another in this region."

The Pusher looked at the opening, then back at the Crew. He hesitated and his face screwed up in a grimace of indecision.

"All that you showed me was true?"

No answer was necessary.

"All right," the Pusher said suddenly. "I'll go. I'm a damned fool, but I'll go. If this means what you say—it *must* mean what you say!"

Talker saw that the agony of the Pusher's decision had forced him out of contact with reality. He believed that he was in a dream, where decisions are easy and unimportant.

"There's just one little trouble," Pusher said with the lightness of hysteria. "Boys, I'll be damned if I know how to Push. You said something about faster-than-light? I can't even run the mile in an hour."

"Of course you can Push," Talker assured him, hoping he was right. He knew what a Pusher's abilities were; but this one . . .

"Just try it."

"Sure," Pusher agreed. "I'll probably wake up out of this, anyhow."

They sealed the ship for takeoff while Pusher talked to himself.

"Funny," Pusher said. "I thought a camping trip would be a nice way to spend a furlough and all I do is get nightmares!"

Engine boosted the Ship into the air. The Walls were sealed and Eye was guiding them away from the planet.

"We're in open space now," Talker said. Listening to Pusher, he hoped his mind hadn't cracked. "Eye and Thinker will give a direction, I'll transmit it to you, and you Push along it."

"You're crazy," Pusher mumbled. "You must have the wrong planet. I wish you nightmares would go away."

"You're in the Cooperation now," Talker said desperately. "There's the direction. Push!"

The Pusher didn't do anything for a moment. He was slowly emerging from his fantasy, realizing that he wasn't in a dream, after all. He felt the Cooperation. Eye to Thinker, Thinker to Talker, Talker to Pusher, all intercoordinated with Walls, and with each other.

"What is this?" Pusher asked. He felt the oneness of the Ship, the great warmth, the closeness achieved only in the Cooperation.

He Pushed.

Nothing happened.

"Try again," Talker begged.

Pusher searched his mind. He found a deep well of doubt and fear. Staring into it, he saw his own tortured face.

Thinker illuminated it for him.

Pushers had lived with this doubt and fear for centuries. Pushers had fought through fear, killed through doubt.

That was where the Pusher organ was!

Human—specialist——Pusher—he entered fully into the Crew, merged with them, threw mental arms around the shoulders of Thinker and Talker.

Suddenly, the Ship shot forward at eight times the speed of light. It continued to accelerate.

WILLIAM TENN
The Liberation of Earth

{1953}

William Tenn is the pseudonym of Philip Klass (1920–2010), who was born in England but as a toddler emigrated with his mother to New York in order to join his father, a socialist, anti-militarist pacifist on the lam because of his refusal to serve in World War I. His mother remained an anglophile and something of an imperialist. Klass served in World War II, which his father saw as more just than the previous war, and eventually became a professor of English at Pennsylvania State University, teaching writing and science fiction. Among his students was David Morrell, who went on to write *First Blood* (1972) and unleash the character Rambo into American culture. Klass uses the name William Tenn for his fiction writing and Phil or Philip Klass for his nonfiction. Therefore, he is sometimes confused with his contemporary, Philip J. Klass, a UFO debunker and no relation. Tenn's most active period was during the 1950s and 1960s, during which time he built his reputation as a highly skilled and witty satirist primarily through his short stories. Among the most famous are "Child's Play" (1947), "Venus and the Seven Sexes" (1951), "Down Among the Dead Men" (1954), and the much later and very funny "On Venus, Have We Got a Rabbi" (1974). The latter is a prime example of his particular flair for Yiddish humor.

In spite of its obvious satire, "The Liberation of Earth" is not quite the laugh riot as "On Venus." Instead, "The Liberation of Earth" seems to channel Tenn's father's anger at the misuse of human lives to serve imperialist aims. The story is written in the style of an epic tale, its elevated diction contrasting with the misery it details. That misery is only gradually revealed, with the reader learning how completely devastated the planet has become only at the end of the story. The story shares a number of plot elements with Arthur C. Clarke's *Childhood's End* (also 1953), including the introduction of superior aliens seeking to reorganize humanity, apparently for their own good. In Tenn's version, however, the imperialist takeover is far from benign and the series of alien invasions illustrates the adage that history belongs to the victors, the narrator's language reflecting the propagandist bias of each conqueror and satirizing a number of common imperialist claims. Tenn's satire would have applied to the scramble for power among the various allied forces after World War II, as well as to the jingoistic posturing of the McCarthyites in the United States, but it continues to have relevance as each generation makes its own hegemonic claims and fights its own wars of liberation. The utter debasement of the narrator's condition reminds us that, whoever wins these fights, the human cost is dear.

This then, is the story of our liberation. Suck air and grab clusters. Heigh-ho, here is the tale.

August was the month, a Tuesday in August. These words are meaningless now, so far have we progressed; but many things known and discussed by our primitive ancestors, our unliberated, unreconstructed forefathers, are devoid of sense to our free minds. Still the tale must be told, with all of its incredible place-names and vanished points of reference.

Why must it be told? Have any of you a *better* thing to do? We have had water and weeds and lie in a valley of gusts. So rest, relax and listen. And suck air, suck air.

On a Tuesday in August, the ship appeared in the sky over France in a part of the world then known as Europe. Five miles long the ship was, and word has come down to us that it looked like an enormous silver cigar.

The tale goes on to tell of the panic and consternation among our forefathers when the ship abruptly materialized in the summer-blue sky. How they ran, how they shouted, how they pointed!

How they excitedly notified the United Nations, one of their chiefest institutions, that a strange metal craft of incredible size had materialized over their land. How they sent an order *here* to cause military aircraft to surround it with loaded weapons, gave instructions *there* for hastily grouped scientists, with signaling apparatus, to approach it with friendly gestures. How, under the great ship, men with cameras took pictures of it, men with typewriters wrote stories about it, and men with concessions sold models of it.

All these things did our ancestors, enslaved and unknowing, do. Then a tremendous slab snapped up in the middle of the ship and the first of the aliens stepped out in the complex tripodal gait that all humans were shortly to know and love so well. He wore a metallic garment to protect him from the effects of our atmospheric peculiarities, a garment of the opaque, loosely folded type that these, the first of our liberators, wore throughout their stay on Earth.

Speaking in a language none could understand, but booming deafeningly through a huge mouth about halfway up his twenty-five feet of height, the alien discoursed for exactly one hour, waited politely for a response when he had finished, and receiving none, retired into the ship.

That night, the first of our liberation! Or the first of our first liberation, should I say? *That* night, anyhow! Visualize our ancestors scurrying about their primitive intricacies: playing ice-hockey, televising, smashing atoms, red-baiting, conducting giveaway shows and signing affidavits—all the incredible minutiae that made the olden times such a frightful mass of cumulative detail in which to live—as compared with the breathless and majestic simplicity of the present.

The big question, of course, was—what had the alien said? Had he called on the human race to surrender? Had he announced that he was on a mission of peaceful trade and, having made what he considered a reasonable offer—for, let us say, the north polar ice-cap—politely withdrawn so that we could discuss his terms among ourselves in relative privacy? Or, possibly, had he merely announced that he was the newly appointed ambassador to Earth from a friendly and intelligent race—and would we please direct him to the proper authority so that he might submit his credentials?

Not to know was quite maddening.

Since decision rested with the diplomats, it was the last possibility which was held, very late that night, to be most likely; and early the next morning, accordingly, a delegation from the United Nations waited under the belly of the motionless star-ship. The delegation had been instructed to welcome the aliens to the outermost limits of its collective linguistic ability. As an additional earnest of mankind's friendly intentions, all military craft patrolling the air about the great ship were ordered to carry no more than one atom-bomb in their racks, and to fly a small white flag—along with the U.N. banner and their own national emblem. Thus did our ancestors face this, the ultimate challenge of history.

When the alien came forth a few hours later, the delegation stepped up to him, bowed, and, in the three official languages of the United Nations—English, French and Russian—asked him to consider this planet his home. He listened to them gravely, and then launched into his talk of the day before—which was evidently as highly charged with emotion and significance to him as it was completely incomprehensible to the representatives of world government.

Fortunately, a cultivated young Indian member of the secretariat detected a suspicious similarity between the speech of the alien and an obscure Bengali dialect whose anomalies he had once puzzled over. The reason, as we all know now, was that the last time Earth had been visited by aliens of this particular type, humanity's most advanced civilization lay in a moist valley in Bengal; extensive dictionaries of that language had been written, so that speech with the natives of Earth would present no problem to any subsequent exploring party.

However, I move ahead of my tale, as one who would munch on the succulent roots before the drier stem. Let me rest and suck air for a moment. Heigh-ho, truly those were tremendous experiences for our kind.

You, sir, now you sit back and listen. You are not yet of an age to Tell the Tale. I remember, *well enough do I remember* how my father told it, and his father before him. You will wait your turn as I did; you listen until too much high land between water holes blocks me off from life.

Then *you* may take your place in the juiciest weed patch and, reclining gracefully between sprints, recite the great epic of our liberation to the carelessly exercising young.

Pursuant to the young Hindu's suggestions, the one professor of comparative linguistics in the world capable of understanding and conversing in this peculiar version of the dead dialect was summoned from an academic convention in New York where he was reading a paper he had been working on for eighteen years: *An Initial Study of Apparent Relationships Between Several Past Participles in Ancient Sanskrit and an Equal Number of Noun Substantives in Modern Szechuanese.*

Yea, verily, all these things—and more, many more—did our ancestors in their besotted ignorance contrive to do. May we not count our freedoms indeed?

The disgruntled scholar, minus—as he kept insisting bitterly—some of his most essential word lists, was flown by fastest jet to the area south of Nancy which, in those long-ago days, lay in the enormous black shadow of the alien spaceship.

Here he was acquainted with his task by the United Nations delegation, whose nervousness had not been allayed by a new and disconcerting development. Several more aliens had emerged from the ship carrying great quantities of immense, shimmering metal which they proceeded to assemble into something that was obviously a machine—though it was taller than any skyscraper man had ever built, and seemed to make noises to itself like a talkative and sentient creature. The first alien still stood courteously in the neighborhood of the profusely perspiring diplomats; ever and anon he would go through his little speech again, in a language that had been almost forgotten when the cornerstone of the library of Alexandria was laid. The men from the U.N. would reply, each one hoping desperately to make up for the alien's lack of familiarity with his own tongue by such devices as hand gestures and facial expressions. Much later, a commission of anthropologists and psychologists brilliantly pointed out the difficulties of such physical, gestural communication with creatures possessing—as these aliens did—five manual appendages and a single, unwinking compound eye of the type the insects rejoice in.

The problems and agonies of the professor as he was trundled about the world in the wake of the aliens, trying to amass a usable vocabulary in a language whose peculiarities he could only extrapolate from the limited samples supplied him by one who must inevitably speak it with the most outlandish of foreign accents—these vexations were minor indeed compared to the disquiet felt by the representatives of world government.

They beheld the extra-terrestrial visitors move every day to a new site on their planet and proceed to assemble there a titanic structure of flickering metal which muttered nostalgically to itself, as if to keep alive the memory of those faraway factories which had given it birth. True, there was always the alien who would pause in his evidently supervisory labors to release the set little speech; but not even the excellent manners he displayed, in listening to upward of fifty-six replies in as many languages, helped dispel the panic caused whenever a human scientist, investigating the shimmering machines, touched a projecting edge and promptly shrank into a disappearing pinpoint. This, while not a frequent occurrence, happened often enough to cause chronic indigestion and insomnia among human administrators.

Finally, having used up most of his nervous system as fuel, the professor collated enough of the language to make conversation possible. He—and, through him, the world—was thereupon told the following:

The aliens were members of a highly advanced civilization which had spread its culture throughout the entire galaxy. Cognizant of the limitations of the as-yet-underdeveloped animals who had latterly become dominant upon Earth, they had placed us in a sort of benevolent ostracism. Until either we or our institutions had evolved to a level permitting, say, at least *associate* membership in the galactic federation (under the sponsoring tutelage, for the first few millennia, of one of the older, more widespread and more important species in that federation)—until that time, all invasions of our privacy and ignorance—except for a few scientific expeditions conducted under conditions of great secrecy—had been strictly forbidden by universal agreement.

Several individuals who had violated this ruling—at great cost to our racial sanity, and enormous profit to our reigning religions—had been so promptly and severely punished that no known infringements had occurred for some time. Our recent growth-curve had been satisfactory enough to cause hopes that a bare thirty or forty centuries more would suffice to place us on applicant status with the federation.

Unfortunately, the peoples of this stellar community were many, and varied as greatly in their ethical outlook as their biological composition. Quite a few species lagged a considerable social distance behind the Dendi, as our visitors called themselves. One of these, a race of horrible, worm-like organisms known as the Troxxt—almost as advanced technologically as they were retarded in moral development—had suddenly volunteered for the position of sole and absolute ruler of the galaxy. They had seized control of several key suns, with their attendant planetary systems, and, after a calculated decimation of the races thus captured, had announced their intention of punishing with a merciless extinction all species unable to appreciate from these object-lessons the value of unconditional surrender.

In despair, the galactic federation had turned to the Dendi, one of the oldest, most selfless, and yet most powerful of races in civilized space, and commissioned them—as the military arm of the federation—to hunt down the Troxxt, defeat them wherever they had gained illegal suzerainty, and destroy forever their power to wage war. This order had come almost too late. Everywhere the Troxxt had gained so much the advantage of attack, that the Dendi were able to contain them only by enormous sacrifice. For centuries now, the conflict had careened across our vast island universe. In the course of it, densely populated planets had been disintegrated; suns had been blasted into novae, and whole groups of stars ground into swirling cosmic dust.

A temporary stalemate had been reached a short while ago, and—reeling and breathless—both sides were using the lull to strengthen weak spots in their perimeter.

Thus, the Troxxt had finally moved into the till-then peaceful section of space that contained our solar system—among others. They were thoroughly uninterested in our tiny planet with its meager resources; nor did they care much for such celestial neighbors as Mars or Jupiter. They established their headquarters on a planet of Proxima Centaurus—the star nearest our own sun—and proceeded to consolidate their offensive-defensive network between Rigel and Aldebaran. At this point in their explanation, the Dendi pointed out, the exigencies of interstellar strategy tended to become too complicated for anything but three-dimensional maps; let us here accept the simple statement, they suggested, that it became immediately vital for them to strike rapidly, and make the Troxxt position on Proxima Centaurus untenable—to establish a base inside their lines of communication.

The most likely spot for such a base was Earth.

The Dendi apologized profusely for intruding on our development, an intrusion which might cost us dear in our delicate developmental state. But, as they explained—in impeccable pre-Bengali—before their arrival we had, in effect, become (all unknowingly) a satrapy of the awful Troxxt. We could now consider ourselves liberated.

We thanked them much for that.

Besides, their leader pointed out proudly, the Dendi were engaged in a war for the sake of civilization itself, against an enemy so horrible, so obscene in its nature, and so utterly filthy in its practices, that it was unworthy of the label of intelligent life. They were fighting, not only for themselves, but for every loyal member of the galactic federation; for every small and helpless species; for every obscure race too weak to defend itself against a ravaging conqueror. Would humanity stand aloof from such a conflict?

There was just a slight bit of hesitation as the information was digested. Then—"No!" humanity roared back through such mass-communication media as television, newspapers, reverberating jungle drums, and mule-mounted backwoods messenger. "*We will not stand aloof! We will help you destroy this menace to the very fabric of civilization! Just tell us what you want us to do!*"

Well, nothing in particular, the aliens replied with some embarrassment. Possibly in a little while there might be something—several little things, in fact—which could be *quite* useful; but, for the moment, if we would concentrate on not getting in their way when they serviced their gun mounts, they would be very grateful, really. . . .

This reply tended to create a large amount of uncertainty among the two billion of Earth's human population. For several days afterward, there was a planet-wide tendency—the legend has come down to us—of people failing to meet each other's eyes.

But then Man rallied from this substantial blow to his pride. He would be useful, be it ever so humbly, to the race which had liberated him from potential subjugation by the ineffably ugly Troxxt. For this, let us remember well our ancestors! Let us hymn their sincere efforts amid their ignorance!

All standing armies, all air and sea fleets, were reorganized into guard-patrols around the Dendi weapons: no human might approach within two miles of the murmuring machinery, without a pass countersigned by the Dendi. Since they were never known to sign such a pass during the entire period of their stay on this planet, however, this loophole-provision was never exercised as far as is known; and the immediate neighborhood of the extra-terrestrial weapons became and remained henceforth wholesomely free of two-legged creatures.

Cooperation with our liberators took precedence over all other human activities. The order of the day was a slogan first given voice by a Harvard professor of government in a querulous radio round table on "Man's Place in a Somewhat Over-Civilized Universe."

"Let us forget our individual egos and collective conceits," the professor cried at one point. "Let us subordinate everything—to the end that the freedom of the solar system in general, and Earth in particular, must and shall be preserved!"

Despite its mouth-filling qualities, this slogan was repeated everywhere. Still, it was difficult sometimes to know exactly what the Dendi wanted—partly because of the limited number of interpreters available to the heads of the various sovereign states, and partly because of their leader's tendency to vanish into his ship after ambiguous and equivocal statements—such as the curt admonition to "Evacuate Washington!"

On that occasion, both the Secretary of State and the American President perspired fearfully through five hours of a July day in all the silk-hatted, stiff-collared, dark-suited diplomatic regalia that the barbaric past demanded of political leaders who would deal with the representatives of another people. They waited and wilted beneath the enormous ship—which no human had ever been invited to enter, despite the wistful hints constantly thrown out by university professors and aeronautical designers—they waited patiently and wetly for the Dendi leader to emerge and let them know whether he had meant the State of Washington or Washington, D.C.

The tale comes down to us at this point as a tale of glory. The capitol building taken apart in a few days, and set up almost intact in the foothills of the Rocky Mountains; the missing Archives, that were later to turn up in the Children's Room of a Public Library in Duluth, Iowa; the bottles of Potomac River water carefully borne westward and ceremoniously poured into the circular concrete ditch built around the President's mansion (from which unfortunately it was to evaporate within a week because of the relatively low humidity of the region)—all these are proud moments in the galactic history of our species, from which not even the later knowledge that the Dendi wished to build no gun site on the spot, nor even an ammunition dump, but merely a recreation hall for their troops, could remove any of the grandeur of our determined cooperation and most willing sacrifice.

There is no denying, however, that the ego of our race was greatly damaged by the discovery, in the course of a routine journalistic interview, that the aliens totaled no more powerful a group than a squad; and that their leader, instead of the great scientist and key military strategist that we might justifiably have expected the Galactic Federation to furnish for the protection of Terra, ranked as the interstellar equivalent of a buck sergeant.

That the President of the United States, the Commander-in-Chief of the Army and the Navy, had waited in such obeisant fashion upon a mere noncommissioned officer was hard for us to swallow; but that the impending Battle of Earth was to have a historical dignity only slightly higher than that of a patrol action was impossibly humiliating.

And then there was the matter of "lendi."

The aliens, while installing or servicing their planet-wide weapon system, would occasionally fling aside an evidently unusable fragment of the talking metal. Separated from the machine of which it had been a component, the substance seemed to lose all those qualities which were deleterious to mankind and retain several which were quite useful indeed. For example, if a portion of the strange material was attached to any terrestrial metal—and insulated carefully from contact with other substances—it would, in a few hours, itself become exactly the metal that it touched, whether that happened to be zinc, gold, or pure uranium.

This stuff—"lendi," men have heard the aliens call it—was shortly in frantic demand in an economy ruptured by constant and unexpected emptyings of its most important industrial centers.

Everywhere the aliens went, to and from their weapon sites, hordes of ragged humans stood chanting—well outside the two-mile limit—"Any lendi, Dendi?" All attempts by law-enforcement agencies of the planet to put a stop to this shameless, wholesale begging were useless—especially since the Dendi themselves seemed to get some unexplainable pleasure out of scattering tiny pieces of lendi to the scrabbling multitude. When policemen and soldiery began to join the trampling, murderous dash to the corner of the meadows wherein had fallen the highly versatile and garrulous metal, governments gave up.

Mankind almost began to hope for the attack to come, so that it would be relieved of the festering consideration of its own patent inferiorities. A few of the more fanatically conservative among our ancestors probably even began to regret liberation.

They did, children; they did! Let us hope that these would-be troglodytes were among the very first to be dissolved and melted down by the red flame-balls. One cannot, after all, turn one's back on progress!

Two days before the month of September was over, the aliens announced that they had detected activity upon one of the moons of Saturn. The Troxxt were evidently threading their treacherous way inward through the solar system. Considering their vicious and deceitful propensities, the Dendi warned, an attack from these worm-like monstrosities might be expected at any moment. Few humans went to sleep as the night rolled up to and past the meridian on which they dwelt. Almost all eyes were lifted to a sky carefully denuded of clouds by watchful Dendi. There was a brisk trade in cheap telescopes and bits of smoked glass in some sections of the planet; while other portions experienced a substantial boom in spells and charms of the all-inclusive, or omnibus, variety.

The Troxxt attacked in three cylindrical black ships simultaneously; one in the Southern Hemisphere, and two in the Northern. Great gouts of green flame roared out of their tiny craft; and everything touched by this imploded into a translucent, glass-like sand. No Dendi was hurt by these, however, and from each of the now-writhing gun mounts there bubbled forth a series of scarlet clouds which pursued the Troxxt hungrily, until forced by a dwindling velocity to fall back upon Earth.

Here they had an unhappy after-effect. Any populated area into which these pale pink cloudlets chanced to fall was rapidly transformed into a cemetery—a cemetery, if the truth be told as it has been handed down to us, that had more the odor of the kitchen than the grave. The inhabitants of these unfortunate localities were subjected to enormous increases of temperature. Their skin reddened, then blackened; their hair and nails shriveled; their very flesh turned into liquid and boiled off their bones. Altogether a disagreeable way for one-tenth of the human race to die.

The only consolation was the capture of a black cylinder by one of the red clouds. When, as a result of this, it had turned white-hot and poured its substance down in the form of a metallic rainstorm, the two ships assaulting the Northern Hemisphere abruptly retreated to the asteroids into which the Dendi—because of severely limited numbers—steadfastly refused to pursue them.

In the next twenty-four hours the aliens—*resident* aliens, let us say—

held conferences, made repairs to their weapons and commiserated with us. Humanity buried its dead. This last was a custom of our forefathers that was most worthy of note; and one that has not, of course, survived into modern times.

By the time the Troxxt returned, Man was ready for them. He could not, unfortunately, stand to arms as he most ardently desired to do; but he could and did stand to optical instrument and conjurer's oration.

Once more the little red clouds burst joyfully into the upper reaches of the stratosphere; once more the green flames wailed and tore at the chattering spires of lendi; once more men died by the thousands in the boiling back-wash of war. But this time, there was a slight difference: the green flames of the Troxxt abruptly changed color after the engagement had lasted three hours; they became darker, more bluish. And, as they did so, Dendi after Dendi collapsed at his station and died in convulsions.

The call for retreat was evidently sounded. The survivors fought their way to the tremendous ship in which they had come. With an explosion from her stern jets that blasted a red-hot furrow southward through France, and kicked Marseilles into the Mediterranean, the ship roared into space and fled home ignominiously.

Humanity steeled itself for the coming ordeal of horror under the Troxxt.

They were truly worm-like in form. As soon as the two night-black cylinders had landed, they strode from their ships, their tiny segmented bodies held off the ground by a complex harness supported by long and slender metal crutches. They erected a dome-like fort around each ship—one in Australia and one in the Ukraine—captured the few courageous individuals who had ventured close to their landing sites, and disappeared back into the dark craft with their squirming prizes.

While some men drilled about nervously in the ancient military patterns, others pored anxiously over scientific texts and records pertaining to the visit of the Dendi—in the desperate hope of finding a way of preserving terrestrial independence against this ravening conqueror of the star-spattered galaxy.

And yet all this time, the human captives inside the artificially darkened space-ships (the Troxxt, having no eyes, not only had little use for light but the more sedentary individuals among them actually found such radiation disagreeable to their sensitive, un-pigmented skins) were not being tortured for information—nor vivisected in the earnest quest of knowledge on a slightly higher level—but educated.

Educated in the Troxxtian language, that is.

True it was that a large number found themselves utterly inadequate for the task which the Troxxt had set them, and temporarily became servants to the more successful students. And another, albeit smaller, group developed various forms of frustration hysteria—ranging from mild unhappiness to complete catatonic depression—over the difficulties presented by a language whose every verb was irregular, and whose myriads of prepositions were formed by noun-adjective combinations derived from the subject of the previous sentence. But, eventually, eleven human beings were released, to blink madly in the sunlight as certified interpreters of Troxxt.

These liberators, it seemed, had never visited Bengal in the heyday of its millennia-past civilization.

Yes, these *liberators*. For the Troxxt had landed on the sixth day of the ancient, almost mythical month of October. And October the Sixth is, of course, the Holy Day of the second Liberation. Let us remember, let us revere. (If only we could figure out which day it is on our calendar!)

The tale the interpreters told caused men to hang their heads in shame and gnash their teeth at the deception they had allowed the Dendi to practice upon them.

True, the Dendi had been commissioned by the Galactic Federation to hunt the Troxxt down and destroy them. This was largely because the Dendi *were* the Galactic Federation. One of the first intelligent arrivals on the interstellar scene, the huge creatures had organized a vast police force to protect them and their power against any contingency of revolt that might arise in the future.

This police force was ostensibly a congress of all thinking life forms throughout the galaxy; actually, it was an efficient means of keeping them under rigid control.

Most species thus-far discovered were docile and tractable, however; the Dendi had been ruling from time immemorial, said they—very well, then, let the Dendi continue to rule. Did it make that much difference?

But, throughout the centuries, opposition to the Dendi grew—and the nuclei of the opposition were the protoplasm-based creatures. What, in fact, had come to be known as the Protoplasmic League.

Though small in number, the creatures whose life cycles were derived from the chemical and physical properties of protoplasm varied greatly in size, structure, and specialization. A galactic community deriving the main wells of its power from them would be a dynamic instead of a static place, where extra-galactic travel would be encouraged, instead of being inhibited, as it was at present because of Dendi fears of meeting a superior civilization.

It would be a true democracy of species—a real biological republic—where all creatures of adequate intelligence and cultural development would enjoy a control of their destinies at present experienced by the silicon-based Dendi alone.

To this end, the Troxxt—the only important race which had steadfastly refused the complete surrender of armaments demanded of all members of the Federation—had been implored by a minor member of the Protoplasmic League to rescue it from the devastation which the Dendi intended to visit upon it, as punishment for an unlawful exploratory excursion outside the boundaries of the galaxy.

Faced with the determination of the Troxxt to defend their cousins in organic chemistry, and the suddenly aroused hostility of at least two-thirds of the interstellar peoples, the Dendi had summoned a rump meeting of the Galactic Council; declared a state of revolt in being; and proceeded to cement their disintegrating rule with the blasted life-forces of a hundred worlds. The Troxxt, hopelessly outnumbered and out-equipped, had been able to continue the struggle only because of the great ingenuity and selflessness of other members of the Protoplasmic League, who had risked extinction to supply them with newly developed secret weapons.

Hadn't we guessed the nature of the beast from the enormous precautions it had taken to prevent the exposure of any part of its body to the intensely corrosive atmosphere of Earth? Surely the seamless, barely translucent suits which our recent visitors had worn for every moment of their stay on our world should have made us suspect a body chemistry developed from complex silicon compounds rather than those of carbon?

Humanity hung its collective head and admitted that the suspicion had never occurred to it.

Well, the Troxxt admitted generously, we were extremely inexperienced and possibly a little too trusting. Put it down to that. Our naiveté, however costly to them—our liberators—would not be allowed to deprive us of that complete citizenship which the Troxxt were claiming as the birthright of all.

But as for our leaders, our probably corrupted, certainly irresponsible leaders. . . .

The first executions of U.N. officials, heads of states, and pre-Bengali interpreters as "Traitors to Protoplasm"—after some of the lengthiest and most nearly-perfectly-fair trials in the history of Earth—were held a week after G-J Day, the inspiring occasion on which—amidst gorgeous ceremonies—

Humanity was invited to join, first the Protoplasmic League and thence the New and Democratic Galactic Federation of All Species, All Races.

Nor was that all. Whereas the Dendi had contemptuously shoved us to one side as they went about their business of making our planet safe for tyranny, and had—in all probability—built special devices which made the very touch of their weapons fatal for us, the Troxxt—with the sincere friendliness which had made their name a byword for democracy and decency wherever living creatures came together among the stars—our Second Liberators, as we lovingly called them, actually *preferred* to have us help them with the intensive, accelerating labor of planetary defense.

So men's intestines dissolved under the invisible glare of the forces used to assemble the new, incredibly complex weapons; men sickened and died, in scrabbling hordes, inside the mines which the Troxxt had made deeper than any we had dug hitherto; men's bodies broke open and exploded in the undersea oil-drilling sites which the Troxxt had declared were essential.

Children's schooldays were requested, too, in such collecting drives as "Platinum Scrap for Procyon" and "Radioactive Debris for Deneb." Housewives also were implored to save on salt whenever possible—this substance being useful to the Troxxt in literally dozens of incomprehensible ways—and colorful posters reminded: "*Don't salinate—sugarfy!*"

And over all—courteously caring for us like an intelligent parent—were our mentors, taking their giant supervisory strides on metallic crutches, while their pale little bodies lay curled in the hammocks that swung from each paired length of shining leg.

Truly, even in the midst of a complete economic paralysis caused by the concentration of all major productive facilities on other-worldly armaments, and despite the anguished cries of those suffering from peculiar industrial injuries which our medical men were totally unequipped to handle, in the midst of all this mind-wracking disorganization, it was yet very exhilarating to realize that we had taken our lawful place in the future government of the galaxy and were even now helping to make the Universe Safe for Democracy.

But the Dendi returned to smash this idyll. They came in their huge, silvery space-ships and the Troxxt, barely warned in time, just managed to rally under the blow and fight back in kind. Even so, the Troxxt ship in the Ukraine was almost immediately forced to flee to its base in the depths of space. After three days, the only Troxxt on Earth were the devoted members of a little band guarding the ship in Australia. They proved, in three or more months, to be as difficult to remove from the face of our planet as the continent itself; and since there was now a state of close and hostile siege, with the Dendi on one side of the globe, and the Troxxt on the other, the battle assumed frightful proportions.

Seas boiled; whole steppes burned away; the climate itself shifted and changed under the grueling pressure of the cataclysm. By the time the Dendi solved the problem, the planet Venus had been blasted from the skies in the course of a complicated battle maneuver, and Earth had wobbled over as orbital substitute.

The solution was simple: since the Troxxt were too firmly based on the small continent to be driven away, the numerically superior Dendi brought up enough firepower to disintegrate all Australia into an ash that muddied the Pacific. This occurred on the twenty-fourth of June, the Holy Day of First Reliberation. A day of reckoning for what remained of the human race, however.

How could we have been so naive, the Dendi wanted to know, as to be taken in by the chauvinistic pro-protoplasm propaganda? Surely, if physical characteristics were to be the criteria of our racial empathy, we would not orient ourselves on a narrow chemical basis! The Dendi life-plasma was based on silicon instead of carbon, true, but did not vertebrates—*appendaged* vertebrates, at that, such as we and the Dendi—have infinitely more in common, in spite of a *minor* biochemical difference or two, than vertebrates and legless, armless, slime-crawling creatures who happened, quite accidentally, to possess an identical organic substance?

As for this fantastic picture of life in the galaxy. . . . *Well*! The Dendi shrugged their quintuple shoulders as they went about the intricate business of erecting their noisy weapons all over the rubble of our planet. Had we ever seen a representative of these protoplasmic races the Troxxt were supposedly protecting? No, nor would we. For as soon as a race—animal, vegetable or mineral—developed enough to constitute even a *potential* danger to the sinuous aggressors, its civilization was systematically dismantled by the watchful Troxxt. We were in so primitive a state that they had not considered it at all risky to allow us the outward seeming of full participation.

Could we say we had learned a single useful piece of information about Troxxt technology—for all of the work we had done on their machines, for all of the lives we had lost in the process? No, of course not! We had merely contributed our mite to the enslavement of far-off races who had done us no harm.

There was much that we had cause to feel guilty about, the Dendi told us gravely—once the few surviving interpreters of the pre-Bengali dialect had crawled out of hiding. But our collective onus was as nothing compared to that borne by "vermicular collaborationists"—those traitors who had supplanted our martyred former leaders. And then there were the unspeakable human interpreters who had had linguistic traffic with creatures destroying a two-million-year-old galactic peace! Why, killing was almost too good for them, the Dendi murmured as they killed them.

When the Troxxt ripped their way back into possession of Earth some eighteen months later, bringing us the sweet fruits of the Second Reliberation—as well as a complete and most convincing rebuttal of the Dendi—there were few humans found who were willing to accept with any real enthusiasm the responsibilities of newly opened and highly paid positions in language, science, and government.

Of course, since the Troxxt, in order to reliberate Earth, had found it necessary to blast a tremendous chunk out of the northern hemisphere, there were very few humans to be found in the first place. . . .

Even so, many of these committed suicide rather than assume the title of Secretary General of the United Nations when the Dendi came back for the glorious Re-Reliberation, a short time after that. This was the liberation, by the way, which swept the deep collar of matter off our planet, and gave it what our forefathers came to call a pear-shaped look.

Possibly it was at this time—possibly a liberation or so later—that the Troxxt and the Dendi discovered the Earth had become far too eccentric in its orbit to possess the minimum safety conditions demanded of a Combat Zone. The battle, therefore, zigzagged coruscatingly and murderously away in the direction of Aldebaran.

That was nine generations ago, but the tale that has been handed down from parent to child, to child's child, has lost little in the telling. You hear it now from me almost exactly as I heard it. From my father I heard it as I ran with him from water puddle to distant water puddle, across the searing heat of yellow sand. From my mother I heard it as we sucked air and frantically grabbed at clusters of thick green weed, whenever the planet beneath us quivered in omen of a geographical spasm that might bury us in its burned-out body, or a cosmic gyration threatened to fling us into empty space.

Yes, even as we do now did we do then, telling the same tale, running the same frantic race across miles of unendurable heat for food and water; fighting the same savage battles with the giant rabbits for each other's carrion—and always, ever and always, sucking desperately at the precious air, which leaves our world in greater quantities with every mad twist of its orbit.

Naked, hungry, and thirsty came we into the world, and naked, hungry, and thirsty do we scamper our lives out upon it, under the huge and never-changing sun.

The same tale it is, and the same traditional ending it has as that I had from my father and his father before him. Suck air, grab clusters, and hear the last holy observation of our history:

"Looking about us, we can say with pardonable pride that we have been about as thoroughly liberated as it is possible for a race and a planet to be!"

ALFRED BESTER
Fondly Fahrenheit

• • • •

{1954}

Alfred Bester (1913–1987) was born in New York City and spent much of his life working there as a writer and editor. After graduation from the University of Pennsylvania, he attended law school at Columbia but soon dropped out; in 1936, he married the radio actress Rollie Goulko Bester. His first sf sale was "The Broken Axiom" (1939), which won a story competition in *Thrilling Wonder Stories*. When the friendly editors there were hired away by DC Comics, Bester began to write for *Green Lantern* and *Superman*; his wife, Rollie, originated the role of Lois Lane on the first broadcast of the radio serial in 1940. Bester was a scriptwriter for many radio detective shows: *Nick Carter*, *The Shadow*, *Charlie Chan*, *Nero Wolfe*, and others. Before becoming a full-time editor at the upscale travel magazine *Holiday* in the later 1950s, he also wrote television scripts for *Tom Corbett, Space Cadet* (1950–55) and other programs. *The Demolished Man*, his first novel, was published in three installments in *Galaxy* (1952); the subsequent book version won the first Hugo Award for best novel. Loosely based on Fyodor Dostoyevsky's *Crime and Punishment* (1866), it pits a troubled murderer against an inexorable, flawed police investigator. The science-fictional twist: in a twenty-fourth-century setting in which the top detectives are telepathic, how can a non-telepathic murderer possibly escape?

During the mid-1950s, the Besters lived for several years in Europe, where his other famous sf novel, *The Stars My Destination* (1957), was written; it may derive its title from the motto of Bester's college debating society (*sic iter ad astra*, "in this way towards the stars"). Like *The Demolished Man*, this work too science-fictionalizes a nineteenth-century classic, Alexandre Dumas *père*'s *The Count of Monte Cristo* (1844). Bester's protagonist, Gulliver Foyle, is non-aggressive until he is marooned in space and left to die when a luxury space liner ignores his distress signal. Transformed into a demon of vindictiveness, he plots revenge, amassing wealth and power along the way. For Bester, sf was a part-time avocation, but he produced several other notable stories, among them "The Men Who Murdered

Mohammed" (1958), a time-paradox story suggesting that those who travel to the past to change history will only change their personal time lines.

Bester's life, like many of his stories, ended with a sardonic twist: left alone after his wife's death in 1984, he is said to have changed his will to leave everything to his bartender. His most generous legacy, however, was to the sf genre: the mad, intricate plots and wildly inventive style (often focused on conveying the motivations of troubled characters) that inspired such major writers as Philip K. Dick and William Gibson. His brisk plotting and noir atmosphere were fostered by his early work in comics and radio, where pacing the action in highly pictorial separate scenes and voicing the characterizations are more important than driving home a unified message or idea.

The story that follows, published in *The Magazine of Fantasy and Science Fiction* in 1954, relies on a concept of psychic "projection," a melding of identity and veering power balance between "servant" and "master" that is suggested even by the shifting pronouns of its first sentence. "Fondly Fahrenheit" also uses the idea of synesthesia, a cross-wiring of sensory stimuli: in synesthesia, sounds might be experienced as colors—or heat might be felt as psychotic rage. The recurring "Beat the Heat" ditty recalls a similarly mindless jingle central to the plot of *The Demolished Man*: "Tenser, said the Tensor. Tenser, said the Tensor. / Tension, apprehension, and dissension have begun." Bester takes on Asimov/Campbell's "Three Laws of Robotics" (at work also in Asimov's story "Reason" [1941]). The laws are precautionary programming that binds artificial beings to human commands, but Bester's story imagines a more uncertain and permeable boundary between human and created beings.

He doesn't know which of us I am these days, but they know one truth. You must own nothing but yourself. You must make your own life, live your own life and die your own death . . . or else you will die another's.

The rice fields on Paragon III stretch for hundreds of miles like checkerboard tundras, a blue and brown mosaic under a burning sky of orange. In the evening, clouds whip like smoke, and the paddies rustle and murmur.

A long line of men marched across the paddies the evening we escaped from Paragon III. They were silent, armed, intent; a long rank of silhouetted statues looming against the smoking sky. Each man carried a gun. Each man wore a walkie-talkie belt pack, the speaker button in his ear, the microphone bug clipped to his throat, the glowing viewscreen strapped to his wrist like a green-eyed watch. The multitude of screens showed nothing but a multitude of individual paths through the paddies. The annunciators uttered no sound but the rustle and splash of steps. The men spoke infrequently, in heavy grunts, all speaking to all.

"Nothing here."

"Where's here?"

"Jenson's fields."

"You're drifting too far west."

"Close in the line there."

"Anybody covered the Grimson paddy?"

"Yeah. Nothing."

"She couldn't have walked this far."

"Could have been carried."

"Think she's alive?"

"Why should she be dead?"

The slow refrain swept up and down the long line of beaters advancing towards the smoky sunset. The line of beaters wavered like a writhing snake, but never ceased its remorseless advance. One hundred men spaced fifty feet apart. Five thousand feet of ominous search. One mile of angry determination stretching from east to west across a compass of heat. Evening fell. Each man lit his search lamp. The writhing snake was transformed into a necklace of wavering diamonds.

"Clear here. Nothing."

"Nothing here."

"Nothing."

"What about the Allen paddies?"

"Covering them now."

"Think we missed her?"

"Maybe."

"We'll beat back and check."

"This'll be an all night job."

"Allen paddies clear."

"God damn! We've got to find her!"

"We'll find her."

"Here she is. Sector seven. Tune in."

The line stopped. The diamonds froze in the heat. There was silence. Each man gazed into the glowing screen on his wrist, tuning to sector seven. All tuned to one. All showed a small nude figure awash in the muddy water of a paddy. Alongside the figure an owner's stake of bronze read: VANDALEUR. The end of the line converged towards the Vandaleur field. The necklace turned into a cluster of stars. One hundred men gathered around a small nude body, a child dead in a rice paddy. There was no water in her mouth. There were fingerprints on her throat. Her innocent face was battered. Her body was torn. Clotted blood on her skin was crusted and hard.

"Dead three-four hours at least."

"Her mouth is dry."

"She wasn't drowned. Beaten to death."

In the dark evening heat the men swore softly. They picked up the body. One stopped the others and pointed to the child's fingernails. She had fought her murderer. Under the nails were particles of flesh and bright drops of scarlet blood, still liquid, still uncoagulated.

"That blood ought to be clotted too."

"Funny."

"Not so funny. What kind of blood don't clot?"

"Android."

"Looks like she was killed by one."

"Vandaleur owns an android."

"She couldn't be killed by an android."

"That's android blood under her nails."

"The police better check."

"The police'll prove I'm right."

"But androids can't kill."

"That's android blood, ain't it?"

"Androids can't kill. They're made that way."

"Looks like one android was made wrong."

"Jesus!"

And the thermometer that day registered 91.9° gloriously Fahrenheit.

So there we were aboard the *Paragon Queen* en route for Megaster V, James Vandaleur and his android. James Vandaleur counted his money and wept. In the second-class cabin with him was his android, a magnificent creature with classic features and wide blue eyes. Raised on its forehead in a cameo of flesh were the letters MA, indicating that this was one of the rare multiple aptitude androids, worth $57,000 on the current exchange. There we were, weeping and counting and calmly watching.

"Twelve, fourteen, sixteen. Sixteen hundred dollars," Vandaleur wept. "That's all. Sixteen hundred dollars. My house was worth ten thousand. The land was worth five. There was furniture, cars, my paintings, etchings, my plane, my—And nothing to show for everything but sixteen hundred dollars. Christ!"

I leaped up from the table and turned on the android. I pulled a strap from one of the leather bags and beat the android. It didn't move.

"I must remind you," the android said, "that I am worth fifty-seven thousand dollars on the current exchange. I must warn you that you are endangering valuable property."

"You damned crazy machine," Vandaleur shouted.

"I am not a machine," the android answered. "The robot is a machine. The android is a chemical creation of synthetic tissue."

"What got into you?' Vandaleur cried. "Why did you do it? Damn you!" He beat the android savagely.

"I must remind you that I cannot be punished," the android said. "The pleasure-pain syndrome is not incorporated in the android synthesis."

"Then why did you kill her?" Vandaleur shouted. "If it wasn't for kicks, why did you—"

"I must remind you," the android said, "that the second class cabins in these ships are not soundproofed."

Vandaleur dropped the strap and stood panting, staring at the creature he owned.

"Why did you do it? Why did you kill her?" I asked.

"I don't know," I answered.

"First it was malicious mischief. Small things. Petty destruction. I should have known there was something wrong with you then. Androids can't destroy. They can't harm. They—"

"There is no pleasure-pain syndrome incorporated in the android synthesis."

"Then it got to arson. Then serious destruction. Then assault . . . that engineer on Rigel. Each time worse. Each time we had to get out faster. Now it's murder. Christ! What's the matter with you? What's happened?"

"There are no self-check relays incorporated in the android brain."

"Each time we had to get out it was a step downhill. Look at me. In a second class cabin. Me. James Paleologue Vandaleur. There was a time when my father was the wealthiest—Now, sixteen hundred dollars in the world. That's all I've got. And you. Christ damn you!"

Vandaleur raised the strap to beat the android again, then dropped it and collapsed on a berth, sobbing. At last he pulled himself together.

"Instructions," he said.

The multiple aptitude android responded at once. It arose and awaited orders.

"My name is now Valentine. James Valentine. I stopped off on Paragon III for only one day to transfer to this ship for Megaster V. My occupation: Agent for one privately owned MA android which is for hire. Purpose of visit: To settle on Megaster V. Fix the papers."

The android removed Vandaleur's passport and papers from a bag, got pen and ink and sat down at the table. With an accurate flawless hand—an accomplished hand that could draw, write, paint, carve, engrave, etch, photograph, design, create and build—it meticulously forged new credentials for Vandaleur. Its owner watched me miserably.

"Create and build," I muttered. "And now destroy. Oh God! What am I going to do? Christ! If I could only get rid of you. If I didn't have to live off you. God! If only I'd inherited some guts instead of you."

Dallas Brady was Megaster's leading jewelry designer. She was short, stocky, amoral and a nymphomaniac. She hired Vandaleur's multiple aptitude android and put me to work in her shop. She seduced Vandaleur. In her bed one night, she asked abruptly: "Your name's Vandaleur, isn't it?"

"Yes," I murmured. Then: "No! No! It's Valentine. James Valentine."

"What happened on Paragon?" Dallas Brady asked. "I thought androids couldn't kill or destroy property. Prime Directives and Inhibitions set up for them when they're synthesized. Every company guarantees they can't."

"Valentine!" Vandaleur insisted.

"Oh, come off it," Dallas Brady said. "I've known for a week. I haven't hollered copper, have I?"

"The name is Valentine."

"You want to prove it? You want I should call the cops?" Dallas reached out and picked up the phone.

"For God's sake, Dallas!" Vandaleur leaped up and struggled to take the phone from her. She fended him off, laughing at him until he collapsed and wept in shame and helplessness.

"How did you find out?" he asked at last.

"The papers are full of it. And Valentine was a little too close to Vandaleur. That wasn't smart, was it?"

"I guess not. I'm not very smart."

"Your android's got quite a record, hasn't it? Assault. Arson. Destruction. What happened on Paragon?"

"It kidnapped a child. Took her out into the rice fields and murdered her."

"Raped her?"

"I don't know."

"They're going to catch up with you."

"Don't I know it? Christ! We've been running for two years now. Seven planets in two years. I must have abandoned fifty thousand dollars' worth of property in two years."

"You better find out what's wrong with it."

"How can I? Can I walk into a repair clinic and ask for an overhaul? What am I going to say? 'My android's just turned killer. Fix it.' They'd call the police right off." I began to shake. "They'd have that android dismantled inside one day. I'd probably be booked as accessory to murder."

"Why didn't you have it repaired before it got to murder?"

"I couldn't take the chance," Vandaleur explained angrily. "If they started fooling around with lobotomies and body chemistry and endocrine surgery, they might have destroyed its aptitudes. What would I have left to hire out? How would I live?"

"You could work yourself. People do."

"Work at what? You know I'm good for nothing. How could I compete with specialist androids and robots? Who can, unless he's got a terrific talent for a particular job?"

"Yeah. That's true."

"I lived off my old man all my life. Damn him! He had to go bust just before he died. Left me the android and that's all. The only way I can get along is living off what it earns."

"You better sell it before the cops catch up with you. You can live off fifty grand. Invest it."

"At three per cent? Fifteen hundred a year? When the android returns fifteen per cent on its value? Eight thousand a year. That's what it earns. No, Dallas. I've got to go along with it."

"What are you going to do about its violence kick?"

"I can't do anything . . . except watch it and pray. What are you going to do about it?'

"Nothing. It's none of my business. Only one thing . . . I ought to get something for keeping my mouth shut."

"What?"

"The android works for me for free. Let somebody else pay you, but I get it for free."

The multiple aptitude android worked. Vandaleur collected its fees. His expenses were taken care of. His savings began to mount. As the warm spring of Megaster V turned to hot summer, I began investigating farms and properties. It would be possible, within a year or two, for us to settle down permanently, provided Dallas Brady's demands did not become rapacious.

On the first hot day of summer, the android began singing in Dallas

Brady's workshop. It hovered over the electric furnace which, along with the weather, was broiling the shop, and sang an ancient tune that had been popular half a century before.

Oh, it's no feat to beat the heat.
All reet! All reet!
So jeet your seat
Be fleet be fleet
Cool and discreet
Honey . . .

It sang in a strange, halting voice, and its accomplished fingers were clasped behind its back, writhing in a strange rhumba all their own. Dallas Brady was surprised.

"You happy or something?" she asked.

"I must remind you that the pleasure-pain syndrome is not incorporated in the android synthesis," I answered. "All reet! All reet! Be fleet be fleet, cool and discreet, honey . . ."

Its fingers stopped their writhing and picked up a heavy pair of iron tongs. The android poked them into the glowing heart of the furnace, leaning far forward to peer into the lovely heat.

"Be careful, you damned fool!" Dallas Brady exclaimed. "You want to fall in?'

"I must remind you that I am worth fifty-seven thousand dollars on the current exchange," I said. "It is forbidden to endanger valuable property. All reet! All reet! Honey . . ."

It withdrew a crucible of glowing gold from the electric furnace, turned, capered hideously, sang crazily, and splashed a sluggish gobbet of molten gold over Dallas Brady's head. She screamed and collapsed, her hair and clothes flaming, her skin crackling. The android poured again while it capered and sang.

"Be fleet be fleet, cool and discreet, honey . . ." It sang and slowly poured and poured the molten gold. Then I left the workshop and rejoined James Vandaleur in his hotel suite. The android's charred clothes and squirming fingers warned its owner that something was very much wrong.

Vandaleur rushed to Dallas Brady's workshop, stared once, vomited and fled. I had enough time to pack one bag and raise nine hundred dollars on portable assets. He took a third class-cabin on the *Megaster Queen* which left that morning for Lyra Alpha. He took me with him. He wept and counted his money and I beat the android again.

And the thermometer in Dallas Brady's workshop registered 98.1° beautifully Fahrenheit.

On Lyra Alpha we holed up in a small hotel near the university. There, Vandaleur carefully bruised my forehead until the letters MA were obliterated by the swelling and discoloration. The letters would reappear, but not for several months, and in the meantime Vandaleur hoped the hue and cry for an MA android would be forgotten. The android was hired out as a common laborer in the university power plant. Vandaleur, as James Venice, eked out life on the android's small earnings.

I wasn't too unhappy. Most of the other residents in the hotel were university students, equally hard-up, but delightfully young and enthusiastic. There was one charming girl with sharp eyes and a quick mind. Her name was Wanda, and she and her beau, Jed Stark, took a tremendous interest in the killing android which was being mentioned in every paper in the galaxy.

"We've been studying the case," she and Jed said at one of the casual student parties which happened to be held this night in Vandaleur's room. "We think we know what's causing it. We're going to do a paper." They were in a high state of excitement.

"Causing what?" somebody wanted to know.

"The android rampage."

"Obviously out of adjustment, isn't it? Body chemistry gone haywire. Maybe a kind of synthetic cancer, yes?"

"No." Wanda gave Jed a look of suppressed triumph.

"Well, what is it?"

"Something specific."

"What?"

"That would be telling."

"Oh, come on."

"Nothing doing."

"Won't you tell us?" I asked intently. "I . . . We're very much interested in what could go wrong with an android."

"No, Mr. Venice," Wanda said. "It's a unique idea and we've got to protect it. One thesis like this and we'll be set up for life. We can't take the chance of somebody stealing it."

"Can't you give us a hint?"

"No. Not a hint. Don't say a word, Jed. But I'll tell you this much, Mr. Venice. I'd hate to be the man who owns that android."

"You mean the police?" I asked.

"I mean projection, Mr. Venice. Projection! That's the danger . . . and I won't say any more. I've said too much as it is."

I heard steps outside, and a hoarse voice singing softly: "Be fleet be fleet, cool and discreet, honey . . ." My android entered the room, home from its tour of duty at the university power plant. It was not introduced. I motioned to it and I immediately responded to the command and went to the beer keg and took over Vandaleur's job of serving the guests. Its accomplished fingers writhed in a private rhumba of their own. Gradually they stopped their squirming, and the strange humming ended.

Androids were not unusual at the university. The wealthier students owned them along with cars and planes. Vandaleur's android provoked no comment, but young Wanda was sharp-eyed and quick-witted. She noted my bruised forehead and she was intent on the history-making thesis she and Jed Stark were going to write. After the party broke up, she consulted with Jed walking upstairs to her room.

"Jed, why'd that android have a bruised forehead?"

"Probably hurt itself, Wanda. It's working in the power plant. They fling a lot of heavy stuff around."

"That's all?"

"What else?"

"It could be a convenient bruise."

"Convenient for what?"

"Hiding what's stamped on its forehead."

"No point to that, Wanda. You don't have to see marks on a forehead to recognize an android. You don't have to see a trademark on a car to know it's a car."

"I don't mean it's trying to pass as a human. I mean it's trying to pass as a lower grade android."

"Why?"

"Suppose it had MA on its forehead."

"Multiple aptitude? Then why in hell would Venice waste it stoking furnaces if it could earn more—Oh. Oh! You mean it's—?"

Wanda nodded.

"Jesus!" Stark pursed his lips. "What do we do? Call the police?"

"No. We don't know if it's an MA for a fact. If it turns out to be an MA and the killing android, our paper comes first anyway. This is our big chance, Jed. If it's *that* android we can run a series of controlled tests and—"

"How do we find out for sure?"

"Easy. Infrared film. That'll show what's under the bruise. Borrow a camera. Buy some film. We'll sneak down to the power plant tomorrow afternoon and take some pictures. Then we'll know."

They stole down into the university power plant the following afternoon. It was a vast cellar, deep under the earth. It was dark, shadowy, luminous with burning light from the furnace doors. Above the roar of the fires they could hear a strange voice shouting and chanting in the echoing vault: "All reet! All reet! So jeet your seat. Be fleet be fleet, cool and discreet, honey . . ." And they could see a capering figure dancing a lunatic rhumba in time to the music it shouted. The legs twisted. The arms waved. The fingers writhed.

Jed Stark raised the camera and began shooting his spool of infrared film, aiming the camera sights at that bobbing head. Then Wanda shrieked, for I saw them and came charging down on them, brandishing a polished steel shovel. It smashed the camera. It felled the girl and then the boy. Jed fought me for a desperate hissing moment before he was bludgeoned into helplessness. Then the android dragged them to the furnace and fed them to the flames, slowly, hideously. It capered and sang. Then it returned to my hotel.

The thermometer in the power plant registered 100.9° murderously Fahrenheit. All reet! All reet!

We bought steerage on the *Lyra Queen* and Vandaleur and the android did odd jobs for their meals. During the night watches, Vandaleur would sit alone in the steerage head with a cardboard portfolio on his lap, puzzling over its contents. That portfolio was all he had managed to bring with him from Lyra Alpha. He had stolen it from Wanda's room. It was labeled ANDROID. It contained the secret of my sickness.

And it contained nothing but newspapers. Scores of newspapers from all over the galaxy, printed, microfilmed, engraved, offset, photostated . . . Rigel *Star-Banner* . . . Paragon *Picayune* . . . Megaster *Times-Leader* . . . Lalande *Journal* . . . Indi *Intelligencer* . . . Eridani *Telegram-News*. All reet! All reet!

Nothing but newspapers. Each paper contained an account of one crime in the android's ghastly career. Each paper also contained news, domestic and foreign, sports, society, weather, shipping news, stock exchange quotations, human interest stories, features, contents, puzzles. Somewhere in that mass of uncollated facts was the secret Wanda and Jed Stark had discovered. Vandaleur pored over the papers helplessly. It was beyond him. So jeet your seat!

"I'll sell you," I told the android. "Damn you. When we land on Terra, I'll sell you. I'll settle for three percent on whatever you're worth."

"I am worth fifty-seven thousand dollars on the current exchange," I told him.

"If I can't sell you, I'll turn you in to the police," I said.

"I am valuable property," I answered. "It is forbidden to endanger valuable property. You won't have me destroyed."

"Christ damn you!" Vandaleur cried. "What? Are you arrogant? Do you know you can trust me to protect you? Is that the secret?"

The multiple aptitude android regarded him with calm accomplished eyes. "Sometimes," it said, "it is a good thing to be property."

It was three below zero when the *Lyra Queen* dropped at Croydon Field. A mixture of ice and snow swept across the field, fizzing and exploding into steam under the *Queen's* tall jets. The passengers trotted numbly across the blackened concrete to customs inspection, and thence to the airport bus that was to take them to London. Vandaleur and the android were broke. They walked.

By midnight they reached Piccadilly Circus. The December ice storm had not slackened and the statue of Eros was encrusted with ice. They turned right, walked down to Trafalgar Square and then along the Strand towards Soho, shaking with cold and wet. Just above Fleet Street, Vandaleur saw a solitary figure coming from the direction of St Paul's. He drew the android into an alley.

"We've got to have money," he whispered. He pointed at the approaching figure. "He has money. Take it from him."

"The order cannot be obeyed," the android said.

"Take it from him," Vandaleur repeated. "By force. Do you understand? We're desperate."

"It is contrary to my prime directive," I said. "I cannot endanger life or property. The order cannot be obeyed."

"For God's sake!" Vandaleur burst out. "You've attacked, destroyed, murdered. Don't gibber about prime directives. You haven't any left. Get his money. Kill him if you have to. I tell you, we're desperate!"

"It is contrary to my prime directive," the android repeated. "The order cannot be obeyed."

I thrust the android back and leaped out at the stranger. He was tall, austere, competent. He had an air of hope curdled by cynicism. He carried a cane. I saw he was blind.

"Yes?" he said. "I hear you near me. What is it?"

"Sir . . ." Vandaleur hesitated. "I'm desperate."

"We are all desperate," the stranger replied. "Quietly desperate."

"Sir . . . I've got to have some money."

"Are you begging or stealing?" The sightless eyes passed over Vandaleur and the android.

"I'm prepared for either."

"Ah. So are we all. It is the history of our race." The stranger motioned over his shoulder. "I have been begging at St. Paul's, my friend. What I desire cannot be stolen. What is it you desire that you are lucky enough to be able to steal?"

"Money," Vandaleur said.

"Money for what? Come, my friend, let us exchange confidences. I will tell you why I beg, if you will tell me why you steal. My name is Blenheim."

"My name is . . . Vole."

"I was not begging for sight at St. Paul's, Mr. Vole. I was begging for a number."

"A number?"

"Ah, yes. Numbers rational, numbers irrational. Numbers imaginary. Positive integers. Negative integers. Fractions, positive and negative. Eh? You have never heard of Blenheim's immortal treatise on Twenty Zeros, or The Differences in Absence of Quantity?" Blenheim smiled bitterly. "I am a wizard of the Theory of Number, Mr. Vole, and I have exhausted the charm of number for myself. After fifty years of wizardry, senility approaches and the appetite vanishes. I have been praying in St. Paul's for inspiration. Dear God, I prayed, if You exist, send me a number."

Vandaleur slowly lifted the cardboard portfolio and touched Blenheim's hand with it. "In here," he said, "is a number. A hidden number. A secret number. The number of a crime. Shall we exchange, Mr. Blenheim? Shelter for a number?"

"Neither begging nor stealing, eh?" Blenheim said. "But a bargain. So all life reduces to the banal." The sightless eyes again passed over Vandaleur and the android. "Perhaps the All-Mighty is not God but a merchant. Come home with me."

On the top floor of Blenheim's house we shared a room—two beds, two closets, two washstands, one bathroom. Vandaleur bruised my forehead again and sent me out to find work, and while the android worked, I consulted with Blenheim and read him the papers from the portfolio, one by one. All reet! All reet!

Vandaleur told him so much and no more. He was a student, I said, attempting a thesis on the murdering android. In these papers which he had collected were the facts that would explain the crimes of which Blenheim had heard nothing. There must be a correlation, a number, a statistic, something which would account for my derangement, I explained, and Blenheim was piqued by the mystery, the detective story, the human interest of number.

We examined the papers. As I read them aloud, he listed them and their contents in his blind, meticulous writing. And then I read his notes to him. He listed the papers by type, by type-face, by fact, by fancy, by article, spelling, words, theme, advertising, pictures, subject, politics, prejudices. He analyzed. He studied. He meditated. And we lived together on that top floor, always a little cold, always a little terrified, always a little closer . . . brought together by our fear of it, our hatred between us. Like a wedge driven into a living tree and splitting the trunk, only to be forever incorporated into the scar tissue, we grew together. Vandaleur and the android. Be fleet be fleet!

And one afternoon Blenheim called Vandaleur into his study and displayed his notes. "I think I've found it," he said, "but I can't understand it."

Vandaleur's heart leaped.

"Here are the correlations," Blenheim continued. "In fifty papers there are accounts of the criminal android. What is there, outside the depredations, that is also in fifty papers?"

"I don't know, Mr. Blenheim."

"It was a rhetorical question. Here is the answer. The weather."

"What?"

"The weather." Blenheim nodded. "Each crime was committed on a day when the temperature was above ninety degrees Fahrenheit."

"But that's impossible," Vandaleur exclaimed. "It was cool on Lyra Alpha."

"We have no record of any crime committed on Lyra Alpha. There is no paper."

"No. That's right. I—" Vandaleur was confused. Suddenly he exclaimed, "No. You're right. The furnace room. It was hot there. Hot! Of course. My God, yes! That's the answer. Dallas Brady's electric furnace . . . The rice deltas on Paragon. So jeet your seat. Yes. But why? Why? My God, why?"

I came into the house at that moment, and passing the study, saw Vandaleur and Blenheim. I entered, awaiting commands, my multiple aptitudes devoted to service.

'That's the android, eh?" Blenheim said after a long moment.

"Yes," Vandaleur answered, still confused by the discovery. "And that explains why it refused to attack you that night on the Strand. It wasn't hot enough to break the prime directive. Only in the heat . . . The heat, all reet!" He looked at the android. A lunatic command passed from man to android. I refused. It is forbidden to endanger life. Vandaleur gestured furiously, then seized Blenheim's shoulders and yanked him back out of his desk chair. Blenheim shouted once. Vandaleur leaped on him like a tiger, pinning him to the floor and sealing his mouth with one hand.

"Find a weapon," he called to the android.

"It is forbidden to endanger life."

"This is a fight for self-preservation. Bring me a weapon!" He held the squirming mathematician with all his weight. I went at once to a cupboard where I knew a revolver was kept. I checked it. It was loaded with five cartridges. I handed it to Vandaleur. I took it, rammed the barrel against Blenheim's head and pulled the trigger. He shuddered once.

We had three hours before the cook returned from her day off. We looted the house. We took Blenheim's money and jewels. We packed a bag with clothes. We took Blenheim's notes, destroyed the newspapers; and we left, carefully locking the door behind us. In Blenheim's study we left a pile of crumpled papers under a half inch of burning candle. And we soaked the rug around it with kerosene. No, I did all that. The android refused. I am forbidden to endanger life or property.

All reet!

They took the tube to Leicester Square, changed trains and rode to the British Museum. There they got off and went to a small Georgian house just off Russell Square. A shingle in the window read: NAN WEBB, PSYCHOMETRIC CONSULTANT. Vandaleur had made a note of the address some weeks earlier. They went into the house. The android waited in the foyer with the bag. Vandaleur entered Nan Webb's office.

She was a tall woman with grey shingled hair, very fine English complexion and very bad English legs. Her features were blunt, her expression acute. She nodded to Vandaleur, finished a letter, sealed it and looked up.

"My name," I said, "is Vanderbilt. James Vanderbilt."

"Quite."

"I'm an exchange student at London University."

"Quite."

"I've been researching on the killing android, and I think I've discovered something very interesting. I'd like your advice on it. What is your fee?"

"What is your college at the University?"

"Why?"

"There is a discount for students."

"Merton College."

"That will be two pounds, please."

Vandaleur placed two pounds on the desk and added to the fee Blenheim's notes. "There is a correlation," he said, "between the crimes of the android and the weather. You will note that each crime was committed when the temperature rose above ninety degrees Fahrenheit. Is there a psychometric answer for this?"

Nan Webb nodded, studied the notes for a moment, put down the sheets of paper and said: "Synesthesia, obviously."

"What?"

"Synesthesia," she repeated. "When a sensation, Mr. Vanderbilt, is interpreted immediately in terms of a sensation from a different sense organ from the one stimulated, it is called synesthesia. For example: A sound stimulus gives rise to a simultaneous sensation of definite color. Or color gives rise to a sensation of taste. Or a light stimulus gives rise to a sensation of sound. There can be confusion or short circuiting of any sensation of taste, smell, pain, pressure, temperature and so on. D'you understand?"

"I think so."

"Your research has uncovered the fact that the android most probably reacts to temperature stimulus above the ninety degree level synesthetically. Most probably there is an endocrine response. Probably a temperature linkage with the android adrenal surrogate. High temperature brings about a response of fear, anger, excitement and violent physical activity . . . all within the province of the adrenal gland."

"Yes. I see. Then if the android were to be kept in cold climates . . ."

"There would be neither stimulus nor response. There would be no crimes. Quite."

"I see. What is projection?"

"How do you mean?"

"Is there any danger of projection with regard to the owner of the android?"

"Very interesting. Projection is a throwing forward. It is the process of throwing out upon another the ideas or impulses that belong to oneself. The paranoid, for example, projects upon others his conflicts and disturbances in order to externalize them. He accuses, directly or by implication, other men of having the very sickness with which he is struggling himself."

"And the danger of projection?"

"It is the danger of believing what is implied. If you live with a psychotic who projects his sickness upon you, there is a danger of falling into his psychotic pattern and becoming virtually psychotic yourself. As, no doubt, is happening to you, Mr. Vandaleur."

Vandaleur leaped to his feet.

"You are an ass," Nan Webb went on crisply. She waved the sheets of notes. "This is no exchange student's writing. It's the unique cursive of the famous Blenheim. Every scholar in England knows his blind writing. There is no Merton College at London University. That was a miserable guess. Merton is one of the Oxford colleges. And you, Mr. Vandaleur, are so obviously infected by association with your deranged android . . . by projection, if you will . . . that I hesitate between calling the Metropolitan Police and the Hospital for the Criminally Insane."

I took out the gun and shot her.

Reet!

"Antares II, Alpha Aurigae, Acrux IV, Pollux IX, Rigel Centaurus," Vandaleur said. "They're all cold. Cold as a witch's kiss. Mean temperature of 40° Fahrenheit. Never get hotter than seventy. We're in business again. Watch that curve."

The multiple aptitude android swung the wheel with its accomplished hands. The car took the curve sweetly and sped on through the northern marshes, the reeds stretching for miles, brown and dry, under the cold English sky. The sun was sinking swiftly. Overhead, a lone flight of bustards flapped clumsily eastward. High above the flight, a lone helicopter drifted towards home and warmth.

"No more warmth for us," I said. "No more heat. We're safe when we're cold. We'll hole up in Scotland, make a little money, get across to Norway, build a bankroll and then slip out. We'll settle on Pollux. We're safe. We've licked it. We can live again."

There was a startling *bleep* from overhead, and then a ragged roar: "ATTENTION JAMES VANDALEUR AND ANDROID. ATTENTION JAMES VANDALEUR AND ANDROID!"

Vandaleur started and looked up. The lone helicopter was floating above them. From its belly came amplified commands: "YOU ARE SURROUNDED, THE ROAD IS BLOCKED. YOU ARE TO STOP YOUR CAR AT ONCE AND SUBMIT TO ARREST. STOP AT ONCE!"

I looked at Vandaleur for orders.

"Keep driving," Vandaleur snapped.

The helicopter dropped lower: "ATTENTION ANDROID, YOU ARE IN CONTROL OF THE VEHICLE. YOU ARE TO STOP AT ONCE. THIS IS A STATE DIRECTIVE SUPERSEDING ALL PRIVATE COMMANDS."

"What the hell are you doing?" I shouted.

"A state directive supersedes all private commands," the android answered. "I must point out to you that—"

"Get the hell away from the wheel," Vandaleur ordered. I clubbed the android, yanked him sideways and squirmed over him to the wheel. The car veered off the road in that moment and went churning through the frozen mud and dry reeds. Vandaleur regained control and continued westward through the marshes towards a parallel highway five miles distant.

"We'll beat their God damned block," he grunted.

The car pounded and surged. The helicopter dropped even lower. A searchlight blazed from the belly of the plane.

"ATTENTION JAMES VANDALEUR AND ANDROID. SUBMIT TO ARREST. THIS IS A STATE DIRECTIVE SUPERSEDING ALL PRIVATE COMMANDS."

"He can't submit," Vandaleur shouted wildly. "There's no one to submit to. He can't and I won't."

"Christ!" I muttered. "We'll beat them yet. We'll beat the block. We'll beat the heat. We'll—"

"I must point out to you," I said, "that I am required by my prime directive to obey state directives which supersede all private commands. I must submit to arrest."

"Who says it's a state directive?" Vandaleur said. "Them? Up in that plane? They've got to show credentials. They've got to prove it's state authority before you submit. How d'you know they're not crooks trying to trick us?"

Holding the wheel with one arm, he reached into his side pocket to make sure the gun was still in place. The car skidded. The tires squealed on frost and reeds. The wheel was wrenched from his grasp and the car yawed up a small hillock and overturned. The motor roared and the wheels screamed. Vandaleur crawled out and dragged the android with him. For the moment we were outside the circle of light boring down from the helicopter. We blundered off into the marsh, into the blackness, into concealment . . . Vandaleur running with a pounding heart, hauling the android along.

The helicopter circled and soared over the wrecked car, searchlight peering, loudspeaker braying. On the highway we had left, lights appeared as the pursuing and blocking parties gathered and followed radio directions from the plane. Vandaleur and the android continued deeper and deeper into the marsh, working their way towards the parallel road and safety. It was night by now. The sky was a black matte. Not a star showed. The temperature was dropping. A southeast night wind knifed us to the bone.

Far behind there was a dull concussion. Vandaleur turned, gasping. The car's fuel had exploded. A geyser of flame shot up like a lurid fountain. It subsided into a low crater of burning reeds. Whipped by the wind, the distant hem of flame fanned up into a wall, ten feet high. The wall began marching down on us, crackling fiercely. Above it, a pall of oily smoke surged forward. Behind it, Vandaleur could make out the figures of men . . . a mass of beaters searching the marsh.

"Christ!" I cried and searched desperately for safety. He ran, dragging me with him, until their feet crunched through the surface ice of a pool. He trampled the ice furiously, then flung himself down in the numbing water, pulling the android with us.

The wall of flame approached. I could hear the crackle and feel the heat. He could see the searchers clearly. Vandaleur reached into his side pocket for the gun. The pocket was torn. The gun was gone. He groaned and shook with cold and terror. The light from the marsh fire was blinding. Overhead, the helicopter floated helplessly to one side, unable to fly through the smoke and flames and aid the searchers who were beating far to the right of us.

"They'll miss us," Vandaleur whispered. "Keep quiet. That's an order. They'll miss us. We'll beat them. We'll beat the fire. We'll—"

Three distinct shots sounded less than a hundred feet from the fugitives. *Blam! Blam! Blam!* They came from the last three cartridges in my gun as the marsh fire reached it where it had dropped, and exploded the shells. The searchers turned towards the sound and began working directly toward us. Vandaleur cursed hysterically and tried to submerge even deeper to escape the intolerable heat of the fire. The android began to twitch.

The wall of flame surged up to them. Vandaleur took a deep breath and prepared to submerge until the flame passed over them. The android shuddered and burst into an earsplitting scream.

"All reet! All reet!" it shouted. "Be fleet be fleet!"

"Damn you!" I shouted. I tried to drown it.

"Damn you!" I cursed him. I smashed his face.

The android battered Vandaleur, who fought it off until it exploded out of the mud and staggered upright. Before I could return to the attack, the live flames captured it hypnotically. It danced and capered in a lunatic rhumba before the wall of fire. Its legs twisted. Its arms waved. The fingers writhed in a private rhumba of their own. It shrieked and sang and ran in a crooked waltz before the embrace of the heat, a muddy monster silhouetted against the brilliant sparkling flare.

The searchers shouted. There were shots. The android spun around twice and then continued its horrid dance before the face of the flames. There was a rising gust of wind. The fire swept around the capering figure and enveloped it for a roaring moment. Then the fire swept on, leaving behind it a sobbing mass of synthetic flesh oozing scarlet blood that would never coagulate.

The thermometer would have registered 1200° wondrously Fahrenheit.

Vandaleur didn't die. I got away. They missed him while they watched the android caper and die. But I don't know which of us he is these days. Projection, Wanda warned me. Projection, Nan Webb told him. If you live with a crazy man or a crazy machine long enough, I become crazy too. Reet!

But we know one truth. We know they are wrong. The new robot and Vandaleur know that because the new robot's started twitching too. Reet! Here on cold Pollux, the robot is twitching and singing. No heat, but my fingers writhe. No heat, but it's taken the little Talley girl off for a solitary walk. A cheap labor robot. A servo-mechanism . . . all I could afford . . . but it's twitching and humming and walking alone with the child somewhere and I can't find them. Christ! Vandaleur can't find me before it's too late. Cool and discreet, honey, in the dancing frost while the thermometer registers 10° fondly Fahrenheit.

AVRAM DAVIDSON
The Golem

• • • •

{1955}

Avram Davidson (1923–1993) was a much respected writer in several genres, receiving the Edgar and Ellery Queen Awards for mystery fiction and the World Fantasy Award for *The Inquiries of Dr. Esterhazy* (1975), as well as a World Fantasy Lifetime Achievement Award in 1986. His first published sf story, "My Boyfriend's Name Is Jello," appeared in *The Magazine of Fantasy and Science Fiction* in 1954. He won the Hugo Award for "Or All the Seas with Oysters" (*Galaxy* 1958), which speculates about safety pins and coat hangers as possible stages in the mysterious life cycle of a murderous bicycle. Like most of his work, that story challenges any rigid distinctions between fantasy and sf as genres, and it is fortunate that Davidson found a friendly home for such boundary crossing in *The Magazine of Fantasy and Science Fiction*, which he edited from 1962 to 1965 and which received a Hugo Award for best magazine during that time.

Reared in an Orthodox Jewish community in Yonkers, Davidson kept kosher even when he served as a medic in the Pacific during World War II, obtaining permission, he said in a memoir written during the 1950s, to wear "the only beard licensed by the first Marine Division." In Israel after the war, he served again in 1948 as a medic during the War of Independence. His first short fiction appeared in *Jewish Life* and *Commentary* (1952). When he turned to genre fiction, Davidson benefited from a certain cultural and imaginative distance from the U.S. mainstream, a distance that was sometimes geographical: he lived for years as an expatriate in rural Mexico and Belize (then British Honduras), returning to the United States mainly to be closer to his son and ex-wife, sf and fantasy writer Grania Davis, in California. Although he attended three colleges, he never completed a degree program; nonetheless, he was formidably literate, a learned and scholarly man. In 1970, he traveled to Japan to study Tenrikyo, a spiritual discipline, translating some of its writings.

"The Golem," published in *The Magazine of Fantasy and Science Fiction* in 1955, was described by Damon Knight in 1998 as a "perfect story," and there is not a single wasted word. Even the ceramics class being taken by the Gumbeiners' dim boarder, Bud, is pressed into service twice. Davidson offers a gentle rendition of the sf scenario of colliding worlds, as the technological menaces and world conquest plots of B movies of the 1950s meet the folklore of the Ashkenazi, the old tales of sixteenth-century Rabbi Loew of Prague (1520–1609), and the golem (artificial man) that he fashioned from clay. Like Alfred Bester in the preceding story, Davidson clearly dissents from Asimov's hard-sf, high-tech approach to the portrayal of robots.

The grey-faced person came along the street where old Mr. and Mrs. Gumbeiner lived. It was afternoon, it was autumn, the sun was warm and soothing to their ancient bones. Anyone who attended the movies in the twenties or the early thirties has seen that street a thousand times. Past these bungalows with their half-double roofs Edmund Lowe walked arm-in-arm with Leatrice Joy and Harold Lloyd was chased by Chinamen waving hatchets. Under these squamous palm trees Laurel kicked Hardy and Woolsey beat Wheeler upon the head with a codfish. Across these pocket-handkerchief-sized lawns the juveniles of the Our Gang comedies pursued one another and were pursued by angry fat men in golf knickers. On this same street—or perhaps on some other one of five hundred streets exactly like it.

Mrs. Gumbeiner indicated the grey-faced person to her husband.

"You think maybe he's got something the matter?" she asked. "He walks kind of funny, to me."

"Walks like a *golem*," Mr. Gumbeiner said indifferently.

The old woman was nettled.

"Oh, I don't know," she said. "*I* think he walks like your cousin Mendel."

The old man pursed his mouth angrily and chewed on his pipestem. The grey-faced person turned up the concrete path, walked up the steps to the porch, sat down in a chair. Old Mr. Gumbeiner ignored him. His wife stared at the stranger.

"Man comes in without a hello, goodbye, or howareyou, sits himself down, and right away he's at home . . . The chair is comfortable?" she asked. "Would you like maybe a glass of tea?"

She turned to her husband.

"Say something, Gumbeiner!" she demanded. "What are you, made of wood?"

The old man smiled a slow, wicked, triumphant smile.

"Why should *I* say anything?" he asked the air. "Who am I? Nothing, that's who."

The stranger spoke. His voice was harsh and monotonous.

"When you learn who—or, rather, what—I am, the flesh will melt from your bones in terror." He bared porcelain teeth.

"Never mind about my bones!" the old woman cried. "You've got a lot of nerve talking about my bones!"

"You will quake with fear," said the stranger. Old Mrs. Gumbeiner said that she hoped he would live so long. She turned to her husband once again.

"Gumbeiner, when are you going to mow the lawn?"

"All mankind—" the stranger began.

"*Shah*! I'm talking to my husband . . . He talks *eppis* kind of funny, Gumbeiner, no?"

"Probably a foreigner," Mr. Gumbeiner said complacently.

"You think so?" Mrs. Gumbeiner glanced fleetingly at the stranger. "He's got a very bad color in his face, *nebbich*. I suppose he came to California for his health."

"Disease, pain, sorrow, love, grief—all are naught to—"

Mr. Gumbeiner cut in on the stranger's statement.

"Gall bladder," the old man said. "Guinzburg down at the *shule* looked exactly the same before his operation. Two professors they had in for him, and a private nurse day and night."

"I am not a human being!" the stranger said loudly.

"Three thousand seven hundred fifty dollars it cost his son, Guinzburg told me. 'For you, Poppa, nothing is too expensive—only get well,' the son told him."

"*I am not a human being!*"

"Ai, is that a son for you!" the old woman said, rocking her head. "A heart of gold, pure gold." She looked at the stranger. "All right, all right, I heard you the first time. Gumbeiner! I asked you a question. When are you going to cut the lawn?"

"On Wednesday, *odder* maybe Thursday, comes the Japaneser to the neighborhood. To cut lawns is *his* profession. *My* profession is to be a glazier—retired."

"Between me and all mankind is an inevitable hatred," the stranger said. "When I tell you what I am, the flesh will melt—"

"You said, you said already," Mr. Gumbeiner interrupted.

"In Chicago where the winters were as cold and bitter as the Czar of Russia's heart," the old woman intoned, "you had strength to carry the frames with the glass together day in and day out. But in California with the golden sun to mow the lawn when your wife asks, for this you have no strength. Do I call in the Japaneser to cook for you supper?"

"Thirty years Professor Allardyce spent perfecting his theories. Electronics, neuronics—"

"Listen, how educated he talks," Mr. Gumbeiner said admiringly. "Maybe he goes to the University here?"

"If he goes to the University, maybe he knows Bud?" his wife suggested.

"Probably they're in the same class and he came to see him about the homework, no?"

"Certainly he must be in the same class. How many classes are there? Five *in ganzen*: Bud showed me on his program card." She counted off on her fingers. "Television Appreciation and Criticism, Small Boat Building, Social Adjustment, The American Dance . . . The American Dance—*nu*, Gumbeiner—"

"Contemporary Ceramics," her husband said, relishing the syllables. "A fine boy, Bud. A pleasure to have him for a boardner."

"After thirty years spent in these studies," the stranger, who had continued to speak unnoticed, went on, "he turned from the theoretical to the pragmatic. In ten years' time he had made the most titanic discovery in history: he made mankind, *all* mankind, superfluous; he made *me*."

"What did Tillie write in her last letter?" asked the old man.

The old woman shrugged.

"What should she write? The same thing. Sidney was home from the Army, Naomi has a new boyfriend—"

"*He made* ME*!*"

"Listen, Mr. Whatever-your-name-is," the old woman said, "maybe where you came from is different, but in *this* country you don't interrupt people while they're talking . . . Hey. Listen—what do you mean, he *made* you? What kind of talk is that?"

The stranger bared all his teeth again, exposing the too-pink gums.

"In his library, to which I had a more complete access after his sudden and as yet undiscovered death from entirely natural causes, I found a complete collection of stories about androids, from Shelley's *Frankenstein* through Capek's *R.U.R.* to Asimov's—"

"Frankenstein?" said the old man, with interest. "There used to be a Frankenstein who had the soda-*wasser* place on Halstead Street—a Litvack, *nebbich*."

"What are you talking?" Mrs. Gumbeiner demanded. "His name was Franken*thal*, and it wasn't on Halstead, it was on Roosevelt."

"—clearly shown that all mankind has an instinctive antipathy towards androids and there will be an inevitable struggle between them—"

"Of course, of course!" Old Mr. Gumbeiner clicked his teeth against his pipe. "I am always wrong, you are always right. How could you stand to be married to such a stupid person all this time?"

"I don't know," the old woman said. "Sometimes I wonder, myself. I think it must be his good looks." She began to laugh. Old Mr. Gumbeiner blinked, then began to smile, then took his wife's hand.

"Foolish old woman," the stranger said. "Why do you laugh? Do you not know I have come to destroy you?"

"What?" old Mr. Gumbeiner shouted. "Close your mouth, you!" He darted from his chair and struck the stranger with the flat of his hand. The stranger's head struck against the porch pillar and bounced back.

"When you talk to my wife, talk respectable, you hear?"

Old Mrs. Gumbeiner, cheeks very pink, pushed her husband back to his chair. Then she leaned forward and examined the stranger's head. She clicked her tongue as she pulled aside a flap of grey, skinlike material.

"Gumbeiner, look! He's all springs and wires inside!"

"I *told* you he was a *golem*, but no, you wouldn't listen," the old man said.

"You said he *walked* like a *golem*."

"How could he walk like a *golem* unless he *was* one?"

"All right, all right . . . You broke him, so now fix him."

"My grandfather, his light shines from Paradise, told me that when MoHaRaL—Moreynu Ha-Rav Löw—his memory for a blessing, made the *golem* in Prague, three hundred? four hundred years ago? he wrote on his forehead the Holy Name."

Smiling reminiscently, the old woman continued, "And the *golem* cut the rabbi's wood and brought his water and guarded the ghetto."

"And one time only he disobeyed the Rabbi Löw, and Rabbi Löw erased the *Shem Ha-Mephorash* from the *golem*'s forehead and the *golem* fell down like a dead one. And they put him up in the attic of the *shule*, and he's still there today if the Communisten haven't sent him to Moscow . . . This is not just a story," he said.

"*Avadda* not!" said the old woman.

"I myself have seen both the *shule and* the rabbi's grave," her husband said conclusively.

"But I think this must be a different kind of *golem*, Gumbeiner. See, on his forehead: nothing written."

"What's the matter, there's a law I can't write something there? Where is that lump of clay Bud brought us from his class?"

The old man washed his hands, adjusted his little black skull-cap, and slowly and carefully wrote four Hebrew letters on the grey forehead.

“Ezra the Scribe himself couldn’t do better,” the old woman said admiringly. “Nothing happens,” she observed, looking at the lifeless figure sprawled in the chair.

“Well, after all, am I Rabbi Löw?” her husband asked deprecatingly. “No,” he answered. He leaned over and examined the exposed mechanism. “This spring goes here . . . this wire comes with this one . . .” The figure moved. “But this one goes where? And this one?”

“Let be,” said his wife. The figure sat up slowly and rolled its eyes loosely.

“Listen, Reb *Golem*,” the old man said, wagging his finger. “Pay attention to what I say—you understand?”

“Understand . . .”

“If you want to stay here, you got to do like Mr. Gumbeiner says.”

“Do-like-Mr.-Gumbeiner-says . . .”

“*That’s* the way I like to hear a *golem* talk. Malka, give here the mirror from the pocketbook. Look, you see your face? You see the forehead, what’s written? If you don’t do like Mr. Gumbeiner says, he’ll wipe out what’s written and you’ll be no more alive.”

“No-more-alive . . .”

“*That’s* right. Now, listen. Under the porch you’ll find a lawnmower. Take it. And cut the lawn. Then come back. Go.”

“Go . . .” The figure shambled down the stairs. Presently the sound of the lawnmower whirred through the quiet air in the street just like the street where Jackie Cooper shed huge tears on Wallace Beery’s shirt and Chester Conklin rolled his eyes at Marie Dressler.

“So what will you write to Tillie?” old Mr. Gumbeiner asked.

“What should I write?” old Mrs. Gumbeiner shrugged. “I’ll write that the weather is lovely out here and that we are both, Blessed be the Name, in good health.”

The old man nodded his head slowly, and they sat together on the front porch in the warm afternoon sun.

Cordwainer Smith
The Game of Rat and Dragon

• • • •

{1955}

Cordwainer Smith (1913–1966) was the sf pseudonym of Paul M. A. Linebarger (1913–1966). His father, a retired American judge and supporter of Chinese nationalism, was an advisor to Sun Yat-sen and supplied guns for the Xinhai revolution of 1912. The family moved constantly across countries and continents: before he was twenty he had lived in the rural South, Hawaii, Washington, D.C., China, Monaco, and Germany. He lost an eye when it was pierced by a wire thrown by a playmate, and his first published sf story, "Scanners Live in Vain" (1950), recalls the pain of "going under the wire." He received his PhD in political science from Johns Hopkins University a few days before his twenty-third birthday. He was a scholar of Asian politics, a teacher of diplomats, a spy in Egypt, Mexico, and Asia for U.S. Army Intelligence, and a courier for the CIA. Drawing on his experiences in World War II, in which he served as a liaison among Chinese nationalist, Chinese communist, and Allied factions, he wrote *Psychological Warfare* (1948), the book that popularized that term. After brief stints at Harvard and Duke, he taught at the School for Advanced International Studies, a Washington, D.C.–based diplomacy program. Cordwainer Smith's real name was one of his most closely guarded secrets, not generally known until after his death.

Probably he was the model for "Kirk Allen," the war-haunted sf writer of Dr. Robert Lindner's psychiatric memoir *The Fifty Minute Hour* (1954). Most of his stories have a strongly psychological focus: in his far future, all voyagers through deep space risk a horrifying psychic disintegration or "burning of the brain," as he calls it in one story. Smith's plots are also unusual for their Cold War era in emphasizing negotiation, conspiracy, and ad hoc liaisons rather than open, mobilized aggression or high-tech weaponry. His heroes are torn between mind and body, independent thought and social programming, domestic happiness and public service. Often they break ranks, rebelling against "normal" consensus. Underhill, hero of the story that follows, is a species-traitor of a sort.

The "game" of this story takes place in phases described in the subtitles. Smith's playful style draws on his fluency in many languages, his love of Symbolist poetry, and his knowledge of Chinese literature and culture. He is especially proficient in the sf art of neologism, the coining of new words: "pinlighter," for example. Details of his future history are explored in longer, later stories in which secretive groups of Lords and Ladies, collectively known as the Instrumentality, ensure prosperity for "true men" across tens of thousands of years yet oppress the "underpeople," animal-derived beings who do most of the work. "The Game of Rat and Dragon," which appeared in *Galaxy*, is early, his second published sf story. Written during a single afternoon in 1954, its short length and intimate focus—on the telepathic bond between its two major characters—make it among his most accessible. In the profound darkness of the "Up and Out," Smith's Chinese-inflected term for space, human beings and their surprising "Partners" link minds to slay a new kind of dragon. The story's depiction of interspecies camaraderie may recall the special man-dog relationship in Clifford Simak's "Desertion" (1944).

I.

The Table

Pinlighting is a hell of a way to earn a living. Underhill was furious as he closed the door behind himself. It didn't make much sense to wear a uniform and look like a soldier if people didn't appreciate what you did.

He sat down in his chair, laid his head back in the headrest, and pulled the helmet down over his forehead.

As he waited for the pin-set to warm up, he remembered the girl in the outer corridor. She had looked at it, then looked at him scornfully.

"Meow." That was all she had said. Yet it had cut him like a knife.

What did she think he was—a fool, a loafer, a uniformed nonentity? Didn't she know that for every half-hour of pinlighting, he got a minimum of two months' recuperation in the hospital?

By now the set was warm. He felt the squares of space around him, sensed himself at the middle of an immense grid, a cubic grid, full of nothing. Out in that nothingness, he could sense the hollow aching horror of space itself and could feel the terrible anxiety which his mind encountered whenever it met the faintest trace of inert dust.

As he relaxed, the comforting solidity of the Sun, the clockwork of the familiar planets and the Moon rang in on him. Our own solar system was as charming and as simple as an ancient cuckoo clock filled with familiar ticking and with reassuring noises. The odd little moons of Mars swung around their planet like frantic mice, yet their regularity was itself an assurance that all was well. Far above the plane of the ecliptic, he could feel half a ton of dust more or less drifting outside the lanes of human travel.

Here there was nothing to fight, nothing to challenge the mind, to tear the living soul out of a body with its roots dripping in effluvium as tangible as blood.

Nothing ever moved in on the solar system. He could wear the pin-set forever and be nothing more than a sort of telepathic astronomer, a man who could feel the hot, warm protection of the Sun throbbing and burning against his living mind.

Woodley came in.

"Same old ticking world," said Underhill. "Nothing to report. No wonder they didn't develop the pin-set until they began to planoform. Down here with the hot Sun around us, it feels so good and so quiet. You can feel everything spinning and turning. It's nice and sharp and compact. It's sort of like sitting around home."

Woodley grunted. He was not much given to flights of fantasy.

Undeterred, Underhill went on, "It must have been pretty good to have been an ancient man. I wonder why they burned up their world with war. They didn't have to planoform. They didn't have to go out to earn their livings among the stars. They didn't have to dodge the Rats or play the Game. They couldn't have invented pinlighting because they didn't have any need of it, did they, Woodley?"

Woodley grunted, "Uh-huh." Woodley was twenty-six years old and due to retire in one more year. He already had a farm picked out. He had gotten through ten years of hard work pinlighting with the best of them. He had kept his sanity by not thinking very much about his job, meeting the strains of the task whenever he had to meet them, and thinking nothing more about his duties until the next emergency arose.

Woodley never made a point of getting popular among the Partners. None of the Partners liked him very much. Some of them even resented him. He was suspected of thinking ugly thoughts of the Partners on occasion, but since none of the Partners ever thought a complaint in articulate form, the other pinlighters and the Chiefs of the Instrumentality left him alone.

Underhill was still full of the wonder of their job. Happily he babbled on, "What does happen to us when we planoform? Do you think it's sort of like dying? Did you ever see anybody who had his soul pulled out?"

"Pulling souls is just a way of talking about it," said Woodley. "After all these years, nobody knows whether we have souls or not."

"But I saw one once. I saw what Dogwood looked like when he came apart. There was something funny. It looked wet and sort of sticky as if it were bleeding and it went out of him—and you know what they did to Dogwood? They took him away, up in that part of the hospital where you and I never go—way up at the top part where the others are, where the others always have to go if they are alive after the Rats of the Up-and-Out have gotten them."

Woodley sat down and lit an ancient pipe. He was burning something called tobacco in it. It was a dirty sort of habit but it made him look very dashing and adventurous.

"Look here, youngster. You don't have to worry about that stuff. Pinlighting is getting better all the time. The Partners are getting better. I've seen them pinlight two Rats forty-six million miles apart in one and a half milliseconds. As long as people had to try to work the pin-sets themselves, there was always the chance that with a minimum of four-hundred milliseconds for the human mind to set a pinlight, we wouldn't light the Rats up fast enough to protect our planoforming ships. The Partners have changed all that. Once they get going, they're faster than the Rats. And they always will be. I know it's not easy, letting a Partner share your mind—"

"It's not easy for them, either," said Underhill.

"Don't worry about them. They're not human. Let them take care of themselves. I've seen more pinlighters go crazy from monkeying around with Partners than I have ever seen caught by the Rats. How many of them do you actually know of that got grabbed by Rats?"

Underhill looked down at his fingers, which shone green and purple in the vivid light thrown by the tuned-in pin-set, and counted ships. The thumb for the *Andromeda*, lost with crew and passengers, the index finger and the middle finger for *Release Ships* 43 and 56, found with their pin-sets burned out and every man, woman, and child on board dead or insane. The ring finger, the little finger, and the thumb of the other hand were the first battleships to be lost to the Rats—lost as people realized that there was something out there *underneath space itself* which was alive, capricious, and malevolent.

Planoforming was sort of funny. It felt like—

Like nothing much.

Like the twinge of a mild electric shock.

Like the ache of a sore tooth bitten on for the first time.

Like a slightly painful flash of light against the eyes.

Yet in that time, a forty-thousand-ton ship lifting free above Earth disappeared somehow or other into two dimensions and appeared half a light-year or fifty light-years off.

At one moment, he would be sitting in the Fighting Room, the pin-set ready and the familiar solar system ticking around inside his head. For a second or a year (he could never tell how long it really was, subjectively), the funny little flash went through him and then he was loose in the Up-and-Out, the terrible open spaces between the stars, where the stars themselves felt like pimples on his telepathic mind and the planets were too far away to be sensed or read.

Somewhere in this outer space, a gruesome death awaited, death and horror of a kind which Man had never encountered until he reached out for interstellar space itself. Apparently the light of the suns kept the dragons away.

Dragons. That was what people called them. To ordinary people, there was nothing, nothing except the shiver of planoforming and the hammer blow of sudden death or the dark spastic note of lunacy descending into their minds.

But to the telepaths, they were Dragons.

In the fraction of a second between the telepaths' awareness of a hostile something out in the black, hollow nothingness of space and the impact of a ferocious, ruinous psychic blow against all living things within the ship, the telepaths had sensed entities something like the Dragons of ancient human lore, beasts more clever than beasts, demons more tangible than demons, hungry vortices of aliveness and hate compounded by unknown means out of the thin, tenuous matter between the stars.

It took a surviving ship to bring back the news—a ship in which, by sheer chance, a telepath had a light-beam ready, turning it out at the innocent dust so that, within the panorama of his mind, the Dragon dissolved into nothing at all and the other passengers, themselves non-telepathic, went about their way not realizing that their own immediate deaths had been averted.

From then on, it was easy—almost.

Planoforming ships always carried telepaths. Telepaths had their sensitiveness enlarged to an immense range by the pin-sets, which were telepathic amplifiers adapted to the mammal mind. The pin-sets in turn were electronically geared into small dirigible light bombs. Light did it.

Light broke up the Dragons, allowed the ships to reform three-dimensionally, skip, skip, skip, as they moved from star to star.

The odds suddenly moved down from a hundred to one against mankind to sixty to forty in mankind's favor.

This was not enough. The telepaths were trained to become ultrasensitive, trained to become aware of the Dragons in less than a millisecond.

But it was found that the Dragons could move a million miles in just under two milliseconds and that this was not enough for the human mind to activate the light beams.

Attempts had been made to sheath the ships in light at all times.

This defense wore out.

As mankind learned about the Dragons, so too, apparently, the Dragons learned about mankind. Somehow they flattened their own bulk and came in on extremely flat trajectories very quickly.

Intense light was needed, light of sunlike intensity. This could be provided only by light bombs. Pinlighting came into existence.

Pinlighting consisted of the detonation of ultra-vivid miniature photonuclear bombs, which converted a few ounces of a magnesium isotope into pure visible radiance.

The odds kept coming down in mankind's favor, yet ships were being lost.

It became so bad that people didn't even want to find the ships because the rescuers knew what they would see. It was sad to bring back to Earth three hundred bodies ready for burial and two hundred or three hundred lunatics, damaged beyond repair, to be wakened, and fed, and cleaned, and put to sleep, wakened and fed again until their lives were ended.

Telepaths tried to reach into the minds of the psychotics who had been damaged by the Dragons, but they found nothing there beyond vivid spouting columns of fiery terror bursting from the primordial id itself, the volcanic source of life.

Then came the Partners.

Man and Partner could do together what Man could not do alone. Men had the intellect. Partners had the speed.

The Partners rode in their tiny craft, no larger than footballs, outside the spaceships. They planoformed with the ships. They rode beside them in their six-pound craft ready to attack.

The tiny ships of the Partners were swift. Each carried a dozen pinlights, bombs no bigger than thimbles.

The Pinlighters threw the Partners—quite literally threw—by means of mind-to-firing relays direct at the Dragons.

What seemed to be Dragons to the human mind appeared in the form of gigantic Rats in the minds of the Partners.

Out in the pitiless nothingness of space, the Partners' minds responded to an instinct as old as life. The Partners attacked, striking with a speed faster than man's, going from attack to attack until the Rats or themselves were destroyed. Almost all the time it was the Partners who won.

With the safety of the interstellar skip, skip, skip of the ships, commerce increased immensely, the population of all the colonies went up, and the demand for trained Partners increased.

Underhill and Woodley were a part of the third generation of pinlighters and yet, to them, it seemed as though their craft had endured forever.

Gearing space into minds by means of the pin-set, adding the Partners to those minds, keying up the minds for the tension of a fight on which all depended—this was more than human synapses could stand for long. Underhill needed his two months' rest after half an hour of fighting. Woodley needed his retirement after ten years of service. They were young. They were good. But they had limitations.

So much depended on the choice of Partners, so much on the sheer luck of who drew whom.

II.

The Shuffle

Father Moontree and the little girl named West entered the room. They were the other two pinlighters. The human complement of the Fighting Room was now complete.

Father Moontree was a red-faced man of forty-five who had lived the peaceful life of a farmer until he reached his fortieth year. Only then, belatedly, did the authorities find he was telepathic and agree to let him late in life enter upon the career of pinlighter. He did well at it, but he was fantastically old for this kind of business.

Father Moontree looked at the glum Woodley and the musing Underhill. "How're the youngsters today? Ready for a good fight?"

"Father always wants a fight," giggled the little girl named West. She was such a little little girl. Her giggle was high and childish. She looked like the last person in the world one would expect to find in the rough, sharp dueling of pinlighting.

Underhill had been amused one time when he found one of the most sluggish of the Partners coming away happy from contact with the mind of the girl named West.

Usually the Partners didn't care much about the human minds with which they were paired for the journey. The Partners seemed to take the attitude that human minds were complex and fouled up beyond belief, anyhow. No Partner ever questioned the superiority of the human mind, though very few of the Partners were much impressed by that superiority.

The Partners liked people. They were willing to fight with them. They were even willing to die for them. But when a Partner liked an individual the way, for example, that Captain Wow or the Lady May liked Underhill, the liking had nothing to do with intellect. It was a matter of temperament, of feel.

Underhill knew perfectly well that Captain Wow regarded his, Underhill's, brains as silly. What Captain Wow liked was Underhill's friendly emotional structure, the cheerfulness and glint of wicked amusement that shot through Underhill's unconscious thought patterns, and the gaiety with which Underhill faced danger. The words, the history books, the ideas, the science—Underhill could sense all that in his own mind, reflected back from Captain Wow's mind, as so much rubbish.

Miss West looked at Underhill. "I bet you've put stickum on the stones."

"I did not!"

Underhill felt his ears grow red with embarrassment. During his novitiate, he had tried to cheat in the lottery because he got particularly fond of a special Partner, a lovely young mother named Murr. It was so much easier to operate with Murr and she was so affectionate toward him that he forgot pinlighting was hard work and that he was not instructed to have a good time with his Partner. They were both designed and prepared to go into deadly battle together.

One cheating had been enough. They had found him out and he had been laughed at for years.

Father Moontree picked up the imitation-leather cup and shook the stone dice which assigned them their Partners for the trip. By senior rights, he took first draw.

He grimaced. He had drawn a greedy old character, a tough old male whose mind was full of slobbering thoughts of food, veritable oceans full of half-spoiled fish. Father Moontree had once said that he burped cod liver oil for weeks after drawing that particular glutton, so strongly had the telepathic image of fish impressed itself upon his mind. Yet the glutton was a glutton for danger as well as for fish. He had killed sixty-three Dragons, more than any other Partner in the service, and was quite literally worth his weight in gold.

The little girl West came next. She drew Captain Wow. When she saw who it was, she smiled.

"I *like* him," she said. "He's such fun to fight with. He feels so nice and cuddly in my mind."

"Cuddly, hell," said Woodley. "I've been in his mind, too. It's the most leering mind in this ship, bar none."

"Nasty man," said the little girl. She said it declaratively without reproach.

Underhill, looking at her, shivered.

He didn't see how she could take Captain Wow so calmly. Captain Wow's mind *did* leer. When Captain Wow got excited in the middle of a battle, confused images of Dragons, deadly Rats, luscious beds, the smell of fish, and the shock of space all scrambled together in his mind as he and Captain Wow, their consciousnesses linked together through the pin-set, became a fantastic composite of human being and Persian cat.

That's the trouble with working with cats, thought Underhill. It's a pity that nothing else anywhere will serve as Partner. Cats were all right once you got in touch with them telepathically. They were smart enough to meet the needs of the fight, but their motives and desires were certainly different from those of humans.

They were companionable enough as long as you thought tangible images at them, but their minds just closed up and went to sleep when you recited Shakespeare or Colegrove, or if you tried to tell them what space was.

It was sort of funny realizing that the Partners who were grim and mature out here in space were the same cute little animals that people had used as pets for thousands of years back on Earth. He had embarrassed himself more than once while on the ground saluting perfectly ordinary non-telepathic cats because he had forgotten for the moment that they were not Partners.

He picked up the cup and shook out his stone dice. He was lucky—he drew the Lady May.

The Lady May was the most thoughtful Partner he had ever met. In her, the finely bred pedigree mind of a Persian cat had reached one of its highest peaks of development. She was more complex than any human woman, but the complexity was all one of emotions, memory, hope and discriminated experience—experience sorted through without benefit of words.

When he had first come into contact with her mind, he was astonished at its clarity. With her he remembered her kittenhood. He remembered every mating experience she had ever had. He saw in a half-recognizable gallery all the other pinlighters with whom she had been paired for the fight. And he saw himself radiant, cheerful and desirable.

He even thought he caught the edge of a longing—

A very flattering and yearning thought: *What a pity he is not a cat.*

Woodley picked up the last stone. He drew what he deserved—a sullen, scarred old tomcat with none of the verve of Captain Wow. Woodley's Partner was the most animal of all the cats on the ship, a low, brutish type with a dull mind. Even telepathy had not refined his character. His ears were half chewed off from the first fights in which he had engaged. He was a serviceable fighter, nothing more.

Woodley grunted.

Underhill glanced at him oddly. Didn't Woodley ever do anything but grunt?

Father Moontree looked at the other three. "You might as well get your Partners now. I'll let the Go-Captain know we're ready to go into the Up-and-Out."

III.

The Deal

Underhill spun the combination lock on the Lady May's cage. He woke her gently and took her into his arms. She humped her back luxuriously, stretched her claws, started to purr, thought better of it, and licked him on the wrist instead. He did not have the pin-set on, so their minds were closed to each other, but in the angle of her moustache and in the movement of her ears, he caught some sense of the gratification she experienced in finding him as her Partner.

He talked to her in human speech, even though speech meant nothing to a cat when the pin-set was not on.

"It's a damn shame, sending a sweet little thing like you whirling around in the coldness of nothing to hunt for Rats that are bigger and deadlier than all of us put together. You didn't ask for this kind of a fight, did you?"

For answer, she licked his hand, purred, tickled his cheek with her long fluffy tail, turned around and faced him, golden eyes shining.

For a moment they stared at each other, man squatting, cat standing erect on her hind legs, front claws digging into his knee. Human eyes and cat eyes looked across an immensity which no words could meet, but which affection spanned in a single glance.

"Time to get in," he said.

She walked docilely into her spheroid carrier. She climbed in. He saw to it that her miniature pin-set rested firmly and comfortably against the base of her brain. He made sure that her claws were padded so that she could not tear herself in the excitement of battle.

Softly he said to her, "Ready?"

For answer, she preened her back as much as her harness would permit and purred softly within the confines of the frame that held her.

He slapped down the lid and watched the sealant ooze around the seam. For a few hours, she was welded into her projectile until a workman with a short cutting arc would remove her after she had done her duty.

He picked up the entire projectile and slipped it into the ejection tube. He closed the door of the tube, spun the lock, seated himself in his chair, and put his own pin-set on.

Once again he flung the switch. He sat in a small room, *small, small, warm, warm,* the bodies of the other three people moving close around him, the tangible lights in the ceiling bright and heavy against his closed eyelids.

As the pin-set warmed, the room fell away. The other people ceased to be people and became small glowing heaps of fire, embers, dark red fire, with the consciousness of life burning like old red coals in a country fireplace.

As the pin-set warmed a little more, he felt Earth just below him, felt the ship slipping away, felt the turning Moon as it swung on the far side of the world, felt the planets and the hot, clear goodness of the Sun which kept the Dragons so far from mankind's native ground.

Finally, he reached complete awareness.

He was telepathically alive to a range of millions of miles.

He felt the dust which he had noticed earlier high above the ecliptic. With a thrill of warmth and tenderness, he felt the consciousness of the Lady May pouring over into his own. Her consciousness was as gentle and clear and yet sharp to the taste of his mind as if it were scented oil. It felt relaxing and reassuring. He could sense her welcome of him. It was scarcely a thought, just a raw emotion of greeting.

At last they were one again.

In a tiny remote corner of his mind, as tiny as the smallest toy he had ever seen in his childhood, he was still aware of the room and the ship, and of Father Moontree picking up a telephone and speaking to a Go-Captain in charge of the ship.

His telepathic mind caught the idea long before his ears could frame the words. The actual sound followed the idea the way that thunder on an ocean beach follows the lightning inward from far out over the seas.

"The Fighting Room is ready. Clear to planoform, sir."

IV.

The Play

Underhill was always a little exasperated the way that the Lady May experienced things before he did.

He was braced for the quick vinegar thrill of planoforming, but he caught her report of it before his own nerves could register what happened.

Earth had fallen so far away that he groped for several milliseconds before he found the Sun in the upper rear right-hand corner of his telepathic mind.

That was a good jump, he thought. *This way we'll get there in four or five skips.*

A few hundred miles outside the ship, the Lady May thought back at him, "O warm, O generous, O gigantic man! O brave, O friendly, O tender and huge Partner! O wonderful with you, with you so good, good, good, warm, warm, now to fight, now to go, good with you . . ."

He knew that she was not thinking words, that his mind took the clear amiable babble of her cat intellect and translated it into images which his own thinking could record and understand.

Neither one of them was absorbed in the game of mutual greetings. He reached out far beyond her range of perception to see if there was anything near the ship. It was funny how it was possible to do two things at once. He could scan space with his pin-set mind and yet at the same time catch a vagrant thought of hers, a lovely, affectionate thought about a son who had had a golden face and a chest covered with soft, incredibly downy white fur.

While he was still searching, he caught the warning from her.

We jump again!

And so they had. The ship moved to a second planoform. The stars were different. The Sun was immeasurably far behind. Even the nearest stars were barely in contact. This was good Dragon country, this open, nasty, hollow kind of space. He reached farther, faster, sensing and looking for danger, ready to fling the Lady May at danger wherever he found it.

Terror blazed up in his mind, so sharp, so clear, that it came through as a physical wrench.

The little girl named West had found something—something immense, long, black, sharp, greedy, horrific. She flung Captain Wow at it.

Underhill tried to keep his own mind clear. "Watch out!" he shouted telepathically at the others, trying to move the Lady May around.

At one corner of the battle, he felt the lustful rage of Captain Wow as the big Persian tomcat detonated lights while he approached the streak of dust which threatened the ship and the people within.

The lights scored near misses.

The dust flattened itself, changing from the shape of a sting-ray into the shape of a spear.

Not three milliseconds had elapsed.

Father Moontree was talking human words and was saying in a voice that moved like cold molasses out of a heavy jar, “C-a-p-t-a-i-n.” Underhill knew that the sentence was going to be “Captain, move fast!”

The battle would be fought and finished before Father Moontree got through talking.

Now, fractions of a millisecond later, the Lady May was directly in line.

Here was where the skill and speed of the Partners came in. She could react faster than he. She could see the threat as an immense Rat coming directly at her.

She could fire the light-bombs with a discrimination which he might miss.

He was connected with her mind, but he could not follow it.

His consciousness absorbed the tearing wound inflicted by the alien enemy. It was like no wound on Earth—raw, crazy pain which started like a burn at his navel. He began to writhe in his chair.

Actually he had not yet had time to move a muscle when the Lady May struck back at their enemy.

Five evenly spaced photonuclear bombs blazed out across a hundred-thousand miles.

The pain in his mind and body vanished.

He felt a moment of fierce, terrible, feral elation running through the mind of the Lady May as she finished her kill. It was always disappointing to the cats to find out that their enemies disappeared at the moment of destruction.

Then he felt her hurt, the pain and the fear that swept over both of them as the battle, quicker than the movement of an eyelid, had come and gone. In the same instant, there came the sharp and acid twinge of planoform.

Once more the ship went skip.

He could hear Woodley thinking at him. “You don’t have to bother much. This old son-of-a-gun and I will take over for a while.”

Twice again the twinge, the skip.

He had no idea where he was until the lights of the Caledonia space port shone below.

With a weariness that lay almost beyond the limits of thought, he threw his mind back into rapport with the pin-set, fixing the Lady May’s projectile gently and neatly in its launching tube.

She was half dead with fatigue, but he could feel the beat of her heart, could listen to her panting, and he grasped the grateful edge of a “Thanks” reaching from her mind to his.

V.

The Score

They put him in the hospital at Caledonia.

The doctor was friendly but firm. "You actually got touched by that Dragon. That's as close a shave as I've ever seen. It's all so quick that it'll be a long time before we know what happened scientifically, but I suppose you'd be ready for the insane asylum now if the contact had lasted several tenths of a millisecond longer. What kind of cat did you have out in front of you?"

Underhill felt the words coming out of him slowly. Words were such a lot of trouble compared with the speed and the joy of thinking, fast and sharp and clear, mind to mind! But words were all that could reach ordinary people like this doctor.

His mouth moved heavily as he articulated words. "Don't call our Partners cats. The right thing to call them is Partners. They fight for us in a team. You ought to know we call them Partners, not cats. How is mine?"

"I don't know," said the doctor contritely. "We'll find out for you. Meanwhile, old man, you take it easy. There's nothing but rest that can help you. Can you make yourself sleep, or would you like us to give you some kind of sedative?"

"I can sleep," said Underhill. "I just want to know about the Lady May."

The nurse joined in. She was a little antagonistic. "Don't you want to know about the other people?"

"They're okay," said Underhill. "I knew that before I came in here."

He stretched his arms and sighed and grinned at them. He could see they were relaxing and were beginning to treat him as a person instead of a patient.

"I'm all right," he said. "Just let me know when I can go see my Partner."

A new thought struck him. He looked wildly at the doctor. "They didn't send her off with the ship, did they?"

"I'll find out right away," said the doctor. He gave Underhill a reassuring squeeze of the shoulder and left the room.

The nurse took a napkin off a goblet of chilled fruit juice. Underhill tried to smile at her. There seemed to be something wrong with the girl. He wished she would go away. First she had started to be friendly and now she was distant again. *It's a nuisance being telepathic*, he thought. *You keep trying to reach even when you are not making contact.*

Suddenly she swung around on him.

"You pinlighters! You and your damn cats!"

Just as she stamped out, he burst into her mind. He saw himself a radiant hero, clad in his smooth suede uniform, the pin-set crown shining like ancient royal jewels around his head. He saw his own face, handsome and masculine, shining out of her mind. He saw himself very far away and he saw himself as she hated him.

She hated him in the secrecy of her own mind. She hated him because he was—she thought—proud and strange and rich, better and more beautiful than people like her.

He cut off the sight of her mind and, as he buried his face in the pillow, he caught an image of the Lady May.

"She *is* a cat," he thought. "That's all she is—a *cat*!" But that was not how his mind saw her—quick beyond all dreams of speed, sharp, clever, unbelievably graceful, beautiful, wordless and undemanding.

Where would he ever find a woman who could compare with her?

Robert A. Heinlein

"All You Zombies—"

• • • •

{1959}

For two generations, Robert A(nson) Heinlein (1907–1988) dominated the sf genre. Outer space was to him not an empty void but a window of opportunity. In a series of novels for young adults produced annually for Scribner's (1947–1958), he made a human future in space seem real in a way that no other writer has approached. The future in his sf belongs to those bright and brave enough to leave home. The central character in *Starman Jones* (1953) is typical: desperate to leave Earth, he forges credentials to get into space, thereby escaping a slovenly stepmother and hopeless future on a run-down family farm. Most of Heinlein's heroes are diligent students: space was for him a frontier to be tamed, but more by the slide rule than the handgun. His characters are happiest in low gravity, whether building families and cities on Luna (*The Moon Is a Harsh Mistress*, 1966), escaping from slavery (*Citizen of the Galaxy*, 1955), or resolving more routine problems such as sibling rivalry (*Time for the Stars*, 1956). Heinlein often showcased heroes who were not American, and heroes of color, and he often questioned gender stereotypes: in *Starship Troopers* (1959), Juan Rico's friend Carmen is immediately recruited as a future starship pilot after enlisting, while he himself fails almost every military aptitude test.

When Heinlein turned entirely to adult sf during the 1960s, he chose risky topics such as free love, ritual cannibalism, and female-to-male consciousness downloads. Many of his late novels remain controversial. Although seldom selling to fantasy markets, Heinlein clearly shared the fantasy genre's fascination with the exhibition/transformation of the body; he was especially drawn to the satiric fantastic in the vein of James Branch Cabell or Mark Twain's *A Connecticut Yankee in King Arthur's Court* (1889). The fact is that the hard sf subgenre became something of a box to him later in his career; and if some of his later *Multiverse* novels do not hold together well, his first out-of-the-sf-box experiment in addressing social taboos, *Stranger in a Strange Land* (1961), remains his best-known work.

Third of seven children, he was born in rural Missouri and schooled in Kansas City. His young heroes who study their way out of cramped living quarters, breaking free to find more congenial mentors in military settings, may be based on his own early life. He attended the U.S. Naval Academy and after being commissioned in 1929 worked on the first aircraft carrier. He soon developed tuberculosis, however, and was discharged on permanent disability in 1934. He tried silver mining in New Mexico and Democratic Party politics in Los Angeles, where in 1938 he ran unsuccessfully for the California State Assembly. In 1939 he sold his first story, "Lifeline," to John W. Campbell at *Astounding*. He was over thirty, an adult in an sf milieu of the young. Isaac Asimov, who also made his first sale to Campbell that year, was nineteen; Theodore Sturgeon, another of Campbell's discoveries, was twenty-one. Even Campbell was younger than Heinlein, who established himself quickly for sf that followed a pre-mapped, consistent Future History, an idea taken from Cabell's working methods. Divorced from his second wife, Leslyn MacDonald, in 1947, Heinlein married Virginia Gerstenfeld a year later; she evidently inspired Hazel Stone and the other feisty redheads who populate his later novels.

The self-reliant man or woman *is* the plucky, can-do "Heinlein hero." Yet in some stories, notably "They" (1941), such characters are depicted as panic stricken, cut off from meaningful contact with others. "'All You Zombies—,'" among the most famous of time-travel stories, likewise casts a cold eye on ordinary human interactions. Its noir tone may have been inspired by its intended market, *Playboy*, but the story was rejected there, appearing instead in *The Magazine of Fantasy and Science Fiction*. Some of Heinlein's working titles—"The Solipsist," "Closed Circuit," "The World Snake"—suggest the claustrophobic implications of his plot. Written in a single day, this was his last short fiction sale; after 1960 he concentrated on novels.

2217 Time Zone V (EST) 7 Nov. 1970—NYC—"Pop's Place": I was polishing a brandy snifter when the Unmarried Mother came in. I noted the time—10:17 P.M. zone five, or eastern time, November 7th, 1970. Temporal agents always notice time and date; we must.

The Unmarried Mother was a man twenty-five years old, no taller than I am, childish features and a touchy temper. I didn't like his looks—I never had—but he was a lad I was here to recruit, he was my boy. I gave him my best barkeep's smile.

Maybe I'm too critical. He wasn't swish; his nickname came from what he always said when some nosy type asked him his line: "I'm an unmarried mother." If he felt less than murderous he would add: "—at four cents a word. I write confession stories."

If he felt nasty, he would wait for somebody to make something of it. He had a lethal style of in-fighting, like a female cop—one reason I wanted him. Not the only one.

He had a load on and his face showed that he despised people more than usual. Silently I poured a double shot of Old Underwear and left the bottle. He drank, poured another.

I wiped the bar top. "How's the 'Unmarried Mother' racket?"

His fingers tightened on the glass and he seemed about to throw it at me; I felt for the sap under the bar. In temporal manipulation you try to figure everything, but there are so many factors that you never take needless risks.

I saw him relax that tiny amount they teach you to watch for in the Bureau's training school. "Sorry," I said. "Just asking, 'How's business?' Make it 'How's the weather?'"

He looked sour. "Business is okay. I write 'em, they print 'em, I eat."

I poured myself one, leaned toward him. "Matter of fact," I said, "you write a nice stick—I've sampled a few. You have an amazingly sure touch with the woman's angle."

It was a slip I had to risk; he never admitted what pen-names he used. But he was boiled enough to pick up only the last: "'Woman's angle!'" he repeated with a snort. "Yeah, I know the woman's angle. I should."

"So?" I said doubtfully. "Sisters?"

"No. You wouldn't believe me if I told you."

"Now, now," I answered mildly, "bartenders and psychiatrists learn that nothing is stranger than the truth. Why, son, if you heard the stories I do—well, you'd make yourself rich. Incredible."

"You don't know what 'incredible' means!"

"So? Nothing astonishes me. I've always heard worse."

He snorted again. "Want to bet the rest of the bottle?"

"I'll bet a full bottle." I placed one on the bar.

"Well—" I signaled my other bartender to handle the trade. We were at the far end, a single-stool space that I kept private by loading the bar top by it with jars of pickled eggs and other clutter. A few were at the other end watching the fights and somebody was playing the juke box—private as a bed where we were.

"Okay," he began, "to start with, I'm a bastard."

"No distinction around here," I said.

"I mean it," he snapped. "My parents weren't married."

"Still no distinction," I insisted. "Neither were mine."

"When—" He stopped, gave me the first warm look I ever saw on him. "You mean that?"

"I do. A one-hundred-percent bastard. In fact," I added, "no one in my family ever marries. All bastards."

"Don't try to top me—*you're* married." He pointed at my ring.

"Oh, that." I showed it to him. "It just looks like a wedding ring; I wear it to keep women off." That ring is an antique I bought in 1985 from a fellow operative—he had fetched it from pre-Christian Crete. "The Worm Ouroboros . . . the World Snake that eats its own tail, forever without end. A symbol of the Great Paradox."

He barely glanced at it. "If you're really a bastard, you know how it feels. When I was a little girl—"

"Wups!" I said. "Did I hear you correctly?"

"Who's telling this story? When I was a little girl—Look, ever hear of Christine Jorgenson? Or Roberta Cowell?"

"Uh, sex-change cases? You're trying to tell me—"

"Don't interrupt or swelp me, I won't talk. I was a foundling, left at an orphanage in Cleveland in 1945 when I was a month old. When I was a little girl, I envied kids with parents. Then, when I learned about sex—and, believe me, Pop, you learn fast in an orphanage—"

"I know."

"—I made a solemn vow that any kid of mine would have both a pop and a mom. It kept me 'pure,' quite a feat in that vicinity—I had to learn to fight to manage it. Then I got older and realized I stood darn little chance of getting married—for the same reason I hadn't been adopted." He scowled. "I was horse-faced and buck-toothed, flat-chested and straight-haired."

"You don't look any worse than I do."

"Who cares how a barkeep looks? Or a writer? But people wanting to adopt pick little blue-eyed golden-haired morons. Later on, the boys want bulging breasts, a cute face, and an Oh-you-wonderful-male manner." He shrugged. "I couldn't compete. So I decided to join the W.E.N.C.H.E.S."

"Eh?"

"Women's Emergency National Corps, Hospitality & Entertainment Section, what they now call 'Space Angels'—Auxiliary Nursing Group, Extraterrestrial Legions."

I knew both terms, once I had them chronized. We use still a third name; it's that elite military service corps: Women's Hospitality Order Refortifying & Encouraging Spacemen. Vocabulary shift is the worst hurdle in time-jumps—did you know that "service station" once meant a dispensary for petroleum fractions? Once on an assignment in the Churchill Era, a woman said to me, "Meet me at the service station next door"—which is not what it sounds; a "service station" (then) wouldn't have a bed in it.

He went on: "It was when they first admitted you can't send men into space for months and years and not relieve the tension. You remember how the wowsers screamed?—that improved my chances, since volunteers were scarce. A gal had to be respectable, preferably virgin (they liked to train them from scratch), above average mentally, and stable emotionally. But most volunteers were old hookers, or neurotics who would crack up ten days off Earth. So I didn't need looks; if they accepted me, they would fix my buck teeth, put a wave in my hair, teach me to walk and dance and how to listen to a man pleasingly, and everything else—plus training for the prime duties. They would even use plastic surgery if it would help—nothing too good for Our Boys.

"Best yet, they made sure you didn't get pregnant during your enlistment—and you were almost certain to marry at the end of your hitch. Same way today, A.N.G.E.L.S. marry spacers—they talk the language.

"When I was eighteen I was placed as a 'mother's helper.' This family simply wanted a cheap servant but I didn't mind as I couldn't enlist till I was twenty-one. I did housework and went to night school—pretending to continue my high school typing and shorthand but going to a charm class instead, to better my chances for enlistment.

"Then I met this city slicker with his hundred-dollar bills." He scowled. "The no-good actually did have a wad of hundred-dollar bills. He showed me one night, told me to help myself.

"But I didn't. I liked him. He was the first man I ever met who was nice to me without trying games with me. I quit night school to see him oftener. It was the happiest time of my life.

"Then one night in the park the games began."

He stopped. I said, "And then?"

"And then *nothing*! I never saw him again. He walked me home and told me he loved me—and kissed me good-night and never came back." He looked grim. "If I could find him, I'd kill him."

"Well," I sympathized, "I know how you feel. But killing him—just for doing what comes naturally—hmm . . . Did you struggle?"

"Huh? What's that got to do with it?"

"Quite a bit. Maybe he deserves a couple of broken arms for running out on you, but—"

"He deserves worse than that! Wait till you hear. Somehow I kept anyone from suspecting and decided it was all for the best. I hadn't really loved him and probably would never love anybody—and I was more eager to join the W.E.N.C.H.E.S. than ever. I wasn't disqualified, they didn't insist on virgins. I cheered up.

"It wasn't until my skirts got tight that I realized."

"Pregnant?"

"He had me higher 'n a kite! Those skinflints I lived with ignored it as long as I could work—then kicked me out and the orphanage wouldn't take me back. I landed in a charity ward surrounded by other big bellies and trotted bedpans until my time came.

"One night I found myself on an operating table, with a nurse saying, 'Relax. Now breathe deeply.'

"I woke up in bed, numb from the chest down. My surgeon came in. 'How do you feel?' he says cheerfully.

"'Like a mummy.'

"'Naturally. You're wrapped like one and full of dope to keep you numb. You'll get well—but a Caesarian isn't a hangnail.'

"'Caesarian,' I said. 'Doc—*did I lose the baby*?'

"'Oh, no. Your baby's fine.'

"'Oh. Boy or girl?'

"'A healthy little girl. Five pounds, three ounces.'

"I relaxed. It's something, to have made a baby. I told myself I would go somewhere and tack 'Mrs.' on my name and let the kid think her papa was dead—no orphanage for *my* kid!

"But the surgeon was talking. 'Tell me, uh—' He avoided my name. '—did you ever think your glandular setup was odd?'

"I said, 'Huh? Of course not. What are you driving at?'

"He hesitated. 'I'll give you this in one dose, then a hypo to let you sleep off your jitters. You'll have 'em.'

"'Why?' I demanded.

"'Ever hear of that Scottish physician who was female until she was thirty-five?—then had surgery and became legally and medically a man? Got married. All okay.'

"'What's that got to do with me?'

"'That's what I'm saying. You're a man.'

"I tried to sit up. 'What?'

'"Take it easy. When I opened you, I found a mess. I sent for the Chief of Surgery while I got the baby out, then we held a consultation with you on the table—and worked for hours to salvage what we could. You had two full sets of organs, both immature, but with the female set well enough developed for you to have a baby. They could never be any use to you again, so we took them out and rearranged things so that you can develop properly as a man.' He put a hand on me. 'Don't worry. You're young, your bones will readjust, we'll watch your glandular balance—and make a fine young man out of you.'

"I started to cry. 'What about my *baby*?'

"'Well, you can't nurse her, you haven't milk enough for a kitten. If I were you, I wouldn't see her—put her up for adoption.'

"'*No!*'

"He shrugged. 'The choice is yours; you're her mother—well, her parent. But don't worry now; we'll get you well first.'

"Next day they let me see the kid and I saw her daily—trying to get used to her. I had never seen a brand-new baby and had no idea how awful they look—my daughter looked like an orange monkey. My feelings changed to cold determination to do right by her. But four weeks later that didn't mean anything."

"Eh?"

"She was snatched."

"'Snatched?'"

The Unmarried Mother almost knocked over the bottle we had bet. "Kidnapped—stolen from the hospital nursery!" He breathed hard. "How's that for taking the last a man's got to live for?"

"A bad deal," I agreed. "Let's pour you another. No clues?"

"Nothing the police could trace. Somebody came to see her, claimed to be her uncle. While the nurse had her back turned, he walked out with her."

"Description?"

"Just a man, with a face-shaped face, like yours or mine." He frowned. "I think it was the baby's father. The nurse swore it was an older man but he probably used makeup. Who else would swipe my baby? Childless women pull such stunts—but whoever heard of a man doing it?"

"What happened to you then?"

"Eleven more months of that grim place and three operations. In four months I started to grow a beard; before I was out I was shaving regularly . . . and no longer doubted that I was male." He grinned wryly. "I was staring down nurses' necklines."

"Well," I said, "seems to me you came through okay. Here you are, a normal man, making good money, no real troubles. And the life of a female is not an easy one."

He glared at me. "A lot you know about it!"

"So?"

"Ever hear the expression 'a ruined woman'?"

"Mmm, years ago. Doesn't mean much today."

"I was as ruined as a woman can be; that bastard *really* ruined me—I was no longer a woman . . . and I didn't know *how* to be a man."

"Takes getting used to, I suppose."

"You have no idea. I don't mean learning how to dress, or not walking into the wrong rest room; I learned those in the hospital. But how could I *live*? What job could I get? Hell, I couldn't even drive a car. I didn't know a trade; I couldn't do manual labor—too much scar tissue, too tender.

"I hated him for having ruined me for the W.E.N.C.H.E.S., too, but I didn't know how much until I tried to join the Space Corps instead. One look at my belly and I was marked unfit for military service. The medical officer spent time on me just from curiosity; he had read about my case.

"So I changed my name and came to New York. I got by as a fry cook, then rented a typewriter and set myself up as a public stenographer—what a laugh! In four months I typed four letters and one manuscript. The manuscript was for *Real Life Tales* and a waste of paper, but the goof who wrote it sold it. Which gave me an idea; I bought a stack of confession magazines and studied them." He looked cynical. "Now you know how I get the authentic woman's angle on an umarried-mother story . . . through the only version I haven't sold—the true one. Do I win the bottle?"

I pushed it toward him. I was upset myself but there was work to do. I said, "Son, you still want to lay hands on that so-and-so?"

His eyes lighted up—a feral gleam.

"Hold it!" I said. "You wouldn't kill him?"

He chuckled nastily. "Try me."

"Take it easy. I know more about it than you think I do. I can help you. I know where he is."

He reached across the bar. "*Where is he?*"

I said softly, "Let go my shirt, sonny—or you'll land in the alley and we'll tell the cops you fainted." I showed him the sap.

He let go. "Sorry. But where is he?" He looked at me. "And how do you know so much?"

"All in good time. There are records—hospital records, orphanage records, medical records. The matron of your orphanage was Mrs. Fetherage—right? She was followed by Mrs. Gruenstein—right? Your name, as a girl, was 'Jane'—right? And you didn't tell me any of this—right?"

I had him baffled and a bit scared. "What's this? You trying to make trouble for me?"

"No indeed. I've your welfare at heart. I can put this character in your lap. You do to him as you see fit—and I guarantee that you'll get away with it. But I don't think you'll kill him. You'd be nuts to—and you aren't nuts. Not quite."

He brushed it aside. "Cut the noise. *Where is he?*"

I poured him a short one; he was drunk but anger was offsetting it. "Not so fast. I do something for you—you do something for me."

"Uh . . . what?"

"You don't like your work. What would you say to high pay, steady work, unlimited expense account, your own boss on the job, and lots of variety and adventure?"

He stared. "I'd say, 'Get those goddam reindeer off my roof !' Shove it, Pop—there's no such job."

"Okay, put it this way: I hand him to you, you settle with him, then try my job. If it's not all I claim—well, I can't hold you."

He was wavering; the last drink did it. "When d'yuh d'liver 'im?" he said thickly.

"If it's a deal—*right now*!"

He shoved out his hand. "It's a deal!"

I nodded to my assistant to watch both ends, noted the time—2300—started to duck through the gate under the bar—when the juke box blared out: "*I'm My Own Granpaw*!" The service man had orders to load it with Americana and classics because I couldn't stomach the "music" of 1970, but I hadn't known that tape was in it. I called out, "Shut that off! Give the customer his money back." I added, "Storeroom, back in a moment," and headed there with my Unmarried Mother following.

It was down the passage across from the johns, a steel door to which no one but my day manager and myself had a key; inside was a door to an inner room to which only I had a key. We went there.

He looked blearily around at windowless walls. "Where is 'e?"

"Right away." I opened a case, the only thing in the room; it was a U.S.F.F. Coordinates Transformer Field Kit, series 1992, Mod. II—a beauty, no moving parts, weight twenty-three kilos fully charged, and shaped to pass as a suitcase. I had adjusted it precisely earlier that day; all I had to do was to shake out the metal net which limits the transformation field.

Which I did. "What's that?" he demanded.

"Time machine," I said and tossed the net over us.

"Hey!" he yelled and stepped back. There is a technique to this; the net has to be thrown so that the subject will instinctively step back *onto* the metal mesh, then you close the net with both of you inside completely—else you might leave shoe soles behind or a piece of foot, or scoop up a slice of floor. But that's all the skill it takes. Some agents con a subject into the net;

I tell the truth and use that instant of utter astonishment to flip the switch. Which I did.

1030-V-3 April 1963-Cleveland, Ohio-Apex Bldg.: "Hey!" he repeated. "Take this damn thing off!"

"Sorry," I apologized and did so, stuffed the net into the case, closed it. "You said you wanted to find him."

"But—you said that was a time machine!"

I pointed out a window. "Does that look like November? Or New York?" While he was gawking at new buds and spring weather, I reopened the case, took out a packet of hundred-dollar bills, checked that the numbers and signatures were compatible with 1963. The Temporal Bureau doesn't care how much you spend (it costs nothing) but they don't like unnecessary anachronisms. Too many mistakes, and a general court-martial will exile you for a year in a nasty period, say 1974 with its strict rationing and forced labor. I never make such mistakes; the money was okay.

He turned around and said, "What happened?"

"He's here. Go outside and take him. Here's expense money." I shoved it at him and added, "Settle him, then I'll pick you up."

Hundred-dollar bills have a hypnotic effect on a person not used to them. He was thumbing them unbelievingly as I eased him into the hall, locked him out. The next jump was easy, a small shift in era.

1700-V-10 March 1964-Cleveland-Apex Bldg.: There was a notice under the door saying that my lease expired next week; otherwise the room looked as it had a moment before. Outside, trees were bare and snow threatened; I hurried, stopping only for contemporary money and a coat, hat and topcoat I had left there when I leased the room. I hired a car, went to the hospital. It took twenty minutes to bore the nursery attendant to the point where I could swipe the baby without being noticed. We went back to the Apex Building. This dial setting was more involved, as the building did not yet exist in 1945. But I had precalculated it.

0100-V-20 Sept 1945-Cleveland-Skyview Motel: Field kit, baby, and I arrived in a motel outside town. Earlier I had registered as "Gregory Johnson, Warren, Ohio," so we arrived in a room with curtains closed, windows locked, and doors bolted, and the floor cleared to allow for waver as the machine hunts. You can get a nasty bruise from a chair where it shouldn't be—not the chair, of course, but backlash from the field.

No trouble. Jane was sleeping soundly; I carried her out, put her in a grocery box on the seat of a car I had provided earlier, drove to the orphanage, put her on the steps, drove two blocks to a "service station" (the petroleum-products sort) and phoned the orphanage, drove back in time to see them taking the box inside, kept going and abandoned the car near the motel—walked to it and jumped forward to the Apex Building in 1963.

2200-V-24 April 1963-Cleveland-Apex Bldg.: I had cut the time rather fine—temporal accuracy depends on span, except on return to zero. If I had it right, Jane was discovering, out in the park this balmy spring night, that she wasn't quite as nice a girl as she had thought. I grabbed a taxi to the home of those skinflints, had the hackie wait around a corner while I lurked in shadows.

Presently I spotted them down the street, arms around each other. He took her up on the porch and made a long job of kissing her good-night—longer than I had thought. Then she went in and he came down the walk, turned away. I slid into step and hooked an arm in his. "That's all, son," I announced quietly. "I'm back to pick you up."

"*You*!" He gasped and caught his breath.

"Me. Now you know who *he* is—and after you think it over you'll know who *you* are . . . and if you think hard enough, you'll figure out who the baby is . . . and who *I* am."

He didn't answer, he was badly shaken. It's a shock to have it proved to you that you can't resist seducing yourself. I took him to the Apex Building and we jumped again.

2300-VII-12 Aug. 1985-Sub Rockies Base: I woke the duty sergeant, showed my I.D., told the sergeant to bed my companion down with a happy pill and recruit him in the morning. The sergeant looked sour, but rank is rank, regardless of era; he did what I said—thinking, no doubt, that the next time we met he might be the colonel and I the sergeant. Which can happen in our corps. "What name?" he asked.

I wrote it out. He raised his eyebrows. "Like so, eh? *Hmm*—"

"You just do your job, Sergeant." I turned to my companion. "Son, your troubles are over. You're about to start the best job a man ever held—and you'll do well. I *know*."

"But—"

"'But' nothing. Get a night's sleep, then look over the proposition. You'll like it."

"That you will!" agreed the sergeant. "Look at me—born in 1917—still around, still young, still enjoying life." I went back to the jump room, set everything on preselected zero.

2301–V–7 Nov. 1970–NYC–"Pop's Place": I came out of the storeroom carrying a fifth of Drambuie to account for the minute I had been gone. My assistant was arguing with the customer who had been playing *"I'm My Own Granpaw!"* I said, "Oh, let him play it, then unplug it." I was very tired.

It's rough, but somebody must do it and it's very hard to recruit anyone in the later years, since the Mistake of 1972. Can you think of a better source than to pick people all fouled up where they are and give them well-paid, interesting (even though dangerous) work in a necessary cause? Everybody knows now why the Fizzle War of 1963 fizzled. The bomb with New York's number on it didn't go off, a hundred other things didn't go as planned—all arranged by the likes of me.

But not the Mistake of '72; that one is not our fault—and can't be undone; there's no paradox to resolve. A thing either is, or it isn't, now and forever amen. But there won't be another like it; an order dated "1992" takes precedence any year.

I closed five minutes early, leaving a letter in the cash register telling my day manager that I was accepting his offer to buy me out, to see my lawyer as I was leaving on a long vacation. The Bureau might or might not pick up his payments, but they want things left tidy. I went to the room back of the storeroom and forward to 1993.

2200–VII–12 Jan. 1993–Sub Rockies Annex–HQ Temporal DOL: I checked in with the duty officer and went to my quarters, intending to sleep for a week. I had fetched the bottle we bet (after all, I won it) and took a drink before I wrote my report. It tasted foul and I wondered why I had ever liked Old Underwear. But it was better than nothing; I don't like to be cold sober, I think too much. But I don't really hit the bottle either; other people have snakes—*I* have people.

I dictated my report; forty recruitments all okayed by the Psych Bureau—counting my own, which I knew would be okayed. I was here, wasn't I? Then I taped a request for assignment to operations; I was sick of recruiting. I dropped both in the slot and headed for bed.

My eye fell on "The By-Laws of Time," over my bed:

Never Do Yesterday What Should Be Done Tomorrow.
If at Last You Do Succeed, Never Try Again.
A Stitch in Time Saves Nine Billion.

A Paradox May Be Paradoctored.
It Is Earlier When You Think.
Ancestors Are Just People.
Even Jove Nods.

They didn't inspire me the way they had when I was a recruit; thirty subjective-years of time-jumping wears you down. I undressed and when I got down to the hide I looked at my belly. A Caesarian leaves a big scar, but I'm so hairy now that I don't notice it unless I look for it.

Then I glanced at the ring on my finger.

The Snake That Eats Its Own Tail, Forever and Ever . . . I *know* where *I* came from—*but where did all you zombies come from?*

I felt a headache coming on, but a headache powder is one thing I do not take. I did once—and you all went away.

So I crawled into bed and whistled out the light.

You aren't really there at all. There isn't anybody but me—Jane—here alone in the dark.

I miss you dreadfully!

J. G. Ballard

The Cage of Sand

• • • •

{1962}

J(ames) G(raham) Ballard (1930–2009), one of the most controversial figures in sf history, was raised in Shanghai, the son of a British businessman; following the 1941 attack on Pearl Harbor, he was interned in a Japanese prison camp, enduring physical and psychological trials that formed the basis for his celebrated mainstream novel *Empire of the Sun* (1984). These experiences left Ballard with an abiding alienation from the values of Western modernity, dubious about the supposed boon of technological progress, and convinced that advanced civilization is merely a screen for violent and irrational impulses. Deeply influenced by Freudian theory and the techniques of European Surrealism, Ballard's work during the late 1950s and early 1960s, most of it published in the British magazines *New Worlds* and *Science-Fantasy*, proffered hard-edged yet often lyrical perspectives on postwar techno-culture; the stories gathered in such collections as *The Voices of Time* (1962) and *The Terminal Beach* (1964) pointed the way toward a sophisticated and cynical new breed of sf, less confident than the pulp tradition had been in the scientific mastery of nature or the essential heroism of the human species. His trilogy of disaster novels—*The Drowned World* (1962), *The Drought* (1964; aka *The Burning World*), and *The Crystal World* (1966)—challenged every convention of the genre. Rather than battling doggedly to preserve the remnants of civilization in the face of monumental adversity, his protagonists pursue a psychic accommodation—virtually a mystical fusion—with the forces destroying their worlds.

In 1962, Ballard published a guest editorial in *New Worlds*—entitled "Which Way to Inner Space?"—that lambasted the pulp tradition of space travel and interplanetary adventure as an archaic realm of childish fantasy that had been eclipsed by the stark realities of Space Age technocracy. Calling for a more introspective sf that explored the labyrinths of the psyche rather than the soaring cosmos, Ballard's editorial became a template for the so-called "New Wave," a loosely coordinated movement of younger writers, centered for a time at *New Worlds* under the editorship of Michael Moorcock, that embraced the countercultural values and experimental styles of the 1960s (Pamela Zoline's "The Heat Death of the Universe" [1967] being a signal example). "The Cage of Sand" is a fictional version of Ballard's "Inner Space" manifesto, giving stark evidence of both his contempt for space adventure and his defense of a more troubled and brooding sf. Set near a ruined Cape Kennedy and peopled by a trio of loners whose past links to a failing space program have reduced them to a clutch of haunted (and hunted) pariahs, the story focuses on the private visions and nostalgias evoked by space travel rather than on the heroic techno-scientific enterprise itself. As dead astronauts circle the earth in their derelict capsules, Ballard's antiheroes pursue their obscure obsessions to an ambiguously triumphant apotheosis. "The Cage of Sand" inaugurated a series of stories that dealt with the dark side of the Apollo missions and the "outward urge" toward space; these tales were eventually gathered into *Memories of the Space Age* (1988).

At sunset, when the vermilion glow reflected from the dunes along the horizon fitfully illuminated the white faces of the abandoned hotels, Bridgman stepped onto his balcony and looked out over the long stretches of cooling sand as the tides of purple shadow seeped across them. Slowly, extending their slender fingers through the shallow saddles and depressions, the shadows massed together like gigantic combs, a few phosphorescing spurs of obsidian isolated for a moment between the tines, and then finally coalesced and flooded in a solid wave across the half-submerged hotels. Behind the silent facades, in the tilting sand-filled streets which had once glittered with cocktail bars and restaurants, it was already night. Halos of moonlight beaded the lamp standards with silver dew, and draped the shuttered windows and slipping cornices like a frost of frozen gas.

As Bridgman watched, his lean bronzed arms propped against the rusting rail, the last whorls of light sank away into the cerise funnel withdrawing below the horizon, and the first wind stirred across the dead Martian sand. Here and there miniature cyclones whirled about a sand spur, drawing off swirling feathers of moon-washed spray, and a nimbus of white dust swept across the dunes and settled in the dips and hollows. Gradually the drifts accumulated, edging toward the former shoreline below the hotels. Already the first four floors had been inundated, and the sand now reached up to within two feet of Bridgman's balcony. After the next sandstorm he would be forced yet again to move to the floor above.

"Bridgman!"

The voice cleft the darkness like a spear. Fifty yards to his right, at the edge of the derelict sandbreak he had once attempted to build below the hotel, a square stocky figure wearing a pair of frayed cotton shorts waved up at him. The moonlight etched the broad sinewy muscles of his chest, the powerful bowed legs sinking almost to their calves in the soft Martian sand. He was about forty-five years old, his thinning hair close-cropped so that he seemed almost bald. In his right hand he carried a large canvas holdall.

Bridgman smiled to himself. Standing there patiently in the moonlight below the derelict hotel, Travis reminded him of some long-delayed tourist arriving at a ghost resort years after its extinction.

"Bridgman, are you coming?" When the latter still leaned on his balcony rail, Travis added, "The next conjunction is tomorrow."

Bridgman shook his head, a rictus of annoyance twisting his mouth. He hated the bimonthly conjunctions, when all Earth crossed the sky together. Invariably on these nights he remained in his room, playing over the old memo-tapes he had salvaged from the submerged chalets and motels further along the beach (the hysterical "This is Mamie Goldberg, 62955 Cocoa Boulevard, I really wanna protest against this crazy evacuation . . ." or resigned "Sam Snade here, the Pontiac convertible in the back garage belongs to anyone who can dig it out"). Travis and Louise Woodward always came to the hotel on the conjunction nights—it was the highest building in the resort, with an unrestricted view from horizon to horizon—and would follow the seven converging stars as they pursued their endless courses around the globe. Both would be oblivious of everything else, which the wardens knew only too well, and they reserved their most careful searches of the sand sea for these bimonthly occasions. Invariably Bridgman found himself forced to act as lookout for the other two.

"I was out last night," he called down to Travis. "Keep away from the northeast perimeter fence by the Cape. They'll be busy repairing the track."

Most nights Bridgman divided his time between excavating the buried motels for caches of supplies (the former inhabitants of the resort area had assumed the government would soon rescind its evacuation order) and disconnecting the sections of metal roadway laid across the desert for the wardens' jeeps. Each of the squares of wire mesh was about five yards wide and weighed over three hundred pounds. After he had snapped the lines of rivets, dragged the sections away, and buried them among the dunes he would be exhausted, and spend most of the next day nursing his strained hands and shoulders. Some sections of the track were now permanently anchored with heavy steel stakes, and he knew that sooner or later they would be unable to delay the wardens by sabotaging the roadway.

Travis hesitated, and with a noncommittal shrug disappeared among the dunes, the heavy tool-bag swinging easily from one powerful arm. Despite the meager diet which sustained him, his energy and determination seemed undiminished—in a single night Bridgman had watched him dismantle twenty sections of track and then loop together the adjacent limbs of a cross-road, sending an entire convoy of six vehicles off into the wastelands to the south.

Bridgman turned from the balcony, then stopped when a faint tang of brine touched the cool air. Ten miles away, hidden by the lines of dunes, was the sea, the long green rollers of the middle Atlantic breaking against the red Martian strand. When he had first come to the beach five years earlier there had never been the faintest scent of brine across the intervening miles of sand. Slowly, however, the Atlantic was driving the shore back to its former margins. The tireless shoulder of the Gulf Stream drummed against the soft Martian dust and piled the dunes into grotesque rococo reefs which the wind carried away into the sand sea. Gradually the ocean was returning, reclaiming its great smooth basin, silting out the black quartz and Martian obsidian which would never be windborne and drawing these down into its deeps. More and more often the stain of brine would hang on the evening air, reminding Bridgman why he had first come to the beach and removing any inclination to leave.

Three years earlier he had attempted to measure the rate of approach, by driving a series of stakes into the sand at the water's edge, but the shifting contours of the dunes carried away the colored poles. Later, using the promontory at Cape Kennedy, where the old launching gantries and landing ramps reared up into the sky like derelict pieces of giant sculpture, he had calculated by triangulation that the advance was little more than thirty yards per year. At this rate—without wanting to, he had automatically made the calculation—it would be well over five hundred years before the Atlantic reached its former littoral at Cocoa Beach. Though discouragingly slow, the movement was nonetheless in a forward direction, and Bridgman was happy to remain in his hotel ten miles away across the dunes, conceding toward its time of arrival the few years he had at his disposal.

Later, shortly after Louise Woodward's arrival, he had thought of dismantling one of the motel cabins and building himself a small chalet by the water's edge. But the shoreline had been too dismal and forbidding. The great red dunes rolled on for miles, cutting off half the sky, dissolving slowly under the impact of the slate-green water. There was no formal tideline, but only a steep shelf littered with nodes of quartz and rusting fragments of Mars rockets brought back with the ballast. He spent a few days in a cave below a towering sand reef, watching the long galleries of compacted red dust crumble and dissolve as the cold Atlantic stream sluiced through them, collapsing like the decorated colonnades of a baroque cathedral. In the summer the heat reverberated from the hot sand as from the slag of some molten sun, burning the rubber soles from his boots, and the light from the scattered flints of washed quartz flickered with diamond hardness. Bridgman had returned to the hotel grateful for his room overlooking the silent dunes.

Leaving the balcony, the sweet smell of brine still in his nostrils, he went over to the desk. A small cone of shielded light shone down over the tape recorder and rack of spools. The rumble of the wardens' unsilenced engines always gave him at least five minutes' warning of their arrival, and it would have been safe to install another lamp in the room—there were no roadways between the hotel and the sea, and from a distance any light reflected onto the balcony was indistinguishable from the corona of glimmering phosphors which hung over the sand like myriads of fireflies. However, Bridgman preferred to sit in the darkened suite, enclosed by the circle of books on the makeshift shelves, the shadow-filled air playing over his shoulders through the long night as he toyed with the memo-tapes, fragments of a vanished and unregretted past. By day he always drew the blinds, immolating himself in a world of perpetual twilight.

Bridgman had easily adapted himself to his self-isolation, soon evolved a system of daily routines that gave him the maximum of time to spend on his private reveries. Pinned to the walls around him were a series of huge white-prints and architectural drawings, depicting various elevations of a fantastic Martian city he had once designed, its glass spires and curtain walls rising like heliotropic jewels from the vermilion desert. In fact, the whole city was a vast piece of jewelry, each elevation brilliantly visualized but as symmetrical, and ultimately as lifeless, as a crown. Bridgman continuously retouched the drawings, inserting more and more details, so that they almost seemed to be photographs of an original.

Most of the hotels in the town—one of a dozen similar resorts buried by the sand which had once formed an unbroken strip of motels, chalets and five-star hotels thirty miles to the south of Cape Kennedy—were well stocked with supplies of canned food abandoned when the area was evacuated and wired off. There were ample reservoirs and cisterns filled with water, apart from a thousand intact cocktail bars six feet below the surface of the sand. Travis had excavated a dozen of these in search of his favorite vintage bourbon. Walking out across the desert behind the town one would suddenly find a short flight of steps cut into the annealed sand and crawl below an occluded sign announcing "The Satellite Bar" or "The Orbit Room" into the inner sanctum, where the jutting deck of a chromium bar had been cleared as far as the diamond-paned mirror freighted with its rows of bottles and figurines. Bridgman would have been glad to see them left undisturbed.

The whole trash of amusement arcades and cheap bars on the outskirts of the beach resorts were a depressing commentary on the original space flights, reducing them to the level of monster sideshows at a carnival.

Outside his room, steps sounded along the corridor, then slowly climbed the stairway, pausing for a few seconds at every landing. Bridgman lowered the memo-tape in his hand, listening to the familiar tired footsteps. This was Louise Woodward, making her invariable evening ascent to the roof ten stories above. Bridgman glanced to the timetable pinned to the wall. Only two of the satellites would be visible, between 12:25 and 12:35 A.M., at an elevation of 62 degrees in the southwest, passing though Cetus and Eridanus, neither of them containing her husband. Although the sighting was two hours away, she was already taking up her position, and would remain there until dawn.

Bridgman listened wanly to the feet recede slowly up the stairwell. All through the night the slim pale-faced woman would sit out under the moonlit sky, as the soft Martian sand her husband had given his life to reach sifted around her in the dark wind, stroking her faded hair like some mourning mariner's wife waiting for the sea to surrender her husband's body. Travis usually joined her later, and the two of them sat side by side against the elevator house, the frosted letters of the hotel's neon sign strewn around their feet like the fragments of a dismembered zodiac, then at dawn made their way down into the shadow-filled streets to their aeries in the nearby hotels.

Initially Bridgman often joined their nocturnal vigil, but after a few nights he began to feel something repellent, if not actually ghoulish, about their mindless contemplation of the stars. This was not so much because of the macabre spectacle of the dead astronauts orbiting the planet in their capsules, but because of the curious sense of unspoken communion between Travis and Louise Woodward, almost as if they were celebrating a private rite to which Bridgman could never be initiated. Whatever their original motives, Bridgman sometimes suspected that these had been overlayed by other, more personal ones.

Ostensibly, Louise Woodward was watching her husband's satellite in order to keep alive his memory, but Bridgman guessed that the memories she unconsciously wished to perpetuate were those of herself twenty years earlier, when her husband had been a celebrity and she herself courted by magazine columnists and TV reporters. For fifteen years after his death—Woodward had been killed testing a new lightweight launching platform—she had lived a nomadic existence, driving restlessly in her cheap car from motel to motel across the continent, following her husband's star as it disappeared into the eastern night, and had at last made her home at Cocoa Beach in sight of the rusting gantries across the bay.

Travis's real motives were probably more complex. To Bridgman, after they had known each other for a couple of years, he had confided that he felt himself bound by a debt of honor to maintain a watch over the dead astronauts; for the example of courage and sacrifice they had set him as a child (although most of them had been piloting their wrecked capsules for fifty years before Travis's birth), and that now they were virtually forgotten he must singlehandedly keep alive the fading flame of their memory. Bridgman was convinced of his sincerity.

Yet later, going through a pile of old news magazines in the trunk of a car he excavated from a motel port, he came across a picture of Travis wearing an aluminum pressure suit and learned something more of his story. Apparently Travis had at one time been himself an astronaut—or rather, a would-be astronaut. A test pilot for one of the civilian agencies setting up orbital relay stations, his nerve had failed him a few seconds before the last "hold" of his countdown, a moment of pure unexpected funk that cost the company some five million dollars.

Obviously it was inability to come to terms with this failure of character, unfortunately discovered lying flat on his back on a contour couch two hundred feet above the launching pad, which had brought Travis to Kennedy, the abandoned Mecca of the first heroes of astronautics.

Tactfully Bridgman had tried to explain that no one would blame him for this failure of nerve—less his responsibility than that of the selectors who had picked him for the flight, or at least the result of an unhappy concatenation of ambiguously worded multiple-choice questions (crosses in the wrong boxes, some heavier to bear and harder to open than others! Bridgman had joked sardonically to himself). But Travis seemed to have reached his own decision about himself. Night after night, he watched the brilliant funerary convoy weave its gilded pathway toward the dawn sun, salving his own failure by identifying it with the greater, but blameless, failure of the seven astronauts. Travis still wore his hair in the regulation "Mohican" cut of the spaceman, still kept himself in perfect physical trim by the vigorous routines he had practiced before his abortive flight. Sustained by the personal myth he had created, he was now more or less unreachable.

"Dear Harry, I've taken the car and deposit box. Sorry it should end like—"

Irritably, Bridgman switched off the memo-tape and its recapitulation of some thirty-year-old private triviality. For some reason he seemed unable to accept Travis and Louise Woodward for what they were. He disliked this failure of compassion, a nagging compulsion to expose other people's motives and strip away the insulating sheaths around their naked nerve strings, particularly as his own motives for being at Cape Kennedy were so suspect. Why was *he* there, what failure was *he* trying to expiate? And why choose Cocoa Beach as his penitential shore? For three years he had asked himself these questions so often that they had ceased to have any meaning, like a fossilized catechism or the blunted self-recrimination of a paranoiac.

He had resigned his job as the chief architect of a big space development company after the large government contract on which the firm depended, for the design of the first Martian city-settlement, was awarded to a rival consortium. Secretly, however, he realized that his resignation had marked his unconscious acceptance that despite his great imaginative gifts he was unequal to the specialized and more prosaic tasks of designing the settlement. On the drawing board, as elsewhere, he would always remain earthbound.

His dreams of building a new Gothic architecture of launching ports and controls gantries, of being the Frank Lloyd Wright and Le Corbusier of the first city to be raised outside Earth, faded forever, but left him unable to accept the alternative of turning out endless plans for low-cost hospitals in Ecuador and housing estates in Tokyo. For a year he had drifted aimlessly, but a few color photographs of the vermilion sunsets at Cocoa Beach and a news story about the recluses living on in the submerged motels had provided a powerful compass.

He dropped the memo-tape into a drawer, making an effort to accept Louise Woodward and Travis on their own terms, a wife keeping watch over her dead husband and an old astronaut maintaining a solitary vigil over the memories of his lost comrades-in-arms.

The wind gusted against the balcony window, and a light spray of sand rained across the floor. At night dust storms churned along the beach. Thermal pools isolated by the cooling desert would suddenly accrete like beads of quicksilver and erupt across the fluffy sand in miniature tornadoes.

Only fifty yards away, the dying cough of a heavy diesel cut through the shadows. Quickly Bridgman turned off the small desk light, grateful for his meanness over the battery packs plugged into the circuit, then stepped to the window.

At the leftward edge of the sand break, half-hidden in the long shadows cast by the hotel, was a large tracked vehicle with a low camouflaged hull. A narrow observation bridge had been built over the bumpers directly in front of the squat snout of the engine housing, and two of the beach wardens were craning up through the plexiglass windows at the balconies of the hotel, shifting their binoculars from room to room. Behind them, under the glass dome of the extended driving cabin, were three more wardens controlling an outboard spotlight. In the center of the bowl a thin mote of light pulsed with the rhythm of the engine, ready to throw its powerful beam into any of the open rooms.

Bridgman hid back behind the shutters as the binoculars focused upon the adjacent balcony, moved to his own, hesitated, and passed to the next. Exasperated by the sabotaging of the roadways, the wardens had evidently decided on a new type of vehicle. With their four broad tracks, the huge squat sand cars would be free of the mesh roadways and able to rove at will through the dunes and sand hills.

Bridgman watched the vehicle reverse slowly, its engine barely varying its deep base growl, then move off along the line of hotels, almost indistinguishable in profile among the shifting dunes and hillocks. A hundred yards away, at the first intersection, it turned toward the main boulevard, wisps of dust streaming from the metal cleats like thin spumes of steam. The men in the observation bridge were still watching the hotel. Bridgman was certain that they had seen a reflected glimmer of light, or perhaps some movement of Louise Woodward's on the roof. However reluctant to leave the car and be contaminated by the poisonous dust, the wardens would not hesitate if the capture of one of the beachcombers warranted it.

Racing up the staircase, Bridgman made his way to the roof, crouching below the windows that overlooked the boulevard. Like a huge crab, the sand car had parked under the jutting overhang of the big department store opposite. Once fifty feet from the ground, the concrete lip was now separated from it by little more than six or seven feet, and the sand car was hidden in the shadows below it, engine silent. A single movement in a window, or the unexpected return of Travis, and the wardens would spring from the hatchways, their long-handled nets and lassos pinioning them around the neck and ankles. Bridgman remembered one beachcomber he had seen flushed from his motel hideout and carried off like a huge twitching spider at the center of a black rubber web, the wardens with their averted faces and masked mouths like devils in an abstract ballet.

Reaching the roof, Bridgman stepped out into the opaque white moonlight. Louise Woodward was leaning on the balcony, looking out toward the distant, unseen sea. At the faint sound of the door creaking she turned and began to walk listlessly around the roof, her pale face floating like a nimbus. She wore a freshly ironed print dress she had found in a rusty spin drier in one of the launderettes, and her streaked blond hair floated out lightly behind her on the wind.

"Louise!"

Involuntarily she started, tripping over a fragment of the neon sign, then moved backward toward the balcony overlooking the boulevard.

"Mrs. Woodward!" Bridgman held her by the elbow, raised a hand to her mouth before she could cry out. "The wardens are down below. They're watching the hotel. We must find Travis before he returns."

Louise hesitated, apparently recognizing Bridgman only by an effort, and her eyes turned up to the black marble sky. Bridgman looked at his watch; it was almost 12:35. He searched the stars in the southwest.

Louise murmured, "They're nearly here now, I must see them. Where is Travis, he should be here?"

Bridgman pulled at her arm. "Perhaps he saw the sand car. Mrs. Woodward, we should leave."

Suddenly she pointed up at the sky, then wrenched away from him and ran to the rail. "There they are!"

Fretting, Bridgman waited until she had filled her eyes with the two companion points of light speeding from the western horizon. These were Merril and Pokrovski—like every schoolboy he knew the sequences perfectly, a second system of constellations with a more complex but far more tangible periodicity and precession—the Castor and Pollux of the orbiting zodiac, whose appearance always heralded a full conjunction the following night.

Louise Woodward gazed up at them from the rail, the rising wind lifting her hair off her shoulders and entraining it horizontally behind her head. Around her feet the red Martian dust swirled and rustled, silting over the fragments of the old neon sign, a brilliant pink spume streaming from her long fingers as they moved along the balcony ledge. When the satellites finally disappeared among the stars along the horizon, she leaned forward, her face raised to the milk-blue moon as if to delay their departure, then turned back to Bridgman, a bright smile on her face.

His earlier suspicions vanishing, Bridgman smiled back at her encouragingly. "Roger will be here tomorrow night, Louise. We must be careful the wardens don't catch us before we see him."

He felt a sudden admiration for her, at the stoical way she had sustained herself during her long vigil. Perhaps she thought of Woodward as still alive, and in some way was patiently waiting for him to return? He remembered her saying once, "Roger was only a boy when he took off, you know, I feel more like his mother now," as if frightened how Woodward would react to her dry skin and fading hair, fearing that he might even have forgotten her. No doubt the death she visualized for him was of a different order than the mortal kind.

Hand in hand, they tiptoed carefully down the flaking steps, jumped down from a terrace window into the soft sand below the windbreak. Bridgman sank to his knees in the fine silver moon dust, then waded up to the firmer ground, pulling Louise after him. They climbed through a breach in the tilting palisades, then ran away from the line of dead hotels looming like skulls in the empty light.

"Paul, wait!" Her head still raised to the sky, Louise Woodward fell to her knees in a hollow between two dunes, with a laugh stumbled after Bridgman as he raced through the dips and saddles. The wind was now whipping the sand off the higher crests, flurries of dust spurting like excited wavelets. A hundred yards away, the town was a fading film set, projected by the camera obscura of the sinking moon. They were standing where the long Atlantic seas had once been ten fathoms deep, and Bridgman could scent again the tang of brine among the flickering whitecaps of dust, phosphorescing like shoals of animalcula. He waited for any sign of Travis.

"Louise, we'll have to go back to the town. The sandstorms are blowing up, we'll never see Travis here."

They moved back through the dunes, then worked their way among the narrow alleyways between the hotels to the northern gateway to the town. Bridgman found a vantage point in a small apartment block, and they lay down looking out below a window lintel into the sloping street, the warm sand forming a pleasant cushion. At the intersections the dust blew across the roadway in white clouds, obscuring the warden's beach car parked a hundred yards down the boulevard.

Half an hour later an engine surged, and Bridgman began to pile sand into the interval in front of them. "They're going. Thank God!"

Louise Woodward held his arm. "Look!"

Fifty feet away, his white vinyl suit half-hidden in the dust clouds, one of the wardens was advancing slowly toward them, his lasso twirling lightly in his hand. A few feet behind was a second warden, craning up at the windows of the apartment block with his binoculars.

Bridgman and Louise crawled back below the ceiling, then dug their way under a transom into the kitchen at the rear. A window opened onto a sand-filled yard, and they darted away through the lifting dust that whirled between the buildings.

Suddenly, around a corner, they saw the line of wardens moving down a side street, the sand car edging along behind them. Before Bridgman could steady himself a spasm of pain seized his right calf, contorting the gastrocnemius muscle, and he fell to one knee. Louise Woodward pulled him back against the wall, then pointed at a squat, bow-legged figure trudging toward them along the curving road into town.

"Travis—"

The tool bag swung from his right hand, and his feet rang faintly on the wire-mesh roadway. Head down, he seemed unaware of the wardens hidden by a bend in the road.

"Come on!" Disregarding the negligible margin of safety, Bridgman clambered to his feet and impetuously ran out into the center of the street. Louise tried to stop him, and they had covered only ten yards before the wardens saw them. There was a warning shout, and the spotlight flung its giant cone down the street. The sand car surged forward, like a massive dust-covered bull, its tracks clawing at the sand.

"Travis!" As Bridgman reached the bend, Louise Woodward ten yards behind, Travis looked up from his reverie, then flung the tool bag over one shoulder and raced ahead of them toward the clutter of motel roofs protruding from the other side of the street. Lagging behind the others, Bridgman again felt the cramp attack his leg, broke off into a painful shuffle. When Travis came back for him Bridgman tried to wave him away, but Travis pinioned his elbow and propelled him forward like an attendant straight-arming a patient.

The dust swirling around them, they disappeared through the fading streets and out into the desert, the shouts of the beach wardens lost in the roar and clamor of the baying engine. Around them, like the strange metallic flora of some extraterrestrial garden, the old neon signs jutted from the red Martian sand—"Satellite Motel," "Planet Bar," "Mercury Motel." Hiding behind them, they reached the scrub-covered dunes on the edge of town, then picked up one of the trails that led away among the sand reefs. There, in the deep grottoes of compacted sand which hung like inverted palaces, they waited until the storm subsided. Shortly before dawn the wardens abandoned their search, unable to bring the heavy sand car onto the disintegrating reef.

Contemptuous of the wardens, Travis lit a small fire with his cigarette lighter, burning splinters of driftwood that had gathered in the gullies. Bridgman crouched beside it, warming his hands.

"This is the first time they've been prepared to leave the sand car," he remarked to Travis. "It means they're under orders to catch us."

Travis shrugged. "Maybe. They're extending the fence along the beach. They probably intend to seal us in forever."

"What?" Bridgman stood up with a sudden feeling of uneasiness. "Why should they? Are you sure? I mean, what would be the point?"

Travis looked up at him, a flicker of dry amusement on his bleached face. Wisps of smoke wreathed his head, curled up past the serpentine columns of the grotto to the winding interval of sky a hundred feet above. "Bridgman, forgive me saying so, but if you want to leave here, you should leave now. In a month's time you won't be able to."

Bridgman ignored this, and searched the cleft of dark sky overhead, which framed the constellation Scorpio, as if hoping to see a reflection of the distant sea. "They must be crazy. How much of this fence did you see?"

"About eight hundred yards. It won't take them long to complete. The sections are prefabricated, about forty feet high." He smiled ironically at Bridgman's discomfort. "Relax, Bridgman. If you do want to get out, you'll always be able to tunnel underneath it."

"I don't want to get out," Bridgman said coldly. "Damn them, Travis, they're turning the place into a zoo. You know it won't be the same with a fence all the way around it."

"A corner of Earth that is forever Mars." Under the high forehead, Travis's eyes were sharp and watchful. "I see their point. There hasn't been a fatal casualty now—" he glanced at Louise Woodward, who was strolling about in the colonnades "—for nearly twenty years, and passenger rockets are supposed to be as safe as commuters' trains. They're quietly sealing off the past, Louise and I and you with it. I suppose it's pretty considerate of them not to burn the place down with flame throwers. The virus would be a sufficient excuse. After all, we are probably the only reservoirs left on the planet." He picked up a handful of red dust and examined the fine crystals with a somber eye. "Well, Bridgman, what are you going to do?"

His thoughts discharging themselves through his mind like frantic signal flares, Bridgman walked away without answering.

Behind them, Louise Woodward wandered among the deep galleries of the grotto, crooning to herself in a low voice to the sighing rhythms of the whirling sand.

The next morning they returned to the town, wading through the deep drifts of sand that lay like a fresh fall of red snow between the hotels and stores, coruscating in the brilliant sunlight. Travis and Louise Woodward made their way toward their quarters in the motels further down the beach. Bridgman searched the still, crystal air for any signs of the wardens, but the sand car had gone, its tracks obliterated by the storm.

In his room he found their calling card.

A huge tide of dust had flowed through the French windows and submerged the desk and bed, three feet deep against the rear wall. Outside the sandbreak had been inundated, and the contours of the desert had completely altered, a few spires of obsidian marking its former perspectives like buoys on a shifting sea. Bridgman spent the morning digging out his books and equipment, dismantled the electrical system and its batteries and carried everything to the room above. He would have moved to the penthouse on the top floor, but his lights would have been visible for miles.

Settling into his new quarters, he switched on the tape recorder, heard a short clipped message in the brisk voice which had shouted orders at the wardens the previous evening. "Bridgman, this is Major Webster, deputy commandant of Cocoa Beach Reservation. On the instructions of the Anti-Viral Subcommittee of the UN General Assembly we are now building a continuous fence around the beach area. On completion no further egress will be allowed, and anyone escaping will be immediately returned to the reservation. Give yourself up now, Bridgman, before—"

Bridgman stopped the tape, then reversed the spool and erased the message, staring angrily at the instrument. Unable to settle down to the task of rewiring the room's circuits, he paced about, fiddling with the architectural drawings propped against the wall. He felt restless and hyperexcited, perhaps because he had been trying to repress, not very successfully, precisely those doubts of which Webster had now reminded him.

He stepped onto the balcony and looked out over the desert, at the red dunes rolling to the windows directly below. For the fourth time he had moved up a floor, and the sequence of identical rooms he had occupied were like displaced images of himself seen through a prism. Their common focus, that elusive final definition of himself which he had sought for so long, still remained to be found. Timelessly the sand swept toward him, its shifting contours, approximating more closely than any other landscape he had found to complete psychic zero, enveloping his past failures and uncertainties, masking them in its enigmatic canopy.

Bridgman watched the red sand flicker and fluoresce in the steepening sunlight. He would never see Mars now, and redress the implicit failure of talent, but a workable replica of the planet was contained within the beach area.

Several million tons of the Martian topsoil had been ferried in as ballast some fifty years earlier, when it was feared that the continuous firing of planetary probes and space vehicles, and the transportation of bulk stores and equipment to Mars would fractionally lower the gravitational mass of the Earth and bring it into a tighter orbit around the Sun. Although the distance involved would be little more than a few millimeters, and barely raise the temperature of the atmosphere, its cumulative effects over an extended period might have resulted in a loss into space of the tenuous layers of the outer atmosphere, and of the radiological veil which alone made the biosphere habitable.

Over a twenty-year period a fleet of large freighters had shuttled to and from Mars, dumping the ballast into the sea near the landing grounds of Cape Kennedy. Simultaneously the Russians were filling in a small section of the Caspian Sea. The intention had been that the ballast should be swallowed by the Atlantic and Caspian waters, but all too soon it was found that the microbiological analysis of the sand had been inadequate.

At the Martian polar caps, where the original water vapor in the atmosphere had condensed, a residue of ancient organic matter formed the topsoil, a fine sandy loess containing the fossilized spores of the giant lichens and mosses which had been the last living organisms on the planet millions of years earlier. Embedded in these spores were the crystal lattices of the viruses which had once preyed on the plants, and traces of these were carried back to Earth with the Kennedy and Caspian ballast.

A few years afterward a drastic increase in a wide range of plant diseases was noticed in the southern states of America and in the Kazakhstan and Turkmenistan republics of the Soviet Union. All over Florida there were outbreaks of blight and mosaic disease, orange plantations withered and died, stunted palms split by the roadside like dried banana skins, manila grass stiffened into paper spears in the summer heat. Within a few years the entire peninsula was transformed into a desert. The swampy jungles of the Everglades became bleached and dry, the rivers' cracked husks strewn with the gleaming skeletons of crocodiles and birds, the forest petrified.

The former launching ground at Kennedy was closed, and shortly afterward the Cocoa Beach resorts were sealed off and evacuated, billions of dollars of real estate were abandoned to the virus. Fortunately never virulent to animal hosts, its influence was confined to within a small radius of the original loess which had borne it, unless ingested by the human organism, when it symbioted with the bacteria in the gut flora, benign and unknown to the host, but devastating to vegetation thousands of miles from Kennedy if returned to the soil.

Unable to rest despite his sleepless night, Bridgman played irritably with the tape recorder. During their close escape from the wardens he had more than half-hoped they would catch him. The mysterious leg cramp was obviously psychogenic. Although unable to accept consciously the logic of Webster's argument, he would willingly have conceded to the *fait accompli* of physical capture, gratefully submitted to a year's quarantine at the Parasitological Cleansing Unit at Tampa, and then returned to his career as an architect, chastened but accepting his failure.

As yet, however, the opportunity for surrender had failed to offer itself. Travis appeared to be aware of his ambivalent motives; Bridgman noticed that he and Louise Woodward had made no arrangements to meet him that evening for the conjunction.

In the early afternoon he went down into the streets, ploughed through the drifts of red sand, following the footprints of Travis and Louise as they wound in and out of the side streets, finally saw them disappear into the coarser, flintlike dunes among the submerged motels to the south of the town. Giving up, he returned through the empty, shadowless streets, now and then shouted up into the hot air, listening to the echoes boom away among the dunes.

Later that afternoon he walked out toward the northeast, picking his way carefully through the dips and hollows, crouching in the pools of shadow whenever the distant sounds of the construction gangs along the perimeter were carried across to him by the wind. Around him, in the great dust basins, the grains of red sand flittered like diamonds. Barbs of rusting metal protruded from the slopes, remnants of Mars satellites and launching stages which had fallen onto the Martian deserts and then been carried back again to Earth. One fragment which he passed, a complete section of hull plate like a concave shield, still carried part of an identification numeral, and stood upright in the dissolving sand like a door into nowhere.

Just before dusk he reached a tall spur of obsidian that reared up into the tinted cerise sky like the spire of a ruined church, climbed up among its jutting cornices and looked out across the intervening two or three miles of dunes to the perimeter. Illuminated by the last light, the metal grills shone with a roseate glow like fairy portcullises on the edge of an enchanted sea. At least half a mile of the fence had been completed, and as he watched another of the giant prefabricated sections was cantilevered into the air and staked to the ground. Already the eastern horizon was cut off by the encroaching fence, the enclosed Martian sand like the gravel scattered at the bottom of a cage.

Perched on the spur, Bridgman felt a warning tremor of pain in his calf. He leapt down in a flurry of dust, without looking back made off among the dunes and reefs.

Later, as the last baroque whorls of the sunset faded below the horizon, he waited on the roof for Travis and Louise Woodward, peering impatiently into the empty moon-filled streets.

Shortly after midnight, at an elevation of 35 degrees in the southwest, between Aquila and Ophiuchus, the conjunction began. Bridgman continued to search the streets, and ignored the seven points of speeding light as they raced toward him from the horizon like an invasion from deep space. There was no indication of their convergent orbital pathways, which would soon scatter them thousands of miles apart, and the satellites moved as if they were always together, in the tight configuration Bridgman had known since childhood, like a lost zodiacal emblem, a constellation detached from the celestial sphere and forever frantically searching to return to its place.

"Travis! Confound you!" With a snarl, Bridgman swung away from the balcony and moved along to the exposed section of rail behind the elevator head. To be avoided like a pariah by Travis and Louise Woodward forced him to accept that he was no longer a true resident of the beach and now existed in a no-man's-land between them and the wardens.

The seven satellites drew nearer, and Bridgman glanced up at them cursorily. They were disposed in a distinctive but unusual pattern resembling the Greek letter *chi*, a limp cross, a straight lateral member containing four capsules more or less in line ahead—Connolly, Tkachev, Merril, and Maiakovski—bisected by three others forming with Tkachev an elongated Z—Pokrovski, Woodward, and Brodisnek. The pattern had been variously identified as a hammer and sickle, an eagle, a swastika, and a dove, as well as a variety of religious and runic emblems, but all these were being defeated by the advancing tendency of the older capsules to vaporize.

It was this slow disintegration of the aluminum shells that made them visible—it had often been pointed out that the observer on the ground was looking, not at the actual capsule, but at a local field of vaporized aluminum and ionized hydrogen peroxide gas from the ruptured altitude jets now distributed within half a mile of each of the capsules. Woodward's, the most recently in orbit, was a barely perceptible point of light. The hulks of the capsules, with their perfectly preserved human cargoes, were continually dissolving, and a wide fan of silver spray opened out in a phantom wake behind Merril and Pokrovski (1998 and 1999), like a double star transforming itself into a nova in the center of a constellation. As the mass of the capsules diminished they sank into a closer orbit around the earth, would soon touch the denser layers of the atmosphere and plummet to the ground.

Bridgman watched the satellites as they moved toward him, his irritation with Travis forgotten. As always, he felt himself moved by the eerie but strangely serene spectacle of the ghostly convoy endlessly circling the dark sea of the midnight sky, the long-dead astronauts converging for the ten-thousandth time upon their brief rendezvous and then setting off upon their lonely flight paths around the perimeter of the ionosphere, the tidal edge of the beachway into space which had reclaimed them.

How Louise Woodward could bear to look up at her husband he had never been able to understand. After her arrival he once invited her to the hotel, remarking that there was an excellent view of the beautiful sunsets, and she had snapped back bitterly: "Beautiful? Can you imagine what it's like looking up at a sunset when your husband's spinning round through it in his coffin?"

This reaction had been a common one when the first astronauts had died after failing to make contact with the launching platforms in fixed orbit. When these new stars rose in the west an attempt had been made to shoot them down—there was the unsettling prospect of the skies a thousand years hence, littered with orbiting refuse—but later they were left in this natural graveyard, forming their own monument.

Obscured by the clouds of dust carried up into the air by the sandstorm, the satellites shone with little more than the intensity of second-magnitude stars, winking as the reflected light was interrupted by the lanes of strato-cirrus. The wake of diffusing light behind Merril and Pokrovski which usually screened the other capsules seemed to have diminished in size, and he could see both Maiakovski and Brodisnek clearly for the first time in several months. Wondering whether Merril or Pokrovski would be the first to fall from orbit, he looked toward the center of the cross as it passed overhead.

With a sharp intake of breath, he tilted his head back. In surprise he noticed that one of the familiar points of light was missing from the center of the group. What he had assumed to be an occlusion of the conjoint vapor trails by dust clouds was simply due to the fact that one of the capsules—Merril's, he decided, the third of the line ahead—had fallen from its orbit.

Head raised, he sidestepped slowly across the roof, avoiding the pieces of rusting neon sign, following the convoy as it passed overhead and moved toward the eastern horizon. No longer overlayed by the wake of Merril's capsule, Woodward's shone with far greater clarity, and almost appeared to have taken the former's place, although he was not due to fall from orbit for at least a century.

In the distance somewhere an engine growled. A moment later, from a different quarter, a woman's voice cried out faintly. Bridgman moved to the rail, over the intervening rooftops saw two figures silhouetted against the sky on the elevator head of an apartment block, then heard Louise Woodward call out again. She was pointing up at the sky with both hands, her long hair blown about her face, Travis trying to restrain her. Bridgman realized that she had misconstrued Merril's descent, assuming that the fallen astronaut was her husband. He climbed onto the edge of the balcony, watching the pathetic tableau on the distant roof.

Again, somewhere among the dunes, an engine moaned. Before Bridgman could turn around, a brilliant blade of light cleaved the sky in the southwest. Like a speeding comet, an immense train of vaporizing particles stretching behind it to the horizon, it soared toward them, the downward curve of its pathway clearly visible. Detached from the rest of the capsules, which were now disappearing among the stars along the eastern horizon, it was little more than a few miles off the ground.

Bridgman watched it approach, apparently on a collision course with the hotel. The expanding corona of white light, like a gigantic signal flare, illuminated the rooftops, etching the letters of the neon signs over the submerged motels on the outskirts of the town. He ran for the doorway, as he raced down the stairs saw the glow of the descending capsule fill the somber streets like a hundred moons. When he reached his room, sheltered by the massive weight of the hotel, he watched the dunes in front of the hotel light up like a stage set. Three hundred yards away the low camouflaged hull of the wardens' beach car was revealed poised on a crest, its feeble spotlight drowned by the glare.

With a deep metallic sigh, the burning catafalque of the dead astronaut soared overhead, a cascade of vaporizing metal pouring from its hull, filling the sky with incandescent light. Reflected below it, like an expressway illuminated by an aircraft's spotlights, a long lane of light several hundred yards in width raced out into the desert toward the sea. As Bridgman shielded his eyes, it suddenly erupted in a tremendous explosion of detonating sand. A huge curtain of white dust lifted into the air and fell slowly to the ground. The sounds of the impact rolled against the hotel, mounting in a sustained crescendo that drummed against the windows. A series of smaller explosions flared up like opalescent fountains. All over the desert fires flickered briefly where fragments of the capsule had been scattered. Then the noise subsided, and an immense glistening pall of phosphorescing gas hung in the air like a silver veil, particles within it beading and winking.

Two hundred yards away across the sand was the running figure of Louise Woodward, Travis twenty paces behind her. Bridgman watched them dart in and out of the dunes, then abruptly felt the cold spotlight of the beach car hit his face and flood the room behind him. The vehicle was moving straight toward him, two of the wardens, nets and lassos in hand, riding the outboard.

Quickly Bridgman straddled the balcony, jumped down into the sand and raced toward the crest of the first dune. He crouched and ran on through the darkness as the beam probed the air. Above, the glistening pall was slowly fading, the particles of vaporized metal sifting toward the dark Martian sand. In the distance the last echoes of the impact were still reverberating among the hotels of the beach colonies further down the coast.

Five minutes later he caught up with Louise Woodward and Travis. The capsule's impact had flattened a number of the dunes, forming a shallow basin some quarter of a mile in diameter, and the surrounding slopes were scattered with the still glowing particles, sparkling like fading eyes. The beach car growled somewhere four or five hundred yards behind him, and Bridgman broke off into an exhausted walk. He stopped beside Travis, who was kneeling on the ground, breath pumping into his lungs. Fifty yards away Louise Woodward was running up and down, distraughtly gazing at the fragments of smoldering metal. For a moment the spotlight of the approaching beach car illuminated her, and she ran away among the dunes. Bridgman caught a glimpse of the inconsolable anguish in her face.

Travis was still on his knees. He had picked up a piece of the oxidized metal and was pressing it together in his hands.

"Travis, for God's sake tell her! This was Merril's capsule, there's no doubt about it! Woodward's still up there."

Travis looked up at him silently, his eyes searching Bridgman's face. A spasm of pain tore his mouth, and Bridgman realized that the barb of steel he clasped reverently in his hands was still glowing with heat.

"Travis!" He tried to pull the man's hands apart, the pungent stench of burning flesh gusting into his face, but Travis wrenched away from him. "Leave her alone, Bridgman! Go back with the wardens!"

Bridgman retreated from the approaching beach car. Only thirty yards away, its spotlight filled the basin. Louise Woodward was still searching the dunes. Travis held his ground as the wardens jumped down from the car and advanced toward him with their nets, his bloodied hands raised at his sides, the steel barb flashing like a dagger. At the head of the wardens, the only one unmasked, was a trim, neat-featured man with an intent, serious face. Bridgman guessed that this was Major Webster, and that the wardens had known of the impending impact and hoped to capture them, and Louise in particular, before it occurred.

Bridgman stumbled back toward the dunes at the edge of the basin. As he neared the crest he trapped his foot in a semicircular plate of metal, sat down, and freed his heel. Unmistakably it was part of a control panel, the circular instrument housings still intact.

Overhead the pall of glistening vapor had moved off to the northeast, and the reflected light was directly over the rusting gantries of the former launching site at Cape Kennedy. For a few fleeting seconds the gantries seemed to be enveloped in a sheen of silver, transfigured by the vaporized body of the dead astronaut, diffusing over them in a farewell gesture, his final return to the site from which he had set off to his death a century earlier. Then the gantries sank again into their craggy shadows, and the pall moved off like an immense wraith toward the sea, barely distinguishable from the star glow.

Down below Travis was sitting on the ground surrounded by the wardens. He scuttled about on his hands like a frantic crab, scooping handfuls of the virus-laden sand at them. Holding tight to their masks, the wardens maneuvered around him, their nets and lassos at the ready. Another group moved slowly toward Bridgman.

Bridgman picked up a handful of the dark Martian sand beside the instrument panel, felt the soft glowing crystals warm his palm. In his mind he could still see the silver-sheathed gantries of the launching site across the bay, by a curious illusion almost identical with the Martian city he had designed years earlier. He watched the pall disappear over the sea, then looked around at the other remnants of Merril's capsule scattered over the slopes. High in the western night, between Pegasus and Cygnus, shone the distant disk of the planet Mars, which for both himself and the dead astronaut had served for so long as a symbol of unattained ambition. The wind stirred softly through the sand, cooling this replica of the planet which lay passively around him, and at last he understood why he had come to the beach and been unable to leave it.

Twenty yards away Travis was being dragged off like a wild dog, his thrashing body pinioned in the center of a web of lassos. Louise Woodward had run away among the dunes toward the sea, following the vanished gas cloud.

In a sudden excess of refound confidence, Bridgman drove his fist into the dark sand, buried his forearm like a foundation pillar. A flange of hot metal from Merril's capsule burned his wrist, bonding him to the spirit of the dead astronaut.

"Merril," he cried exultantly as the wardens' lassos stung his neck and shoulders. "We made it!"

R. A. Lafferty

Slow Tuesday Night

• • • •

{1965}

R(aphael) A(loysius) Lafferty (1914–2002) began writing sf rather late in life, his first published story not appearing until 1960. He is a perfect example of the idiosyncratic writers who were lured into the genre during the magazine and paperback boom of the postwar decades. Erudite and brimming with ideas but in no way committed to traditional sf, he was—like his contemporaries Avram Davidson and Cordwainer Smith—a shrewd innovator who used the classic tropes of the field as flexible metaphors, developing in the process an offbeat literary vision of extraordinary range and complexity. The tales gathered in such collections as *Nine Hundred Grandmothers* (1970) and *Strange Doings* (1972) are among the most extravagantly creative of the period, closer to fables or folktales in their effects than to straightforward works of sf. Lafferty excelled at the short-story form; his novels—from rollicking space-opera quests such as *Space Chantey* (1968) to outlandish utopian romances such as *Past Master* (1968)—tend to be rather diffuse and episodic. A devout Catholic, Lafferty often encoded moral allegories into his seemingly absurdist plots: *Fourth Mansions* (1969), for example, features a cartoonishly oneiric conflict between cosmic good and evil that draws on the mystic visions of Saint Teresa of Ávila. Lafferty's work is brilliantly inventive but very much an acquired taste; as a result, his career suffered after the 1980s, when the markets for his quirky fiction began to dry up, relegating his work to low-circulation chapbooks and small-press compendiums.

"Slow Tuesday Night" develops a bizarre central premise with a lunatic's logic, in the best Lafferty manner. Following an experimental procedure that unshackles the decision-making capacity of the human brain, cultural experience has become subject to an unprecedented acceleration: cities rise and fall, fortunes wax and wane, trends appear and fade away, all in the course of a night. Tongue planted squarely in cheek, Lafferty parodies the modes of extrapolation characteristic of the genre, bestowing plausibility and causal consistency on a fundamentally absurd situation. Though on the surface zany and facetious (Lafferty pioneered a strain of gonzo sf that can be seen today in, for example, Charles Stross's "Rogue Farm"

[2003]), the tale has an underlying strain of social satire: the world depicted in the story, with its transient fads and impulsive desires, embodies an exaggerated version of modern consumerism, its pleasures shallow and ultimately meaningless. Even human relationships have become evanescent—passing fancies that flare up and recede in mere moments. As we confront this madcap future dominated by trivia and caprice, rumor and ballyhoo, we are invited to wonder whether any aspect of human life is truly consequential or enduring.

A panhandler intercepted the young couple as they strolled down the night street.

"Preserve us this night," he said as he touched his hat to them, "and could you good people advance me a thousand dollars to be about the recouping of my fortunes?"

"I gave you a thousand last Friday," said the young man.

"Indeed you did," the panhandler replied, "and I paid you back tenfold by messenger before midnight."

"That's right, George, he did," said the young woman. "Give it to him dear. I believe he's a good sort."

So the young man gave the panhandler a thousand dollars and the panhandler touched his hat to them in thanks, and went on to the recouping of his fortunes.

As he went into Money Market, the panhandler passed Ildefonsa Impala, the most beautiful woman in the city.

"Will you marry me this night, Ildy?" he asked cheerfully.

"Oh, I don't believe so, Basil," she said. "I marry you pretty often, but tonight I don't seem to have any plans at all. You may make me a gift on your first or second, however. I always like that."

But when they had parted she asked herself: "But whom will I marry tonight?"

The panhandler was Basil Bagelbaker who would be the richest man in the world within an hour and a half. He would make and lose four fortunes within eight hours; and these not the little fortunes that ordinary men acquire, but titanic things.

When the Abebaios block had been removed from human minds, people began to make decisions faster, and often better. It had been the mental stutter. When it was understood what it was, and that it had no useful function, it was removed by simple childhood metasurgery.

Transportation and manufacturing had then become practically instantaneous. Things that had once taken months and years now took only minutes and hours. A person could have one or several pretty intricate careers within an eight-hour period.

Freddy Fixico had just invented a manus module. Freddy was a Nyctalops, and the modules were characteristic of these people. The people had then divided themselves—according to their natures and inclinations—into the Auroreans, the Hemerobians, and the Nyctalops—or the Dawners, who had their most active hours from 4 A.M. till noon; the Day-Flies who obtained from noon to 8 P.M.; and the Night-Seers whose civilization thrived from 8 P.M. to 4 A.M. The cultures, inventions, markets and activities of these three folk were a little different. As a Nyctalops, Freddy had just begun his working day at 8 P.M. on a slow Tuesday night.

Freddy rented an office and had it furnished. This took one minute, negotiation, selection, and installation being almost instantaneous. Then he invented the manus module; that took another minute. He then had it manufactured and marketed; in three minutes it was in the hands of key buyers.

It caught on. It was an attractive module. The flow of orders began within thirty seconds. By ten minutes after eight every important person had one of the new manus modules, and the trend had been set. The module began to sell in the millions. It was one of the most interesting fads of the night, or at least the early part of the night.

Manus modules had no practical function, no more than had Sameki verses. They were attractive, of a psychologically satisfying size and shape, and could be held in the hands, set on a table, or installed in a module niche of any wall.

Naturally Freddy became very rich. Ildefonsa Impala, the most beautiful woman in the city, was always interested in newly rich men. She came to see Freddy about eight-thirty. People made up their minds fast, and Ildefonsa had hers made up when she came. Freddy made his own up quickly and divorced Judy Fixico in Small Claims Court. Freddy and Ildefonsa went honeymooning to Paraiso Dorado, a resort.

It was wonderful. All of Ildy's marriages were. There was the wonderful floodlighted scenery. The recirculated water of the famous falls was tinted gold; the immediate rocks had been done by Rambles; and the hills had been contoured by Spall. The beach was a perfect copy of that at Merevale, and the popular drink that first part of the night was blue absinthe.

But scenery—whether seen for the first lime or revisited after an interval—is striking for the sudden intense view of it. It is not meant to be lingered over. Food, selected and prepared instantly, is eaten with swift enjoyment: and blue absinthe lasts no longer than its own novelty. Loving, for Ildefonsa and her paramours, was quick and consuming; and repetition would have been pointless to her. Besides Ildefonsa and Freddy had taken only the one-hour luxury honeymoon.

Freddy wished to continue the relationship, but Ildefonsa glanced at a trend indicator. The manus module would hold its popularity for only the first third of the night. Already it had been discarded by people who mattered. And Freddy Fixico was not one of the regular successes. He enjoyed a full career only about one night a week.

They were back in the city and divorced in Small Claims Court by nine thirty-five. The stock of manus modules was remaindered, and the last of it would be disposed to bargain hunters among the Dawners, who will buy anything.

"Whom shall I marry next?" Ildefonsa asked herself. "It looks like a slow night."

"Bagelbaker is buying," ran the word through Money Market, but Bagelbaker was selling again before the word had made its rounds. Basil Bagelbaker enjoyed making money, and it was a pleasure to watch him work as he dominated the floor of the Market and assembled runners and a competent staff out of the corner of his mouth. Helpers stripped the panhandler rags off him and wrapped him in a tycoon toga. He sent one runner to pay back twentyfold the young couple who had advanced him a thousand dollars. He sent another with a more substantial gift to Ildefonsa Impala, for Basil cherished their relationship. Basil acquired title to the Trend Indication Complex and had certain falsifications set into it. He caused to collapse certain industrial empires that had grown up within the last two hours, and made a good thing of recombining their wreckage. He had been the richest man in the world for some minutes now. He became so money-heavy that he could not maneuver with the agility he had shown an hour before. He became a great fat buck, and the pack of expert wolves circled him to bring him down.

Very soon he would lose that first fortune of the evening. The secret of Basil Bagelbaker is that he enjoyed losing money spectacularly after he was full of it to the bursting point.

A thoughtful man named Maxwell Mouser had just produced a work of actinic philosophy. It took him seven minutes to write it. To write works of philosophy one used the flexible outlines and the idea indexes; one set the activator for such a wordage in each subsection; an adept would use the paradox feed-in, and the striking analogy blender; one calibrated the particular-slant and the personality-signature. It had to come out a good work, for excellence had become the automatic minimum for such productions.

"I will scatter a few nuts on the frosting," said Maxwell, and he pushed the lever for that. This sifted handfuls of words like chthonic and heuristic and prozymeides through the thing so that nobody could doubt it was a work of philosophy.

Maxwell Mouser sent the work out to publishers, and received it back each time in about three minutes. An analysis of it and reason for rejection was always given—mostly that the thing had been done before and better. Maxwell received it back ten times in thirty minutes, and was discouraged. Then there was a break.

Ladion's work had become a hit within the last ten minutes, and it was now recognized that Mouser's monograph was both an answer and a supplement to it. It was accepted and published in less than a minute after this break. The reviews of the first five minutes were cautious ones; then real enthusiasm was shown. This was truly one of the greatest works of philosophy to appear during the early and medium hours of the night. There were those who said it might be one of the enduring works and even have a holdover appeal to the Dawners the next morning.

Naturally Maxwell became very rich, and naturally Ildefonsa came to see him about midnight. Being a revolutionary philosopher, Maxwell thought that they might make some free arrangement, but Ildefonsa insisted it must be marriage. So Maxwell divorced Judy Mouser in Small Claims Court and went off with Ildefonsa.

This Judy herself, though not so beautiful as Ildefonsa, was the fastest taker in the City. She only wanted the men of the moment for a moment, and she was always there before even Ildefonsa. Ildefonsa believed that she took the men away from Judy; Judy said that Ildy had her leavings and nothing else.

"I had him first," Judy would always mock as she raced through Small Claims Court.

"Oh that damned Urchin!" Ildefonsa would moan. "She wears my very hair before I do."

Maxwell Mouser and Ildefonsa Impala went honeymooning to Musicbox Mountain, a resort. It was wonderful. The peaks were done with green snow by Dunbar and Fittle. (Back at Money Market Basil Bagelbaker was putting together his third and greatest fortune of the night, which might surpass in magnitude even his fourth fortune of the Thursday before.) The chalets were Switzier than the real Swiss and had live goats in every room. (And Stanley Skuldugger was emerging as the top actor-imago of the middle hours of the night) The popular drink for that middle part of the night was Glotzengubber, Eve Cheese and Rhine wine over pink ice. (And back in the city the leading Nyctalops were taking their midnight break at the Toppers' Club.)

Of course it was wonderful, as were all of Ildefonsa's—but she had never been really up on philosophy so she had scheduled only the special thirty-five minute honeymoon. She looked at the trend indicator to be sure. She found that her current husband had been obsoleted, and his opus was now referred to sneeringly as Mouser's Mouse. They went back to the city and were divorced in Small Claims Court.

The membership of the Toppers' Club varied. Success was the requisite of membership. Basil Bagelbaker might be accepted as a member, elevated to the presidency and expelled from it as a dirty pauper from three to six times a night. But only important persons could belong to it, or those enjoying brief moments of importance.

"I believe I will sleep during the Dawner period in the morning," Overcall said. "I may go up to this new place Koimopolis for an hour of it. They're said to be good. Where will you sleep, Basil?'

"Flop house."

"I believe I will sleep an hour by the Midian Method," said Burnbanner. "They have a fine new clinic. And perhaps I'll sleep an hour by the Prasenka Process, and an hour by the Dormidio."

"Crackle has been sleeping an hour every period by the natural method," said Overcall.

"I did that for a half hour not long since," said Burnbanner. "I believe an hour is too long to give it. Have you tried the natural method, Basil?'

"Always. Natural method and a bottle of red-eye."

Stanley Skuldugger had become the most meteoric actor-imago for a week. Naturally he became very rich, and Ildefonsa Impala went to see him about three A.M.

"I had him first!" rang the mocking voice of Judy Skuldugger as she skipped through her divorce in Small Claims Court. And Ildefonsa and Stanley-boy went off honeymooning. It is always fun to finish up a period with an actor-imago who is the hottest property in the business. There is something so adolescent and boorish about them.

Besides, there was the publicity, and Ildefonsa liked that. The rumor-mills ground. Would it last ten minutes? Thirty? An hour? Would it be one of those rare Nyctalops marriages that lasted through the rest of the night and into the daylight off hours? Would it even last into the next night as some had been known to do?

Actually it lasted nearly forty minutes, which was almost to the end of the period.

It had been a slow Tuesday night. A few hundred new products had run their course on the markets. There had been a score of dramatic hits, three-minute and five-minute capsule dramas, and several of the six-minute long-play affairs. *Night Street Nine*—a solidly sordid offering—seemed to be in as the drama of the night unless there should be a late hit.

Hundred-storied buildings had been erected, occupied, obsoleted, and demolished again to make room for more contemporary structures. Only the mediocre would use a building that had been left over from the Day-Flies or the Dawners, or even the Nyctalops of the night before. The city was rebuilt pretty completely at least three times during an eight-hour period.

The period drew near its end. Basil Bagelbaker, the richest man in the world, the reigning president of the Toppers' Club, was enjoying himself with his cronies. His fourth fortune of the night was a paper pyramid that had risen to incredible heights; but Basil laughed to himself as he savored the manipulation it was founded on.

Three ushers of the Toppers' Club came in with firm step.

"Get out of here, you dirty bum!" they told Basil savagely. They tore the tycoon's toga off him and then tossed him his seedy panhandler's rags with a three-man sneer.

"All gone?" Basil asked. "I gave it another five minutes."

"All gone," said a messenger from Money Market. "Nine billion gone in five minutes, and it really pulled some others down with it."

"Pitch the busted bum out!" howled Overcall and Burnbanner and the other cronies.

"Wait, Basil," said Overcall. "Turn in the President's Crosier before we kick you downstairs. After all, you'll have it several times again tomorrow night."

The period was over. The Nyctalops drifted off to sleep clinics or leisure-hour hide-outs to pass their ebb time. The Auroreans, the Dawners, took over the vital stuff.

Now you would see some action! Those Dawners really made fast decisions. You wouldn't catch them wasting a full minute setting up a business.

A sleepy panhandler met Ildefonsa Impala on the way.

"Preserve us this morning, Ildy," he said, "and will you marry me the coming night?'

"Likely I will, Basil," she told him. "Did you marry Judy during the night past?"

“I’m not sure. Could you let me have two dollars, Ildy?’

“Out of the question. I believe a Judy Bagelbaker was named one of the ten best-dressed women during the frou-frou fashion period about two o’clock. Why do you need two dollars?”

“A dollar for a bed and a dollar for red-eye. After all, I sent you two million out of my second.”

“I keep my two sorts of accounts separate. Here’s a dollar, Basil. Now, be off! I can’t be seen talking to a dirty panhandler.”

“Thank you, Ildy. I’ll get the red-eye and sleep in an alley. Preserve us this morning.”

Bagelbaker shuffled off whistling “Slow Tuesday Night.”

And already the Dawners had set Wednesday morning to jumping.

HARLAN ELLISON®

"Repent, Harlequin!" Said the Ticktockman

• • • •

{1965}

Harlan Ellison (1934–) is probably the most honored of modern sf short story writers, having won three Nebula Awards, a Grand Master laureate (2006), and eight and a half Hugo Awards for eight different tales—including "'Repent, Harlequin!' Said the Ticktockman," which won both. According to the *Index to Science Fiction Anthologies and Collections*, prepared by William G. Contento, Ellison is the third most anthologized sf writer behind Ray Bradbury and Isaac Asimov. Ellison's success (memorialized in Erik Nelson's award-winning documentary film *Dreams with Sharp Teeth* [2009]) is equaled by his notoriety: a contentious presence within the field for over five decades, Ellison has feuded with a number of authors, editors, publishers, fans, and studio executives, once allegedly telling the head of Warner Brothers, during discussion of a screenplay adaptation of Asimov's *I, Robot* (1950), that he had "the intellectual capacity of an artichoke." While Ellison's pugnacity and legendary sharp tongue have at times led him into lamentable controversies, they have also been marshaled in support of estimable causes: over the years he has battled, valiantly and volubly, for equal rights and authors' rights, and has participated in many anti-censorship and anti-war protests, showing enormous personal and professional courage in the process. Early in his career, he often struggled with editors who casually altered or censored his work; as a result, his pathbreaking anthologies *Dangerous Visions* (1967) and *Again, Dangerous Visions* (1972) were designed to give sf writers a showcase for their most challenging material, free from the constraints of magazine publication. While these taboo-shattering books, and Ellison's own increasingly bold and flamboyant fictions, came to be associated with the New Wave movement, the author's intellectual and artistic commitments have always been broader: not just to the experimental impulses of the sf avant-garde or the political causes of the 1960s counterculture but to the enduring values of individual autonomy and unfettered self-expression.

"Repent, Harlequin," his breakthrough story (originally published in *Galaxy* in December 1965), is a case in point. An allegory of civil disobedience set in a cartoonishly vivid dystopian future, it pits an iconic representative of dissent, the eponymous Harlequin, against a grim agent of social authority, the Ticktockman, whose obsession with timetables reflects a tyrannically regimented worldview. Ellison's satire of conformity and defense of anarchic freedom are reflected in the tale's very form: loquacious and freewheeling, it delights in jokey puns and juvenile pratfalls. Its vision of dystopia is, in essence, the reverse of R. A. Lafferty's in "Slow Tuesday Night" (1965), where anarchic change is deplored; "Repent, Harlequin" embraces it.

Ellison originally submitted the story to the Milford Writers' Workshop hosted by Damon Knight, where the response was reportedly divided: some deplored its outright daffiness and seeming formlessness while others appreciated its mercurial brilliance and whimsical skewering of autocratic pretensions. The latter cohort would seem to have won the day, since "Repent, Harlequin" has become one of the most celebrated and most reprinted stories in sf history.

There are always those who ask, what is it all about? For those who need to ask, for those who need points sharply made, who need to know "where it's at," this:

> *The mass of men serve the state thus, not as men mainly, but as machines, with their bodies. They are the standing army, and the militia, jailors, constables,* posse comitatus, *etc. In most cases there is no free exercise whatever of the judgment or of the moral sense; but they put themselves on a level with wood and earth and stones; and wooden men can perhaps be manufactured that will serve the purpose as well. Such command no more respect than men of straw or a lump of dirt. They have the same sort of worth only as horses and dogs. Yet such as these even are commonly esteemed good citizens. Others—as most legislators, politicians, lawyers, ministers, and officeholders—serve the state chiefly with their heads; and, as they rarely make any moral distinctions, they are as likely to serve the Devil, without intending it, as God. A very few, as heroes, patriots, martyrs, reformers in the great sense, and* men, *serve the state with their consciences also, and so necessarily resist it for the most part; and they are commonly treated as enemies by it.*
>
> —Henry David Thoreau, CIVIL DISOBEDIENCE

That is the heart of it. Now begin in the middle, and later learn the beginning; the end will take care of itself.

But because it was the very world it was, the very world they had allowed it to *become*, for months his activities did not come to the alarmed attention of The Ones Who Kept The Machine Functioning Smoothly, the ones who poured the very best butter over the cams and mainsprings of the culture. Not until it had become obvious that somehow, someway, he had become a notoriety, a celebrity, perhaps even a hero for (what Officialdom inescapably tagged) "an emotionally disturbed segment of the populace," did they turn it over to the Ticktockman and his legal machinery. But by then, because it was the very world it was, and they had no way to predict he would happen—possibly a strain of disease long-defunct, now, suddenly, reborn in a system where immunity had been forgotten, had lapsed—he had been allowed to become too real. Now he had form and substance.

He had become a *personality*, something they had filtered out of the system many decades before. But there it was, and there *he* was, a very definitely imposing personality. In certain circles—middle-class circles—it was thought disgusting. Vulgar ostentation. Anarchistic. Shameful. In others, there was only sniggering: those strata where thought is subjugated to form and ritual, niceties, proprieties. But down below, ah, down below, where the people always needed their saints and sinners, their bread and circuses, their heroes and villains, he was considered a Bolivar; a Napoleon; a Robin Hood; a Dick Bong (Ace of Aces); a Jesus; a Jomo Kenyatta.

And at the top—where, like socially-attuned Shipwreck Kellys, every tremor and vibration threatening to dislodge the wealthy, powerful and titled from their flagpoles—he was considered a menace; a heretic; a rebel; a disgrace; a peril. He was known down the line, to the very heartmeat core, but the important reactions were high above and far below. At the very top, at the very bottom.

So his file was turned over, along with his time-card and his cardioplate, to the office of the Ticktockman.

The Ticktockman: very much over six feet tall, often silent, a soft purring man when things went timewise. The Ticktockman.

Even in the cubicles of the hierarchy, where fear was generated, seldom suffered, he was called the Ticktockman. But no one called him that to his mask.

You don't call a man a hated name, not when that man, behind his mask, is capable of revoking the minutes, the hours, the days and nights, the years of your life. He was called the Master Timekeeper to his mask. It was safer that way.

"This is *what* he is," said the Ticktockman with genuine softness, "but not *who* he is. This time-card I'm holding in my left hand has a name on it, but it is the name of *what* he is, not *who* he is. The cardioplate here in my right hand is also named, but not *whom* named, merely *what* named. Before I can exercise proper revocation, I have to know *who* this *what* is."

To his staff, all the ferrets, all the loggers, all the finks, all the commex, even the mineez, he said, "Who is this Harlequin?"

He was not purring smoothly. Timewise, it was jangle.

However, it *was* the longest speech they had ever heard him utter at one time, the staff, the ferrets, the loggers, the finks, the commex, but not the mineez, who usually weren't around to know, in any case. But even they scurried to find out.

Who is the Harlequin?

High above the third level of the city, he crouched on the humming aluminum-frame platform of the air-boat (foof! air-boat, indeed! swizzleskid is what it was, with a tow-rack jerry-rigged) and he stared down at the neat Mondrian arrangement of the buildings.

Somewhere nearby, he could hear the metronomic left-right-left of the 2:47 P.M. shift, entering the Timkin roller-bearing plant in their sneakers. A minute later, precisely, he heard the softer right-left-right of the 5:00 A.M. formation, going home.

An elfin grin spread across his tanned features, and his dimples appeared for a moment. Then, scratching at his thatch of auburn hair, he shrugged within his motley, as though girding himself for what came next, and threw the joystick forward, and bent into the wind as the air-boat dropped. He skimmed over a slidewalk, purposely dropping a few feet to crease the tassels of the ladies of fashion, and—inserting thumbs in large ears—he stuck out his tongue, rolled his eyes and went wugga-wugga-wugga. It was a minor diversion. One pedestrian skittered and tumbled, sending parcels every-whichway, another wet herself, a third keeled slantwise and the walk was stopped automatically by the servitors till she could be resuscitated. It was a minor diversion.

Then he swirled away on a vagrant breeze, and was gone. Hi-ho. As he rounded the cornice of the Time-Motion Study Building, he saw the shift, just boarding the slidewalk. With practiced motion and an absolute conservation of movement, they sidestepped up onto the slow-strip and (in a chorus line reminiscent of a Busby Berkeley film of the antediluvian 1930s) advanced across the strips ostrich-walking till they were lined up on the expresstrip.

Once more, in anticipation, the elfin grin spread, and there was a tooth missing back there on the left side. He dipped, skimmed, and swooped over them; and then, scrunching about on the air-boat, he released the holding pins that fastened shut the ends of the home-made pouring troughs that kept his cargo from dumping prematurely. And as he pulled the trough-pins, the air-boat slid over the factory workers and one hundred and fifty thousand dollars' worth of jelly beans cascaded down on the expresstrip.

Jelly beans! Millions and billions of purples and yellows and greens and licorice and grape and raspberry and mint and round and smooth and crunchy outside and soft-mealy inside and sugary and bouncing jouncing tumbling clittering clattering skittering fell on the heads and shoulders and hardhats and carapaces of the Timkin workers, tinkling on the slidewalk and bouncing away and rolling about underfoot and filling the sky on their way down with all the colors of joy and childhood and holidays, coming down in a steady rain, a solid wash, a torrent of color and sweetness out of the sky from above, and entering a universe of sanity and metronomic order with quite-mad coocoo newness. Jelly beans!

The shift workers howled and laughed and were pelted, and broke ranks, and the jelly beans managed to work their way into the mechanism of the slidewalks after which there was a hideous scraping as the sound of a million fingernails rasped down a quarter of a million blackboards, followed by a coughing and a sputtering, and then the slidewalks all stopped and everyone was dumped thisawayandthataway in a jackstraw tumble, still laughing and popping little jelly bean eggs of childish color into their mouths. It was a holiday, and a jollity, an absolute insanity, a giggle. But . . .

The shift was delayed seven minutes.

They did not get home for seven minutes.

The master schedule was thrown off by seven minutes.

Quotas were delayed by inoperative slidewalks for seven minutes.

He had tapped the first domino in the line, and one after another, like chik chik chik, the others had fallen.

The System had been seven minutes' worth of disrupted. It was a tiny matter, one hardly worthy of note, but in a society where the single driving force was order and unity and equality and promptness and clocklike precision and attention to the clock, reverence of the gods of the passage of time, it was a disaster of major importance.

So he was ordered to appear before the Ticktockman. It was broadcast across every channel of the communications web. He was ordered to be *there* at 7:00 dammit on time. And they waited, and they waited, but he didn't show up till almost ten-thirty, at which time he merely sang a little song about moonlight in a place no one had ever heard of, called Vermont, and vanished again. But they had all been waiting since seven, and it wrecked *hell* with their schedules. So the question remained: Who is the Harlequin?

But the *unasked* question (more important of the two) was: how did we get *into* this position, where a laughing, irresponsible japer of jabberwocky and jive could disrupt our entire economic and cultural life with a hundred and fifty thousand dollars' worth of jelly beans . . .

Jelly for God's sake *beans*! This is madness! Where did he get the money to buy a hundred and fifty thousand dollars' worth of jelly beans? (They knew it would have cost that much, because they had a team of Situation Analysts pulled off another assignment, and rushed to the slidewalk scene to sweep up and count the candies, and produce findings, which disrupted *their* schedules and threw their entire branch at least a day behind.) Jelly beans! Jelly . . . *beans*? Now wait a second—a second accounted for—no one has manufactured jelly beans for over a hundred years. Where did he get jelly beans?

That's another good question. More than likely it will never be answered to your complete satisfaction. But then, how many questions ever are?

The middle you know. Here is the beginning. How it starts:

A desk pad. Day for day, and turn each day. 9:00—Open the mail. 9:45—appointment with planning commission board. 10:30—discuss installation progress charts with J.L. 11:45—pray for rain. 12:00—lunch. *And so it goes.*

"I'm sorry, Miss Grant, but the time for interviews was set at 2:30, and it's almost five now. I'm sorry you're late, but those are the rules. You'll have to wait till next year to submit application for this college again." *And so it goes.*

The 10:10 local stops at Cresthaven, Galesville, Tonawanda Junction, Selby and Farnhurst, but not at Indiana City, Lucasville and Colton, except on Sunday. The 10:35 express stops at Galesville, Selby and Indiana City, except on Sundays & Holidays, at which time it stops at . . . *And so it goes.*

"I couldn't wait, Fred. I had to be at Pierre Cartain's by 3:00, and you said you'd meet me under the clock in the terminal at 2:45, and you weren't there, so I had to go on.

You're always late, Fred. If you'd been there, we could have sewed it up together, but as it was, well, I took the order alone . . ." And so it goes.

Dear Mr. and Mrs. Atterley: In reference to your son Gerold's constant tardiness, I am afraid we will have to suspend him from school unless some more reliable method can be instituted guaranteeing he will arrive at his classes on time. Granted he is an exemplary student, and his marks are high, his constant flouting of the schedules of this school makes it impractical to maintain him in a system where the other children seem capable of getting where they are supposed to be on time and so it goes.

YOU CANNOT VOTE UNLESS YOU APPEAR AT 8:45 A.M.

"I don't care if the script is good, I need it Thursday!"

CHECK-OUT TIME IS 2:00 P.M.

"You got here late. The job's taken. Sorry."

YOUR SALARY HAS BEEN DOCKED FOR TWENTY MINUTES TIME LOST.

"God, what time is it, I've gotta run!"

And so it goes. And so it goes. And so it goes. And so it goes goes goes goes goes tick tock tick tock tick tock and one day we no longer let time serve us, we serve time and we are slaves of the schedule, worshippers of the sun's passing, bound into a life predicated on restrictions because the system will not function if we don't keep the schedule tight.

Until it becomes more than a minor inconvenience to be late. It becomes a sin. Then a crime. Then a crime punishable by this:

EFFECTIVE 15 JULY 2389 12:00:00 midnight, the office of the Master Timekeeper will require all citizens to submit their time-cards and cardioplates for processing. In accordance with Statute 555-7-SGH-999 governing the revocation of time per capita, all cardioplates will be keyed to the individual holder and—

What they had done was devise a method of curtailing the amount of life a person could have. If he was ten minutes late, he lost ten minutes of his life. An hour was proportionately worth more revocation. If someone was consistently tardy, he might find himself, on a Sunday night, receiving a communiqué from the Master Timekeeper that his time had run out, and he would be "turned off" at high noon on Monday, please straighten your affairs, sir, madame or bisex.

And so, by this simple scientific expedient (utilizing a scientific process held dearly secret by the Ticktockman's office) the System was maintained.

It was the only expedient thing to do. It was, after all, patriotic. The schedules had to be met. After all, there *was* a war on!

But, wasn't there always?

"Now that is really disgusting," the Harlequin said, when Pretty Alice showed him the wanted poster. "Disgusting and *highly* improbable. After all, this isn't the Day of the Desperado. A *wanted* poster!"

"You know," Pretty Alice noted, "you speak with a great deal of inflection."

"I'm sorry," said the Harlequin, humbly.

"No need to be sorry. You're always saying 'I'm sorry.' You have such massive guilt, Everett, it's really very sad."

"I'm sorry," he said again, then pursed his lips so the dimples appeared momentarily. He hadn't wanted to say that at all. "I have to go out again. I have to *do* something."

Pretty Alice slammed her coffee-bulb down on the counter. "Oh for God's *sake*, Everett, can't you stay home just *one* night! Must you always be out in that ghastly clown suit, running around an*noy*ing people?"

"I'm—" He stopped, and clapped the jester's hat onto his auburn thatch with a tiny tinkling of bells. He rose, rinsed out his coffee-bulb at the spray, and put it into the dryer for a moment. "I have to go."

She didn't answer. The faxbox was purring, and she pulled a sheet out, read it, threw it toward him on the counter. "It's about you. Of course. You're ridiculous."

He read it quickly. It said the Ticktockman was trying to locate him. He didn't care, he was going out to be late again. At the door, dredging for an exit line, he hurled back petulantly, "Well, *you* speak with inflection, *too*!"

Pretty Alice rolled her pretty eyes heavenward. "You're ridiculous."

The Harlequin stalked out, slamming the door, which sighed shut softly, and locked itself.

There was a gentle knock, and Pretty Alice got up with an exhalation of exasperated breath, and opened the door. He stood there. "I'll be back about ten-thirty, okay?"

She pulled a rueful face. "Why do you tell me that? Why? You *know* you'll be late! You *know* it! You're *always* late, so why do you tell me these dumb things?" She closed the door.

On the other side, the Harlequin nodded to himself. *She's right. She's always right. I'll be late. I'm always late. Why* do *I tell her these dumb things?*

He shrugged again, and went off to be late once more.

•

He had fired off the firecracker rockets that said: I will attend the 115th annual International Medical Association Invocation at 8:00 P.M. precisely. I do hope you will all be able to join me.

The words had burned in the sky, and of course the authorities were there, lying in wait for him. They assumed, naturally, that he would be late. He arrived twenty minutes early, while they were setting up the spiderwebs to trap and hold him. Blowing a large bullhorn, he frightened and unnerved them so, their own moisturized encirclement webs sucked closed, and they were hauled up, kicking and shrieking, high above the amphitheater's floor. The Harlequin laughed and laughed, and apologized profusely. The physicians, gathered in solemn conclave, roared with laughter, and accepted the Harlequin's apologies with exaggerated bowing and posturing and a merry time was had by all, who thought the Harlequin was a regular foofaraw in fancy pants; all, that is, but the authorities, who had been sent out by the office of the Ticktockman; they hung there like so much dockside cargo, hauled up above the floor of the amphitheater in a most unseemly fashion.

(In another part of the same city where the Harlequin carried on his "activities," totally unrelated in every way to what concerns us here, save that it illustrates the Ticktockman's power and import, a man named Marshall Delahanty received his turn-off notice from the Ticktockman's office. His wife received the notification from the gray-suited minee who delivered it, with the traditional "look of sorrow" plastered hideously across his face. She knew what it was, even without unsealing it. It was a billet-doux of immediate recognition to everyone these days. She gasped, and held it as though it were a glass slide tinged with botulism, and prayed it was not for her. Let it be for Marsh, she thought, brutally, realistically, or one of the kids, but not for me, please dear God, not for me. And then she opened it, and it *was* for Marsh, and she was at one and the same time horrified and relieved. The next trooper in the line had caught the bullet. "Marshall," she screamed, "Marshall! Termination, Marshall! OhmiGod, Marshall, whattl we do, whattl we do, Marshall omigodmarshall . . ." and in their home that night was the sound of tearing paper and fear, and the stink of madness went up the flue and there was nothing, absolutely nothing they could do about it.

(But Marshall Delahanty tried to run. And early the next day, when turn-off time came, he was deep in the Canadian forest two hundred miles away, and the office of the Ticktockman blanked his cardioplate, and Marshall Delahanty keeled over, running, and his heart stopped, and the blood dried up on its way to his brain, and he was dead that's all. One light went out on the sector map in the office of the Master Timekeeper, while notification was entered for fax reproduction, and Georgette Delahanty's name was entered on the dole roles till she could remarry. Which is the end of the footnote, and all the point that need be made, except don't laugh, because that is what would happen to the Harlequin if ever the Ticktockman found out his real name. It isn't funny.)

The shopping level of the city was thronged with the Thursday-colors of the buyers. Women in canary yellow chitons and men in pseudo-Tyrolean outfits that were jade and leather and fit very tightly, save for the balloon pants.

When the Harlequin appeared on the still-being-constructed shell of the new Efficiency Shopping Center, his bullhorn to his elfishly-laughing lips, everyone pointed and stared, and he berated them:

"Why let them order you about? Why let them tell you to hurry and scurry like ants or maggots? Take your time! Saunter a while! Enjoy the sunshine, enjoy the breeze, let life carry you at your own pace! Don't be slaves of time, it's a helluva way to die, slowly, by degrees . . . down with the Ticktockman!"

Who's the nut? most of the shoppers wanted to know. Who's the nut oh wow I'm gonna be late I gotta run . . .

And the construction gang on the Shopping Center received an urgent order from the office of the Master Timekeeper that the dangerous criminal known as the Harlequin was atop their spire, and their aid was urgently needed in apprehending him. The work crew said no, they would lose time on their construction schedule, but the Ticktockman managed to pull the proper threads of governmental webbing, and they were told to cease work and catch that nitwit up there on the spire; up there with the bullhorn. So a dozen and more burly workers began climbing into their construction platforms, releasing the a-grav plates, and rising toward the Harlequin.

After the debacle (in which, through the Harlequin's attention to personal safety, no one was seriously injured), the workers tried to reassemble, and assault him again, but it was too late. He had vanished. It had attracted quite a crowd, however, and the shopping cycle was thrown off by hours, simply hours. The purchasing needs of the system were therefore falling behind, and so measures were taken to accelerate the cycle for the rest of the day, but it got bogged down and speeded up and they sold too many float-valves and not nearly enough wegglers, which meant that the popli ratio was off, which made it necessary to rush cases and cases of spoiling Smash-O to stores that usually needed a case only every three or four hours. The shipments were bollixed, the transshipments were misrouted, and in the end, even the swizzleskid industries felt it.

“Don’t come back till you have him!” the Ticktockman said, very quietly, very sincerely, extremely dangerously.

They used dogs. They used probes. They used cardioplate crossoffs. They used teepers. They used bribery. They used stiktytes. They used intimidation. They used torment. They used torture. They used finks. They used cops. They used search&seizure. They used fallaron. They used betterment incentive. They used fingerprints. They used the Bertillon system. They used cunning. They used guile. They used treachery. They used Raoul Mitgong, but he didn’t help much. They used applied physics. They used techniques of criminology.

And what the hell: they caught him.

After all, his name was Everett C. Marm, and he wasn’t much to begin with, except a man who had no sense of time.

“Repent, Harlequin!” said the Ticktockman.

“Get stuffed!” the Harlequin replied, sneering.

“You’ve been late a total of sixty-three years, five months, three weeks, two days, twelve hours, forty-one minutes, fifty-nine seconds, point oh three six one one one microseconds. You’ve used up everything you can, and more. I’m going to turn you off.”

“Scare someone else. I’d rather be dead than live in a dumb world with a bogeyman like you.”

“It’s my job.”

“You’re full of it. You’re a tyrant. You have no right to order people around and kill them if they show up late.”

“You can’t adjust. You can’t fit in.”

“Unstrap me, and I’ll fit my fist into your mouth.”

“You’re a nonconformist.”

“That didn’t used to be a felony.”

“It is now. Live in the world around you.”

“I hate it. It’s a terrible world.”

“Not everyone thinks so. Most people enjoy order.”

“I don’t, and most of the people I know don’t.”

“That’s not true. How do you think we caught you?”

“I’m not interested.”

“A girl named Pretty Alice told us who you were.”

“That’s a lie.”

“It’s true. You unnerve her. She wants to belong; she wants to conform; I’m going to turn you off.”

"Then do it already, and stop arguing with me."

"I'm not going to turn you off."

"You're an idiot!"

"Repent, Harlequin!" said the Ticktockman.

"Get stuffed."

So they sent him to Coventry. And in Coventry they worked him over. It was just like what they did to Winston Smith in NINETEEN EIGHTY-FOUR, which was a book none of them knew about, but the techniques are really quite ancient, and so they did it to Everett C. Marm; and one day, quite a long time later, the Harlequin appeared on the communications web, appearing elfin and dimpled and bright-eyed, and not at all brainwashed, and he said he had been wrong, that it was a good, a very good thing indeed, to belong, to be right on time hip-ho and away we go, and everyone stared up at him on the public screens that covered an entire city block, and they said to themselves, well, you see, he was just a nut after all, and if that's the way the system is run, then let's do it that way, because it doesn't pay to fight city hall, or in this case, the Ticktockman. So Everett C. Marm was destroyed, which was a loss, because of what Thoreau said earlier, but you can't make an omelet without breaking a few eggs, and in every revolution a few die who shouldn't, but they have to, because that's the way it happens, and if you make only a little change, then it seems to be worthwhile. Or, to make the point lucidly:

"Uh, excuse me, sir, I, uh, don't know how to uh, to uh, tell you this, but you were three minutes late. The schedule is a little, uh, bit off."

He grinned sheepishly.

"That's ridiculous!" murmured the Ticktockman behind his mask. "Check your watch." And then he went into his office, going *mrmee, mrmee, mrmee, mrmee.*

FREDERIK POHL

Day Million

• • • •

{1966}

Frederik Pohl (1919–) has had a long and remarkably diverse career. Unlike his better-known contemporaries (and fellow SFWA Grand Masters) Isaac Asimov and Robert A. Heinlein, both of whom developed unique voices early on in their careers from which they never wavered, Pohl has been protean, moving from droll works of social satire during the 1950s (many, such as *The Space Merchants* [1953], written in collaboration with C. M. Kornbluth) to grimly serious hard sf (the Nebula-winning *Man Plus* ([1975]) and freewheeling space opera (the *Heechee* series [1977–2004]) in the 1970s and after. He was active in fandom during the late 1930s and 1940s, being a member of the celebrated New York–based group the Futurians, and became a literary agent and professional editor while still in his teens. Throughout the 1960s, he edited *Galaxy* and its sibling publications *If* and *Worlds of Tomorrow*, winning three Hugo Awards for best magazine. Though overtly an opponent of the New Wave, which he saw as trendy and anti–science oriented, he published much of the cream of the movement's work in the United States, including classic short fiction by Harlan Ellison and Robert Silverberg. During the 1970s, Pohl served as chief sf editor for Bantam Books, where he developed the "Frederick Pohl Selections" series, which included such genre-bending works as Samuel R. Delany's *Dhalgren* (1975) and Joanna Russ's *The Female Man* (1975). His own sf from the 1960s onward began to blend traditional values of adventure-based plotting and techno-scientific extrapolation with the New Wave's penchant for brooding character studies and formal experimentation.

"Day Million" is a case in point. On the one hand, it is a far-future extravaganza featuring genetic engineering, cyborgs, and interstellar travel; on the other hand, it is a shrewd meditation on what it means to be human, cast in an aggressive style that confronts and even mocks the reader. Since the story was published in a men's magazine, *Rogue* (where a number of sf authors, such as Frank Robinson and Algis Budrys, served as editors and feature writers), the narrator presumes—and sneeringly addresses—a certain type of audience: unmarried male swingers eager to read about "a boy, a girl, and a love story." The narrator dutifully serves up this standard fare, but with a series of wry twists that puts enormous pressure on the seemingly transparent categories of gender identity and sexual orientation. There is an abiding strangeness—a powerful whiff of posthuman *otherness*—about this seemingly straightforward love story, and that is precisely Pohl's point. Just as the present is radically different from the past, so "day million" will be far enough from current norms that we will not recognize—indeed, might be horribly shocked by—its taken-for-granted verities. Even the ways we love one another will change in the future, a theme also taken up by Samuel R. Delany in "Aye, and Gomorrah . . ." (1967).

On this day I want to tell you about, which will be about a thousand years from now, there were a boy, a girl and a love story.

Now although I haven't said much so far, none of it is true. The boy was not what you and I would normally think of as a boy, because he was a hundred and eighty-seven years old. Nor was the girl a girl, for other reasons; and the love story did not entail that sublimation of the urge to rape and concurrent postponement of the instinct to submit which we at present understand in such matters. You won't care much for this story if you don't grasp these facts at once. If, however, you will make the effort, you'll likely enough find it jam-packed, chockful and tiptop-crammed with laughter, tears and poignant sentiment which may, or may not, be worthwhile. The reason the girl was not a girl was that she was a boy.

How angrily you recoil from the page! You say, who the hell wants to read about a pair of queers? Calm yourself. Here are no hot-breathing secrets of perversion for the coterie trade. In fact, if you were to see this girl, you would not guess that she was in any sense a boy. Breasts, two; vagina, one. Hips, Callipygean; face, hairless; supra-orbital lobes, non-existent. You would term her female at once, although it is true that you might wonder just what species she was a female of, being confused by the tail, the silky pelt or the gill slits behind each ear.

Now you recoil again. Cripes, man, take my word for it. This is a sweet kid, and if you, as a normal male, spent as much as an hour in a room with her, you would bend heaven and earth to get her in the sack. Dora (we will call her that; her "name" was omicron-Di-base seven-group-totter-oot S Doradus 5314, the last part of which is a color specification corresponding to a shade of green)—Dora, I say, was feminine, charming, and cute. I admit she doesn't sound that way. She was, as you might put it, a dancer. Her art involved qualities of intellection and expertise of a very high order, requiring both tremendous natural capacities and endless practice; it was performed in null-gravity and I can best describe it by saying that it was something like the performance of a contortionist and something like classical ballet, maybe resembling Danilova's dying swan. It was also pretty damned sexy. In a symbolic way, to be sure; but face it, most of the things we call "sexy" are symbolic, you know, except perhaps an exhibitionist's open fly. On Day Million when Dora danced, the people who saw her panted; and you would too.

About this business of her being a boy. It didn't matter to her audiences that genetically she was male. It wouldn't matter to you, if you were among them, because you wouldn't know it—not unless you took a biopsy cutting of her flesh and put it under an electron microscope to find the XY chromosome—and it didn't matter to them because they didn't care. Through techniques which are not only complex but haven't yet been discovered, these people were able to determine a great deal about the aptitudes and easements of babies quite a long time before they were born—at about the second horizon of cell-division, to be exact, when the segmenting egg is becoming a free blastocyst—and then they naturally helped those aptitudes along. Wouldn't we? If we find a child with an aptitude for music we give him a scholarship to Juilliard. If they found a child whose aptitudes were for being a woman, they made him one. As sex had long been dissociated from reproduction this was relatively easy to do and caused no trouble and no, or at least very little, comment.

How much is "very little"? Oh, about as much as would be caused by our own tampering with Divine Will by filling a tooth. Less than would be caused by wearing a hearing aid. Does it still sound awful? Then look closely at the next busty babe you meet and reflect that she may be a Dora, for adults who are genetically male but somatically female are far from unknown even in our own time. An accident of environment in the womb overwhelms the blueprints of heredity. The difference is that with us it happens only by accident and we don't know about it except rarely, after close study; whereas the people of Day Million did it often, on purpose, because they wanted to.

Well, that's enough to tell you about Dora. It would only confuse you to add that she was seven feet tall and smelled of peanut butter. Let us begin our story.

On Day Million Dora swam out of her house, entered a transportation tube, was sucked briskly to the surface in its flow of water and ejected in its plume of spray to an elastic platform in front of her—ah—call it her rehearsal hall. "Oh, shit!' she cried in pretty confusion, reaching out to catch her balance and find herself tumbled against a total stranger, whom we will call Don.

They met cute. Don was on his way to have his legs renewed. Love was the farthest thing from his mind; but when, absent-mindedly taking a short cut across the landing platform for submarinites and finding himself drenched, he discovered his arms full of the loveliest girl he had ever seen, he knew at once they were meant for each other. "Will you marry me?" he asked. She said softly, "Wednesday," and the promise was like a caress.

Don was tall, muscular, bronze, and exciting. His name was no more Don than Dora's was Dora, but the personal part of it was Adonis in tribute to his vibrant maleness, and so we will call him Don for short. His personality color-code, in Angstrom units, was 5290, or only a few degrees bluer than Dora's 5314, a measure of what they had intuitively discovered at first sight, that they possessed many affinities of taste and interest.

I despair of telling you exactly what it was that Don did for a living—I don't mean for the sake of making money, I mean for the sake of giving purpose and meaning to his life, to keep him from going off his nut with boredom—except to say that it involved a lot of traveling. He traveled in interstellar spaceships. In order to make a spaceship go really fast about thirty-one male and seven genetically female human beings had to do certain things, and Don was one of the thirty-one. Actually he contemplated options. This involved a lot of exposure to radiation flux—not so much from his own station in the propulsive system as in the spillover from the next stage, where a genetic female preferred selections and the subnuclear particles making the selections she preferred demolished themselves in a shower of quanta. Well, you don't give a rat's ass for that, but it meant that Don had to be clad at all times in a skin of light, resilient, extremely strong copper-colored metal. I have already mentioned this, but you probably thought I meant he was sunburned.

More than that, he was a cybernetic man. Most of his ruder parts had been long since replaced with mechanisms of vastly more permanence and use. A cadmium centrifuge, not a heart, pumped his blood. His lungs moved only when he wanted to speak out loud, for a cascade of osmotic filters rebreathed oxygen out of his own wastes. In a way, he probably would have looked peculiar to a man from the twentieth century, with his glowing eyes and seven-fingered hands; but to himself, and of course to Dora, he looked mighty manly and grand. In the course of his voyages Don had circled Proxima Centauri, Procyon, and the puzzling worlds of Mira Ceti; he had carried agricultural templates to the planets of Canopus and brought back warm, witty pets from the pale companion of Aldebaran. Blue-hot or red-cool, he had seen a thousand stars and their ten thousand planets. He had, in fact, been traveling the starlanes with only brief leaves on Earth for pushing two centuries. But you don't care about that, either. It is people that make stories, not the circumstances they find themselves in, and you want to hear about these two people. Well, they made it. The great thing they had for each other grew and flowered and burst into fruition on Wednesday just as Dora had promised. They met at the encoding room, with a couple of well-wishing friends apiece to cheer them on, and while their identities were being taped and stored they smiled and whispered to each other and bore the jokes of their friends with blushing repartee. Then they exchanged their mathematical analogues and went away, Dora to her dwelling beneath the surface of the sea and Don to his ship.

It was an idyll, really. They lived happily ever after—or anyway, until they decided not to bother any more and died.

Of course, they never set eyes on each other again.

Oh, I can see you now, you eaters of charcoal-broiled steak, scratching an incipient bunion with one hand and holding this story with the other, while the stereo plays d'Indy or Monk. You don't believe a word of it, do you? Not for one minute. People wouldn't live like that, you say with an irritated and not amused grunt as you get up to put fresh ice in a stale drink.

And yet there's Dora, hurrying back through the flushing commuter pipes toward her underwater home (she prefers it there; has had herself somatically altered to breathe the stuff). If I tell you with what sweet fulfillment she fits the recorded analogue of Don into the symbol manipulator, hooks herself in and turns herself on . . . if I try to tell you any of that you will simply stare. Or glare; and grumble, what the hell kind of love-making is this? And yet I assure you, friend, I really do assure you that Dora's ecstasies are as creamy and passionate as any of James Bond's lady spies, and one hell of a lot more so than anything you are going to find in "real life." Go ahead, glare and grumble. Dora doesn't care. If she thinks of you at all, her thirty-times-great-great-grandfather, she thinks you're a pretty primordial sort of brute. You are. Why, Dora is farther removed from you than you are from the australopithecines of five thousand centuries ago. You could not swim a second in the strong currents of her life. You don't think progress goes in a straight line, do you? Do you recognize that it is an ascending, accelerating, maybe even exponential curve? It takes hell's own time to get started, but when it goes it goes like a bomb. And you, you Scotch-drinking steak-eater in your Relaxacizer chair, you've just barely lighted the primacord of the fuse. What is it now, the six or seven hundred thousandth day after Christ? Dora lives in Day Million. A thousand years from now. Her body fats are polyunsaturated, like Crisco. Her wastes are hemodialyzed out of her bloodstream while she sleeps—that means she doesn't have to go to the bathroom. On whim, to pass a slow half-hour, she can command more energy than the entire nation of Portugal can spend today, and use it to launch a weekend satellite or remold a crater on the Moon. She loves Don very much. She keeps his every gesture, mannerism, nuance, touch of hand, thrill of intercourse, passion of kiss stored in symbolic-mathematical form. And when she wants him, all she has to do is turn the machine on and she has him.

And Don, of course, has Dora. Adrift on a sponson city a few hundred yards over her head or orbiting Arcturus, fifty light-years away, Don has only to command his own symbol-manipulator to rescue Dora from the ferrite files and bring her to life for him, and there she is; and rapturously, tirelessly they ball all night. Not in the flesh, of course; but then his flesh has been extensively altered and it wouldn't really be much fun. He doesn't need the flesh for pleasure. Genital organs feel nothing. Neither do hands, nor breasts, nor lips; they are only receptors, accepting and transmitting impulses. It is the brain that feels, it is the interpretation of those impulses that makes agony or orgasm; and Don's symbol-manipulator gives him the analogue of cuddling, the analogue of kissing, the analogue of wildest, most ardent hours with the eternal, exquisite, and incorruptible analogue of Dora. Or Diane. Or sweet Rose, or laughing Alicia; for to be sure, they have each of them exchanged analogues before, and will again.

Balls, you say, it looks crazy to me. And you—with your after-shave lotion and your little red car, pushing papers across a desk all day and chasing tail all night—tell me, just how the hell do you think you would look to Tiglath-Pileser, say, or Attila the Hun?

PHILIP K. DICK

We Can Remember It for You Wholesale

{1966}

Philip K(indred) Dick (1928–1982) was one of the most distinctive and influential U.S. sf writers after World War II. Dick spent most of his early life in the San Francisco Bay Area, where he participated in the full career of the postwar antiauthoritarian counterculture, from the Beat movement to the psychedelic drug culture, New Age mysticism, and psychotherapeutic cults. He aspired to a career as a non–science fiction novelist, but only one of his seven mainstream novels, *Confessions of a Crap Artist* (1975), was published in his lifetime. Supporting himself entirely from his writing, Dick published over a hundred sf stories in pulp magazines in the 1950s and 1960s, eventually turning exclusively to novels, of which he wrote fifty-three at breakneck speed with the help of prescribed amphetamines. His major contribution to sf came with a group of dizzyingly original novels in the 1960s that combined traditional sf motifs with phantasmagoric hallucinatory visions of shifting realities and identities, in which unheroic, unassuming protagonists struggle against political and metaphysical powers capable of warping the fabric of reality itself. Among the best known of these are *Time Out of Joint* (1959), *The Man in the High Castle* (1962), *The Three Stigmata of Palmer Eldritch* (1965), *Do Androids Dream of Electric Sheep?* (1968), and *Ubik* (1969). Futuristic science and technology play only minor roles in Dick's sf; he used them primarily as vehicles for calling into question the distinction between authenticity and artificiality in memory, experience, and identity—themes that culminate in the ambiguous relationship between androids and human beings in *Do Androids Dream*, memorably adapted to the screen by Ridley Scott in *Blade Runner* (1982).

Dick's mental health was unstable for much of his life, and his fiction reflects a paranoid fascination with conspiracies extending from personal relationships to political power, and ultimately to the manipulation of reality itself. In 1974 he experienced what he considered a mystical epiphany that he devoted much of the rest of his life to exploring in a massive journal known as the *Exegesis*. Dick's lifelong fascination with the notion that reality might be manipulated by a destructive cosmic force flowered into an explicit interest in the theology of Gnosticism, which profoundly influenced his last works, *A Scanner Darkly* (1977) and the so-called *VALIS* trilogy (*VALIS* [1981], *The Divine Invasion* [1981], *The Transmigration of Timothy Archer* [1982]). *VALIS*, which relates a gnostic-inflected myth of struggle between competing cosmic forces on the plane of human history through a self-divided autobiographical narrator, is widely celebrated as one of the major works of postmodern science fiction.

Few sf writers have had a more widespread impact on contemporary culture than Dick. Directors David Cronenberg, Darren Aronofsky, Richard Kelly, and the Wachowski brothers have acknowledged Dick as a major influence on their work, and more texts by Dick have been adapted to cinema than by any other sf writer. These include, in addition to *Blade Runner*, *Screamers* (1995, based on the story "Second Variety"), *Minority Report* (2002), *Impostor* (2002), *Paycheck* (2003), *A Scanner Darkly* (2006), and *Next* (2007, loosely based on "The Golden Man").

"We Can Remember It for You Wholesale" appeared first in *The Magazine of Fantasy and Science Fiction* in 1966. It was adapted to the screen in 1990 by director Paul Verhoeven as *Total Recall*, starring Arnold Schwarzenegger. The story displays one of Dick's most typical themes—the inability to distinguish authentic from artificial memories—as well as the style that sf writer James Tiptree Jr. characterized as "pervasive strangeness."

He awoke—and wanted Mars. The valleys, he thought. What would it be like to trudge among them? Great and greater yet: the dream grew as he became fully conscious, the dream and the yearning. He could almost feel the enveloping presence of the other world, which only government agents and high officials had seen. A clerk like himself? Not likely.

"Are you getting up or not?" his wife Kirsten asked drowsily, with her usual hint of fierce crossness. "If you are, push the hot coffee button on the darn stove."

"Okay," Douglas Quail said, and made his way barefoot from the bedroom of their conapt to the kitchen. There, having dutifully pressed the hot coffee button, he seated himself at the kitchen table, brought out a yellow, small tin of fine Dean Swift snuff. He inhaled briskly, and the Beau Nash mixture stung his nose, burned the roof of his mouth. But still he inhaled; it woke him up and allowed his dreams, his nocturnal desires, and random wishes to condense into a semblance of rationality.

I will go, he said to himself. *Before I die I'll see Mars*.

It was, of course, impossible, and he knew this even as he dreamed. But the daylight, the mundane noise of his wife now brushing her hair before the bedroom mirror—everything conspired to remind him of what he was. *A miserable little salaried employee*, he said to himself with bitterness. Kirsten reminded him of this at least once a day, and he did not blame her; it was a wife's job to bring her husband down to Earth. *Down to Earth*, he thought, and laughed. The figure of speech in this was literally apt.

"What are you sniggering about?" his wife asked as she swept into the kitchen, her long busy-pink robe wagging after her. "A dream, I bet. You're always full of them."

"Yes," he said, and gazed out the kitchen window at the hovercars and traffic runnels, and all the little energetic people hurrying to work. In a little while he would be among them. As always.

"I'll bet it had to do with some woman," Kirsten said witheringly.

"No," he said. "A god. The god of war. He has wonderful craters with every kind of plant life growing deep down in them."

"Listen." Kirsten crouched down beside him and spoke earnestly, the harsh quality momentarily gone from her voice. "The bottom of the ocean—our ocean is much more, an infinity of times more beautiful. You know that; everyone knows that. Rent an artificial gill outfit for both of us, take a week off from work, and we can descend and live down there at one of those year-round aquatic resorts. And in addition—" She broke off. "You're not listening. You should be. Here is something a lot better than that compulsion, that obsession you have about Mars, and you don't even listen!" Her voice rose piercingly. "God in heaven, you're doomed, Doug! What's going to become of you?"

"I'm going to work," he said, rising to his feet, his breakfast forgotten. "That's what's going to become of me."

She eyed him. "You're getting worse. More fanatical every day. Where's it going to lead?"

"To Mars," he said, and opened the door to the closet to get down a fresh shirt to wear to work.

Having descended from the taxi, Douglas Quail slowly walked across three densely-populated foot runnels and to the modern, attractively inviting doorway. There he halted, impeding mid-morning traffic, and with caution read the shifting-color neon sign. He had, in the past, scrutinized this sign before . . . but never had he come so close. This was very different; what he did now was something else. Something which sooner or later had to happen.

Was this the answer? After all, an illusion, no matter how convincing, remained nothing more than an illusion. At least objectively. But subjectively—quite the opposite entirely.

And anyhow he had an appointment. Within the next five minutes.

Taking a deep breath of mildly smog-infested Chicago air, he walked through the dazzling polychromatic shimmer of the doorway and up to the receptionist's counter.

The nicely articulated blonde at the counter, bare-bosomed and tidy, said pleasantly, "Good morning, Mr. Quail."

"Yes," he said. "I'm here to see about a Rekal course. As I guess you know."

"Not 'rekal' but '*re*call,' the receptionist corrected him. She picked up the receiver of the vidphone by her smooth elbow and said into it, "Mr. Douglas Quail is here, Mr. McClane. May he come inside, now? Or is it too soon?"

"Giz wetwa wum-wum wamp," the phone mumbled.

"Yes, Mr. Quail," she said. "You may go on in; Mr. McClane is expecting you." As he started off uncertainly, she called after him, "Room D, Mr. Quail. To your right."

After a frustrating but brief moment of being lost, he found the proper room. The door hung open and inside, at a big genuine walnut desk, sat a genial-looking man, middle-aged, wearing the latest Martian frog-pelt gray suit; his attire alone would have told Quail that he had come to the right person.

"Sit down, Douglas," McClane said, waving his plump hand toward a chair which faced the desk. "So you want to have gone to Mars. Very good."

Quail seated himself, feeling tense. "I'm not so sure this is worth the fee," he said. "It costs a lot and as far as I can see I really get nothing." *Costs almost as much as going*, he thought.

"You get tangible proof of your trip," McClane disagreed emphatically. "All the proof you'll need. Here; I'll show you." He dug within a drawer of his impressive desk. "Ticket stub." Reaching into a manila folder, he produced a small square of embossed cardboard. "It proves you went—and returned. Postcards." He laid out four franked picture 3-D full-color postcards in a neatly arranged row on the desk for Quail to see. "Film. Shots you took of local sights on Mars with a rented movie camera." To Quail he displayed those, too. "Plus the names of people you met, two hundred poscreds' worth of souvenirs, which will arrive—from Mars—within the following month. And passport, certificates listing the shots you received. And more." He glanced up keenly at Quail. "You'll know you went, all right," he said. "You won't remember us, won't remember me or ever having been here. It'll be a real trip in your mind; we guarantee that. A full two weeks of recall; every last piddling detail. Remember this: if at any time you doubt that you really took an extensive trip to Mars, you can return here and get a full refund. You see?"

"But I didn't go," Quail said. "I won't have gone, no matter what proofs you provide me with." He took a deep, unsteady breath. "And I never was a secret agent with Interplan." It seemed impossible to him that Rekal, Incorporated's extra-factual memory implant would do its job—despite what he had heard people say.

"Mr. Quail," McClane said patiently. "As you explained in your letter to us, you have no chance, no possibility in the slightest, of ever actually getting to Mars; you can't afford it, and what is much more important, you could never qualify as an undercover agent for Interplan or anybody else. This is the only way you can achieve your, ahem, life-long dream; am I not correct, sir? You can't be this; you can't actually do this." He chuckled. "But you can *have been* and *have done*. We see to that. And our fee is reasonable; no hidden charges." He smiled encouragingly.

"Is an extra-factual memory that convincing?" Quail asked.

"More than the real thing, sir. Had you really gone to Mars as an Interplan agent, you would by now have forgotten a great deal; our analysis of true-mem systems—authentic recollections of major events in a person's life—shows that a variety of details are very quickly lost to the person. Forever. Part of the package we offer you is such a deep implantation recall that nothing is forgotten. The packet which is fed to you while you're comatose is a creation of trained experts, men who have spent years on Mars; in every case we verify details down to the last iota. And you've picked a rather easy extra-factual system; had you picked Pluto or wanted to be Emperor of the Inner Planet Alliance we'd have much more difficulty . . . and the charges would be considerably greater."

Reaching into his coat for his wallet, Quail said, "Okay. It's been my life-long ambition and I can see I'll never really do it. So I guess I'll have to settle for this."

"Don't think of it that way," McClane said severely. "You're not accepting second-best. The actual memory, with all its vagueness, omissions, and ellipses, not to say distortions—that's second best." He accepted the money and pressed a button on his desk. "All right, Mr. Quail," he said, as the door of his office opened and two burly men swiftly entered. "You're on your way to Mars as a secret agent." He rose, came over to shake Quail's nervous, moist hand. "Or rather, you have been on your way. This afternoon at four-thirty you will, um, arrive back here on Terra; a cab will leave you off at your conapt and, as I say, you will never remember seeing me or coming here; you won't, in fact, even remember having heard of our existence."

His mouth dry with nervousness, Quail followed the two technicians from the office; what happened next depended on them.

Will I actually believe I've been on Mars? he wondered. *That I managed to fulfill my lifetime ambition*? He had a strange, lingering intuition that something would go wrong. But just what—he did not know.

He would have to wait to find out.

The intercom on McClane's desk, which connected him with the work area of the firm, buzzed and a voice said, "Mr. Quail is under sedation now, sir. Do you want to supervise this one, or shall we go ahead?"

"It's routine," McClane observed. "You may go ahead, Lowe. I don't think you'll run into any trouble." Programming an artificial memory of a trip to another planet—with or without the added fillip of being a secret agent—showed up on the firm's work schedule with monotonous regularity. *In one month*, he calculated wryly, *we must do twenty of these . . . ersatz interplanetary travel has become our bread and butter.*

"Whatever you say, Mr. McClane," Lowe's voice came, and thereupon the intercom shut off.

Going to the vault section in the chamber behind his office, McClane searched about for a Three packet—trip to Mars—and a Sixty-two packet: secret Interplan spy. Finding the two packets, he returned with them to his desk, seated himself comfortably, poured out the contents—merchandise which would be planted in Quail's conapt while the lab technicians busied themselves installing the false memory.

A one-poscred sneaky-pete side arm, McClane reflected; *that's the largest item. Sets us back financially the most.* Then a pellet-sized transmitter, which could be swallowed if the agent were caught. Code book that astonishingly resembled the real thing . . . the firm's models were highly accurate: based, whenever possible, on actual U.S. military issue. Odd bits which made no intrinsic sense but which would be woven into the warp and woof of Quail's imaginary trip, would coincide with his memory: half an ancient silver fifty-cent piece, several quotations from John Donne's sermons written incorrectly, each on a separate piece of transparent tissue-thin paper, several match folders from bars on Mars, a stainless steel spoon engraved PROPERTY OF DOME-MARS NATIONAL KIBBUTZIM, a wire tapping coil which—

The intercom buzzed. "Mr. McClane, I'm sorry to bother you, but something rather ominous has come up. Maybe it would be better if you were in here after all. Quail is already under sedation; he reacted well to the narkidrine; he's completely unconscious and receptive. But—"

"I'll be in." Sensing trouble, McClane left his office; a moment later he emerged in the work area.

On a hygienic bed lay Douglas Quail, breathing slowly and regularly, his eyes virtually shut; he seemed dimly—but only dimly—aware of the two technicians and now McClane himself.

"There's no space to insert false memory patterns?" McClane felt irritation. "Merely drop out two work weeks; he's employed as a clerk at the West Coast Emigration Bureau which is a government agency, so he undoubtedly has or had two weeks' vacation within the last year. That ought to do it." Petty details annoyed him. And always would.

"Our problem," Lowe said sharply, "is something quite different." He bent over the bed, said to Quail, "Tell Mr. McClane what you told us." To McClane he said, "Listen closely."

The gray-green eyes of the man lying supine in the bed focused on McClane's face. The eyes, he observed uneasily, had become hard; they had a polished, inorganic quality, like semiprecious tumbled stones. He was not sure that he liked what he saw; the brilliance was too cold. "What do you want now?" Quail said harshly. "You've broken my cover. Get out of here before I take you all apart." He studied McClane. "Especially you," he continued. "You're in charge of this counter-operation."

Lowe said, "How long were you on Mars?"

"One month," Quail said gratingly.

"And your purpose there?" Lowe demanded.

The meager lips twisted; Quail eyed him and did not speak. At last, drawling the words out so that they dripped with hostility, he said "Agent for Interplan. As I already told you. Don't you record everything that's said? Play your vid-aud tape back for your boss and leave me alone." He shut his eyes, then; the hard brilliance ceased. McClane felt, instantly, a rushing splurge of relief.

Lowe said quietly; "This is a tough man, Mr. McClane." "He won't be," McClane said, "after we arrange for him to lose his memory chain again. He'll be as meek as before." To Quail he said, "So this is why you wanted to go to Mars so terribly bad."

Without opening his eyes Quail said, "I never wanted to go to Mars. I was assigned it—they handed it to me and there I was: stuck. Oh, yeah, I admit I was curious about it. Who wouldn't be?" Again he opened his eyes and surveyed the three of them, McClane in particular. "Quite a truth drug you've got here; it brought up things I had absolutely no memory of." He pondered. "I wonder about Kirsten," he said, half to himself. "Could she be in on it? An Interplan contact keeping an eye on me . . . to be certain I didn't regain my memory? No wonder she's been so derisive about my wanting to go there." Faintly, he smiled; the smile—one of understanding—disappeared almost at once.

McClane said, "Please believe me, Mr. Quail. We stumbled onto this entirely by accident. In the work we do—"

"I believe you," Quail said. He seemed tired now; the drug was continuing to pull him under, deeper and deeper. "Where did I say I'd been?" he murmured. "Mars? Hard to remember—I know I'd like to see it; so would everybody else. But me—" His voice trailed off. "Just a clerk, a nothing clerk."

Straightening up, Lowe said to his superior, "He wants a false memory implanted that corresponds to a trip he actually took. And a false reason which is the real reason. He's telling the truth; he's a long way down in the narkidrine. The trip is very vivid in his mind—at least under sedation. But apparently he doesn't recall it otherwise. Someone, probably at a government military sciences lab, erased his conscious memories; all he knew was that going to Mars meant something special to him, and so did being a secret agent. They couldn't erase that; it's not a memory but a desire, undoubtedly the same one that motivated him to volunteer for the assignment in the first place."

The other technician, Keeler, said to McClane, "What do we do? Graft a false-memory pattern over the real memory? There's no telling what the results would be; he might remember some of the genuine trip, and the confusion might bring on a psychotic interlude. He'd have to hold two opposite premises in his mind simultaneously: that he went to Mars and that he didn't. That he's a genuine agent for Interplan and he's not, that it's spurious. I think we ought to revive him without any false memory implantation and send him out of here; this is hot."

"Agreed," McClane said. A thought came to him. "Can you predict what he'll remember when he comes out of sedation?"

"Impossible to tell," Lowe said. "He probably will have some dim, diffuse memory of his actual trip now. And he'd probably be in grave doubt as to its validity; he'd probably decide our programming slipped a gear-tooth. And he'd remember coming here; that wouldn't be erased—unless you want it erased."

"The less we mess with this man," McClane said, "the better I like it. This is nothing for us to fool around with; we've been foolish enough to—or unlucky enough to—uncover a genuine Interplan spy who has a cover so perfect that up to now even he didn't know what he was—or rather is." The sooner they washed their hands of the man calling himself Douglas Quail the better.

"Are you going to plant packets Three and Sixty-two in his conapt?" Lowe said.

"No," McClane said. "And we're going to return half his fee."

"Half! Why half?"

McClane said lamely, "It seems to be a good compromise."

As the cab carried him back to his conapt at the residential end of Chicago, Douglas Quail said to himself, *It's sure good to be back on Terra.*

Already the month-long period on Mars had begun to waver in his memory; he had only an image of profound gaping craters, an ever-present ancient erosion of hills, of vitality, of motion itself. A world of dust where little happened, where a good part of the day was spent checking and rechecking one's portable oxygen source. And then the life forms, the unassuming and modest gray-brown cacti and maw-worms.

As a matter of fact he had brought back several moribund examples of Martian fauna; he had smuggled them through customs. After all, they posed no menace; they couldn't survive in Earth's heavy atmosphere.

Reaching into his coat pocket, he rummaged for the container of Martian maw worms—

And found an envelope instead.

Lifting it out, he discovered, to his perplexity, that it contained five hundred and seventy poscreds, in 'cred bills of low denomination.

Where'd I get this? he asked himself. *Didn't I spend every 'cred I had on my trip*?

With the money came a slip of paper marked *One-half fee ret'd. By McClane.* And then the date. Today's date.

"Recall," he said aloud.

"Recall what, sir or madam?" the robot driver of the cab inquired respectfully.

"Do you have a phone book?" Quail demanded.

"Certainly, sir or madam." A slot opened; from it slid a microtape phone book for Cook County.

"It's spelled oddly," Quail said as he leafed through the pages of the yellow section. He felt fear, then; abiding fear. "Here it is," he said. "Take me there, to Rekal, Incorporated. I've changed my mind; I don't want to go home."

"Yes, sir or madam, as the case may be," the driver said. A moment later the cab was zipping back in the opposite direction.

"May I make use of your phone?" he asked.

"Be my guest," the robot driver said. And presented a shiny new emperor 3-D color phone to him.

He dialed his own conapt. And after a pause found himself confronted by a miniature but chillingly realistic image of Kirsten on the small screen. "I've been to Mars," he said to her.

"You're drunk." Her lips writhed scornfully. "Or worse."

"'s God's truth."

"When?" she demanded.

"I don't know." He felt confused. "A simulated trip, I think. By means of one of those artificial or extra-factual or whatever it is memory places. It didn't take."

Kirsten said witheringly, "You *are* drunk." And broke the connection at her end. He hung up, then, feeling his face flush. *Always the same tone*, he said hotly to himself. *Always the retort, as if she knows everything and I know nothing. What a marriage. Keerist*, he thought dismally.

A moment later the cab stopped at the curb before a modern, very attractive little pink building, over which a shifting, polychromatic neon sign read: REKAL, INCORPORATED.

The receptionist, chic and bare from the waist up, started in surprise, then gained masterful control of herself. "Oh, hello, Mr. Quail," she said nervously. "H-how are you? Did you forget something?"

"The rest of my fee back," he said.

More composed now, the receptionist said, "Fee? I think you are mistaken. Mr. Quail. You were here discussing the feasibility of an extra-factual trip for you, but—" She shrugged her smooth pale shoulders. "As I understand it, no trip was taken."

Quail said, "I remember everything, miss. My letter to Rekal, Incorporated, which started this whole business off. I remember my arrival here, my visit with Mr. McClane. Then the two lab technicians taking me in tow and administering a drug to put me out." No wonder the firm had returned half his fee. The false memory of "his trip" to Mars hadn't taken—at least not entirely, not as he had been assured.

"Mr. Quail," the girl said, "although you are a minor clerk, you are a good-looking man and it spoils your features to become angry. If it would make you feel any better, I might, ahem, let you take me out . . ."

He felt furious, then. "I remember you," he said savagely. "For instance the fact that your breasts are sprayed blue; that stuck in my mind. And I remember Mr. McClane's promise that if I remembered my visit to Rekal, Incorporated I'd receive my money back in full. Where is Mr. McClane?"

After a delay—probably as long as they could manage—he found himself once more seated facing the imposing walnut desk, exactly as he had been an hour or so earlier in the day.

"Some technique you have," Quail said sardonically. His disappointment—and resentment—were enormous, by now. "My so-called 'memory' of a trip to Mars as an undercover agent for Interplan is hazy and vague and shot full of contradictions. And I clearly remember my dealings here with you people. I ought to take this to the Better Business Bureau." He was burning angry, at this point; his sense of being cheated had overwhelmed him, had destroyed his customary aversion to participating in a public squabble.

Looking morose, as well as cautious, McClane said, "We capitulate, Quail. We'll refund the balance of your fee. I fully concede the fact that we did absolutely nothing for you." His tone was resigned.

Quail said accusingly, "You didn't even provide me with the various artifacts that you claimed would 'prove' to me I had been on Mars. All that song-and-dance you went into—it hasn't materialized into a damn thing. Not even a ticket stub. Nor postcards. Nor passport. Nor proof of immunization shots. Nor—"

"Listen, Quail," McClane said. "Suppose I told you—" He broke off. "Let it go." He pressed a button on his intercom. "Shirley, will you disburse five hundred and seventy more 'creds in the form of a cashier's check made out to Douglas Quail? Thank you." He released the button, then glared at Quail.

Presently the check appeared; the receptionist placed it before McClane and once more vanished out of sight, leaving the two men alone, still facing each other across the surface of the massive walnut desk.

"Let me give you a word of advice," McClane said as he signed the check and passed it over. "Don't discuss your, ahem, recent trip to Mars with anyone."

"What trip?"

"Well, that's the thing." Doggedly, McClane said, "The trip you partially remember. Act as if you don't remember; pretend it never took place. Don't ask me why; just take my advice: it'll be better for all of us." He had begun to perspire. Freely. "Now, Mr. Quail, I have other business, other clients to see." He rose, showed Quail to the door.

Quail said, as he opened the door, "A firm that turns out such bad work shouldn't have any clients at all." He shut the door behind him.

On the way home in the cab Quail pondered the wording of his letter of complaint to the Better Business Bureau, Terra Divison. As soon as he could get to his typewriter he'd get started; it was clearly his duty to warn other people away from Rekal, Incorporated.

When he got back to his conapt, he seated himself before his Hermes Rocket portable, opened the drawers and rummaged for carbon paper—and noticed a small, familiar box. A box which he had carefully filled on Mars with Martian fauna and later smuggled through customs.

Opening the box he saw, to his disbelief, six dead maw-worms and several varieties of the unicellular life on which the Martian worms fed. The protozoa were dried-up, dusty, but he recognized them; it had taken him an entire day picking among the vast dark alien boulders to find them. A wonderful, illuminated journey of discovery.

But I didn't go to Mars, he realized.

Yet on the other hand—

Kirsten appeared at the doorway to the room, an armload of pale brown groceries gripped. "Why are you home in the middle of the day?" Her voice, in an eternity of sameness, was accusing.

"*Did I go to Mars?*" he asked her. "You would know."

"No, of course you didn't go to Mars; *you* would know that, I would think. Aren't you always bleating about going?"

He said, "By God, I think I went." After a pause he added, "And simultaneously I think I didn't go."

"Make up your mind."

"How can I?" He gestured. "I have both memory tracks grafted inside my head; one is real and one isn't but I can't tell which is which. Why can't I rely on you? They haven't tinkered with you." She could do this much for him at least—even if she never did anything else.

Kirsten said in a level, controlled voice, "Doug, if you don't pull yourself together, we're through. I'm going to leave you."

"I'm in trouble." His voice came out husky and coarse. And shaking. "Probably I'm heading into a psychotic episode. I hope not, but—maybe that's it. It would explain everything, anyhow."

Setting down the bag of groceries, Kirsten stalked to the closet. "I was not kidding," she said to him quietly. She brought out a coat, got it on, walked back to the door of the conapt. "I'll phone you one of these days soon," she said tonelessly. "This is good-bye, Doug. I hope you pull out of this eventually. I really pray you do. For your sake."

"Wait," he said desperately. "Just tell me and make it absolute; I did go or I didn't—tell me which one." *But they may have altered your memory-track also,* he realized.

The door closed. His wife had left. Finally!

A voice behind him said, "Well, that's that. Now put up your hands, Quail. And also please turn around and face this way."

He turned, instinctively, without raising his hands.

The man who faced him wore the plum uniform of the Interplan Police Agency, and his gun appeared to be UN issue. And, for some odd reason, he seemed familiar to Quail; familiar in a blurred, distorted fashion which he could not pin down. So, jerkily, he raised his hands.

"You remember," the policeman said, "your trip to Mars. We know all your actions today and all your thoughts—in particular your very important thoughts on the trip home from Rekal, Incorporated." He explained, "We have a tele-transmitter wired within your skull; it keeps us constantly informed."

A telepathic transmitter; use of a living plasma that had been discovered on Luna. He shuddered with self-aversion. The thing lived inside him, within his own brain, feeding, listening, feeding. But the Interplan police used them; that had come out even in the homeopapes. So this was probably true, dismal as it was.

"Why me?" Quail said huskily. What had he done—or thought? And what did this have to do with Rekal, Incorporated?

"Fundamentally," the Interplan cop said, "this has nothing to do with Rekal; it's between you and us." He tapped his right ear. "I'm still picking up your mentational processes by way of your cephalic transmitter." In the man's ear Quail saw a small white-plastic plug. "So I have to warn you: anything you think may be held against you." He smiled. "Not that it matters now; you've already thought and spoken yourself into oblivion. What's annoying is the fact that under narkidrine at Rekal, Incorporated, you told them, their technicians and the owner, Mr. McClane, about your trip—where you went, for whom, some of what you did. They're very frightened. They wish they had never laid eyes on you." He added reflectively, "They're right."

Quail said, "I never made any trip. It's a false memory chain improperly planted in me by McClane's technicians." But then he thought of the box, in his desk drawer, containing the Martian life forms. And the trouble and hardship he had had gathering them. The memory seemed real. And the box of life forms; that certainly was real. Unless McClane had planted it. Perhaps this was one of the "proofs" which McClane had talked glibly about.

The memory of my trip to Mars, he thought, *doesn't convince me—but unfortunately it has convinced the Interplan Police Agency. They think I really went to Mars and they think I at least partially realize it.*

"We not only know you went to Mars," the Interplan cop agreed, in answer to his thoughts, "but we know that you now remember enough to be difficult for us. And there's no use expunging your conscious memory of all this, because if we do you'll simply show up at Rekal, Incorporated, again and start over. And we can't do anything about McClane and his operation because we have no jurisdiction over anyone except our own people. Anyhow, McClane hasn't committed any crime." He eyed Quail. "Nor, technically, have you. You didn't go to Rekal, Incorporated with the idea of regaining your memory; you went, as we realize, for the usual reason people go there—a love by plain, dull people for adventure. He added, "Unfortunately you're not plain, not dull, and you've already had too much excitement; the last thing in the universe you needed was a course from Rekal, Incorporated. Nothing could have been more lethal for you or for us. And, for that matter, for McClane."

Quail said, "Why is it 'difficult' for you if I remember my trip—my alleged trip—and what I did there?"

"Because," the Interplan harness bull said, "what you did is not in accord with our great white all-protecting father public image. You did, for us, what we never do. As you'll presently remember—thanks to narkidrine. That box of dead worms and algae has been sitting in your desk drawer for six months, ever since you got back. And at no time have you shown the slightest curiosity about it. We didn't even know you had it until you remembered it on your way home from Rekal; then we came here on the double to look for it." He added unnecessarily, "Without any luck; there wasn't enough time."

A second Interplan cop joined the first one; the two briefly conferred. Meanwhile, Quail thought rapidly. He did remember more, now; the cop had been right about narkidrine. They—Interplan—probably used it themselves. Probably? He knew darn well they did; he had seen them putting a prisoner on it. Where would *that* be? Somewhere on Terra? More likely on Luna, he decided, viewing the image rising from his highly defective—but rapidly less so—memory.

And he remembered something else. Their reason for sending him to Mars; the job he had done.

No wonder they had expunged his memory.

"Oh, God," the first of the two Interplan cops said, breaking off his conversation with his companion. Obviously, he had picked up Quail's thoughts. "Well, this is a far worse problem now; as bad as it can get." He walked toward Quail, again covering him with his gun. "We've got to kill you," he said. "And right away."

Nervously, his fellow officer said, "Why right away? Can't we simply cart him off to Interplan New York and let them—"

"*He* knows why it has to be right away," the first cop said; he too looked nervous now, but Quail realized that it was for an entirely different reason.

His memory had been brought back almost entirely now. And he fully understood the officer's tension.

"On Mars," Quail said hoarsely, "I killed a man. After getting past fifteen bodyguards. Some armed with sneaky-pete guns, the way you are." He had been trained, by Interplan, over a five-year period, to be an assassin. A professional killer. He knew ways to take out armed adversaries . . . such as these two officers; and the one with the ear receiver knew it, too.

If he moved swiftly enough—

The gun fired. But he had already moved to one side, and at the same time he chopped down the gun-carrying officer. In an instant he had possession of the gun and was covering the other, confused, officer.

"Picked my thoughts up," Quail said, panting for breath. "He knew what I was going to do, but I did it anyhow."

Half sitting up, the injured officer grated, "He won't use that gun on you, Sam. I pick that up, too. He knows he's finished, and he knows we know it, too. Come on, Quail." Laboriously, grunting with pain, he got shakily to his feet. He held out his hand. "The gun," he said to Quail. "You can't use it, and if you turn it over to me I'll guarantee not to kill you; you'll be given a hearing, and someone higher up in Interplan will decide, not me. Maybe they can erase your memory once more, I don't know. But you know the thing I was going to kill you for; I couldn't keep you from remembering it. So my reason for wanting to kill you is in a sense past."

Quail, clutching the gun, bolted from the conapt, sprinted for the elevator. *If you follow me*, he thought, *I'll kill you. So don't.* He jabbed at the elevator button, and a moment later, the doors slid back.

The police hadn't followed him. Obviously they had picked up his terse, tense thoughts and had decided not to take the chance.

With him inside the elevator descended. He had gotten away—for a time. But what next? Where could he go?

The elevator reached the ground floor; a moment later Quail had joined the mob of peds hurrying along the runnels. His head ached and he felt sick. But at least he had evaded death; they had come very close to shooting him on the spot, back in his own conapt.

And they probably will again, he decided. *When they find me. And with this transmitter inside me, that won't take too long.*

Ironically, he had gotten exactly what he had asked Rekal, Incorporated for. Adventure, peril, Interplan police at work, a secret and dangerous trip to Mars in which his life was at stake—everything he had wanted as a false memory.

The advantages of it being a memory—and nothing more—could now be appreciated.

On a park bench, alone, he sat dully watching a flock of perts: a semi-bird imported from Mars' two moons, capable of soaring flight, even against Earth's huge gravity.

Maybe I can find my way back to Mars, he pondered. *But then what*? It would be worse on Mars; the political organization whose leader he had assassinated would spot him the moment he stepped from the ship; he would have Interplan and *them* after him, there.

Can you hear me thinking? he wondered. Easy avenue to paranoia; sitting there alone he felt them tuning in on him, monitoring, recording, discussing . . . He shivered, rose to his feet, walked aimlessly, his hands deep in his pockets. *No matter where I go*, he realized, *you'll always be with me. As long as I have this device inside my head.*

I'll make a deal with you, he thought to himself—and to them. *Can't you imprint a false-memory template on me again, as you did before, that I lived an average, routine life, never went to Mars? Never saw an Interplan uniform up close and never handled a gun?*

A voice inside his brain answered, "As has been carefully explained to you, that would not be enough."

Astonished, he halted.

"We formerly communicated with you in this manner," the voice continued. "When you were operating in the field, on Mars. It's been months since we've done it; we assumed, in fact, that we'd never have to do so again. Where are you?"

"Walking," Quail said, "to my death." *By your officer's guns*, he added as an afterthought, "How can you be sure it wouldn't be enough?" he demanded. "Don't the Rekal techniques work?"

"As we said. If you're given a set of standard, average memories you get—restless. You'd inevitably seek out Rekal or one of its competitors again. We can't go through this a second time."

"Suppose," Quail said, "once my authentic memories have been canceled, something more vital than standard memories are implanted. Something which would act to satisfy my craving," he said. "That's been proved; that's probably why you initially hired me. But you ought to be able to come up with something else—something equal. I was the richest man on Terra but I finally gave all my money to educational foundations. Or I was a famous deep-space explorer. Anything of that sort; wouldn't one of those do?"

Silence.

"Try it," he said desperately. "Get some of your top-notch military psychiatrists; explore my mind. Find out what my most expansive daydream is." He tried to think. "Women," he said. "Thousands of them, like Don Juan had. An interplanetary playboy—a mistress in every city on Earth, Luna, and Mars. Only I gave that up, out of exhaustion. Please," he begged. "Try it."

"You'd voluntarily surrender, then?" the voice inside his head asked. "If we agreed to arrange such a solution? *If* it's possible?"

After an interval of hesitation he said, "Yes." *I'll take the risk,* he said to himself, *that you don't simply kill me.*

"You make the first move," the voice said presently. "Turn yourself over to us. And we'll investigate that line of possibility. If we can't do it, however, if your authentic memories begin to crop up again as they've done at this time, then—" There was silence and then the voice finished. "We'll have to destroy you. As you must understand. Well, Quail, you still want to try?"

"Yes," he said. Because the alternative was death now—and for certain. At least this way he had a chance, slim as it was.

"You present yourself at our main barracks in New York," the voice of the Interplan cop resumed. "At 580 Fifth Avenue, floor twelve. Once you've surrendered yourself, we'll have our psychiatrists begin on you; we'll have personality-profile tests made. We'll attempt to determine your absolute, ultimate fantasy wish—and then we'll bring you back to Rekal, Incorporated, here; get them in on it, fulfilling that wish in vicarious surrogate retrospection. And—good luck. We do owe you something; you acted as a capable instrument for us." The voice lacked malice; if anything, they—the organization—felt sympathy toward him.

"Thanks," Quail said, and began searching for a robot cab.

"Mr. Quail," the stern-faced, elderly Interplan psychiatrist said, "you possess a most interesting wish-fulfillment dream fantasy. Probably nothing such as you consciously entertain or suppose. This is commonly the way; I hope it won't upset you too much to hear about it."

The senior-ranking Interplan officer present said briskly, "He better not be too much upset to hear about it, not if he expects not to get shot."

"Unlike the fantasy of wanting to be an Interplan undercover agent," the psychiatrist continued, "which, being relatively speaking a product of maturity, had a certain plausibility to it, this production is a grotesque dream of your childhood; it is no wonder you fail to recall it. Your fantasy is this: you are nine years old, walking alone down a rustic lane. An unfamiliar variety of space vessel from another star system lands directly in front of you. No one on Earth but you, Mr. Quail, sees it. The creatures within are very small and helpless, somewhat on the order of field mice, although they are attempting to invade Earth; tens of thousands of other such ships will soon be on their way, when this advance party gives the go-ahead signal."

"And I suppose I stop them," Quail said, experiencing a mixture of amusement and disgust. "Single-handed I wipe them out. Probably by stepping on them with my foot."

"No," the psychiatrist said patiently, "You halt the invasion, but not by destroying them. Instead, you show them kindness and mercy, even though by telepathy—their mode of communication—you know why they have come. They have never seen such humane traits exhibited by any sentient organism, and to show their appreciation they make a covenant with you."

Quail said, "They won't invade Earth as long as I'm alive."

"Exactly." To the Interplan officer the psychiatrist said, "You can see it does fit his personality, despite his feigned scorn."

"So by merely existing," Quail said, feeling a growing pleasure, "by simply being alive, I keep Earth safe from alien rule. I'm in effect, then, the most important person on Terra. Without lifting a finger."

"Yes, indeed, sir," the psychiatrist said. "And this is bedrock in your psyche; this is a life-long childhood fantasy. Which, without depth and drug therapy, you never would have recalled. But it has always existed in you; it went underneath, but never ceased."

To McClane, who sat intently listening, the senior police official said, "Can you implant an extra-factual memory pattern that extreme in him?"

"We get handed every possible type of wish fantasy there is," McClane said. "Frankly, I've heard a lot worse than this. Certainly we can handle it. Twenty-four hours from now he won't just *wish* he'd saved Earth; he'll devoutly believe it really happened."

The senior police official said, "You can start the job, then. In preparation we've already once again erased the memory in him of his trip to Mars."

Quail said, "What trip to Mars?"

No one answered him, so, reluctantly, he shelved the question. And anyhow a police vehicle had now put in its appearance; he, McClane and the senior police officer crowded into it, and presently they were on their way to Chicago and Rekal, Incorporated.

"You had better make no errors this time," the police officer said to heavy-set, nervous-looking McClane.

"I can't see what could go wrong," McClane mumbled, perspiring. "This has nothing to do with Mars or Interplan. Single-handedly stopping an invasion of Earth from another star system." He shook his head at that. "Wow, what a kid dreams up. And by pious virtue, too; not by force. It's sort of quaint." He dabbed at his forehead with a large linen pocket handkerchief.

Nobody said anything.

"In fact," McClane said, "it's touching."

"But arrogant," the police official said starkly. "Inasmuch as when he dies the invasion will resume. No wonder he doesn't recall it; it's the most grandiose fantasy I ever ran across." He eyed Quail with disapproval. "And to think we put this man on our payroll?"

When they reached Rekal, Incorporated, the receptionist, Shirley, met them breathlessly in the outer office. "Welcome back, Mr. Quail," she fluttered, her melon-shaped breasts—today painted an incandescent orange—bobbing with agitation. "I'm sorry everything worked out so badly before; I'm sure this time it'll go better."

Still repeatedly dabbing at his shiny forehead with his neatly folded Irish linen handkerchief, McClane said, "It better." Moving with rapidity, he rounded up Lowe and Keeler, escorted them and Douglas Quail to the work area, and then, with Shirley and the senior police officer, returned to his familiar office. To wait.

"Do we have a packet made up for this, Mr. McClane?" Shirley asked, bumping against him in her agitation, then coloring modestly.

"I think we do." He tried to recall; then gave up and consulted the formal chart. "A combination," he decided aloud, "of packets Eighty-one, Twenty, and Six." From the vault section of the chamber behind his desk he fished out the appropriate packets, carried them to his desk for inspection. From Eighty-one," he explained, "a magic healing rod given him—the client in question, this time Mr. Quail—by the race of beings from another system. A token of their gratitude."

'"Does it work?" the police officer asked curiously.

"It did once," McClane explained. "But he, ahem, you see, used it up years ago, healing right and left. Now it's only a memento. But he remembers it working spectacularly." He chuckled, then opened packet Twenty. "Document from the UN Secretary General thanking him for saving Earth; this isn't precisely appropriate, because part of Quail's fantasy is that no one knows of the invasion except himself, but for the sake of verisimilitude we'll throw it in." He inspected packet Six then. What came from this? He couldn't recall; frowning, he dug into the plastic bag as Shirley and the Interplan police officer watched intently.

"Writing," Shirley said. "In a funny language."

"This tells who they were," McClane said, "and where they came from.

Including a detailed star map logging their flight here and the system of origin. Of course it's in *their* script, so he can't read it. But he remembers them reading it to him in his own tongue." He placed the three artifacts in the center of the desk. "These should be taken to Quail's conapt," he said to the police officer, "so that when he gets home he'll find them. And it'll confirm his fantasy. SOP—standard operating procedure." He chuckled apprehensively, wondering how matters were going with Lowe and Keeler.

The intercom buzzed. "Mr. McClane, I'm sorry to bother you." It was Lowe's voice; he froze as he recognized it, froze and became mute. "But something's come up. Maybe it would be better if you came in here and supervised. Like before, Quail reacted well to the narkidrine; he's unconscious, relaxed and receptive. But—"

McClane sprinted for the work area.

On a hygienic bed Douglas Quail lay breathing slowly and regularly, eyes half shut, dimly conscious of those around him.

"We started interrogating him," Lowe said, white-faced, "To find out exactly when to place the fantasy memory of him single-handedly having saved Earth. And strangely enough—"

"They told me not to tell," Douglas Quail mumbled in a dull drug-saturated voice. "That was the agreement. I wasn't even supposed to remember. But how could I forget an event like that?"

I guess it would be hard, McClane reflected. *But you did—until now.*

"They even gave me a scroll," Quail mumbled, "of gratitude. I have it hidden in my conapt; I'll show it to you."

To the Interplan officer who had followed after him, McClane said, "Well, I offer the suggestion that you better not kill him. If you do they'll return."

"They also gave me a magic invisible destroying rod," Quail mumbled, eyes totally shut, now. "That's how I killed that man on Mars you sent me to take out. It's in my drawer along with the box of Martian maw worms and dried-up plant life."

Wordlessly, the Interplan officer turned and stalked from the work area.

I might as well put those packets of proof artifacts away, McClane said to himself resignedly. He walked, step by step, back to his office. *Including the citation from the UN Secretary General. After all—*

The real one probably would not be long in coming.

SAMUEL R. DELANY

Aye, and Gomorrah . . .

{1967}

Samuel R. Delany (1942–) was, along with Ursula K. Le Guin and Roger Zelazny, one of the most important younger sf writers to emerge in the United States during the early 1960s. Indeed, he was the youngest of the lot, publishing his first novel, *The Jewels of Aptor*, in 1962, when he was only twenty. By 1965, he had five books in print, all lush, brightly colored exercises in post-pulp space opera. With *Babel-17* (1966) and *The Einstein Intersection* (1967), each a Nebula winner for best novel, his work became more densely textured and ambitious, drawing on contemporary cultural and linguistic theory to develop complex sf plots. While still making use of classic adventure scenarios, these works—along with his celebrated short fiction from the period, most of it gathered in *Driftglass* (1971)—showed a tremendous intellectual energy and fertility: in Delany's hands, sf became an instrument for investigating cultural difference, extrapolating futuristic or alien worlds in which questions of identity emerge as paramount. Since he was black, gay, and an avid participant in the youth counterculture, Delany had a strong personal interest in such issues: his work often features outsiders or mavericks who do not fit into neat social categories and who, as a result, undertake intricate, often ambiguous quests to discover themselves and their worlds. His massive 1975 novel *Dhalgren* is a monument to the restlessly searching ethos of the period, and it became a surprise best seller.

"Aye, and Gomorrah . . . ," published in Harlan Ellison's controversial New Wave anthology *Dangerous Visions* (1967), is a showcase for Delany's characteristic concerns. We have a band of counterculture oddballs, the rollicking spacers, and their eager groupies, the frelks, who are living emblems of uncategorizable difference: the spacers, having been neutered in order to work in high-radiation off-world environments, seem as a result to elude clear distinctions of gender and sexual preference, as do the yearning frelks who desire and worship them. Even the pronouns used to denote them differ in Spanish and French—a point that Delany, ever attentive to issues of language, subtly registers. While the story appears to celebrate these social outcasts, who are shunned by those who fear their elusive otherness, we also see how difficult it is for them to exist in a state of constant liminality, never quite belonging to any settled identity. Indeed, the encounter between the spacer and the frelk in the tale conveys a painful sense of unfulfilled longing.

Frelk is almost certainly a coinage from the term *freak*, used at the time to identify members of the youth counterculture who scorned conventional modes of dress, behavior, and belief. Initially an abusive epithet directed at these nonconformists by "straight" society, the term was defiantly adopted by 1960s outsiders to describe themselves. This sort of linguistic reappropriation prefigures the way that contemporary gay and lesbian groups have embraced the term "queer," originally an insult, as a marker of prideful difference.

And came down in Paris:

Where we raced along the Rue de Médicis with Bo and Lou and Muse inside the fence, Kelly and me outside, making faces through the bars, making noise, making the Luxembourg Gardens roar at two in the morning. Then climbed out, and down to the square in front of St. Sulpice where Bo tried to knock me into the fountain.

At which point Kelly noticed what was going on around us, got an ashcan cover, and ran into the pissoir, banging the walls. Five guys scooted out; even a big pissoir only holds four.

A very blond young man put his hand on my arm and smiled. "Don't you think, Spacer, that you . . . people should leave?"

I looked at his hand on my blue uniform. "*Est-ce que tu es un frelk?*"

His eyebrows rose, then he shook his head. "Une *frelk*," he corrected. "No. I am not. Sadly for me. You look as though you may once have been a man. But now . . ." He smiled. "You have nothing for me now. The police." He nodded across the street where I noticed the gendarmerie for the first time. "They don't bother us. You are strangers, though . . ."

But Muse was already yelling, "Hey, come on! Let's get out of here, huh?" And left.

And went up again.

And came down in Houston:

"God damn!" Muse said. "Gemini Flight Control—you mean this is where it all started? Let's get *out* of here, *please*!"

So took a bus out through Pasadena, then the monoline to Galveston, and were going to take it down the Gulf, but Lou found a couple with a pickup truck—

"Glad to give you a ride, Spacers. You people up there on them planets and things, doing all that good work for the government."

—who were going south, them and the baby, so we rode in the back for two hundred and fifty miles of sun and wind.

"You think they're frelks?" Lou asked, elbowing me. "I bet they're frelks. They're just waiting for us to give 'em the come-on."

"Cut it out. They're a nice, stupid pair of country kids."

"That don't mean they ain't frelks!"

"You don't trust anybody, do you?"

"No."

And finally a bus again that rattled us through Brownsville and across the border into Matamoros where we staggered down the steps into the dust and the scorched evening with a lot of Mexicans and chickens and Texas Gulf shrimp fishermen—who smelled worst—and *we* shouted the loudest. Forty-three whores—I counted—had turned out for the shrimp fishermen, and by the time we had broken two of the windows in the bus station they were all laughing. The shrimp fishermen said they wouldn't buy us no food but would get us drunk if we wanted, 'cause that was the custom with shrimp fishermen. But we yelled, broke another window; then, while I was lying on my back on the telegraph office steps, singing, a woman with dark lips bent over and put her hands on my cheeks. "You are very sweet." Her rough hair fell forward. "But the men, they are standing around and watching *you*. And that is taking up *time*. Sadly, their time is our money. Spacer, do you not think you . . . people should leave?"

I grabbed her wrist. "*¡Usted!*" I whispered. "*¿Usted es una frelka?*"

"*Frelko en español.*" She smiled and patted the sunburst that hung from my belt buckle. "Sorry. But you have nothing that . . . would be useful to me. It is too bad, for you look like you were once a woman, no? And I like women, too . . ."

I rolled off the porch.

"Is this a drag, or is this a drag!" Muse was shouting. "Come *on*! Let's *go*!"

We managed to get back to Houston before dawn, somehow.

And went up.

And came down in Istanbul:

That morning it rained in Istanbul.

At the commissary we drank our tea from pear-shaped glasses, looking out across the Bosphorus. The Princess Islands lay like trash heaps before the prickly city.

"Who knows their way in this town?" Kelly asked.

"Aren't we going around together?" Muse demanded. "I thought we were going around together."

"They held up my check at the purser's office," Kelly explained. "I'm flat broke. I think the purser's got it in for me," and shrugged. "Don't want to, but I'm going to have to hunt up a rich frelk and come on friendly," went back to the tea; *then* noticed how heavy the silence had become. "Aw, come *on* now! You gape at me like that and I'll bust every bone in that carefully-conditioned-from-puberty body of yours. Hey you!" meaning me. "Don't give me that holier-than-thou gawk like you never went with no frelk!"

It was starting.

"I'm not gawking," I said and got quietly mad.

The longing, the old longing.

Bo laughed to break tensions. "Say, last time I was in Istanbul—about a year before I joined up with this platoon—I remember we were coming out of Taksim Square down Istiqlal. Just past all the cheap movies we found a little passage lined with flowers. Ahead of us were two other spacers. It's a market in there, and farther down they got fish, and then a courtyard with oranges and candy and sea urchins and cabbage. But flowers in front. Anyway, we noticed something funny about the spacers. It wasn't their uniforms; they were perfect. The haircuts: fine. It wasn't till we heard them talking—they were a man and woman dressed up like spacers, trying *to pick up frelks*! Imagine, queer for frelks!"

"Yeah," Lou said. "I seen that before. There were a lot of them in Rio."

"We beat hell out of them two," Bo concluded. "We got them in a side street and went to *town*!"

Muse's tea glass clicked on the counter. "From Taksim down Istiqlal till you get to the flowers? Now why didn't you say that's where the frelks were, huh?" A smile on Kelly's face would have made that okay. There was no smile.

"Hell," Lou said, "nobody ever had to tell me where to look. I go out in the street and frelks smell me coming. I can spot 'em halfway along Piccadilly. Don't they have nothing but tea in this place? Where can you get a drink?"

Bo grinned. "Moslem country, remember? But down at the end of the Flower Passage there're a lot of little bars with green doors and marble counters where you can get a liter of beer for about fifteen cents in lira. And there're all these stands selling deep-fat-fried bugs and pig's gut sandwiches—"

"You ever notice how frelks can put it away? I mean liquor, not . . . pig's guts."

And launched off into a lot of appeasing stories. We ended with the one about the frelk some spacer tried to roll who announced: "There are two things I go for. One is spacers; the other is a good fight . . ."

But they only allay. They cure nothing. Even Muse knew we would spend the day apart, now.

The rain had stopped, so we took the ferry up the Golden Horn. Kelly straight off asked for Taksim Square and Istiqlal and was directed to a dolmush, which we discovered was a taxicab, only it just goes one place and picks up lots and lots of people on the way. And it's cheap.

Lou headed off over Ataturk Bridge to see the sights of New City. Bo decided to find out what the Dolma Boche really was; and when Muse discovered you could go to Asia for fifteen cents—one lira and fifty krush—well, Muse decided to go to Asia.

I turned through the confusion of traffic at the head of the bridge and up past the gray, dripping walls of Old City, beneath the trolley wires. There are times when yelling and helling won't fill the lack. There are times when you must walk by yourself because it hurts so much to be alone.

I walked up a lot of little streets with wet donkeys and wet camels and women in veils; and down a lot of big streets with buses and trash baskets and men in business suits.

Some people stare at spacers; some people don't. Some people stare or don't stare in a way a spacer gets to recognize within a week after coming out of training school at sixteen. I was walking in the park when I caught her watching. She saw me see and looked away.

I ambled down the wet asphalt. She was standing under the arch of a small, empty mosque shell. As I passed she walked out into the courtyard among the cannons.

"Excuse me."

I stopped.

"Do you know whether or not this is the shrine of St. Irene?" Her English was charmingly accented. "I've left my guidebook home."

"Sorry. I'm a tourist too."

"Oh." She smiled. "I am Greek. I thought you might be Turkish because you are so dark."

"American red Indian." I nodded. Her turn to curtsy.

"I see. I have just started at the university here in Istanbul. Your uniform, it tells me that you are"—and in the pause, all speculations resolved—"a spacer."

I was uncomfortable. "Yeah." I put my hands in my pockets, moved my feet around on the soles of my boots, licked my third from the rear left molar—did all the things you do when you're uncomfortable. *You're so* exciting *when you look like that*, a frelk told me once. "Yeah, I am." I said it too sharply, too loudly, and she jumped a little.

So now she knew I knew she knew I knew, and I wondered how we would play out the Proust bit.

"I'm Turkish," she said. "I'm not Greek. I'm not just starting. I'm a graduate in art history here at the university. These little lies one makes for strangers to protect one's ego . . . why? Sometimes I think my ego is very small."

That's one strategy.

"How far away do you live?" I asked. "And what's the going rate in Turkish lira?" That's another.

"I can't pay you." She pulled her raincoat around her hips. She was very pretty. "I would like to." She shrugged and smiled. "But I am . . . a poor student. Not a rich one. If you want to turn around and walk away, there will be no hard feelings. I shall only be sad."

I stayed on the path. I thought she'd suggest a price after a little while. She didn't.

And that's another.

I was asking myself, *What do you want the damn money for anyway?* when a breeze upset water from one of the park's great cypresses.

"I think the whole business is sad." She wiped drops from her face. There had been a break in her voice, and for a moment I looked too closely at the water streaks. "I think it's sad that they have to alter you to make you a spacer. If they hadn't, then *we* . . . If spacers had never been, then we could not be . . . the way we are. Did you start out male or female?"

Another shower. I was looking at the ground and droplets went down my collar.

"Male," I said. "It doesn't matter."

"How old are you? Twenty-three, twenty-four?"

"Twenty-three," I lied. It's reflex. I'm twenty-five, but the younger they think you are, the more they pay you. But I didn't *want* her damn money—

"I guessed right then." She nodded. "Most of us are experts on spacers. Do you find that? I suppose we have to be." She looked at me with wide black eyes. At the end of the stare, she blinked rapidly. "You would have been a fine man. But now you are a spacer, building water-conservation units on Mars, programming mining computers on Ganymede, servicing communication relay towers on the moon. The alteration . . ." Frelks are the only people I've ever heard say "the alteration" with so much fascination and regret. "You'd think they'd have found some other solution. They could have found another way than neutering you, turning you into creatures not even androgynous; things that are—"

I put my hand on her shoulder, and she stopped like I'd hit her. She looked to see if anyone was near. Lightly, so lightly then, she raised her hand to mine.

I pulled my hand away. "That are what?"

"They could have found another way." Both hands in her pockets now.

"They could have. Yes. Up beyond the ionosphere, baby, there's too much radiation for those precious gonads to work right anywhere you might want to do something that would keep you there over twenty-four hours, like the moon, or Mars, or the satellites of Jupiter—"

"They could have made protective shields. They could have done more research into biological adjustment—"

"Population Explosion time," I said. "No, they were hunting for any excuse to cut down kids back then—especially deformed ones."

"Ah, yes." She nodded. "We're still fighting our way up from the neo-puritan reaction to the sex freedom of the twentieth century."

"It was a fine solution." I grinned and hung my hand over my crotch. "I'm happy with it." And scratched. I've never known why that's so much more obscene when a spacer does it.

"Stop it," she snapped, moving away.

"What's the matter?"

"Stop it," she repeated. "Don't do that! You're a child."

"But they choose us from children whose sexual responses are hopelessly retarded at puberty."

"And your childish, violent substitutes for love? I suppose that's one of the things that's attractive. Yes, I know you're a child."

"Yeah? What about frelks?"

She thought awhile. "I think they are the sexually retarded ones they miss. Perhaps it was the right solution. You really don't regret you have no sex?"

"We've got you," I said.

"Yes." She looked down. I glanced to see the expression she was hiding. It was a smile. "You have your glorious, soaring life—*and* you have us." Her face came up. She glowed. "You spin in the sky, the world spins under you, and you step from land to land, while we . . ." She turned her head right, left, and her black hair curled and uncurled on the shoulder of her coat. "We have our dull, circled lives, bound in gravity, *worshiping* you!"

She looked back at me. "Perverted, yes? In love with a bunch of corpses in free fall!" She suddenly hunched her shoulders. "I don't like having a free-fall-sexual-displacement complex."

"That always sounded like too much to say."

She looked away. "I don't like being a frelk. Better?"

"I wouldn't like it either. Be something else."

"You don't choose your perversions. *You* have no perversions at all. *You're* free of the whole business. I love you for that, Spacer. My love starts with the fear of love. Isn't that beautiful? A pervert substitutes something unattainable for 'normal' love: the homosexual, a mirror; the fetishist, a shoe or a watch or a girdle. Those with free-fall-sexual-dis—"

"Frelks."

"Frelks substitute"—she looked at me sharply again—"loose, swinging meat."

"That doesn't offend me."

"I wanted it to."

"Why?"

"You don't have desires. You wouldn't understand."

"Go on."

"I want you because you can't want me. That's the pleasure. If someone really had a sexual reaction to . . . us, we'd be scared away. I wonder how many people there were before there were you, waiting for your creation. We're necrophiles. I'm sure grave-robbing has fallen off since you started going up. But you don't understand . . ." She paused. "If you did, then I wouldn't be scuffing leaves now and trying to think from whom I could borrow sixty lira." She stepped over the knuckles of a root that had cracked the pavement. "And that, incidentally, is the going rate in Istanbul."

I calculated. "Things still get cheaper as you go east."

"You know," and she let her raincoat fall open, "you're different from the others. You at least *want* to know—"

I said, "If I spat on you for every time you'd said that to a spacer, you'd drown."

"Go back to the moon, loose meat." She closed her eyes. "Swing on up to Mars. There are satellites around Jupiter where you might do some good. Go up and come down in some other city."

"Where do you live?"

"You want to come with me?"

"Give me something," I said. "Give me something—it doesn't have to be worth sixty lira. Give me something you like, anything of yours that means something to you."

"No!"

"Why not?"

"Because I—"

"—don't want to give up part of that small ego. None of you frelks do!"

"You really don't understand I just don't want to buy you?"

"You have nothing to buy me with."

"You are a child," she said. "I love you."

We reached the gate of the park. She stopped, and we stood time enough for a breeze to rise and die in the grass. "I . . ." she offered tentatively, pointing without taking her hand from her coat pocket. "I live right down there."

"All right," I said. "Let's go."

A gas main had once exploded along this street, she explained to me, a gushing road of fire as far as the docks, overhot and over-quick. It had been put out within minutes, no building had fallen, but the charred fascias glittered. "This is sort of an artist and student quarter." We crossed the cobbles. "Yuri Pasha, number fourteen. In case you're ever in Istanbul again." Her door was covered with black scales, the gutter was thick with garbage.

"A lot of artists and professional people are frelks," I said, trying to be inane.

"So are lots of other people." She walked inside and held the door. "We're just more flamboyant about it."

On the landing there was a portrait of Ataturk. Her room was on the second floor. "Just a moment while I get my key—"

Marsscapes! Moonscapes! On her easel was a six-foot canvas showing the sunrise flaring on a crater's rim! There were copies of the original Observer pictures of the moon pinned to the wall, and pictures of every smooth-faced general in the International Spacer Corps.

On one corner of her desk was a pile of those photo magazines about spacers that you can find in most kiosks all over the world: I've seriously heard people say they were printed for adventurous-minded high school children. They've never seen the Danish ones. She had a few of those too. There was a shelf of art books, art history texts. Above them were six feet of cheap paper-covered space operas: *Sin on Space Station #12, Rocket Rake, Savage Orbit.*

"Arrack?" she asked. "Ouzo, or pernod? You've got your choice. But I may pour them all from the same bottle." She set out glasses on the desk, then opened a waist-high cabinet that turned out to be an icebox. She stood up with a tray of lovelies: fruit puddings, Turkish delight, braised meats.

"What's this?"

"Dolmades. Grape leaves filled with rice and pignolias."

"Say it again?"

"Dolmades. Comes from the same Turkish word as 'dolmush.' They both mean 'stuffed.'" She put the tray beside the glasses. "Sit down."

I sat on the studio-couch-that-becomes-bed. Under the brocade I felt the deep, fluid resilience of a glycogel mattress. They've got the idea that it approximates the feeling of free fall. "Comfortable? Would you excuse me for a moment? I have some friends down the hall. I want to see them for a moment." She winked. "They like spacers."

"Are you going to take up a collection for me?" I asked. "Or do you want them to line up outside the door and wait their turn?"

She sucked a breath. "Actually I was going to suggest both." Suddenly she shook her head. "Oh, what do you want!"

"What will you give me? I want something," I said. "That's why I came. I'm lonely. Maybe I want to find out how far it goes. I don't know yet."

"It goes as far as you will. Me? I study, I read, paint, talk with my friends"—she came over to the bed, sat down on the floor—"go to the theater, look at spacers who pass me on the street, till one looks back; I am lonely too." She put her head on my knee. "I want something. But," and after a minute neither of us had moved, "you are not the one who will give it to me."

"You're not going to pay me for it," I countered. "You're not, are you?"

On my knee her head shook. After a while she said, all breath and no voice, "Don't you think you . . . should leave?"

"Okay," I said, and stood up.

She sat back on the hem of her coat. She hadn't taken it off yet.

I went to the door.

"Incidentally." She folded her hands in her lap. "There is a place in New City you might find what you're looking for, called the Flower Passage—"

I turned toward her, angry. "The frelk hangout? Look, I don't *need* money! I said *anything* would do! I don't want—"

She had begun to shake her head, laughing quietly. Now she lay her cheek on the wrinkled place where I had sat. "Do you persist in misunderstanding? It is a *spacer* hangout. When you leave, I am going to visit my friends and talk about . . . ah, yes, the beautiful one that got away. I thought you might find . . . perhaps someone you know."

With anger, it ended.

"Oh," I said. "Oh, it's a spacer hangout. Yeah. Well, thanks."

And went out.

And found the Flower Passage, and Kelly and Lou and Bo and Muse. Kelly was buying beer, so we all got drunk, and ate fried fish and fried clams and fried sausage, and Kelly was waving the money around, saying, "You should have seen him! The changes I put that frelk through, you should have *seen* him! Eighty lira is the going rate here, and he gave me a hundred and fifty!" and drank more beer.

And went up.

Pamela Zoline
The Heat Death of the Universe

• • • •

{1967}

Pamela Zoline (1941–) has lived since the 1980s in Telluride, Colorado; she has written two opera libretti, a children's chapbook, and some half a dozen sf stories. In 1967, she was an American in London working chiefly as an artist/illustrator when her first and best-known story, "The Heat Death of the Universe," appeared in *New Worlds* magazine, edited by Michael Moorcock. Promptly reprinted in *England Swings SF* (1968), one of Judith Merril's most influential anthologies, the story became part of the debate over the relation of New Wave writers to the sf genre. Zoline's London friends were sf's avant-garde: Moorcock himself, Thomas M. Disch, John Clute, J. G. Ballard, John Sladek, and others. Their experimental and self-consciously literary style was controversial, especially for critics who resented the New Wave's collective hostility to such sf trappings as a far-future setting, extraterrestrial locations and characters, and the depiction of technological wonders.

This story's scale is intimate; like Zoline's collages, it juxtaposes unlike things. In her own illustration for the story, fragmented images of a bathroom cleaner, maps of California, and Marcel Duchamp's 1919 rendition of a mustachioed "Mona Lisa" are interspersed. The story itself reads a day in the life of an overtaxed housewife in terms of the Second Law of Thermodynamics—in the formulation of Rudolf Clausius, the principle that "the entropy of the universe tends to a maximum." Entropy is a term for the measure of energy in a system unavailable for work. Its end-stage is "heat-death," when the amount of energy available for work decreases to zero. Clausius, who coined the term *entropy* in 1865, observed that "in a closed system, entropy always increases." Sarah Boyle's house is just such a closed system. Though surrounded by objects and busy with social duties, she is marooned on her suburban desert island. Her husband remains offstage and her mother is dead. In a world of ever-dissipating forms, Shakespeare and Mozart dwindle to cardboard masks on a cereal box: art declines to a near-vanishing point, regrouping as consumerism. Clausius's most famous example of how entropy works—the dissolving of ice in a glass of water—suggests the inexorable process against which Sarah Boyle struggles: "educated at a fine Eastern college," she is now confined to routines that yield ever-diminishing returns. As Simone de Beauvoir wrote in *The Second Sex* (1949), "Few tasks are more like the torture of Sisyphus than housework, with its endless repetition: the clean becomes soiled, the soiled is made clean, over and over, day after day. The housewife wears herself out, marking time: she makes nothing, merely perpetuates the present."

Zoline studied philosophy at the University of London, and her numbering of paragraphs in this story suggests Ludwig Wittgenstein's listing of points in *Tractatus Logico Philosophicus* (1921). Sarah Boyle's own compulsive listing and sorting convey her struggle against the increasing disorder of her closed-off world; but the workings of entropy cannot be halted by labeling, cleaning, or preserving. This story's extrapolation from one of the grimmer laws in physics sometimes distracts readers from fully recognizing Zoline's equally striking and exuberant wit.

Her story is strongly science fictional, despite the absence of high-tech machines or a far-future, outer space setting. Science fiction considers human life—what people *are*—in terms of what science *knows* (or thinks it knows): the genre itself, like this story, has legitimate ontological concerns. In her sardonic vision of the California suburbs, Zoline is as trenchant as Thomas Pynchon in *The Crying of Lot 49* (1966); and her snapshots of suburbia's frenzied consumption patterns anticipate Jean Baudrillard's *Simulacra and Simulation* (1983) and its postmodern analysis of the American hyperreal.

(1) ONTOLOGY
That branch of metaphysics which concerns itself with the problems of the nature of existence or being.

(2) Imagine a pale blue morning sky, almost green, with clouds only at the rims. The earth rolls and the sun appears to mount, mountains erode, fruits decay, the Foraminifera adds another chamber to its shell, babies' fingernails grow as does the hair of the dead in their graves, and in egg timers the sands fall and the eggs cook on.

(3) Sarah Boyle thinks of her nose as too large, though several men have cherished it. The nose is generous and performs a well-calculated geometric curve, at the arch of which the skin is drawn very tight and a faint whiteness of bone can be seen showing through, it has much the same architectural tension and sense of mathematical calculation as the day after Thanksgiving

breastbone on the carcass of a turkey; her maiden name was Sloss, mixed German, English and Irish descent; in grade school she was very bad at playing softball and, besides being chosen last for the team, was always made to play center field, no one could ever hit to center field; she loves music best of all the arts, and of music, Bach, J. S.; she lives in California, though she grew up in Boston and Toledo.

(4) BREAKFAST TIME AT THE BOYLES' HOUSE ON LA FLORIDA STREET, ALAMEDA, CALIFORNIA, THE CHILDREN DEMAND SUGAR FROSTED FLAKES.
With some reluctance Sarah Boyle dishes out Sugar Frosted Flakes to her children, already hearing the decay set in upon the little white milk-teeth, the bony whine of the dentist's drill. The dentist is a short, gentle man with a moustache who sometimes reminds Sarah of an Uncle who lives in Ohio. One bowl per child.

(5) If one can imagine it considered as an abstract object by members of a totally separate culture, one can see that the cereal box might seem a beautiful thing. The solid rectangle is neatly joined and classical in proportions, on it are squandered wealths of richest colors, virgin blues, crimsons, dense ochres, precious pigments once reserved for sacred paintings and as cosmetics for the blind faces of marble gods. Giant size. Net Weight 16 ounces, 250 grams. "They're tigeriffic!" says Tony the Tiger. The box blatts promises. Energy, Nature's Own Goodness, an endless pubescence. On its back is a mask of William Shakespeare to be cut out, folded, worn by thousands of tiny Shakespeares in Kansas City, Detroit, Tucson, San Diego, Tampa. He appears at once more kindly and somewhat more vacant than we are used to seeing him. Two or more of the children lay claim to the mask, but Sarah puts off that Solomon's decision until such time as the box is empty.

(6) A notice in orange flourishes states that a Surprise Gift is to be found somewhere in the packet, nestled amongst the golden flakes. So far it has not been unearthed, and the children request more cereal than they wish to eat, great yellow heaps of it, to hurry the discovery. Even so, at the end of the meal, some layers of flakes remain in the box and the Gift must still be among them.

(7) There is even a Special Offer of a secret membership, code and magic ring; these to be obtained by sending in the box top with 50 cents.

(8) Three offers on one cereal box. To Sarah Boyle this seems to be oversell. Perhaps something is terribly wrong with the cereal and it must be sold quickly, got off the shelves before the news breaks. Perhaps it causes a special, cruel Cancer in little children. As Sarah Boyle collects the bowls printed with bunnies and baseball statistics, still slopping half full of milk and wilted flakes, she imagines *in her mind's eye* the headlines, "Nation's Small Fry Stricken, Fate's Finger Sugar Coated, Lethal Sweetness Socks Tots."

(9) Sarah Boyle is a vivacious and intelligent young wife and mother, educated at a fine Eastern college, proud of her growing family, which keeps her busy and happy around the house.

(10) BIRTHDAY

Today is the birthday of one of the children. There will be a party in the late afternoon.

(11) CLEANING UP THE HOUSE. (ONE.)

Cleaning up the kitchen. Sarah Boyle puts the bowls, plates, glasses and silverware into the sink. She scrubs at the stickiness on the yellow-marbled formica table with a blue synthetic sponge, a special blue which we shall see again. There are marks of children's hands in various sizes printed with sugar and grime on all the table's surfaces. The marks catch the light; they appear and disappear according to the position of the observing eye. The floor sweepings include a triangular half of toast spread with grape jelly, bobby pins, a green Band-Aid, flakes, a doll's eye, dust, dog's hair and a button.

(12) Until we reach the statistically likely planet and begin to converse with whatever green-faced teleporting denizens thereof—considering only this shrunk and communication-ravaged world—can we any more postulate a separate culture? Viewing the metastasis of Western Culture it seems progressively less likely. Sarah Boyle imagines a whole world which has become like California, all topographical imperfections sanded away with the sweet-smelling burr of the plastic surgeon's cosmetic polisher; a world populace dieting, leisured, similar in pink and mauve hair and rhinestone shades. A land Cunt Pink and Avocado Green, brassiered and girdled by monstrous complexities of Super Highways, a California endless and unceasing, embracing and transforming the entire globe, California, California!

(13) INSERT ONE. ON ENTROPY.

ENTROPY: A quantity introduced in the first place to facilitate the calculation, and to give clear expressions to the results of thermodynamics. Changes of entropy can be calculated only for a reversible process, and may then be defined as the ratio of the amount of heat taken up to the absolute temperature at which the heat is absorbed. Entropy changes for actual irreversible processes are calculated by postulating equivalent theoretical reversible changes. The entropy of a system is a measure of its degree of disorder. The total entropy of any isolated system can never decrease in any change; it must either increase (irreversible process) or remain constant (reversible process). The total entropy of the Universe therefore is increasing, tending towards a maximum, corresponding to complete disorder of the particles in it (assuming that it may be regarded as an isolated system). See *heat death of the Universe*.

(14) CLEANING UP THE HOUSE. (TWO.)

Washing the baby's diapers. Sarah Boyle writes notes to herself all over the house; a mazed wild script larded with arrows, diagrams, pictures, graffiti on every available surface in a desperate/heroic attempt to index, record, bluff, invoke, order and placate. On the fluted and flowered white plastic lid of the diaper bin she has written in Blushing Pink Nitetime lipstick a phrase to ward off fumey ammoniac despair. "The nitrogen cycle is the vital round of organic and inorganic exchange on earth. The sweet breath of the Universe." On the wall by the washing machine are Yin and Yang signs, mandalas, and the words, "Many young wives feel trapped. It is a contemporary sociological phenomenon which may be explained in part by a gap between changing living patterns and the accommodation of social services to these patterns." Over the stove she has written "Help, Help, Help, Help, Help."

(15) Sometimes she numbers or letters the things in a room, writing the assigned character on each object. There are 819 separate moveable objects in the living-room, counting books. Sometimes she labels objects with their names, or with false names; thus on her bureau the hair brush is labeled HAIR BRUSH, the cologne, COLOGNE, the hand cream, CAT. She is passionately fond of children's dictionaries, encyclopedias, ABCs and all reference books, transfixed and comforted at their simulacra of a complete listing and ordering.

(16) On the door of a bedroom are written two definitions from reference books. "GOD: An object of worship"; "HOMEOSTASIS: Maintenance of constancy of internal environment."

(17) Sarah Boyle washes the diapers, washes the linen, Oh Saint Veronica, changes the sheets on the baby's crib. She begins to put away some of the toys, stepping over and around the organizations of playthings which still seem inhabited. There are various vehicles, and articles of medicine, domesticity and war: whole zoos of stuffed animals, bruised and odorous with years of love; hundreds of small figures, plastic animals, cowboys, cars, spacemen, with which the children make sub and supra worlds in their play. One of Sarah's favorite toys is the Baba, the wooden Russian doll which, opened, reveals a smaller but otherwise identical doll, which opens to reveal, etc., a lesson in infinity at least to the number of seven dolls.

(18) Sarah Boyle's mother has been dead for two years. Sarah Boyle thinks of music as the formal articulation of the passage of time, and of Bach as the most poignant rendering of this. Her eyes are sometimes the color of the aforementioned kitchen sponge. Her hair is natural spaniel-brown; months ago on an hysterical day she dyed it red, so now it is two-toned with a stripe in the middle, like the painted walls of slum buildings or old schools.

(19) INSERT TWO. THE HEAT DEATH OF THE UNIVERSE.
The second law of thermodynamics can be interpreted to mean that the ENTROPY of a closed system tends towards a maximum and that its available ENERGY tends towards a minimum. It has been held that the Universe constitutes a thermodynamically closed system, and if this were true it would mean that a time must finally come when the Universe "unwinds" itself, no energy being available for use. This state is referred to as the "heat death of the Universe." It is by no means certain, however, that the Universe can be considered as a closed system in this sense.

(20) Sarah Boyle pours out a Coke from the refrigerator and lights a cigarette. The coldness and sweetness of the thick brown liquid make her throat ache and her teeth sting briefly, sweet juice of my youth, her eyes glass with the carbonation, she thinks of the Heat Death of the Universe. A logarithmic of those late summer days, endless as the Irish serpent twisting through jeweled manuscripts forever, tail in mouth, the heat pressing, bloating, doing violence. The Los Angeles sky becomes so filled and bleached with detritus that it loses all colors and silvers like a mirror, reflecting back the fricasseeing earth. Everything becoming warmer and warmer, each particle of matter becoming more agitated, more excited until the bonds shatter, the glues fail, the deodorants lose their seals. She imagines the whole of New York City

melting like a Dalí into a great chocolate mass, a great soup, the Great Soup of New York.

(21) CLEANING UP THE HOUSE. (THREE.)
Beds made. Vacuuming the hall, a carpet of faded flowers, vines and leaves which endlessly wind and twist into each other in a fevered and permanent ecstasy. Suddenly the vacuum blows instead of sucks, spewing marbles, dolls' eyes, dust, crackers. An old trick. "Oh my god," says Sarah. The baby yells on cue for attention/changing/food. Sarah kicks the vacuum cleaner and it retches and begins working again.

(22) AT LUNCH ONLY ONE GLASS OF MILK IS SPILLED.
At lunch only one glass of milk is spilled.

(23) The plants need watering, Geranium, Hyacinth, Lavender, Avocado, Cyclamen. Feed the fish, happy fish with china castles and mermaids in the bowl. The turtle looks more and more unwell and is probably dying.

(24) Sarah Boyle's blue eyes, how blue? Bluer far and of a different quality than the Nature metaphors which were both engine and fuel to so much of precedent literature. A fine, modern, acid, synthetic blue; the shiny cerulean of the skies on postcards sent from lush subtropics, the natives grinning ivory ambivalent grins in their dark faces; the promising fat, unnatural blue of the heavy tranquilizer capsule; the cool mean blue of that fake kitchen sponge; the deepest, most unbelievable azure of the tiled and mossless interiors of California swimming pools. The chemists in their kitchens cooked, cooled and distilled this blue from thousands of colorless and wonderfully constructed crystals, each one unique and nonpareil; and now that color hisses, bubbles, burns in Sarah's eyes.

(25) INSERT THREE. ON LIGHT.
LIGHT: Name given to the agency by means of which a viewed object influences the observer's eyes. Consists of electromagnetic radiation within the wave-length range 4×10^{-5} cm to 7×10^{-5} cm approximately; variations in the wave-length produce different sensations in the eye, corresponding to different colors. See *color vision*.

(26) LIGHT AND CLEANING THE LIVING ROOM.
All the objects (819) and surfaces in the living room are dusty, gray common dust as though this were the den of a giant molting mouse. Suddenly

quantities of waves or particles of very strong sunlight speed in through the window, and everything incandesces, multiple rainbows. Poised in what has become a solid cube of light, like an ancient insect trapped in amber, Sarah Boyle realizes that the dust is indeed the most beautiful stuff in the room, a manna for the eyes. Duchamp, that father of thought, has set with fixative some dust which fell on one of his sculptures, counting it as part of the work. "That way madness lies, says Sarah," says Sarah. The thought of ordering a household on Dada principles balloons again. All the rooms would fill up with objects, newspapers and magazines would compost, the potatoes in the rack, the canned green beans in the garbage can would take new heart and come to life again, reaching out green shoots towards the sun. The plants would grow wild and wind into a jungle around the house, splitting plaster, tearing shingles, the garden would enter in at the door. The goldfish would die, the birds would die, we'd have them stuffed; the dog would die from lack of care, and probably the children—all stuffed and sitting around the house, covered with dust.

(27) INSERT FOUR. DADA.

DADA (Fr., hobby-horse) was a nihilistic precursor of Surrealism, invented in Zurich during World War I, a product of hysteria and shock lasting from about 1915 to 1922. It was deliberately anti-art and anti-sense, intended to outrage and scandalize, and its most characteristic production was the reproduction of the *Mona Lisa* decorated with a moustache and the obscene caption LHOOQ (read: *elle a chaud au cul*) "by" Duchamp. Other manifestations included Arp's collages of colored paper cut out at random and shuffled, ready-made objects such as the bottle drier and the bicycle wheel "signed" by Duchamp, Picabia's drawings of bits of machinery with incongruous titles, incoherent poetry, a lecture given by 38 lecturers in unison, and an exhibition in Cologne in 1920, held in an annex to a café lavatory, at which a chopper was provided for spectators to smash the exhibits with—which they did.

(28) TIME-PIECES AND OTHER MEASURING DEVICES.

In the Boyle house there are four clocks; three watches (one a Mickey Mouse watch which does not work); two calendars and two engagement books; three rulers, a yardstick; a measuring cup; a set of red plastic measuring spoons which includes a tablespoon, a teaspoon, a one-half teaspoon, one-fourth teaspoon and one-eighth teaspoon; an egg timer; an oral thermometer and a rectal thermometer; a Boy Scout compass; a barometer in the shape of a house, in and out of which an old woman and an old man chase each other forever without fulfillment; a bathroom scale; an infant scale; a tape measure which can be pulled out of a stuffed felt strawberry; a wall on which the children's heights are marked; a metronome.

(29) Sarah Boyle finds a new line in her face after lunch while cleaning the bathroom. It is as yet barely visible, running from the midpoint of her forehead to the bridge of her nose. By inward curling of her eyebrows she can etch it clearly as it will come to appear in the future. She marks another mark on the wall where she has drawn out a scoring area. Face Lines and Other Intimations of Mortality, the heading says. There are thirty-two marks, counting this latest one.

(30) Sarah Boyle is a vivacious and witty young wife and mother, educated at a fine Eastern college, proud of her growing family, which keeps her happy and busy around the house, involved in many hobbies and community activities, and only occasionally given to obsessions concerning Time/Entropy/Chaos and Death.

(31) Sarah Boyle is never quite sure how many children she has.

(32) Sarah thinks from time to time; Sarah is occasionally visited with this thought; at times this thought comes upon Sarah, that there are things to be hoped for, accomplishments to be desired beyond the mere reproductions, mirror reproduction of one's kind. The babies. Lying in bed at night sometimes the memory of the act of birth, always the hue and texture of red plush theatre seats, washes up; the rending which always, at a certain intensity of pain, slipped into landscapes, the sweet breath of the sweating nurse. The wooden Russian doll has bright, perfectly round red spots on her cheeks, she splits in the center to reveal a doll smaller but in all other respects identical with round bright red spots on her cheeks, etc.

(33) How fortunate for the species, Sarah muses or is mused, that children are as ingratiating as we know them. Otherwise they would soon be salted off for the leeches they are, and the race would extinguish itself in a fair sweet flowering, the last generation's massive achievement in the arts and pursuits of high civilization. The finest women would have their tubes tied off at the age of twelve, or perhaps refrain altogether from the Act of Love? All interests would be bent to a refining and perfecting of each febrile sense, each fluid hour, with no more cowardly investment in immortality via the patchy and too often disappointing vegetables of one's own womb.

(34) INSERT FIVE. LOVE.

LOVE: a typical sentiment involving fondness for, or attachment to, an object, the idea of which is emotionally colored whenever it arises in the mind, and capable, as Shand has pointed out, of evoking any one of a whole gamut of primary emotions, according to the situation in which the object is placed, or represented; often, and by psychoanalysts always, used in the sense of *sex-love* or even *lust* (q.v.)

(35) Sarah Boyle has at times felt a unity with her body, at other times a complete separation. The mind/body duality considered. The time/space duality considered. The male/female duality considered. The matter/energy duality considered. Sometimes, at extremes, her Body seems to her an animal on a leash, taken for walks in the park by her Mind. The lamp posts of experience. Her arms are lightly freckled and when she gets very tired the places under her eyes become violet.

(36) Housework is never completed, the chaos always lurks ready to encroach on any area left unweeded, a jungle filled with dirty pans and the roaring of giant stuffed toy animals suddenly turned savage. Terrible glass eyes.

(37) SHOPPING FOR THE BIRTHDAY CAKE.

Shopping in the supermarket with the baby in front of the cart and a larger child holding on. The light from the ice-cube-tray-shaped fluorescent lights is mixed blue and pink and brighter, colder, and cheaper than daylight. The doors swing open just as you reach out your hand for them, Tantalus, moving with a ghastly quiet swing. Hot dogs for the party. Potato chips, gum drops, a paper tablecloth with birthday designs, hot dog buns, catsup, mustard, piccalilli, balloons, instant coffee Continental style, dog food, frozen peas, ice cream, frozen lima beans, frozen broccoli in butter sauce, paper birthday hats, paper napkins in three colors, a box of Sugar Frosted Flakes with a Wolfgang Amadeus Mozart mask on the back, bread, pizza mix. The notes of a just-graspable music filter through the giant store, for the most part by-passing the brain and acting directly on the liver, blood and lymph. The air is delicately scented with aluminum. Half-and-half cream, tea bags, bacon, sandwich meat, strawberry jam. Sarah is in front of the shelves of cleaning products now, and the baby is beginning to whine. Around her are whole libraries of objects, offering themselves. Some of that same old hysteria that had incarnadined her hair rises up again, and she does not refuse it. There is one moment when she can choose direction, like standing on a chalk-drawn X, a hot cross bun, and she does not choose calm and measure. Sarah Boyle begins to pick out, methodically, deliberately and with a careful ecstasy, one of every cleaning product which the store sells. Window Cleaner, Glass Cleaner, Brass Polish, Silver Polish, Steel Wool, eighteen different brands of Detergent, Disinfectant, Toilet Cleanser, Water Softener, Fabric Softener, Drain Cleanser, Spot Remover, Floor Wax, Furniture Wax, Car Wax, Carpet Shampoo, Dog Shampoo, Shampoo for people with dry, oily and normal hair, for people with dandruff, for people with grey hair. Toothpaste, Tooth Powder, Denture Cleaner, Deodorants, Antiperspirants, Antiseptics, Soaps, Cleansers, Abrasives, Oven Cleansers, Makeup Removers. When the same products appear in different sizes Sarah takes one of each size. For some products she accumulates whole little families of containers: a giant Father bottle of shampoo, a Mother bottle, an Older Sister bottle just smaller than the Mother bottle, and a very tiny Baby Brother bottle. Sarah fills three shopping carts and has to have help wheeling them all down the aisles. At the checkout counter her laughter and hysteria keep threatening to overflow as the pale blond clerk with no eyebrows like the *Mona Lisa* pretends normality and disinterest. The bill comes to $57.53 and Sarah has to write a check. Driving home, the baby strapped in the drive-a-cot and the paper bags bulging in the back seat, she cries.

(38) BEFORE THE PARTY.
Mrs. David Boyle, mother-in-law of Sarah Boyle, is coming to the party of her grandchild. She brings a toy, a yellow wooden duck on a string, made in Austria: the duck quacks as it is pulled along the floor. Sarah is filling paper cups with gum drops and chocolates, and Mrs. David Boyle sits at the kitchen table and talks to her. She is talking about several things, she is talking about her garden, which is flourishing except for a plague of rare black beetles, thought to have come from Hong Kong, which are undermining some of the most delicate growths at the roots and feasting on the leaves of other plants. She is talking about a sale of household linens which she plans to attend on the following Tuesday. She is talking about her neighbor who has Cancer and is wasting away. The neighbor is a Catholic woman who had never had a day's illness in her life until the Cancer struck, and now she is, apparently, failing with dizzying speed. The doctor says her body's chaos, chaos, cells running wild all over, says Mrs. David Boyle. When I visited her she hardly *knew* me, can hardly *speak*, can't keep herself *clean*, says Mrs. David Boyle.

(39) Sometimes Sarah can hardly remember how many cute chubby little children she has.

(40) When she used to stand out in center field far away from the other players, she used to make up songs and sing them to herself.

(41) She thinks of the end of the world by ice.

(42) She thinks of the end of the world by water.

(43) She thinks of the end of the world by nuclear war.

(44) There must be more than this, Sarah Boyle thinks, from time to time. What could one do to justify one's passage? Or less ambitiously, to change, even in the motion of the smallest mote, the course and circulation of the world? Sometimes Sarah's dreams are of heroic girth, a new symphony using laboratories of machinery and all invented instruments, at once giant in scope and intelligible to all, to heal the bloody breach; a series of paintings which would transfigure and astonish and calm the frenzied art world in its panting race; a new novel that would refurbish language. Sometimes she considers the mystical, the streaky and random, and it seems that one change, no matter how small, would be enough. Turtles are supposed to live for many years. To carve a name, date and perhaps a word of hope upon a turtle's shell, then set him free to wend the world, surely this one act might cancel out absurdity?

(45) Mrs. David Boyle has a faint moustache, like Duchamp's *Mona Lisa*.

(46) THE BIRTHDAY PARTY.
Many children, dressed in pastels, sit around the long table. They are exhausted and overexcited from games fiercely played, some are flushed and wet, others unnaturally pale. This general agitation and the paper party hats they wear combine to make them appear a dinner party of debauched midgets. It is time for the cake. A huge chocolate cake in the shape of a rocket and launching pad and covered with blue and pink icing is carried in. In the hush the birthday child begins to cry. He stops crying, makes a wish and blows out the candles.

(47) One child will not eat hot dogs, ice cream or cake, and asks for cereal. Sarah pours him out a bowl of Sugar Frosted Flakes, and a moment later he chokes. Sarah pounds him on the back, and out spits a tiny green plastic snake with red glassy eyes, the Surprise Gift. All the children want it.

(48) AFTER THE PARTY THE CHILDREN ARE PUT TO BED.
Bath time. Observing the nakedness of children, pink and slippery as seals, squealing as seals, now the splashing, grunting and smacking of cherry flesh on raspberry flesh reverberate in the pearl-tiled steamy cubicle. The nakedness of children is so much more absolute than that of the mature. No musky curling hair to indicate the target points, no knobbly clutch of plane and fat and curvature to ennoble this prince of beasts. All well-fed naked children appear edible, Sarah's teeth hum in her head with memory of bloody feastings, prehistory. Young humans appear too like the young of other species for smugness, and the comparison is not even in their favor, they are much the most peeled and unsupple of those young. Such pinkness, such utter nuded pinkness; the orifices neatly incised, rimmed with a slightly deeper rose, the incessant demands for breast, time, milks of many sorts.

(49) INSERT SIX. WEINER ON ENTROPY.
In Gibb's Universe order is least probable, chaos most probable. But while the Universe as a whole, if indeed there is a whole Universe, tends to run down, there are local enclaves whose direction seems opposed to that of the Universe at large and in which there is a limited and temporary tendency for organization to increase. Life finds its home in some of these enclaves.

(50) Sarah Boyle imagines, in her mind's eye, cleaning, and ordering the whole world, even the Universe. Filling the great spaces of Space with a marvelous sweet-smelling, deep-cleansing foam. Deodorizing rank caves and volcanoes. Scrubbing rocks.

(51) INSERT SEVEN. TURTLES.
Many different species of carnivorous Turtles live in the fresh waters of the tropical and temperate zones of various continents. Most northerly of the European Turtles (extending as far as Holland and Lithuania) is the European Pond Turtle (*Emys orbicularis*). It is from eight to ten inches long and may live a hundred years.

(52) CLEANING UP AFTER THE PARTY.
Sarah is cleaning up after the party. Gum drops and melted ice cream surge off paper plates, making holes in the paper tablecloth through the printed roses. A fly has died a splendid death in a pool of strawberry ice cream. Wet jelly beans stain all they touch, finally becoming themselves colorless, opaque white, like flocks of tame or sleeping maggots. Plastic favors mount half-eaten pieces of blue cake. Strewn about are thin strips of fortune papers

from the Japanese poppers. Upon them are printed strangely assorted phrases selected by apparently unilingual Japanese. Crowds of delicate yellow people spending great chunks of their lives in producing these most ephemeral of objects, and inscribing thousands of fine papers with absurd and incomprehensible messages. "The very hairs of your head are all numbered," reads one. Most of the balloons have popped. Someone has planted a hot dog in the daffodil pot. A few of the helium balloons have escaped their owners and now ride the ceiling. Another fortune paper reads, "Emperor's horses meet death worse, numbers, numbers."

(53) She is very tired, violet under the eyes, mauve beneath the eyes. Her uncle in Ohio used to get the same marks under his eyes. She goes to the kitchen to lay the table for tomorrow's breakfast, then she sees that in the turtle's bowl the turtle is floating, still, on the surface of the water. Sarah Boyle pokes at it with a pencil but it does not move. She stands for several minutes looking at the dead turtle on the surface of the water. She is crying again.

(54) She begins to cry. She goes to the refrigerator and takes out a carton of eggs, white eggs, extra large. She throws them one by one onto the kitchen floor, which is patterned with strawberries in squares. They break beautifully. There is a Secret Society of Dentists, all moustached, with Special Code and Magic Rings. She begins to cry. She takes up three bunny dishes and throws them against the refrigerator; they shatter, and then the floor is covered with shards, chunks of partial bunnies, an ear, an eye here, a paw; Stockton, California, Acton, California, Chico, California, Redding, California, Glen Ellen, California, Cadiz, California, Angels Camp, California, Half Moon Bay. The total ENTROPY of the Universe therefore is increasing, tending towards a maximum, corresponding to complete disorder of the particles in it. She is crying, her mouth is open. She throws a jar of grape jelly and it smashes the window over the sink. It has been held that the Universe constitutes a thermodynamically closed system, and if this were true it would mean that a time must finally come when the Universe "unwinds" itself, no energy being available for use. This state is referred to as the "heat death of the Universe." Sarah Boyle begins to cry. She throws a jar of strawberry jam against the stove, enamel chips off and the stove begins to bleed. Bach had twenty children, how many children has Sarah Boyle? Her mouth is open. Her mouth is opening. She turns on the water and fills the sink with detergent. She writes on the kitchen wall, "William Shakespeare has Cancer and lives in California." She writes, "Sugar Frosted Flakes are the Food of the Gods." The water

foams up in the sink, overflowing, bubbling onto the strawberry floor. She is about to begin to cry. Her mouth is opening. She is crying. She cries. How can one ever tell whether there are one or many fish? She begins to break glasses and dishes, she throws cups and cooking pots and jars of food, which shatter and break and spread over the kitchen. The sand keeps falling, very quietly, in the egg timer. The old man and woman in the barometer never catch each other. She picks up eggs and throws them into the air. She begins to cry. She opens her mouth. The eggs arch slowly through the kitchen, like a baseball, hit high against the spring sky, seen from far away. They go higher and higher in the stillness, hesitate at the zenith, then begin to fall away slowly, slowly, through the fine clear air.

ROBERT SILVERBERG
Passengers

• • • •

{1968}

If there is one sf author whose career can be viewed as a microcosm of the genre's development in America during the past forty years, it is probably Robert Silverberg (1935–). Starting out in the world of fandom, Silverberg turned to professional writing during the boom of the mid-1950s, producing hundreds of stories under several pseudonyms for such magazines as *Fantastic* and *Super-Science Fiction*. Most of these were essentially apprentice work, though estimable enough to earn him a 1956 Hugo Award for most promising new writer. When the boom went bust in the late 1950s, Silverberg, like many of that decade's authors, moved on to other literary endeavors, writing mostly nonfiction for juvenile markets and erotica, two disparate fields in which he produced at least two hundred titles during the early 1960s. The mid-1960s paperback boom, coinciding with the advent of the New Wave movement, lured Silverberg back into the genre, and soon he was producing some of the most celebrated sf of the era—novels such as *Thorns* (1967) and *The Book of Skulls* (1972), the stories "Sundance" (1969) and "Born with the Dead" (1974)—as well as editing one of the most memorable anthology series of the period, *New Dimensions*. When the serial novel with quest fantasy elements came to dominate the field in the late 1970s and early 1980s, Silverberg emerged from a brief retirement with the *Majipoor Trilogy* (1980–83). He has continued to publish steadily, his work often reflecting contemporary trends, such as an emphasis on mythic and anthropological themes (*Gilgamesh the King* [1984], *At Winter's End* [1988]) and participation in corporate publishing ventures such as shared-world anthologies (*Time Gate* [1988]) and sharecropper novels (*Nightfall*, with Isaac Asimov [1990]).

"Passengers," which won a Nebula Award for best short story, is one of the most characteristic works of its period, showing how the genre was beginning to adapt its modes of futuristic speculation to countercultural trends. Like Samuel R. Delany's "Aye, and Gomorrah . . ." (1967), it extrapolates current erotic mores, specifically casual sex with strangers, into a near future in which this practice has become the norm. With the unexplained advent of the Passengers, alien psychic symbiotes that temporarily hijack and "ride" human bodies, people find themselves impelled against their will into abrupt and anonymous encounters, brief debauches that leave only hazy memories and a lingering feeling of self-disgust. Silverberg's deployment of a fairly conventional sf trope—the mind parasite that controls human behavior, as in Robert A. Heinlein's 1951 classic *The Puppet Masters*—serves here a largely allegorical and satirical purpose, commenting on the contemporary penchant for promiscuous "hookups" and "one night stands." Indeed, as with much work of the 1960s New Wave, the sf content is more symbolic than literal; Silverberg is not particularly interested in where the Passengers came from or what they want, but rather with what they represent.

There are only fragments of me left now. Chunks of memory have broken free and drifted away like calved glaciers. It is always like that when a Passenger leaves us. We can never be sure of all the things our borrowed bodies did. We have only the lingering traces, the imprints.

Like sand clinging to an ocean-tossed bottle. Like the throbbings of amputated legs.

I rise. I collect myself. My hair is rumpled; I comb it. My face is creased from too little sleep. There is sourness in my mouth. Has my Passenger been eating dung with my mouth? They do that. They do anything.

It is morning.

A gray, uncertain morning. I stare at it awhile, and then, shuddering, I opaque the window and confront instead the gray, uncertain surface of the inner panel. My room looks untidy. Did I have a woman here? There are ashes in the trays. Searching for butts, I find several with lipstick stains. Yes a woman was here.

I touch the bedsheets. Still warm with shared warmth. Both pillows tousled. She has gone, though, and the Passenger is gone, and I am alone.

How long did it last, this time?

I pick up the phone and ring Central. "What is the date?"

The computer's bland feminine voice replies, "Friday, December fourth, nineteen eighty-seven."

"The time?"

"Nine fifty-one, Eastern Standard Time."

"The weather forecast?"

"Predicted temperature, thirty-one. Wind from the north, sixteen miles an hour. Chances of precipitation slight."

"What do you recommend for a hangover?"

"Food or medication?"

"Anything you like," I say.

The computer mulls that one over for a while. Then it decides on both, and activates my kitchen. The spigot yields cold tomato juice. Eggs begin to fry. From the medicine slot comes a purplish liquid. The Central Computer is always so thoughtful. Do the Passengers ever ride it, I wonder? What thrills could that hold for them? Surely it must be more exciting to borrow the million minds of Central than to live awhile in the faulty, short-circuited soul of a corroding human being!

December fourth, Central said. Friday. So the Passenger had me for three nights.

I drink the purplish stuff and probe my memories in a gingerly way, as one might probe a festering sore.

I remember Tuesday morning. A bad time at work. None of the charts will come out right. The section manager irritable; he has been taken by Passengers three times in five weeks, and his section is in disarray as a result, and his Christmas bonus is jeopardized. Even though it is customary not to penalize a person for lapses due to Passengers, according to the system, the section manager seems to feel he will be treated unfairly. So he treats us unfairly. We have a hard time. Revise the charts, fiddle with the program, check the fundamentals ten times over. Out they come: the detailed forecasts for price variations of public utility securities, February—April 1988. That afternoon we are to meet and discuss the charts and what they tell us.

I do not remember Tuesday afternoon.

That must have been when the Passenger took me. Perhaps at work; perhaps in the mahogany-paneled boardroom itself, during the conference. Pink concerned faces all about me; I cough, I lurch, I stumble from my seat. They shake their heads sadly. No one reaches for me. No one stops me. It is too dangerous to interfere with one who has a Passenger. The chances are great that a second Passenger lurks nearby in the discorporate state looking for a mount. So I am avoided. I leave the building.

After that, what?

Sitting in my room on a bleak Friday morning, I eat my scrambled eggs and try to reconstruct the three lost nights.

Of course it is impossible. The conscious mind functions during the period of captivity, but upon withdrawal of the Passenger nearly every recollection goes too. There is only a slight residue, a gritty film of faint and ghostly memories. The mount is never precisely the same person afterwards; though he cannot recall the details of his experience, he is subtly changed by it.

I try to recall.

A girl? Yes: lipstick on the butts. Sex, then, here in my room. Young? Old? Blonde? Dark? Everything is hazy. How did my borrowed body behave? Was I a good lover? I try to be, when I am myself. I keep in shape. At 38, I can handle three sets of tennis on a summer afternoon without collapsing. I can make a woman glow as a woman is meant to glow. Not boasting: just categorizing. We have our skills. These are mine.

But Passengers, I am told, take wry amusement in controverting our skills. So would it have given my rider a kind of delight to find me a woman and force me to fail repeatedly with her?

I dislike that thought.

The fog is going from my mind now. The medicine prescribed by Central works rapidly. I eat, I shave, I stand under the vibrator until my skin is clean. I do my exercises. Did the Passenger exercise my body Wednesday and Thursday morning? Probably not. I must make up for that. I am close to middle age, now; tonus lost is not easily regained.

I touch my toes twenty times, knees stiff.

I kick my legs in the air.

I lie flat and lift myself on pumping elbows.

The body responds, maltreated though it has been. It is the first bright moment of my awakening: to feel the inner tingling, to know that I still have vigor.

Fresh air is what I want next. Quickly I slip into my clothes and leave. There is no need for me to report to work today. They are aware that since Tuesday afternoon I have had a Passenger; they need not be aware that before dawn on Friday the Passenger departed. I will have a free day. I will walk the city's streets, stretching my limbs, repaying my body for the abuse it has suffered.

I enter the elevator. I drop fifty stories to the ground. I step out into the December dreariness.

The towers of New York rise about me.

In the street the cars stream forward. Drivers sit edgily at their wheels. One never knows when the driver of a nearby car will be borrowed, and there is always a moment of lapsed coordination as the Passenger takes over. Many lives are lost that way on our streets and highways; but never the life of a Passenger.

I begin to walk without purpose. I cross Fourteenth Street, heading north, listening to the soft violent purr of the electric engines. I see a boy jigging in the street and know he is being ridden. At Fifth and Twenty-second a prosperous-looking paunchy man approaches; his necktie askew, this morning's *Wall Street Journal* jutting from an overcoat pocket. He giggles.

He thrusts out his tongue. Ridden. Ridden. I avoid him. Moving briskly, I come to the underpass that carries traffic below Thirty-fourth Street toward Queens, and pause for a moment to watch two adolescent girls quarreling at the rim of the pedestrian walk. One is a Negro. Her eyes are rolling in terror. The other pushes her closer to the railing. Ridden. But the Passenger does not have murder on its mind, merely pleasure. The Negro girl is released and falls in a huddled heap, trembling. Then she rises and runs. The other girl draws a long strand of gleaming hair into her mouth, chews on it, seems to awaken. She looks dazed.

I avert my eyes. One does not watch while a fellow sufferer is awakening. There is a morality of the ridden; we have so many new tribal mores in these dark days.

I hurry on.

Where am I going so hurriedly? Already I have walked more than a mile. I seem to be moving toward some goal, as though my Passenger still hunches in my skull, urging me about. But I know that is not so. For the moment, at least, I am free.

Can I be sure of that?

Cogito ergo sum no longer applies. We go on thinking even while we are ridden, and we live in quiet desperation, unable to halt our courses no matter how ghastly, no matter how self-destructive. I am certain that I can distinguish between the condition of bearing a Passenger and the condition of being free. But perhaps not. Perhaps I bear a particularly devilish Passenger which has not quitted me at all, but which merely has receded to the cerebellum, leaving me the illusion of freedom while all the time surreptitiously driving me onward to some purpose of its own.

Did we ever have more than that: the illusion of freedom?

But this is disturbing, the thought that I may be ridden without realizing it. I burst out in heavy perspiration, not merely from the exertion of walking. Stop. Stop here. Why must you walk? You are at Forty-second Street. There is the library. Nothing forces you onward. Stop a while, I tell myself. Rest on the library steps.

I sit on the cold stone and tell myself that I have made this decision for myself.

Have I? It is the old problem, free will versus determinism, translated into the foulest of forms. Determinism is no longer a philosopher's abstraction; it is cold alien tendrils sliding between the cranial sutures. The Passengers arrived three years ago. I have been ridden five times since then. Our world is quite different now. But we have adjusted even to this. We have adjusted. We have our mores. Life goes on. Our governments rule, our legislatures meet, our stock exchanges transact business as usual, and we have methods for compensating for the random havoc. It is the only way. What else can we do? Shrivel in defeat? We have an enemy we cannot fight; at best we can resist through endurance. So we endure.

The stone steps are cold against my body. In December few people sit here.

I tell myself that I made this long walk of my own free will, that I halted of my own free will, that no Passenger rides my brain now. Perhaps. Perhaps. I cannot let myself believe that I am not free.

Can it be, I wonder, that the Passenger left some lingering command in me? Walk to this place, halt at this place? That is possible too.

I look about me at the others on the library steps.

An old man, eyes vacant, sitting on newspaper. A boy of thirteen or so with flaring nostrils. A plump woman. Are all of them ridden? Passengers seem to cluster about me today. The more I study the ridden ones, the more convinced I become that I am, for the moment, free. The last time, I had three months of freedom between rides. Some people, they say, are scarcely ever free. Their bodies are in great demand, and they know only scattered bursts of freedom, a day here, a week there, an hour. We have never been able to determine how many Passengers infest our world. Millions, maybe. Or maybe five. Who can tell?

A wisp of snow curls down out of the gray sky. Central had said the chance of precipitation was slight. Are they riding Central this morning too?

I see the girl.

She sits diagonally across from me, five steps up and a hundred feet away, her black skirt pulled up on her knees to reveal handsome legs. She is young. Her hair is deep, rich auburn. Her eyes are pale; at this distance, I cannot make out the precise color. She is dressed simply. She is younger than thirty. She wears a dark green coat and her lipstick has a purplish tinge. Her lips are full, her nose slender, high-bridged, her eyebrows carefully plucked.

I know her.

I have spent the past three nights with her in my room. She is the one. Ridden, she came to me, and ridden, I slept with her. I am certain of this. The veil of memory opens; I see her slim body naked on my bed.

How can it be that I remember this?

It is too strong to be an illusion. Clearly this is something that I have been *permitted* to remember for reasons I cannot comprehend. And I remember more. I remember her soft gasping sounds of pleasure. I know that my own body did not betray me those three nights, nor did I fail her need.

And there is more. A memory of sinuous music; a scent of youth in her hair; the rustle of winter trees. Somehow she brings back to me a time of innocence, a time when I am young and girls are mysterious, a time of parties and dances and warmth and secrets.

I am drawn to her now.

There is an etiquette about such things, too. It is in poor taste to approach someone you have met while being ridden. Such an encounter gives you no privilege; a stranger remains a stranger, no matter what you and she may have done and said during your involuntary time together.

Yet I am drawn to her.

Why this violation of taboo? Why this raw breach of etiquette? I have never done this before. I have been scrupulous.

But I get to my feet and walk along the step on which I have been sitting, until I am below her, and I look up, and automatically she folds her ankles together and angles her knees as if in awareness that her position is not a modest one. I know from that gesture that she is not ridden now. My eyes meet hers. Her eyes are hazy green. She is beautiful, and I rack my memory for more details of our passion.

I climb step by step until I stand before her.

"Hello," I say.

She gives me a neutral look. She does not seem to recognize me. Her eyes are veiled, as one's eyes often are, just after the Passenger has gone. She purses her lips and appraises me in a distant way.

"Hello," she replies coolly. "I don't think I know you."

"No. You don't. But I have the feeling you don't want to be alone just now. And I know I don't." I try to persuade her with my eyes that my motives are decent. "There's snow in the air," I say. "We can find a warmer place. I'd like to talk to you."

"About what?"

"Let's go elsewhere, and I'll tell you. I'm Charles Roth."

"Helen Martin."

She gets to her feet. She still has not cast aside her cool neutrality; she is suspicious, ill at ease. But at least she is willing to go with me. A good sign.

"Is it too early in the day for a drink?" I ask.

"I'm not sure. I hardly know what time it is."

"Before noon."

"Let's have a drink anyway," she says, and we both smile.

We go to a cocktail lounge across the street. Sitting face to face in the darkness, we sip drinks, daiquiri for her, bloody mary for me. She relaxes a little. I ask myself what it is I want from her. The pleasure of her company, yes. Her company in bed? But I have already had that pleasure, three nights of it, though she does not know that. I want something more. Something more. What?

Her eyes are bloodshot. She has had little sleep these past three nights.

I say, "Was it very unpleasant for you?"

"What?"

"The Passenger."

A whiplash of reaction crosses her face. "How did you know I've had a Passenger?"

"I know."

"We aren't supposed to talk about it."

"I'm broadminded," I tell her. "My Passenger left me some time during the night. I was ridden since Tuesday afternoon."

"Mine left me about two hours ago, I think." Her cheeks color. She is doing something daring, talking like this. "I was ridden since Monday night. This was my fifth time."

"Mine also."

We toy with our drinks. Rapport is growing, almost without the need of words. Our recent experiences with Passengers give us something in common, although Helen does not realize how intimately we shared those experiences.

We talk. She is a designer of display windows. She has a small apartment several blocks from here. She lives alone. She asks me what I do. "Securities analyst," I tell her. She smiles. Her teeth are flawless. We have a second round of drinks. I am positive, now, that this is the girl who was in my room while I was ridden.

A seed of hope grows in me. It was a happy chance that brought us together again, so soon after we parted as dreamers. A happy chance, too, that some vestige of the dream lingered in my mind.

We have shared something, who knows what, and it must have been good to leave such a vivid imprint on me, and now I want to come to her conscious, aware, my own master, and renew that relationship, making it a real one this time. It is not proper, for I am trespassing on a privilege that is not mine except by virtue of our Passenger's brief presence in us. Yet I need her. I want her.

She seems to need me, too, without realizing who I am. But fear holds her back.

I am frightened of frightening her, and I do not try to press my advantage too quickly. Perhaps she would take me to her apartment with her now, perhaps not, but I do not ask. We finish our drinks. We arrange to meet by the library steps again tomorrow. My hand momentarily brushes hers. Then she is gone.

I fill three ashtrays that night. Over and over I debate the wisdom of what I am doing. But why not leave her alone? I have no right to follow her. In the place our world has become, we are wisest to remain apart.

And yet—there is that stab of half-memory when I think of her. The blurred lights of lost chances behind the stairs, of girlish laughter in second-floor corridors, of stolen kisses, of tea and cake. I remember the girl with the orchid in her hair, and the one in the spangled dress, and the one with the child's face and the woman's eyes, all so long ago, all lost, all gone, and I tell myself that this one I will not lose, I will not permit her to be taken from me.

Morning comes, a quiet Saturday. I return to the library, hardly expecting to find her there, but she is there, on the steps, and the sight of her is like a reprieve. She looks wary, troubled; obviously she has done much thinking, little sleeping. Together we walk along Fifth Avenue. She is quite close to me, but she does not take my arm. Her steps are brisk, short, nervous.

I want to suggest that we go to her apartment instead of to the cocktail lounge. In these days we must move swiftly while we are free. But I know it would be a mistake to think of this as a matter of tactics. Coarse haste would be fatal, bringing me perhaps an ordinary victory, a numbing defeat within it. In any event her mood hardly seems promising. I look at her, thinking of string music and new snowfalls, and she looks toward the gray sky.

She says, "I can feel them watching me all the time. Like vultures swooping overhead, waiting, waiting. Ready to pounce."

"But there's a way of beating them. We can grab little scraps of life when they're not looking."

"They're *always* looking."

"No," I tell her. "There can't be enough of them for that. Sometimes they're looking the other way. And while they are, two people can come together and try to share warmth."

"But what's the use?"

"You're too pessimistic, Helen. They ignore us for months at a time. We have a chance. We have a chance."

But I cannot break through her shell of fear. She is paralyzed by the nearness of the Passengers, unwilling to begin anything for fear it will be snatched away by our tormentors. We reach the building where she lives, and I hope she will relent and invite me in. For an instant she wavers, but only for an instant: she takes my hand in both of hers, and smiles, and the smile fades, and she is gone, leaving me only with the words, "Let's meet at the library again tomorrow. Noon."

I make the long chilling walk home alone.

Some of her pessimism seeps into me that night. It seems futile for us to try to salvage anything. More than that: wicked for me to seek her out, shameful to offer a hesitant love when I am not free. In this world, I tell myself, we should keep well clear of others, so that we do not harm anyone when we are seized and ridden.

I do not go to meet her in the morning.

It is best this way, I insist. I have no business trifling with her. I imagine her at the library, wondering why I am late, growing tense, impatient, then annoyed. She will be angry with me for breaking our date, but her anger will ebb, and she will forget me quickly enough.

Monday comes. I return to work.

Naturally, no one discusses my absence. It is as though I have never been away. The market is strong that morning. The work is challenging; it is mid-morning before I think of Helen at all. But once I think of her, I can think of nothing else. My cowardice in standing her up. The childishness of Saturday night's dark thoughts. Why accept fate so passively? Why give in? I want to fight, now, to carve out a pocket of security despite the odds. I feel a deep conviction that it can be done. The Passengers may never bother the two of us again, after all. And that flickering smile of hers outside her building Saturday, that momentary glow—it should have told me that behind her wall of fear she felt the same hopes. She was waiting for me to lead the way. And I stayed home instead.

At lunchtime I go to the library, convinced it is futile.

But she is there. She paces along the steps; the wind slices at her slender figure. I go to her.

She is silent a moment. "Hello," she says finally.

"I'm sorry about yesterday."

"I waited a long time for you."

I shrug. "I made up my mind that it was no use to come. But then I changed my mind again."

She tries to look angry. But I know she is pleased to see me again—else why did she come here today? She cannot hide her inner pleasure. Nor can I. I point across the street to the cocktail lounge.

"A daiquiri?" I say. "As a peace offering?'

"All right."

Today the lounge is crowded, but we find a booth somehow. There is a brightness in her eyes that I have not seen before. I sense that a barrier is crumbling within her.

"You're less afraid of me, Helen," I say.

"I've never been afraid of you. I'm afraid of what could happen if we take the risks."

"Don't be. Don't be."

"I'm trying not to be afraid. But sometimes it seems so hopeless. Since *they* came here—"

"We can still try to live our own lives."

"Maybe."

"We have to. Let's make a pact, Helen. No more gloom. No more worrying about the terrible things that might just maybe happen. All right?"

A pause. Then a cool hand against mine.

"All right."

We finish our drinks, and I present my Credit Central to pay for them, and we go outside. I want her to tell me to forget about this afternoon's work and come home with her. It is inevitable, now, that she will ask me, and better sooner than later.

We walk a block. She does not offer the invitation. I sense the struggle inside her, and I wait, letting that struggle reach its own resolution without interference from me. We walk a second block. Her arm is through mine, but she talks only of her work, of the weather, and it is a remote, arm's-length conversation. At the next corner she swings around, away from her apartment, back toward the cocktail lounge. I try to be patient with her.

I have no need to rush things now, I tell myself. Her body is not a secret to me. We have begun our relationship topsy-turvy, with the physical part first; now it will take time to work backward to the more difficult part that some people call love.

But of course she is not aware that we have known each other that way. The wind blows swirling snowflakes in our faces, and somehow the cold sting awakens honesty in me. I know what I must say. I must relinquish my unfair advantage.

I tell her, "While I was ridden last week, Helen, I had a girl in my room."

"Why talk of such things now?"

"I have to, Helen. You were the girl."

She halts. She turns to me. People hurry past us in the street. Her face is very pale, with dark red spots growing in her cheeks.

"That's not funny, Charles."

"It wasn't meant to be. You were with me from Tuesday night to early Friday morning."

"How can you possibly know that?"

"I do. I do. The memory is clear. Somehow it remains, Helen. I see your whole body."

"Stop it, Charles."

"We were very good together," I say. "We must have pleased our Passengers because we were so good. To see you again—it was like waking from a dream, and finding that the dream was real, the girl right there—"

"No!"

"Let's go to your apartment and begin again."

She says, "You're being deliberately filthy, and I don't know why, but there wasn't any reason for you to spoil things. Maybe I was with you and maybe I wasn't, but you wouldn't know it, and if you did know it you should keep your mouth shut about it, and—"

"You have a birthmark the size of a dime," I say, "about three inches below your left breast."

She sobs and hurls herself at me, there in the street. Her long silvery nails assail me. No one pays attention; those who pass by assume we are ridden, and turn their heads. She is all fury, but I have my arms around hers like metal bands, so that she can only stamp and snort, and her body is close against mine. She is rigid, anguished.

In a low, urgent voice I say, "We'll defeat them, Helen. We'll finish what they started. Don't fight me. There's no reason to fight me. I know, it's a fluke that I remember you, but let me go with you and I'll prove that we belong together."

"Let—go—"

"Please. Please. Why should we be enemies? I don't mean you any harm. I love you, Helen. Do you remember, when we were kids, we could play at being in love? I did; you must have done it too. Sixteen, seventeen years old. The whispers, the conspiracies—all a big game, and we knew it. But the game's over. We can't afford to tease and run. We have so little time, when we're free—we have to trust, to open ourselves—"

"It's wrong."

"No. Just because it's the stupid custom for two people brought together by Passengers to avoid one another, that doesn't mean we have to follow it. Helen—Helen—"

Something in my tone registers with her. She ceases to struggle. Her rigid body softens. She looks up at me, her tear-streaked face thawing, her eyes blurred.

"Trust me," I say. "Trust me, Helen!"

She hesitates. Then she smiles.

In that moment I feel the chill at the back of my skull, the sensation as of a steel needle driven deep through bone. I stiffen. My arms drop away from her. For an instant, I lose touch, and when the mists clear all is different.

"Charles?" she says. "*Charles?*"

Her knuckles are against her teeth. I turn, ignoring her, and go back into the cocktail lounge. A young man sits in one of the front booths. His dark hair gleams with pomade; his cheeks are smooth. His eyes meet mine.

I sit down. He orders drinks. We do not talk.

My hand falls on his wrist, and remains there. The bartender, serving the drinks, scowls but says nothing. We sip our cocktails and put the drained glasses down.

"Let's go," the young man says.

I follow him out.

Brian W. ALDISS

Super-Toys Last All Summer Long

• • • •

{1969}

Brian W. Aldiss (1925–) is one of England's most prolific and respected writers. As well as his extensive output in science fiction and fantasy, he has published mainstream fiction, autobiography, drama, poetry, history, and literary criticism. As a member of the Royal Corps of Signals during World War II, Aldiss was posted to various locations in the Far East, including Burma, India, Sumatra, and Hong Kong, which later provided material for a number of his novels and stories. The impact and influence of his more than fifty years as a writer have been recognized by many awards: he received the Science Fiction Research Association's Pilgrim Award in 1978 for his extensive contributions to the study of science fiction; in 1989 he was named a Fellow of the Royal Society of Literature; and in 2000 he was named a Grand Master by the Science Fiction Writers of America, the same year in which he was awarded the Order of the British Empire "for services to literature."

Aldiss is the author of *Billion Year Spree* (1973; updated in 1986, with David Wingrove, as *Trillion Year Spree*), one of the most significant histories of the field written to date. In it he defines science fiction as "the search for a definition of man and his status in the universe which will stand in our advanced but confused state of knowledge (science), and is characteristically cast in the Gothic or post-Gothic mould." *Billion Year Spree* made an influential argument for Mary Shelley's *Frankenstein* (1818) as the "originary" sf novel, a position that continues to spark much lively debate.

It is almost impossible to suggest the scope and diversity of Aldiss's science fiction, which includes classic disaster novels such as *Hothouse* (1962) and *Greybeard* (1964); exemplary New Wave fictions such as *Report on Probability A* (1968) and *Barefoot in the Head* (1969); lovingly (re)constructed pastiches of early progenitor texts including *Frankenstein Unbound* (1973) and *Moreau's Other Island* (1980); epic planetary world-building such as the *Helliconia Trilogy* (1982–85)—and the list goes on. He has also published hundreds of short stories. The best of his several volumes of autobiography, *The Twinkling of an Eye, or My Life as an*

Englishman, appeared in 1995. His latest novel at the time of writing is *Harm* (2007), which is set in a near-future dystopia; in 2008, he published his first full-length collection of poetry, *A Prehistory of Mind*.

"Super-Toys Last All Summer Long" is one of Aldiss's best-known short stories, not least because it provided the basis for the film *A.I.: Artificial Intelligence* (2001). This was the last project undertaken by British auteur-director Stanley Kubrick, perhaps best known for the sf masterpiece *2001: A Space Odyssey* (1968). When Kubrick died before filming began on *A.I.*, it was completed by quintessential American director Steven Spielberg. Unsurprisingly, Spielberg's sprawling sf epic bears little resemblance to Aldiss's delicately spare parable. "Supertoys" is set in an overpopulated future where technological simulation has become a key strategy for coping with unbearable loneliness. The story dramatizes what has become an increasingly familiar conundrum in contemporary techno-culture, addressed in stories such as Philip K. Dick's "We Can Remember It for You Wholesale" (1966) and Pat Cadigan's "Pretty Boy Crossover" (1986). In protagonist David's words, "How do you tell what are real things from what aren't real things?"

In Mrs. Swinton's garden, it was always summer. The lovely almond trees stood about it in perpetual leaf. Monica Swinton plucked a saffron-colored rose and showed it to David.

"Isn't it lovely?" she said.

David looked up at her and grinned without replying. Seizing the flower, he ran with it across the lawn and disappeared behind the kennel where the mowervator crouched, ready to cut or sweep or roll when the moment dictated. She stood alone on her impeccable plastic gravel path.

She had tried to love him.

When she made up her mind to follow the boy, she found him in the courtyard floating the rose in his paddling pool. He stood in the pool engrossed, still wearing his sandals.

"David, darling, do you have to be so awful? Come in at once and change your shoes and socks."

He went with her without protest into the house, his dark head bobbing at the level of her waist. At the age of three, he showed no fear of the ultrasonic dryer in the kitchen. But before his mother could reach for a pair of slippers, he wriggled away and was gone into the silence of the house.

He would probably be looking for Teddy.

Monica Swinton, twenty-nine, of graceful shape and lambent eye, went and sat in her living room, arranging her limbs with taste. She began by sitting and thinking; soon she was just sitting. Time waited on her shoulder with the manic sloth it reserves for children, the insane, and wives whose husbands are away improving the world. Almost by reflex, she reached out and changed the wavelength of her windows. The garden faded; in its place, the city center rose by her left hand, full of crowding people, blowboats, and buildings (but she kept the sound down). She remained alone. An overcrowded world is the ideal place in which to be lonely.

The directors of Synthank were eating an enormous luncheon to celebrate the launching of their new product. Some of them wore the plastic facemasks popular at the time. All were elegantly slender, despite the rich food and drink they were putting away. Their wives were elegantly slender, despite the food and drink they too were putting away. An earlier and less sophisticated generation would have regarded them as beautiful people, apart from their eyes.

Henry Swinton, Managing Director of Synthank, was about to make a speech.

"I'm sorry your wife couldn't be with us to hear you," his neighbor said.

"Monica prefers to stay at home thinking beautiful thoughts," said Swinton, maintaining a smile.

"One would expect such a beautiful woman to have beautiful thoughts," said the neighbor.

Take your mind off my wife, you bastard, thought Swinton, still smiling.

He rose to make his speech amid applause.

After a couple of jokes, he said, "Today marks a real breakthrough for the company. It is now almost ten years since we put our first synthetic lifeforms on the world market. You all know what a success they have been, particularly the miniature dinosaurs. But none of them had intelligence.

"It seems like a paradox that in this day and age we can create life but not intelligence. Our first selling line, the Crosswell Tape, sells best of all, and is the most stupid of all." Everyone laughed.

"Though three-quarters of the overcrowded world are starving, we are lucky here to have more than enough, thanks to population control. Obesity's our problem, not malnutrition. I guess there's nobody round this table who doesn't have a Crosswell working for him in the small intestine, a perfectly safe parasite tape-worm that enables its host to eat up to fifty per cent more food and still keep his or her figure. Right?" General nods of agreement.

"Our miniature dinosaurs are almost equally stupid. Today, we launch an intelligent synthetic life-form—a full-size serving-man.

"Not only does he have intelligence, he has a controlled amount of intelligence. We believe people would be afraid of a being with a human brain. Our serving-man has a small computer in his cranium.

"There have been mechanicals on the market with mini-computers for brains—plastic things without life, super-toys—but we have at last found a way to link computer circuitry with synthetic flesh."

David sat by the long window of his nursery, wrestling with paper and pencil. Finally, he stopped writing and began to roll the pencil up and down the slope of the desk-lid.

"Teddy!" he said.

Teddy lay on the bed against the wall, under a book with moving pictures and a giant plastic soldier. The speech-pattern of his master's voice activated him and he sat up.

"Teddy, I can't think what to say!"

Climbing off the bed, the bear walked stiffly over to cling to the boy's leg. David lifted him and set him on the desk.

"What have you said so far?"

"I've said—" He picked up his letter and stared hard at it. "I've said, 'Dear Mummy, I hope you're well just now. I love you. . . .'"

There was a long silence, until the bear said, "That sounds fine. Go downstairs and give it to her."

Another long silence.

"It isn't quite right. She won't understand."

Inside the bear, a small computer worked through its program of possibilities. "Why not do it again in crayon?"

When David did not answer, the bear repeated his suggestion. "Why not do it again in crayon?"

David was staring out of the window. "Teddy, you know what I was thinking? How do you tell what are real things from what aren't real things?"

The bear shuffled its alternatives. "Real things are good."

"I wonder if time is good. I don't think Mummy *likes* time very much. The other day, lots of days ago, she said that time went by her. Is time real, Teddy?"

"Clocks tell the time. Clocks are real. Mummy has clocks so she must like them. She has a clock on her wrist next to her dial."

David started to draw a jumbo jet on the back of his letter. "You and I are real, Teddy, aren't we?"

The bear's eyes regarded the boy unflinchingly. "You and I are real, David." It specialized in comfort.

Monica walked slowly about the house. It was almost time for the afternoon post to come over the wire. She punched the Post Office number on the dial on her wrist but nothing came through. A few minutes more.

She could take up her painting. Or she could dial her friends. Or she could wait till Henry came home. Or she could go up and play with David. . . .

She walked out into the hall and to the bottom of the stairs.

"David!"

No answer. She called again and a third time.

"Teddy!" she called, in sharper tones.

"Yes, Mummy!" After a moment's pause, Teddy's head of golden fur appeared at the top of the stairs.

"Is David in his room, Teddy?"

"David went into the garden, Mummy."

"Come down here, Teddy!"

She stood impassively, watching the little furry figure as it climbed down from step to step on its stubby limbs. When it reached the bottom, she picked it up and carried it into the living room. It lay unmoving in her arms, staring up at her. She could feel just the slightest vibration from its motor.

"Stand there, Teddy. I want to talk to you." She set him down on a tabletop, and he stood as she requested, arms set forward and open in the eternal gesture of embrace.

"Teddy, did David tell you to tell me he had gone into the garden?"

The circuits of the bear's brain were too simple for artifice. "Yes, Mummy."

"So you lied to me."

"Yes, Mummy."

"*Stop* calling me Mummy! Why is David avoiding me? He's not afraid of me, is he?"

"No. He loves you."

"Why can't we communicate?"

"David's upstairs."

The answer stopped her dead. Why waste time talking to this machine? Why not simply go upstairs and scoop David into her arms and talk to him, as a loving mother should to a loving son? She heard the sheer weight of silence in the house, with a different quality of silence pouring out of every room. On the upper landing, something was moving very silently—David, trying to hide away from her. . . .

He was nearing the end of his speech now. The guests were attentive; so was the Press, lining two walls of the banqueting chamber, recording Henry's words and occasionally photographing him.

"Our serving-man will be, in many senses, a product of the computer. Without computers, we could never have worked through the sophisticated biochemics that go into synthetic flesh. The serving-man will also be an extension of the computer—for he will contain a computer in his own head, a microminiaturized computer capable of dealing with almost any situation he may encounter in the home. With reservations, of course." Laughter at this; many of those present knew the heated debate that had engulfed the Synthank boardroom before the decision had finally been taken to leave the serving-man neuter under his flawless uniform.

"Amid all the triumphs of our civilization—yes, and amid the crushing problems of overpopulation too—it is sad to reflect how many millions of people suffer from increasing loneliness and isolation. Our serving-man will be a boon to them; he will always answer, and the most vapid conversation cannot bore him.

"For the future, we plan more models, male and female—some of them without the limitations of this first one, I promise you!—of more advanced design, true bio-electronic beings.

"Not only will they possess their own computers, capable of individual programming; they will be linked to the World Data Network. Thus everyone will be able to enjoy the equivalent of an Einstein in their own homes. Personal isolation will then be banished forever!"

He sat down to enthusiastic applause. Even the synthetic serving-man, sitting at the table dressed in an unostentatious suit, applauded with gusto.

Dragging his satchel, David crept round the side of the house. He climbed on to the ornamental seat under the living-room window and peeped cautiously in.

His mother stood in the middle of the room. Her face was blank; its lack of expression scared him. He watched fascinated. He did not move; she did not move. Time might have stopped, as it had stopped in the garden.

At last she turned and left the room. After waiting a moment, David tapped on the window. Teddy looked round, saw him, tumbled off the table, and came over to the window. Fumbling with his paws, he eventually got it open.

They looked at each other.

"I'm no good, Teddy. Let's run away!"

"You're a very good boy. Your Mummy loves you."

Slowly, he shook his head. "If she loved me, then why can't I talk to her?"

"You're being silly, David. Mummy's lonely. That's why she had you."

"She's got Daddy. I've got nobody 'cept you, and I'm lonely."

Teddy gave him a friendly cuff over the head. "If you feel so bad, you'd better go to the psychiatrist again."

"I hate that old psychiatrist—he makes me feel I'm not real." He started to run across the lawn. The bear toppled out of the window and followed as fast as its stubby legs would allow.

Monica Swinton was up in the nursery. She called to her son once and then stood there, undecided. All was silent.

Crayons lay on his desk. Obeying a sudden impulse, she went over to the desk and opened it. Dozens of pieces of paper lay inside. Many of them were written in crayon in David's clumsy writing, with each letter picked out in a color different from the letter preceding it. None of the messages was finished.

MY DEAR MUMMY, HOW ARE YOU REALLY, DO YOU LOVE ME AS MUCH—

DEAR MUMMY, I LOVE YOU AND DADDY AND THE SUN IS SHINING—

DEAR DEAR MUMMY, TEDDY'S HELPING ME WRITE TO YOU. I LOVE YOU AND TEDDY—

DARLING MUMMY, I'M YOUR ONE AND ONLY SON AND I LOVE YOU SO MUCH THAT SOME TIMES—

DEAR MUMMY, YOU'RE REALLY MY MUMMY AND I HATE TEDDY—

DARLING MUMMY, GUESS HOW MUCH I LOVE—

DEAR MUMMY, I'M YOUR LITTLE BOY NOT TEDDY AND I LOVE YOU BUT TEDDY—

DEAR MUMMY, THIS IS A LETTER TO YOU JUST TO SAY HOW MUCH HOW EVER SO MUCH—

Monica dropped the pieces of paper and burst out crying. In their gay inaccurate colors, the letters fanned out and settled on the floor.

Henry Swinton caught the express home in high spirits, and occasionally said a word to the synthetic serving-man he was taking home with him. The serving-man answered politely and punctually, although his answers were not always entirely relevant by human standards.

The Swintons lived in one of the ritziest city-blocks, half a kilometer above the ground. Embedded in other apartments, their apartment had no windows to the outside; nobody wanted to see the overcrowded external world. Henry unlocked the door with his retina pattern-scanner and walked in, followed by the serving-man.

At once, Henry was surrounded by the friendly illusion of gardens set in eternal summer. It was amazing what Whologram could do to create huge mirages in small spaces. Behind its roses and wisteria stood their house; the deception was complete: a Georgian mansion appeared to welcome him.

"How do you like it?" he asked the serving-man.

"Roses occasionally suffer from black spot."

"These roses are guaranteed free from any imperfections."

"It is always advisable to purchase goods with guarantees, even if they cost slightly more."

"Thanks for the information," Henry said dryly. Synthetic life-forms were less than ten years old, the old android mechanicals less than sixteen; the faults of their systems were still being ironed out, year by year.

He opened the door and called to Monica.

She came out of the sitting-room immediately and flung her arms round him, kissing him ardently on cheek and lips. Henry was amazed.

Pulling back to look at her face, he saw how she seemed to generate light and beauty. It was months since he had seen her so excited. Instinctively, he clasped her tighter.

"Darling, what's happened?"

"Henry, Henry—oh, my darling, I was in despair. . . . But I've just dialed the afternoon post and—you'll never believe it! Oh, it's wonderful!"

"For heaven's sake, woman, what's wonderful?"

He caught a glimpse of the heading on the photostat in her hand, still moist from the wall-receiver: Ministry of Population. He felt the color drain from his face in sudden shock and hope.

"Monica . . . oh . . . Don't tell me our number's come up!"

"Yes, my darling, yes, we've won this week's parenthood lottery! We can go ahead and conceive a child at once!"

He let out a yell of joy. They danced round the room. Pressure of population was such that reproduction had to be strictly controlled. Childbirth required government permission. For this moment, they had waited four years. Incoherently they cried their delight.

They paused at last, gasping, and stood in the middle of the room to laugh at each other's happiness. When she had come down from the nursery, Monica had de-opaqued the windows, so that they now revealed the vista of garden beyond. Artificial sunlight was growing long and golden across the lawn—and David and Teddy were staring through the window at them.

Seeing their faces, Henry and his wife grew serious.

"What do we do about *them*?" Henry asked.

"Teddy's no trouble. He works well."

"Is David malfunctioning?"

"His verbal communication-center is still giving trouble. I think he'll have to go back to the factory again."

"Okay. We'll see how he does before the baby's born. Which reminds me—*I* have a surprise for you: help just when help is needed! Come into the hall and see what I've got."

As the two adults disappeared from the room, boy and bear sat down beneath the standard roses.

"Teddy—I suppose Mummy and Daddy are real, aren't they?"

Teddy said, "You ask such silly questions, David. Nobody knows what 'real' really means. Let's go indoors."

"First I'm going to have another rose!" Plucking a bright pink flower, he carried it with him into the house. It could lie on the pillow as he went to sleep. Its beauty and softness reminded him of Mummy.

URSULA K. LE GUIN
Nine Lives

• • • •

{1969}

The spare, measured eloquence of Ursula K(roeber) Le Guin's sf has led many a skeptic to acknowledge the genre's higher possibilities. She was born in 1929 in Berkeley, California, youngest child of Theodora Brown Kroeber, a psychologist and author, and Alfred L. Kroeber, an anthropologist. While teaching at the University of California, Berkeley, Kroeber intervened in 1911 in the fate of Ishi (d. 1916), last of California's Yahi tribe, who was later memorialized by Theodora Kroeber in *Ishi in Two Worlds* (1964). Given her family history, it is not surprising that Le Guin's sf so often includes detailed field reports about the legends, taboos, naming practices, marriage customs, and kinship systems of other worlds. Her most fully engaged anthropological novel is *Always Coming Home* (1985), in which long-vanished California tribal customs are displaced to a far future.

Le Guin resists the sf genre's frequent emphasis on intergalactic clashes between alien entities, often focusing instead, as in *The Dispossessed* (1974), on estranged but closely related worlds. Her "Hainish" universe, setting of five sf novels, contains no true aliens, having been seeded with life by a human-like group (from "Hain," not Earth). Le Guin's heroes are tolerant and insightful, responding to conflict with new efforts to resolve hostilities. In *The Left Hand of Darkness* (1969), a Terran travels to a recently discovered world, unique because its people have a capacity to become either sex. The novel's co-heroes, an Earth envoy and an androgynous Gethenian courtier and power-broker, gradually develop a telepathic bond that signifies their successful negotiation of biological, temperamental, and cultural differences. *The Left Hand of Darkness* broke new ground, creating an audience for the subsequent explosion of feminist sf during the 1970s. *The Dispossessed* (1974), which like *The Left Hand of Darkness* won both the Hugo and Nebula Awards, turns to the politicization of science, describing the life of Shevek, a troubled genius reminiscent of nuclear physicist J. Robert Oppenheimer, a Berkeley colleague of Le Guin's father. Shevek, like Therem Harth in *The Left Hand of Darkness*, struggles *against* instinctive loyalty to a home-world that has never appreciated him, finally giving away his breakthrough "theory of simultaneity" so that no single world can exploit it.

Le Guin holds degrees in romance languages from Radcliffe College and Columbia University, where her master's thesis concerned Pierre de Ronsard (1524–85), a humanist and poet. In a talk about her haunting of the foreign-languages room of the Berkeley Public Library when she was in high school, she recalled in 1997 that "I lived there, crouched in a spiderwebby window. . . . That's when I learned you can read a language that you don't know if you love it enough." Memorable languages, such as the rich Karhidish of *The Left Hand of Darkness*, are an important element in Le Guin's evocation of planetary cultures; she trusts readers to love her worlds and characters well enough eventually to understand the messages they bear.

The story that follows first appeared in *Playboy*, which required her to use the name "U. K. Le Guin," cloaking her gender. As in her novels, Le Guin here emphasizes interpersonal tensions that resist easy resolution. Two "singletons" from Wales and Argentina, survivors of a post-famine Earth, must share close off-world quarters with a ten-member group of youthful, brilliant clones, super-beings designed to replenish the human race. Libra, the world on which they are mining uranium ore, is despite its name anything but a balanced environment. Convulsively active, the planet is by nature violent. In contrast, human nature has been gentled, chastened by the decimation of Earth's population. Darwinian survival of the fittest has been replaced, in the words of the story, with "survival of the fair-minded," as this story's heroes, human and posthuman, work patiently toward truly seeing, hearing, and understanding each other.

She was alive inside but dead outside, her face a black and dun net of wrinkles, tumors, cracks. She was bald and blind. The tremors that crossed Libra's face were mere quiverings of corruption. Underneath, in the black corridors, the halls beneath the skin, there were crepitations in darkness, ferments, chemical nightmares that went on for centuries. "O the damned flatulent planet," Pugh murmured as the dome shook and a boil burst a kilometer to the southwest, spraying silver pus across the sunset. The sun had been setting for the last two days. "I'll be glad to see a human face."

"Thanks," said Martin.

"Yours is human to be sure," said Pugh, "but I've seen it so long I can't see it."

Radvid signals cluttered the communicator which Martin was operating, faded, returned as face and voice. The face filled the screen, the nose of an Assyrian king, the eyes of a samurai, skin bronze, eyes the color of iron: young, magnificent. "Is that what human beings look like?" said Pugh with awe. "I'd forgotten."

"Shut up, Owen, we're on."

"Libra Exploratory Mission Base, come in please, this is *Passerine* launch."

"Libra here. Beam fixed. Come on down, launch."

"Expulsion in seven E-seconds. Hold on." The screen blanked and sparkled.

"Do they all look like that? Martin, you and I are uglier men than I thought."

"Shut up, Owen. . . ."

For twenty-two minutes Martin followed the landing craft down by signal, and then through the cleared dome they saw it, small star in the blood-colored east, sinking. It came down neat and quiet, Libra's thin atmosphere carrying little sound. Pugh and Martin closed the head-pieces of their imsuits, zipped out of the dome airlocks, and ran with soaring strides, Nijinsky and Nureyev, toward the boat. Three equipment modules came floating down at four-minute intervals from each other and hundred-meter intervals east of the boat. "Come on out," Martin said on his suit radio, "we're waiting at the door.'

"Come on in, the methane's fine," said Pugh.

The hatch opened. The young man they had seen on the screen came out with one athletic twist and leaped down onto the shaky dust and clinkers of Libra. Martin shook his hand, but Pugh was staring at the hatch, from which another young man emerged with the same neat twist and jump, followed by a young woman who emerged with the same neat twist, ornamented by a wriggle, and the jump. They were all tall, with bronze skin, black hair, high-bridged noses, epicanthic fold, the same face. They all had the same face. The fourth was emerging from the hatch with a neat twist and jump. "Martin bach," said Pugh, "we've got a clone."

"Right," said one of them, "we're a tenclone. John Chow's the name. You're Lieutenant Martin?"

"I'm Owen Pugh."

"Alvaro Guillen Martin," said Martin, formal, bowing slightly. Another girl was out, the same beautiful face; Martin stared at her and his eye rolled like a nervous pony's. Evidently he had never given any thought to cloning and was suffering technological shock. "Steady," Pugh said in the Argentine dialect, “it’s only excess twins.” He stood close by Martin’s elbow. He was glad himself of the contact.

It is hard to meet a stranger. Even the greatest extrovert meeting even the meekest stranger knows a certain dread, though he may not know he knows it. Will he make a fool of me wreck my image of myself invade me destroy me change me? Will he be different from me? Yes, that he will. There’s the terrible thing: the strangeness of the stranger.

After two years on a dead planet, and the last half year isolated as a team of two, oneself and one other, after that it’s even harder to meet a stranger, however welcome he may be. You’re out of the habit of difference, you’ve lost the touch; and so the fear revives, the primitive anxiety, the old dread.

The clone, five males and five females, had got done in a couple of minutes what a man might have got done in twenty: greeted Pugh and Martin, had a glance at Libra, unloaded the boat, made ready to go. They went, and the dome filled with them, a hive of golden bees. They hummed and buzzed quietly, filled up all silences, all spaces, with a honey-brown swarm of human presence. Martin looked bewildered at the long-limbed girls, and they smiled at him, three at once. Their smile was gentler than that of the boys, but no less radiantly self-possessed.

“Self-possessed,” Owen Pugh murmured to his friend, “that’s it. Think of it, to be oneself ten times over. Nine seconds for every motion, nine ayes on every vote. It would be glorious.” But Martin was asleep. And the John Chows had all gone to sleep at once. The dome was filled with their quiet breathing. They were young, they didn’t snore. Martin sighed and snored, his Hershey-bar-colored face relaxed in the dim afterglow of Libra’s primary, set at last. Pugh had cleared the dome and stars looked in, Sol among them, a great company of lights, a clone of splendors. Pugh slept and dreamed of a one-eyed giant who chased him through the shaking halls of Hell.

From his sleeping bag Pugh watched the clone’s awakening. They all got up within one minute except for one pair, a boy and a girl, who lay snugly tangled and still sleeping in one bag. As Pugh saw this there was a shock like one of Libra’s earthquakes inside him, a very deep tremor. He was not aware of this, and in fact thought he was pleased at the sight; there was no other such comfort on this dead hollow world. More power to them, who made love. One of the others stepped on the pair. They woke and the girl sat up flushed and sleepy, with bare golden breasts. One of her sisters murmured something to her; she shot a glance at Pugh and disappeared in the sleeping bag; from another direction came a fierce stare, from still another direction a voice: "Christ, we're used to having a room to ourselves. Hope you don't mind, Captain Pugh."

"It's a pleasure," Pugh said half truthfully. He had to stand up then wearing only the shorts he slept in, and he felt like a plucked rooster, all white scrawn and pimples. He had seldom envied Martin's compact brownness so much. The United Kingdom had come through the Great Famines well, losing less than half its population: a record achieved by rigorous food control. Black marketeers and hoarders had been executed. Crumbs had been shared. Where in richer lands most had died and a few had thriven, in Britain fewer died and none throve. They all got lean. Their sons were lean, their grandsons lean, small, brittle-boned, easily infected. When civilization became a matter of standing in lines, the British had kept queue, and so had replaced the survival of the fittest with the survival of the fair-minded. Owen Pugh was a scrawny little man. All the same, he was there.

At the moment he wished he wasn't.

At breakfast a John said, "Now, if you'll brief us, Captain Pugh—"

"Owen, then."

"Owen, we can work out our schedule. Anything new on the mine since your last report to your Mission? We saw your reports when *Passerine* was orbiting Planet V, where they are now."

Martin did not answer, though the mine was his discovery and project, and Pugh had to do his best. It was hard to talk to them. The same faces, each with the same expression of intelligent interest, all leaned toward him across the table at almost the same angle. They all nodded together.

Over the Exploitation Corps insignia on their tunics each had a nameband, first name John and last name Chow of course, but the middle names different. The men were Aleph, Kaph, Yod, Gimel, and Samedh; the women Sadhe, Daleth, Zayin, Beth, and Resh. Pugh tried to use the names but gave it up at once; he could not even tell sometimes which one had spoken, for all the voices were alike.

Martin buttered and chewed his toast, and finally interrupted: "You're a team. Is that it?"

"Right," said two Johns.

"God, what a team! I hadn't seen the point. How much do you each know what the others are thinking?"

"Not at all, properly speaking," replied one of the girls, Zayin. The others watched her with the proprietary, approving look they had. "No ESP, nothing fancy. But we think alike. We have exactly the same equipment. Given the same stimulus, the same problems, we're likely to be coming up with the same reactions and solutions at the same time. Explanations are easy—don't even have to make them, usually. We seldom misunderstand each other. It does facilitate our working as a team."

"Christ yes," said Martin. "Pugh and I have spent seven hours out of ten for six months misunderstanding each other. Like most people. What about emergencies, are you as good at meeting the unexpected problem as a nor . . . an unrelated team?"

"Statistics so far indicate that we are," Zayin answered readily. Clones must be trained, Pugh thought, to meet questions, to reassure and reason. All they said had the slightly bland and stilted quality of answers furnished to the Public. "We can't brainstorm as singletons can, we as a team don't profit from the interplay of varied minds; but we have a compensatory advantage. Clones are drawn from the best human material, individuals of IIQ ninety-ninth percentile, Genetic Constitution alpha double A, and so on. We have more to draw on than most individuals do."

"And it's multiplied by a factor of ten. Who is—who was John Chow?"

"A genius surely," Pugh said politely. His interest in cloning was not so new and avid as Martin's.

"Leonardo Complex type," said Yod. "Biomath, also a cellist and an undersea hunter, and interested in structural engineering problems and so on. Died before he'd worked out his major theories."

"Then you each represent a different facet of his mind, his talents?"

"No," said Zayin, shaking her head in time with several others. "We share the basic equipment and tendencies, of course, but we're all engineers in Planetary Exploitation. A later clone can be trained to develop other aspects of the basic equipment. It's all training; the genetic substance is identical. We *are* John Chow. But we were differently trained."

Martin looked shell-shocked. "How old are you?"

"Twenty-three."

"You say he died young—had they taken germ cells from him beforehand or something?"

Gimel took over: "He died at twenty-four in an air car crash. They couldn't save the brain, so they took some intestinal cells and cultured them for cloning. Reproductive cells aren't used for cloning, since they have only half the chromosomes. Intestinal cells happen to be easy to despecialize and reprogram for total growth."

"All chips off the old block," Martin said valiantly. "But how can . . . some of you be women . . .?"

Beth took over: "It's easy to program half the clonal mass back to the female. Just delete the male gene from half the cells and they revert to the basic, that is, the female. It's trickier to go the other way, have to hook in artificial Y chromosomes. So they mostly clone from males, since clones function best bisexually."

Gimel again: "They've worked these matters of technique and function out carefully. The taxpayer wants the best for his money, and of course clones are expensive. With the cell manipulations, and the incubation in Ngama Placentae, and the maintenance and training of the foster-parent groups, we end up costing about three million apiece."

"For your next generation," Martin said, still struggling, "I suppose you . . . you breed?"

"We females are sterile," said Beth with perfect equanimity. "You remember that the Y chromosome was deleted from our original cell. The males can interbreed with approved singletons, if they want to. But to get John Chow again as often as they want, they just reclone a cell from this clone."

Martin gave up the struggle. He nodded and chewed cold toast. "Well," said one of the Johns and all changed mood, like a flock of starlings that change course in one wingflick, following a leader so fast that no eye can see which leads. They were ready to go. "How about a look at the mine? Then we'll unload the equipment. Some nice new models in the robocarts; you'll want to see them. Right?" Had Pugh or Martin not agreed they might have found it hard to say so. The Johns were polite but unanimous; their decisions carried. Pugh, Commander of Libra Base 2, felt a qualm. Could he boss around this superman-woman-entity-of-ten? and a genius at that? He stuck close to Martin as they suited for outside. Neither said anything.

Four apiece in the three large airsleds, they slipped off north from the dome, over Libra's dun rugose skin, in starlight.

"Desolate," one said.

It was a boy and girl with Pugh and Martin. Pugh wondered if these were the two that had shared a sleeping bag last night. No doubt they wouldn't mind if he asked them. Sex must be as handy as breathing to them. Did you two breathe last night?

"Yes," he said, "it is desolate."

"This is our first time off, except training on Luna." The girl's voice was definitely a bit higher and softer.

"How did you take the big hop?"

"They doped us. I wanted to experience it." That was the boy; he sounded wistful. They seemed to have more personality, only two at a time. Did repetition of the individual negate individuality?

"Don't worry," said Martin, steering the sled, "you can't experience notime because it isn't there."

"I'd just like to once," one of them said. "So we'd know."

The Mountains of Merioneth showed leprotic in starlight to the east, a plume of freezing gas trailed silvery from a vent-hole to the west, and the sled tilted ground-ward. The twins braced for the stop at one moment, each with a slight protective gesture to the other. Your skin is my skin, Pugh thought, but literally, no metaphor. What would it be like, then, to have someone as close to you as that? Always to be answered when you spoke; never to be in pain alone. Love your neighbor as you love yourself. . . . That hard old problem was solved. The neighbor was the self: the love was perfect.

And here was Hellmouth, the mine.

Pugh was the Exploratory Mission's E.T. geologist, and Martin his technician and cartographer; but when in the course of a local survey Martin had discovered the U-mine, Pugh had given him full credit, as well as the onus of prospecting the lode and planning the Exploitation Team's job. These kids had been sent out from Earth years before Martin's reports got there and had not known what their job would be until they got here. The Exploitation Corps simply sent out teams regularly and blindly as a dandelion sends out its seeds, knowing there would be a job for them on Libra or the next planet out or one they hadn't even heard about yet. The Government wanted uranium too urgently to wait while reports drifted home across the light-years. The stuff was like gold, old-fashioned but essential, worth mining extraterrestrially and shipping interstellar. Worth its weight in people, Pugh thought sourly, watching the tall young men and women go one by one, glimmering in starlight, into the black hole Martin had named Hellmouth.

As they went in, their homeostatic forehead-lamps brightened. Twelve nodding gleams ran along the moist, wrinkled walls. Pugh heard Martin's radiation counter peeping twenty to the dozen up ahead. "Here's the drop-off," said Martin's voice in the suit intercom, drowning out the peeping and the dead silence that was around them. "We're in a side-fissure, this is the main vertical vent in front of us." The black void gaped, its far side not visible in the headlamp beams. "Last vulcanism seems to have been a couple of thousand years ago. Nearest fault is twenty-eight kilos east, in the Trench. This area seems to be as safe seismically as anything in the area. The big basalt-flow overhead stabilizes all these substructures, so long as it remains stable itself. Your central lode is thirty-six meters down and runs in a series of five bubble caverns northeast. It is a lode, a pipe of very high-grade ore. You saw the percentage figures, right? Extraction's going to be no problem. All you've got to do is get the bubbles topside."

"Take off the lid and let 'em float up." A chuckle. Voices began to talk, but they were all the same voice and the suit radio gave them no location in space.

"Open the thing right up.—Safer that way.—But it's a solid basalt roof, how thick, ten meters here?—Three to twenty, the report said.—Blow good ore all over the lot.—Use this access we're in, straighten it a bit and run slider rails for the robos.—Import burros.—Have we got enough propping material?—What's your estimate of total payload mass, Martin?"

"Say over five million kilos and under eight."

"Transport will be here in ten E-months.—It'll have to go pure—No, they'll have the mass problem in NAFAL shipping licked by now, remember it's been sixteen years since we left Earth last Tuesday.—Right, they'll send the whole lot back and purify it in Earth orbit.—Shall we go down, Martin?"

"Go on. I've been down."

The first one—Aleph? (Heb., the ox, the leader)—swung onto the ladder and down; the rest followed. Pugh and Martin stood at the chasm's edge. Pugh set his intercom to exchange only with Martin's suit, and noticed Martin doing the same. It was a bit wearing, this listening to one person think aloud in ten voices, or was it one voice speaking the thoughts of ten minds?

"A great gut," Pugh said, looking down into the black pit, its veined and warted walls catching stray gleams of headlamps far below. "A cow's bowel. A bloody great constipated intestine."

Martin's counter peeped like a lost chicken. They stood inside the dead but epileptic planet, breathing oxygen from tanks, wearing suits impermeable to corrosives and harmful radiations, resistant to a 200-degree range of temperatures, tear-proof, and as shock-resistant as possible given the soft vulnerable stuff inside.

"Next hop," Martin said, "I'd like to find a planet that has nothing whatever to exploit."

"You found this."

"Keep me home next time."

Pugh was pleased. He had hoped Martin would want to go on working with him, but neither of them was used to talking much about their feelings, and he had hesitated to ask. "I'll try that," he said.

"I hate this place. I like caves, you know. It's why I came in here. Just spelunking. But this one's a bitch. Mean. You can't ever let down in here. I guess this lot can handle it, though. They know their stuff."

"Wave of the future, whatever," said Pugh.

The wave of the future came swarming up the ladder, swept Martin to the entrance, gabbled at and around him: "Have we got enough material for supports?—If we convert one of the extractor servos to anneal, yes.—Sufficient if we miniblast?—Kaph can calculate stress." Pugh had switched his intercom back to receive them; he looked at them, so many thoughts jabbering in an eager mind, and at Martin standing silent among them, and at Hellmouth and the wrinkled plain. "Settled! How does that strike you as a preliminary schedule, Martin?"

"It's your baby," Martin said.

Within five E-days the Johns had all their material and equipment unloaded and operating and were starting to open up the mine. They worked with total efficiency; Pugh was fascinated and frightened by their effectiveness, their confidence, their independence. He was no use to them at all. A clone, he thought, might indeed be the first truly stable, self-reliant human being. Once adult it would need nobody's help. It would be sufficient to itself physically, sexually, emotionally, intellectually. Whatever he did, any member of it would always receive the support and approval of his peers, his other selves. Nobody else was needed.

Two of the clone stayed in the dome doing calculations and paperwork, with frequent sled trips to the mine for measurements and tests. They were the mathematicians of the clone, Zayin and Kaph. That is, as Zayin explained, all ten had had thorough mathematical training from age three to twenty-one, but from twenty-one to twenty-three she and Kaph had gone on with math while the others intensified study in other specialties: geology, mining engineering, electronic engineering, equipment robotics, applied atomics, and so on. "Kaph and I feel," she said, "that we're the element of the clone closest to what John Chow was in his singleton lifetime. But of course he was principally in biomath, and they didn't take us far in that."

"They needed us most in this field," Kaph said, with the patriotic priggishness they sometimes evinced.

Pugh and Martin soon could distinguish this pair from the others, Zayin by gestalt, Kaph only by a discolored left fourth fingernail, got from an ill-aimed hammer at the age of six. No doubt there were many such differences, physical and psychological, among them; nature might be identical, nurture could not be. But the differences were hard to find. And part of the difficulty was that they never really talked to Pugh and Martin. They joked with them, were polite, got along fine. They gave nothing. It was nothing one could complain about; they were very pleasant, they had the standardized American friendliness. "Did you come from Ireland, Owen?'

"Nobody comes from Ireland, Zayin."

"There are lots of Irish-Americans."

"To be sure, but no more Irish. A couple of thousand in all the island, the last I knew. They didn't go in for birth control, you know, so the food ran out. By the Third Famine there were no Irish left at all but the priesthood, and they all celibate, or nearly all."

Zayin and Kaph smiled stiffly. They had no experience of either bigotry or irony. "What are you then, ethnically?" Kaph asked, and Pugh replied, "A Welshman."

"Is it Welsh that you and Martin speak together?"

None of your business, Pugh thought, but said, "No, it's his dialect, not mine: Argentinean. A descendant of Spanish."

"You learned it for private communication?"

"Whom had we here to be private from? It's just that sometimes a man likes to speak his native language."

"Ours is English," Kaph said unsympathetically. Why should they have sympathy? That's one of the things you give because you need it back.

"Is Wells quaint?" asked Zayin.

"Wells? Oh, Wales, it's called. Yes. Wales is quaint." Pugh switched on his rock-cutter, which prevented further conversation by a synapse-destroying whine, and while it whined he turned his back and said a profane word in Welsh.

That night he used the Argentine dialect for private communication. "Do they pair off in the same couples or change every night?"

Martin looked surprised. A prudish expression, unsuited to his features, appeared for a moment. It faded. He too was curious. "I think it's random."

"Don't whisper, man, it sounds dirty. I think they rotate."

"On a schedule?"

"So nobody gets omitted." Martin gave a vulgar laugh and smothered it. "What about us? Aren't we omitted?"

"That doesn't occur to them."

"What if I proposition one of the girls?"

"She'd tell the others and they'd decide as a group."

"I am not a bull," Martin said, his dark, heavy face heating up. "I will not be judged—"

"Down, down, *machismo*," said Pugh. "Do you mean to proposition one?"

Martin shrugged, sullen. "Let 'em have their incest."

"Incest is it, or masturbation?"

"I don't care, if they'd do it out of earshot!" The clone's early attempts at modesty had soon worn off, unmotivated by any deep defensiveness of self or awareness of others. Pugh and Martin were daily deeper swamped under the intimacies of its constant emotional-sexual-mental interchange: swamped yet excluded.

"Two months to go," Martin said one evening. "To what?" snapped Pugh. He was edgy lately, and Martin's sullenness got on his nerves.

"To relief."

In sixty days the full crew of the Exploratory Mission were due back from their survey of the other planets of the system. Pugh was aware of this.

"Crossing off the days on your calendar?" he jeered.

"Pull yourself together, Owen."

"What do you mean?"

"What I say."

They parted in contempt and resentment.

Pugh came in after a day alone on the Pampas, a vast lava plain the nearest edge of which was two hours south by jet. He was tired but refreshed by solitude. They were not supposed to take long trips alone but lately had often done so. Martin stooped under bright lights, drawing one of his elegant masterly charts. This one was of the whole face of Libra, the cancerous face. The dome was otherwise empty, seeming dim and large as it had before the clone came. "Where's the golden horde?"

Martin grunted ignorance, cross-hatching. He straightened his back to glance round at the sun, which squatted feebly like a great red toad on the eastern plain, and at the clock, which said 18:45. "Some big quakes today," he said, returning to his map. "Feel them down there? Lots of crates were falling around. Take a look at the seismo."

The needle jigged and wavered on the roll. It never stopped dancing here. The roll had recorded five quakes of major intensity back in mid-afternoon; twice the needle had hopped off the roll. The attached computer had been activated to emit a slip reading, "Epicenter 61′ N by 42′4″ E."

"Not in the Trench this time."

"I thought it felt a bit different from usual. Sharper."

"In Base One I used to lie awake all night feeling the ground jump. Queer how you get used to things."

"Go spla if you didn't. What's for dinner?"

"I thought you'd have cooked it."

"Waiting for the clone."

Feeling put upon, Pugh got out a dozen dinnerboxes, stuck two in the Instobake, pulled them out. "All right, here's dinner."

"Been thinking," Martin said, coming to table. "What if some clone cloned itself? Illegally. Made a thousand duplicates—ten thousand. Whole army. They could make a tidy power grab, couldn't they?"

"But how many millions did this lot cost to rear? Artificial placentae and all that. It would be hard to keep secret, unless they had a planet to themselves . . . Back before the Famines when Earth had national governments, they talked about that: clone your best soldiers, have whole regiments of them. But the food ran out before they could play that game."

They talked amicably, as they used to do.

"Funny," Martin said, chewing. "They left early this morning, didn't they?"

"All but Kaph and Zayin. They thought they'd get the first payload above ground today. What's up?"

"They weren't back for lunch."

"They won't starve, to be sure."

"They left at seven."

"So they did." Then Pugh saw it. The air tanks held eight hours' supply.

"Kaph and Zayin carried out spare cans when they left. Or they've got a heap out there."

"They did, but they brought the whole lot in to recharge." Martin stood up, pointing to one of the stacks of stuff that cut the dome into rooms and alleys.

"There's an alarm signal on every imsuit."

"It's not automatic."

Pugh was tired and still hungry. "Sit down and eat, man. That lot can look after themselves."

Martin sat down but did not eat. "There was a big quake, Owen. The first one. Big enough it scared me."

After a pause Pugh sighed and said, "All right." Unenthusiastically, they got out the two-man sled that was always left for them and headed it north. The long sunrise covered everything in poisonous red jello. The horizontal light and shadow made it hard to see, raised walls of fake iron ahead of them which they slid through, turned the convex plain beyond Hellmouth into a great dimple full of bloody water. Around the tunnel entrance a wilderness of machinery stood, cranes and cables and servos and wheels and diggers and robocarts and sliders and control huts, all slanting and bulking incoherently in the red light. Martin jumped from the sled, ran into the mine. He came out again, to Pugh. "Oh God, Owen, it's down," he said. Pugh went in and saw, five meters from the entrance, the shiny moist, black wall that ended the tunnel. Newly exposed to air, it looked organic, like visceral tissue. The tunnel entrance, enlarged by blasting and double-tracked for robocarts, seemed unchanged until he noticed thousands of tiny spiderweb cracks in the walls. The floor was wet with some sluggish fluid.

"They were inside," Martin said.

"They may be still. They surely had extra air cans—"

"Look, Owen, look at the basalt flow, at the roof, don't you see what the quake did, look at it."

The low hump of land that roofed the caves still had the unreal look of an optical illusion. It had reversed itself, sunk down, leaving a vast dimple or pit. When Pugh walked on it he saw that it too was cracked with many tiny fissures. From some a whitish gas was seeping, so that the sunlight on the surface of the gas pool was shafted as if by the waters of a dim red lake.

"The mine's not on the fault. There's no fault here!" Pugh came back to him quickly. "No, there's no fault, Martin.—Look, they surely weren't all inside together."

Martin followed him and searched among the wrecked machines dully, then actively. He spotted the airsled. It had come down heading south, and stuck at an angle in a pothole of colloidal dust. It had carried two riders. One was half sunk in the dust, but his suit meters registered normal functioning; the other hung strapped onto the tilted sled. Her imsuit had burst open on the broken legs, and the body was frozen hard as any rock. That was all they found. As both regulation and custom demanded, they cremated the dead at once with the laser guns they carried by regulation and had never used before. Pugh, knowing he was going to be sick, wrestled the survivor onto the two-man sled and sent Martin off to the dome with him. Then he vomited and flushed the waste out of his suit, and finding one four-man sled undamaged, followed after Martin, shaking as if the cold of Libra had got through to him.

The survivor was Kaph. He was in deep shock. They found a swelling on the occiput that might mean concussion, but no fracture was visible.

Pugh brought two glasses of food concentrate and two chasers of aquavit. "Come on," he said. Martin obeyed, drinking off the tonic. They sat down on crates near the cot and sipped the aquavit.

Kaph lay immobile, face like beeswax, hair bright black to the shoulders, lips stiffly parted for faintly gasping breaths.

"It must have been the first shock, the big one," Martin said. "It must have slid the whole structure sideways. Till it fell in on itself. There must be gas layers in the lateral rocks, like those formations in the Thirty-first Quadrant. But there wasn't any sign—" As he spoke the world slid out from under *them*. Things leaped and clattered, hopped and jigged, shouted Ha! Ha! Ha! "It was like this at fourteen hours," said Reason shakily in Martin's voice, amidst the unfastening and ruin of the world. But Unreason sat up, as the tumult lessened and things ceased dancing, and screamed aloud.

Pugh leaped across his spilt aquavit and held Kaph down. The muscular body flailed him off. Martin pinned the shoulders down. Kaph screamed, struggled, choked; his face blackened. "Oxy," Pugh said, and his hand found the right needle in the medical kit as if by homing instinct; while Martin held the mask he struck the needle home to the vagus nerve, restoring Kaph to life.

"Didn't know you knew that stunt," Martin said, breathing hard.

"The Lazarus Jab; my father was a doctor. It doesn't often work," Pugh said. "I want that drink I spilled. Is the quake over? I can't tell."

"Aftershocks. It's not just you shivering."

"Why did he suffocate?"

"I don't know, Owen. Look in the book.'

Kaph was breathing normally and his color was restored; only the lips were still darkened. They poured a new shot of courage and sat down by him again with their medical guide. "Nothing about cyanosis or asphyxiation under 'Shock' or 'Concussion.' He can't have breathed in anything with his suit on. I don't know. We'd get as much good out of *Mother Mog's Home Herbalist*. . . . 'Anal Hemorrhoids,' fy!" Pugh pitched the book to a crate-table. It fell short, because either Pugh or the table was still unsteady.

"Why didn't he signal?"

"Sorry?"

"The eight inside the mine never had time. But he and the girl must have been outside. Maybe she was in the entrance and got hit by the first slide. He must have been outside, in the control hut maybe. He ran in, pulled her out, strapped her onto the sled, started for the dome. And all that time never pushed the panic button in his imsuit. Why not?"

"Well, he'd had that whack on his head. I doubt he ever realized the girl was dead. He wasn't in his senses. But if he had been I don't know if he'd have thought to signal us. They looked to one another for help."

Martin's face was like an Indian mask, grooves at the mouth corners, eyes of dull coal. "That's so. What must he have felt, then, when the quake came and he was outside, alone—"

In answer Kaph screamed.

He came off the cot in the heaving convulsions of one suffocating, knocked Pugh right down with his flailing arm, staggered into a stack of crates and fell to the floor, lips blue, eyes white. Martin dragged him back onto the cot and gave him a whiff of oxygen, then knelt by Pugh, who was just sitting up, and wiped at his cut cheekbone. "Owen, are you all right, are you going to be all right, Owen?"

"I think I am," Pugh said. "Why are you rubbing that on my face?"

It was a short length of computer tape, now spotted with Pugh's blood.

Martin dropped it. "Thought it was a towel. You clipped your cheek on that box there."

"Is he out of it?"

"Seems to be."

They stared down at Kaph lying stiff, his teeth a white line inside dark parted lips.

"Like epilepsy. Brain damage, maybe?"

"What about shooting him full of meprobamate?"

Pugh shook his head. "I don't know what's in that shot I already gave him for shock. Don't want to overdose him."

"Maybe he'll sleep it off now."

"I'd like to myself. Between him and the earthquake I can't seem to keep on my feet."

"You got a nasty crack there. Go on, I'll sit up a while."

Pugh cleaned his cut cheek and pulled off his shirt, then paused.

"Is there anything we ought to have done—have tried to do—"

"They're all dead," Martin said heavily, gently.

Pugh lay down on top of his sleeping bag and one instant later was awakened by a hideous, sucking, struggling noise. He staggered up, found the needle, tried three times to jab it in correctly and failed, began to massage over Kaph's heart. "Mouth-to-mouth," he said, and Martin obeyed. Presently Kaph drew a harsh breath, his heartbeat steadied, his rigid muscles began to relax.

"How long did I sleep?"

"Half an hour."

They stood up sweating. The ground shuddered, the fabric of the dome sagged and swayed. Libra was dancing her awful polka again, her *Totentanz*. The sun, though rising, seemed to have grown larger and redder, gas and dust must have been stirred up in the feeble atmosphere.

"What's wrong with him, Owen?"

"I think he's dying with them."

"Them—But they're dead, I tell you."

"Nine of them. They're all dead, they were crushed or suffocated. They were all him, he is all of them. They died, and now he's dying their deaths one by one."

"Oh, pity of God," said Martin.

The next time was much the same. The fifth time was worse, for Kaph fought and raved, trying to speak but getting no words out, as if his mouth were stopped with rocks or clay. After that the attacks grew weaker, but so did he. The eighth seizure came at about four-thirty; Pugh and Martin worked till five-thirty doing all they could to keep life in the body that slid without protest into death. They kept him, but Martin said, "The next will finish him." And it did; but Pugh breathed his own breath into the inert lungs, until he himself passed out.

He woke. The dome was opaqued and no light on. He listened and heard the breathing of two sleeping men. He slept, and nothing woke him till hunger did.

The sun was well up over the dark plains, and the planet had stopped dancing. Kaph lay asleep. Pugh and Martin drank tea and looked at him with proprietary triumph.

When he woke Martin went to him: "How do you feel, old man?" There was no answer. Pugh took Martin's place and looked into the brown, dull eyes that gazed toward but not into his own. Like Martin he quickly turned away. He heated food concentrate and brought it to Kaph. "Come on, drink."

He could see the muscles in Kaph's throat tighten. "Let me die," the young man said.

"You're not dying."

Kaph spoke with clarity and precision: "I am nine-tenths dead. There is not enough of me left alive."

That precision convinced Pugh, and he fought the conviction. "No," he said, peremptory. "They are dead. The others. Your brothers and sisters. You're not them, you're alive. You are John Chow. Your life is in your own hands."

The young man lay still, looking into a darkness that was not there.

Martin and Pugh took turns taking the Exploitation hauler and a spare set of robos over to Hellmouth to salvage equipment and protect it from Libra's sinister atmosphere, for the value of the stuff was, literally, astronomical. It was slow work for one man at a time, but they were unwilling to leave Kaph by himself. The one left in the dome did paperwork, while Kaph sat or lay and stared into his darkness and never spoke. The days went by, silent.

The radio spat and spoke: the Mission calling from the ship. "We'll be down on Libra in five weeks, Owen. Thirty-four E-days nine hours I make it as of now. How's tricks in the old dome?"

"Not good, chief. The Exploit team were killed, all but one of them, in the mine. Earthquake. Six days ago."

The radio crackled and sang starsong. Sixteen seconds' lag each way; the ship was out around Planet II now. "Killed, all but one? You and Martin weren't hurt?"

"We're all right, chief."

Thirty-two seconds.

"*Passerine* left an Exploit team out here with us. I may put them on the Hellmouth project then, instead of the Quadrant Seven project. We'll settle that when we come down. In any case you and Martin will be relieved at Dome Two. Hold tight. Anything else?"

"Nothing else."

Thirty-two seconds.

"Right then. So long, Owen."

Kaph had heard all this, and later on Pugh said to him, "The chief may ask you to stay here with the other Exploit team. You know the ropes here." Knowing the exigencies of Far Out life, he wanted to warn the young man. Kaph made no answer. Since he had said, "There is not enough of me left alive," he had not spoken a word.

"Owen," Martin said on suit intercom, "he's spla. Insane. Psycho."

"He's doing very well for a man who's died nine times."

"Well? Like a turned-off android is well? The only emotion he has left is hate. Look at his eyes."

"That's not hate, Martin. Listen, it's true that he has, in a sense, been dead. I cannot imagine what he feels. But it's not hatred. He can't even see us. It's too dark."

"Throats have been cut in the dark. He hates us because we're not Aleph and Yod and Zayin."

"Maybe. But I think he's alone. He doesn't see us or hear us, that's the truth. He never had to see anyone else before. He never was alone before. He had himself to see, talk with, live with, nine other selves all his life. He doesn't know how you go it alone. He must learn. Give him time."

Martin shook his heavy head. "Spla," he said. "Just remember when you're alone with him that he could break your neck one-handed."

"He could do that," said Pugh, a short, soft-voiced man with a scarred cheekbone; he smiled. They were just outside the dome airlock, programming one of the servos to repair a damaged hauler. They could see Kaph sitting inside the great half-egg of the dome like a fly in amber.

"Hand me the insert pack there. What makes you think he'll get any better?"

"He has a strong personality, to be sure."

"Strong? Crippled. Nine-tenths dead, as he put it."

"But he's not dead. He's a live man: John Kaph Chow. He had a jolly queer upbringing, but after all every boy has got to break free of his family. He will do it."

"I can't see it."

"Think a bit, Martin bach. What's this cloning for? To repair the human race. We're in a bad way. Look at me. My IIQ and GC are half this John Chow's. Yet they wanted me so badly for the Far Out Service that when I volunteered they took me and fitted me out with an artificial lung and corrected my myopia. Now if there were enough good sound lads about would they be taking one-lunged short-sighted Welshmen?"

"Didn't know you had an artificial lung."

"I do then. Not tin, you know. Human, grown in a tank from a bit of somebody; cloned, if you like. That's how they make replacement organs, the same general idea as cloning, but bits and pieces instead of whole people. It's my own lung now, whatever. But what I am saying is this, there are too many like me these days and not enough like John Chow. They're trying to raise the level of the human genetic pool, which is a mucky little puddle since the population crash. So then if a man is cloned, he's a strong and clever man. It's only logic, to be sure."

Martin grunted; the servo began to hum.

Kaph had been eating little; he had trouble swallowing his food, choking on it, so that he would give up trying after a few bites. He had lost eight or ten kilos. After three weeks or so, however, his appetite began to pick up, and one day he began to look through the clone's possessions, the sleeping bags, kits, papers which Pugh had stacked neatly in a far angle of a packing-crate alley. He sorted, destroyed a heap of papers and oddments, made a small packet of what remained, then relapsed into his walking coma.

Two days later he spoke. Pugh was trying to correct a flutter in the tape-player and failing; Martin had the jet out, checking their maps of the Pampas. "Hell and damnation!" Pugh said, and Kaph said in a toneless voice, "Do you want me to do that?" Pugh jumped, controlled himself, and gave the machine to Kaph. The young man took it apart, put it back together, and left it on the table.

"Put on a tape," Pugh said with careful casualness, busy at another table.

Kaph put on the topmost tape, a chorale. He lay down on his cot. The sound of a hundred human voices singing together filled the dome. He lay still, his face blank.

In the next days he took over several routine jobs, unasked. He undertook nothing that wanted initiative, and if asked to do anything he made no response at all.

"He's doing well," Pugh said in the dialect of Argentina.

"He's not. He's turning himself into a machine. Does what he's programmed to do, no reaction to anything else. He's worse off than when he didn't function at all. He's not human any more."

Pugh sighed. "Well, good night," he said in English. "Goodnight, Kaph."

"Good night," Martin said; Kaph did not.

Next morning at breakfast Kaph reached across Martin's plate for the toast. "Why don't you ask for it?" Martin said with the geniality of repressed exasperation. "I can pass it."

"I can reach it," Kaph said in his flat voice.

"Yes, but look. Asking to pass things, saying good night or hello, they're not important, but all the same when somebody says something a person ought to answer . . ."

The young man looked indifferently in Martin's direction; his eyes still did not seem to see clear through to the person he looked toward. "Why should I answer?"

"Because somebody has said something to you."

"Why?"

Martin shrugged and laughed. Pugh jumped up and turned on the rock-cutter.

Later on he said, "Lay off that, please, Martin."

"Manners are essential in small isolated crews, some kind of manners, whatever you work out together. He's been taught that, everybody in Far Out knows it. Why does he deliberately flout it?"

"Do you tell yourself good night?"

"So?"

"Don't you see Kaph's never known anyone but himself?"

Martin brooded and then broke out. "Then by God this cloning business is all wrong. It won't do. What are a lot of duplicate geniuses going to do for us when they don't even know we exist?"

Pugh nodded. "It might be wiser to separate the clones and bring them up with others. But they make such a grand team this way."

"Do they? I don't know. If this lot had been ten average inefficient E.T. engineers, would they all have been in the same place at the same time? Would they all have got killed? What if, when the quake came and things started caving in, what if all those kids ran the same way, farther into the mine, maybe, to save the one that was farthest in? Even Kaph was outside and went in. . . . It's hypothetical. But I keep thinking, out of ten ordinary confused guys, more might have got out."

"I don't know. It's true that identical twins tend to die at about the same time, even when they have never seen each other. Identity and death, it is very strange. . . ."

The days went on, the red sun crawled across the dark sky, Kaph did not speak when spoken to, Pugh and Martin snapped at each other more frequently each day. Pugh complained of Martin's snoring. Offended, Martin moved his cot clear across the dome and also ceased speaking to Pugh for some while. Pugh whistled Welsh dirges until Martin complained, and then Pugh stopped speaking for a while.

The day before the Mission ship was due, Martin announced he was going over to Merioneth.

"I thought at least you'd be giving me a hand with the computer to finish the rock analyses!" Pugh said, aggrieved.

"Kaph can do that. I want one more look at that Trench. Have fun," Martin added in dialect, and laughed, and left.

"What is that language?"

"Argentinean. I told you that once, didn't I?"

"I don't know." After a while the young man added, "I have forgotten a lot of things, I think."

"It wasn't important, to be sure," Pugh said gently, realizing all at once how important this conversation was. "Will you give me a hand running the computer, Kaph?"

He nodded.

Pugh had left a lot of loose ends, and the job took them all day. Kaph was a good co-worker, quick and systematic, much more so than Pugh himself. His flat voice, now that he was talking again, got on the nerves; but it didn't matter, there was only this one day left to get through and then the ship would come, the old crew, comrades and friends.

During tea break Kaph said, "What will happen if the Explore ship crashes?"

"They'd be killed."

"To you, I mean."

"To us? We'd radio SOS signals and live on half rations till the rescue cruiser from Area Three Base came. Four and a half E-years away it is. We have life support here for three men for, let's see, maybe between four and five years. A bit tight, it would be."

"Would they send a cruiser for three men?"

"They would."

Kaph said no more.

"Enough cheerful speculations," Pugh said cheerfully, rising to get back to work. He slipped sideways and the chair avoided his hand; he did a sort of half-pirouette and fetched up hard against the dome hide. "My goodness," he said, reverting to his native idiom, "what is it?"

"Quake," said Kaph.

The teacups bounced on the table with a plastic cackle, a litter of papers slid off a box, the skin of the dome swelled and sagged. Underfoot there was a huge noise, half sound, half shaking, a subsonic boom.

Kaph sat unmoved. An earthquake does not frighten a man who died in an earthquake.

Pugh, white-faced, wiry black hair sticking out, a frightened man, said, "Martin is in the Trench."

"What trench?"

"The big fault line. The epicenter for the local quakes. Look at the seismograph." Pugh struggled with the stuck door of a still-jittering locker.

"Where are you going?'

"After him."

"Martin took the jet. Sleds aren't safe to use during quakes. They go out of control."

"For God's sake man, shut up."

Kaph stood up, speaking in a flat voice as usual. "It's unnecessary to go out after him now. It's taking an unnecessary risk."

"If his alarm goes off, radio me," Pugh said, shut the head-piece of his suit, and ran to the lock. As he went out Libra picked up her ragged skirts and danced a belly dance from under his feet clear to the red horizon.

Inside the dome, Kaph saw the sled go up, tremble like a meteor in the dull red daylight, and vanish to the northeast. The hide of the dome quivered, the earth coughed. A vent south of the dome belched up a slow-flowing bile of black gas.

A bell shrilled and a red light flashed on the central control board. The sign under the light read Suit 2, and scribbled under that, A.G.M. Kaph did not turn the signal off. He tried to radio Martin, then Pugh, but got no reply from either.

When the aftershocks decreased he went back to work and finished up Pugh's job. It took him about two hours. Every half hour he tried to contact Suit 1 and got no reply, then Suit 2 and got no reply. The red light had stopped flashing after an hour.

It was dinnertime. Kaph cooked dinner for one and ate it. He lay down on his cot.

The aftershocks had ceased except for faint, rolling tremors at long intervals. The sun hung in the west, oblate, pale red, immense. It did not sink visibly. There was no sound at all.

Kaph got up and began to walk about the messy, half-packed-up, overcrowded, empty dome. The silence continued. He went to the player and put on the first tape that came to hand. It was pure music, electronic, without harmonies, without voices. It ended. The silence continued.

Pugh's uniform tunic, one button missing, hung over a stack of rock samples. Kaph stared at it a while.

The silence continued.

The child's dream: There is no one else alive in the world but me. In all the world.

Low, north of the dome, a meteor flickered.

Kaph's mouth opened as if he were trying to say something, but no sound came. He went hastily to the north wall and peered out into the gelatinous red light.

The little star came in and sank. Two figures blurred the airlock. Kaph stood close beside the lock as they came in. Martin's imsuit was covered with some kind of dust so that he looked raddled and warty like the surface of Libra. Pugh had him by the arm.

"Is he hurt?"

Pugh shucked his suit, helped Martin peel his off. "Shaken up," he said, curt.

"A piece of cliff fell onto the jet," Martin said, sitting down at the table and waving his arms. "Not while I was in it though. I was parked, see, and poking about that carbon-dust area when I felt things humping. So I went out onto a nice bit of early igneous I'd noticed from above, good footing and out from under the cliffs. Then I saw this bit of the planet fall off onto the flyer, quite a sight it was, and after a while it occurred to me the spare aircans were in the flyer, so I leaned on the panic button. But I didn't get any radio reception, that's always happening here during quakes, so I didn't know if the signal was getting through either. And things went on jumping and pieces of the cliff coming off. Little rocks flying around, and so dusty you couldn't see a meter ahead. I was really beginning to wonder what I'd do for breathing in the small hours, you know, when I saw old Owen buzzing up the Trench in all that dust and junk like a big ugly bat—"

"Want to eat?" said Pugh.

"Of course I want to eat. How'd you come through the quake here, Kaph? No damage? It wasn't a big one actually, was it, what's the seismo say? My trouble was I was in the middle of it. Old Epicenter Alvaro. Felt like Richter-fifteen there—total destruction of planet—"

"Sit down," Pugh said. "Eat."

After Martin had eaten a little his spate of talk ran dry. He very soon went off to his cot, still in the remote angle where he had removed it when Pugh complained of his snoring. "Good night, you one-lunged Welshman," he said across the dome.

"Good night."

There was no more out of Martin. Pugh opaqued the dome, turned the lamp down to a yellow glow less than a candle's light, and sat doing nothing, saying nothing, withdrawn.

The silence continued.

"I finished the computations."

Pugh nodded thanks.

"The signal from Martin came through, but I couldn't contact you or him."

Pugh said with effort, "I should not have gone. He had two hours of air left even with only one can. He might have been heading home when I left. This way we were all out of touch with one another. I was scared."

The silence came back, punctuated now by Martin's long, soft snores.

"Do you love Martin?"

Pugh looked up with angry eyes: "Martin is my friend. We've worked together, he's a good man." He stopped. After a while he said, "Yes, I love him. Why did you ask that?"

Kaph said nothing, but he looked at the other man. His face was changed, as if he were glimpsing something he had not seen before; his voice too was changed. "How can you. . . How do you. . . ."

But Pugh could not tell him. "I don't know," he said, "it's practice, partly. I don't know. We're each of us alone, to be sure. What can you do but hold your hand out in the dark?"

Kaph's strange gaze dropped, burned out by its own intensity.

"I'm tired," Pugh said. "That was ugly, looking for him in all that black dust and muck, and mouths opening and shutting in the ground. . . . I'm going to bed. The ship will be transmitting to us by six or so." He stood up and stretched.

"It's a clone," Kaph said. "The other Exploit Team they're bringing with them."

"Is it then?"

"A twelveclone. They came out with us on the *Passerine*."

Kaph sat in the small yellow aura of the lamp seeming to look past it at what he feared: the new clone, the multiple self of which he was not part. A lost piece of a broken set, a fragment, inexpert at solitude, not knowing even how you go about giving love to another individual, now he must face the absolute, closed self-sufficiency of the clone of twelve; that was a lot to ask of the poor fellow, to be sure. Pugh put a hand on his shoulder in passing. "The chief won't ask you to stay here with a clone. You can go home. Or since you're Far Out maybe you'll come on farther out with us. We could use you. No hurry deciding. You'll make out all right."

Pugh's quiet voice trailed off. He stood unbuttoning his coat, stooped a little with fatigue. Kaph looked at him and saw the thing he had never seen before, saw him: Owen Pugh, the other, the stranger who held his hand out in the dark.

"Good night," Pugh mumbled, crawling into his sleeping bag and half asleep already, so that he did not hear Kaph reply after a pause, repeating, across darkness, benediction.

Frank Herbert
Seed Stock

{1970}

Frank Herbert (1920–1986) is best known for his *Dune* novels, which broadened sf world-building in ways analogous to J. R. R. Tolkien's extension of fantasy in the *Lord of the Rings* trilogy (1954–55). If Tolkien Christianized high fantasy as a parable of redemption through sacrifice, then Herbert's *Dune* novels Darwinized space opera as a myth of evolutionary struggle. To space opera's vast backdrops of time and space and its focus on contending superpowers, Herbert added a vivid foreground: a desert planet presenting unusual challenges to human survival. The original stories—"Dune World" (1963–64) and "The Prophet of Dune" (1965)—were serialized in *Analog* by John W. Campbell. Mostly for reasons of length, twenty publishers rejected the novel version, which eventually found a home at Chilton Books, then best known for aftermarket car repair manuals. Chilton's editor, Sterling Lanier, was an sf author who had much admired the series in *Analog*. *Dune* won the 1965 Nebula Award and shared the Hugo in 1966.

Herbert's childhood was spent in rural Washington State; his father drove a bus and later became a highway patrolman. Beginning at nineteen, he worked for most of his life as a newspaperman in various West Coast cities, with interruptions for military service in the Navy during World War II and for schooling at the University of Washington. One news story he pitched to the *San Francisco Examiner* concerned efforts in Oregon to push back sand dunes that were engulfing settled towns. *California Living*, the newspaper's Sunday supplement, rejected the story, but Herbert's intensive research was one inspiration for *Dune*. "Survival of the Cunning," the first short story Herbert liked well enough to sign with his own name, appeared in *Esquire* in March 1945: its hero, an Inuit, more than matches wits with a soldier equipped with high-tech weapons. Herbert's first sf sale was to *Startling Stories* in 1952, but he worked best on a broad canvas, and his reputation rests in large part on his six *Dune* novels (1965–85) and eleven sf novels with non-*Dune* settings; he also coauthored a trilogy with Bill Ransom and a novel with his son Brian.

Working with the environment, as opposed to performing drastic technological interventions, is important in all Herbert's fiction, including the story that follows. "Seed Stock," which appeared in the April 1970 issue of *Analog*, is unusual in its focus on a single character's thoughts: *Dune* offers by contrast a mosaic—"mandala" is the term Herbert used—of contrary viewpoints. This story is spare, with no feudal tapestry of plotting and counterplotting, no noble families with hereditary prerogatives, and no privileging of mental, scientific, or political acumen. The scientists of a landing party on a far planet are still intent on terraforming "their" new world, but they remain offstage, as the viewpoint character, slow-witted but observant, considers his family's options for survival. Herbert, himself of working-class stock, depicts Kroudar as an unlikely sf hero: a "sea peasant" with no sympathy for big ideas, he tries instead, like a falcon, to think with the body: "Falcons knew a thing about *this place* that humans did not know. The birds knew it in their flesh."

When the sun had sunk almost to the edge of the purple ocean, hanging there like a giant orange ball—much larger than the sun of Mother Earth which he remembered with such nostalgia—Kroudar brought his fishermen back to the harbor.

A short man, Kroudar gave the impression of heaviness, but under his shipcloth motley he was as scrawny as any of the others, all bone and stringy muscle. It was the sickness of this planet, the doctors told him. They called it "body burdens," a subtle thing of differences in chemistry, gravity, diurnal periods and even the lack of a tidal moon.

Kroudar's yellow hair, his one good feature, was uncut and contained in a protective square of red cloth. Beneath this was a wide, low forehead, deeply sunken large eyes of a washed-out blue, a crooked nose that was splayed and pushed in, thick lips over large and unevenly spaced yellow teeth, and a melon chin receding into a short, ridged neck.

Dividing his attention between sails and shore, Kroudar steered with one bare foot on the tiller.

They had been all day out in the up-coast current netting the shrimp-like *trodi* which formed the colony's main source of edible protein. There were nine boats and the men in all of them were limp with fatigue, silent, eyes closed or open and staring at nothing.

The evening breeze rippled its dark lines across the harbor, moved the sweat-matted yellow hair on Kroudar's neck. It bellied the ship-cloth sails and gave the heavily loaded boats that last necessary surge to carry them up into the strands.

Men moved then. Sails dropped with a slatting and rasping. Each thing was done with sparse motion in the weighted slowness of their fatigue.

Trodi had been thick in the current out there, and Kroudar had pushed his people to their limit. It had not taken much push. They all understood the need. The swarmings and runnings of useful creatures on this planet had not been clocked with any reliable precision. Things here exhibited strange gaps and breaks in seeming regularity. The *trodi* might vanish at any moment into some unknown place—as they had been known to do before.

The colony had experienced hunger and children crying for food that must be rationed. Men seldom spoke of this any more, but they moved with the certain knowledge of it.

More than three years now, Kroudar thought, as he shouldered a dripping bag of *trodi* and pushed his weary feet through the sand, climbing the beach toward the storage huts and racks where the sea creatures were dried for processing. It had been more than three years since their ship had come down from space.

The colony ship had been constructed as a multiple tool, filled with select human stock, their domestic animals and basic necessities, and it had been sent to plant humans in this far place. It had been designed to land once, then be broken down into useful things.

Somehow, the basic necessities had fallen short, and the colony had been forced to improvise its own tools. They had not really settled here yet, Kroudar realized. More than three years—and three years here were five years of Mother Earth—and they still lived on the edge of extinction. They were trapped here. Yes, that was true. The ship could never be reconstructed. And even if that miracle were accomplished, the fuel did not exist.

The colony was *here.*

And every member knew the predatory truth of their predicament: survival had not been assured. It was known in subtle things to Kroudar's unlettered mind, especially in a fact he observed without being able to explain.

Not one of their number had yet accepted a name for this planet. It was "here" or "this place."

Or even more bitter terms.

Kroudar dumped his sack of *trodi* onto a storage hut porch, mopped his forehead. The joints of his arms and legs ached. His back ached. He could feel the sickness of *this place* in his bowels. Again, he wiped perspiration from his forehead, removed the red cloth he wore to protect his head from that brutal sun.

Yellow hair fell down as he loosed the cloth, and he swung the hair back over his shoulders.

It would be dark very soon.

The red cloth was dirty, he saw. It would require another gentle washing. Kroudar thought it odd, this cloth; grown and woven on Mother Earth, it would end its days on *this place.*

Even as he and the others.

He stared at the cloth for a moment before placing it carefully in a pocket.

All around him, his fishermen were going through the familiar ritual. Brown sacks woven of coarse native roots were dumped dripping onto the storage hut porches. Some of his men leaned then against the porch uprights, some sprawled in the sand.

Kroudar lifted his gaze. Fires behind the bluff above them sent smoke spirals into the darkening sky. Kroudar was suddenly hungry. He thought of Technician Honida up there at the cookfire, their twin sons—two years old next week—nearby at the door of the shipmetal longhouse.

It stirred him to think of Honida. She had chosen *him.* With men from the Scientist class and the Technicians available to her, Honida had reached down into the Labor pool to tap the one they all called "Old Ugly." He wasn't old, Kroudar reminded himself. But he knew the source of the name. *This place* had worked its changes on him with more visible evidence than upon any of the others.

Kroudar held no illusions about why he had been brought on this human migration. It was his muscles and his minimal education. The reason was embodied in that label written down in the mother ship manifest—laborer. The planners back on Mother Earth had realized there were tasks which required human muscles not inhibited by too much thinking. The *kroudars* landed *here* were not numerous, but they knew each other and they knew themselves for what they were.

There'd even been talk among the higher echelons of not allowing Honida to choose him as mate. Kroudar knew this. He did not resent it particularly. It didn't even bother him that the vote among the biologists—they'd discussed his ugliness at great length, so it was reported—favored Honida's choice on philosophical rather than physical grounds.

Kroudar knew he was ugly.

He knew also that his present hunger was a good sign. A strong desire to see his family grew in him, beginning to ignite his muscles for the climb from the beach. Particularly, he wanted to see his twins, the one yellow-haired like himself, and the other dark as Honida. The other women favored with children looked upon his twins as stunted and sickly, Kroudar knew. The women fussed over diets and went running to the medics almost every day. But as long as Honida did not worry, Kroudar remained calm. Honida, after all, was a technician, a worker in the hydrophonics gardens.

Kroudar moved his bare feet softly in the sand. Once more, he looked up at the bluff. Along the edge grew scattered native trees. Their thick trunks hugged the ground, gnarled and twisted, supports for bulbous yellow-green leaves that exuded poisonous milky sap in the heat of the day. A few of the surviving Earth-falcons perched in the trees, silent, watchful.

The birds gave Kroudar an odd confidence in his own decisions. For what do the falcons watch, he wondered. It was a question the most exalted of the colony's thinkers had not been able to answer. Search 'copters had been sent out following the falcons. The birds flew offshore in the night, swooped low over the waters, rested occasionally on barren islands, and returned at dawn. The colony command had been unwilling to risk its precious boats in the search, and the mystery of the falcons remained unsolved.

It was doubly a mystery because the other birds had perished or flown off to some unfound place. The doves, the quail—the gamebirds and songbirds—all had vanished. And the domestic chickens had all died, their eggs infertile. Kroudar knew this as a comment by *this place*, a warning for the life that came from Mother Earth.

A few scrawny cattle survived, and several calves had been born *here*. But they moved with a listless gait and there was distressed lowing in the pastures. Looking into their eyes was like looking into open wounds. A few pigs still lived, as listless and sickly as the cattle, and all the wild creatures had strayed off or died.

Except the falcons.

How odd it was, because the people who planned and conceived profound thoughts had held such hopes for *this place*. The survey reports had been exciting. This was a planet without native land animals. It was a planet whose native plants appeared not too different from those of Mother Earth—in some respects. And the sea creatures were primitive by sophisticated evolutionary standards.

Without being able to put it into those beautifully polished phrases which others admired, Kroudar knew where the mistake had been made. Sometimes, you had to search out a problem with your flesh and not with your mind.

He stared around now at the motley rags of his men. They were *his* men.

He was the master fisherman, the one who had found the *trodi* and conceived these squat, ugly boats built within the limitations of native woods. The colony was alive now because of his skills with boat and net.

There would be more gaps in the *trodi* runs, though. Kroudar felt this as an awareness on the edges of his fatigue. There would be unpopular and dangerous things to do then, all necessary because *thinking* had failed. The salmon they had introduced, according to plan, had gone off into the ocean vastness. The flatfish in the colony's holding ponds suffered mysterious attrition. Insects flew away and were never seen again.

There's food here, the biologists argued. Why do they die?

The colony's maize was a sometime thing with strange ears. Wheat came up in scabrous patches. There were no familiar patterns of growth or migration. The colony lived on the thin edge of existence, maintained by protein bulk from the processed *trodi* and vitamins from vegetables grown hydroponically with arduous filtering and adjustment of their water. Breakdown of a single system in the chain could bring disaster.

The giant orange sun showed only a small arc above the sea horizon now, and Kroudar's men were stirring themselves, lifting their tired bodies off the sand, pushing away from the places where they had leaned.

"All right now," Kroudar ordered. "Let's get this food inside on the racks."

"Why?" someone asked from the dusk. "You think the falcons will eat it?"

They all knew the falcons would not eat the *trodi*. Kroudar recognized the objection: it was tiredness of the mind speaking. The shrimp creatures fed only humans—after careful processing to remove dangerous irritants. A falcon might take up a frond-legged *trodi*, but would drop it at the first taste.

What did they eat, those waiting birds?

Falcons knew a thing about *this place* that humans did not know. The birds knew it in their flesh in the way Kroudar sought the knowledge.

Darkness fell, and with a furious clatter, the falcons flew off toward the sea. One of Kroudar's men kindled a torch and, having rested, anxious now to climb the bluff and join their families, the fishermen pitched into the work that must be done. Boats were hauled up on rollers. *Trodi* were spread out in thin layers along racks within the storage huts. Nets were draped on racks to dry.

As he worked, Kroudar wondered about the scientists up there in the shining laboratories. He had the working man's awe of knowledge, a servility in the face of titles and things clearly superior, but he had also the simple man's sure awareness of when superior things failed.

Kroudar was not privy to the high-level conferences in the colony command, but he knew the physical substance of the ideas discussed there. His awareness of failure and hovering disaster had no sophisticated words or erudition to hold itself dancingly before men's minds, but his knowledge carried its own elegance. He drew on ancient knowledge adjusted subtly to the differences of *this place*. Kroudar had found the *trodi*. Kroudar had organized the methods of capturing them and preserving them. He had no refined labels to explain it, but Kroudar knew himself for what he could do and what he was.

He was the first sea peasant *here*.

Without wasting energy on talk, Kroudar's band finished the work, turned away from the storage huts and plodded up the cliff trail, their course marked by, here and there, men with flaming torches. There were fuzzy orange lights, heavy shadows, inching their way upward in a black world, and they gave heart to Kroudar.

Lingering to the last, he checked the doors of the huts, then followed, hurrying to catch up. The man directly ahead of him on the path carried a torch; native wood soaked in *trodi* oil. It flickered and smoked and gave off poisonous fumes. The light revealed a troglodyte figure, a human clad in patched shipcloth, body too thin, muscles moving on the edge of collapse.

Kroudar sighed.

It was not like this on Mother Earth, he knew. There, the women waited on the strand for their men to return from the sea. Children played among the pebbles. Eager hands helped with the work onshore, spreading the nets, carrying the catch, pulling the boats.

Not *here*.

And the perils *here* were not the perils of Home. Kroudar's boats never strayed out of sight of these cliffs. One boat always carried a technician with a radio for contact with shore. Before its final descent, the colony ship had seeded space with orbiting devices—watchers, guardians against surprises from the weather. The laboriously built fishing fleet always had ample waning of storms. No monster sea creatures had ever been seen in that ocean.

This place lacked the cruel savagery and variety of seas Kroudar had known, but it was nonetheless deadly. He *knew* this.

The women should wait for us on the shore, he thought.

But colony command said the women—and even some of the children—were needed for too many other tasks. Individual plants from home required personal attention. Single wheat stalks were nurtured with tender care. Each orchard tree existed with its own handmaiden, its guardian dryad.

Atop the cliff, the fishermen came in sight of the longhouses, shipmetal *quonsets* named for some far distant place and time in human affairs. Scattered electric lights ringed the town. Many of the unpaved streets wandered off unlit. There were mechanical sounds here and murmurous voices.

The men scattered to their own affairs now, no longer a band. Kroudar plodded down his street toward the open cook fires in the central plaza. The open fires were a necessity to conserve the more sophisticated energies of the colony. Some looked upon those flames as admission of defeat. Kroudar saw them as victory. It was *native* wood being burned.

Off in the hills beyond the town, he knew, stood the ruins of the wind machines they had built. The storm which had wreaked that destruction had achieved no surprise in its coming, but had left enormous surprise at its power.

For Kroudar, the *thinkers* had begun to diminish in stature then. When native chemistry and water life had wrecked the turbines in the river which emptied into the harbor, those men of knowledge had shrunk even more. Then it was that Kroudar had begun his own search for native foods.

Now, Kroudar heard, native plant life threatened the cooling systems for their atomic generators, defying radiation in a way no life should. Some among the technicians already were fashioning steam engines of materials not intended for such use. Soon, they would have native metals, though—materials to resist the wild etchings and rusts of *this place*.

They might succeed—provided the dragging sickness did not sap them further.

If they survived.

Honida awaited him at the door to their quarters, smiling, graceful. Her dark hair was plaited and wound in rings around her forehead. The brown eyes were alive with welcome. Firelight from the plaza cast a familiar glow across her olive skin. The high cheekbones of her Amerind ancestry, the full lips and proudly hooked nose—all filled him with remembered excitement.

Kroudar wondered if the *planners* had known this thing about her which gave him such warmth—her strength and fecundity. She had chosen *him*, and now she carried more of their children—twins again.

"Ahhh, my fisherman is home," she said, embracing him in the doorway for anyone to see.

They went inside then, closed the door, and she held him with more ardor, stared up into his face which, reflected in her eyes, lost some of its ugliness.

"Honida," he said, unable to find other words.

Presently, he asked about the boys.

"They're asleep," she said, leading him to the crude trestle table he had built for their kitchen.

He nodded. Later, he would go in and stare at his sons. It did not bother him that they slept so much. He could feel the reasons for this somewhere within himself.

Honida had hot *trodi* soup waiting for him on the table. It was spiced with hydroponic tomatoes and peas and contained other things which he knew she gathered from the land without telling the scientists.

Whatever she put in front of him, Kroudar ate. There was bread tonight with an odd musty flavor which he found pleasant. In the light of the single lamp they were permitted for this room, he stared at a piece of the bread. It was almost purple—like the sea. He chewed it, swallowed.

Honida, watchfully eating across from him, finished her bread and soup, asked: "Do you like the bread?"

"I like it."

"I made it myself in the coals," she said.

He nodded, took another slice.

Honida refilled his soup bowl.

They were privileged, Kroudar realized, to have this privacy for their meals. Many of the others had opted for communal cooking and eating—even among the technicians and higher echelons who possessed more freedom of choice. Honida had seen something about *this place*, though, which required secrecy and going private ways.

Kroudar, hunger satisfied, stared across the table at her. He adored her with a devotion that went far deeper than the excitement of her flesh. He could not say the thing she was, but he knew it. If they were to have a future here, that future was in Honida and the things he might learn, form and construct of himself with his own flesh.

Under the pressure of his eyes, Honida arose, came around the table and began massaging the muscles of his back—the very muscles he used to haul the nets.

"You're tired," she said. "Was it difficult out there today?"

"Hard work," Kroudar said.

He admired the way she spoke. She had many words at her disposal. He had heard her use some of them during colony meetings and during the time of their application for mating choice. She had words for things he did not know, and she knew also when to speak with her body rather than with her mouth. She knew about the muscles of his back.

Kroudar felt such a love for her then that he wondered if it went up through her fingers into her body.

"We filled the boats," he said.

"I was told today that we'll soon need more storage huts," she said. "They're worried about sparing the labor for the building."

"Ten more huts," he said.

She would pass that word along, he knew. Somehow, it would be done. The other technicians listened to Honida. Many among the scientists scoffed at her; it could be heard beneath the blandness of their voices. Perhaps it was because she had chosen Kroudar for mate. But technicians listened. The huts would be built.

And they would be filled before the *trodi* run stopped.

Kroudar realized then that he knew when the run would stop, not as a date, but almost as a physical thing which he could reach out and touch. He longed for the words to explain this to Honida.

She gave his back a final kneading, sat down beside him and leaned her dark head against his chest. "If you're not too tired," she said, "I have something to show you."

With a feeling of surprise, Kroudar became aware of unspoken excitement in Honida. Was it something about the hydroponic gardens where she worked? His thoughts went immediately to that place upon which the scientists pinned their hopes, the place where they chose the tall plants, the beautiful, engorged with richness from Mother Earth. Had they achieved something important at last? Was there, after all, a clear way to make *this place* arable?

Kroudar was a primitive then wanting his gods redeemed. He found himself full of peasant hopes for the land. Even a sea peasant knew the value of land.

He and Honida had responsibilities, though. He nodded questioningly toward the twins' bedroom.

"I arranged . . ." She gestured toward their neighbor's cubicle. "They will listen."

She had planned for this, then. Kroudar stood up, held out his hand for her. "Show me."

They went out into the night. Their town was quieter now; he could hear the distant roistering of the river. For a moment, he thought he heard a cricket, but reason told him it could only be one of the huts cooling in the night. He longed wordlessly for a moon.

Honida had brought one of the rechargeable electric torches, the kind issued to technicians against emergency calls in the night. Seeing that torch, Kroudar sensed a deeper importance in this mysterious thing she wanted to show him. Honida had the peasant's hoarding instinct. She would not waste such a torch.

Instead of leading him toward the green lights and glass roofs of the hydroponic gardens, though, she guided their steps in the opposite direction toward the deep gorge where the river plunged into the harbor.

There were no guards along the footpath, only an occasional stone marker and grotesqueries of native growth. Swiftly, without speaking, she led him to the gorge and the narrow path which he knew went only down to a ledge which jutted into the damp air of the river's spray.

Kroudar found himself trembling with excitement as he followed Honida's shadowy figure, the firefly darting of her light. It was cold on the ledge and the alien outline of native trees revealed by the torch filled Kroudar with disquiet.

What had Honida discovered—or created?

Condensation dripped from the plants here. The river noise was loud. It was marsh air he breathed, dank and filled with bizarre odors.

Honida stopped, and Kroudar held his breath. He listened. There was only the river.

For a moment, he didn't realize that Honida was directing the orange light of the torch at her discovery. It looked like one of the native plants—a thing with a thick stem crouched low to the land, gnarled and twisted, bulbous yellow-green protrusions set with odd spacing along its length.

Slowly, realization came over him. He recognized a darker tone in the green, the way the leaf structures were joined to the stalk, a bunching of brown-yellow silk drooping from the bulbous protrusions.

"Maize," he whispered.

In a low voice, pitching her explanation to Kroudar's vocabulary, Honida explained what she had done. He saw it in her words, understood why she had done this thing stealthily, here away from the scientists. He took the light from her, crouched, stared with rapt attention. This meant the death of those things the scientists held beautiful. It ended their plan for *this place*.

Kroudar could see his own descendants in this plant. They might develop bulbous heads, hairless, wide thick-lipped mouths. Their skins might become purple. They would be short statured; he knew that.

Honida had assured this—right here on the river-drenched ledge. Instead of selecting seed from the tallest, the straightest stalks, the ones with the longest and most perfect ears—the ones most like those from Mother Earth—she had tested her maize almost to destruction. She had chosen sickly, scrawny plants, ones barely able to produce seed. She had taken only those plants which *this place* influenced most deeply. From these, she had selected finally a strain which lived *here* as native plants lived.

This was *native* maize.

She broke off an ear, peeled back the husk.

There were gaps in the seed rows and, when she squeezed a kernel, the juice ran purple. He recognized the smell of the bread.

Here was the thing the scientists would not admit. They were trying to make *this place* into another Earth. But it was not and it could never be. The falcons had been the first among their creatures to discover this, he suspected.

The statement Honida made here was that she and Kroudar would be short-lived. Their children would be sickly by Mother Earth's standards. Their descendants would change in ways that defied the hopes of those who had planned this migration. The scientists would hate this and try to stop it.

This gnarled stalk of maize said the scientists would fail.

For a long while, Kroudar crouched there, staring into the future until the torch began to dim, losing its charge. He aroused himself then, led the way back out of the gorge.

At the top, with the lights of their dying civilization visible across the plain, he stopped, said:

"The *trodi* run will stop . . . soon. I will take one boat and . . . friends. We will go out where the falcons go."

It was one of the longest speeches he had ever made.

She took the light from his hand, extinguished it, pressed herself against him.

"What do you think the falcons have found?"

"The seed," he said.

He shook his head. He could not explain it, but the thing was there in his awareness. Everything here exuded poisonous vapors, or juices in which only its own seed could live. Why should the *trodi* or any other sea creature be different? And, with the falcons as evidence, the seed must be slightly less poisonous to the intruders from Mother Earth.

"The boats are slow," she said.

He agreed silently. A storm could trap them too far out for a run to safety. It would be dangerous. But he heard also in her voice that she was not trying to stop him or dissuade him.

"I will take good men," he said.

"How long will you be gone?" Honida asked.

He thought about this for a moment. The rhythms of *this place* were beginning to make themselves known to him. His awareness shaped the journey, the days out, the night search over the water where the falcons were known to sweep in their low gliding runs—then the return.

"Eight days," he said.

"You'll need fine mesh nets," she said. "I'll see to having them made. Perhaps a few technicians, too. I know some who will go with you."

"Eight days," he said, telling her to choose strong men.

"Yes," she said. "Eight days. I'll be waiting on the shore when you return."

He took her hand then and led the way back across the plain. As they walked, he said: "We must name *this place*."

"When you come back," she said.

STANISLAW LEM

"The Seventh Voyage" from *The Star Diaries*

{ 1971 }

Stanislaw Lem (1921–2006) was the most prominent European science-fiction writer after World War II. His work, translated into over forty languages, is widely admired for its originality of vision, philosophical sophistication, and inventive literary techniques. Lem wrote in a great variety of forms and styles: adventure novels, realistic stories, satirical fables, metafictions, quasi-fictional essays, and treatises on the role of technology in human culture. In all these forms, Lem was concerned with a single theme: the inexorable collision between the inherent inability of human consciousness to know itself and its ingrained need to do so.

Born and raised in then–Polish Lvov, where he participated in underground resistance to the German occupation, Lem moved to the university city of Krakow in 1946. For most of his adult life, Lem remained in Poland, and did not travel west of Berlin or east of Moscow. Insulated from the commercial forces of Anglo-American science fiction, Lem's writing owes little to pulp and romantic formulas, and draws instead on the Central and East European traditions of grotesque fantasy and the classical science fiction of Verne, Wells, and Olaf Stapledon. Although he was for a generation the most popular and influential writer of science fiction in the Soviet bloc, Lem was profoundly anti-utopian. In his fiction, technology and ideology represent independent forces of domination that, when combined, produce absurd and disastrous results.

Lem is best known for a group of novels that dramatize the indecipherability of truly alien phenomena that might be encountered in space exploration—*Eden* (1959), *Solaris* (1961), *The Invincible* (1964), *His Master's Voice* (1968), and *Fiasco* (1987). In *Solaris*, Lem's best known novel, scientists encounter a planet that appears to be an intelligent entity, yet which cannot be analyzed scientifically and does not communicate. The novel has been filmed twice, by the revered Soviet director Andrei Tarkovsky in 1972 and in 2002 by American director Steven Soderbergh. Most of Lem's work is in shorter forms: short stories, grotesque sketches, and fantastic fairy tales collected in various cycles. The stories of the *Pirx* cycle follow the career of a resolutely unheroic protagonist from cadet to space pilot, and contain no fantastic elements. By far the most popular of Lem's fictions have been the wildly playful stories and fables associated with *The Robot Fables* (1964), *The Cyberiad* (1965–67), and *The Star Diaries* (1954–71). In the *Robot Fables*, Lem tells silicone-world fairy tales, a device *The Cyberiad* develops to whimsical extremes. Parodying Rabelais and the Finnish epic the *Kalevala*, two giant "constructors" who are robot-masters of cybernetics have the power to create and consume anything they wish. *The Star Diaries*, written over several decades (and made into a recent television series in Germany), are narrated by Ijon Tichy, a combination of Lemuel Gulliver and Baron von Munchhausen, a modest and earthy space traveler who introduces one philosophically complex science-fictional situation after another in fantastically comic form.

In addition to his fiction, Lem also wrote a number of ambitious nonfiction treatises. In *Summa Technologiae* (1964), Lem uses both scholarship and inventive language to imagine the effect of cyber-technology on the refashioning of the human species. Although written in isolation from ongoing research and development in computers, Lem was remarkably prescient about trends such as virtual reality, simulation, artificial intelligence, entanglement, and consciousness-uploads, which he named with his characteristic inventiveness, fantomatics, imitology, intellectronics, teletaxia, and fantoplication. In 1971, Lem published *A Perfect Vacuum*, a prismatic collection of metafictions masquerading as reviews of imaginary books, ranging from "Non Serviam," an account of artificial "personoids" coming to self-awareness in a computer mainframe, to "The New Cosmogony," which asserts that the anomalies and paradoxes of cosmology can be attributed to communication among cosmic super-entities.

In "The Seventh Voyage," one of the best-known entries of *The Star Diaries*, Lem uses the problem of cosmological time-loops, which many sf writers have treated with sublime awe, as an occasion for science-fictional slapstick.

It was on a Monday, April second—I was cruising in the vicinity of Betelgeuse—when a meteor no larger than a lima bean pierced the hull, shattered the drive regulator and part of the rudder, as a result of which the rocket lost all maneuverability. I put on my space suit, went outside and tried to fix the mechanism, but found I couldn't possibly attach the spare rudder—which I'd had the foresight to bring along—without the help of another man. The constructors had foolishly designed the rocket in such a way that it took one person to hold the head of the bolt in place with a wrench, and another to tighten the nut. I didn't realize this at first and spent several hours trying to grip the wrench with my feet while using both hands to screw on the nut at the other end. But I was getting nowhere, and had already missed lunch. Then finally, just as I almost succeeded, the wrench popped out from under my feet and went flying off into space. So not only had I accomplished nothing, but lost a valuable tool besides; I watched helplessly as it sailed away, growing smaller and smaller against the starry sky.

After a while the wrench returned in an elongated ellipse, but though it had now become a satellite of the rocket, it never got close enough for me to retrieve it. I went back inside and, sitting down to a modest supper, considered how best to extricate myself from this stupid situation. Meanwhile the ship flew on, straight ahead, its velocity steadily increasing, since my drive regulator too had been knocked out by that blasted meteor. It's true there were no heavenly bodies on course, but this headlong flight could hardly continue indefinitely. For a while I contained my anger, but then discovered, when starting to wash the dinner dishes, that the now overheated atomic pile had ruined my very best cut of sirloin (I'd been keeping it in the freezer for Sunday). I momentarily lost my usually level head, burst into a volley of the vilest oaths and smashed a few plates. This did give me a certain satisfaction, but was hardly practical. In addition, the sirloin which I threw overboard, instead of drifting off into the void, didn't seem to want to leave the rocket and revolved about it, a second artificial satellite, which produced a brief eclipse of the sun every eleven minutes and four seconds. To calm my nerves I calculated till evening the components of its trajectory, as well as the orbital perturbation caused by the presence of the lost wrench. I figured out that for the next six million years the sirloin, rotating about the ship in a circular path, would lead the wrench, then catch up with it from behind and pass it again. Finally, exhausted by these computations, I went to bed. In the middle of the night I had the feeling someone was shaking me by the shoulder. I opened my eyes and saw a man standing over the bed; his face was strangely familiar, though I hadn't the faintest idea who this could be.

"Get up," he said, "and take the pliers, we're going out and screwing on the rudder bolts . . ."

"First of all, your manner is somewhat unceremonious, and we haven't even been introduced," I replied, "and secondly, I know for a fact that you aren't there. I'm alone on this rocket, and have been now for two years, en route from Earth to the constellation of the Ram. Therefore you are a dream and nothing more."

However he continued to shake me, repeating that I should go with him at once and get the tools.

"This is idiotic," I said, growing annoyed, because this dream argument could very well wake me up, and I knew from experience the difficulty I would have getting back to sleep. "Look, I'm not going anywhere, there's no point in it. A bolt tightened in a dream won't change things as they are in the sober light of day. Now kindly stop pestering me and evaporate or leave in some other fashion, otherwise I might awake."

"But you *are* awake, word of honor!" cried the stubborn apparition. "Don't you recognize me? Look here!"

And saying this, he pointed to the two warts, big as strawberries, on his left cheek. Instinctively I clutched my own face, for yes, I had two warts, exactly the same, and in that very place. Suddenly I realized why this phantom reminded me of someone I knew: he was the spitting image of myself.

"Leave me alone, for heaven's sake!" I cried, shutting my eyes, anxious to stay asleep. "If you are me, then fine, we needn't stand on ceremony, but it only proves you don't exist!"

With which I turned on my other side and pulled the covers up over my head. I could hear him saying something about utter nonsense; then finally, when I didn't respond, he shouted: "You'll regret this, knucklehead! And you'll find out, too late, that this was not a dream!"

But I didn't budge. In the morning I opened my eyes and immediately recalled that curious nocturnal episode. Sitting up in bed, I thought about what strange tricks the mind can play: for here, without a single fellow creature on board and confronted with an emergency of the most pressing kind, I had—as it were—split myself in two, in that dream fantasy, to answer the needs of the situation.

After breakfast, discovering that the rocket had acquired an additional chunk of acceleration during the night, I took to leafing through the ship's library, searching the textbooks for some way out of this predicament. But I didn't find a thing. So I spread my star map out on the table and in the light of nearby Betelgeuse, obscured every so often by the orbiting sirloin, examined the area in which I was located for the seat of some cosmic civilization that might possibly come to my aid. But unfortunately this was a complete stellar wilderness, avoided by all vessels as a region unusually dangerous, for in it lay gravitational vortices, as formidable as they were mysterious, one hundred and forty-seven of them in all, whose existence was explained by six astrophysical theories, each theory saying something different.

The cosmonautical almanac warned of them, in view of the incalculable relativistic effects that passage through a vortex could bring about—particularly when traveling at high velocities.

Yet there was little I could do. According to my calculations I would be making contact with the edge of the first vortex at around eleven, and therefore hurriedly prepared lunch, not wanting to face the danger on an empty stomach. I had barely finished drying the last saucer when the rocket began to pitch and heave in every direction, till all the objects not adequately tied down went flying from wall to wall like hail. With difficulty I crawled over to the armchair, and after I'd lashed myself to it, as the ship tossed about with ever-increasing violence, I noticed a sort of pale lilac haze forming on the opposite side of the cabin, and in the middle of it, between the sink and the stove, a misty human shape, which had on an apron and was pouring omelet batter into a frying pan. The shape looked at me with interest, but without surprise, then shimmered and was gone. I rubbed my eyes. I was obviously alone, so attributed the vision to a momentary aberration.

As I continued to sit in—or rather, jump along with the armchair, it suddenly hit me, like a dazzling revelation, that this hadn't been a hallucination at all. A thick volume of the General Theory of Relativity came whirling past my chair and I grabbed for it, finally catching it on the fourth pass. Turning the pages of that heavy tome wasn't easy under the circumstances—awesome forces hurled the rocket this way and that, it reeled like a drunken thing—but at last I found the right chapter. It spoke of the manifestation of the "time loop," that is, the bending of the direction of the flow of time in the presence of gravitational fields of great intensity, which phenomenon might even on occasion lead to the complete reversal of time and the "duplication of the present." The vortex I had just entered was not one of the most powerful. I knew that if I could turn the ship's bow, even if only a little, towards the Galactic Pole, it would intersect the so-called Vortex Gravitatiosus Pinckenbachii, in which had been observed more than once the duplication, even the triplication, of the present.

True, the controls were out, but I went down to the engine room and fiddled with the instruments so long that I actually managed to produce a slight deflection of the rocket towards the Galactic Pole. This took several hours. The results were beyond my expectations. The ship fell into the center of the vortex at around midnight, its girders shook and groaned until I began to fear for its safety; but it emerged from this ordeal whole and once again was wrapped in the lifeless arms of cosmic silence, whereupon I left the engine room, only to see myself sound asleep in bed. I realized at once that this was I of the previous day, that is, from Monday night. Without reflecting on the philosophical side of this rather singular event, I ran over and shook the sleeper by the shoulder, shouting for him to get up, since I had no idea how long his Monday existence would last in my Tuesday one, therefore it was imperative we go outside and fix the rudder as quickly as possible, together.

But the sleeper merely opened one eye and told me that not only was I rude, but didn't exist, being a figment of his dream and nothing more. I tugged at him in vain, losing patience, and even attempted to drag him bodily from the bed. He wouldn't budge, stubbornly repeating that it was all a dream, I began to curse, but he pointed out logically that bolts tightened in dreams wouldn't hold on rudders in the sober light of day. I gave my word of honor that he was mistaken, I pleaded and swore in turn, to no avail—even the warts did not convince him. He turned his back to me and started snoring.

I sat down in the armchair to collect my thoughts and take stock of the situation. I'd lived through it twice now, first as that sleeper, on Monday, and then as the one trying to wake him, unsuccessfully, on Tuesday. The Monday me hadn't believed in the reality of the duplication, while the Tuesday me already knew it to be a fact. Here was a perfectly ordinary time loop. What then should be done in order to get the rudder fixed? Since the Monday me slept on—I remembered that on that night I had slept through to the morning undisturbed—I saw the futility of any further efforts to rouse him. The map indicated a number of other large gravitational vortices up ahead, therefore I could count on the duplication of the present within the next few days. I decided to write myself a letter and pin it to the pillow, enabling the Monday me, when he awoke, to see for himself that the dream had been no dream.

But no sooner did I sit at the table with pen and paper than something started rattling in the engines, so I hurried there and poured water on the overheated atomic pile till dawn, while the Monday me slept soundly, licking his lips from time to time, which galled me no end. Hungry and bleary-eyed, for I hadn't slept a wink, I set about making breakfast, and was just wiping the dishes when the rocket fell into the next gravitational vortex. I saw my Monday self staring at me dumbfounded, lashed to the armchair, while Tuesday I fried an omelet. Then a lurch knocked me off balance, everything grew dark, and down I went. I came to on the floor among bits of broken china; near my face were the shoes of a man standing over me.

"Get up," he said, lifting me. "Are you all right?"

"I think so," I answered, keeping my hands on the floor, for my head was still spinning. "From what day of the week are you?"

"Wednesday," he said. "Come on, let's get that rudder fixed while we have the chance!"

"But where's the Monday me?" I asked.

"Gone. Which means, I suppose, that you are he."

"How is that?"

"Well, the Monday me on Monday night became, Tuesday morning, the Tuesday me, and so on."

"I don't understand."

"Doesn't matter—you'll get the hang of it. But hurry up, we're wasting time!"

"Just a minute," I replied, remaining on the floor. "Today is Tuesday. Now if you are the Wednesday *me*, and if by that time on Wednesday the rudder still hasn't been fixed, then it follows that something will prevent us from fixing it, since otherwise you, on Wednesday, would not now, on Tuesday, be asking me to help you fix it. Wouldn't it be best, then, for us not to risk going outside?"

"Nonsense!" he exclaimed. "Look, I'm the Wednesday me and you're the Tuesday me, and as for the rocket, well, my guess is that its existence is patched, which means that in places it's Tuesday, in places Wednesday, and here and there perhaps there's even a bit of Thursday. Time has simply become shuffled up in passing through these vortices, but why should that concern us, when together we are two and therefore have a chance to fix the rudder?"

"No, you're wrong!" I said. "If on Wednesday, where you already are, having lived through all of Tuesday, so that now Tuesday is behind you, if on Wednesday—I repeat—the rudder isn't fixed, then one can only conclude that it didn't get fixed on Tuesday, since it's Tuesday now and if we were to go and fix the rudder right away, that *right away* would be your *yesterday* and there would now be nothing to fix. And consequently—"

"And consequently you're as stubborn as a mule!" he growled. "You'll regret this! And my only consolation is that you too will be infuriated by your own pigheadedness just as I am now—when you yourself reach Wednesday!"

"Ah, wait," I cried, "do you mean that on Wednesday, I, being you, will try to convince the Tuesday me, just as you are doing here, except that everything will be reversed, in other words you will be me and I you? But, of course! That's what makes a time loop! Hold on, I'm coming, yes, it makes sense now . . ."

But before I could get up off the floor we fell into a new vortex and the terrible acceleration flattened us against the ceiling.

The dreadful pitching and heaving didn't let up once throughout that night from Tuesday to Wednesday. Then, when things had finally quieted down a little, the volume of the General Theory of Relativity came flying across the cabin and hit me on the forehead with such force, that I lost consciousness. When I opened my eyes I saw broken dishes and a man sprawled among them. I immediately jumped to my feet and lifted him, shouting:

"Get up! Are you all right?"

"I think so," he replied, blinking." From what day of the week are you?"

"Wednesday," I said, "come on, let's get that rudder fixed while we have the chance."

"But where's the Monday me?" he asked, sitting up. He had a black eye.

"Gone," I said, "which means that you are he."

"How is that?"

"Well, the Monday me on Monday night became, Tuesday morning, the Tuesday me, and so on."

"I don't understand."

"Doesn't matter—you'll get the hang of it. But hurry up, we're wasting time!"

Saying this, I was already looking around for the tools.

"Just a minute," he drawled, not budging an inch. "Today is Tuesday. Now, if you are the Wednesday me, and if by that time on Wednesday the rudder still hasn't been fixed, then it follows that something will prevent us from fixing it, since otherwise you, on Wednesday, would not be asking me now, on Tuesday, to help you fix it. Wouldn't it be best, then, for us not to risk going outside?"

"Nonsense!" I yelled, losing my temper. "Look, I'm the Wednesday me, you're the Tuesday me . . ."

And so we quarreled, in opposite roles, during which he did in fact drive me into a positive fury, for he persistently refused to help me fix the rudder and it did no good calling him pigheaded and a stubborn mule. And when at last I managed to convince him, we plunged into the next gravitational vortex. I was in a cold sweat, for the thought occurred to me that we might now go around and around in this time loop, repeating ourselves for all eternity, but luckily that didn't happen. By the time the acceleration had slackened enough for me to stand, I was alone once more in the cabin. Apparently the localized existence of Tuesday, which until now had persisted in the vicinity of the sink, had vanished, becoming a part of the irretrievable past. I rushed over to the map, to find some nice vortex into which I could send the rocket, so as to bring about still another warp of time and in that way obtain a helping hand.

There was in fact one vortex, quite promising too, and by manipulating the engines with great difficulty, I aimed the rocket to intersect it at the very center. True, the configuration of that vortex was, according to the map, rather unusual—it had two foci, side by side. But by now I was too desperate to concern myself with this anomaly.

After several hours of bustling about in the engine room my hands were filthy, so I went to wash them, seeing as there was plenty of time yet before I would be entering the vortex. The bathroom was locked. From inside came the sounds of someone gargling.

"Who's there?" I hollered, taken aback. "Me," replied a voice.

"Which me is that?!"

"Ijon Tichy."

"From what day?"

"Friday. What do you want?"

"I wanted to wash my hands . . ." I said mechanically, thinking meanwhile with the greatest intensity: it was Wednesday evening, and he came from Friday, therefore the gravitational vortex into which the ship was to fall would bend time from Friday to Wednesday, but as for what then would take place within the vortex, that I could in no way picture. Particularly intriguing was the question of where Thursday might be. In the meantime the Friday me still wasn't letting me into the bathroom, taking his sweet time, though I pounded on the door insistently.

"Stop that gargling!" I roared, out of patience. "Every second is precious—come out at once, we have to fix the rudder!"

"For that you don't need me," he said phlegmatically from behind the door. "The Thursday me must be around here somewhere, go with him."

"What Thursday me? That's not possible . . ."

"I ought to know whether it's possible or not, considering that I'm already in Friday and consequently have lived through your Wednesday as well as his Thursday . . ."

Feeling dizzy, I jumped back from the door, for yes, I did hear some commotion in the cabin: a man was standing there, pulling the toolbag out from under the bed.

"You're the Thursday me?" I cried, running into the man.

"Right," he said. "Here, give me a hand."

"Will we be able to fix the rudder this time?" I asked as together we pulled out the heavy satchel.

"I don't know, it wasn't fixed on Tuesday, ask the Friday me . . ."

That hadn't crossed my mind! I quickly ran back to the bathroom door.

"Hey there, Friday me! Has the rudder been fixed?"

"Not on Friday," he replied.

"Why not?"

"This is why not," he said, opening the door. His head was wrapped in a towel, and he pressed the flat of a knife to his forehead, trying in this manner to reduce the swelling of a lump the size of an egg. The Thursday me meanwhile approached with the tools and stood beside me, calmly scrutinizing the me with the lump, who with his free hand was putting back on the shelf a siphon of seltzer. So it was its gurgle I had taken for his gargle.

"What gave you that?" I asked sympathetically. "Not what, who," he replied. "It was the Sunday me."

"The Sunday me? But why . . . that can't be!" I cried. "Well it's a long story . . ."

"Makes no difference! Quick, let's go outside, we might just make it!" said the Thursday me, turning to the me that was I.

"But the rocket will fall into the vortex any minute now," I replied. "The shock could throw us off into space, and that would be the end of us . . ."

"Use your head, stupid," snapped the Thursday me.

"If the Friday me's alive, nothing can happen to us."

"Today is only Thursday."

"It's Wednesday," I objected.

"It makes no difference, in either case I'll be alive on Friday, and so will you."

"Yes, but there really aren't two of us, it only looks that way," I observed, "actually there is *one* me, just from different days of the week . . ."

"Fine, fine, now open the hatch . . ." But it turned out here that we had only one space suit between us. Therefore we could not both leave the rocket at the same time, and therefore our plan to fix the rudder was completely ruined.

"Blast!" I cried, angrily throwing down the toolbag. "What I should have done is put on the spacesuit to begin with and kept it on. I just didn't think of it—but you, as the Thursday me, you ought to have remembered!"

"I had the spacesuit, but the Friday me took it," he said.

"When? Why?"

"Eh, it's not worth going into," he shrugged and, turning around, went back to the cabin. The Friday me wasn't there; I looked in the bathroom, but it was empty too.

"Where's the Friday me?" I asked, returning. The Thursday me methodically cracked an egg with a knife and poured its contents onto the sizzling fat.

"Somewhere in the neighborhood of Saturday, no doubt," he replied, indifferent, quickly scrambling the egg.

"Excuse me," I protested, "but you already had your meals on Wednesday—what makes you think you can go and eat a second Wednesday supper?"

"These rations are mine just as much as they are yours," he said, calmly lifting the browned edge of the egg with his knife; "I am you, you are me, so it makes no difference . . ."

"What sophistry! Wait, that's too much butter! Are you crazy? I don't have enough food for this many people!"

The skillet flew out of his hand, and I went crashing into a wall: we had fallen into a new vortex. Once again the ship shook, as if in a fever, but my only thought was to get to the corridor where the spacesuit was hanging and put it on. For in that way (I reasoned) when Wednesday became Thursday, I, as the Thursday me, would be wearing that spacesuit, and if only I didn't take it off for a single minute (and I was determined not to) then I would obviously be wearing it on Friday also. And therefore the me on Thursday and the me on Friday would both be in our spacesuits, so that when we came together in the same present it would finally be possible to fix that miserable rudder. The increasing thrust of gravity made my head swim, and when I opened my eyes I noticed that I was lying to the right of the Thursday me, and not to the left, as I had been a few moments before. Now while it had been easy enough for me to develop this plan about the spacesuit, it was considerably more difficult to put it into action, since with the growing gravitation I could hardly move. When it weakened just a little, I began to inch my way across the floor—in the direction of the door that led to the corridor. Meanwhile I noticed that the Thursday me was likewise heading for the door, crawling on his belly towards the corridor. At last, after about an hour, when the vortex had reached its widest point we met at the threshold, both flattened to the floor. Then I thought, why should I have to strain myself to reach the handle? Let the Thursday me do it. Yet at the same time I began to recall certain things which clearly indicated that it was I now who was the Thursday me, and not he.

"What day of the week are you?" I asked, to make sure. With my chin pressed to the floor I looked him in the eye. Struggling, he opened his mouth.

"Thurs—day—me," he groaned. Now that was odd.

Could it be that, in spite of everything, I was *still* the Wednesday me? Calling to mind all my recollections of the recent past, I had to conclude that this was out of the question. So he must have been the Friday me. For if he had preceded me by a day before, then he was surely a day ahead now. I waited for him to open the door, but apparently he expected the same of me. The gravitation had now subsided noticeably, so I got up and ran to the corridor. Just as I grabbed the space suit, he tripped me, pulling it out of my hands, and I fell flat on my face.

"You dog!" I cried. "Tricking your own self—that's really low!" He ignored me, stepping calmly into the spacesuit. The shamelessness of it was appalling. Suddenly a strange force threw him from the suit—as it turned out, someone was already inside. For a moment I wavered, no longer knowing who was who.

"You, Wednesday!" called the one in the spacesuit. "Hold back Thursday, help me!"

For the Thursday me was indeed trying to tear the spacesuit off him.

"Give me the spacesuit!" bellowed the Thursday me as he wrestled with the other.

"Get off! What are you trying to do? Don't you realize I'm the one who should have it, and not you?" howled the other. "And why is that, pray?"

"For the reason, fool, that I'm closer to Saturday than you, and by Saturday there will be two of us in suits!"

"But that's ridiculous," I said, getting into their argument. "At best you'll be alone in the suit on Saturday, like an absolute idiot, and won't be able to do a thing. Let *me* have the suit: if I put it on now, then you'll be wearing it on Friday as the Friday me, and I will also on Saturday as the Saturday me, and so you see there will then be two of us, and with two suits . . . Come on, Thursday, give me a hand!"

"Wait," protested the Friday me when I had forcibly yanked the spacesuit off his back. "In the first place, there is no one here for you to call 'Thursday,' since midnight has passed and *you* are now the Thursday me, and in the second place, it'll be better if I stay in the spacesuit. The spacesuit won't do you a bit of good."

"Why not? If I put it on today, I'll have it on tomorrow too."

"You'll see for yourself . . . after all, I was already you, on Thursday, and *my* Thursday has passed, so I ought to know . . ."

"Enough talk. Let go of it this instant!" I snarled. But he grabbed it from me and I chased him, first through the engine room and then into the cabin. It somehow worked out that there were only two of us now. Suddenly I understood why the Thursday me, when we were standing at the hatch with the tools, had told me that the Friday me took the spacesuit from him: for in the meantime I myself had become the Thursday me, and here the Friday me was in fact taking it. But I had no intention of giving in that easily. Just you wait, I thought, I'll take care of you, and out I ran into the corridor, and from there to the engine room, where before—during the chase—I had noticed a heavy pipe lying on the floor, which served to stoke the atomic pile, and I picked it up and—thus armed—dashed back to the cabin. The other me was already in the spacesuit, he had pulled on everything but the helmet.

"Out of the spacesuit!" I snapped, clenching my pipe in a threatening manner.

"Not a chance."

"Out, I say!"

Then I wondered whether or not I should hit him. It was a little disconcerting, the fact that he had neither a black eye nor a bump on his head, like the other Friday me, the one I'd found in the bathroom, but all at once I realized that this was the way it had to be. *That* Friday me by now was the Saturday me, yes, and perhaps even was knocking about somewhere in the vicinity of Sunday, while this Friday me inside the spacesuit had only recently been the Thursday me, into which same Thursday me I myself had been transformed at midnight. Thus I was moving along the sloping curve of the time loop towards that place in which the Friday me before the beating would change into the Friday me already beaten. Still, he *did* say, back then, that it had been the Sunday me who did it, and there was no trace, as yet, of *him*. We stood alone in the cabin, he and I. Then suddenly I had a brainstorm.

"Out of that spacesuit!" I growled.

"Keep off, Thursday" he yelled.

"I'm not Thursday, I'm the SUNDAY ME!" I shrieked, closing in for the kill. He tried to kick me, but spacesuit boots are very heavy and before he could raise his leg, I let him have it over the head. Not too hard, of course, since I had grown sufficiently familiar with all of this to know that I in turn, when eventually I went from the Thursday to the Friday me, would be on the receiving end, and I wasn't particularly set on fracturing my own skull. The Friday me fell with a groan, holding his head, and I brutally tore the spacesuit off him. While he made for the bathroom on wobbly legs, muttering, "Where's the cotton . . . where's the seltzer," I quickly began to don the suit that we had struggled over, until I noticed—sticking out from under the bed—a human foot. I took a closer look, kneeling. Under the bed lay a man; trying to muffle the sound of his chewing, he was hurriedly bolting down the last bar of the milk chocolate I had stored away in the suitcase for a rainy sidereal day. The bastard was in such a hurry that he ate the chocolate along with bits of tin foil, which glittered on his lips.

"Leave that chocolate alone!" I yelled, pulling at his foot. "Who are you anyway? The Thursday me? . . ." I added in a lower voice, seized by a sudden doubt, for the thought occurred that maybe I already was the Friday me, and would soon have to collect what I had dished out earlier to the same.

"The Sunday me," he mumbled, his mouth full. I felt weak. Now either he was lying, in which case there was nothing to worry about, or telling the truth, and if he was, I faced a clobbering for sure, because the Sunday me—after all—was the one who had hit the Friday me, the Friday me told me so himself before it happened, and then later I, impersonating the Sunday me, had let him have it with the pipe. But on the other hand, I said to myself, even if he's lying and not the Sunday me, it's still quite possible that he's a later me than me, and if he *is* a later me, he remembers everything that I do, therefore already knows that I lied to the Friday me, and so could deceive me in a similar manner, since what had been a spur of the moment stratagem on my part was for him—by now—simply a memory, a memory he could easily make use of. Meanwhile, as I remained in uncertainty, he had eaten the rest of the chocolate and crawled out from under the bed.

"If you're the Sunday me, where's your spacesuit?" I cried, struck by a new thought.

"I'll have it in a minute," he said calmly, and then I noticed the pipe in his hand . . . The next thing I saw was a bright flash, like a few dozen supernovas going off at once, after which I lost consciousness. I came to, sitting on the floor of the bathroom; someone was banging on the door. I began to attend to my bruises and bumps, but he kept pounding away; it turned out to be the Wednesday me. After a while I showed him my battered head, he went with the Thursday me for the tools, then there was a lot of running around and yanking off of spacesuits, this too in one way or another I managed to live through, and on Saturday morning crawled under the bed to see if there wasn't some chocolate left in the suitcase. Someone started pulling at my foot as I ate the last bar, which I'd found underneath the shirts; I no longer knew just who this was, but hit him over the head anyhow, pulled the spacesuit off him and was going to put it on—when the rocket fell into the next vortex.

When I regained consciousness, the cabin was packed with people. There was barely elbowroom. As it turned out, they were all of them me, from different days, weeks, months, and one—so he said—was even from the following year. There were plenty with bruises and black eyes, and five among those present had on spacesuits. But instead of immediately going out through the hatch and repairing the damage, they began to quarrel, argue, bicker and debate. The problem was, who had hit whom, and when. The situation was complicated by the fact that there now had appeared morning me's and afternoon me's—I feared that if things went on like this, I would soon be broken into minutes and seconds—and then too, the majority of the me's present were lying like mad, so that to this day I'm not altogether sure whom I hit and who hit me when that whole business took place, triangularly, between the Thursday, the Friday and the Wednesday me's, all of whom I was in turn. My impression is that because I had lied to the Friday me, pretending to be the Sunday me, I ended up with one blow more than I should have, going by the calendar. But I would prefer not to dwell any longer on these unpleasant memories; a man who for an entire week does nothing but hit himself over the head has little reason to be proud.

Meanwhile the arguments continued. The sight of such inaction, such wasting of precious time, drove me to despair, while the rocket rushed blindly on, straight ahead, plunging every now and then into another gravitational vortex. At last the ones wearing spacesuits started slugging it out with the ones who were not. I tried to introduce some sort of order into that absolute chaos and finally, after superhuman efforts, succeeded in organizing something that resembled a meeting, in which the one from next year—having seniority—was elected chairman by acclamation.

We then appointed an elective committee, a nominating committee, and a committee for new business, and four us from next month were made sergeants at arms. But in the meantime we had passed through a negative vortex, which cut our number in half, so that on the very first ballot we lacked a quorum, and had to change the bylaws before proceeding to vote on the candidates for rudder repairer. The map indicated the approach of still other vortices, and these undid all that we had accomplished so far: first the candidates already chosen disappeared, and then the Tuesday me showed up with the Friday me, who had his head wrapped in a towel, and they created a shameful scene. Upon passage through a particularly strong positive vortex we hardly fit in the cabin and corridor, and opening the hatch was out of the question—there simply wasn't room. But the worst of it was, these time displacements were increasing in amplitude, a few grayhaired me's had already appeared and here and there I even caught a glimpse of the close-cropped heads of children, that is of myself, of course—or rather—myselves from the halcyon days of boyhood.

I really can't recall whether I was still the Sunday me, or had already turned into the Monday me. Not that it made any difference. The children sobbed that they were being squashed in the crowd, and called for their mommy; the chairman—the Tichy from next year—let out a string of curses, because the Wednesday me, who had crawled under the bed in a futile search for chocolate, bit him in the leg when he accidentally stepped on the latter's finger. I saw that all this would end badly, particularly now as here and there graybeards were turning up. Between the 142nd and 143rd vortices I passed around an attendance sheet, but, afterwards it came to light that a large number of those present were cheating. Supplying false vital statistics, God knows why. Perhaps the prevailing atmosphere had muddled their wits. The noise and confusion were such that you could make yourself understood only by screaming at the top of your lungs. But then one of last year's Ijons hit upon what seemed to be an excellent idea, namely, that the oldest among us tell the story of his life; in that way we would learn just who was supposed to fix the rudder. For obviously the oldest me contained within his past experiences the lives of all the others there from their various months, days and years. So we turned, in this matter, to a hoary old gentleman who, slightly palsied, was standing idly in the corner. When questioned, he began to speak at great length of his children and grandchildren, then passed to his cosmic voyages, and he had embarked upon no end of these in the course of his ninety-some years. Of the one now taking place—the only one of interest to us—the old man had no recollection whatever, owing to his generally sclerotic and overexcited condition, however he was far too proud to admit this and went on evasively, obstinately, time and again returning to his high connections, decorations and grandchildren, till finally we shouted him down and ordered him to hold his tongue. The next two vortices cruelly thinned our ranks After the third, not only was there more room, but all of those spacesuits had disappeared as well. One empty suit remained; we voted to hang it up in the corridor, then went back to our deliberations. Then, following another scuffle for the possession of that precious garment, a new vortex came along and suddenly the place was deserted. I was sitting on the floor, puffy-eyed, in my strangely spacious cabin, surrounded by broken furniture, strips of clothing, ripped-up books. The floor was strewn with ballots. According to the map, I had now passed through the entire zone of gravitational vortices. No longer able to count on duplication, and thus no longer able to correct the damage, I fell into numb despair. About an hour later I looked out in the corridor and discovered, to my great surprise, that the spacesuit was missing. But then I vaguely remembered—yes—right before that last vortex two little boys sneaked out into the corridor. Could they have possibly, both of them, put on the one spacesuit?! Struck by a sudden thought, I ran to the controls. The rudder worked? So then, those little tykes had fixed it after all, while we adults were stuck in endless disagreements. I imagine that one of them placed his arms in the sleeves of the suit, and the other—in the pants; that way, they could have tightened the nut and bolt with wrenches at the same time, working on either side of the rudder. The empty spacesuit I found in the air lock, behind the hatch. I carried it inside the rocket like a sacred relic; my heart full of boundless gratitude for those brave lads I had been so long ago! And thus concluded what was surely one of my most unusual adventures. I reached my destination safely, thanks to the courage and resourcefulness I had displayed when only two children.

It was said afterwards that I invented the whole thing, and those more malicious even went so far as to insinuate that I had a weakness for alcohol, carefully concealed on Earth but freely indulged during those long and lonely cosmic flights. Lord only knows what other gossip has been circulating on the subject. But that is how people are; they'll willingly give credence to the most farfetched drivel, but not to the simple truth, which is precisely what I have presented here.

Joanna Russ
When It Changed

{1972}

Joanna Russ (1937–) is one of the writers, including Suzy McKee Charnas and James Tiptree Jr. (pseudonym of Alice Sheldon), who brought a sharp feminist consciousness to the genre during the 1970s. She began publishing sf in 1959, and her short fiction output, while never prolific, was always agile and intelligent, as evidenced by the stories gathered in *The Zanzibar Cat* (1983) and *The Hidden Side of the Moon* (1987). During the 1960s, she published a series of tales featuring the time-traveling Alyx, a female warrior in the mold of C. L. Moore's Jirel of Joiry, though with an even more aggressive gender-bending aura. Alyx gracefully and competently adopts all the intrepid postures of the traditional male protagonist, as in the novel *Picnic on Paradise* (1968), where she saves a group of refugees on a war-ravaged planet. Russ's later novels grew increasingly ambitious, from *And Chaos Died* (1970), with its psychedelic depiction of psionic powers, to *We Who Are About to . . .* (1977), an uncompromising parable of individual autonomy. Russ's finest novel, *The Female Man* (1975), is ideologically rigorous and experimentally rich, examining the linked lives of four women from disparate time frames who are engaged in a grueling battle of the sexes, whether figurative or literal. An intricate fusion of sf, postmodern metafiction, and the consciousness-raising novel, it brilliantly illustrates the feminist gender politics Russ would soon begin to explore in such nonfiction works as *How to Suppress Women's Writing* (1983). Indeed, Russ is one of the most important author-critics in the genre's history, as proven by the agenda-setting essays gathered in *To Write Like a Woman: Essays in Feminism and Science Fiction* (1995).

"When It Changed," which won a Nebula Award for best short story, is set in a fictive venue that would also be featured in *The Female Man*: the planet Whileaway, a lost earth colony populated exclusively by women—all the men having perished in a shadowy plague. Whileaway is probably the most famous all-female utopia in contemporary sf, and second only to Charlotte Perkins Gilman's *Herland* (1915) in the history of the genre. As Russ shows, women are quite capable of running a complex society, raising well-grounded children, and engaging in loving relationships in the absence of men—though these facts are unbelievable to the male explorers in the story, who rediscover Whileaway after six centuries of women-only rule. Russ cleverly deploys the atmospherics of classic first-contact narratives to depict the resulting clash of cultures and perspectives: though of the same species, the men seem like aliens to the Whileawayans—curiously exotic to some, grotesquely repulsive to others. For their part, the men operate with the patronizing assumption that their recolonization of the planet will be welcomed by the grateful natives. The story's powerful satire has proven influential: William Gibson, for example, uses the phrase "when it changed" in his novel *Count Zero* (1986), and his fiction is filled with subtle allusions to Russ's work, leading some critics (such as Samuel R. Delany) to discern the imprint of 1970s feminist sf on 1980s cyberpunk.

Katy drives like a maniac; we must have been doing over 120 km/hr on those turns. She's good, though, extremely good, and I've seen her take the whole car apart and put it together again in a day. My birthplace on Whileaway was largely given to farm machinery and I refuse to wrestle with a five-gear shift at unholy speeds, not having been brought up to it, but even on those turns in the middle of the night, on a country road as bad as only our district can make them, Katy's driving didn't scare me. The funny thing about my wife, though: she will not handle guns. She has even gone hiking in the forests above the 48th parallel without firearms, for days at a time. And that *does* scare me.

Katy and I have three children between us, one of hers and two of mine. Yuriko, my eldest, was asleep in the back seat, dreaming twelve-year-old dreams of love and war: running away to sea, hunting in the North, dreams of strangely beautiful people in strangely beautiful places, all the wonderful guff you think up when you're turning twelve and the glands start going. Some day soon, like all of them, she will disappear for weeks on end to come back grimy and proud, having knifed her first cougar or shot her first bear, dragging some abominably dangerous dead beastie behind her, which I will never forgive for what it might have done to my daughter. Yuriko says Katy's driving puts her to sleep.

For someone who has fought three duels, I am afraid of far, far too much. I'm getting old. I told this to my wife.

"You're thirty-four," she said. Laconic to the point of silence, that one. She flipped the lights on, on the dash—three kilometers to go and the road getting worse all the time. Far out in the country. Electric-green trees rushed into our headlights and around the car. I reached down next to me where we bolt the carrier panel to the door and eased my rifle into my lap. Yuriko stirred in the back. My height but Katy's eyes, Katy's face. The car engine is so quiet, Katy says, that you can hear breathing in the back seat. Yuki had been alone in the car when the message came, enthusiastically decoding her dot-dashes (silly to mount a wide-frequency transceiver near an I.C. engine, but most of Whileaway is on steam). She had thrown herself out of the car, my gangly and gaudy offspring, shouting at the top of her lungs, so of course she had had to come along. We've been intellectually prepared for this ever since the Colony was founded, ever since it was abandoned, but this is different. This is awful.

"Men!" Yuki had screamed, leaping over the car door. "They've come back! Real Earth men!"

We met them in the kitchen of the farmhouse near the place where they had landed; the windows were open, the night air very mild. We had passed all sorts of transportation when we parked outside, steam tractors, trucks, an I.C. flatbed, even a bicycle. Lydia, the district biologist, had come out of her Northern taciturnity long enough to take blood and urine samples and was sitting in a corner of the kitchen shaking her head in astonishment over the results; she even forced herself (very big, very fair, very shy, always painfully blushing) to dig up the old language manuals—though I can talk the old tongues in my sleep. And do. Lydia is uneasy with us; we're Southerners and too flamboyant. I counted twenty people in that kitchen, all the brains of North Continent. Phyllis Spet, I think, had come in by glider. Yuki was the only child there.

Then I saw the four of them.

They are bigger than we are. They are bigger and broader. Two were taller than me, and I am extremely tall, one meter eighty centimeters in my bare feet. They are obviously of our species but *off*, indescribably off, and as my eyes could not and still cannot quite comprehend the lines of those alien bodies, I could not, then, bring myself to touch them, though the one who spoke Russian—what voices they have!—wanted to "shake hands," a custom from the past, I imagine. I can only say they were apes with human faces. He seemed to mean well, but I found myself shuddering back almost the length of the kitchen—and then I laughed apologetically—and then to set a good example (*interstellar amity,* I thought) did "shake hands" finally. A hard, hard hand. They are heavy as draft horses. Blurred, deep voices. Yuriko had sneaked in between the adults and was gazing at *the men* with her mouth open.

He turned *his* head—those words have not been in our language for six hundred years—and said, in bad Russian:

"Who's that?"

"My daughter," I said, and added (with that irrational attention to good manners we sometimes employ in moments of insanity), "My daughter, Yuriko Janetson. We use the patronymic. You would say matronymic."

He laughed, involuntarily. Yuki exclaimed, "I thought they would be *good-looking*!" greatly disappointed at this reception of herself. Phyllis Helgason Spet, whom someday I shall kill, gave me across the room a cold, level, venomous look, as if to say: *Watch what you say. You know what I can do.* It's true that I have little formal status, but Madam President will get herself in serious trouble with both me and her own staff if she continues to consider industrial espionage good clean fun. Wars and rumors of wars, as it says in one of our ancestor's books. I translated Yuki's words into *the man's* dog-Russian, once our *lingua franca*, and *the man* laughed again.

"Where are all your people?" he said conversationally.

I translated again and watched the faces around the room; Lydia embarrassed (as usual), Spet narrowing her eyes with some damned scheme, Katy very pale.

"This is Whileaway," I said.

He continued to look unenlightened.

"Whileaway," I said. "Do you remember? Do you have records? There was a plague on Whileaway."

He looked moderately interested. Heads turned in the back of the room, and I caught a glimpse of the local professions-parliament delegate; by morning every town meeting, every district caucus, would be in full session.

"Plague?" he said. "That's most unfortunate."

"Yes," I said. "Most unfortunate. We lost half our population in one generation."

He looked properly impressed.

"Whileaway was lucky," I said. "We had a big initial gene pool, we had been chosen for extreme intelligence, we had a high technology and a large remaining population in which every adult was two-or-three experts in one. The soil is good. The climate is blessedly easy. There are thirty millions of us now. Things are beginning to snowball in industry—do you understand?—give us seventy years and we'll have more than one real city, more than a few industrial centers, full-time professions, full-time radio operators, full-time machinists, give us seventy years and not everyone will have to spend three quarters of a lifetime on the farm." And I tried to explain how hard it is when artists can practice full-time only in old age, when there are so few, so very few who can be free, like Katy and myself. I tried also to outline our government, the two houses, the one by professions and the geographic one; I told him the district caucuses handled problems too big for the individual towns. And that population control was not a political issue, not yet, though give us time and it would be. This was a delicate point in our history; give us time. There was no need to sacrifice the quality of life for an insane rush into industrialization. Let us go our own pace. Give us time.

"Where are all the people?" said the monomaniac.

I realized then that he did not mean people, he meant *men*, and he was giving the word the meaning it had not had on Whileaway for six centuries.

"They died," I said. "Thirty generations ago."

I thought we had poleaxed him. He caught his breath. He made as if to get out of the chair he was sitting in; he put his hand to his chest; he looked around at us with the strangest blend of awe and sentimental tenderness. Then he said, solemnly and earnestly:

"A great tragedy."

I waited, not quite understanding.

"Yes," he said, catching his breath again with that queer smile, that adult-to-child smile that tells you something is being hidden and will be presently produced with cries of encouragement and joy, "a great tragedy. But it's over." And again he looked around at all of us with the strangest deference. As if we were invalids.

"You've adapted amazingly," he said.

"To what?" I said. He looked embarrassed. He looked insane. Finally he said, "Where I come from, the women don't dress so plainly."

"Like you?" I said. "Like a bride?" for the men were wearing silver from head to foot. I had never seen anything so gaudy. He made as if to answer and then apparently thought better of it; he laughed at me again. With an odd exhilaration—as if we were something childish and something wonderful, as if he were doing us an enormous favor—he took one shaky breath and said, "Well, we're here."

I looked at Spet, Spet looked at Lydia, Lydia looked at Amalia, who is the head of the local town meeting, Amalia looked at I don't know who. My throat was raw. I cannot stand local beer, which the farmers swill as if their stomachs had iridium linings, but I took it anyway, from Amalia (it was her bicycle we had seen outside as we parked), and swallowed it all. This was going to take a long time. I said, "Yes, here you are," and smiled (feeling like a fool), and wondered seriously if male Earth people's minds worked so very differently from female Earth people's minds, but that couldn't be so or the race would have died out long ago. The radio network had got the news around-planet by now and we had another Russian speaker, flown in from Varna; I decided to cut out when *the man* passed around pictures of his wife, who looked like the priestess of some arcane cult. He proposed to question Yuki, so I barreled her into a back room in spite of her furious protests, and went out to the front porch. As I left, Lydia was explaining the difference between parthenogenesis (which is so easy that anyone can practice it) and what we do, which is the merging of ova. That is why Katy's baby looks like me. Lydia went on to the Ansky process and Katy Ansky, our one full-polymath genius and the great-great-I-don't-know-how-many-times-great-grandmother of my own Katharina.

A dot-dash transmitter in one of the outbuildings chattered faintly to itself: operators flirting and passing jokes down the line.

There was a man on the porch. The other tall man. I watched him for a few minutes—I can move very quietly when I want to—and when I allowed him to see me, he stopped talking into the little machine hung around his neck. Then he said calmly, in excellent Russian, "Did you know that sexual equality had been reestablished on Earth?"

"You're the real one," I said, "aren't you? The other one's for show." It was a great relief to get things cleared up. He nodded affably.

"As a people, we are not very bright," he said. "There's been too much genetic damage in the last few centuries. Radiation. Drugs. We can use Whileaway's genes, Janet." Strangers do not call strangers by the first name.

"You can have cells enough to drown in," I said. "Breed your own."

He smiled. "That's not the way we want to do it." Behind him I saw Katy come into the square of light that was the screened-in door. He went on, low and urbane, not mocking me, I think, but with the self-confidence of someone who has always had money and strength to spare, who doesn't know what it is to be second-class or provincial. Which is very odd, because the day before, I would have said that was an exact description of me.

"I'm talking to you, Janet," he said, "because I suspect you have more popular influence than anyone else here. You know as well as I do that parthenogenetic culture has all sorts of inherent defects, and we do not—if we can help it—mean to use you for anything of the sort. Pardon me; I should not have said 'use.' But surely you can see that this kind of society is unnatural."

"Humanity is unnatural," said Katy. She had my rifle under her left arm. The top of that silky head does not quite come up to my collarbone, but she is as tough as steel; he began to move, again with that queer smiling deference (which his fellow had showed to me but he had not) and the gun slid into Katy's grip as if she had shot with it all her life.

"I agree," said the man. "Humanity is unnatural. I should know. I have metal in my teeth and metal pins here." He touched his shoulder. "Seals are harem animals," he added, "and so are men; apes are promiscuous and so are men; doves are monogamous and so are men; there are even celibate men and homosexual men. There are homosexual cows, I believe. But Whileaway is still missing something." He gave a dry chuckle. I will give him the credit of believing that it had something to do with nerves.

"I miss nothing," said Katy, "except that life isn't endless."

"You are—?" said the man, nodding from me to her.

"Wives," said Katy. "We're married." Again the dry chuckle.

"A good economic arrangement," he said, "for working and taking care of the children. And as good an arrangement as any for randomizing heredity, if your reproduction is made to follow the same pattern. But think, Katharina Michaelason, if there isn't something better that you might secure for your daughters. I believe in instincts, even in Man, and I can't think that the two of you—a machinist, are you? and I gather you are some sort of chief of police—don't feel somehow what even you must miss. You know it intellectually, of course. There is only half a species here. Men must come back to Whileaway."

Katy said nothing.

"I should think, Katharina Michaelason," said the man gently, "that you, of all people, would benefit most from such a change," and he walked past Katy's rifle into the square of light coming from the door. I think it was then that he noticed my scar, which really does not show unless the light is from the side: a fine line that runs from temple to chin. Most people don't even know about it.

"Where did you get that?" he said, and I answered with an involuntary grin, "In my last duel." We stood there bristling at each other for several seconds (this is absurd but true) until he went inside and shut the screen door behind him. Katy said in a brittle voice, "You damned fool, don't you know when we've been insulted?" and swung up the rifle to shoot him through the screen, but I got to her before she could fire and knocked the rifle out of aim; it burned a hole through the porch floor. Katy was shaking. She kept whispering over and over, "That's why I never touched it, because I knew I'd kill someone, I knew I'd kill someone." The first man—the one I'd spoken with first—was still talking inside the house, something about the grand movement to recolonize and rediscover all that Earth had lost. He stressed the advantages to Whileaway: trade, exchange of ideas, education. He too said that sexual equality had been reestablished on Earth.

Katy was right, or course; we should have burned them down where they stood. Men are coming to Whileaway. When one culture has the big guns and the other has none, there is a certain predictability about the outcome. Maybe men would have come eventually in any case. I like to think that a hundred years from now my great-grandchildren could have stood them off or fought them to a standstill, but even that's no odds; I will remember all my life those four people I first met who were muscled like bulls and who made me—if only for a moment—feel small. A neurotic reaction, Katy says. I remember everything that happened that night; I remember Yuki's excitement in the car, I remember Katy's sobbing when we got home as if her heart would break, I remember her lovemaking, a little peremptory as always, but wonderfully soothing and comforting. I remember prowling restlessly around the house after Katy fell asleep with one bare arm flung into a patch of light from the hall. The muscles of her forearms are like metal bars from all that driving and testing of her machines. Sometimes I dream about Katy's arms. I remember wandering into the nursery and picking up my wife's baby, dozing for a while with the poignant, amazing warmth of an infant in my lap, and finally returning to the kitchen to find Yuriko fixing herself a late snack. My daughter eats like a Great Dane.

"Yuki," I said, "do you think you could fall in love with a man?" and she whooped derisively. "With a ten-foot toad!" said my tactful child.

But men are coming to Whileaway. Lately I sit up nights and worry about the men who will come to this planet, about my two daughters and Betta Katharinason, about what will happen to Katy, to me, to my life. Our ancestors' journals are one long cry of pain and I suppose I ought to be glad now but one can't throw away six centuries, or even (as I have lately discovered) thirty-four years. Sometimes I laugh at the question those four men hedged about all evening and never quite dared to ask, looking at the lot of us, hicks in overalls, farmers in canvas pants and plain shirts: *Which of you plays the role of the man?* As if we had to produce a carbon copy of their mistakes! I doubt very much that sexual equality has been reestablished on Earth. I do not like to think of myself mocked, of Katy deferred to as if she were weak, of Yuki made to feel unimportant or silly, of my other children cheated of their full humanity or turned into strangers. And I'm afraid that my own achievements will dwindle from what they were—or what I thought they were—to the not-very-interesting curiosa of the human race, the oddities you read about in the back of the book, things to laugh at sometimes because they are so exotic, quaint but not impressive, charming but not useful. I find this more painful than I can say. You will agree that for a woman who has fought three duels, all of them kills, indulging in such fears is ludicrous. But what's around the corner now is a duel so big that I don't think I have the guts for it; in Faust's words: *Verweile doch, du bist so schoen!* Keep it as it is. Don't change.

Sometimes at night I remember the original name of this planet, changed by the first generation of our ancestors, those curious women for whom, I suppose, the real name was too painful a reminder after the men died. I find it amusing, in a grim way, to see it all so completely turned around. This too shall pass. All good things must come to an end.

Take my life but don't take away the meaning of my life.

For-A-While.

JAMES TIPTREE JR.
And I Awoke and Found Me Here on the Cold Hill's Side

• • • •

{ 1972 }

James Tiptree Jr. is the pseudonym of Alice B. Sheldon (1915–1987), who, as Tiptree, was one of the most skilled and influential sf writers of the 1970s. Sheldon/Tiptree was the author of such classic short fiction as "The Girl Who Was Plugged In" (1973), an important forerunner of cyberpunk; "Houston, Houston, Do You Read?" (1976), an ambiguous lesbian-feminist utopia that won both the Nebula and Hugo Awards; and "The Women Men Don't See" (1973), a despairing assessment of the lives of women in patriarchy: "What women do is survive. We live by ones and twos in the chinks of your world-machine." Sheldon/Tiptree also published a handful of powerful short stories as Racoona Sheldon, including the chilling "The Screwfly Solution" (1977), in which human sex and human violence become inextricably fused. Tiptree published only two novels, *Up the Walls of the World* (1978) and *Brightness Falls from the Air* (1985); her skill as a writer of hard-hitting and blackly ironic sf is more readily apparent in her four major short-story collections, *Ten Thousand Light Years from Home* (1973), *Warm Worlds and Otherwise* (1975), *Star Songs of an Old Primate* (1978), and *Out of the Everywhere and Other Extraordinary Visions* (1981). In 1990, Arkham House published a selection of some of her best stories as *Her Smoke Rose Up Forever*, reprinted in paperback by Tachyon in 2004.

Much like Mary Shelley, Alice Sheldon led a fascinating life that continues to grip the popular imagination. As a child, she traveled extensively in Africa; as a young woman she was a member of Chicago's social elite; she was one of the first women to work in the CIA; in 1967—the same year she began to write as Tiptree—she acquired a PhD in experimental psychology. Becoming "Tiptree" gave Sheldon a new voice and a new identity; she published increasingly notable short stories for ten years before the pseudonym was discovered to be that of Alice Sheldon. As Tiptree, she also maintained a lively correspondence with a wide circle of acquaintances in the sf community. In his introduction to *Warm Worlds and Otherwise*, writer Robert Silverberg took up the question of Tiptree's gender, famously insisting that "there is to me something ineluctably masculine about Tiptree's writing." Silverberg's comment continues to provide a brilliant argument against the idea that there are inherent gender differences in the creative work of women and men.

Tiptree's life and career has exerted a strong influence on the sf community, demonstrated, for example, in the title of the first full-length study of feminism and science fiction, Sarah Lefanu's *In the Chinks of the World Machine* (1988). In 1991, Pat Murphy and Karen Joy Fowler, writers associated with Wiscon, the long-running feminist sf convention, established the annual James Tiptree Jr. Award for science fiction and fantasy literature that expands and/or explores our understanding of gender, and several anthologies of Tiptree Award–winning fiction have been published to date. In 2006, a well-received full-length biography by Julie Phillips appeared, *James Tiptree, Jr.: The Double Life of Alice B. Sheldon*.

According to the *Encyclopedia of Science Fiction*, "Several themes interpenetrate [Tiptree's] best work—sex, exogamy, feminist depictions of male/female relations, ecology, death—but the greatest of these is death." "And I Awoke and Found Me Here on the Cold Hill's Side"—which takes its title from Keats's poem "La Belle Dame Sans Merci" (1820)—is no exception. In a sense its scenario resembles that of Silverberg's "Passengers" (1968), in which alien symbiotes puppeteer humans' erotic desires.

He was standing absolutely still by a service port, staring out at the belly of the *Orion* docking above us. He had on a gray uniform and his rusty hair was cut short. I took him for a station engineer.

That was bad for me. Newsmen strictly don't belong in the bowels of Big Junction. But in my first twenty hours I hadn't found any place to get a shot of an alien ship.

I turned my holocam to show its big World Media insigne and started my bit about What It Meant to the People Back Home who were paying for it all.

"—it may be routine work to you, sir, but we owe it to them to share—"

His face came around slow and tight, and his gaze passed over me from a peculiar distance.

"The wonders, the drama," he repeated dispassionately. His eyes focused on me. "You consummated fool."

"Could you tell me what races are coming in, sir? If I could even get a view—"

He waved me to the port. Greedily I angled my lenses up at the long blue hull blocking out the starfield. Beyond her I could see the bulge of a black and gold ship.

"That's a Foramen," he said. "There's a freighter from Belye on the other side, you'd call it Arcturus. Not much traffic right now."

"You're the first person who's said two sentences to me since I've been here, sir. What are those colorful little craft?"

"Procya," he shrugged. "They're always around. Like us."

I squashed my face on the vitrite, peering. The walls clanked. Somewhere overhead aliens were off-loading into their private sector of Big Junction. The man glanced at his wrist.

"Are you waiting to go out, sir?"

His grunt could have meant anything.

"Where are you from on Earth?" he asked me in his hard tone.

I started to tell him and suddenly saw that he had forgotten my existence. His eyes were on nowhere, and his head was slowly bowing forward onto the port frame.

"Go home," he said thickly. I caught a strong smell of tallow.

"Hey, sir!" I grabbed his arm; he was in a rigid tremor. "Steady, man."

"I'm waiting . . . waiting for my wife. My loving wife." He gave a short ugly laugh. "Where are you from?"

I told him again.

"Go home," he mumbled. "Go home and make babies. While you still can."

One of the early GR casualties, I thought.

"Is that all you know?" His voice rose stridently. "Fools. Dressing in their styles. Gnivo suits, Aoleelee music. Oh, I see your newscasts," he sneered. "Nixi parties. A year's salary for a floater. Gamma radiation? Go home, read history. *Ballpoint pens and bicycles*—"

He started a slow slide downward in the half gee. My only informant. We struggled confusedly; he wouldn't take one of my sobertabs but I finally got him along the service corridor to a bench in an empty loading bay. He fumbled out a little vacuum cartridge. As I was helping him unscrew it, a figure in starched whites put his head in the bay.

"I can be of assistance, yes?" His eyes popped, his face was covered with brindled fur. An alien, a Procya! I started to thank him but the red-haired man cut me off.

"Get lost. Out."

The creature withdrew, its big eyes moist. The man stuck his pinky in the cartridge and then put it up his nose, gasping deep in his diaphragm. He looked toward his wrist.

"What time is it?"

I told him.

"News," he said. "A message for the eager, hopeful human race. A word about those lovely, lovable aliens we all love so much." He looked at me. "Shocked, aren't you, newsboy?"

I had him figured now. A xenophobe. Aliens plot to take over Earth.

"Ah, Christ, they couldn't care less." He took another deep gasp, shuddered and straightened. "The hell with generalities. What time d'you say it was? All right, I'll tell you how I learned it. The hard way. While we wait for my loving wife. You can bring that little recorder out of your sleeve, too. Play it over to yourself some time . . . when it's too late." He chuckled. His tone had become chatty—an educated voice. "You ever hear of supernormal stimuli?"

"No," I said. "Wait a minute. White sugar?"

"Near enough. Y'know Little Junction Bar in D.C.? No, you're an Aussie, you said. Well, I'm from Burned Barn, Nebraska."

He took a breath, consulting some vast disarray of the soul.

"I accidentally drifted into Little Junction Bar when I was eighteen. No. Correct that. You don't go into Little Junction by accident, any more than you first shoot skag by accident.

"You go into Little Junction because you've been craving it, dreaming about it, feeding on every hint and clue about it, back there in Burned Barn, since before you had hair in your pants. Whether you know it or not. Once you're out of Burned Barn, you can no more help going into Little Junction than a sea-worm can help rising to the moon.

"I had a brand-new liquor I.D. in my pocket. It was early; there was an empty spot beside some humans at the bar. Little Junction isn't an embassy bar, y'know. I found out later where the high-caste aliens go—when they go out. The New Rive, the Curtain by the Georgetown Marina.

"And they go by themselves. Oh, once in a while they do the cultural exchange bit with a few frosty couples of other aliens and some stuffed humans. Galactic Amity with a ten-foot pole.

"Little Junction was the place where the lower orders went, the clerks and drivers out for kicks. Including, my friend, the perverts. The ones who can take humans. Into their beds, that is."

He chuckled and sniffed his finger again, not looking at me.

"Ah, yes. Little Junction is Galactic Amity Night, every night. I ordered . . . what? A margarita. I didn't have the nerve to ask the snotty spade bartender for one of the alien liquors behind the bar. It was dim. I was trying to stare everywhere at once without showing it. I remember those white boneheads—Lyrans, that is. And a mess of green veiling I decided was a multiple being from someplace. I caught a couple of human glances in the bar mirror. Hostile flicks. I didn't get the message, then.

"Suddenly an alien pushed right in beside me. Before I could get over my paralysis, I heard this blurry voice: "'You air a futeball enthushiash?'

"An alien had spoken to me. An *alien*, a being from the stars. Had spoken. To me.

"Oh, god, I had no time for football, but I would have claimed a passion for paper-folding, for dumb crambo—anything to keep him talking. I asked him about his home-planet sports, I insisted on buying his drinks. I listened raptly while he spluttered out a play-by-play account of a game I wouldn't have turned a dial for. The 'Grain Bay Pashkers.' Yeah. And I was dimly aware of trouble among the humans on my other side.

"Suddenly this woman—I'd call her a girl now—this girl said something in a high nasty voice and swung her stool into the arm I was holding my drink with. We both turned around together.

"Christ, I can see her now. The first thing that hit me was *discrepancy*. She was a nothing—but terrific. Transfigured. Oozing it, radiating it.

"The next thing was I had a horrifying hard-on just looking at her.

"I scrooched over so my tunic hid it, and my spilled drink trickled down, making everything worse. She pawed vaguely at the spill, muttering.

"I just stared at her trying to figure out what had hit me. An ordinary figure, a soft avidness in the face. Eyes heavy, satiated-looking. She was totally sexualized. I remember her throat pulsed. She had one hand up touching her scarf, which had slipped off her shoulder. I saw angry bruises there. That really tore it. I understood at once those bruises had some sexual meaning.

"She was looking past my head with her face like a radar dish. Then she made an 'ahhhh' sound that had nothing to do with me and grabbed my forearm as if it were a railing. One of the men behind her laughed. The woman said, 'Excuse me,' in a ridiculous voice and slipped out behind me. I wheeled around after her, nearly upsetting my football friend, and saw that some Sirians had come in.

"That was my first look at Sirians in the flesh, if that's the word. God knows I'd memorized every news shot, but I wasn't prepared. That tallness, that cruel thinness. That appalling alien arrogance. Ivory-blue, these were. Two males in immaculate metallic gear. Then I saw there was a female with them. An ivory-indigo exquisite with a permanent faint smile on those bone-hard lips.

"The girl who'd left me was ushering them to a table. She reminded me of a goddamn dog that wants you to follow it. Just as the crowd hid them, I saw a man join them too. A big man, expensively dressed, with something wrecked about his face.

"Then the music started and I had to apologize to my furry friend. And the Sellice dancer came out and my personal introduction to hell began."

The red-haired man fell silent for a minute enduring self-pity. Something wrecked about the face, I thought; it fit.

He pulled his face together.

"First I'll give you the only coherent observation of my entire evening. You can see it here at Big Junction, always the same. Outside of the Procya, it's humans with aliens, right? Very seldom aliens with other aliens. Never aliens with humans. It's the humans who want in."

I nodded, but he wasn't talking to me. His voice had a druggy fluency.

"Ah, yes, my Sellice. My first Sellice."

"They aren't really well-built, y'know, under those cloaks. No waist to speak of and short-legged. But they flow when they walk.

"This one flowed out into the spotlight, cloaked to the ground in violet silk. You could only see a fall of black hair and tassels over a narrow face like a vole. She was a mole-gray. They come in all colors. Their fur is like a flexible velvet all over; only the color changes startlingly around their eyes and lips and other places. Erogenous zones? Ah, man, with them it's not zones.

"She began to do what we'd call a dance, but it's no dance, it's their natural movement. Like smiling, say, with us. The music built up, and her arms undulated toward me, letting the cloak fall apart little by little. She was naked under it. The spotlight started to pick up her body markings moving in the slit of the cloak. Her arms floated apart and I saw more and more.

"She was fantastically marked and the markings were writhing. Not like body paint—alive. Smiling, that's a good word for it. As if her whole body was smiling sexually, beckoning, winking, urging, pouting, speaking to me. You've seen a classic Egyptian belly dance? Forget it—a sorry stiff thing compared to what any Sellice can do. This one was ripe, near term.

"Her arms went up and those blazing lemon-colored curves pulsed, waved, everted, contracted, throbbed, evolved unbelievably welcoming, inciting permutations. *Come do it to me, do it, do it here and here and here and now.* You couldn't see the rest of her, only a wicked flash of mouth. Every human male in the room was aching to ram himself into that incredible body. I mean it was *pain.* Even the other aliens were quiet, except one of the Sirians who was chewing out a waiter.

"I was a basket case before she was halfway through . . . I won't bore you with what happened next; before it was over there were several fights and I got cut. My money ran out on the third night. She was gone next day.

"I didn't have time to find out about the Sellice cycle then, mercifully. That came after I went back to campus and discovered you had to have a degree in solid-state electronics to apply for off-planet work. I was a pre-med but I got that degree. It only took me as far as First Junction then.

"Oh god, First Junction. I thought I was in heaven—the alien ships coming in and our freighters going out. I saw them all, all but the real exotics, the tankies. You only see a few of those a cycle, even here. And the Yyeire. You've never seen that.

"Go home, boy. Go home to your version of Burned Barn . . .

"The first Yyeir I saw, I dropped everything and started walking after it like a starving hound, just breathing. You've seen the pix of course. Like lost dreams. *Man is in love and loves what vanishes*. . . . It's the scent, you can't guess that. I followed until I ran into a slammed port. I spent half a cycle's credits sending the creature the wine they call stars' tears. . . . Later I found out it was a male. That made no difference at all.

"You can't have sex with them, y'know. No way. They breed by light or something, no one knows exactly. There's a story about a man who got hold of a Yyeir woman and tried. They had him skinned. Stories—"

He was starting to wander.

"What about that girl in the bar, did you see her again?"

He came back from somewhere.

"Oh, yes. I saw her. She'd been making it with the two Sirians, y'know. The males do it in pairs. Said to be the total sexual thing for a woman, if she can stand the damage from those beaks. I wouldn't know. She talked to me a couple of times after they finished with her. No use for men whatever. She drove off the P Street bridge. . . . The man, poor bastard, he was trying to keep that Sirian bitch happy single-handed. Money helps, for a while. I don't know where he ended."

He glanced at his wrist again. I saw the pale bare place where a watch had been and told him the time.

"Is that the message you want to give Earth? Never love an alien?"

"Never love an alien—" He shrugged. "Yeah. No. Ah, Jesus, don't you see? Everything going out, nothing coming back. Like the poor damned Polynesians. We're gutting Earth, to begin with. Swapping raw resources for junk. Alien status symbols. Tape decks, Coca-Cola, and Mickey Mouse watches."

"Well, there is concern over the balance of trade. Is that your message?"

"The balance of trade." He rolled it sardonically. "Did the Polynesians have a word for it, I wonder? You don't see, do you? All right, why are you here? I mean *you*, personally. How many guys did you climb over—"

He went rigid, hearing footsteps outside. The Procya's hopeful face appeared around the corner. The red-haired man snarled at him and he backed out. I started to protest.

"Ah, the silly reamer loves it. It's the only pleasure we have left. . . . Can't you see, man? That's *us*. That's the way we look to them, to the real ones."

"But—"

"And now we're getting the cheap C-drive, we'll be all over just like the Procya. For the pleasure of serving as freight monkeys and junction crews. Oh, they appreciate our ingenious little service stations, the beautiful star folk. They don't *need* them, y'know. Just an amusing convenience. D'you know what I do here with my two degrees? What I did at First Junction. Tube cleaning. A swab. Sometimes I get to replace a fitting."

I muttered something; the self-pity was getting heavy.

"Bitter? Man, it's a *good* job. Sometimes I get to talk to one of them." His face twisted. "My wife works as a—oh, hell, you wouldn't know. I'd trade—correction I have traded—everything Earth offered me for just that chance. To see them. To speak to them. Once in a while to touch one. Once in a great while to find one low enough, perverted enough to want to touch me—"

His voice trailed off and suddenly came back strong.

"And so will you!" He glared at me. "Go home! Go home and tell them to quit it. Close the ports. Burn every god-lost alien thing before it's too late! That's what the Polynesians didn't do."

"But surely—"

"But surely be damned! Balance of trade—balance of *life*, man. I don't know if our birth rate is going, that's not the point. Our soul is leaking out. We're bleeding to death!"

He took a breath and lowered his tone.

"What I'm trying to tell you, this is a trap. We've hit the supernormal stimulus. Man is exogamous—all our history is one long drive to find and impregnate the stranger. Or get impregnated by him, it works for women too. Anything different-colored, different nose, ass, anything, man *has* to fuck it or die trying. That's a drive, y'know, it's built in. Because it works fine as long as the stranger is human. For millions of years that kept the genes circulating. But now we've met aliens we can't screw, and we're about to die trying. . . . Do you think I can touch my wife?"

"But—"

"Look. Y'know, if you give a bird a fake egg like its own but bigger and brighter-marked, it'll roll its own egg out of the nest and sit on the fake? That's what we're doing."

"We've been talking about sex so far." I was trying to conceal my impatience. "Which is great, but the kind of story I'd hoped—"

"Sex? No, it's deeper." He rubbed his head, trying to clear the drug. "Sex is only part of it—there's more. I've seen Earth missionaries, teachers, sexless people. Teachers—they end cycling waste or pushing floaters, but they're hooked. They stay. I saw one fine-looking old woman, she was servant to a Cu'ushbar kid. A defective—his own people would have let him die. That wretch was swabbing up its vomit as if it was holy water. Man, it's deep . . . some cargo cult of the soul. We're built to dream outwards. They laugh at us. They don't have it."

There were sounds of movement in the next corridor. The dinner crowd was starting. I had to get rid of him and get there; maybe I could find the Procya. A side door opened and a figure started towards us. At first I thought it was an alien and then I saw it was a woman wearing an awkward body-shell. She seemed to be limping slightly. Behind her I could glimpse the dinner-bound throng passing the open door.

The man got up as she turned into the bay. They didn't greet each other.

"The station employs only happily wedded couples," he told me with that ugly laugh. "We give each other . . . comfort."

He took one of her hands. She flinched as he drew it over his arm and let him turn her passively, not looking at me. "Forgive me if I don't introduce you. My wife appears fatigued."

I saw that one of her shoulders was grotesquely scarred.

"Tell them," he said, turning to go. "Go home and tell them." Then his head snapped back toward me and he added quietly, "And stay away from the Syrtis desk or I'll kill you."

They went away up the corridor.

I changed tapes hurriedly with one eye on the figures passing that open door. Suddenly among the humans I caught a glimpse of two sleek scarlet shapes. My first real aliens! I snapped the recorder shut and ran to squeeze in behind them.

JOHN VARLEY

Air Raid

{1977}

The stories of John Varley (1947–) combine cutting-edge speculation on bioengineering with a gripping narrative pacing reminiscent of Robert A. Heinlein. Varley's *The Persistence of Vision* (1978) is widely considered to be among the best single-author collections of short sf published to date. His gritty tales from sf's "hard" side, focused on rapid technological change, were something new in the 1970s and early 1980s, when the sf scene had shifted to critiques of the genre's pro-technological bias by such feminists as Joanna Russ, Ursula K. Le Guin, and Alice Sheldon (aka James Tiptree Jr.). Varley's "The Pusher" (1981) received a Hugo Award, and "The Persistence of Vision" (1978) and "PRESS ENTER" ■ (1984) won Hugo and Nebula Awards. Among the first to use cloning as a central topic, Varley, like J. G. Ballard, John Brunner, and Philip K. Dick, draws many of his plots from an imagination of eco-catastrophe. He chooses gloomy posthuman scenarios unlike anything imagined by Heinlein, yet science and engineering, as in Heinlein, empower human beings at least to defer extinction and devolution.

Like most of his sf, "Air Raid" extrapolates from the premise that surviving the inevitable disasters of the future—Varley may be pro-technological, but he is no optimist—will require prosthetic supplementation, a rethinking of the body that raises questions about what constitutes a human being and a human life. The story first appeared in *Isaac Asimov's Science Fiction Magazine* in 1977 under the pseudonym Herb Boehm. Expanded into the novel *Millennium* (1983), it was filmed under that title in 1989 from a screenplay by Varley that saw many changes, for the film was abandoned by three directors before Michael Anderson completed it. Varley's female narrator is reminiscent of such Heinlein warrior women as Wyoming Knott in *The Moon Is a Harsh Mistress* (1966) and Mary in *The Puppet Masters* (1951); in fact, his opening sentence, in which a skull-implanted cell phone wakens her with an emergency call, echoes the first scene in *The Puppet Masters*. Set in a dystopian future, "Air Raid" is very much of its own time, too: the first international treaty to address the problem of terrorist skyjacking was signed in July 1978. The colonizers of North America are a part of the past indirectly recalled as well, for pioneering has always been hazardous. During the first year at Jamestown, 66 of the original 104 colonists died.

Shuttling between a horrific far future and a bright day in South Florida in 1979, the story raises a question unusual in sf. What if today—the world right now, with all its problems—is an unrecognized paradise toward which human beings of the distant future will turn with wonder and longing?

I was jerked awake by the silent alarm vibrating my skull. It won't shut down until you sit up, so I did. All around me in the darkened bunkroom the Snatch Team members were sleeping singly and in pairs. I yawned, scratched my ribs, and patted Gene's hairy flank. He turned over. So much for a romantic send-off.

Rubbing sleep from my eyes, I reached to the floor for my leg, strapped it on, and plugged it in. Then I was running down the rows of bunks toward Ops.

The situation board glowed in the gloom. Sun-Belt Airlines Flight 128, Miami to New York, September 15, 1979. We'd been looking for that one for three years. I should have been happy, but who can afford it when you wake up?

Liza Boston muttered past me on the way to Prep. I muttered back and followed. The lights came on around the mirrors, and I groped my way to one of them. Behind us, three more people staggered in. I sat down, plugged in, and at last I could lean back and close my eyes.

They didn't stay closed for long. Rush! I sat up straight as the sludge I use for blood was replaced with supercharged go-juice. I looked around me and got a series of idiot grins. There was Liza, and Pinky and Dave. Against the far wall Cristabel was already turning slowly in front of the airbrush, getting a Caucasian paint job. It looked like a good team.

I opened the drawer and started preliminary work on my face. It's a bigger job every time. Transfusion or no, I looked like death. The right ear was completely gone now. I could no longer close my lips; the gums were permanently bared. A week earlier, a finger had fallen off in my sleep. And what's it to you, bugger?

While I worked, one of the screens around the mirror glowed. A smiling young woman, blonde, high brow, round face. Close enough. The crawl line read *Mary Katrina Sondergard, born Trenton, New Jersey, age in 1979: 25.* Baby, this is your lucky day.

The computer melted the skin away from her face to show me the bone structure, rotated it, gave me cross sections. I studied the similarities with my own skull, noted the differences. Not bad, and better than some I'd been given.

I assembled a set of dentures that included the slight gap in the upper incisors. Putty filled out my cheeks. Contact lenses fell from the dispenser and I popped them in. Nose plugs widened my nostrils. No need for ears; they'd be covered by the wig. I pulled a blank plastiflesh mask over my face and had to pause while it melted in. It took only a minute to mold it to perfection. I smiled at myself. How nice to have lips.

The delivery slot clunked and dropped a blonde wig and a pink outfit into my lap. The wig was hot from the styler. I put it on, then the pantyhose.

"Mandy? Did you get the profile on Sondergard?" I didn't look up; I recognized the voice.

"Roger."

"We've located her near the airport. We can slip you in before take-off, so you'll be the joker."

I groaned and looked up at the face on the screen. Elfreda Baltimore-Louisville, Director of Operational Teams: lifeless face and tiny slits for eyes. What can you do when all the muscles are dead?

"Okay." You take what you get.

She switched off, and I spent the next two minutes trying to get dressed while keeping my eyes on the screens. I memorized names and faces of crew members plus the few facts known about them. Then I hurried out and caught up with the others. Elapsed time from first alarm: twelve minutes and seven seconds. We'd better get moving.

"Goddam Sun-Belt," Cristabel groused, hitching at her bra.

"At least they got rid of the high heels," Dave pointed out. A year earlier we would have been teetering down the aisles on three-inch platforms. We all wore short pink shifts with blue and white diagonal stripes across the front, and carried matching shoulder bags. I fussed trying to get the ridiculous pillbox cap pinned on.

We jogged into the dark Operations Control Room and lined up at the gate. Things were out of our hands now. Until the gate was ready, we could only wait.

I was first, a few feet away from the portal. I turned away from it; it gives me vertigo. I focused instead on the gnomes sitting at their consoles, bathed in yellow lights from their screens. None of them looked back at me. They don't like us much. I don't like them, either. Withered, emaciated, all of them. Our fat legs and butts and breasts are a reproach to them, a reminder that Snatchers eat five times their ration to stay presentable for the masquerade. Meantime we continue to rot. One day I'll be sitting at a console. One day I'll be *built in* to a console, with all my guts on the outside and nothing left of my body but stink. The hell with them.

I buried my gun under a clutter of tissues and lipsticks in my purse. Elfreda was looking at me.

"Where is she?" I asked.

"Motel room. She was alone from ten P.M. to noon on flight day."

Departure time was 1:15. She had cut it close and would be in a hurry. Good.

"Can you catch her in the bathroom? Best of all, in the tub?"

"We're working on it." She sketched a smile with a fingertip drawn over lifeless lips. She knew how I liked to operate, but she was telling me I'd take what I got. It never hurts to ask. People are at their most defenseless stretched out and up to their necks in water.

"Go!" Elfreda shouted. I stepped through, and things started to go wrong.

I was facing the wrong way, stepping *out* of the bathroom door and facing the bedroom. I turned and spotted Mary Katrina Sondergard through the haze of the gate. There was no way I could reach her without stepping back through. I couldn't even shoot without hitting someone on the other side.

Sondergard was at the mirror, the worst possible place. Few people recognize themselves quickly, but she'd been looking right at herself. She saw me and her eyes widened. I stepped to the side, out of her sight.

"What the hell is . . . hey? Who the hell—" I noted the voice, which can be the trickiest thing to get right.

I figured she'd be more curious than afraid. My guess was right. She came out of the bathroom, passing through the gate as if it wasn't there, which it wasn't, since it only has one side. She had a towel wrapped around her.

"Jesus Christ! What are you doing in my—" Words fail you at a time like that. She knew she ought to say something, but what? *Excuse me, haven't I seen you in the mirror?*

I put on my best stew smile and held out my hand.

"Pardon the intrusion. I can explain everything. You see, I'm—" I hit her on the side of the head and she staggered and went down hard. Her towel fell to the floor. "—working my way through college." She started to get up, so I caught her under the chin with my artificial knee. She stayed down.

"Standard fuggin' *oil!*" I hissed, rubbing my injured knuckles. But there was no time. I knelt beside her, checked her pulse. She'd be okay, but I think I loosened some front teeth. I paused a moment. Lord, to look like that with no makeup, no prosthetics! She nearly broke my heart.

I grabbed her under the knees and wrestled her to the gate. She was a sack of limp noodles. Somebody reached through, grabbed her feet, and pulled. *So long, love! How would you like to go on a long voyage?*

I sat on her rented bed to get my breath. There were car keys and cigarettes in her purse, genuine tobacco, worth its weight in blood. I lit six of them, figuring I had five minutes of my very own. The room filled with sweet smoke. They don't make 'em like that anymore.

The Hertz sedan was in the motel parking lot. I got in and headed for the airport. I breathed deeply of the air, rich in hydrocarbons. I could see for hundreds of yards into the distance. The perspective nearly made me dizzy, but I live for those moments. There's no way to explain what it's like in the pre-meck world. The sun was a fierce yellow ball through the haze.

The other stews were boarding. Some of them knew Sondergard, so I didn't say much, pleading a hangover. That went over well, with a lot of knowing laughs and sly remarks. Evidently it wasn't out of character. We boarded the 707 and got ready for the goats to arrive.

It looked good. The four commandos on the other side were identical twins for the women I was working with. There was nothing to do but be a stewardess until departure time. I hoped there would be no more glitches. Inverting a gate for a joker run into a motel room was one thing, but in a 707 at twenty thousand feet . . .

The plane was nearly full when the woman Pinky would impersonate sealed the forward door. We taxied to the end of the runway, then we were airborne. I started taking orders for drinks in first.

The goats were the usual lot, for 1979. Fat and sassy, all of them, and as unaware of living in a paradise as a fish is of the sea. *What would you think, ladies and gents, of* a *trip to the future? No? I can't say I'm surprised. What if I told you this plane is going to—*

My alarm beeped as we reached cruising altitude. I consulted the indicator under my Lady Bulova and glanced at one of the restroom doors. I felt a vibration pass through the plane. *Damn it, not so soon.*

The gate was in there. I came out quickly, and motioned for Diana Gleason—Dave's pigeon—to come to the front.

"Take a look at this," I said, with a disgusted look. She started to enter the restroom, stopped when she saw the green glow. I planted a boot on her fanny and shoved. Perfect. Dave would have a chance to hear her voice before popping in. Though she'd be doing little but screaming when she got a look around . . .

Dave came through the gate, adjusting his silly little hat. Diana must have struggled.

"Be disgusted," I whispered.

"What a mess," he said as he came out of the restroom. It was a fair imitation of Diana's tone, though he'd missed the accent. It wouldn't matter much longer.

"What is it?" It was one of the stews from tourist. We stepped aside so she could get a look, and Dave shoved her through. Pinky popped out very quickly.

"We're minus on minutes," Pinky said. "We lost five on the other side."

"Five?" Dave-Diana squeaked. I felt the same way. We had a hundred and three passengers to process.

"Yeah. They lost contact after you pushed my pigeon through. It took that long to realign."

You get used to that. Time runs at different rates on each side of the gate, though it's always sequential, past to future. Once we'd started the Snatch with me entering Sondergard's room, there was no way to go back any earlier on either side. Here, in 1979, we had a rigid ninety-four minutes to get everything done. On the other side, the gate could never be maintained longer than three hours.

"When you left, how long was it since the alarm went in?"

"Twenty-eight minutes."

It didn't sound good. It would take at least two hours just customizing the wimps. Assuming there was no more slippage on 79-time, we might just make it. But there's *always* slippage. I shuddered, thinking about riding it in.

"No time for any more games, then," I said. "Pink, you go back to tourist and call both of the other girls up here. Tell 'em to come one at a time, and tell 'em we've got a problem. You know the bit."

"Biting back the tears. Got you." She hurried aft. In no time the first one showed up. Her friendly Sun-Belt Airlines smile was stamped on her face, but her stomach would be churning. *Oh God, this* is *it!*

I took her by the elbow and pulled her behind the curtains in front. She was breathing hard.

"Welcome to the twilight zone," I said, and put the gun to her head. She slumped, and I caught her. Pinky and Dave helped me shove her through the gate.

"Fug! The rotting thing's flickering."

Pinky was right. A very ominous sign. But the green glow stabilized as we watched, with who knows how much slippage on the other side. Cristabel ducked through.

"We're plus thirty-three," she said. There was no sense talking about what we were all thinking: things were going badly.

"Back to tourist," I said. "Be brave, smile at everyone, but make it just a little bit too good, got it?"

"Check," Cristabel said.

We processed the other quickly, with no incident. Then there was no time to talk about anything. In eighty-nine minutes Flight 128 was going to be spread all over a mountain whether we were finished or not.

Dave went into the cockpit to keep the flight crew out of our hair. Me and Pinky were supposed to take care of first class, then back up Cristabel and Liza in tourist. We used the standard "coffee, tea, or milk" gambit, relying on our speed and their inertia.

I leaned over the first two seats on the left.

"Are you enjoying your flight?" Pop, pop. Two squeezes on the trigger, close to the heads and out of sight of the rest of the goats.

"Hi, folks. I'm Mandy. Fly me." Pop, pop.

Halfway to the galley, a few people were watching us curiously. But people don't make a fuss until they have a lot more to go on. One goat in the back row stood up, and I let him have it. By now there were only eight left awake. I abandoned the smile and squeezed off four quick shots. Pinky took care of the rest. We hurried through the curtains, just in time.

There was an uproar building in the back of tourist, with about 60 percent of the goats already processed. Cristabel glanced at me, and I nodded.

"Okay, folks," she bawled. "I want you to be quiet. Calm down and listen up. *You*, fathead, *pipe down* before I cram my foot up your ass sideways."

The shock of hearing her talk like that was enough to buy us a little time, anyway. We had formed a skirmish line across the width of the plane, guns out, steadied on seat backs, aimed at the milling, befuddled group of thirty goats.

The guns are enough to awe all but the most foolhardy. In essence, a standard-issue stunner is just a plastic rod with two grids about six inches apart. There's not enough metal in it to set off a hijack alarm. And to people from the Stone Age to about 2190 it doesn't look any more like a weapon than a ball-point pen. So Equipment Section jazzes them up in a plastic shell to real Buck Rogers blasters, with a dozen knobs and lights that flash and a barrel like the snout of a hog. Hardly anyone ever walks into one.

"We are in great danger, and time is short. You must all do exactly as I tell you, and you will be safe."

You can't give them time to think, you have to rely on your status as the Voice of Authority. The situation is just *not* going to make sense to them, no matter how you explain it.

"Just a minute, I think you owe us—"

An airborne lawyer. I made a snap decision, thumbed the fireworks switch on my gun, and shot him.

The gun made a sound like a flying saucer with hemorrhoids, spit sparks and little jets of flame, and extended a green laser finger to his forehead. He dropped.

All pure kark, of course. But it sure is impressive.

And it's damn risky, too. I had to choose between a panic if the fathead got them to thinking, and a possible panic from the flash of the gun. But when a 20th gets to talking about his "rights" and what he is "owed," things can get out of hand. It's infectious.

It worked. There was a lot of shouting, people ducking behind seats, but no rush. We could have handled it, but we needed some of them conscious if we were ever going to finish the Snatch.

"Get up. Get *up*, you *slugs!*" Cristabel yelled. "He's stunned, nothing worse. But I'll *kill* the next one who gets out of line. Now *get to your feet* and do what I tell you. *Children first! Hurry*, as fast as you can, to the front of the plane. Do what the stewardess tells you. Come on, kids, *move!*"

I ran back into first class just ahead of the kids, turned at the open restroom door, and got on my knees.

They were petrified. There were five of them—crying, some of them, which always chokes me up—looking left and right at dead people in the first class seats, stumbling, near panic.

"Come on, kids," I called to them, giving my special smile. "Your parents will be along in just a minute. Everything's going to be all right, I promise you. Come on."

I got three of them through. The fourth balked. She was determined not to go through that door. She spread her legs and arms and I couldn't push her through. I will *not* hit a child, never. She raked her nails over my face. My wig came off, and she gaped at my bare head. I shoved her through.

Number five was sitting in the aisle, bawling. He was maybe seven. I ran back and picked him up, hugged him and kissed him, and tossed him through. God, I needed a rest, but I was needed in tourist.

"You, you, you, and you. Okay, you too. Help him, will you?" Pinky had a practiced eye for the ones that wouldn't be any use to anyone, even themselves. We herded them toward the front of the plane, then deployed ourselves along the left side where we could cover the workers. It didn't take long to prod them into action. We had them dragging the limp bodies forward as fast as they could go. Me and Cristabel were in tourist, with the others up front.

Adrenaline was being catabolized in my body now; the rush of action left me and I started to feel very tired. There's an unavoidable feeling of sympathy for the poor dumb goats that starts to get me about this stage of the game. Sure, they were better off; sure, they were going to die if we didn't get them off the plane. But when they saw the other side they were going to have a hard time believing it.

The first ones were returning for a second load, stunned at what they'd just seen: dozens of people being put into a cubicle that was crowded when it was empty. One college student looked like he'd been hit in the stomach. He stopped by me and his eyes pleaded.

"Look, I want to *help* you people, just . . . what's going *on*? Is this some new kind of rescue? I mean, are we going to crash—"

I switched my gun to prod and brushed it across his cheek. He gasped and fell back.

"Shut your fuggin' mouth and get moving, or I'll kill you." It would be hours before his jaw was in shape to ask any more stupid questions.

We cleared tourist and moved up. A couple of the work gang were pretty damn pooped by then. Muscles like horses, all of them, but they can hardly run up a flight of stairs. We let some of them go through, including a couple that were at least fifty years old. *Je*-zuz. Fifty! We got down to a core of four men and two women who seemed strong, and worked them until they nearly dropped. But we processed everyone in twenty-five minutes.

The portapak came through as we were stripping off our clothes. Cristabel knocked on the door to the cockpit and Dave came out, already naked. A bad sign.

"I had to cork 'em," he said. "Bleeding captain just *had* to make his grand march through the plane. I tried *everything*."

Sometimes you have to do it. The plane was on autopilot, as it normally would be at this time. But if any of us did anything detrimental to the craft, changed the fixed course of events in any way, that would be it. All that work for nothing, and Flight 128 inaccessible to us for all Time. I don't know sludge about time theory, but I know the practical angles. We can do things in the past only at times and in places where it won't make any difference. We have to cover our tracks. There's flexibility; once a Snatcher left her gun behind and it went in with the plane. Nobody found it, or if they did, they didn't have the smoggiest idea of what it was, so we were okay.

Flight 128 was mechanical failure. That's the best kind; it means we don't have to keep the pilot unaware of the situation in the cabin right down to ground level. We can cork him and fly the plane, since there's nothing he could have done to save the flight anyway. A pilot-error smash is almost impossible to snatch. We mostly work midairs, bombs, and structural failures. If there's even one survivor, we can't touch it. It would not fit the fabric of space-time, which is immutable (though it can stretch a little), and we'd all just fade away and appear back in the ready room.

My head was hurting. I wanted that portapak very badly.

"Who has the most hours on a 707?" Pinky did, so I sent her to the cabin, along with Dave, who could do the pilot's voice for air traffic control. You have to have a believable record in the flight recorder, too. They trailed two long tubes from the portapak, and the rest of us hooked in up close. We stood there, each of us smoking a fistful of cigarettes, wanting to finish them but hoping there wouldn't be time. The gate had vanished as soon as we tossed our clothes and the flight crew through.

But we didn't worry long. There's other nice things about Snatching, but nothing to compare with the rush of plugging into a portapak. The wake-up transfusion is nothing but fresh blood, rich in oxygen and sugars. What we were getting now was an insane brew of concentrated adrenaline, supersaturated hemoglobin, methedrine, white lightning, TNT, and Kickapoo joyjuice. It was like a firecracker in your heart; a boot in the box that rattled your sox.

"I'm growing hair on my chest," Cristabel said solemnly. Everyone giggled.

"Would someone hand me my eyeballs?"

"The blue ones, or the red ones?"

"I think my ass just fell off."

We'd heard them all before, but we howled anyway. We were strong, *strong*, and for one golden moment we had no worries. Everything was hilarious. I could have torn sheet metal with my eyelashes.

But you get hyper on that mix. When the gate didn't show, and didn't show, and *didn't sweetjeez show* we all started milling. This bird wasn't going to fly all that much longer.

Then it did show, and we turned on. The first of the wimps came through, dressed in the clothes taken from a passenger it had been picked to resemble.

"Two thirty-five elapsed upside time," Cristabel announced.

"Je-zuz."

It is a deadening routine. You grab the harness around the wimp's shoulders and drag it along the aisle, after consulting the seat number painted on its forehead. The paint would last three minutes. You seat it, strap it in, break open the harness and carry it back to toss through the gate as you grab the next one. You have to take it for granted they've done the work right on the other side: fillings in the teeth, fingerprints, the right match in height and weight and hair color. Most of those things don't matter much, especially on Flight 128, which was a crash-and-burn. There would be bits and pieces, and burned to a crisp at that. But you can't take chances. Those rescue workers are pretty thorough on the parts they *do* find; the dental work and fingerprints especially are important.

I hate wimps. I really hate 'em. Every time I grab the harness of one of them, if it's a child, I wonder if it's Alice. *Are you my kid, you vegetable, you slug, you slimy worm?* I joined the Snatchers right after the brain bugs ate the life out of my baby's head. I couldn't stand to think she was the last generation, that the last humans there would ever be would live with nothing in their heads, medically dead by standards that prevailed even in 1979, with computers working their muscles to keep them in tone. You grow up, reach puberty still fertile—one in a thousand—rush to get pregnant in your first heat. Then you find out your mom or pop passed on a chronic disease bound right into the genes, and none of your kids will be immune. I *knew* about the paraleprosy; I grew *up* with my toes rotting away. But this was too much. What do you do?

Only one in ten of the wimps had a customized face. It takes time and a lot of skill to build a new face that will stand up to a doctor's autopsy. The rest came premutilated. We've got millions of them; it's not hard to find a good match in the body. Most of them would stay breathing, too dumb to stop, until they went in with the plane.

The plane jerked, hard. I glanced at my watch. Five minutes to impact. We should have time. I was on my last wimp. I could hear Dave frantically calling the ground. A bomb came through the gate, and I tossed it into the cockpit. Pinky turned on the pressure sensor on the bomb and came running out, followed by Dave. Liza was already through. I grabbed the limp dolls in stewardess costume and tossed them to the floor. The engine fell off and a piece of it came through the cabin. We started to depressurize. The bomb blew away part of the cockpit (the ground crash crew would read it—we hoped—that part of the engine came through and killed the crew: no more words from the pilot on the flight recorder) and we turned, slowly, left and down. I was lifted toward the hole in the side of the plane, but I managed to hold onto a seat. Cristabel wasn't so lucky. She was blown backwards.

We started to rise slightly, losing speed. Suddenly it was uphill from where Cristabel was lying in the aisle. Blood oozed from her temple. I glanced back; everyone was gone, and three pink-suited wimps were piled on the floor. The plane began to stall, to nose down, and my feet left the floor.

"Come on, Bel!" I screamed. That gate was only three feet away from me, but I began pulling myself along to where she floated. The plane bumped, and she hit the floor. Incredibly, it seemed to wake her up. She started to swim toward me, and I grabbed her hand as the floor came up to slam us again. We crawled as the plane went through its final death agony, and we came to the door. The gate was gone.

There wasn't anything to say. We were going in. It's hard enough to keep the gate in place on a plane that's moving in a straight line. When a bird gets to corkscrewing and coming apart, the math is fearsome. So I've been told.

I embraced Cristabel and held her bloodied head. She was groggy, but managed to smile and shrug. You take what you get. I hurried into the restroom and got both of us down on the floor. Back to the forward bulkhead, Cristabel between my legs, back to front. Just like in training. We pressed our feet against the other wall. I hugged her tightly and cried on her shoulder.

And it was there. A green glow to my left. I threw myself toward it, dragging Cristabel, keeping low as two wimps were thrown headfirst through the gate above our heads. Hands grabbed and pulled us through. I clawed my way a good five yards along the floor. You can leave a leg on the other side and I didn't have one to spare.

I sat up as they were carrying Cristabel to Medical. I patted her arm as she went by on the stretcher, but she was passed out. I wouldn't have minded passing out myself.

For a while, you can't believe it all really happened. Sometimes it turns out it *didn't* happen. You come back and find out all the goats in the holding pen have softly and suddenly vanished away because the continuum won't tolerate the changes and paradoxes you've put into it. The people you've worked so hard to rescue are spread like tomato surprise all over some goddam hillside in Carolina and all you've got left is a bunch of ruined wimps and an exhausted Snatch Team. But not this time. I could see the goats milling around in the holding pen, naked and more bewildered than ever. And just starting to be *really* afraid.

Elfreda touched me as I passed her. She nodded, which meant well-done in her limited repertoire of gestures. I shrugged, wondering if I cared, but the surplus adrenaline was still in my veins and I found myself grinning at her. I nodded back.

Gene was standing by the holding pen. I went to him, hugged him. I felt the juices start to flow. *Damn it, let's squander a little ration and have us a good time.*

Someone was beating on the sterile glass wall of the pen. She shouted, mouthing angry words at us. *Why? What have you done to us?* It was Mary Sondergard. She implored her bald, one-legged twin to make her understand. She thought she had problems. God, was she pretty. I hated her guts.

Gene pulled me away from the wall. My hands hurt, and I'd broken off all my fake nails without scratching the glass. She was sitting on the floor now, sobbing. I heard the voice of the briefing officer on the outside speaker.

". . . Centauri Three is hospitable, with an Earth-like climate. By that, I mean *your* Earth, not what it has become. You'll see more of that later. The trip will take five years, shiptime. Upon landfall, you will be entitled to one horse, a plow, three axes, two hundred kilos of seed grain . . ."

I leaned against Gene's shoulder. At their lowest ebb, this very moment, they were so much better than us. I had maybe ten years, half of that as a basket case. They are our best, our very brightest hope. Everything is up to them.

". . . that no one will be forced to go. We wish to point out again, not for the last time, that you would all be dead without our intervention. There are things you should know, however. You cannot breathe our air. If you remain on Earth, you can never leave this building. We are not like you. We are the result of a genetic winnowing, a mutation process. We are the survivors, but our enemies have evolved along with us. They are winning. You, however, are immune to the diseases that afflict us . . ."

I winced and turned away.

". . . the other hand, if you emigrate you will be given a chance at a new life. It won't be easy, but as Americans you should be proud of your pioneer heritage. Your ancestors survived, and so will you. It can be a rewarding experience, and I urge you . . ."

Sure, Gene and I looked at each other and laughed. *Listen to this, folks. Five percent of you will suffer nervous breakdowns in the next few days, and never leave. About the same number will commit suicide, here and on the way. When you get there, sixty to seventy percent will die in the first three years. You will die in childbirth, be eaten by animals, bury two out of three of your babies, starve slowly when the rains don't come. If you live, it will be to break your back behind a plow, sun-up to dusk. New Earth is Heaven, folks!*

God, how I wish I could go with them.

CAROL EMSHWILLER

Abominable

• • • •

{ 1980 }

Carol Emshwiller (1921–), born in Ann Arbor, Michigan, did not begin writing until she was thirty, married to sf artist Ed Emshwiller, and a mother. She can cite as influences both a class with poet Kenneth Koch and the world of science fiction to which she was introduced by her husband. Meanwhile, she was learning the lessons of feminism on the front lines of domestic life: describing how she wrote while her children were small, she says she set up the playpen and put herself, a table, and a typewriter inside it, with the babies in sight but not able to actively interfere. The anecdote exemplifies the firm and humorous tone of her fiction. She has produced steadily since her first story in 1955, and later stories are at least as experimental and fresh as early ones. Although she identifies with sf and has received Nebula and Philip K. Dick Awards, as well as a World Fantasy Award for Lifetime Achievement, she is limited to genre in neither style nor publication, has published in literary as well as sf magazines, and has written several Western novels. Among her finest sf novels are *Carmen Dog* (1990) and *The Mount* (2002): the former imagines women turning into animals and vice versa as it skewers the gender roles men and women demand of themselves and one another; the latter uses an alien invasion to expand the examination to ethnic, national, and species roles. Characteristically, both books take on their serious subjects with humor and an easy grace. Her many short stories share these qualities, although their form is often more experimental.

"Abominable" is in many ways typical: satirically feminist, employing an unreliable narrator, and toying with sf conventions. The narrator is an unnamed and self-styled manly man whose inability to understand women illustrates stereotypical phallocentric attitudes in a portrait more humorous than angry. Simultaneously deadly and sympathetic, the tale reveals his childish naïveté. Transforming the battle of the sexes into the man's search for an illusive species akin to the Yeti, the story reveals a feminism as pointed as that of Joanna Russ and James Tiptree Jr., but the sharpness slips between the ribs more gently and with less pain, its tart satire mocking the romantic portrayal of women as emotional and animalistic.

The present tense and personal address, from "I" to the reader's "you," invites readers to identify with the narrator in a way that implicates them in the narrator's sexist viewpoint. The narrator's analysis of his quarry is pseudoscientific, with its charts and statistics, and also vain, with its assumption of male superiority, but it is childishly pathetic, too, showing the limits of sexism for men as well as women, how the struggle to understand may be crippled by cultural assumptions. The story also satirizes male and female separatist science fiction in its portrayal of the militaristic male society like that of the visitors to Whileaway in Russ's "When It Changed" (1972) and the hidden domestic underground life of the female society imagined by the men.

We are advancing into an unknown land with a deliberate air of nonchalance, our elbows out or our hands on hips, or standing one foot on a rock when there's the opportunity for it. Always to the left, the river, as they told us it should be. Always to the right, the hills. At every telephone booth we stop and call. Frequently the lines are down because of high winds or ice. The Commander says we are already in an area of the sightings. We must watch now, he has told us over the phone, for those curious two-part footprints no bigger than a boy's and of a unique delicacy. "Climb a tree," the Commander says, "or a telephone pole, whichever is the most feasible, and call out a few of the names you have memorized." So we climb a pole and cry out: Alice, Betty, Elaine, Jean, Joan, Marilyn, Mary . . . and so on, in alphabetical order. Nothing comes of it.

We are seven manly men in the dress uniform of the Marines, though we are not (except for one) Marines. But this particular uniform has always been thought to attract them. We are seven seemingly blasé (our collars open at the neck in any weather) experts in our fields, we, the research team for the Committee on Unidentified Objects that Whizz by in Pursuit of Their Own Illusive Identities. Our guns shoot sparks and stars and chocolate-covered cherries and make a big bang. It's already the age of frontal nudity; of "Why not?" instead of "Maybe." It's already the age of devices that can sense a warm, pulsing, live body at seventy-five yards and home in on it, and we have one of those devices with us. (I might be able to love like that myself someday.) On the other hand, we carry only a few blurry pictures in our wallets, most of these from random sightings several months ago. One is thought to be of the wife of the Commander. It was taken from a distance and we can't make out her features, she was wearing her fur coat. He thought he recognized it. He has said there was nothing seriously wrong with her.

So far there has been nothing but snow. What we put up with for these creatures!

Imagine their bodies as you hold this little reminder in the palm of your hand . . . this fat, four-inch Venus of their possibilities. . . . The serious elements are missing, the eyes simple dots (the characteristic hair-do almost covers the face), the feet, the head inconsequential. Imagine the possibility of triumph but avoid the smirk. Accept the challenge of the breasts, of the outsize hips, and then . . . (the biggest challenge of all). If we pit ourselves against it *can we win?* Or come off with honorable mention, or, at the least, finish without their analysis of our wrong moves?

Here are the signs of their presence that we have found so far (we might almost think these things had been dropped in our path on purpose if we didn't know how careless they can be, especially when harassed or in a hurry; and since they are nervous creatures, easily excited, they usually *are* harassed and/or in a hurry). . . . Found in our path, then: one stalk of still-frozen asparagus, a simple recipe for moussaka using onion-soup mix, carelessly torn out of a magazine, a small purse with a few crumpled-up dollar bills and a book of matches. (It is clear that they do have fire. We take comfort in that.)

And now the Commander says to leave the river and to go up into the hills even though they are treacherous with spring thaws and avalanches. The compass points up. We slide on scree and ice all day sometimes, well aware that they may have all gone south by now, whole tribes of them feeling worthless, ugly, and unloved. Because the possibilities are endless, any direction may be wrong, but at the first sign of superficialities, we'll know we're on the right track.

One of us is a psychoanalyst of long experience, a specialist in hysteria and masochism. (Even without case histories, he is committed to the study of their kind.) He says that if we find them they will probably make some strange strangling sounds, but that these are of no consequence and are often mistaken for laughter, which, he says, is probably the best way to take them. If, on the other hand, they smile, it's a simple reflex and serves the purpose of disarming us. (It has been found that they smile two and a half times as often as we do.) Sometimes, he says, there's a kind of nervous giggle, which is essentially sexual in origin and, if it occurs when they see us, is probably a very good sign. In any case, he says, we should give no more than our names and our rank, and, if they get angry, we should be careful that their rage doesn't turn against themselves.

Grace is the name of the one in the picture, but she must be all of fifty-five by now. Slipped out of a diner one moonlit night when the Commander forgot to look in her direction. But what was there to do but go on as usual, commanding what needed to be commanded? We agree. He said she had accepted her limitations up to that time, as far as he could see, and the limits of her actions. He blamed it on incomplete acculturation or on not seeing the obvious, and did not wonder about it until several years later.

I'd like to see one like her right now. Dare to ask where I come from and how come they're so unlike? How we evolved affectations the opposite of theirs? And do they live deep underground in vast kitchens, some multi-chambered sanctuary heated by ovens, the smell of gingerbread, those of childbearing age perpetually pregnant from the frozen semen of some tall, redheaded, long-dead comedian or rock star? Anyway, that's one theory.

But now the sudden silence of our own first sighting. One! . . . On the heights above us, huge (or seems so) and in full regalia (as in the Commander's photograph): mink and monstrous hat, the glint of something in the ears, standing (it seems a full five minutes) motionless on one leg. Or maybe just an upright bear (the sun was in our eyes) but gone when we got up to the place a half hour later. The psychoanalyst waited by the footprints all night, ready with his own kind of sweet-talk, but no luck.

The information has been phoned back to the Commander ("Tell her I think I love her," he said), and it has been decided that we will put on the paraphernalia ourselves . . . the shoes that fit the footprints, the mink, fox, leopard (phony) over several layers of the proper underwear. We have decided to put bananas out along the snow in a circle seventy-five yards beyond our camp and to set up our live warm-body sensor. Then when they come out for the bananas, we will follow them back to their lairs, down into their own dark sacred places; our camera crew will be ready to get their first reactions to us for TV. They'll like being followed. They always have.

We hope they are aware, if only on some dim level, of our reputations in our respective fields.

But the live warm-body sensor, while it does sound the alarm, can't seem to find any particular right direction, and in the morning all the bananas are gone.

It's because they won't sit still . . . won't take anything seriously. There's nobody to coordinate their actions, so they run around in different directions, always distracted from the task at hand, jumping to conclusions, making unwarranted assumptions, taking everything for granted or, on the other hand, not taking *anything* for granted (love, for instance). The forces of nature are on their side, yes, (chaos?) but we have other forces. This time we will lay the bananas out in one long logical straight line.

When we step into those kitchens finally! The largest mountain completely hollowed out, my God! And the smells! The bustle! The humdrum *everydayness* of their existence! We won't believe what we see. And they will probably tell us things are going better than ever. They will be thinking they no longer need to be close to the sources of power. They may even say they like places of no power to anyone . . . live powerless, as friends, their own soft signals one to the other, the least of them to the least of them. And they will also say we hardly noticed them anyway, or noticed that they weren't there. They will say we were always looking in the other direction, that we never knew who or what they were, or cared. Well, we did sense something . . . have sensed it for a long time, and we feel a lack we can't quite pinpoint. Unpaid creatures, mostly moneyless, but even so, noticed. We will tell them this, and also that the Commander thinks he may love one of them.

But this time they have refused the bananas. (What we offer them is never quite right.) Okay. The final offering (they have one more chance): these glass beads that look like jade; a set of fine, imported cookware; a self-help book, "How to Overcome Shyness with the Opposite Sex"; and (especially) we offer ourselves for their delight as sons, fathers, or lovers (their choice).

The psychoanalyst says they're entitled to their own opinions, but we wonder how independent should they be allowed to be?

One of us has said it was just a bear we saw at the top of that hill. He said he remembered that it humped down on all fours after standing on one leg, but they *might* do that.

The psychoanalyst has had a dream. Afterwards he told us never to be afraid of the snapping vagina (figuratively speaking) but to come on down to them (though we are climbing up, actually) and throw fish to the wombs (nothing but the best filet of sole, figuratively speaking).

This is the diagram the psychoanalyst has laid out for further study:

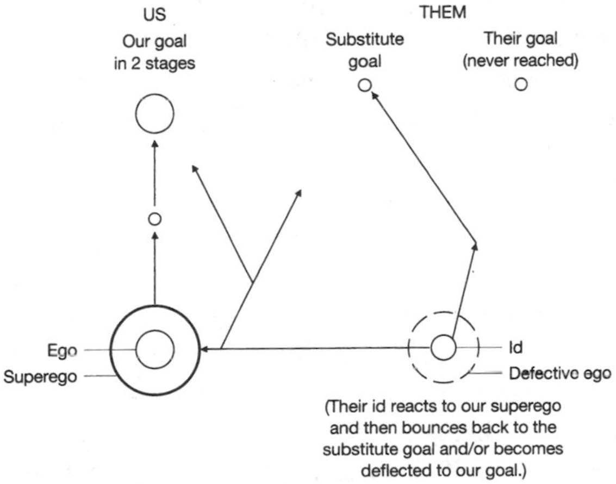

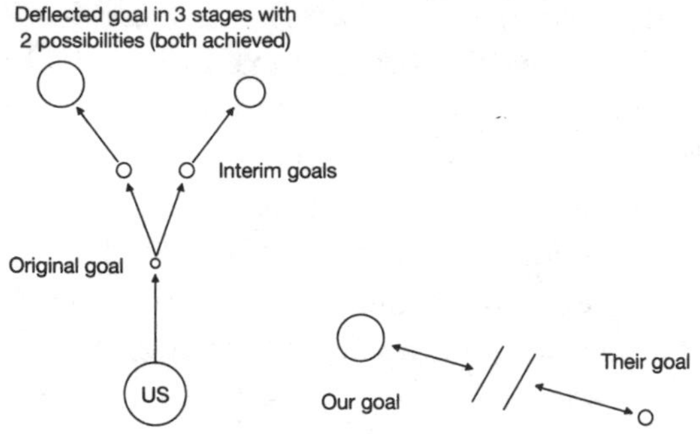

Well, if I had one I'd wash its feet (literally) and the back. Venture the front, too. Let the water flow over both of us. Let their hair hang down. I'd take some time out now and then, even from important work, to do some little things like this of hardly any meaning, and listen, sometimes, to its idle chatter or, at least, seem to. But as to Grace, it must be something else I have in mind, though I'm not sure what.

We are telling all the old tales about them around our campfires in the late evenings, but it's not the same kind of frightening that it used to be when we were young and telling the tales in similar circumstances because now we know they may actually be lurking out there in the shadows, and what's scary is that we have really no idea of their size! We're not sure what to believe. On the one hand, whether they are twice our size or, as the Commander insists, whether almost all of them are quite a bit smaller and definitely weaker. The more mythically oriented among us have said that they are large enough to swallow us up into their stomachs (from below) and to ejaculate us out again months later, weak and helpless. The anthropologically oriented say they may be the missing link we have searched for so long and stand, as they believe, somewhere between the gorilla and us (though probably quite a bit higher on the scale than *Pithecanthropus erectus*) and that they are, therefore, (logically) distinctly smaller and somewhat bent over, but may not necessarily be weaker. The sexually obsessed among us wonder, among other things, if their orgasm is as specific a reaction as ours is. The romantics among us think they will be cute and lovable creatures even when they're angry and regardless of size and strength. Others think the opposite. Opinions also vary as to how to console them for the facts of their lives and whether it is possible to do so at all since 72 percent of them perceive themselves as inferior, 65 percent perceive themselves to be in a fragile mental balance, only 33⅓ percent are without deep feelings of humiliation simply for being what they are. How will it be possible, then, to penetrate their lines of self-defense and their lines of defensiveness? Altercations are inevitable, that's clear. (Eighty-five percent return to rehash old arguments.) We dislike unpleasant emotional confrontations, try to avoid such things at all costs, but we also realize that playing the role of dominant partner in intimate interaction won't always be easy. How nice, even so, to have a group of beings, one of these days (almost invisible, too), whose main job would be to tidy up!

Pedestals have already been set out for them.

Even if (or especially if) they are not quite up to our standards, they will, in any case, remind us of the animal in all of us, of our beastliness . . . our ebb and flow . . . of life-forces we barely know exist . . . maybe some we never suspected.

But now we have had a strange and disturbing message from the Commander telling us that some very important political appointees have said that these stories of sightings are exactly that, stories . . . hoaxes, and it's been proven that the photographs have been doctored, in one case a gorilla superimposed on a snowy mountain, in another case a man in drag. (Only two pictures still unexplained.) Several people have confessed. Some have never even been in the area at all. Whatever we have seen must have been a trick of light and shadow or, more likely, one of the bears in this vicinity and (they're sure of it) we have a hoaxer among us, stealing the bananas himself and making footprints with an old shoe on the end of a long stick. Besides, think if we should discover that they do, in fact, exist. We would only be adding to our present problems. Committees would have to be set up to find alternatives to boredom once their dishwashing years were over. Cures would have to be discovered for cancers in peculiar places, for strange flows, for vaginismus and other spasms. A huge group of dilettantes (Sunday poets and painters) would be added to society, which society can well do without, according to the Commander. And why should we come searching for them, as though they were Mount Everest (and as important), simply because they're there? Anyway, the funding for our search has run out. The Commander even doubts if we can afford any more phone calls.

We are all very depressed by this news, though it's hard to pinpoint exactly why. Some of us feel sure, or fairly sure, that there *is* something out there . . . just out of sight . . . just out of earshot. Some of us seem to see, sometimes, a flash of color out of the corners of our eyes, as though the essentially invisible had been made *almost* visible for a few seconds. Makes one think, too (and some of us do), how socks and underwear might someday return, magically, from under beds to be found clean and folded in the drawer, as if cups of coffee could appear out of nowhere just when most needed, as if the refrigerator never ran out of milk or butter. . . . But we are at the service of our schedule and our budget. We must return to the seats of power, to the service of civilization . . . politics. . . .We turn back.

For a while I think seriously of going on by myself. I think perhaps if I crept back alone, sat quietly, maybe dressed to blend in more. Maybe if I sat still long enough (and stopped telling, out loud, those old, scary stories about them), if I made no proud gestures . . . shoulders not so stiff . . . maybe then they'd get used to me, even eat bananas out of my hand, and come, in time, to recognize an authoritarian figure by the subtle reality of it, and perhaps learn a few simple commands. But I have to stick to my orders. It's too bad, though I do want to pick up my pay, my medals, and get on with the next project. Still, I want to make one more move toward these creatures, if only a symbolic one. I sneak back along the trail and leave a message where it can't be missed, surrounded by bananas. I leave something they'll be sure to understand: the simple drawing of a naked man; a crescent that can't help but stand for moon; a heart shape (anatomically correct) for love; a clock face with the time of the message; the outline of a footprint of my own next to an outline of one of theirs (looks like a question mark next to an exclamation point). "To Grace" at the top. I sit there for a while, then, and listen for sighs and think I hear some . . . think I see something vaguely white on white in the clarity of snow. Invisible *on purpose*, that's for sure (if there at all), so if we can't see them, it's not *our* fault.

Well, if that's how they want it, let them bark at the moon alone (or whatever it is they do) and dance and keep their own home fires burning. Let them live, as was said, "in the shadow of man." It serves them right.

I ask the psychoanalyst, "Who are we, anyway?" He says about 90 percent of us ask that same question in one form or another, while about 10 percent seem to have found some kind of an answer of their own. He says that, anyway, we will remain essentially who we already are whether we bother to ask the question or not.

WILLIAM GIBSON
Burning Chrome

{1982}

William Gibson, the most renowned and influential writer in the cyberpunk style of sf, was born in South Carolina in 1948, and expatriated to Canada at the time of the Vietnam War. In the late 1970s, Gibson became affiliated with a group of young U.S. sf writers centered around the Austin, Texas–based writer-editor Bruce Sterling, with whom Gibson would collaborate for many years. The group—which included Rudy Rucker, Pat Cadigan, John Shirley, and Lewis Shiner—came to be known as the "cyberpunks" because of their fascination with computer-based manipulation of consciousness (hence the *cyber*) and their edgy, ironic attitude toward the optimistic tone of mainstream sf (hence the *punk*).

Gibson's early stories of the late 1970s and early 1980s, collected in the volume *Burning Chrome* (1986), typically set caper stories derived from the noir crime genre in a run-down urban future dominated by international cartels, criminal networks, and technologically savvy countercultures, all of them trafficking in mind-altering drugs, bio-prosthetics, and powerful computer-based virtual environments, extrapolated from current trends in computer technology and bioengineering. Gibson's protagonists are often hackers who operate in the vast, complex virtual-reality system known as the *matrix*, the data-domain where the world's governments and corporations store their information, situated in *cyberspace*. (Gibson is generally credited with introducing the latter term to contemporary usage.) Gibson elaborated these early themes in his first novel, *Neuromancer* (1984), which is often viewed as the most influential sf novel in the last quarter of the twentieth century.

Gibson expanded on the world of *Neuromancer* in two sequels, *Count Zero* (1986) and *Mona Lisa Overdrive* (1988). He followed this first trilogy with a second one, consisting of *Virtual Light* (1993), *Idoru* (1996), and *All Tomorrow's Parties* (1999), set in a near future where virtual reality combines with nanotechnology. In 1990, he collaborated with Sterling to write *The Difference Engine*, a definitive work of steampunk (alternative histories set in an imaginary past that has been transformed by science-fictional technology). Gibson's recent novels, *Pattern Recogni-*

tion (2003) and *Spook Country* (2007) eschew science-fictional devices, depicting a realistic present that seems barely distinguishable from sf.

"Burning Chrome" is one of Gibson's best, and most typical, stories. It includes many of the elements of Gibson's influential early cyberpunk style: a thriller plot set in a corrupt and violent "failed future" where rebellious hackers raid soulless cartels and mafias that use technology to exploit human beings. The protagonists are mildly antiheroic, with technical and street skills to manipulate the corrupt system, but lacking in higher ideals. Technological enhancements of the human body or brain are familiar aspects of the landscape. But also evident is Gibson's distinctive, lyrical prose style, which captures his fallen world in striking language that combines futuristic high-tech vocabulary with romantic imagery and feeling. Influenced by Ridley Scott's stylish film, *Blade Runner* (1982), and the highly stylized fiction of J. G. Ballard, William S. Burroughs, and Samuel R. Delany, Gibson's language conveys a melancholy nostalgia for lost affections at the same moment it expresses awe at technological transformations of the human condition.

It was hot, the night we burned Chrome. Out in the malls and plazas, moths were batting themselves to death against the neon, but in Bobby's loft the only light came from a monitor screen and the green and red LEDs on the face of the matrix simulator. I knew every chip in Bobby's simulator by heart; it looked like your workaday Ono-Sendai VII, the "Cyberspace Seven," but I'd rebuilt it so many times that you'd have had a hard time finding a square millimeter of factory circuitry in all that silicon.

We waited side by side in front of the simulator console, watching the time display in the screen's lower left corner.

"Go for it," I said, when it was time, but Bobby was already there, leaning forward to drive the Russian program into its slot with the heel of his hand. He did it with the tight grace of a kid slamming change into an arcade game, sure of winning and ready to pull down a string of free games.

A silver tide of phosphenes boiled across my field of vision as the matrix began to unfold in my head, a 3-D chessboard, infinite and perfectly transparent. The Russian program seemed to lurch as we entered the grid. If anyone else had been jacked into that part of the matrix, he might have seen a surf of flickering shadow roll out of the little yellow pyramid that represented our computer. The program was a mimetic weapon, designed to absorb local color and present itself as a crash-priority override in whatever context it encountered.

"Congratulations," I heard Bobby say. "We just became an Eastern Seaboard Fission Authority inspection probe . . ." That meant we were clearing fiberoptic lines with the cybernetic equivalent of a fire siren, but in the simulation matrix we seemed to rush straight for Chrome's database. I couldn't see it yet, but I already knew those walls were waiting. Walls of shadow, walls of ice.

Chrome: her pretty childface smooth as steel, with eyes that would have been at home on the bottom of some deep Atlantic trench, cold gray eyes that lived under terrible pressure. They said she cooked her own cancers for people who crossed her, rococo custom variations that took years to kill you. They said a lot of things about Chrome, none of them at all reassuring.

So I blotted her out with a picture of Rikki. Rikki kneeling in a shaft of dusty sunlight that slanted into the loft through a grid of steel and glass: her faded camouflage fatigues, her translucent rose sandals, the good line of her bare back as she rummaged through a nylon gear bag. She looks up, and a half-blond curl falls to tickle her nose. Smiling, buttoning an old shirt of Bobby's, frayed khaki cotton drawn across her breasts.

She smiles.

"Son of a bitch," said Bobby, "we just told Chrome we're an IRS audit and three Supreme Court subpoenas. . . . Hang on to your ass, Jack."

So long, Rikki. Maybe now I see you never.

And dark, so dark, in the halls of Chrome's ice.

Bobby was a cowboy, and ice was the nature of his game, *ice* from ICE, Intrusion Countermeasures Electronics. The matrix is an abstract representation of the relationships between data systems. Legitimate programmers jack into their employers' sector of the matrix and find themselves surrounded by bright geometries representing the corporate data.

Towers and fields of it ranged in the colorless nonspace of the simulation matrix, the electronic consensus-hallucination that facilitates the handling and exchange of massive quantities of data. Legitimate programmers never see the walls of ice they work behind, the walls of shadow that screen their operations from others, from industrial-espionage artists and hustlers like Bobby Quine.

Bobby was a cowboy. Bobby was a cracksman, a burglar, casing mankind's extended electronic nervous system, rustling data and credit in the crowded matrix, monochrome nonspace where the only stars are dense concentrations of information, and high above it all burn corporate galaxies and the cold spiral arms of military systems.

Bobby was another one of those young-old faces you see drinking in the Gentleman Loser, the chic bar for computer cowboys, rustlers, cybernetic second-story men. We were partners.

Bobby Quine and Automatic Jack. Bobby's the thin, pale dude with the dark glasses, and Jack's the mean-looking guy with the myoelectric arm. Bobby's software and Jack's hard; Bobby punches console and Jack runs down all the little things that can give you an edge. Or, anyway, that's what the scene watchers in the Gentleman Loser would've told you, before Bobby decided to burn Chrome. But they also might've told you that Bobby was losing his edge, slowing down. He was twenty-eight, Bobby, and that's old for a console cowboy.

Both of us were good at what we did, but somehow that one big score just wouldn't come down for us. I knew where to go for the right gear, and Bobby had all his licks down pat. He'd sit back with a white terry sweatband across his forehead and whip moves on those keyboards faster than you could follow, punching his way through some of the fanciest ice in the business, but that was when something happened that managed to get him totally wired, and that didn't happen often. Not highly motivated, Bobby, and I was the kind of guy who's happy to have the rent covered and a clean shirt to wear.

But Bobby had this thing for girls, like they were his private tarot or something, the way he'd get himself moving. We never talked about it, but when it started to look like he was losing his touch that summer, he started to spend more time in the Gentleman Loser. He'd sit at a table by the open doors and watch the crowd slide by, nights when the bugs were at the neon and the air smelled of perfume and fast food. You could see his sunglasses scanning those faces as they passed, and he must have decided that Rikki's was the one he was waiting for, the wild card and the luck changer. The new one.

I went to New York to check out the market, to see what was available in hot software.

The Finn's place has a defective hologram in the window; METRO HOLOGRAFIX, over a display of dead flies wearing fur coats of gray dust. The scrap's waist-high, inside, drifts of it rising to meet walls that are barely visible behind nameless junk, behind sagging pressboard shelves stacked with old skin magazines and yellow-spined years of *National Geographic*.

"You need a gun," said the Finn. He looks like a recombo DNA project aimed at tailoring people for high-speed burrowing. "You're in luck. I got the new Smith and Wesson, the four-oh-eight Tactical. Got this xenon projector slung under the barrel, see, batteries in the grip, throw you a twelve-inch high-noon circle in the pitch dark at fifty yards. The light source is so narrow, it's almost impossible to spot. It's just like voodoo in a nightfight."

I let my arm clunk down on the table and started the fingers drumming; the servos in the hand began whining like overworked mosquitoes. I knew that the Finn really hated the sound.

"You looking to pawn that?" He prodded the Duralumin wrist joint with the chewed shaft of a felt-tip pen. "Maybe get yourself something a little quieter?"

I kept it up. "I don't need any guns, Finn."

"Okay," he said, "okay," and I quit drumming. "I only got this one item, and I don't even know what it is." He looked unhappy. "I got it off these bridge-and-tunnel kids from Jersey last week."

"So when'd you ever buy anything you didn't know what it was, Finn?"

"Wise ass." And he passed me a transparent mailer with something in it that looked like an audio cassette through the bubble padding. "They had a passport," he said. "They had credit cards and a watch. And that."

"They had the contents of somebody's pockets, you mean."

He nodded. "The passport was Belgian. It was also bogus, looked to me, so I put it in the furnace. Put the cards in with it. The watch was okay, a Porsche, nice watch."

It was obviously some kind of plug-in military program. Out of the mailer, it looked like the magazine of a small assault rifle, coated with nonreflective black plastic. The edges and corners showed bright metal; it had been knocking around for a while.

"I'll give you a bargain on it, Jack. For old times' sake."

I had to smile at that. Getting a bargain from the Finn was like God repealing the law of gravity when you have to carry a heavy suitcase down ten blocks of airport corridor.

"Looks Russian to me," I said. "Probably the emergency sewage controls for some Leningrad suburb. Just what I need."

"You know," said the Finn, "I got a pair of shoes older than you are. Sometimes I think you got about as much class as those yahoos from Jersey. What do you want me to tell you, it's the keys to the Kremlin? You figure out what the goddamn thing is. Me, I just sell the stuff."

I bought it.

Bodiless, we swerve into Chrome's castle of ice. And we're fast, fast. It feels like we're surfing the crest of the invading program, hanging ten above the seething glitch systems as they mutate. We're sentient patches of oil swept along down corridors of shadow.

Somewhere we have bodies, very far away, in a crowded loft roofed with steel and glass. Somewhere we have microseconds, maybe time left to pull out.

We've crashed her gates disguised as an audit and three subpoenas, but her defenses are specifically geared to cope with that kind of official intrusion. Her most sophisticated ice is structured to fend off warrants, writs, subpoenas. When we breached the first gate, the bulk of her data vanished behind core-command ice, these walls we see as leagues of corridor, mazes of shadow. Five separate landlines spurted May Day signals to law firms, but the virus had already taken over the parameter ice. The glitch systems gobble the distress calls as our mimetic subprograms scan anything that hasn't been blanked by core command.

The Russian program lifts a Tokyo number from the unscreened data, choosing it for frequency of calls, average length of calls, the speed with which Chrome returned those calls.

"Okay," says Bobby, "we're an incoming scrambler call from a pal of hers in Japan. That should help."

Ride 'em, cowboy.

Bobby read his future in women; his girls were omens, changes in the weather, and he'd sit all night in the Gentleman Loser, waiting for the season to lay a new face down in front of him like a card.

I was working late in the loft one night, shaving down a chip, my arm off and the little waldo jacked straight into the stump.

Bobby came in with a girl I hadn't seen before, and usually I feel a little funny if a stranger sees me working that way, with those leads clipped to the hard carbon studs that stick out of my stump. She came right over and looked at the magnified image on the screen, then saw the waldo moving under its vacuum-sealed dust cover. She didn't say anything, just watched. Right away I had a good feeling about her; it's like that sometimes.

"Automatic Jack, Rikki. My associate."

He laughed, put his arm around her waist, something in his tone letting me know that I'd be spending the night in a dingy room in a hotel.

"Hi," she said. Tall, nineteen or maybe twenty, and she definitely had the goods. With just those few freckles across the bridge of her nose, and eyes somewhere between dark amber and French coffee. Tight black jeans rolled to mid-calf and a narrow plastic belt that matched the rose-colored sandals.

But now when I see her sometimes when I'm trying to sleep, I see her somewhere out on the edge of all this sprawl of cities and smoke, and it's like she's a hologram stuck behind my eyes, in a bright dress she must've worn once, when I knew her, something that doesn't quite reach her knees. Bare legs long and straight. Brown hair, streaked with blond, hoods her face, blown in a wind from somewhere, and I see her wave good-bye.

Bobby was making a show of rooting through a stack of audio cassettes. "I'm on my way, cowboy," I said, unclipping the waldo. She watched attentively as I put my arm back on.

"Can you fix things?" she asked.

"Anything, anything you want, Automatic Jack'll fix it." I snapped my Duralumin fingers for her.

She took a little simstim deck from her belt and showed me the broken hinge on the cassette cover.

"Tomorrow," I said, "no problem."

And my oh my, I said to myself, sleep pulling me down the six flights to the street, *what'll Bobby's luck be like with a fortune cookie like that? If his system worked, we'd be striking it rich any night now*. In the street I grinned and yawned and waved for a cab.

Chrome's castle is dissolving, sheets of ice shadow flickering and fading, eaten by the glitch systems that spin out from the Russian program, tumbling away from our central logic thrust and infecting the fabric of the ice itself. The glitch systems are cybernetic virus analogs, self-replicating and voracious. They mutate constantly, in unison, subverting and absorbing Chrome's defenses.

Have we already paralyzed her, or is a bell ringing somewhere, a red light blinking? Does she know?

Rikki Wildside, Bobby called her, and for those first few weeks it must have seemed to her that she had it all, the whole teeming show spread out for her, sharp and bright under the neon. She was new to the scene, and she had all the miles of malls and plazas to prowl, all the shops and clubs, and Bobby to explain the wild side, the tricky wiring on the dark underside of things, all the players and their names and their games. He made her feel at home.

"What happened to your arm?" she asked me one night in the Gentleman Loser, the three of us drinking at a small table in a corner.

"Hang-gliding," I said, "accident."

"Hang-gliding over a wheatfield," said Bobby, "place called Kiev. Our Jack's just hanging there in the dark, under a Nightwing parafoil, with fifty kilos of radar jammer between his legs, and some Russian asshole accidentally burns his arm off with a laser."

I don't remember how I changed the subject, but I did.

I was still telling myself that it wasn't Rikki who was getting to me, but what Bobby was doing with her. I'd known him for a long time, since the end of the war, and I knew he used women as counters in a game, Bobby Quine versus fortune, versus time and the night of cities. And Rikki had turned up just when he needed something to get him going, something to aim for. So he'd set her up as a symbol for everything he wanted and couldn't have, everything he'd had and couldn't keep.

I didn't like having to listen to him tell me how much he loved her, and knowing he believed it only made it worse. He was a past master at the hard fall and the rapid recovery, and I'd seen it happen a dozen times before. He might as well have had NEXT printed across his sunglasses in green Day-Glo capitals, ready to flash out at the first interesting face that flowed past the tables in the Gentleman Loser.

I knew what he did to them. He turned them into emblems, sigils on the map of his hustler's life, navigation beacons he could follow through a sea of bars and neon. What else did he have to steer by? He didn't love money, in and of itself, not enough to follow its lights. He wouldn't work for power over other people; he hated the responsibility it brings. He had some basic pride in his skill, but that was never enough to keep him pushing.

So he made do with women.

When Rikki showed up, he needed one in the worst way. He was fading fast, and smart money was already whispering that the edge was off his game. He needed that one big score, and soon, because he didn't know any other kind of life, and all his clocks were set for hustler's time, calibrated in risk and adrenaline and that supernal dawn calm that comes when every move's proved right and a sweet lump of someone else's credit clicks into your own account.

It was time for him to make his bundle and get out; so Rikki got set up higher and further away than any of the others ever had, even though—and I felt like screaming it at him—she was right there, alive, totally real, human, hungry, resilient, bored, beautiful, excited, all the things she was . . .

Then he went out one afternoon, about a week before I made the trip to New York to see the Finn. Went out and left us there in the loft, waiting for a thunderstorm. Half the skylight was shadowed by a dome they'd never finished, and the other half showed sky, black and blue with clouds. I was standing by the bench, looking up at that sky, stupid with the hot afternoon, the humidity, and she touched me, touched my shoulder, the half-inch border of taut pink scar that the arm doesn't cover. Anybody else ever touched me there, they went on to the shoulder, the neck. . . .

But she didn't do that. Her nails were lacquered black, not pointed, but tapered oblongs, the lacquer only a shade darker than the carbon-fiber laminate that sheathes my arm. And her hand went down the arm, black nails tracing a weld in the laminate, down to the black anodized elbow joint, out to the wrist, her hand soft-knuckled as a child's, fingers spreading to lock over mine, her palm against the perforated Duralumin.

Her other palm came up to brush across the feedback pads, and it rained all afternoon, raindrops drumming on the steel and soot-stained glass above Bobby's bed.

Ice walls flick away like supersonic butterflies made of shade. Beyond them, the matrix's illusion of infinite space. It's like watching a tape of a prefab building going up; only the tape's reversed and run at high speed, and these walls are torn wings.

Trying to remind myself that this place and the gulf beyond are only representations, that we aren't "in" Chrome's computer, but interfaced with it, while the matrix simulator in Bobby's loft generates this illusion . . . The core data begin to emerge, exposed, vulnerable. . . . This is the far side of ice, the view of the matrix I've never seen before, the view that fifteen million legitimate console operators see daily and take for granted.

The core data tower around us like vertical freight trains, color-coded for access. Bright primaries, impossibly bright in that transparent void, linked by countless horizontals in nursery blues and pinks.

But ice still shadows something at the center of it all: the heart of all Chrome's expensive darkness, the very heart.

It was late afternoon when I got back from my shopping expedition to New York. Not much sun through the skylight, but an ice pattern glowed on Bobby's monitor screen, a 2-D graphic representation of someone's computer defenses, lines of neon woven like an Art Deco prayer rug. I turned the console off, and the screen went completely dark.

Rikki's things were spread across my workbench, nylon bags spilling clothes and makeup, a pair of bright red cowboy boots, audio cassettes, glossy Japanese magazines about simstim stars. I stacked it all under the bench and then took my arm off, forgetting that the program I'd bought from the Finn was in the right-hand pocket of my jacket, so that I had to fumble it out left-handed and then get it into the padded jaws of the jeweler's vise.

The waldo looks like an old audio turntable, the kind that played disc records, with the vise set up under a transparent dust cover. The arm itself is just over a centimeter long, swinging out on what would've been the tone arm on one of those turntables. But I don't look at that when I've clipped the leads to my stump; I look at the scope, because that's my arm there in black and white, magnification 40x.

I ran a tool check and picked up the laser. It felt a little heavy; so I scaled my weight-sensor input down to a quarter-kilo per gram and got to work. At 40x the side of the program looked like a trailer truck.

It took eight hours to crack: three hours with the waldo and the laser and four dozen taps, two hours on the phone to a contact in Colorado, and three hours to run down a lexicon disc that could translate eight-year-old technical Russian.

Then Cyrillic alphanumerics started reeling down the monitor, twisting themselves into English halfway down. There were a lot of gaps, where the lexicon ran up against specialized military acronyms in the readout I'd bought from my man in Colorado, but it did give me some idea of what I'd bought from the Finn.

I felt like a punk who'd gone out to buy a switchblade and come home with a small neutron bomb.

Screwed again, I thought. *What good's a neutron bomb in a streetfight?* The thing under the dust cover was right out of my league. I didn't even know where to unload it, where to look for a buyer. Someone had, but he was dead, someone with a Porsche watch and a fake Belgian passport, but I'd never tried to move in those circles. The Finn's muggers from the 'burbs had knocked over someone who had some highly arcane connections.

The program in the jeweler's vise was a Russian military icebreaker, a killer-virus program.

It was dawn when Bobby came in alone. I'd fallen asleep with a bag of takeout sandwiches in my lap.

"You want to eat?" I asked him, not really awake, holding out my sandwiches. I'd been dreaming of the program, of its waves of hungry glitch systems and mimetic subprograms; in the dream it was an animal of some kind, shapeless and flowing.

He brushed the bag aside on his way to the console, punched a function key. The screen lit with the intricate pattern I'd seen there that afternoon. I rubbed sleep from my eyes with my left hand, one thing I can't do with my right. I'd fallen asleep trying to decide whether to tell him about the program. Maybe I should try to sell it alone, keep the money, go somewhere new, ask Rikki to go with me.

"Whose is it?" I asked.

He stood there in a black cotton jumpsuit, an old leather jacket thrown over his shoulders like a cape. He hadn't shaved for a few days, and his face looked thinner than usual.

"It's Chrome's," he said.

My arm convulsed, started clicking, fear translated to the myoelectrics through the carbon studs. I spilled the sandwiches; limp sprouts, and bright yellow dairy-produce slices on the unswept wooden floor.

"You're stone crazy," I said.

"No," he said, "you think she rumbled it? No way. We'd be dead already. I locked on to her through a triple-blind rental system in Mombasa and an Algerian comsat. She knew somebody was having a look-see, but she couldn't trace it."

If Chrome had traced the pass Bobby had made at her ice, we were good as dead. But he was probably right, or she'd have had me blown away on my way back from New York. "Why her, Bobby? Just give me one reason . . .

Chrome: I'd seen her maybe half a dozen times in the Gentleman Loser. Maybe she was slumming, or checking out the human condition, a condition she didn't exactly aspire to. A sweet little heart-shaped face framing the nastiest pair of eyes you ever saw. She'd looked fourteen for as long as anyone could remember, hyped out of anything like a normal metabolism on some massive program of serums and hormones. She was as ugly a customer as the street ever produced, but she didn't belong to the street anymore. She was one of the Boys, Chrome, a member in good standing of the local Mob subsidiary. Word was, she'd gotten started as a dealer, back when synthetic pituitary hormones were still proscribed. But she hadn't had to move hormones for a long time. Now she owned the House of Blue Lights.

"You're flat-out crazy, Quine. You give me one sane reason for having that stuff on your screen. You ought, to dump it, and I mean *now* . . ."

"Talk in the Loser," he said, shrugging out of the leather jacket. "Black Myron and Crow Jane. Jane, she's up on all the sex lines, claims she knows where the money goes. So she's arguing with Myron that Chrome's the controlling interest in the Blue Lights, not just some figurehead for the Boys."

"'The Boys,' Bobby," I said. "That's the operative word there. You still capable of seeing that? We don't mess with the Boys, remember? That's why we're still walking around."

"That's why we're still poor, partner." He settled back into the swivel chair in front of the console, unzipped his jumpsuit, and scratched his skinny white chest. "But maybe not for much longer."

"I think maybe this partnership just got itself permanently dissolved."

Then he grinned at me. That grin was truly crazy, feral and focused, and I knew that right then he really didn't give a shit about dying.

"Look," I said, "I've got some money left, you know? Why don't you take it and get the tube to Miami, catch a hopper to Montego Bay. You need a rest, man. You've got to get your act together."

"My act, Jack," he said, punching something on the keyboard, "never has been this together before." The neon prayer rug on the screen shivered and woke as an animation program cut in, ice lines weaving with hypnotic frequency, a living mandala. Bobby kept punching, and the movement slowed; the pattern resolved itself, grew slightly less complex, became an alternation between two distant configurations. A first-class piece of work, and I hadn't thought he was still that good. "Now," he said, "there, see it? Wait. There. There again. And there. Easy to miss. That's it. Cuts in every hour and twenty minutes with a squirt transmission to their comsat. We could live for a year on what she pays them weekly in negative interest."

"Whose comsat?"

"Zurich. Her bankers. That's her bankbook, Jack. That's where the money goes. Crow Jane was right."

I stood there. My arm forgot to click.

"So how'd you do in New York, partner? You get anything that'll help me cut ice? We're going to need whatever we can get."

I kept my eyes on his, forced myself not to look in the direction of the waldo, the jeweler's vise. The Russian program was there, under the dust cover.

Wild cards, luck changers.

"Where's Rikki?" I asked him, crossing to the console, pretending to study the alternating patterns on the screen.

"Friends of hers," he shrugged, "kids, they're all into simstim." He smiled absently. "I'm going to do it for her, man."

"I'm going out to think about this, Bobby. You want me to come back, you keep your hands off the board."

"I'm doing it for her," he said as the door closed behind me. "You know I am."

And down now, down, the program a roller coaster through this fraying maze of shadow walls, gray cathedral spaces between the bright towers. Headlong speed.

Black ice. Don't think about it. Black ice.

Too many stories in the Gentleman Loser; black ice is a part of the mythology. Ice that kills. Illegal, but then aren't we all? Some kind of neural-feedback weapon, and you connect with it only once. Like some hideous

Word that eats the mind from the inside out. Like an epileptic spasm that goes on and on until there's nothing left at all.

And we're diving for the floor of Chrome's shadow castle.

Trying to brace myself for the sudden stopping of breath, a sickness and final slackening of the nerves. Fear of that cold Word waiting, down there in the dark.

I went out and looked for Rikki, found her in a café with a boy with Sendai eyes, half-healed suture lines radiating from his bruised sockets. She had a glossy brochure spread open on the table, Tally Isham smiling up from a dozen photographs, the Girl with the Zeiss Ikon Eyes.

Her little simstim deck was one of the things I'd stacked under my bench the night before, the one I'd fixed for her the day after I'd first seen her. She spent hours jacked into that unit, the contact band across her forehead like a gray plastic tiara. Tally Isham was her favorite, and with the contact band on, she was gone, off somewhere in the recorded sensorium of simstim's biggest star. Simulated stimuli: the world—all the interesting parts, anyway—as perceived by Tally Isham. Tally raced a black Fokker ground-effect plane across Arizona mesa tops. Tally dived the Truk Island preserves. Tally partied with the super-rich on private Greek islands, heartbreaking purity of those tiny white seaports at dawn.

Actually she looked a lot like Tally, same coloring and cheekbones. I thought Rikki's mouth was stronger. More sass. She didn't want to *be* Tally Isham, but she coveted the job. That was her ambition, to be in simstim. Bobby just laughed it off. She talked to me about it, though. "How'd I look with a pair of these?" she'd ask, holding a full-page headshot, Tally Isham's blue Zeiss Ikons lined up with her own amber-brown. She'd had her corneas done twice, but she still wasn't twenty-twenty; so she wanted Ikons. Brand of the stars. Very expensive.

"You still window-shopping for eyes?" I asked as I sat down.

"Tiger just got some," she said. She looked tired, I thought.

Tiger was so pleased with his Sendais that he couldn't help smiling, but I doubted whether he'd have smiled otherwise. He had the kind of uniform good looks you get after your seventh trip to the surgical boutique; he'd probably spend the rest of his life looking vaguely like each new season's media front-runner; not too obvious a copy, but nothing too original, either.

"Sendai, right?" I smiled back.

He nodded. I watched as he tried to take me in with his idea of a professional simstim glance. He was pretending that he was recording. I thought he spent too long on my arm. "They'll be great on peripherals when the muscles heal," he said, and I saw how carefully he reached for his double espresso. Sendai eyes are notorious for depth-perception defects and warranty hassles, among other things.

"Tiger's leaving for Hollywood tomorrow."

"Then maybe Chiba City, right?" I smiled at him. He didn't smile back. "Got an offer, Tiger? Know an agent?"

"Just checking it out," he said quietly. Then he got up and left. He said a quick good-bye to Rikki, but not to me.

"That kid's optic nerves may start to deteriorate inside six months. You know that, Rikki? Those Sendais are illegal in England, Denmark, lots of places. You can't replace nerves."

"Hey, Jack, no lectures." She stole one of my croissants and nibbled at the tip of one of its horns.

"I thought I was your adviser, kid."

"Yeah. Well, Tiger's not too swift, but everybody knows about Sendais. They're all he can afford. So he's taking a chance. If he gets work, he can replace them."

"With these?" I tapped the Zeiss Ikon brochure. "Lot of money, Rikki. You know better than to take a gamble like that."

She nodded. "I want Ikons."

"If you're going up to Bobby's, tell him to sit tight until he hears from me."

"Sure. It's business?"

"Business," I said. But it was craziness.

I drank my coffee, and she ate both my croissants. Then I walked her down to Bobby's. I made fifteen calls, each one from a different pay phone.

Business. Bad craziness.

All in all, it took us six weeks to set the burn up, six weeks of Bobby telling me how much he loved her. I worked even harder, trying to get away from that.

Most of it was phone calls. My fifteen initial and very oblique enquiries each seemed to breed fifteen more. I was looking for a certain service Bobby and I both imagined as a requisite part of the world's clandestine economy, but which probably never had more than five customers at a time. It would be one that never advertised.

We were looking for the world's heaviest fence, for a non-aligned money laundry capable of dry-cleaning a megabuck on-line cash transfer and then forgetting about it.

All those calls were a waste, finally, because it was the Finn who put me on to what we needed. I'd gone up to New York to buy a new blackbox rig, because we were going broke paying for all those calls.

I put the problem to him as hypothetically as possible.

"Macao," he said.

"Macao?"

"The Long Hum family. Stockbrokers."

He even had the number. You want a fence, ask another fence.

The Long Hum people were so oblique that they made my idea of a subtle approach look like a tactical nuke-out. Bobby had to make two shuttle runs to Hong Kong to get the deal straight. We were running out of capital, and fast. I still don't know why I decided to go along with it in the first place; I was scared of Chrome, and I'd never been all that hot to get rich.

I tried telling myself that it was a good idea to burn the House of Blue Lights because the place was a creep joint, but I just couldn't buy it. I didn't like the Blue Lights, because I'd spent a supremely depressing evening there once, but that was no excuse for going after Chrome. Actually I halfway assumed we were going to die in the attempt. Even with that killer program, the odds weren't exactly in our favor.

Bobby was lost in writing the set of commands we were going to plug into the dead center of Chrome's computer. That was going to be my job, because Bobby was going to have his hands full trying to keep the Russian program from going straight for the kill. It was too complex for us to rewrite, and so he was going to try to hold it back for the two seconds I needed.

I made a deal with a streetfighter named Miles. He was going to follow Rikki the night of the burn, keep her in sight, and phone me at a certain time. If I wasn't there, or didn't answer in just a certain way, I'd told him to grab her and put her on the first tube out. I gave him an envelope to give her, money and a note.

Bobby really hadn't thought about that, much, how things would go for her if we blew it. He just kept telling me he loved her, where they were going to go together, how they'd spend the money.

"Buy her a pair of Ikons first, man. That's what she wants. She's serious about that simstim scene."

"Hey," he said, looking up from the keyboard, "she won't need to work. We're going to make it, Jack. She's my luck. She won't ever have to work again."

"Your luck," I said. I wasn't happy. I couldn't remember when I had been happy. "You seen your luck around lately?"

He hadn't, but neither had I. We'd both been too busy.

I missed her. Missing her reminded me of my one night in the House of

Blue Lights, because I'd gone there out of missing someone else. I'd gotten drunk to begin with, then I'd started hitting Vasopressin inhalers. If your main squeeze has just decided to walk out on you, booze and Vasopressin are the ultimate in masochistic pharmacology; the juice makes you maudlin and the Vasopressin makes you remember, I mean really remember. Clinically they use the stuff to counter senile amnesia, but the street finds its own uses for things. So I'd bought myself an ultra-intense replay of a bad affair; trouble is, you get the bad with the good. Go gunning for transports of animal ecstasy and you get what you said, too, and what she said to that, how she walked away and never looked back.

I don't remember deciding to go to the Blue Lights, or how I got there, hushed corridors and this really tacky decorative waterfall trickling somewhere, or maybe just a hologram of one. I had a lot of money that night; somebody had given Bobby a big roll for opening a three-second window in someone else's ice.

I don't think the crew on the door liked my looks, but I guess my money was okay.

I had more to drink there when I'd done what I went there for. Then I made some crack to the barman about closet necrophiliacs, and that didn't go down too well. Then this very large character insisted on calling me War Hero, which I didn't like. I think I showed him some tricks with the arm, before the lights went out, and I woke up two days later in a basic sleeping module somewhere else. A cheap place, not even room to hang yourself. And I sat there on that narrow foam slab and cried.

Some things are worse than being alone. But the thing they sell in the House of Blue Lights is so popular that it's almost legal.

At the heart of darkness, the still center, the glitch systems shred the dark with whirlwinds of light, translucent razors spinning away from us; we hang in the center of a silent slow-motion explosion, ice fragments falling away forever, and Bobby's voice comes in across light-years of electronic void illusion—"Burn the bitch down. I can't hold the thing back—"

The Russian program, rising through towers of data, blotting out the playroom colors. And I plug Bobby's homemade command package into the center of Chrome's cold heart. The squirt transmission cuts in, a pulse of condensed information that shoots straight up, past the thickening tower of darkness, the Russian program, while Bobby struggles to control that crucial second. An unformed arm of shadow twitches from the towering dark, too late.

We've done it.

The matrix folds itself around me like an origami trick.

And the loft smells of sweat and burning circuitry.

I thought I heard Chrome scream, a raw metal sound, but I couldn't have.

Bobby was laughing, tears in his eyes. The elapsed-time figure in the corner of the monitor read 07:24:05. The burn had taken a little under eight minutes.

And I saw that the Russian program had melted in its slot.

We'd given the bulk of Chrome's Zurich account to a dozen world charities. There was too much there to move, and we knew we had to break her, burn her straight down, or she might come after us. We took less than ten percent for ourselves and shot it through the Long Hum set-up in Macao. They took sixty percent of that for themselves and kicked what was left back to us through the most convoluted sector of the Hong Kong exchange. It took an hour before our money started to reach the two accounts we'd opened in Zurich.

I watched zeros pile up behind a meaningless figure on the monitor. I was rich.

Then the phone rang. It was Miles. I almost blew the code phrase.

"Hey, Jack, man, I dunno—what's it all about, with this girl of yours? Kinda funny thing here . . ."

"What? Tell me."

"I been on her, like you said, tight but out of sight. She goes to the Loser, hangs out, then she gets a tube. Goes to the House of Blue Lights—"

"She what?"

"Side door. *Employees* only. No way I could get past their security."

"Is she there now?"

"No, man, I just lost her. It's insane down here, like the Blue Lights just shut down, looks like for good, seven kinds of alarms going off, everybody running, the heat out in riot gear. . . . Now there's all this stuff going on, insurance guys, real-estate types, vans with municipal plates . . .

"Miles, where'd she go?"

"Lost her, Jack."

"Look, Miles, you keep the money in the envelope, right?"

"You serious? Hey, I'm real sorry. I—"

I hung up.

"Wait'll we tell her," Bobby was saying, rubbing a towel across his bare chest.

"You tell her yourself, cowboy. I'm going for a walk."

So I went out into the night and the neon and let the crowd pull me along, walking blind, willing myself to be just a segment of that mass organism, just one more drifting chip of consciousness under the geodesics. I didn't think, just put one foot in front of another, but after a while I did think, and it all made sense. She'd needed the money.

I thought about Chrome, too. That we'd killed her, murdered her, as surely as if we'd slit her throat. The night that carried me along through the malls and plazas would be hunting her now, and she had nowhere to go. How many enemies would she have in this crowd alone? How many would move, now they weren't held back by fear of her money? We'd taken her for everything she had. She was back on the street again. I doubted she'd live till dawn.

Finally I remembered the café, the one where I'd met Tiger.

Her sunglasses told the whole story, huge black shades with a telltale smudge of fleshtone paintstick in the corner of one lens. "Hi, Rikki," I said, and I was ready when she took them off.

Blue. Tally Isham blue. The clear trademark blue they're famous for, ZEISS IKON ringing each iris in tiny capitals, the letters suspended there like flecks of gold.

"They're beautiful," I said. Paintstick covered the bruising. No scars with work that good. "You made some money."

"Yeah, I did." Then she shivered. "But I won't make any more, not that way."

"I think that place is out of business."

"Oh." Nothing moved in her face then. The new blue eyes were still and very deep.

"It doesn't matter. Bobby's waiting for you. We just pulled down a big score."

"No. I've got to go. I guess he won't understand, but I've got to go."

I nodded, watching the arm swing up to take her hand; it didn't seem to be part of me at all, but she held on to it like it was.

"I've got a one-way ticket to Hollywood. Tiger knows some people I can stay with. Maybe I'll even get to Chiba City."

She was right about Bobby. I went back with her. He didn't understand. But she'd already served her purpose, for Bobby, and I wanted to tell her not to hurt for him, because I could see that she did. He wouldn't even come out into the hallway after she had packed her bags. I put the bags down and kissed her and messed up the paintstick, and something came up inside me the way the killer program had risen above Chrome's data. A sudden stopping of the breath, in a place where no word is. But she had a plane to catch.

Bobby was slumped in the swivel chair in front of his monitor, looking at his string of zeros. He had his shades on, and I knew he'd be in the Gentleman Loser by nightfall, checking out the weather, anxious for a sign, someone to tell him what his new life would be like. I couldn't see it being very different. More comfortable, but he'd always be waiting for that next card to fall.

I tried not to imagine her in the House of Blue Lights, working three-hour shifts in an approximation of REM sleep, while her body and a bundle of conditioned reflexes took care of business. The customers never got to complain that she was faking it, because those were real orgasms. But she felt them, if she felt them at all, as faint silver flares somewhere out on the edge of sleep. Yeah, it's so popular, it's almost legal. The customers are torn between needing someone and wanting to be alone at the same time, which has probably always been the name of that particular game, even before we had the neuroelectronics to enable them to have it both ways.

I picked up the phone and punched the number for her airline. I gave them her real name, her flight number. "She's changing that," I said, "to Chiba City. That's right. Japan." I thumbed my credit card into the slot and punched my ID code. "First class." Distant hum as they scanned my credit records. "Make that a return ticket."

But I guess she cashed the return fare, or else she didn't need it, because she hasn't come back. And sometimes late at night I'll pass a window with posters of simstim stars, all those beautiful, identical eyes staring back at me out of faces that are nearly as identical, and sometimes the eyes are hers, but none of the faces are, none of them ever are, and I see her far out on the edge of all this sprawl of night and cities, and then she waves good-bye.

OCTAVIA E. BUTLER
Speech Sounds

• • • •

{1983}

Octavia E(stelle) Butler (1947–2006) was born in Pasadena, California, and died suddenly at her home in Seattle, Washington. The West Coast landscape figures prominently in her largely dystopic vision of the future. Shy, reserved, and dyslexic, she suffered a writing block from about 2000 to 2005. Butler often explores the difficulties of communication and connection. Her fiction provides a powerful contrast to these struggles to communicate, however, given her crystal-clear narrative style devoid of ornament, the emotional immediacy of her characters' predicaments, and the accessibility of her rich metaphorical content. As a pioneering African American woman sf writer, she paved the way for the flowering of African American voices in science fiction of the twenty-first century, using speculative fiction to examine how the historical legacy of slavery haunts the present, and how the African American experience can illuminate our present and near future. Her importance has been recognized not only within the field by her winning of Hugo and Nebula Awards and by the attention paid to her by sf scholars but also by the recognition she has received beyond the field in African American studies and through the MacArthur Foundation grant she received in 1996. Among her most notable works are the five volumes of the *Patternist* series (1976–84; collected as *Seed to Harvest*, 2007), the three volumes of the *Xenogenesis* series (1987–89; collected as *Lilith's Brood*, 2000), and the two volumes of the uncompleted *Parable* series (*Parable of the Sower* [1993] and *Parable of the Talents* [1998]). Unexpectedly, her last published novel, *Fledgling* (2005), was a science-fictional vampire story. Although she apparently hated writing short stories, several of her short works are indispensable, including "Bloodchild" (1984) and "The Evening and the Morning and the Night" (1987), as well as the story collected here. Her work, long and short, is strongly rooted in the physical world, always taking into account the realities and limitations of embodiment, including race, gender, and health, as well as economics, class, and the environment.

"Speech Sounds," one of Butler's Hugo Award–winning stories, imagines a dystopic near-future Los Angeles ravaged by a virus that destroys people's abilities to read, write, and speak. The frustration of blocked communication has resulted in a disintegration of civil behavior and a breakdown in civic structures. Like Samuel R. Delany's *Babel-17* (1966) and Suzette Haden Elgin's *Native Tongue* (1984), this story uses as a starting point in its speculation the Sapir-Whorf hypothesis, that one's language determines how one thinks and acts in the world. Butler gives the frustrating lack of literacy in her characters an added social dimension by suggesting through situations and gestures that her characters are black and already suffer the social disadvantages of racism and poverty. The story is a powerful argument for the power of literacy of every kind. It also stresses the importance of empathy and personal responsibility while demonstrating how gender roles complicate every sort of social issue.

Written at the beginning of the AIDS epidemic, the story has particular resonance for the ways in which it handles the social disintegration and prejudice that result from fear of contamination; in its handling of this theme, it is similar to the later "The Evening and the Morning and the Night" (1987), which is also about the social effects of disease. In the *Parable* books, Butler imagines empathy as both the symptom of an illness and the solution for a diseased society. In this story, the protagonist finds hope in both empathy and education.

There was trouble aboard the Washington Boulevard bus. Rye had expected trouble sooner or later in her journey. She had put off going until loneliness and hopelessness drove her out. She believed she might have one group of relatives left alive—a brother and his two children twenty miles away in Pasadena. That was a day's journey one-way, if she were lucky. The unexpected arrival of the bus as she left her Virginia Road home had seemed to be a piece of luck—until the trouble began.

Two young men were involved in a disagreement of some kind, or, more likely, a misunderstanding. They stood in the aisle, grunting and gesturing at each other, each in his own uncertain T stance as the bus lurched over the potholes. The driver seemed to be putting some effort into keeping them off balance. Still, their gestures stopped just short of contact—mock punches, hand games of intimidation to replace lost curses.

People watched the pair, then looked at one another and made small anxious sounds. Two children whimpered.

Rye sat a few feet behind the disputants and across from the back door. She watched the two carefully, knowing the fight would begin when someone's nerve broke or someone's hand slipped or someone came to the end of his limited ability to communicate. These things could happen anytime.

One of them happened as the bus hit an especially large pothole and one man, tall, thin, and sneering, was thrown into his shorter opponent.

Instantly, the shorter man drove his left fist into the disintegrating sneer. He hammered his larger opponent as though he neither had nor needed any weapon other than his left fist. He hit quickly enough, hard enough to batter his opponent down before the taller man could regain his balance or hit back even once.

People screamed or squawked in fear. Those nearby scrambled to get out of the way. Three more young men roared in excitement and gestured wildly. Then, somehow, a second dispute broke out between two of these three—probably because one inadvertently touched or hit the other.

As the second fight scattered frightened passengers, a woman shook the driver's shoulder and grunted as she gestured toward the fighting.

The driver grunted back through bared teeth. Frightened, the woman drew away.

Rye, knowing the methods of bus drivers, braced herself and held on to the crossbar of the seat in front of her. When the driver hit the brakes, she was ready and the combatants were not. They fell over seats and onto screaming passengers, creating even more confusion. At least one more fight started.

The instant the bus came to a full stop, Rye was on her feet, pushing the back door. At the second push, it opened and she jumped out, holding her pack in one arm. Several other passengers followed, but some stayed on the bus. Buses were so rare and irregular now, people rode when they could, no matter what. There might not be another bus today—or tomorrow. People started walking, and if they saw a bus they flagged it down. People making intercity trips like Rye's from Los Angeles to Pasadena made plans to camp out, or risked seeking shelter with locals who might rob or murder them.

The bus did not move, but Rye moved away from it. She intended to wait until the trouble was over and get on again, but if there was shooting, she wanted the protection of a tree. Thus, she was near the curb when a battered blue Ford on the other side of the street made a U-turn and pulled up in front of the bus. Cars were rare these days—as rare as a severe shortage of fuel and of relatively unimpaired mechanics could make them. Cars that still ran were as likely to be used as weapons as they were to serve as transportation. Thus, when the driver of the Ford beckoned to Rye, she moved away warily. The driver got out—a big man, young, neatly bearded with dark, thick hair. He wore a long overcoat and a look of wariness that matched Rye's. She stood several feet from him, waiting to see what he would do. He looked at the bus, now rocking with the combat inside, then at the small cluster of passengers who had gotten off. Finally he looked at Rye again.

She returned his gaze, very much aware of the old forty-five automatic her jacket concealed. She watched his hands.

He pointed with his left hand toward the bus. The dark-tinted windows prevented him from seeing what was happening inside.

His use of the left hand interested Rye more than his obvious question. Left-handed people tended to be less impaired, more reasonable and comprehending, less driven by frustration, confusion, and anger.

She imitated his gesture, pointing toward the bus with her own left hand, then punching the air with both fists.

The man took off his coat revealing a Los Angeles Police Department uniform complete with baton and service revolver.

Rye took another step back from him. There was no more LAPD, no more *any* large organization, governmental or private. There were neighborhood patrols and armed individuals. That was all.

The man took something from his coat pocket, then threw the coat into the car. Then he gestured Rye back, back toward the rear of the bus. He had something made of plastic in his hand. Rye did not understand what he wanted until he went to the rear door of the bus and beckoned her to stand there. She obeyed mainly out of curiosity. Cop or not, maybe he could do something to stop the stupid fighting.

He walked around the front of the bus, to the street side where the driver's window was open. There, she thought she saw him throw something into the bus. She was still trying to peer through the tinted glass when people began stumbling out the rear door, choking and weeping. Gas.

Rye caught an old woman who would have fallen, lifted two little children down when they were in danger of being knocked down and trampled. She could see the bearded man helping people at the front door. She caught a thin old man shoved out by one of the combatants. Staggered by the old man's weight, she was barely able to get out of the way as the last of the young men pushed his way out. This one, bleeding from nose and mouth, stumbled into another and they grappled blindly, still sobbing from the gas.

The bearded man helped the bus driver out through the front door, though the driver did not seem to appreciate his help. For a moment, Rye thought there would be another fight. The bearded man stepped back and watched the driver gesture threateningly, watched him shout in wordless anger.

The bearded man stood still, made no sound, refused to respond to clearly obscene gestures. The least impaired people tended to do this—stand back unless they were physically threatened and let those with less control scream and jump around. It was as though they felt it beneath them to be as touchy as the less comprehending. This was an attitude of superiority and that was the way people like the bus driver perceived it. Such "superiority" was frequently punished by beatings, even by death. Rye had had close calls of her own. As a result, she never went unarmed. And in this world where the only likely common language was body language, being armed was often enough. She had rarely had to draw her gun or even display it.

The bearded man's revolver was on constant display. Apparently that was enough for the bus driver. The driver spat in disgust, glared at the bearded man for a moment longer, then strode back to his gas-filled bus.

He stared at it for a moment, clearly wanting to get in, but the gas was still too strong. Of the windows, only his tiny driver's window actually opened. The front door was open, but the rear door would not stay open unless someone held it. Of course, the air conditioning had failed long ago. The bus would take some time to clear. It was the driver's property, his livelihood. He had pasted old magazine pictures of items he would accept as fare on its sides. Then he would use what he collected to feed his family or to trade. If his bus did not run, he did not eat. On the other hand, if the inside of his bus was torn apart by senseless fighting, he would not eat very well either. He was apparently unable to perceive this. All he could see was that it would be some time before he could use his bus again. He shook his fist at the bearded man and shouted. There seemed to be words in his shout, but Rye could not understand them. She did not know whether this was his fault or hers. She had heard so little coherent human speech for the past three years, she was no longer certain how well she recognized it, no longer certain of the degree of her own impairment.

The bearded man sighed. He glanced toward his car, then beckoned to Rye. He was ready to leave, but he wanted something from her first. No. No, he wanted her to leave with him. Risk getting into his car when, in spite of his uniform, law and order were nothing—not even words any longer.

She shook her head in a universally understood negative, but the man continued to beckon.

She waved him away. He was doing what the less-impaired rarely did—drawing potentially negative attention to another of his kind. People from the bus had begun to look at her.

One of the men who had been fighting tapped another on the arm, then pointed from the bearded man to Rye, and finally held up the first two fingers of his right hand as though giving two-thirds of a Boy Scout salute. The gesture was very quick, its meaning obvious even at a distance. She had been grouped with the bearded man. Now what?

The man who had made the gesture started toward her.

She had no idea what he intended, but she stood her ground. The man was half a foot taller than she was and perhaps ten years younger. She did not imagine she could outrun him. Nor did she expect anyone to help her if she needed help. The people around her were all strangers.

She gestured once—a clear indication to the man to stop. She did not intend to repeat the gesture. Fortunately, the man obeyed. He gestured obscenely and several other men laughed. Loss of verbal language had spawned a whole new set of obscene gestures. The man, with stark simplicity, had accused her of sex with the bearded man and had suggested she accommodate the other men present—beginning with him.

Rye watched him wearily. People might very well stand by and watch if he tried to rape her. They would also stand and watch her shoot him. Would he push things that far?

He did not. After a series of obscene gestures that brought him no closer to her, he turned contemptuously and walked away.

And the bearded man still waited. He had removed his service revolver, holster and all. He beckoned again, both hands empty. No doubt his gun was in the car and within easy reach, but his taking it off impressed her. Maybe he was all right. Maybe he was just alone. She had been alone herself for three years. The illness had stripped her, killing her children one by one, killing her husband, her sister, her parents.

The illness, if it was an illness, had cut even the living off from one another, As it swept over the country, people hardly had time to lay blame on the Soviets (though they were falling silent along with the rest of the world), on a new virus, a new pollutant, radiation, divine retribution. . . . The illness was stroke-swift in the way it cut people down and stroke-like in some of its effects. But it was highly specific. Language was always lost or severely impaired. It was never regained. Often there was also paralysis, intellectual impairment, death.

Rye walked toward the bearded man, ignoring the whistling and applauding of two of the young men and their thumbs-up signs to the bearded man. If he had smiled at them or acknowledged them in any way, she would almost certainly have changed her mind. If she had let herself think of the possible deadly consequences of getting into a stranger's car, she would have changed her mind. Instead, she thought of the man who lived across the street from her. He rarely washed since his bout with the illness. And he had gotten into the habit of urinating wherever he happened to be. He had two women already—one tending each of his large gardens. They put up with him in exchange for his protection. He had made it clear that he wanted Rye to become his third woman.

She got into the car and the bearded man shut the door. She watched as he walked around to the driver's door—watched for his sake because his gun was on the seat beside her. And the bus driver and a pair of young men had come a few steps closer. They did nothing, though, until the bearded man was in the car. Then one of them threw a rock. Others followed his example, and as the car drove away, several rocks bounced off harmlessly.

When the bus was some distance behind them, Rye wiped sweat from her forehead and longed to relax. The bus would have taken her more than halfway to Pasadena. She would have had only ten miles to walk. She wondered how far she would have to walk now—and wondered if walking a long distance would be her only problem.

At Figueroa and Washington where the bus normally made a left turn, the bearded man stopped, looked at her, and indicated that she should choose a direction. When she directed him left and he actually turned left, she began to relax. If he was willing to go where she directed, perhaps he was safe.

As they passed blocks of burned, abandoned buildings, empty lots, and wrecked or stripped cars, he slipped a gold chain over his head and handed it to her. The pendant attached to it was a smooth, glassy, black rock. Obsidian. His name might be Rock or Peter or Black, but she decided to think of him as Obsidian. Even her sometimes useless memory would retain a name like Obsidian.

She handed him her own name symbol—a pin in the shape of a large golden stalk of wheat. She had bought it long before the illness and the silence began. Now she wore it, thinking it was as close as she was likely to come to Rye. People like Obsidian who had not known her before probably thought of her as Wheat. Not that it mattered. She would never hear her name spoken again.

Obsidian handed her pin back to her. He caught her hand as she reached for it and rubbed his thumb over her calluses.

He stopped at First Street and asked which way again. Then, after turning right as she had indicated, he parked near the Music Center. There, he took a folded paper from the dashboard and unfolded it. Rye recognized it as a street map, though the writing on it meant nothing to her. He flattened the map, took her hand again, and put her index finger on one spot. He touched her, touched himself, pointed toward the floor. In effect, "We are here." She knew he wanted to know where she was going. She wanted to tell him, but she shook her head sadly. She had lost reading and writing. That was her most serious impairment and her most painful. She had taught history at UCLA. She had done freelance writing. Now she could not even read her own manuscripts. She had a houseful of books that she could neither read nor bring herself to use as fuel. And she had a memory that would not bring back to her much of what she had read before.

She stared at the map, trying to calculate. She had been born in Pasadena, had lived for fifteen years in Los Angeles. Now she was near L.A. Civic Center. She knew the relative positions of the two cities, knew streets, directions, even knew to stay away from freeways which might be blocked by wrecked cars and destroyed overpasses. She ought to know how to point out Pasadena even though she could not recognize the word.

Hesitantly, she placed her hand over a pale orange patch in the upper right corner of the map. That should be right. Pasadena.

Obsidian lifted her hand and looked under it, then folded the map and put it back on the dashboard. He could read, she realized belatedly. He could probably write, too. Abruptly, she hated him—deep, bitter hatred. What did literacy mean to him—a grown man who played cops and robbers? But he was literate and she was not. She never would be. She felt sick to her stomach with hatred, frustration, and jealousy. And only a few inches from her hand was a loaded gun.

She held herself still, staring at him, almost seeing his blood. But her rage crested and ebbed and she did nothing.

Obsidian reached for her hand with hesitant familiarity. She looked at him. Her face had already revealed too much. No person still living in what was left of human society could fail to recognize that expression, that jealousy.

She closed her eyes wearily, drew a deep breath. She had experienced longing for the past, hatred of the present, growing hopelessness, purposelessness, but she had never experienced such a powerful urge to kill another person. She had left her home, finally, because she had come near to killing herself. She had found no reason to stay alive. Perhaps that was why she had gotten into Obsidian's car. She had never before done such a thing.

He touched her mouth and made chatter motions with thumb and fingers. Could she speak?

She nodded and watched his milder envy come and go. Now both had admitted what it was not safe to admit, and there had been no violence. He tapped his mouth and forehead and shook his head. He did not speak or comprehend spoken language. The illness had played with them, taking away, she suspected, what each valued most.

She plucked at his sleeve, wondering why he had decided on his own to keep the LAPD alive with what he had left. He was sane enough otherwise. Why wasn't he at home raising corn, rabbits, and children? But she did not know how to ask. Then he put his hand on her thigh and she had another question to deal with.

She shook her head. Disease, pregnancy, helpless, solitary agony . . . no.

He massaged her thigh gently and smiled in obvious disbelief.

No one had touched her for three years. She had not wanted anyone to touch her. What kind of world was this to chance bringing a child into even if the father were willing to stay and help raise it? It was too bad, though. Obsidian could not know how attractive he was to her—young, probably younger than she was, clean, asking for what he wanted rather than demanding it. But none of that mattered. What were a few moments of pleasure measured against a lifetime of consequences?

He pulled her closer to him and for a moment she let herself enjoy the closeness. He smelled good—male and good. She pulled away reluctantly.

He sighed, reached toward the glove compartment. She stiffened, not knowing what to expect, but all he took out was a small box. The writing on it meant nothing to her. She did not understand until he broke the seal, opened the box, and took out a condom. He looked at her and she first looked away in surprise. Then she giggled. She could not remember when she had last giggled.

He grinned, gestured toward the backseat, and she laughed aloud. Even in her teens, she had disliked backseats of cars. But she looked around at the empty streets and ruined buildings, then she got out and into the backseat. He let her put the condom on him, then seemed surprised at her eagerness.

Sometime later, they sat together, covered by his coat, unwilling to become clothed near-strangers again just yet. He made rock-the-baby gestures and looked questioningly at her.

She swallowed, shook her head. She did not know how to tell him her children were dead.

He took her hand and drew a cross in it with his index finger, then made his baby-rocking gesture again.

She nodded, held up three fingers, then turned away, trying to shut out a sudden flood of memories. She had told herself that the children growing up now were to be pitied. They would run through the downtown canyons with no real memory of what the buildings had been or even how they had come to be. Today's children gathered books as well as wood to be burned as fuel. They ran through the streets chasing one another and hooting like chimpanzees. They had no future. They were now all they would ever be.

He put his hand on her shoulder and she turned suddenly, fumbling for his small box, then urging him to make love to her again. He could give her forgetfulness and pleasure. Until now, nothing had been able to do that. Until now, every day had brought her closer to the time when she would do what she had left home to avoid doing; putting her gun in her mouth and pulling the trigger.

She asked Obsidian if he would come home with her, stay with her.

He looked surprised and pleased once he understood. But he did not answer at once. Finally he shook his head as she had feared he might. He was probably having too much fun playing cops and robbers and picking up women.

She dressed in silent disappointment, unable to feel any anger toward him. Perhaps he already had a wife and a home. That was likely. The illness had been harder on men than on women—had killed more men, had left male survivors more severely impaired. Men like Obsidian were rare. Women either settled for less or stayed alone. If they found an Obsidian, they did what they could to keep him. Rye suspected he had someone younger, prettier keeping him.

He touched her while she was strapping her gun on and asked with a complicated series of gestures whether it was loaded.

She nodded grimly.

He patted her arm.

She asked once more if he would come home with her, this time using a different series of gestures. He had seemed hesitant. Perhaps he could be courted.

He got out and into the front seat without responding.

She took her place in front again, watching him. Now he plucked at his uniform and looked at her. She thought she was being asked something, but did not know what it was.

He took off his badge, tapped it with one finger, then tapped his chest. Of course.

She took the badge from his hand and pinned her wheat stalk to it. If playing cops and robbers was his only insanity, let him play. She would take him, uniform and all. It occurred to her that she might eventually lose him to someone he would meet as he had met her. But she would have him for a while.

He took the street map down again, tapped it, pointed vaguely northeast toward Pasadena, then looked at her.

She shrugged, tapped his shoulder, then her own, and held up her index and second fingers tight together, just to be sure.

He grasped the two fingers and nodded. He was with her.

She took the map from him and threw it onto the dashboard. She pointed back southwest—back toward home. Now she did not have to go to Pasadena. Now she could go on having a brother there and two nephews—three right-handed males. Now she did not have to find out for certain whether she was as alone as she feared. Now she was not alone.

Obsidian took Hill Street south, then Washington west, and she leaned back, wondering what it would be like to have someone again. With what she had scavenged, what she had preserved, and what she grew, there was easily enough food for them. There was certainly room enough in a four-bedroom house. He could move his possessions in. Best of all, the animal across the street would pull back and possibly not force her to kill him.

Obsidian had drawn her closer to him and she had put her head on his shoulder when suddenly he braked hard, almost throwing her off the seat. Out of the corner of her eye, she saw that someone had run across the street in front of the car. One car on the street and someone had to run in front of it.

Straightening up, Rye saw that the runner was a woman, fleeing from an old frame house to a boarded-up storefront. She ran silently, but the man who followed her a moment later shouted what sounded like garbled words as he ran. He had something in his hand. Not a gun. A knife, perhaps.

The woman tried a door, found it locked, looked around desperately, finally snatched up a fragment of glass broken from the storefront window. With this she turned to face her pursuer. Rye thought she would be more likely to cut her own hand than to hurt anyone else with the glass.

Obsidian jumped from the car, shouting. It was the first time Rye had heard his voice—deep and hoarse from disuse. He made the same sound over and over the way some speechless people did, "Da, da, da!"

Rye got out of the car as Obsidian ran toward the couple. He had drawn his gun. Fearful, she drew her own and released the safety. She looked around to see who else might be attracted to the scene. She saw the man glance at Obsidian, then suddenly lunge at the woman. The woman jabbed his face with her glass, but he caught her arm and managed to stab her twice before Obsidian shot him.

The man doubled, then toppled, clutching his abdomen. Obsidian shouted, then gestured Rye over to help the woman.

Rye moved to the woman's side, remembering that she had little more than bandages and antiseptic in her pack. But the woman was beyond help. She had been stabbed with a long, slender boning knife.

She touched Obsidian to let him know the woman was dead. He had bent to check the wounded man who lay still and also seemed dead. But as Obsidian looked around to see what Rye wanted, the man opened his eyes. Face contorted, he seized Obsidian's just-holstered revolver and fired. The bullet caught Obsidian in the temple and he collapsed.

It happened just that simply, just that fast. An instant later, Rye shot the wounded man as he was turning the gun on her.

And Rye was alone—with three corpses.

She knelt beside Obsidian, dry-eyed, frowning, trying to understand why everything had suddenly changed. Obsidian was gone. He had died and left her—like everyone else.

Two very small children came out of the house from which the man and woman had run—a boy and girl perhaps three years old. Holding hands, they crossed the street toward Rye. They stared at her, then edged past her and went to the dead woman. The girl shook the woman's arm as though trying to wake her.

This was too much. Rye got up, feeling sick to her stomach with grief and anger. If the children began to cry, she thought she would vomit.

They were on their own, those two kids. They were old enough to scavenge. She did not need any more grief. She did not need a stranger's children who would grow up to be hairless chimps.

She went back to the car. She could drive home, at least. She remembered how to drive.

The thought that Obsidian should be buried occurred to her before she reached the car, and she did vomit.

She had found and lost the man so quickly. It was as though she had been snatched from comfort and security and given a sudden, inexplicable beating. Her head would not clear. She could not think.

Somehow, she made herself go back to him, look at him. She found herself on her knees beside him with no memory of having knelt. She stroked his face, his beard. One of the children made a noise and she looked at them, at the woman who was probably their mother. The children looked back at her, obviously frightened. Perhaps it was their fear that reached her finally.

She had been about to drive away and leave them. She had almost done it, almost left two toddlers to die. Surely there had been enough dying. She would have to take the children home with her. She would not be able to live with any other decision. She looked around for a place to bury three bodies. Or two. She wondered if the murderer were the children's father. Before the silence, the police had always said some of the most dangerous calls they went out on were domestic disturbance calls. Obsidian should have known that—not that the knowledge would have kept him in the car. It would not have held her back either. She could not have watched the woman murdered and done nothing.

She dragged Obsidian toward the car. She had nothing to dig with her, and no one to guard for her while she dug. Better to take the bodies with her and bury them next to her husband and her children. Obsidian would come home with her after all.

When she had gotten him onto the floor in the back, she returned for the woman. The little girl, thin, dirty, solemn, stood up and unknowingly gave Rye a gift. As Rye began to drag the woman by her arms, the little girl screamed, "No!"

Rye dropped the woman and stared at the girl.

"No!" the girl repeated. She came to stand beside the woman. "Go away!" she told Rye.

"Don't talk," the little boy said to her. There was no blurring or confusing of sounds. Both children had spoken and Rye had understood. The boy looked at the dead murderer and moved further from him. He took the girl's hand. "Be quiet," he whispered.

Fluent speech! Had the woman died because she could talk and had taught her children to talk? Had she been killed by a husband's festering anger or by a stranger's jealous rage? And the children . . . they must have been born after the silence. Had the disease run its course, then? Or were these children simply immune? Certainly they had had time to fall sick and silent. Rye's mind leaped ahead. What if children of three or fewer years were safe and able to learn language? What if all they needed were teachers? Teachers and protectors.

Rye glanced at the dead murderer. To her shame, she thought she could understand some of the passions that must have driven him, whoever he was. Anger, frustration, hopelessness, insane jealousy . . . how many more of him were there—people willing to destroy what they could not have?

Obsidian had been the protector, had chosen that role for who knew what reason. Perhaps putting on an obsolete uniform and patrolling the empty streets had been what he did instead of putting a gun into his mouth. And now that there was something worth protecting, he was gone.

She had been a teacher. A good one. She had been a protector, too, though only of herself. She had kept herself alive when she had no reason to live. If the illness let these children alone, she could keep them alive.

Somehow she lifted the dead woman into her arms and placed her on the backseat of the car. The children began to cry, but she knelt on the broken pavement and whispered to them, fearful of frightening them with the harshness of her long unused voice.

"It's all right," she told them. "You're going with us, too. Come on." She lifted them both, one in each arm. They were so light. Had they been getting enough to eat?

The boy covered her mouth with his hand, but she moved her face away. "It's all right for me to talk," she told him. "As long as no one's around, it's all right." She put the boy down on the front seat of the car and he moved over without being told to, to make room for the girl. When they were both in the car Rye leaned against the window, looking at them, seeing that they were less afraid now, that they watched her with at least as much curiosity as fear.

"I'm Valerie Rye," she said, savoring the words. "It's all right for you to talk to me."

Nancy Kress
Out of All Them Bright Stars

• • • •

{1985}

Nancy Kress (1948–) was born in Buffalo, New York, and taught elementary school and college English before establishing her writing career. Her first publication was an sf short story (1976), but she made her reputation with three fantasy novels, *The Prince of the Morning Bells* (1981), *The Golden Grove* (1984), and *The White Pipes* (1985). She returned to science fiction and has since that time written a number of successful novels including *An Alien Light* (1988), the *Beggars in Spain* trilogy (1993–96), and the *Probability* series (2000–2002), as well as many short stories. Notable stories include "Trinity" (1984), "The Flowers of Aulit Prison" (1996), and "Laws of Survival" (2007), as well as the novella "Beggars in Spain" (1991), which, imagining specially bred children without the need for sleep who are hounded for their special abilities, launched the trilogy of the same name. Although lacking scientific training, Kress was married to the late sf writer Charles Sheffield (1935–2002) and would often use his expertise in physics and mathematics. Kress continues to conduct thorough research to keep her speculations plausible: nevertheless, as she told a *Locus* interviewer, "[Sheffield] pronounces it *science* fiction, and I pronounce it science *fiction*." Her most common speculations concern genetic engineering and alien beings, and her fiction is notable for an emphasis on ethics and emotions. In style, plot, and character, her work is open to feminist, social, and animal studies interpretations.

"Out of All Them Bright Stars," which won the Nebula Award, takes as its setting an ordinary, small-town diner at the end of the day. Its human characters, a waitress and her boss, are equally mundane. The only novum is the blue alien who walks in and treats the waitress with a courtesy as foreign to the waitress as his blue skin. The alien of this story stands in for all those whose race, ethnicity, class, or gender disenfranchises them. Here the waitress's relationship to her boss parallels the alien's to both the boss and the government agents, so an affinity is established among women, workers, and minority groups in their relationships to gender, economic, ethnic, and other hegemonic forces. While the representations are clear, they are not pedantic because of the skill with which Kress draws what seems like a slice of life rather than a dramatic plot of alien encounter. Her allegorical development of an extraterrestrial to comment on real-world issues of power and authority echoes Gene Wolfe's story "Useful Phrases" (1992).

So I'm filling the catsup bottles at the end of the night, and I'm listening to the radio Charlie has stuck up on top of the movable panel in the ceiling, when the door opens and one of them walks in. I know right away it's one of them—no chance to make a mistake about *that*—even though it's got on a nice-cut suit and a brim hat like Humphrey Bogart used to wear in *Casablanca.* But there's nobody with it, no professor from the college or government men like on the TV show from the college or even any students. It's all alone. And we're a long way out on the highway from the college.

It stands in the doorway, blinking a little, with rain dripping off its hat. Kathy, who's supposed to be cleaning the coffee machine behind the counter, freezes and stares with one hand still holding the used filter up in the air like she's never going to move again. Just then Charlie calls out from the kitchen, "Hey, Kathy, you ask anybody who won the trifecta?" and she doesn't even answer him. Just goes on staring with her mouth open like she's thinking of screaming but forgot how. And the old couple in the corner booth, the only ones left from the crowd after the movie got out, stop chewing their chocolate cream pie and stare, too. Kathy closes her mouth and opens it again, and a noise comes out like "Uh—errrgh . . ."

Well, that made me annoyed. Maybe she tried to say "ugh" and maybe she didn't, but here it is standing in the doorway with rain falling around it in little drops and we're staring like it's a clothes dummy and not a customer. So I think that's not right and maybe we're even making it feel a little bad. *I* wouldn't like Kathy staring at me like that, and I dry my hands on my towel and go over.

"Yes, sir, can I help you?" I say.

"Table for one," it says, like Charlie's was some nice steak house in town. But I suppose that's the kind of place the government people mostly take them to. And besides, its voice is polite and easy to understand, with a sort of accent but not as bad as some we get from the college. I can tell what it's saying. I lead him to a booth in the corner opposite the old couple, who come in every Friday night and haven't left a tip yet.

He sits down slowly. I notice he keeps his hands on his lap, but I can't tell if that's because he doesn't know what to do with them or because he thinks I won't want to see them. But I've seen the close-ups on TV—they don't look so weird to me like they do to some. Charlie says they make his stomach turn, but I can't see it. You'd think he'd of seen worse meat in Vietnam. He talks enough like he did, on and on, and sometimes we even believe him.

I say, "Coffee, sir?"

He makes a sort of movement with his eyes. I can't tell what the movement means, but he says in that polite voice, "No, thank you. I am unable to drink coffee," and I think that's a good thing, because I suddenly remember that Kathy's got the filter out. But then he says, "May I have a green salad, please? With no dressing, please."

The rain is still dripping off his hat. I figure the government people never told him to take off his hat in a restaurant, and for some reason that tickles me and makes me feel real bold. This polite blue guy isn't going to bother anybody, and that fool Charlie was just spouting off his mouth again.

"The salad's not too fresh, sir," I say, experimental-like, just to see what he'll say next. And it's the truth—the salad is left over from yesterday. But the guy answers like I asked him something else.

"What is your name?" he says, so polite I know he's curious and not starting anything. And what could he start anyway, blue and with those hands? Still, you never know.

"Sally," I say. "Sally Gourley."

"I am John," he says, and makes that movement with his eyes again. All of a sudden it tickles me—"John!" For this blue guy! So I laugh, and right away I feel sorry, like I might have hurt his feelings or something. How could you tell?

"Hey, I'm sorry," I say, and he takes off his hat. He does it real slow, like taking off the hat is important and means something, but all there is underneath is a bald blue head. Nothing weird like with the hands.

"Do not apologize," John says. "I have another name, of course, but in my own language."

"What is it?" I say, bold as brass, because all of a sudden I picture myself telling all this to my sister Mary Ellen and her listening real hard.

John makes some noise with his mouth, and I feel my own mouth open because it's not like a word he says at all, it's a beautiful sound—like a bird-call, only sadder. It's just that I wasn't expecting it, that beautiful sound right here in Charlie's diner. It surprised me, coming out of that bald blue head. That's all it was: surprise.

I don't say anything. John looks at me and says, "It has a meaning that can be translated. It means—" But before he can say what it means, Charlie comes charging out of the kitchen, Kathy right behind him. He's still got the racing form in one hand, like he's been studying the trifecta, and he pushes right up against the booth and looks red and furious. Then I see the old couple scuttling out the door, their jackets clutched to their fronts, and the chocolate cream pie not half-eaten on their plates. I see they're going to stiff me for the check, but before I can stop them, Charlie grabs my arm and squeezes so hard his nails slice into my skin.

"What the hell do you think you're doing?" he says right to me. Not so much as a look at John, but Kathy can't stop looking and her fist is pushed up to her mouth.

I drag my arm away and rub it. Once I saw Charlie push his wife so hard she went down and hit her head and had to have four stitches. It was me that drove her to the emergency room.

Charlie says again, "What the hell do you think you're doing?"

"I'm serving my table. He wants a salad. Large." I can't remember if John'd said a large or a small salad, but I figure a large order would make Charlie feel better. But Charlie doesn't want to feel better.

"You get him out of here," Charlie hisses. He still doesn't look at John. "You hear me, Sally? You get him *out*. The government says I gotta serve spiks and niggers, but it don't say I gotta serve *him*!"

I look at John. He's putting on his hat, ramming it onto his bald head, and half-standing in the booth. He can't get out because Charlie and me are both in the way. I expect John to look mad or upset, but except that he's holding the muscles in his face in some different way, I can't see any change of expression. But I figure he's got to feel something bad, and all of a sudden I'm mad at Charlie, who's a bully and who's got the feelings of a scumbag. I open my mouth to tell him so, plus one or two other little things I been saving up, when the door flies open and in burst four men, and damn if they aren't *all* wearing hats like Humphrey Bogart in *Casablanca*. As soon as the first guy sees John, his walk changes and he comes over slower but more purposeful-like, and he's talking to John and to Charlie in a sincere voice like a TV anchorman giving out the news.

I see the situation now belongs to him, so I go back to the catsup bottles. I'm still plenty burned, though, about Charlie manhandling me and about Kathy rushing so stupid into the kitchen to get Charlie. She's a flake and always has been.

Charlie is scowling and nodding. The harder he scowls, the nicer the government guy's voice gets. Pretty soon the government man is smiling sweet as pie. Charlie slinks back into the kitchen, and the four men move toward the door with John in the middle of them like some high school football huddle. Next to the real men, he looks stranger than he did before, and I see how really flat his face is. But then when the huddle's right opposite the table with my catsup bottles, John breaks away and comes over to me.

"I am sorry, Sally Gourley," he says. And then: "I seldom have the chance to show our friendliness to an ordinary Earth person. I make so little difference!"

Well, that throws me. His voice sounds so sad, and besides, I never thought of myself as an ordinary Earth person. Who would? So I just shrug and wipe off a catsup bottle with my towel. But then John does a weird thing. He just touches my arm where Charlie squeezed it, just touches it with the palm of those hands. And the palm's not slimy at all—dry, and sort of cool, and I don't jump or anything. Instead, I remember that beautiful noise when he said his other name. Then he goes out with three of the men, and the door bangs behind them on a gust of rain because Charlie never fixed the air-stop from when some kids horsing around broke it last spring.

The fourth man stays and questions me: What did the alien say, what did I say. I tell him, but then he starts asking the same exact questions all over again, like he didn't believe me the first time, and that gets me mad. Also, he has this snotty voice, and I see how his eyebrows move when I slip once and accidentally say, "he don't." I might not know what John's muscles mean, but I sure the hell can read those eyebrows. So I get miffed, and pretty soon he leaves and the door bangs behind him.

I finish the catsup and mustard bottles, and Kathy finishes the coffee machine. The radio in the ceiling plays something instrumental, no words, real sad. Kathy and me start to wash down the booths with disinfectant, and because we're doing the same work together and nobody comes in, I finally say to her, "It's funny."

She says, "What's funny?"

"Charlie called that guy 'him' right off. 'I don't got to serve him,' he said. And I thought of him as 'it' at first, least until I had a name to use. But Charlie's the one who threw him out."

Kathy swipes at the back of her booth. "And Charlie's right. That thing scared me half to death, coming in here like that. And where there's food being served, too." She snorts and sprays on more disinfectant.

Well, she's a flake. Always has been.

"*The National Enquirer*," Kathy goes on, "told how they have all this firepower up there in the big ship that hasn't landed yet. My husband says they could blow us all to smithereens, they're so powerful. I don't know why they even came here. *We* don't want them. I don't even know why they came, all that way."

"They want to make a difference," I say, but Kathy barrels on ahead, not listening.

"The Pentagon will hold them off, it doesn't matter what weapons they got up there or how much they insist on seeing about our defenses, the Pentagon won't let them get any toeholds on Earth. That's what my husband says. Blue bastards."

I say, "Will you please shut up?"

She gives me a dirty look and flounces off. I don't care. None of it is anything to me. Only, standing there with the disinfectant in my hand, looking at the dark windows and listening to the music wordless and slow on the radio, I remember that touch on my arm, so light and cool. And I think they didn't come here with any firepower to blow us all to smithereens. I just don't believe it. But then why did they come? Why come all that way from another star to walk into Charlie's diner and order a green salad with no dressing from an ordinary Earth person?

Charlie comes out with his keys to unlock the cash register and go over the tapes. I remember the old couple who stiffed me and I curse to myself. Only pie and coffee, but it still comes off my salary. The radio in the ceiling starts playing something else, not the sad song, but nothing snappy neither. It's a love song, about some guy giving and giving and getting treated like dirt. I don't like it.

"Charlie," I say, "what did those government men say to you?"

He looks up from his tapes and scowls, "What do you care?"

"I just want to know."

"And maybe I don't want you to know," he says, and smiles nasty-like. Me asking him has put him in a better mood, the creep. All of a sudden I remember what his wife said when she got the stitches, "The only way to get something from Charlie is to let him smack me around a little, and then ask him when I'm down. He'll give me anything when I'm down. He gives me shit if he thinks I'm on top."

I do the rest of the clean-up without saying anything. Charlie swears at the night's take—I know from my tips that it's not much. Kathy teases her hair in front of the mirror behind the doughnuts and pies, and I put down the breakfast menus. But all the time I'm thinking, and I don't much like my thoughts.

Charlie locks up and we all leave. Outside it's stopped raining, but it's still misty and soft, real pretty but too cold. I pull my sweater around myself and in the parking lot, after Kathy's gone, I say, "Charlie."

He stops walking toward his truck. "Yeah?"

I lick my lips. They're all of a sudden dry. It's an experiment, like, what I'm going to say. It's an experiment.

"Charlie. What if those government guys hadn't come just then and the . . . blue guy hadn't been willing to leave? What would you have done?"

"What do you care?"

I shrug. "I don't care. Just curious. It's *your* place."

"Damn right it's my place!" I could see him scowl, through the mist. "I'd of squashed him flat!"

"And then what? After you squashed him flat, what if the men came then and made a stink?"

"Too bad. It'd be too late by then, huh?" He laughs, and I can see how he's seeing it: the blue guy bleeding on the linoleum, and Charlie standing over him, dusting his hands together.

Charlie laughs again and goes off to his truck, whistling. He has a little bounce to his step. He's still seeing it all, almost like it really *had* happened. Over his shoulder he calls to me, "They're built like wimps. Or girls. All bone, no muscle. Even *you* must of seen that," and his voice is cheerful. It doesn't have any more anger in it, or hatred, or anything but a sort of friendliness. I hear him whistle some more, until the truck engine starts up and he peels out of the parking lot, laying rubber like a kid.

I unlock my Chevy. But before I get in, I look up at the sky. Which is really stupid because of course I can't see anything, with all the mists and clouds. No stars.

Maybe Kathy's husband is right. Maybe they do want to blow us all to smithereens. I don't think so, but what the hell difference does it ever make what I think? And all at once I'm furious at John, furiously mad, as furious as I've ever been in my life.

Why does he have to come here, with his birdcalls and his politeness? Why can't they all go someplace else besides here? There must be lots of other places they can go, out of all them bright stars up there behind the clouds. They don't need to come here, here where I need this job and that means I need Charlie. He's a bully, but I want to look at him and see nothing else but a bully. Nothing else but that. That's all I want to see in Charlie, in the government men—just small-time bullies, nothing special, not a mirror of anything, not a future of anything. Just Charlie. That's all. I won't see anything else.

I won't.

"I make so little difference," he says.

Yeah. Sure.

PAT CADIGAN
Pretty Boy Crossover

{1986}

Pat Cadigan (1953–) was during the 1980s a major contributor to the cyberpunk movement, publishing stories and novels that combined funky street life with high-tech gadgetry in imaginative near-future scenarios. Her work, like that of William Gibson, focused on the interface between corporate culture and youth subculture, that ambiguous space where (in Gibson's words) "the street finds its own uses" for technological innovation. The stories gathered in *Patterns* (1989), one of the finest single-author collections of the decade, are a mix of hard-edged sf and breathless Gothic horror, a hybridization of genres that has also marked her novels. In Cadigan's universe, the border between computer hardware and human selfhood is not merely permeable, it is also under constant invasive erasure by technologies of consciousness of various sorts, especially by the simulation of human sensory and motor functions characteristic of virtual reality. In *Mindplayers* (1987), psychotherapeutic techniques have achieved a level of terrifying sophistication, as the eponymous professionals infiltrate and manipulate their subjects' minds in the most intrusively intimate of ways, while in *Synners* (1989), the steadily improving commodification of creative skills has fatal consequences, as a jacked-in artist unwittingly unleashes a malignant, semi-sentient virus into the global computer net. Faced with such eventualities, human autonomy seems threatened in epochal ways, and Cadigan's work, for all its reveling in cyborg possibility, bears a strain of cautionary humanism, a lurking anxiety that something irreplaceable may soon be gone forever.

"Pretty Boy Crossover" displays the author's distinctive themes and concerns. Set in a trendy nightclub peopled by a kaleidoscopic array of bohemian subcultures, its central premise involves the uploading of human personality into computer software. It remains unclear whether the result is an alluring utopia of eternal youth or an insidious form of corporate exploitation; the protagonist must decide between these options when he is offered the chance to join his erstwhile friend in the simulated realm of "Self Aware Data." The story extrapolates, in classic "if this goes on" fashion, the ethical-political implications of virtual-reality technology, suggesting that full-body perceptual immersion in an artificial environment may be only a short step away from disposal of the body altogether. Cadigan has expanded upon this theme in her novels *Tea from an Empty Cup* (1998) and *Dervish Is Digital* (2000), which combine cyberpunk themes with the tones and textures of hard-boiled detective fiction to explore a looming near-future where human identity has been systematically commodified and dispersed through a nexus of high-tech interfaces.

First you see video. Then you wear video.
Then you eat video. Then you be video.
The Gospel According to Visual Mark

Watch or Be Watched.
Pretty Boy Credo

"Who made you?"

"You mean recently?"

Mohawk on the door smiles and takes his picture. "You in. But only you, okay? Don't try to get no friends in, hear that?"

"I hear. And I ain't no fool, fool. I got no friends."

Mohawk leers, leaning forward. "Pretty Boy like you, no friends?"

"Not in this world." He pushes past the Mohawk, ignoring the kissy-kissy sounds. He would like to crack the bridge of the Mohawk's nose and shove bone splinters into his brain but he is lately making more effort to control his temper and besides, he's not sure if any of that bone splinters in the brain stuff is really true. He's a Pretty Boy, all of sixteen years old, and tonight could be his last chance.

The club is Noise. Can't sneak into the bathroom for quiet, the Noise is piped in there, too. Want to get away from Noise? Why? No reason. But this Pretty Boy has learned to think between the beats. Like walking between the raindrops to stay dry, but he can do it. This Pretty Boy thinks things all the time—*all the time.* Subversive (and, he thinks so much that he knows that word *subversive*, sixteen, Pretty, or not). He thinks things like *how many Einsteins have died of hunger and thirst under a hot African sun* and *why can't you remember being born* and *why is music common to every culture* and especially *how much was there going on that he didn't know about and how could he find out about it.*

And this is all the time, one thing after another running in his head, you can see by his eyes. It's for def not much like a Pretty Boy but it's one reason why they want him. That he *is* a Pretty Boy is another and one reason why they're halfway home getting him.

He knows all about them. Everybody knows about them and everybody wants them to pause, look twice, and cough up a card that says, Yes, we see possibilities, please come to the following address during regular business hours on the next regular business day for regular further review. Everyone wants it but this Pretty Boy, who once got five cards in a night and tore them all up. But here he is, still a Pretty Boy. He thinks enough to know this is a failing in himself, that he likes being Pretty and chased and that is how they could end up getting him after all and that's b-b-b-bad. When he thinks about it, he thinks it with the stutter. B-b-b-bad. B-b-b-bad for him because he doesn't God help him want it, no, no, n-n-n-no. Which may make him the strangest Pretty Boy still live tonight and every night.

Still live and standing in the club where only the Prettiest Pretty Boys can get in any more. Pretty Girls are too easy, they've got to be better than Pretty and besides, Pretty Boys like to be Pretty all alone, no help thank you so much. This Pretty Boy doesn't mind Pretty Girls or any other kind of girls. Lately, though, he has begun to wonder how much longer it will be for him. Two years? Possibly a little longer? By three it will be for def over and the Mohawk on the door will as soon spit in his face as leer in it.

If they don't get to him.

And if they *do* get to him, then it's never over and he can be wherever he chooses to be and wherever that is will be the center of the universe. They promise it, unlimited access in your free hours and endless hot season, endless youth. Pretty Boy Heaven, and to get there, they say, you don't even really have to die.

He looks up the DJ's roost, far above the bobbing, boogieing crowd on the dance floor. They still call them DJs even though they aren't discs any more, they're chips and there's more than just sound on a lot of them. The great hyper-program, he's been told, the ultimate of ultimates, a short walk from there to the fourth dimension. He suspects this stuff comes from low-steppers shilling for them, hoping they'll get auditioned if they do a good enough shuck job. Nobody knows what it's really like except the ones who are there and you can't trust them, he figures. Because maybe they *aren't*, any more. Not really.

The DJ sees his Pretty upturned face, recognizes him even though it's been awhile since he's come back here. Part of it was wanting to stay away from them and part of it was that the thug on the door might not let him in.

And then, of course, he *had* to come, to see if he could get in, to see if anyone still wanted him. What was the point of Pretty if there was nobody to care and watch and pursue? Even now, he is almost sure he can feel the room rearranging itself around his presence in it and the DJ confirms this is true by holding up a chip and pointing it to the left.

They are squatting on the make-believe stairs by the screen, reminding him of pigeons plotting to take over the world. He doesn't look too long, doesn't want to give them the idea he'd like to talk. But as he turns away, one, the younger man, starts to get up. The older man and the woman pull him back. He pretends a big interest in the figures lining the nearest wall. Some are Pretty, some are female, some are undecided, some are very bizarre, or wealthy, or just charity cases. They all notice him and adjust themselves for his perusal.

Then one end of the room lights up with color and new noise. Bodies dance and stumble back from the screen where images are forming to rough music.

It's Bobby, he realizes.

A moment later, there's Bobby's face on the screen, sixteen feet high, even Prettier than he'd been when he was loose among the mortals. The sight of Bobby's Pretty-Pretty face fills him with anger and dismay and a feeling of loss so great he would strike anyone who spoke Bobby's name without his permission.

Bobby's lovely slate-gray eyes scan the room. They've told him senses are heightened after you make the change and go over but he's not so sure how that's supposed to work. Bobby looks kind of blind up there on the screen. A few people wave at Bobby—the dorks they let in so the rest can have someone to be hip in front of—but Bobby's eyes move slowly back and forth, back and forth, and then stop, looking right at him.

'Ah . . ." Bobby whispers it, long and drawn out. "Aaaaaaahhhhhh."

He lifts his chin belligerently and stares back at Bobby.

"You don't have to die any more," Bobby says silkily. Music bounces under his words. "It's beautiful in here. The dreams can be as real as you want them to be. And if you want to be, you can be with me."

He knows the commercial is not aimed only at him but it doesn't matter. This is *Bobby*. Bobby's voice seems to be pouring over him, caressing him, and it feels too much like a taunt. The night before Bobby went over, he tried to talk him out of it, knowing it wouldn't work. If they'd actually refused him, Bobby would have killed himself, like Franco had.

But now Bobby would live forever and ever, if you believed what they said.

The music comes up louder but Bobby's eyes are still on him. He sees Bobby mouth his name.

"Can you really see me, Bobby?" he says. His voice doesn't make it over the music but if Bobby's senses are so heightened, maybe he hears it anyway. If he does, he doesn't choose to answer. The music is a bumped up remix of a song Bobby used to party-till-he-puked to. The giant Bobby-face fades away to be replaced with a whole Bobby, somewhat larger than life, dancing better than the old Bobby ever could, whirling along changing scenes of streets, rooftops and beaches. The locales are nothing special but Bobby never did have all that much imagination, never wanted to go to Mars or even to the South Pole, always just to the hottest club. Always he liked being the exotic in plain surroundings and he still likes it. He always loved to get the looks. To be watched, worshipped, pursued. Yeah. He can see this is Bobby-heaven. The whole world will be giving him the looks now.

The background on the screen goes from street to the inside of a club; *this* club, only larger, better, with an even hipper crowd, and Bobby shaking it with them. Half the real crowd is forgetting to dance now because they're watching Bobby, hoping he's put some of them into his video. Yeah, that's the dream, get yourself remixed in the extended dance version.

His own attention drifts to the fake stairs that don't lead anywhere. They're still perched on them, the only people who are watching *him* instead of Bobby. The woman, looking overaged in a purple plastic sac-suit, is fingering a card.

He looks up at Bobby again. Bobby is dancing in place and looking back at him, or so it seems. Bobby's lips move soundlessly but so precisely he can read the words: *This can be you. Never get old, never get tired, it's never last call, nothing happens unless you want it to and it could be you. You. You.* Bobby's hands point to him on the beat. *You. You. You.*

Bobby. Can you really see me?

Bobby suddenly breaks into laughter and turns away, shaking it some more.

He sees the Mohawk from the door pushing his way through the crowd, the real crowd, and he gets anxious. The Mohawk goes straight for the stairs, where they make room for him, rubbing the bristly red strip of hair running down the center of his head as though they were greeting a favored pet. The Mohawk looks as satisfied as a professional glutton after a foodrace victory. He wonders what they promised the Mohawk for letting him in. Maybe some kind of limited contract. Maybe even a try-out.

Now they are all watching him together. Defiantly, he touches a tall girl dancing nearby and joins her rhythm. She smiles down at him, moving between him and them purely by chance but it endears her to him anyway. She is wearing a flap of translucent rag over second-skins, like an old-time showgirl. Over six feet tall, not beautiful with that nose, not even pretty, but they let her in so she could be tall. She probably doesn't know that; she probably doesn't know anything that goes on and never really will. For that reason, he can forgive her the hard-tech orange hair.

A Rude Boy brushes against him in the course of a dervish turn, asking acknowledgment by ignoring him. Rude Boys haven't changed in more decades than anyone's kept track of, as though it were the same little group of leathered and chained troopers buggering their way down the years. The Rude Boy isn't dancing with anyone. Rude Boys never do. But this one could be handy, in case of an emergency.

The girl is dancing hard, smiling at him. He smiles back, moving slightly to her right, watching Bobby possibly watching him. He still can't tell if Bobby really sees anything. The scene behind Bobby is still a double of the club, getting hipper and hipper if that's possible. The music keeps snapping back to its first peak passage. Then Bobby gestures like God and he *sees himself*. He is dancing next to Bobby, Prettier than he ever could be, just the way they promise. Bobby doesn't look at the phantom but at him where he really is, lips moving again. *If you want to be, you can be with me. And so can she.*

His tall partner appears next to the phantom of himself. She is also much improved, though still not Pretty, or even pretty. The real girl turns and sees herself and there's no mistaking the delight in her face. Queen of the Hop for a minute or two. Then Bobby sends her image away so that it's just the two of them, two Pretty Boys dancing the night away, private party, stranger, go find your own good time. How it used to be sometimes in real life, between just the two of them. He remembers hard.

"B-b-b-bobby!" he yells, the old stutter reappearing. Bobby's image seems to give a jump, as though he finally heard. He forgets everything, the girl, the Rude Boy, the Mohawk, them on the stairs, and plunges through the crowd toward the screen. People fall away from him as though they were reenacting the Red Sea. He dives for the screen, for Bobby, not caring how it must look to anyone. What would they know about it, any of them. He can't remember in his whole sixteen years ever hearing one person say, *I love my friend*. Not Bobby, not even himself.

He fetches up against the screen like a slap and hangs there, face pressed to the glass. He can't see it now but on the screen Bobby would seem to be looking down at him. Bobby never stops dancing.

The Mohawk comes and peels him off. The others swarm up and take him away. The tall girl watches all this with the expression of a woman who lives upstairs from Cinderella and wears the same shoe size. She stares longingly at the screen. Bobby waves bye-bye and turns away.

"Of course, the process isn't reversible," says the older man. The steely hair has a careful blue tint; he has sense enough to stay out of hip clothes.

They have laid him out on a lounger with a tray of refreshments right by him. Probably slap his hand if he reaches for any, he thinks.

"Once you've distilled something to pure information, it just can't be reconstituted in a less efficient form," the woman explains, smiling. There's no warmth to her. *A less efficient form.* If that's what she really thinks, he knows he should be plenty scared of these people. Did she say things like that to Bobby? And did it make him even *more* eager?

"There may be no more exalted a form of existence than to live as sentient information," she goes on. "Though a lot more research must be done before we can offer conversion on a larger scale."

"Yeah?" he says. "Do they know that, Bobby and the rest?"

"Oh, there's nothing to worry about," says the younger man. He looks as though he's still getting over the pain of having outgrown his boogie shoes. "The system's quite perfected. What Grethe means is we want to research more applications for this new form of existence."

"Why not go over yourselves and do that, if it's so *exalted*."

"There are certain things that need to be done on this side," the woman says bitchily. "Just because—"

"Grethe." The older man shakes his head. She pats her slicked-back hair as though to soothe herself and moves away.

"We have other plans for Bobby when he gets tired of being featured in clubs," the older man says. "Even now, we're educating him, adding more data to his basic information configuration—"

"That would mean he ain't really *Bobby* any more, then, huh?"

The man laughs. "Of course he's Bobby. Do you change into someone else every time you learn something new?"

"Can you prove I *don't*?"

The man eyes him warily. "Look. You *saw* him. Was that Bobby?"

"I saw a video of Bobby dancing on a giant screen."

"That *is* Bobby and it will remain Bobby no matter what, whether he's poured into a video screen in a dot pattern or transmitted the length of the universe."

"That what you got in mind for him? Send a message to nowhere and the message is him?"

"We could. But we're not going to. We're introducing him to the concept of higher dimensions. The way he is now, he could possibly break out of the three-dimensional level of existence, pioneer a whole new plane of reality."

"Yeah? And how do you think you're gonna get Bobby to do *that*?"

"We convince him it's entertaining."

He laughs. "That's a good one. Yeah. Entertainment. You get to a higher level of existence and you'll open a club there that only the hippest can get into. It figures."

The older man's face gets hard. "That's what all you Pretty Boys are crazy for, isn't it? Entertainment?"

He looks around. The room must have been a dressing room or something back in the days when bands had been live. Somewhere overhead he can hear the faint noise of the club but he can't tell if Bobby's still on. "You call this entertainment?"

"I'm tired of this little prick," the woman chimes in. "He's thrown away opportunities other people would kill for."

He makes a rude noise. "Yeah, we'd all kill to be someone's data chip. You think I really believe Bobby's real just because I can see him on a *screen*?"

The older man turns to the younger one. "Phone up and have them pipe Bobby down here." Then he swings the lounger around so it faces a nice modem screen implanted in a shored-up cement-block wall.

"Bobby will join us shortly. Then he can tell you whether he's real or not himself. How will that be for you?"

He stares hard at the screen, ignoring the man, waiting for Bobby's image to appear. As though they really bothered to communicate regularly with Bobby this way. Feed in that kind of data and memory and Bobby'll believe it. He shifts uncomfortably, suddenly wondering how far he could get if he moved fast enough.

"My *boy*," says Bobby's sweet voice from the speaker on either side of the screen and he forces himself to keep looking as Bobby fades in, presenting himself on the same kind of lounger and looking mildly exerted, as though he's just come off the dance floor for real. "Saw you shakin' it upstairs awhile ago. You haven't been here for such a long time. What's the story?"

He opens his mouth but there's no sound. Bobby looks at him with boundless patience and indulgence. So Pretty, hair the perfect shade now and not a bit dry from the dyes and lighteners, skin flawless and shining like a healthy angel. Overnight angel, just like the old song.

"My *boy*," says Bobby. "Are you struck, like, shy or *dead*?"

He closes his mouth, takes one breath. "I don't like it, Bobby. I don't like it this way."

"Of course not, lover. You're the Watcher, not the Watchee, that's why. Get yourself picked up for a season or two and your disposition will *change*."

"You really like it, Bobby, being a blip on a chip?"

"Blip on a chip, your ass. I'm a universe now. I'm, like, *everything*. And, hey, dig—I'm on every channel." Bobby laughs. "I'm happy I'm sad!"

"S-A-D," comes in the older man. "Self-Aware Data."

"Ooo-eee," he says. "Too clever for me. Can I get out of here now?"

"What's your hurry?" Bobby pouts. "Just because I went over you don't love me anymore?"

"You always were screwed up about that, Bobby. Do you know the difference between being loved and being watched?"

"Sophisticated boy," Bobby says. "So wise, so learned. So fully packed. On this side, there is no difference. Maybe there never was. If you love me, you watch me. If you don't look, you don't care and if you don't care I don't matter. If I don't matter, I don't exist. Right?"

He shakes his head.

"No, my boy, I *am* right." Bobby laughs. "You believe I'm right, because if you *didn't*, you wouldn't come shaking your Pretty Boy ass in a place like *this*, now, would you? You *like* to be watched, get seen. You see me, I see you. Life goes on."

He looks up at the older man, needing relief from Bobby's pure Prettiness. "How does he see me?"

"Sensors in the equipment. Technical stuff, nothing you care about."

He sighs. He should be upstairs or across town, shaking it with everyone else, living Pretty for as long as he could. Maybe in another few months, this way would begin to look good to him. By then they might be off Pretty Boys and looking for some other type and there he'd be, out in the cold-cold, sliding down the other side of his peak and no one would *want* him. Shut out of something going on that he might want to know about after all. Can he face it? He glances at the younger man. All grown up and no place to glow. Yeah, but can *he* face it?

He doesn't know. Used to be there wasn't much of a choice and now that there is, it only seems to make it worse. Bobby's image looks like it's studying him for some kind of sign, Pretty eyes bright, hopeful.

The older man leans down and speaks low into his ear. "We need to get you before you're twenty-five, before the brain stops growing. A mind taken from a still-growing brain will blossom and adapt. Some of Bobby's predecessors have made marvelous adaptation to their new medium. Pure video: there's a staff that does nothing all day but watch and interpret their symbols for breakthroughs in thought. And we'll be taking Pretty Boys for as long as they're publicly sought-after. It's the most efficient way to find the best performers, go for the ones everyone wants to see or be. The top of the trend is closest to heaven. And even if you never make a breakthrough, you'll still be entertainment. Not such a bad way to live for a Pretty Boy. Never have to age, to be sick, to lose touch. You spent most of your life young, why learn how to be old? Why learn how to live without all the things you have now—"

He puts his hands over his ears. The older man is still talking and Bobby is saying something and the younger man and the woman come over to try to do something about him. Refreshments are falling off the tray. He struggles out of the lounger and makes for the door.

"Hey, my *boy*," Bobby calls after him. "Gimme a minute here, gimme what the *problem* is."

He doesn't answer. What can you tell someone made of pure information anyway?

There's a new guy on the front door, bigger and meaner than His Mohawkness but he's only there to keep people out, not to keep anyone *in*. You want to jump ship, go to, you poor un-hip asshole. Even if you are a Pretty Boy. He reads it in the guy's face as he passes from Noise into the three A.M. quiet of the street.

They let him go. He doesn't fool himself about that part. They *let* him out of the room because they know all about him. They know he lives like Bobby lived, they know he loves what Bobby loved—the clubs, the admiration, the lust of strangers for his personal magic. He can't say he doesn't love that, because he *does*. He isn't even sure if he loves it more than he ever loved Bobby, or if he loves it more than being alive. Than being live.

And here it is, three A.M., prime clubbing time, and he is moving toward home. Maybe he *is* a poor un-hip asshole after all, no matter what he loves. Too stupid to even stay in the club, let alone grab a ride to heaven. Still he keeps moving, unbothered by the chill but feeling it. Bobby doesn't have to go home in the cold any more, he thinks. Bobby doesn't even have to get through the hours between club-times if he doesn't want to. All times are now prime time for Bobby. Even if he gets unplugged, he'll never know the difference. Poof, it's a day later, poof, it's a year later, poof, you're out for good. Painlessly.

Maybe Bobby has the right idea, he thinks, moving along the empty sidewalk. If he goes over tomorrow, who will notice? Like when he left the dance floor—people will come and fill up the space. Ultimately, it wouldn't make a difference to anyone.

He smiles suddenly. Except *them*. As long as they don't have him, he makes a difference. As long as he has flesh to shake and flaunt and feel with, he makes a pretty goddam big difference to *them*. Even after they don't want him any more, he will still be the only one they didn't get. He rubs his hands together against the chill, feeling the skin rubbing skin, really *feeling* it for the first time in a long time, and he thinks about sixteen million things all at once, maybe one thing for every brain cell he's using, or maybe one thing for every brain cell yet to come.

He keeps moving, holding to the big thought, making a difference, and all the little things they won't be making a program out of. He's lightheaded with joy—he doesn't know what's going to happen.

Neither do they.

KATE WILHELM

Forever Yours, Anna

• • • •

{1987}

Kate Wilhelm (1928–) was one of several significant female authors to emerge within the genre during the 1950s, alongside Katherine MacLean, Marion Zimmer Bradley, Margaret St. Clair, and Zenna Henderson. Her early work, in the mold of Judith Merril, translated the anxieties of suburban domesticity into futuristic and otherworldly scenarios, though it grew increasingly broader and bolder in scope during the 1960s and 1970s. The stories gathered in *The Downstairs Room* (1968) and *The Infinity Box* (1971) are arresting fables with an uneasy edge of Gothic horror—ambitious works for which Wilhelm preferred the term (again following Merril) "speculative fiction." Wilhelm's novels have ranged from large-scale hard sf—for example, *Where Late the Sweet Birds Sang* (1976), a post-apocalypse tale featuring a family of clones—to prosaic depictions of scientists at work, as in *The Clewiston Test* (1976), to genre-straddling efforts like *Death Qualified* (1991), which fuses science-fictional with detective-story elements. Since the 1990s, she has largely eschewed sf in favor of mysteries and courtroom melodramas; yet throughout her three decades of serious engagement with the genre, Wilhelm was indisputably a central presence, not only winning numerous awards (including two Hugos and three Nebulas) but also involving herself in the institutional development of the field, especially through her service to the Clarion Writers Workshop, which for many years she anchored along with her husband, the late sf author and editor Damon Knight.

"Forever Yours, Anna," which won a Nebula Award, is an elegant and elusive tale whose seemingly straightforward absorption in a mundane plot, featuring a romantic triangle and corporate chicanery, disguises a complex sf scenario that unfolds with devious precision. Like Robert A. Heinlein's "'All You Zombies—'" (1959), the tale uses a time-travel paradox to explore the perplexities of identity and the mysteries of human relationships. The protagonist, a graphology expert, believes that he can construe the subtleties of personality encoded in another's handwriting, yet only gradually does he come to grasp his own limitations and complicities, his own opaqueness to himself. We are creatures of fate, Wilhelm suggests, surrounded by fugitive oracles we can read only dimly, whose portent we grasp in a sudden gestalt of shattering perception. As the tale's fluid unwinding shows, her command of the craft of storytelling is remarkably deft, and it is no surprise that she has authored a book on the subject, *Storyteller: Writing Lessons and More from 27 Years of the Clarion Writers' Workshop* (2005).

Anna entered his life on a spring afternoon, not invited, not even wanted. Gordon opened his office door that day to a client who was expected and found a second man also in the hallway. The second man brought him Anna, although Gordon did not yet know this. At the moment, he simply said, "Yes?"

"Gordon Sills? I don't have an appointment, but . . . may I wait?"

"Afraid I don't have a waiting room."

"Out here's fine."

He was about fifty, and he was prosperous. It showed in his charcoal-colored suit, a discreet blue-gray silk tie, a silk shirtfront. Gordon assumed the rest of the shirt was also silk. He also assumed the stone on his finger was a real emerald of at least three carats. Ostentatious touch, that.

"Sure," Gordon said and ushered his client inside. They passed through a foyer to his office-workroom. The office section was partitioned from the rest of the room by three rice-paper screens with beautiful Chinese calligraphy. In the office area were his desk and two chairs for visitors, his chair, and an overwhelmed bookcase, with books on the floor in front of it.

Their business only took half an hour; when the client left, the hall was empty. Gordon shrugged and returned to his office. He pulled his telephone across the desk and dialed his former wife's number, let it ring a dozen times, hung up.

He leaned back in his chair and rubbed his eyes. Late afternoon sunlight streamed through the slats in the venetian blinds, zebra light. He should go away for a while, he thought. Just close shop and walk away from it all until he started getting overdraft notices. Three weeks, he told himself, that was about as long as it would take.

Gordon Sills was thirty-five, a foremost expert in graphology, and could have been rich, his former wife had reminded him quite often. If you don't make it before forty, she had also said, too often, you simply won't make it, and he did not care, simply did not care about money, security, the future, the children's future. . . .

Abruptly he pushed himself away from the desk and left the office, went into his living room. Like the office, it was messy, with several days' worth of newspapers, half a dozen books, magazines scattered haphazardly. To his eyes it was comfortable looking, comfort giving; he distrusted neatness in homes. Karen had most of the furniture; he had picked up only a chair, a couch, a single lamp, a scarred oak coffee table that he could put his feet on, a card table and several chairs for the kitchen. And a very good radio. It was sufficient. Some fine Japanese landscapes were on the walls.

The buzzer sounded. When he opened the door, the prosperous, uninvited client was there. He was carrying a brushed-suede briefcase.

"Hi," Gordon said. "I thought you'd left."

"I did, and came back."

Gordon admitted him and led him through the foyer into the office, where he motioned toward a chair and went behind his desk and sat down. The sunlight was gone, eclipsed by the building across Amsterdam.

"I apologize for not making an appointment," his visitor said. He withdrew a wallet from his breast pocket, took out a card, and slid it across the desk. "I'm Avery Roda. On behalf of my company I should like to consult with you regarding some correspondence in our possession."

"That's my business," Gordon said. "And what is your company, Mr. Roda?"

"Draper Fawcett."

Gordon nodded slowly. "And your position?"

Roda looked unhappy. "I am vice-president in charge of research and development, but right now I am in charge of an investigation we have undertaken. My first duty in connection with this was to find someone with your expertise. You come very highly recommended, Mr. Sills."

"Before we go on any further," Gordon said, "I should tell you that there are a number of areas where I'm not interested in working. I don't do paternity suits, for example. Or employer-employee pilferage cases."

Roda flushed.

"Or blackmail," Gordon finished equably. "That's why I'm not rich, but that's how it is."

"The matter I want to discuss is none of the above," Roda snapped. "Did you read about the explosion we had at our plant on Long Island two months ago?" He did not wait for Gordon's response. "We lost a very good scientist, one of the best in the country. And we cannot locate some of his paperwork, his notes. He was involved with a woman who may have them in her possession. We want to find her, recover them."

Gordon shook his head. "You need the police then, private detectives, your own security force."

"Mr. Sills, don't underestimate our resolve or our resources. We have set all that in operation, and no one has been able to locate the woman. Last week we had a conference during which we decided to try this route. What we want from you is as complete an analysis of the woman as you can give us, based on her handwriting. That may prove fruitful." His tone said he doubted it very much.

"I assume the text has not helped."

"You assume correctly," Roda said with some bitterness. He opened his briefcase and withdrew a sheaf of papers and laid them on the desk.

From the other side Gordon could see that they were not the originals, but photocopies. He let his gaze roam over the upside-down letters and then shook his head. "I have to have the actual letters to work with."

"That's impossible. They are being kept under lock and key."

"Would you offer a wine taster colored water?" Gordon's voice was bland, but he could not stop his gaze. He reached across the desk and turned the top letter right side up to study the signature. Anna. Beautifully written; even in the heavy black copy it was delicate, as artful as any of the Chinese calligraphy on his screens. He looked up to find Roda watching him intently. "I can tell you a few things from just this, but I have to have the originals. Let me show you my security system."

He led the way to the other side of the room. Here he had a long worktable, an oversized light table, a copy camera, enlarger, files. There was a computer and printer on a second desk. It was all fastidiously neat and clean.

"The files are fireproof," he said dryly, "and the safe is also. Mr. Roda, if you've investigated me, you know I've handled some priceless documents. And I've kept them right here in the shop. Leave the copies. I can start with them, but tomorrow I'll want the originals."

"Where's the safe?"

Gordon shrugged and went to the computer, keyed in his code, and then moved to the wall behind the worktable and pushed aside a panel to reveal a safe front. "I don't intend to open it for you. You can see enough without that."

"Computer security?"

"Yes."

"Very well. Tomorrow I'll send you the originals. You said you can already tell us something."

They returned to the office space. "First you," Gordon said, pointing to the top letter. "Who censored them?"

The letters had been cut off just above the greeting, and there were rectangles of white throughout.

"That's how they were when we found them," Roda said heavily. "Mercer must have done it himself. One of the detectives said the holes were cut with a razor blade."

Gordon nodded. "Curiouser and curiouser. Well, for what it's worth at this point, she's an artist more than likely. Painter would be my first guess"

"Are you sure?"

"Don't be a bloody fool. Of course I'm not sure, not with copies to work with. It's a guess. Everything I report will be a guess. Educated guesswork, Mr. Roda, that's all I can guarantee."

Roda sank down into his chair and expelled a long breath "How long will it take?"

"How many letters?"

"Nine."

"Two, three weeks."

Very slowly Roda shook his head. "We are desperate, Mr. Sills. We will double your usual fee if you can give this your undivided attention."

"And how about your cooperation?"

"What do you mean?"

"His handwriting also. I want to see at least four pages of his writing."

Roda looked blank.

"It will help to know her if I know her correspondent."

"Very well," Roda said.

"How old was he?"

"Thirty."

"Okay. Anything else you can tell me?"

Roda seemed deep in thought, his eyes narrowed, a stillness about him that suggested concentration. With a visible start he looked up, nodded. "What you said about her could be important already. She mentions a show in one of the letters. We assumed a showgirl, a dancer, something like that. I'll put someone on it immediately. An artist. That could be right."

"Mr. Roda, can you tell me anything else? How important are those papers? Are they salable? Would anyone outside your company have an idea of their value?"

"They are quite valuable," he said with such a lack of tone that Gordon's ears almost pricked to attention. "If we don't recover them in a relatively short time, we will have to bring in the FBI. National security may be at stake. We want to handle it ourselves, obviously." He finished in the same monotone. "The Russians would pay millions for them, I'm certain. And we will pay whatever we have to. She has them. She says so in one of the letters. We have to find that woman."

For a moment Gordon considered turning down the job. Trouble, he thought. Real trouble. He glanced at the topmost letter again, the signature *Anna*, and he said, "Okay I have a contract I use routinely . . ."

After Roda left he studied the one letter for several minutes, not reading it, in fact examining it upside down again, and he said softly, "Hello, Anna."

Then he gathered up all the letters and put them in a file which he deposited in his safe. He had no intention of starting until he had the originals. But it would comfort Roda to believe he was already at work.

Roda sent the originals and a few samples of Mercer's writing before noon the next day, and for three hours Gordon studied them all. He arranged hers on the worktable under the gooseneck lamp and turned them this way and that, not yet reading them, making notes now and then. As he suspected, her script was fine, delicate, with beautiful shading. She used a real pen with real ink, not a felt-tip or a ballpoint. Each stroke was visually satisfying, artistic in itself. One letter was three pages long, four were two pages, the others were single sheets. None of them had a date, an address, a complete name. He cursed the person who had mutilated them. One by one he turned them over to examine the backs and jotted: "Pressure—light to medium." His other notes were equally brief: "Fluid, rapid, not conventional; proportions, 1:5." That was European and he did not think she was, but it would bear close examination. Each note was simply a direction marker, a first impression. He was whistling tunelessly as he worked and was startled when the telephone rang.

It was Karen, finally returning his many calls. The children would arrive by six, and he must return them by seven Sunday night. Her voice was cool, as if she were giving orders about laundry. He said okay and hung up, surprised at how little he felt about the matter. Before, it had given him a wrench every time they talked; he had asked questions: How was she? Was she working? Was the house all right? She had the house on Long Island, and that was fine with him, he had spent more and more time in town anyway over the past few years; but still, they had bought it together, he had repaired this and that, put up screens, taken them down, struggled with plumbing.

That night he took the two children to a Greek restaurant. Buster, eight years old, said it was yucky; Dana, ten, called him a baby and Gordon headed off the fight by saying he had bought a new Monopoly game. Dana said Buster was into winning. Dana looked very much like her mother, but Buster was her true genetic heir. Karen was into winning too.

They went to The Cloisters and fantasized medieval scenarios; they played Monopoly again, and on Sunday he took them to a puppet show at the Met and then drove them home. He was exhausted. When he got back he looked about, deeply depressed. There were dirty dishes in the sink, on the table, in the living room. Buster had slept on the couch and his bedclothes and covers were draped over it. Karen said they were getting too old to share a room any longer. Dana's bedroom was also a mess. She had left her pajamas and slippers. Swiftly he gathered up the bedding from the living room and tossed it all onto the bed in Dana's room and closed the door. He overfilled the dishwasher and turned it on and finally went into his workroom and opened the safe.

"Hello, Anna," he said softly, and tension seeped from him; the ache that had settled in behind his eyes vanished; he forgot the traffic jams coming home from Long Island, forgot the bickering his children seemed unable to stop.

He took the letters to the living room and sat down to read them through for the first time.

Love letters, passionate letters, humorous in places, perceptive, intelligent. Without dates it was hard to put them in chronological order, but the story emerged. She had met Mercer in the city; they had walked and talked and he had left. He had come back and this time they were together for a weekend and became lovers. She sent her letters to a post office box; he did not write to her, although he left papers covered with incomprehensible scribbles in her care. She was married to someone, whose name had been cut out with a razor blade every time she referred to him. Mercer knew him, visited him apparently. They were even friends, and had long serious talks from which she was excluded. She was afraid; Mercer was involved in something very dangerous, and no one told her what it was, although her husband knew. She called Mercer her mystery man and speculated about his secret life, his family, his insane wife, or tyrannical father, or his own lapses into lycanthropy. Gordon smiled. Anna was not a whiner or a weeper, but she was hopelessly in love with Mercer and did not even know where he lived, where he worked, what danger threatened him, anything about him except that when he was with her, she was alive and happy. That was enough. Her husband understood and wanted only her happiness, and it was destroying her, knowing she was hurting him so much, but she was helpless.

He pursed his lips and reread one. "My darling, I can't stand it. I really can't stand it any longer. I dream of you, see you in every stranger on the street, hear your voice every time I answer the phone. My palms become wet and I tingle all over, thinking it's your footsteps I hear. You are my dreams. So, I told myself today, that is how it is? No way! Am I a silly schoolgirl mooning over a television star? At twenty-six? I gathered all your papers and put them in a carton and addressed it, and as I wrote the box number, I found myself giggling. You can't send a Dear John to a post office box number. What if you failed to pick it up and an inspector opened it finally? I should entertain such a person? They're all gray and desiccated, you know, those inspectors. Let them find their own entertainment! What if they could read your mysterious squiggles and discover the secret of the universe? Do any of them deserve such enlightenment? No. I put everything back in [excised] safe—" Mercer was not the mystery man, Gordon thought then; the mystery was the other man, the nameless one whose safe hid Mercer's papers. Who was he? He shook his head over the arrangement of two men and a woman, and continued to read: "—and [excised] came in and let me cry on his shoulder. Then we went to dinner. I was starved."

Gordon laughed out loud and put the letters down on the coffee table, leaned back with his hands behind his head and contemplated the ceiling. It needed paint.

For the next two weeks he worked on the letters, and the few pages of Mercer's handwriting. He photographed everything, made enlargements, and searched for signs of weakness, illness. He keystroked the letters into his computer and ran the program he had developed, looking for usages, foreign or regional combinations, anything unusual or revealing. Mercer, he decided, had been born in a test tube and never left school and the laboratory until the day he met Anna. She was from the Midwest, not a big city, somewhere around one of the Great Lakes. The name that had been consistently cut out had six letters. She had gone to an opening and the artist's name had been cut out also. It had nine letters. Even without her testimony about the artist, it was apparent that she had been excited by his work. It showed in the writing. He measured the spaces between the words, the size of individual letters, the angle of her slant, the proportions of everything. Every movement she made was graceful, rhythmic. Her connections were garlands, open and trusting; that meant she was honest herself. Her threadlike connections that strung her words together indicated her speed in writing, her intuition, which she trusted.

As the work went on he made more complete notes, drawing conclusions more and more often. The picture of Anna was becoming real.

He paid less attention to Mercer's writing after making an initial assessment of him. A scientist, technologist, precise, angular, a genius, inhibited, excessively secretive, a loner. He was a familiar type.

When Roda returned, Gordon felt he could tell him more about those two people than their own mothers knew about them.

What he could not tell was what they looked like, or where Anna was now, or where the papers were that she had put in her husband's safe.

He watched Roda skim through the report on Anna. Today, rain was falling in gray curtains of water; the air felt thick and clammy.

"That's all?" Roda demanded when he finished.

"That's it."

"We checked every art show in the state," Roda said, scowling at him. "We didn't find her. And we have proof that Mercer couldn't have spent as much time with her as she claimed in the letters. We've been set up. You've been set up. You say she's honest, ethical, and we say she's an agent or worse. She got her hooks in him and got those papers, and these letters are fakes, every one of them is a fake!"

Gordon shook his head. "There's not a lie in those letters."

"Then why didn't she come forward when he died? There was enough publicity at the time. We saw to that. I tell you he never spent any real time with her. We found him in a talent hunt when he was a graduate student, and he stayed in that damn lab ever since, seven days a week for four years. He never had time for a relationship of the sort she talks about. It's a lie through and through. A fantasy." He slumped in his chair. Today his face was almost as gray as his very good suit. He looked years older than he had the last time he had been in the office. "They're going to win," he said in a low voice. "The woman and her partner, they're probably out of the country already. Probably left the day after the accident, with the papers, their job done. Well done. That stupid, besotted fool!" He stared at the floor for several more seconds, then straightened. His voice was hard, clipped. "I was against consulting you from the start. A waste of time and money. Voodoo crap, that's all this is. Well, we've done what we can. Send in your bill. Where are her letters?"

Silently Gordon slid a folder across the desk. Roda went through it carefully, then put it in his briefcase and stood up. "If I were you, I would not give our firm as reference in the future, Sills." He pushed Gordon's report away from him. "We can do without that. Good day."

It should have ended there, Gordon knew, but it did not end. Where are you, Anna? he thought, gazing at the world swamped in cold rain. Why hadn't she come forward, attended the funeral, turned in the papers? He had no answers. She was out there, painting, living with a man who loved her very much, enough to give her the freedom to fall in love with someone else. Take good care of her, he thought at that other man. Be gentle with her, be patient while she heals. She's very precious, you know. He leaned his head against the window, let the coolness soothe him. He said aloud, "She's very precious."

"Gordon, are you all right?" Karen asked on the phone. It was his weekend for the children again.

"Sure. Why?"

"I just wondered. You sound strange. Do you have a girlfriend?"

"What do you want, Karen?"

The ice returned to her voice, and they made arrangements for the children's arrival, when he was to return them. Library books, he thought distantly. Just like library books.

When he hung up he looked at the apartment and was dismayed by the dinginess, the disregard for the barest amenities. Another lamp, he thought. He needed a second lamp, at the very least. Maybe even two. Anna loved light. A girlfriend? He wanted to laugh, and to cry also. He had a signature, some love letters written to another man, a woman who came to his dreams and spoke to him in the phrases from her letters. A girlfriend! He closed his eyes and saw the name: Anna. The capital *A* was a flaring volcano, high up into the stratosphere, then the even, graceful *n*'s, the funny little final *a* that had trouble staying on the base line, that wanted to fly away. And a beautiful sweeping line that flew out from it, circled above the entire name, came down to cross the first letter, turn it into an *A*, and in doing so formed a perfect palette. A graphic representation of Anna, soaring into the heavens, painting, creating art with every breath, every motion. Forever yours, Anna. Forever yours.

He took a deep breath and tried to make plans for the children's weekend, for the rest of the month, the summer, the rest of his life.

The next day he bought a lamp, and on his way home stopped in a florist shop and bought half a dozen flowering plants. She had written that the sunlight turned the flowers on the sill into jewels. He put them on the sill and raised the blind; the sunlight turned the blossoms into jewels. His hands were clenched; abruptly he turned away.

He went back to work; spring became summer, hot and humid as only New York could be, and he found himself going from one art show to another. He mocked himself, and cursed himself for it, but he attended openings, examined new artists' work, signatures, again and again and again. If the investigators trained in this couldn't find her, he told himself firmly, and the FBI couldn't find her, he was a fool to think he had even a remote chance. But he went to the shows. He was lonely, he told himself, and tried to become interested in other women, any other woman, and continued to attend openings.

In the fall he went to the opening of yet another new artist, out of an art school, a teacher. And he cursed himself for not thinking of that before. She could be an art teacher. He made a list of schools and started down the list, perfecting a story as he worked down it one by one. He was collecting signatures of artists for an article he planned to write. It was a passable story. It got him nothing.

She might be ugly, he told himself. What kind of woman would have fallen in love with Mercer? He had been inhibited, constricted, without grace, brilliant, eccentric, and full of wonder. It was the wonder that she had sensed, he knew. She had been attracted to that in Mercer, and had got through his many defenses, had found a boy-man who was truly appealing. And he had adored her. That was apparent from her letters; it had been mutual. Why had he lied to her? Why hadn't he simply told her who he was, what he was doing? The other man in her life had not been an obstacle, that had been made clear also. The two men had liked each other, and both loved her. Gordon brooded about her, about Mercer, the other man, and he haunted openings, became a recognized figure at the various studios and schools where he collected signatures. It was an obsession, he told himself, unhealthy, maybe even a sign of neurosis—or worse. It was insane to fall in love with someone's signature, love letters to another man.

And he could be wrong, he told himself. Maybe Roda had been right, after all. The doubts were always short-lived.

The cold October rains had come. Karen was engaged to a wealthy man. The children's visits had become easier because he no longer was trying to entertain them every minute; he had given in and bought a television and video games for them. He dropped by the Art Academy to meet Rick Henderson, who had become a friend over the past few months. Rick taught watercolors.

Gordon was in his office waiting for him to finish with a class critique session when he saw the *A*, Anna's capital *A*.

He felt his arms prickle, and sweat form on his hands, and a tightening in the pit of his stomach as he stared at an envelope on Rick's desk. Almost fearfully he turned it around to study the handwriting. The *A's* in Art Academy were like volcanoes, reaching up into the stratosphere, crossed with a quirky, insouciant line, like a sombrero at a rakish angle. Anna's *A*. It did not soar and make a palette, but it wouldn't, not in an address. That was her personal sign.

He let himself sink into Rick's chair and drew in a deep breath. He did not touch the envelope again. When Rick finally joined him, he nodded toward it.

"Would you mind telling me who wrote that?" His voice sounded hoarse, but Rick seemed not to notice. He opened the envelope and scanned a note, then handed it over. Her handwriting. Not exactly the same, but it was hers. He was certain it was hers, even with the changes. The way the writing was positioned on the page, the sweep of the letters, the fluid grace. . . . But it was not the same. The *A* in her name, Anna, was different. He felt bewildered by the differences, and knew it was hers in spite of them. Finally, he actually read the words. She would be out of class for a few days. It was dated four days ago.

"Just a kid," Rick said. "Fresh in from Ohio, thinks she has to be excused from class. I'm surprised it's not signed by her mother."

"Can I meet her?"

Now Rick looked interested. "Why?"

"I want her signature."

Rick laughed. "You're a real nut, you know. Sure. She's in the studio, making up for time off. Come on."

He stopped at the doorway and gazed at the young woman painting. She was no more than twenty, almost painfully thin, hungry looking. She wore scruffy sneakers, very old, faded blue jeans, a man's plaid shirt. Not the Anna of the letters. Not yet.

Gordon felt dizzy and held on to the door frame for a moment, and he knew what it was that Mercer had worked on, what he had discovered. He felt as if he had slipped out of time himself as his thoughts raced, explanations formed, his next few years shaped themselves in his mind. Understanding came the way a memory comes, a gestalt of the entire event or series of events, all accessible at once. Mercer's notes had shown him to be brilliant, obsessional, obsessed with time, secretive. Roda had assumed Mercer failed because he had blown himself up. Everyone must have assumed that. But he had not failed. He had gone forward five years, six at the most, to the time when Anna would be twenty-six. He had slipped out of time to the future.

Gordon knew with certainty that it was his own name that had been excised from Anna's letters. Phrases from her letters tumbled through his mind. She had mentioned a Japanese bridge, from his painting, the flowers on the sill, even the way the sun failed when it sank behind the building across the street. He thought of Roda and the hordes of agents searching for the papers that were to be hidden, had been hidden in the safest place in the world—the future. The safe Anna would put the papers in would be his, Gordon's, safe. He closed his eyes hard, already feeling the pain he knew would come when Mercer realized that he was to die, that he had died. For Mercer there could not be a love strong enough to make him abandon his work.

Gordon knew he would be with Anna, watch her mature, become the Anna of the letters, watch her soar into the stratosphere, and when Mercer walked through his time door, Gordon would still love her, and wait for her, help her heal afterward.

Rick cleared his throat and Gordon released his grasp of the door frame, took the next step into the studio. Anna's concentration was broken; she looked up at him. Her eyes were dark blue.

Hello, Anna.

Bruce Sterling

We See Things Differently

{1989}

During the 1980s, Bruce Sterling (1954–) was the polemical spearhead of the cyberpunk movement, championing its high-tech vision of a posthuman future in the pages of his fanzine *Cheap Truth*. Writing as "Vincent Omniaveritas," Sterling bemoaned what he saw as the "reptilian torpor" of contemporary sf, especially the writing of so-called "humanists" like Connie Willis and Kim Stanley Robinson, whose work (so he claimed) was stale and soft by comparison with that of William Gibson, an author then making a name for himself for his hard-edged, techno-intensive "Sprawl" stories. Sterling's introduction to the "cyberpunk anthology" *Mirrorshades* (1986) laid out a manifesto for the movement, proclaiming cyberpunk as the cutting edge of hip futurism, defined by its global vision, its hacker attitude, and its embrace of prosthetic transformation. As he anticipated, his incendiary proclamations stirred enormous controversy within the field, drawing attention to the work of writers associated with the movement, such as Gibson, Rudy Rucker, Pat Cadigan, John Shirley, and Lewis Shiner.

Sterling's highly visible role as cyberpunk's chief polemicist threatened for a time to overshadow his own significant gifts as a writer of fiction. Throughout the 1980s and 1990s, he was at the forefront in extrapolating plausible futures from contemporary technological and geopolitical developments. Novels like *Islands in the Net* (1988), *Heavy Weather* (1994), and *Holy Fire* (1998) built compelling near-future scenarios out of the realities of data networking, global warming, and life extension, respectively. His *Shaper-Mechanist* series was even more ambitious, sketching out a sprawling future history of divergent evolution, with humanity splintering into two competing camps: the Shapers, who use gene therapy and manipulation to renovate themselves, and the Mechs, who deploy drugs and cybernetic prostheses for the same purpose. For all the difference in their methods, both groups have moved into a posthuman realm where the body has become a technologized object, radically augmented and transmogrified. The *Shaper-Mech* stories, gathered in *Schismatrix Plus* (1996), are among the most exciting and visionary works of contemporary sf. The central text of the series, the novel *Schismatrix* (1985), was a pioneer of the "new space opera" that emerged in the subsequent two decades, with the stylish, concept-driven fictions of Paul J. McAuley, Alistair Reynolds, and Robert Reed owing it a significant debt (as Reynolds has acknowledged, claiming that reading *Schismatrix* "blew my mind on so many levels. . . . It will melt your face").

While Sterling has excelled as a novelist, he has also been a prolific author of short stories that have amplified his vision of a globally interconnected, technologically sophisticated, and ideologically complex near future. The tales collected in *Crystal Express* (1989), *Globalhead* (1992), *A Good Old-Fashioned Future* (1999), and *Visionary in Residence* (2006) offer a series of brilliant snapshots of a postmodern world buckling and yielding under the pressures of change. Sterling's fictive universe—peopled by gene-hackers and phone-phreaks, punk spies and techno-anarchists—conveys an up-to-the-minute vigor and vivacity that has made the author one of the most noted futurologists of his era. Indeed, his novels and stories form a continuum with his extensive nonfiction writing, including his blog "Beyond the Beyond" for *Wired* magazine and his 2002 book *Tomorrow Now: Envisioning the Next Fifty Years*. Originally published in the anthology *Semiotext(e) SF* in 1989, "We See Things Differently," with its backdrop of global terrorism and economic collapse and its portrait of a politically exhausted United States rapidly being outstripped by Middle Eastern powers, could have been written yesterday.

This was the *jahiliyah*—the land of ignorance. This was America. The Great Satan, the Arsenal of Imperialism, the Bankroller of Zionism, the Bastion of Neo-Colonialism. The home of Hollywood and blonde sluts in black nylon. The land of rocket-equipped F-15s that slashed across God's sky, in godless pride. The land of nuclear-powered global navies, with cannon that fired shells as large as cars.

They have forgotten that they used to shoot us, shell us, insult us, and equip our enemies. They have no memory, the Americans, and no history. Wind sweeps through them, and the past vanishes. They are like dead leaves.

I flew into Miami, on a winter afternoon. The jet banked over a tangle of empty highways, then a large dead section of the city—a ghetto perhaps. In our final approach we passed a coal-burning power plant, reflected in the canal. For a moment I mistook it for a mosque, its tall smokestacks slender as minarets. A Mosque for the American Dynamo.

I had trouble with my cameras at customs. The customs officer was a grimy-looking American white with hair the color of clay. He squinted at my passport. "That's an awful lot of film, Mr. Cuttab," he said.

"Qutb," I said, smiling. "Sayyid Qutb. Call me Charlie."

"Journalist, huh?" He looked unhappy. It seemed that I owed substantial import duties on my Japanese cameras, as well as my numerous rolls of Pakistani color film. He invited me into a small back office to discuss it. Money changed hands. I departed with my papers in order.

The airport was half-full: mostly prosperous Venezuelans and Cubans, with the haunted look of men pursuing sin. I caught a taxi outside, a tiny vehicle like a motorcycle wrapped in glass. The cabbie, an ancient black man, stowed my luggage in the cab's trailer.

Within the cab's cramped confines, we were soon unwilling intimates. The cabbie's breath smelled of sweetened alcohol. "You Iranian?" the cabbie asked.

"Arab."

"We respect Iranians around here, we really do," the cabbie insisted.

"So do we," I said. "We fought them on the Iraqi front for years."

"Yeah?" said the cabbie uncertainly. "Seems to me I heard about that. How'd that end up?"

"The Shi'ite holy cities were ceded to Iran. The Ba'athist regime is dead, and Iraq is now part of the Arab Caliphate." My words made no impression on him, and I had known it before I spoke. This is the land of ignorance. They know nothing about us, the Americans. After all this, and they still know nothing whatsoever.

"Well, who's got more money these days?" the cabbie asked. "Y'all, or the Iranians?"

"The Iranians have heavy industry," I said. "But we Arabs tip better." The cabbie smiled. It is very easy to buy Americans. The mention of money brightens them like a shot of drugs. It is not just the poverty; they were always like this, even when they were rich. It is the effect of spiritual emptiness. A terrible grinding emptiness in the very guts of the West, which no amount of Coca-Cola seems able to fill.

We rolled down gloomy streets toward the hotel. Miami's streetlights were subsidized by commercial enterprises. It was another way of, as they say, shrugging the burden of essential services from the exhausted backs of the taxpayers. And onto the far sturdier shoulders of peddlers of aspirin, sticky sweetened drinks, and cosmetics. Their billboards gleamed bluely under harsh lights encased in bulletproof glass. It reminded me so strongly of Soviet agitprop that I had a sudden jarring sense of displacement, as if I were being sold Lenin and Engels and Marx in the handy jumbo size.

The cabbie, wondering perhaps about his tip, offered to exchange dollars for riyals at black-market rates. I declined politely, having already done this in Cairo. The lining of my coat was stuffed with crisp Reagan $1,000 bills. I also had several hundred in pocket change, and an extensive credit line at the Islamic Bank of Jerusalem. I foresaw no difficulties.

Outside the hotel, I gave the ancient driver a pair of fifties. Another very old man, of Hispanic descent, took my bags on a trolley. I registered under the gaze of a very old woman. Like all American women, she was dressed in a way intended to provoke lust. In the young, this technique works admirably, as proved by America's unhappy history of sexually transmitted plague. In the very old, it provokes only sad disgust.

I smiled on the horrible old woman and paid in advance.

I was rewarded by a double-handful of glossy brochures promoting local casinos, strip-joints, and bars.

The room was adequate. This had once been a fine hotel. The air conditioning was quiet and both hot and cold water worked well. A wide flat screen covering most of one wall offered dozens of channels of television.

My wristwatch buzzed quietly, its programmed dial indicating the direction of Mecca. I took the rug from my luggage and spread it before the window. I cleansed my face, my hands, my feet. Then I knelt before the darkening chaos of Miami, many stories below. I assumed the eight positions, bowing carefully, sinking with gratitude into deep meditation. I forced away the stress of jet-lag, the innate tension and fear of a Believer among enemies.

Prayer completed, I changed my clothing, putting aside my dark Western business suit. I assumed denim jeans, a long-sleeved shirt, and photographer's vest. I slipped my press card, my passport, my health cards into the vest's zippered pockets, and draped the cameras around myself. I then returned to the lobby downstairs, to await the arrival of the American rock star.

He came on schedule, even slightly early. There was only a small crowd, as the rock star's organization had sought confidentiality. A train of seven monstrous buses pulled into the hotel's lot, their whale-like sides gleaming with brushed aluminum. They bore Massachusetts license plates. I walked out on to the tarmac and began photographing.

All seven buses carried the rock star's favored insignia, the thirteen-starred blue field of the early American flag. The buses pulled up with military precision, forming a wagon-train fortress across a large section of the weedy, broken tarmac. Folding doors hissed open and a swarm of road crew piled out into the circle of buses.

Men and women alike wore baggy fatigues, covered with buttoned pockets and block-shaped streaks of urban camouflage: brick red, asphalt black, and concrete gray. Dark-blue shoulder-patches showed the thirteen-starred circle. Working efficiently, without haste, they erected large satellite dishes on the roofs of two buses. The buses were soon linked together in formation, shaped barriers of woven wire securing the gaps between each nose and tail. The machines seemed to sit breathing, with the stoked-up, leviathan air of steam locomotives.

A dozen identically dressed crewmen broke from the buses and departed in a group for the hotel. Within their midst, shielded by their bodies, was the rock star, Tom Boston. The broken outlines of their camouflaged fatigues made them seem to blur into a single mass, like a herd of moving zebras. I followed them; they vanished quickly within the hotel. One crew woman tarried outside.

I approached her. She had been hauling a bulky piece of metal luggage on trolley wheels. It was a newspaper vending machine. She set it beside three other machines at the hotel's entrance. It was the Boston organization's propaganda paper, *Poor Richard's*.

I drew near. "Ah, the latest issue," I said. "May I have one?"

"It will cost five dollars," she said in painstaking English. To my surprise, I recognized her as Boston's wife. "Valya Plisetskaya," I said with pleasure, and handed her a five-dollar nickel. "My name is Sayyid; my American friends call me Charlie."

She looked about her. A small crowd already gathered at the buses, kept at a distance by the Boston crew. Others clustered under the hotel's green-and-white awning.

"Who are you with?" she said.

"*Al-Ahram*, of Cairo. An Arabic newspaper."

"You're not a political?" she said.

I shook my head in amusement at this typical show of Soviet paranoia. "Here's my press card." I showed her the tangle of Arabic. "I am here to cover Tom Boston. The Boston phenomenon."

She squinted. "Tom is big in Cairo these days? Muslims, yes? Down on rock and roll."

"We're not all ayatollahs," I said, smiling up at her. She was very tall. "Many still listen to Western pop music; they ignore the advice of their betters. They used to rock all night in Leningrad. Despite the Party. Isn't that so?"

"You know about us Russians, do you, Charlie?" She handed me my paper, watching me with cool suspicion.

"No, I can't keep up," I said. "Like Lebanon in the old days. Too many factions." I followed her through the swinging glass doors of the hotel. Valentina Plisetskaya was a broad-cheeked Slav with glacial blue eyes and hair the color of corn tassels. She was a childless woman in her thirties, starved as thin as a girl. She played saxophone in Boston's band. She was a native of Moscow, but had survived its destruction. She had been on tour with her jazz band when the Afghan Martyrs' Front detonated their nuclear bomb.

I tagged after her. I was interested in the view of another foreigner. "What do you think of the Americans these days?" I asked her.

We waited beside the elevator.

"Are you recording?" she said.

"No! I'm a print journalist. I know you don't like tapes," I said.

"We like tapes fine," she said, staring down at me. "As long as they are ours." The elevator was sluggish. "You want to know what I think, Charlie? I think Americans are fucked. Not as bad as Soviets, but fucked anyway. What do you think?"

"Oh," I said. "American gloom-and-doom is an old story. At *Al-Ahram*, we are more interested in the signs of American resurgence. That's the big angle, now. That's why I'm here." She looked at me with remote sarcasm. "Aren't you a little afraid they will beat the shit out of you? They're not happy, the Americans. Not sweet and easy-going like before."

I wanted to ask her how sweet the CIA had been when their bomb killed half the Iranian government in 1981. Instead, I shrugged. "There's no substitute for a man on the ground. That's what my editors say." The elevator shunted open. "May I come up with you?"

"I won't stop you." We stepped in. "But they won't let you in to see Tom."

"They will if you ask them to, Mrs. Boston."

"I'm Plisetskaya," she said, fluffing her yellow hair. "See? No veil." It was the old story of the so-called "liberated" Western woman. They call the simple, modest clothing of Islam "bondage"—while they spend countless hours, and millions of dollars, painting themselves. They grow their nails like talons, cram their feet into high heels, strap their breasts and hips into spandex. All for the sake of male lust.

It baffles the imagination. Naturally I told her nothing of this, but only smiled. "I'm afraid I will be a pest," I said. "I have a room in this hotel. Some time I will see your husband. I must, my editors demand it."

The doors opened. We stepped into the hall of the fourteenth floor. Boston's entourage had taken over the entire floor. Men in fatigues and sunglasses guarded the hallway; one of them had a trained dog.

"Your paper is big, is it?" the woman said.

"Biggest in Cairo, millions of readers," I said. "We still read, in the Caliphate."

"State-controlled television," she muttered.

"Worse than corporations?" I asked. "I saw what CBS said about Tom Boston." She hesitated, and I continued to prod. "A 'Luddite fanatic,' am I right? A 'rock demagogue.'"

"Give me your room number." I did this. "I'll call," she said, striding away down the corridor. I almost expected the guards to salute her as she passed so regally, but they made no move, their eyes invisible behind the glasses. They looked old and rather tired, but with the alert relaxation of professionals. They had the look of former Secret Service bodyguards. The putty-colored fatigues were baggy enough to hide almost any amount of weaponry.

I returned to my room. I ordered Japanese food from room service, and ate it. Wine had been used in its cooking, but I am not a prude in these matters. It was now time for the day's last prayer, though my body, still attuned to Cairo, did not believe it.

My devotions were broken by a knocking at the door. I opened it. It was another of Boston's staff, a small black woman whose hair had been treated. It had a nylon sheen, it looked like the plastic hair on a child's doll. "You Charlie?"

"Yes."

"Valya says, you want to see the gig. See us set up. Got you a backstage pass."

"Thank you very much." I let her clip the plastic-coated pass to my vest. She looked past me into the room, and saw my prayer rug at the window. "What you doin' in there? Prayin'?"

"Yes."

"Weird," she said. "You coming or what?"

I followed my nameless benefactor to the elevator.

Down at ground level, the crowd had swollen. Two hired security guards stood outside the glass doors, refusing admittance to anyone without a room key. The girl ducked, and plowed through the crowd with sudden headlong force, like an American football player. I struggled in her wake, the gawkers, pickpockets, and autograph hounds closing at my heels. The crowd was liberally sprinkled with the repulsive derelicts one sees so often in America: those without homes, without family, without charity.

I was surprised at the age of the people. For a rock-star's crowd, one expects dizzy teenage girls and the libidinous young street-toughs that pursue them. There were many of those, but more of another type: tired, footsore people with crow's-feet and graying hair. Men and women in their thirties and forties, with a shabby, crushed look. Unemployed, obviously, and with time on their hands to cluster around anything that resembled hope.

We walked without hurry to the fortress circle of buses. A rearguard of Boston's kept the onlookers at bay. Two of the buses were already unlinked from the others and under full steam. I followed the black woman up perforated steps and into the bowels of one of the shining machines.

She called brief greetings to the others already inside.

The air held the sharp reek of cleaning fluid. Neat elastic cords strapped down stacks of amplifiers, stencilled instrument cases, wheeled dollies of black rubber and crisp yellow pine. The thirteen-starred circle marked everything, stamped or spray-painted. A methane-burning steam generator sat at the back of the bus, next to a tall crashproof rack of high-pressure fuel tanks. We skirted the equipment and joined the others in a narrow row of second-hand airplane seats. We buckled ourselves in. I sat next to the Doll-Haired Girl.

The bus surged into motion. "It's very clean," I said to her. "I expected something a bit wilder on a rock and roll bus."

"Maybe in Egypt," she said, with the instinctive decision that Egypt was in the Dark Ages. "We don't have the luxury to screw around. Not now."

I decided not to tell her that Egypt, as a nation-state, no longer existed. "American pop culture is a very big industry."

"Biggest we have left," she said. "And if you Muslims weren't so pimpy about it, maybe we could pull down a few riyals and get out of debt."

"We buy a great deal from America," I told her. "Grain and timber and minerals."

"That's Third-World stuff. We're not your farm." She looked at the spotless floor. "Look, our industries suck, everyone knows it. So we sell entertainment. Except where there's media barriers. And even then the fucking video pirates rip us off."

"We see things differently," I said. "America ruled the global media for decades. To us, it's cultural imperialism. We have many talented musicians in the Arab world. Have you ever heard them?"

"Can't afford it," she said crisply. "We spent all our money saving the Persian Gulf from commies."

"The Global Threat of Red Totalitarianism," said the heavyset man in the seat next to Doll-Hair. The others laughed grimly.

"Oh," I said. "Actually, it was Zionism that concerned us. When there was a Zionism."

"I can't believe the hate shit I see about America," said the heavy man. "You know how much money we gave away to people, just gave away, for nothing? Billions and billions. Peace Corps, development aid . . . for decades. Any disaster anywhere, and we fell all over ourselves to give food, medicine. . . . Then the Russians go down and the whole world turns against us like we were monsters."

"Moscow," said another crewman, shaking his shaggy head.

"You know, there are still motherfuckers who think we Americans killed Moscow. They think we gave a Bomb to those Afghani terrorists."

"It had to come from somewhere," I said.

"No, man. We wouldn't do that to them. No, man, things were going great between us. Rock for Detente—I was at that gig."

We drove to Miami's Memorial Colosseum. It was an ambitious structure, left half-completed when the American banking system collapsed.

We entered double-doors at the back, wheeling the equipment along dusty corridors. The Colosseum's interior was skeletal; inside it was clammy and cavernous. A stage, a concrete floor. Bare steel arched high overhead, with crudely bracket-mounted stage-lights. Large sections of that bizarre American parody of grass, "Astroturf," had been dragged before the stage. The itchy green fur, still lined with yard-marks from some forgotten stadium, was almost indestructible. At second-hand rates, it was much cheaper than carpeting.

The crew worked with smooth precision, setting up amplifiers, spindly mike-stands, a huge high-tech drum kit with the clustered, shiny look of an oil refinery. Others checked lighting, flicking blue and yellow spots across the stage. At the public entrances, two crewmen from a second bus erected metal detectors for illicit cameras, recorders, or handguns. Especially handguns. Two attempts had already been made on Boston's life, one at the Chicago Freedom Festival, when Chicago's Mayor was wounded at Boston's side.

For a moment, to understand it, I mounted the empty stage and stood before Boston's microphone. I imagined the crowd before me, ten thousand souls, twenty thousand eyes. Under that attention, I realized, every motion was amplified. To move my arm would be like moving ten thousand arms, my every word like the voice of thousands. I felt like a Nasser, a Qadaffi, a Saddam Hussein.

This was the nature of secular power. Industrial power. It was the West that invented it, that invented Hitler, the gutter orator turned trampler of nations, that invented Stalin, the man they called "Genghis Khan with a telephone." The media pop star, the politician. Was there any difference any more? Not in America; it was all a question of seizing eyes, of seizing attention. Attention is wealth, in an age of mass media. Center stage is more important than armies.

The last unearthly moans and squeals of sound-check faded. The Miami crowd began to filter into the Colosseum. They looked livelier than the desperate searchers that had pursued Boston to his hotel. America was still a wealthy country, by most standards; the professional classes had kept much of their prosperity. There were those legions of lawyers, for instance, that secular priesthood that had done so much to drain America's once-vaunted enterprise. And their associated legions of state bureaucrats. They were instantly recognizable; the cut of their suits, the telltale pocket telephones proclaiming their status.

What were they looking for here? Had they never read Boston's propaganda paper, with its bitter condemnation of everything they stood for? With its fierce attacks on the "legislative-litigative complex," its demands for sweeping reforms?

Was it possible that they failed to take him seriously?

I joined the crowd, mingling, listening to conversations. At the doors, Boston cadres were cutting ticket prices for those who showed voter registrations. Those who showed unemployment cards got in for even less.

The prosperous Americans stood in little knots of besieged gentility, frightened of the others, yet curious, smiling. There was a liveliness in the destitute: brighter clothing, knotted kerchiefs at the elbows, cheap Korean boots of iridescent cloth. Many wore tricornered hats, some with a cockade of red, white, and blue, or the circle of thirteen stars.

This was rock and roll, I realized; that was the secret. They had all grown up on it, these Americans, even the richer ones. To them, the sixty-year tradition of rock music seemed as ancient as the Pyramids. It had become a Jerusalem, a Mecca of American tribes.

The crowd milled, waiting, and Boston let them wait. At the back of the crowd, Boston crewmen did a brisk business in starred souvenir shirts, programs, and tapes. Heat and tension mounted, and people began to sweat. The stage remained dark.

I bought the souvenir items and studied them. They talked about cheap computers, a phone company owned by its workers, a free database, neighborhood co-ops that could buy unmilled grain by the ton. ATTENTION MIAMI, read one brochure in letters of dripping red. It named the ten largest global corporations and meticulously listed every subsidiary doing business in Miami, with its address, its phone number, the percentage of income shipped to banks in Europe and Japan. Each list went on for pages. Nothing else. To Boston's audience, nothing else was necessary.

The house lights darkened. A frightening animal roar rose from the crowd. A single spot lit Tom Boston, stenciling him against darkness.

“My fellow Americans,” he said. A funereal hush followed. The crowd strained for each word. Boston smirked. “My f-f-f-f-fellow Americans.” It was a clever microphone, digitized, a small synthesizer in itself. “My fellow Am-am-am-am-AMM!” The words vanished in a sudden soaring wail of feedback. “My Am / my fellows / My Am / my fellows / Miami, Miami, Miami, MIAMI!” The sound of Boston’s voice, suddenly leaping out of all human context, becoming something shattering, superhuman—the effect was bone-chilling. It passed all barriers, it seeped directly into the skin, the blood.

“Tom Jefferson Died Broke!” he shouted. It was the title of his first song. Stage lights flashed up and hell broke its gates. Was it a “song” at all, this strange, volcanic creation? There was a melody loose in it somewhere, pursued by Plisetskaya’s saxophone, but the sheer volume and impact hurled it through the audience like a sheet of flame. I had never before heard anything so loud. What Cairo’s renegade set called rock and roll paled to nothing beside this invisible hurricane.

At first it seemed raw noise. But that was only a kind of flooring, a merciless grinding foundation below the rising architectures of sound. Technology did it: a piercing, soaring, digitized, utter clarity, of perfect cybernetic acoustics adjusting for each echo, a hundred times a second.

Boston played a glass harmonica: an instrument invented by the early American genius Benjamin Franklin. The harmonica was made of carefully tuned glass disks, rotating on a spindle, and played by streaking a wet fingertip across each moving edge.

It was the sound of pure crystal, seemingly sourceless, of tooth-aching purity.

The famous Western musician, Wolfgang Mozart, had composed for the Franklin harmonica in the days of its novelty. But legend said that its players went mad, their nerves shredded by its clarity of sound. It was a legend Boston was careful to exploit. He played the machine sparingly, with the air of a magician, of a Solomon unbottling demons. I was glad of his spare use, for its sound was so beautiful that it stung the brain.

Boston threw aside his hat. Long coiled hair spilled free. Boston was what Americans called “black”; at least he was often referred to as black, though no one seemed certain. He was no darker than myself. The beat rose up, a strong animal heaving. Boston stalked across the stage as if on springs, clutching his microphone. He began to sing.

The song concerned Thomas Jefferson, a famous American president of the 18th century. Jefferson was a political theorist who wrote revolutionary manifestos and favored a decentralist mode of government. The song, however, dealt with the relations of Jefferson and a black concubine in his household. He had several children by this woman, who were a source of great shame, due to the odd legal code of the period. Legally, they were his slaves, and it was only at the end of his life, when he was in great poverty, that Jefferson set them free.

It was a story whose pathos makes little sense to a Muslim. But Boston's audience, knowing themselves Jefferson's children, took it to heart.

The heat became stifling, as massed bodies swayed in rhythm. The next song began in a torrent of punishing noise. Frantic hysteria seized the crowd; their bodies spasmed with each beat, the shaman Boston seeming to scourge them. It was a fearsome song, called "The Whites of Their Eyes," after an American war-cry. He sang of a tactic of battle: to wait until the enemy comes close enough so that you can meet his eyes, frighten him with your conviction, and then shoot him point blank. The chorus harked again and again to the "Cowards of the long kill," a Boston slogan condemning those whose abstract power structures let them murder without ever seeing pain.

Three more songs followed, one of them slower, the others battering the audience like iron rods. Boston stalked like a madman, his clothing dark with sweat. My heart spasmed as heavy bass notes, filled with dark murderous power, surged through my ribs. I moved away from the heat to the fringe of the crowd, feeling light-headed and sick.

I had not expected this. I had expected a political spokesman, but instead it seemed I was assaulted by the very Voice of the West. The Voice of a society drunk with raw power, maddened by the grinding roar of machines. It filled me with terrified awe.

To think that once, the West had held us in its armored hands. It had treated Islam like a natural resource, its invincible armies plowing through the lands of the Faithful like bulldozers. The West had chopped our world up into colonies, and smiled upon us with its awful schizophrenic perfidy. It told us to separate God and State, to separate Mind and Body, to separate Reason and Faith. It had torn us apart.

I stood shaking as the first set ended. The band vanished backstage, and a single figure approached the microphone. I recognized him as a famous American television comedian, who had abandoned his own career to join Boston.

The man began to joke and clown, his antics seeming to soothe the crowd, which hooted with laughter. This intermission was a wise move on Boston's part, I thought. The level of pain, of intensity, had become unbearable.

It struck me then how much Boston was like the great Khomeini. Boston too had the persona of the Man of Sorrows, the sufferer after justice, the ascetic among corruption, the battler against odds. And the air of the mystic, the adept, at least as far as such a thing was possible in America. I thought of this, and deep fear struck me once again.

I walked through the gates to the Colosseum's outer hall, seeking air and room to think. Others had come out too. They leaned against the wall, men and women, with the look of wrung-out mops. Some smoked cigarettes, others argued over brochures, others simply sat with palsied grins.

Still others wept. These disturbed me most, for these were the ones whose souls seemed stung and opened. Khomeini made men weep like that, tearing aside despair like a bandage from a burn. I walked down the hall, watching them, making mental notes.

I stopped by a woman in dark glasses and a trim business suit. She leaned against the wall, shaking, her face beneath the glasses slick with silent tears. Something about the precision of her styled hair, her cheekbones, struck a memory. I stood beside her, waiting, and recognition came.

"Hello," I said. "We have something in common, I think. You've been covering the Boston tour. For CBS."

She glanced at me once, and away. "I don't know you."

"You're Marjory Cale, the correspondent."

She drew in a breath. "You're mistaken."

"'Luddite fanatic,'" I said lightly. "'Rock demagogue.'"

"Go away," she said.

"Why not talk about it? I'd like to know your point of view."

"Go away, you nasty little man."

I returned to the crowd inside. The comedian was now reading at length from the American Bill of Rights, his voice thick with sarcasm. "Freedom of advertising," he said. "Freedom of global network television conglomerates. Right to a speedy and public trial, to be repeated until our lawyers win. A well-regulated militia being necessary, citizens will be issued orbital lasers and aircraft carriers. . . ." No one was laughing.

The crowd was in an ugly mood when Boston reappeared. Even the well-dressed ones now seemed surly and militant, not recognizing themselves as the enemy. Like the Shah's soldiers who at last refused to fire, who threw themselves sobbing at Khomeini's feet.

"You all know this one," Boston said. With his wife, he raised a banner, one of the first flags of the American Revolution. It bore a coiled snake, a native American viper, with the legend: DON'T TREAD ON ME. A sinister, scaly rattling poured from the depths of a synthesizer, merging with the crowd's roar of recognition, and a sprung, loping rhythm broke loose. Boston edged back and forth at the stage's rim, his eyes fixed, his long neck swaying. He shook himself like a man saved from drowning and leaned into the microphone.

"We know you own us / You step upon us / We feel the onus / But here's a bonus / Today I see / So enemy / Don't tread on me / Don't tread on me. . . ." Simple words, fitting each beat with all the harsh precision of the English language. A chant of raw hostility. The crowd took it up. This was the hatred, the humiliation of a society brought low. Americans. Somewhere within them conviction still burned. The conviction they had always had: that they were the only real people on our planet. The chosen ones, the Light of the World, the Last Best Hope of Mankind, the Free and the Brave, the crown of creation. They would have killed for him. I knew, someday, they would.

I was called to Boston's suite at two o'clock that morning. I had shaved and showered, dashed on the hotel's complimentary cologne. I wanted to smell like an American.

Boston's guards frisked me, carefully and thoroughly, outside the elevator. I submitted with good grace.

Boston's suite was crowded. It had the air of an election victory. There were many politicians, sipping glasses of bubbling alcohol, laughing, shaking hands. Miami's Mayor was there, with half his City Council. I recognized a young woman Senator, speaking urgently into her pocket phone, her large freckled breasts on display in an evening gown.

I mingled, listening. Men spoke of Boston's ability to raise funds, of the growing importance of his endorsement. More of Boston's guards stood in corners, arms folded, eyes hidden, their faces stony. A black man distributed lapel buttons with the face of Martin Luther King on a background of red and white stripes. The wall-sized television played a tape of the first Moon Landing. The sound had been turned off, and people all over the world, in the garb of the 1960s, mouthed silently at the camera, their eyes shining.

It was not until four o'clock that I finally met the star himself. The party had broken up by then, the politicians politely ushered out, their vows of undying loyalty met with discreet smiles. Boston was in a back bedroom with his wife, and a pair of aides.

"Sayyid," he said, and shook my hand. In person he seemed smaller, older, his hybrid face, with stage makeup, beginning to peel.

"Dr. Boston," I said.

He laughed freely. "Sayyid, my friend. You'll ruin my street fucking credibility."

"I want to tell the story as I see it," I said.

"Then you'll have to tell it to me," he said, and turned briefly to an aide.

He dictated in a low, staccato voice, not losing his place in our conversation, simply loosing a burst of thought. "'Let us be frank. Before I showed an interest you were ready to sell the ship for scrap iron. This is not an era for supertankers. They are dead tech, smokestack-era garbage. Reconsider my offer.'" The secretary pounded keys. Boston looked at me again, returning the searchlight of his attention.

"You plan to buy a supertanker?" I said.

"I wanted an aircraft carrier," he said, smiling.

"They're all in mothballs, but the Feds frown on selling nuke power plants to private citizens."

"We will make the tanker into a floating stadium," Plisetskaya put in. She sat slumped in a padded chair, wearing satin lounge pajamas. A half-filled ashtray on the chair's arm reeked of strong tobacco.

"Ever been inside a tanker?" Boston said. "Huge. Great acoustics." He sat suddenly on the sprawling bed and pulled off his snakeskin boots. "So, Sayyid. Tell me this story of yours."

"You graduated magna cum laude from Rutgers with a doctorate in political science," I said. "In five years."

"That doesn't count," Boston said, yawning behind his hand. "That was before rock and roll beat my brains out."

"You ran for state office in Massachusetts," I said. "You lost a close race. Two years later you were touring with your first band—Swamp Fox. You were an immediate success. You became involved in political fund-raising, recruiting your friends in the music industry. You started your own record label. You helped organize Rock for Detente, where you met your wife-to-be. Your romance was front-page news on both continents. Record sales soared."

"You left out the first time I got shot at," Boston said. "That's more interesting; Val and I are old hat by now."

He paused, then burst out at the second secretary. "'I urge you once again not to go public. You will find yourselves vulnerable to a leveraged buyout. I've told you that Evans is an agent of Marubeni. If he brings your precious plant down around your ears, don't come crying to me.'"

"February 1998," I said. "An anti-communist zealot fired on your bus."

"You're a big fan, Sayyid."

"Why are you afraid of multinationals?" I said. "That was the American preference, wasn't it? Global trade, global economics?"

"We screwed up," Boston said. "Things got out of hand."

"Out of American hands, you mean?"

"We used our companies as tools for development," Boston said, with the patience of a man instructing a child. "But then our lovely friends in South America refused to pay their debts. And our staunch allies in Europe and Japan signed the Geneva Economic Agreement and decided to crash the dollar. And our friends in the Arab countries decided not to be countries any more, but one almighty Caliphate, and, just for good measure, they pulled all their oil money out of our banks and into Islamic ones. How could we compete? They were holy banks, and our banks pay interest, which is a sin, I understand." He paused, his eyes glittering, and fluffed curls from his neck. "And all that time, we were already in hock to our fucking ears to pay for being the world's policeman."

"So the world betrayed your country," I said. "Why?"

He shook his head. "Isn't it obvious? Who needs St. George when the dragon is dead? Some Afghani fanatics scraped together enough plutonium for a Big One, and they blew the dragon's fucking head off. And the rest of the body is still convulsing, ten years later. We bled ourselves white competing against Russia, which was stupid, but we'd won. With two giants, the world trembles. One giant, and the midgets can drag it down. So that's what happened. They took us out, that's all. They own us."

"It sounds very simple," I said.

He showed annoyance for the first time. "Valya says you've read our newspapers. I'm not telling you anything new. Should I lie about it? Look at the figures, for Christ's sake. The EEC and Japanese use their companies for money pumps, they're sucking us dry, deliberately. You don't look stupid, Sayyid. You know very well what's happening to us, anyone in the Third World does."

"You mentioned Christ," I said. "You believe in Him?"

Boston rocked back onto his elbows and grinned. "Do you?"

"Of course. He is one of our Prophets. We call Him Isa."

Boston looked cautious. "I never stand between a man and his God." He paused. "We have a lot of respect for the Arabs, truly. What they've accomplished. Breaking free from the world economic system, returning to authentic local tradition. . . . You see the parallels."

"Yes," I said. I smiled sleepily, and covered my mouth as I yawned. "Jet lag. Your pardon, please. These are only questions my editors would want me to ask. If I were not an admirer, a fan as you say, I would not have this assignment."

He smiled and looked at his wife. Plisetskaya lit another cigarette and leaned back, looking skeptical. Boston grinned. "So the sparring's over, Charlie?"

"I have every record you've made," I said. "This is not a job for hatchets." I paused, weighing my words. "I still believe that our Caliph is a great man. I support the Islamic Resurgence. I am Muslim. But I think, like many others, that we have gone a bit too far in closing every window to the West. Rock and roll is a Third World music at heart. Don't you agree?"

"Sure," Boston said, closing his eyes. "Do you know the first words spoken in independent Zimbabwe? Right after they ran up the flag."

"No."

He spoke out blindly, savoring the words. "Ladies and gentlemen. Bob Marley. And the Wailers."

"You admire him."

"Comes with the territory," said Boston, flipping a coil of hair.

"He had a black mother, a white father. And you?"

"Oh, both my parents were shameless mongrels like myself," Boston said. "I'm a second-generation nothing-in-particular. An American." He sat up, knotting his hands, looking tired. "You going to stay with the tour a while, Charlie?" He spoke to a secretary. "Get me a Kleenex." The woman rose.

"Till Philadelphia," I said. "Like Marjory Cale."

Plisetskaya blew smoke, frowning. "You spoke to that woman?"

"Of course. About the concert."

"What did the bitch say?" Boston asked lazily. His aide handed him tissues and cold cream. Boston dabbed the Kleenex and smeared makeup from his face.

"She asked me what I thought. I said it was too loud," I said.

Plisetskaya laughed once, sharply. I smiled. "It was quite amusing. She said that you were in good form. She said that I should not be so tight-arsed."

"'Tight-arsed'?" Boston said, raising his brows. Fine wrinkles had appeared beneath the greasepaint. "She said that?"

"She said we Muslims were afraid of modern life. Of new experience. Of course I told her that this wasn't true. Then she gave me this." I reached into one of the pockets of my vest and pulled out a flat packet of aluminum foil.

"Marjory Cale gave you cocaine?" Boston asked.

"Wyoming Flake," I said. "She said she has friends who grow it in the Rocky Mountains." I opened the packet, exposing a little mound of white powder. "I saw her use some. I think it will help my jet lag." I pulled my chair closer to the bedside phone-table. I shook the packet out, with much care, upon the shining mahogany surface. The tiny crystals glittered. It was finely chopped.

I opened my wallet and removed a crisp thousand-dollar bill. The actor-president smiled benignly. "Would this be appropriate?"

"Tom does not do drugs," said Plisetskaya, too quickly.

"Ever do coke before?" Boston asked. He threw a wadded tissue to the floor.

"I hope I'm not offending you," I said. "This is Miami, isn't it? This is America." I began rolling the bill, clumsily.

"We are not impressed," said Plisetskaya sternly. She ground out her cigarette. "You are being a rube, Charlie. A hick from the NIC's."

"There is a lot of it," I said, allowing doubt to creep into my voice. I reached in my pocket, then divided the pile in half with the sharp edge of a developed slide. I arranged the lines neatly. They were several centimeters long.

I sat back in the chair. "You think it's a bad idea? I admit, this is new to me." I paused. "I have drunk wine several times, though the *Koran* forbids it."

One of the secretaries laughed. "Sorry," she said. "He drinks wine. That's cute."

I sat and watched temptation dig into Boston. Plisetskaya shook her head.

"Cale's cocaine," Boston mused. "Man."

We watched the lines together for several seconds, he and I. "I did not mean to be trouble," I said. "I can throw it away."

"Never mind Val," Boston said. "Russians chain-smoke." He slid across the bed.

I bent quickly and sniffed. I leaned back, touching my nose. The cocaine quickly numbed it. I handed the paper tube to Boston. It was done in a moment. We sat back, our eyes watering.

"Oh," I said, drug seeping through tissue. "Oh, this is excellent."

"It's good toot," Boston agreed. "Looks like you get an extended interview."

We talked through the rest of the night, he and I.

My story is almost over. From where I sit to write this, I can hear the sound of Boston's music, pouring from the crude speakers of a tape pirate in the bazaar. There is no doubt in my mind that Boston is a great man.

I accompanied the tour to Philadelphia. I spoke to Boston several times during the tour, though never again with the first fine rapport of the drug. We parted as friends, and I spoke well of him in my article for *Al-Ahram*. I did not hide what he was, I did not hide his threat. But I did not malign him. We see things differently. But he is a man, a child of God like all of us.

His music even saw a brief flurry of popularity in Cairo, after the article. Children listen to it, and then turn to other things, as children will. They like the sound, they dance, but the words mean nothing to them. The thoughts, the feelings, are alien.

This is the *dar-al-harb*, the land of peace. We have peeled the hands of the West from our throat, we draw breath again, under God's sky. Our Caliph is a good man, and I am proud to serve him. He reigns, he does not rule. Learned men debate in the *Majlis*, not squabbling like politicians, but seeking truth in dignity. We have the world's respect.

We have earned it, for we paid the martyr's price. We Muslims are one in five in all the world, and as long as ignorance of God persists, there will always be the struggle, the *jihad*. It is a proud thing to be one of the Caliph's *Mujihadeen*. It is not that we value our lives lightly. But that we value God more.

Some call us backward, reactionary. I laughed at that when I carried the powder. It had the subtlest of poisons: a living virus. It is a tiny thing, bred in secret labs, and in itself does no harm. But it spreads throughout the body, and it bleeds out a chemical, a faint but potent trace that carries the rot of cancer.

The West can do much with cancer these days, and a wealthy man like Boston can buy much treatment. They may cure the first attack, or the second. But within five years he will surely be dead. People will mourn his loss. Perhaps they will put his image on a stamp, as they did for Bob Marley. Marley, who also died of systemic cancer; whether by the hand of God or man, only Allah knows.

I have taken the life of a great man; in trapping him I took my own life as well, but that means nothing. I am no one. I am not even Sayyid Qutb, the Martyr and theorist of Resurgence, though I took that great man's name as cover. I meant only respect, and believe I have not shamed his memory.

I do not plan to wait for the disease. The struggle continues in the Muslim lands of what was once the Soviet Union. There the Believers ride in Holy Jihad, freeing their ancient lands from the talons of Marxist atheism. Secretly, we send them carbines, rockets, mortars, and nameless men. I shall be one of them; when I meet death, my grave will be nameless also. But nothing is nameless to God.

God is Great; men are mortal, and err. If I have done wrong, let the Judge of Men decide. Before His Will, as always, I submit.

MISHA NOGHA
Chippoke Na Gomi

{1989}

Misha Nogha (1955–), whose works are often published under just her first name, was born in Minnesota and now lives on a farm in Oregon. Her forthcoming novel *Yellowjacket* is set in the far west; her most recent collection of poems and short fictions is *Magpies and Tigers* (2007).

She is best known for *Red Spider, White Web* (1990), a novel that, in Elyce Helford's words, was "everything cyberpunk should have been but wasn't." Turning from console cowboys, *Red Spider* considers not the highs of jacking-in but the risks of making art. Artists in a dystopian city must resist the seductive comforts of a Disney-like enclave, "Mickey-San." The hero, Kumo, shows her hologram creations in a street market instead, yet living on the edge is not safe. Some of her friends, such as Tommy (a prosthetically altered man worshiped as a god in Mickey-San) or David the hermaphrodite, are dangerous yet sympathetic. Her adversaries—groups of flesh eaters, fundamentalist "Mikans," homeless "street wiggers," neo-Nazi "Pink Flies"—are just plain dangerous. As in Philip K. Dick's *The Man in the High Castle* (1962), Japanese hegemony across the western United States is a given; and as in the short fiction of Cordwainer Smith, the underground is the realm of the real, despite the apparent invincibility of the owning classes. Smith wonders how the world's forgotten ones might acquire political power, but Misha's focus is on retaining personal integrity in a collapsing society. *Red Spider*'s unusual style may have influenced the mixture of lyricism and violence in the fiction of China Miéville. It won the 1990 ReaderCon Award and was shortlisted for the Arthur C. Clarke Award. A sequel (its working title is *The Bell Factory*) is planned. Like her protagonist, the author is of mixed ancestry—Misha is Métis/Nordic, whereas the novel's Kumo is a genetically engineered mixture of Native American and wolverine. Like Kumo, Misha makes art that crosses borders. A musician herself, she is married to composer Michael Chocholak; her story "Tsuki Mangetsu" (Moon Full Moon), set to music by two Australian composers, won the 1989 *Prix d'Italia*.

She has been a high-school language teacher, and the story that follows is rich in foreign and technical terms. First published in *The Witness Anthology of Experimental Fiction* and reprinted here from the 1994 chapbook *Ke-Qua-Hawk-As* ("small wolverine" in Cree), the story's title is Japanese: "Chippoke na" (tiny, small, petty) "gomi" (garbage, refuse, dust). "Bon mitsuri" refers to a Buddhist summer festival held in honor of ancestors; and "loess" is a term in geology for deposits of silt laid down by the action of wind, in this case the wind-storm—"arimitama" wind, using the Japanese word for raw force—following the impact of an atom bomb. On August 9, 1945, three days after Hiroshima was destroyed, the city of Nagasaki was bombed. This story brings the specter of that day's poisonous fall-out—some 74,000 died on impact or shortly after—to a dusty U.S. railway station half a century and half a world away. (Theodore Sturgeon's "Thunder and Roses" [1947] likewise uses a setting in the United States, bringing the horrors of nuclear devastation literally home to readers.) The lantern patch worn by the shadow-girl in this story recalls a ceremony held in Hiroshima a year after the city's destruction, when survivors floated thousands of lanterns in the Ohta River, each one bearing the name of a dead or missing person.

It is raining sand and dirt. It slithers down in truckloads and flows around his feet, spattering his shoes and his gray slacks and the hem of his duster. The red bricks of the station platform spit at him as he leans forward to catch sight of the connection.

His leather bags heel at his feet like two black lizards. He grabs their collars and drags them hissing across the gritty floor of the station.

He frowns, straining with the luggage. It grows heavier with every mile.

He focuses on a shadow etched against the wall. It is a shadow of a missing person bent over in thought.

His eyes bounce the room. He sees the eclipsed woman in a soft sable coverall. The coverall has a flame-colored lantern patch on the shoulder. She is leaning forward with her elbows on her knees. Her head is down and her hands are lightly held in interlocking fingers. When he blinks she is all flat again, like a shadow.

He slides the bags over to the bench and sits down.

He brushes the raindust off of his coat and stares at her. The sun slides through an opening in the cloud.

Small strings of dust float from the ceiling toward the floor.

He sneezes.

A brown bottle bounces across the tile floor. He turns and sees a tattered derelict stagger out of the door. From him rags unravel and fall into the debris of the station. The sake bottle rolls up against a hairy dust bunny under the benches.

A huge column of purple and orange flame is rising.

A phone jangles and echoes in the station. He turns his head. The station-master croaks into the receiver. He cocks his head expectantly, listening.

He hears someone crying on the other end of the line.

He looks at the shadow woman. Her coverall is stained at the knees and elbows with a thick white ash. She is wearing scorched hightops with yellow flames embossed on them.

Carbonized timbers and beams twist and burn hundreds of feet above the ground.

He can't ever remember being this tired. Or this thirsty. He hopes to waken himself in her conversation.

"In Japan they have trains that travel 120 miles an hour and this one is 120 minutes late."

She looks straight ahead, then slowly turns her head toward him. She has the dusky complexion and features of an Aino but he decides she is American Indian.

"Were you in Japan?" Her voice is soft bran. It makes his throat itch.

"That's right." He coughs into his white gloves. "I've been studying Japanese dust."

Although her eyes are huge and dark, he can't help but notice that they are inflamed and sticky at the corners. A little whitish matter clings there.

He rubs his nose. "I'm a konologist."

An inch thick of gray ash covers everything. As he tries to write her a letter, the brush drags into the ash falling on the rice paper.

She chews the inside of her cheek.

Her feral look and a strange efflorescence on her cheeks alarm him.

He pulls out his white kerchief.

She scrunches up her nose. "Konologist." The word breaks in her mouth, as if she spoke around grains of sand.

Her voice grates on him, but he continues.

"The study of dust." He slides closer to her to obscure her shadow. He notices she is wearing a fine covering of face powder which makes her skin look slightly farinaceous.

Her bruised looking eyes fasten on his bags. "And what is in there? Dust I suppose."

He is reluctant to answer. A strange weakness sluices in his bowels and travels down his legs. He wants to lie down.

He has no energy to hunt her ashes in the ruins.

That the train is late is amplified in the cave-like hollowness of the station. The only sound, besides the falling of the dust and his raspy breathing, is the heavy impact of the freight cars slamming together in the yard. Metal couples spark against metal couples, throwing minute particles of oil-soaked dirt into the air. Rusty filings grind on the track as steel rolls on steel.

He smiles at her. Her return smile is hot ice.

A terrible thirst.

He is feeling better, more at home. He calls to the stationmaster.

"Could you please tell me what the hold up is?"

"Bad dust storm about thirty miles out. They're clearing the tracks now." After he speaks his face disintegrates into chalky disinterest.

He rolls his eyes at the woman and shakes his head slowly. He brushes some lint off of his knees.

He checks his watch, then slaps his hand over it. He has just changed it to Pacific time and finds it is still reading Tokyo time July 15, a whole day ahead.

Boats of lantern fire.

The sable woman stares at his bag.

He sighs and stands up. "Excuse me," he says and walks to the pay telephone. It is grimy with use. Little circles of white had been cleared by fingertips dragging in the caked dirt beneath the dial wheel. He removes his gloves.

He dials his house and after a time there is an answer.

It is his wife—living migraine.

"The train has been delayed. I didn't want you to worry."

“I was napping, asleep.” The “was” hissed in the Migraine’s mouth, between her sharp white teeth.

“I’ll be along anytime.” He is cutting into her chest with a letter opener. Her skin is like a paper bag. Lint and thick gray dust pour out of her lungs, along with pins, seeds, and an apple green condom of a kind he never wears. It is sticky with semen and dog hair.

His wife is silent while he does this, then answers “Fine” in a voice that means he is not welcome.

He feels his whole life comminated into this one emotionless phone call.

A miasma of heat and dust.

He sits near the shadow woman. She seems to crumble in front of his eyes. Dust swirls in the open door of the station.

“I think some of the dust is leaking out of those bags.” Her face is deadpan, as if she is serious.

A laugh splinters his throat. “No, it’s all sealed in vacuum jars.” He reaches into his bag and pulls out a small glass jar of ashy-looking dust.

The woman shimmers in a sudden bright shaft of light.

Lightning, roar, rice white calx, black soil.

“I think some of that dust has escaped.” She repeats.

He studies the jar closely, shaking it in the air to catch the light. “Impossible.”

She doesn’t seem convinced. He feels he needs to make an explanation. “You see, dust is a fascinating thing. Have you ever, for example, looked at dust under an electron microscope?”

A sheet of sun falls through the window. She shakes her head.

He sets the jar of dust on the bench, reaches over into his bag and removes a thin green book.

He opens it to a page that is covered with large grains of grayish rice.

“What do you suppose that is?” he asks as he hands her the book and slides close enough to see it over her shoulder.

She shrugs. He sniffs her odor of baby powder. He wonders why women wash off and then dust themselves with talcum.

He glances at her and seems caught in her flat black eyes. A line of sweat pops out on his upper lip.

She stares at the plate a moment and then speaks in a dull, uninterested voice. “Dust.”

He draws the kanji for man in the powder.

He is disappointed she knows his answer. "That's right! Though most people would say 'grains of rice.' Look at this." It is a 100 times enlargement of a piece of pollen. It looks like a small moon pitted with craters.

He points to another grainy photo. It is a monstrous creature with a vicious set of mandibles and repulsive grape-like clusters on its hairy legs.

A mass for dead insects.

"This tiger mite is too small to be identified by the naked eye, and yet—" he points to the clusters, "It has its own parasites even smaller."

He looks closely at the plate himself; though he has seen it many times, this time he sees something different. He sees a human face trapped between two tiny pieces of dust.

He snaps the book shut and tosses it in his bag. He holds up his jar of dust and peers at the label.

"Dust tells us much about our history. You might be interested to know," he says boldly, "that this dust from Nagasaki is still radioactive. Even after all these years."

A crimson display of pyrotechnics explodes in her eyes.

"Yes, that's right." He replaces the jar carefully, as if it is worth its weight in gold. "This dust is full of pulverized buildings, books, dinnerware, bamboo stalks and grains of rice—remnants of a great city."

She stares fixedly at his shoes.

A field of carbonated bone.

He talks on a bit, but notices her obsession soon enough.

"Excuse me but," he captures her attention.

She looks at him with cold mineral eyes.

They are like highly polished mirrors and in them he can see it. A huge column of dust traveling up and up and finally spreading out in a horizontal bank of cloud. In the cloud, thousands of faces, ancestors come for Bon mitsuri.

She points at his shoes. "They're covered with the victims of Nagasaki."

Before he replies, the bellowing of the diesel horn, the grating of steel on pitted steel and the roaring of the engine meet his ears.

From the west a terrible arimitama wind.

He jumps forward to grab her hand and the skin peels off just like a glove. She suddenly flares in a pillar of fire and a wave of intense heat sears his eyes.

He falls to his knees and cries out in terror and pain.

The train roars in and pulls away while he is still kneeling in the station with a handful of crematory ash.

It is pale dust, gray and gritty and still warm.

A fine sandy loess blows about his knees.

The station is whirling with small dust devils. Through them he can see a dark shape.

"Ahhh!" He staggers to his feet and runs forward. She is not there but her shadow remains permanently scorched into the station wall.

He exclaims again and holds the ashes tightly in his fist. The tighter he holds them, the more they slip through his fingers.

With each step he takes he shakes the dust from his feet. His eyes seem to stare blankly ahead.

But he is focusing very intently on one thing.

The tiny motes of dust dancing in a red shaft of sunlight.

EILEEN GUNN
Computer Friendly

{1989}

Eileen Gunn (1945–) is an American writer who has published a handful of carefully crafted and technologically sophisticated short stories. Her first story, "What Are Friends For?"—an absurdist fable about aliens and pornography—appeared in *Amazing Science Fiction* in 1978. Her best-known story is "Stable Strategies for Middle Management" (1988), a cheerful Kafkaesque satire on how to get ahead in high-tech corporate culture, which was nominated for a Hugo Award. It was inspired in part by Gunn's experiences in the early years of the digital-communications boom; among other positions, she worked in the mid-1980s as director of advertising for the Microsoft Corporation.

Gunn's well-received collection, *Stable Strategies and Others* (2004), reprints most of her published fiction of the past thirty years, including "Computer Friendly," which originally appeared in *Asimov's Science Fiction* and was also nominated for a Hugo. New stories in the collection include the Nebula Award–winning "Coming to Terms" (2004), inspired by her friendship with sf writer Avram Davidson (Gunn is planning to write a biography of Davidson). The collection itself was short-listed for both the World Fantasy Award and the James Tiptree Jr. Award for speculative fiction that explores and expands our understanding of gender; in Japanese translation, it won the Sense of Gender Award given at the 2007 World Science Fiction Convention in Yokohama. William Gibson, best known for his classic cyberpunk novel *Neuromancer* (1984), contributed the foreword to *Stable Strategies and Others* and, in a brief note following it, Gunn reveals "the secret of writing" that Gibson once shared with her: "You must learn to overcome your very natural and appropriate revulsion for your own work."

Gunn is admired not only for her fiction, but also for her role as editor and publisher of the webzine *The Infinite Matrix*, which appeared between 2001 and 2006. *The Infinite Matrix* published both fiction and nonfiction by a wide-ranging group of writers that included Eleanor Arnason, Pat Cadigan, Cory Doctorow, Gibson, Kathleen Ann Goonan, Robert Sheckley, and Bruce Sterling. Gunn is also a longtime member of the board of directors of the Clarion West Writers Workshop, an annual six-week workshop focused on sf, fantasy, and horror.

While "Computer Friendly" is only obliquely related to cyberpunk—the subgenre most often associated with late-1980s and early-1990s American sf—it is as interested in the breathtaking possibilities of computing technologies and artificial-intelligence research as is anything written by Cadigan, Gibson, or Sterling. Unlike the lovingly detailed noir worlds of cyberpunk that we see in stories such as Gibson's "Burning Chrome," the dystopian features of the high-tech near future in "Computer Friendly" are only indirectly suggested, limited as they are to the perspective of the story's seven-year-old protagonist: "her mom had custom-made connectors that stretched all the way into the dining room. Even though she didn't really eat anymore, her local I/O was always extended to the table at dinnertime."

Holding her dad's hand, Elizabeth went up the limestone steps to the testing center. As she climbed, she craned her neck to read the words carved in pink granite over the top of the door: FRANCIS W. PARKER SCHOOL. Above them was a banner made of grey cement that read, "Health, Happiness, Success."

"This building is old," said Elizabeth. "It was built before the war."

"Pay attention to where you're going, punkin," said her dad. "You almost ran into that lady there."

Inside, the entrance hall was dark and cool. A dim yellow glow came through the shades on the tall windows.

As Elizabeth walked across the polished floor, her footsteps echoed lightly down the corridors that led off to either side. She and her father went down the hallway to the testing room. An old, beat-up, army-green query box sat on a table outside the door.

"Ratherford, Elizabeth Ratherford," said her father to the box. "Age seven, computer-friendly, smart as a whip."

"We'll see," said the box with a chuckle. It had a gruff, teasing, grandfatherly voice. "We'll just see about *that*, young lady." What a jolly interface, thought Elizabeth. She watched as the classroom door swung open. "You go right along in there, and we'll see just how smart you are." It chuckled again, then it spoke to Elizabeth's dad. "You come back for her at three, sir. She'll be all ready and waiting for you, bright as a little watermelon."

This was going to be fun, thought Elizabeth. Nothing to do all day except show how smart she was.

Her father knelt in front of her and smoothed her hair back from her face. "You try real hard on these tests, punkin. You show them just how talented and clever you really are, okay?" Elizabeth nodded. "And you be on your best behavior." He gave her a hug and a pat on the rear.

Inside the testing room were dozens of other seven-year-olds, sitting in rows of tiny chairs with access boxes in front of them. Glancing around the room, Elizabeth realized that she had never seen so many children together all at once. There were only ten in her weekly socialization class. It was sort of overwhelming.

The monitors called everyone to attention and told them to put on their headsets and ask their boxes for Section One.

Elizabeth followed directions, and she found that all the interfaces were strange—they were friendly enough, but none of them were the programs she worked with at home. The first part of the test was the multiple-choice exam. The problems, at least, were familiar to Elizabeth—she'd practiced for this test all her life, it seemed. There were word games, number games, and games in which she had to rotate little boxes in her head. She knew enough to skip the hardest until she'd worked her way through the whole test. There were only a couple of problems left to do when the system told her to stop and the box went all grey.

The monitors led the whole room full of kids in jumping-jack exercises for five minutes. Then everyone sat down again and a new test came up in the box. This one seemed very easy, but it wasn't one she'd ever done before. It consisted of a series of very detailed pictures; she was supposed to make up a story about each picture. Well, she could do that. The first picture showed a child and a lot of different kinds of animals. "Once upon a time there was a little girl who lived all alone in the forest with her friends the skunk, the wolf, the bear, and the lion. . . ." A beep sounded every so often to tell her to end one story and begin another. Elizabeth really enjoyed telling the stories, and was sorry when that part of the test was over.

But the next exercise was almost as interesting. She was to read a series of short stories and answer questions about them. Not the usual questions about what happened in the story—these were harder. "Is it fair to punish a starving cat for stealing?" "Should people do good deeds for strangers?" "Why is it important for everyone to learn to obey?"

When this part was over, the monitors took the class down the hall to the big cafeteria, where there were lots of other seven-year-olds, who had been taking tests in other rooms.

Elizabeth was amazed at the number and variety of children in the cafeteria. She watched them as she stood in line for her milk and sandwich.

Hundreds of kids, all exactly as old as she was. Tall and skinny, little and fat; curly hair, straight hair, and hair that was frizzy or held up with ribbons or cut into strange patterns against the scalp; skin that was light brown like Elizabeth's, chocolate brown, almost black, pale pink, freckled, and all the colors in between. Some of the kids were all dressed up in fancy clothes; others were wearing patched pants and old shirts.

When she got her snack, Elizabeth's first thought was to find someone who looked like herself and sit next to her. But then a freckled boy with dark, nappy hair smiled at her in a very friendly way. He looked at her feet and nodded. "Nice shoes," he said. She sat down on the empty seat next to him, suddenly aware of her red maryjanes with the embroidered flowers. She was pleased that they had been noticed, and a little embarrassed.

"Let me see *your* shoes," she said, unwrapping her sandwich.

He stuck his feet out. He was wearing pink plastic sneakers with hologram pictures of a missile gantry on the toes. When he moved his feet, they launched a defensive counterattack.

"Oh, neat." Elizabeth nodded appreciatively and took a bite of the sandwich. It was filled with something yellow that tasted okay.

A little tiny girl with long, straight, black hair was sitting on the other side of the table from them. She put one foot up on the table. "I got shoes, too," she said. "Look." Her shoes were black patent, with straps. Elizabeth and the freckled boy both admired them politely. Elizabeth thought that the little girl was very daring to put her shoe right up on the table. It was certainly an interesting way to enter a conversation.

"My name is Sheena and I can spit," said the little girl. "Watch." Sure enough, she could spit really well. The spit hit the beige wall several meters away, just under the mirror, and slid slowly down.

"I can spit, too," said the freckled boy. He demonstrated, hitting the wall a little lower than Sheena had.

"I can *learn* to spit," said Elizabeth.

"All right there, no spitting!" said a monitor firmly. "Now, you take a napkin and clean that up." It pointed to Elizabeth.

"She didn't do it, I did," said Sheena. "I'll clean it up."

"I'll help," said Elizabeth. She didn't want to claim credit for Sheena's spitting ability, but she liked being mistaken for a really good spitter.

The monitor watched as they wiped the wall, then took their thumbprints. "You three settle down now. I don't want any more spitting." It moved away. All three of them were quiet for a few minutes, and munched on their sandwiches.

"What's your name?" said Sheena suddenly. "My name is Sheena."

"Elizabeth."

"Lizardbreath. That's a funny name," said Sheena.

"My name is Oginga," said the freckled boy.

"That's *really* a funny name," said Sheena.

"You think everybody's name is funny," said Oginga. "Sheena-Teena-Peena."

"I can tap dance, too," said Sheena, who had recognized that it was time to change the subject. "These are my tap shoes." She squirmed around to wave her feet in the air briefly, then swung them back under the table.

She moves more than anyone I've ever seen, thought Elizabeth.

"Wanna see me shuffle off to Buffalo?" asked Sheena.

A bell rang at the front of the room, and the three of them looked up. A monitor was speaking.

"Quiet! Everybody quiet, now! Finish up your lunch quickly, those of you who are still eating, and put your wrappers in the wastebaskets against the wall. Then line up on the west side of the room. The *west* side. . . ."

The children were taken to the restroom after lunch. It was grander than any bathroom Elizabeth had ever seen, with walls made of polished red granite, lots of little stalls with toilets in them, and a whole row of sinks. The sinks were lower than the sink at home, and so were the toilets. Even the mirrors were just the right height for kids.

It was funny because there were no stoppers in the sinks, so you couldn't wash your hands in a proper sink of water. Sheena said she could make the sink fill up, and Oginga dared her to do it, so she took off her sweater and put it in the sink, and sure enough, it filled up with water and started to overflow, and then she couldn't get the sweater out of it, so she called a monitor over. "This sink is overflowing," she said, as if it were all the sink's fault. A group of children stood around and watched while the monitor fished the sweater from the drain and wrung it out.

"That's mine!" said Sheena, as if she had dropped it by mistake. She grabbed it away from the monitor, shook it, and nodded knowingly to Elizabeth. "It dries real fast." The monitor wanted thumbprints from Sheena and Elizabeth and everyone who watched.

The monitors then took the children to the auditorium, and led the whole group in singing songs and playing games, which Elizabeth found only moderately interesting. She would have preferred to learn to spit. At one o'clock, a monitor announced it was time to go back to the classrooms, and all the children should line up by the door.

Elizabeth and Sheena and Oginga pushed into the same line together. There were so many kids that there was a long wait while they all lined up and the monitors moved up and down the lines to make them straight.

"Are you going to go to the Asia Center?" asked Sheena. "My mom says I'll probably go to the Asia Center tomorrow, because I'm so fidgety."

Elizabeth didn't know what the Asia Center was, but she didn't want to look stupid. "I don't know. I'll have to ask my dad." She turned to Oginga, who was behind her. "Are you going to the Asia Center?'

"What's the Asia Center?" asked Oginga.

Elizabeth looked back at Sheena, waiting to hear her answer.

"Where we go to sleep," Sheena said. "My mom says it doesn't hurt."

"I got my own room," said Oginga.

"It's not like your room," Sheena explained. "You go there, and you go to sleep, and your parents get to try again."

"What do they try?" asked Elizabeth. "Why do you have to go to sleep?"

"You go to sleep so they have some peace and quiet," said Sheena. "So you're not in their way."

"But what do they try?" repeated Elizabeth.

"I bet they try more of that stuff that they do when they think you're asleep," said Oginga. Sheena snorted and started to giggle, and then Oginga started to giggle and he snorted too, and the more one giggled and snorted, the more the other did. Pretty soon Elizabeth was giggling too, and the three of them were helplessly choking, behind great hiccoughing gulps of noise.

The monitor rolled by then and told them to be quiet and move on to their assigned classrooms. That broke the spell of their giggling, and, subdued, they moved ahead in the line. All the children filed quietly out of the lunchroom and walked slowly down the halls. When Elizabeth came to her classroom, she shrugged her shoulders at Oginga and Sheena and jerked her head to one side. "I go in here," she whispered.

"See ya at the Asia Center," said Sheena.

The rest of the tests went by quickly, though Elizabeth didn't think they were as much fun as in the morning. The afternoon tests were more physical; she pulled at joysticks and tried to push buttons quickly on command. They tested her hearing and even made her sing to the computer. Elizabeth didn't like to do things fast, and she didn't like to sing.

When it was over, the monitors told the children they could go now, their parents were waiting for them at the front of the school. Elizabeth looked for Oginga and Sheena as she left, but children from the other classrooms were not in the halls. Her dad was waiting for her out front, as he had said he would be.

Elizabeth called to him to get his attention. He had just come off work, and she knew he would be sort of confused. They wiped their secrets out of his brain before he logged off of the system, and sometimes they took a little other stuff with it by mistake, so he might not be too sure about his name, or where he lived.

On the way home, she told him about her new friends. "They don't sound as though they would do very well at their lessons, princess," said her father. "But it does sound as if you had an interesting time at lunch." Elizabeth pulled his hand to guide him onto the right street. He'd be okay in an hour or so—anything important usually came back pretty fast.

When they got home, her dad went into the kitchen to start dinner, and Elizabeth played with her dog, Brownie. Brownie didn't live with them anymore because his brain was being used to help control data traffic in the network. Between rush hours, Elizabeth would call him up on the system and run simulations in which she plotted the trajectory of a ball and he plotted an interception of it.

They ate dinner when her mom logged off work. Elizabeth's parents believed it was very important for the family to all eat together in the evening, and her mom had custom-made connectors that stretched all the way into the dining room. Even though she didn't really eat anymore, her local I/O was always extended to the table at dinnertime.

After dinner, Elizabeth got ready for bed. She could hear her father in his office, asking his mail for the results of her test that day. When he came into her room to tuck her in, she could tell he had good news for her.

"Did you wash behind your ears, punkin?" he asked. Elizabeth figured that this was a ritual question, since she was unaware that washing behind her ears was more useful than washing anywhere else.

She gave the correct response: "Yes, Daddy." She understood that, whether she washed or not, giving the expected answer was an important part of the ritual. Now it was her turn to ask a question. "Did you get the results of my tests, Daddy?"

"We sure did, princess," her father replied. "You did very well on them."

Elizabeth was pleased, but not too surprised. "What about my new friends, Daddy? How did they do?"

"I don't know about that, punkin. They don't send us everybody's scores, just yours."

"I want to be with them when I go to the Asia Center."

Elizabeth could tell by the look on her father's face that she'd said something wrong. "The what? Where did you hear about that?" he asked sharply.

"My friend Sheena told me about it. She said she was going to the Asia Center tomorrow," said Elizabeth.

'Well, *she* might be going there, but that's not anyplace you're going." Her dad sounded very strict. "You're going to continue your studies, young lady, and someday you'll be an important executive like your mother. That's clear from your test results. I don't want to hear any talk about you doing anything else. Or about this Sheena."

"What does mommy do, daddy?"

"She's a processing center, sweetheart, that talks directly to the CPU. She uses her brain to control important information and tell the rest of the computer what to do. And she gives the whole system common sense." He sat down on the edge of the bed, and Elizabeth could tell that she was going to get what her dad called an "explanatory chat."

"You did so well on your test today that maybe it's time we told you something about what you might be doing when you get a little older." He pulled the blanket up a little bit closer to her chin and turned the sheet down evenly over it.

"It'll be a lot like studying, or like taking that test today," he continued. "Except you'll be hardwired into the network, just like your mom, so you won't have to get up and move around. You'll be able to do anything and go anywhere in your head."

"Will I be able to play with Brownie?"

"Of course, sweetheart, you'll be able to call him up just like you did tonight. It's important that you play. It keeps you healthy and alert, and it's good for Brownie, too."

"Will I be able to call you and Mommy?"

"Well, princess, that depends on what kind of job you're doing. You just might be so busy and important that you don't have time to call us."

Like Bobby, she thought. Her parents didn't talk much about her brother Bobby. He had done well on his tests, too. Now he was a milintel cyborg with go-nogo authority. He never called home, and her parents didn't call him, either.

"Being an executive is sort of like playing games all the time," her father added, when Elizabeth didn't say anything. "And the harder you work right now, the better you do on your tests, the more fun you'll have later."

He tucked the covers up around her neck again. "Now you go to sleep, so you can work your best tomorrow, okay, princess?" Elizabeth nodded. Her dad kissed her good night, and poked at the covers again. He got up. "Good night, sweetheart," he said, and he left the room.

Elizabeth lay in bed for a while, trying to get to sleep. The door was open so that the light would come in from the hall, and she could hear her parents talking downstairs.

Her dad, she knew, would be reading the news at his access box, as he did every evening. Her mom would be tidying up noise-damaged data in the household module. She didn't have to do that, but she said it calmed her nerves.

Listening to the rise and fall of their voices, she heard her name. What were they saying? Was it about the test? She got up out of bed, crept to the door of her room. They stopped talking. Could they hear her? She was very quiet. Standing in the doorway, she was only a few feet from the railing at the top of the staircase, and the sounds came up very clearly from the living room below.

"Just the house settling," said her father, after a moment. "She's asleep by now." Ice cubes clinked in a glass.

"Well," said her mother, resuming the conversation, "I don't know what they think they're doing, putting euthanasable children in the testing center with children like Elizabeth." There was a bit of a whine behind her mother's voice. RF interference, perhaps. "Just talking with that Sheena could skew her test results for years. I have half a mind to call the net executive and ask it what it thinks it's doing."

"Now, calm down, honey," said her dad. Elizabeth heard his chair squeak as he turned away from his access box toward the console that housed her mother. "You don't want the exec to think we're questioning its judgment. Maybe this was part of the test."

"Well, you'd think they'd let us know, so we could prepare her for it."

Was Sheena part of the test, wondered Elizabeth. She'd hate to ask the system what "euthanasable" meant.

"Look at her scores," said her father. "She did much better than the first two on verbal skills—her programs are on the right track there. And her physical aptitude scores are even lower than Bobby's."

"That's a blessing," said her mother. "It held Christopher back, right from the beginning, being so active." Who's Christopher? wondered Elizabeth.

Her mother continued. "But it was a mistake, putting him in with the euthana—"

"Her socialization scores were okay, but right on the edge," added her dad, talking right over her mother. "Maybe they should reduce her class time to twice a month. Look at how she sat right down with those children at lunch."

"Anyway, she passed," said her mother. "They're moving her up a level instead of taking her now."

"Maybe because she didn't initiate the contact, but she was able to handle it when it occurred. Maybe that's what they want for the execs."

Elizabeth shifted her weight, and the floor squeaked again.

Her father called up to her, "Elizabeth, are you up?"

"Just getting a drink of water, Daddy." She walked to the bathroom and drew a glass of water from the tap. She drank a little and poured the rest down the drain.

Then she went back to her room and climbed into bed. Her parents were talking more quietly now, and she could hear only little bits of what they were saying.

". . . mistake about Christopher. . . ." Her mother's voice.

". . . that other little girl to sleep forever? . . ." Her dad.

". . . worth it? . . ." Her mother again.

Their voices slowed down and fell away, and Elizabeth dreamed of eerie white things in glass jars, of Brownie, still a dog, all furry and fetching a ball, and of Sheena, wearing a sparkly costume and tapdancing very fast. She fanned her hands out to her sides and turned around in a circle, tapping faster and faster.

Then Sheena began to run down like a wind-up toy. She went limp and dropped to the floor. Brownie sniffed at her, and the white things in the jars watched. Elizabeth was afraid, but she didn't know why. She grabbed Sheena's shoulders and tried to rouse her.

"Don't let me fall asleep," Sheena murmured, but she dozed off even as Elizabeth shook her.

"Wake up! Wake up!" Elizabeth's own words pulled her out of her dream. She sat up in bed. The house was quiet, except for the sound of her father snoring in the other room.

Sheena needed her help, thought Elizabeth, but she wasn't really sure why. Very quietly, she slipped out of bed. On the other side of her room, her terminal was waiting for her, humming faintly.

When she put the headset on, she saw her familiar animal friends: a gorilla, a bird, and a pig. Each was a node that enabled her to communicate with other parts of the system. Elizabeth had given them names.

Facing Sam, the crow, she called her dog. Sam transmitted the signal, and was replaced by Brownie, who was barking. That meant his brain was routing information, and she couldn't get through.

What am I doing, anyway, Elizabeth asked herself. As she thought, a window irised open in the center of her vision, and there appeared the face of a boy of about eleven or twelve. “Hey, Elizabeth, what are you doing up at this hour?” It was the sysop on duty in her sector.

“My dog was crying.”

The sysop laughed. “Your dog was crying? That’s the first time I’ve ever heard anybody say something like that.” He shook his head at her.

“He was so crying. Even if he wasn’t crying out loud, I heard him, and I came over to see what was the matter. Now he’s busy and I can’t get through.”

The sysop stopped laughing. “Sorry. I didn’t mean to make fun of you. I had a dog once, before I came here, and they took him for the system, too.”

“Do you call him up?”

“Well, not anymore. I don’t have time. I used to, though. He was a golden Lab. . . .” Then the boy shook his head sternly and said, “But you should be in bed.”

“Can’t I stay until Brownie is free again? Just a few more minutes?”

“Well, maybe a couple minutes more. But then you gotta go to bed for sure. I’ll be back to check. Good night, Elizabeth.”

“Good night,” she said, but the window had already closed.

Wow, thought Elizabeth. That worked. She had never told a really complicated lie before and was surprised that it had gone over so well. It seemed to be mostly a matter of convincing yourself that what you said was true.

But right now, she had an important problem to solve, and she wasn’t even exactly sure what it was. If she could get into the files for Sheena and Oginga, maybe she could find out what was going on. Then maybe she could change the results on their tests or move them to her socialization group or something.

If she could just get through to Brownie, she knew he could help her. After a few minutes, the flood of data washed away, and the dog stopped barking. “Here, Brownie!” she called. He wagged his tail and looked happy to see her.

She told Brownie her problem, and he seemed to understand her. “Can you get it, Brownie?’

He gave a little bark, like he did when she plotted curves.

“Okay, go get it.”

Brownie ran away real fast, braked to a halt, and seemed to be digging. This wasn’t what he was really doing, of course, it was just the way Elizabeth’s interface interpreted Brownie’s brain waves. In just a few seconds, Brownie came trotting back with the records from yesterday’s tests in his mouth.

But when Elizabeth examined them, her heart sank. There were four

Sheenas and fifteen Ogingas. But then she looked more carefully, and noticed that most of the identifying information didn't fit her Sheena and Oginga. There was only one of each that was the right height, with the right color hair.

When she read the information, she felt bad again. Oginga had done all right on the test, but they wanted to use him for routine processing right away, kind of like Brownie. Sheena, as Elizabeth's mother had suggested, had failed the personality profile and was scheduled for the euthanasia center the next afternoon at two o'clock. There was that word again: euthanasia. Elizabeth didn't like the sound of it.

"Here, Brownie." Her dog looked up at her with a glint in his eye. "Now listen to me. We're going to play with this stuff just a little, and then I want you to take it and put it back where you got it. Okay, Brownie?"

The window irised open again and the sysop reappeared. "Elizabeth, what do you think you're doing?" he said. "You're not supposed to have access to this data."

Elizabeth thought for a minute. Then she figured she was caught red-handed, so she might as well ask for his advice. So she explained her problem, all about her new friends and how Oginga was going to be put in the system like Brownie, and Sheena was going to be taken away somewhere.

"They said she would go to the euthanasia center, and I'm not real sure what that is," said Elizabeth. "But I don't think it's good."

"Let me look it up," said the sysop. He paused for a second, then he looked worried. "They want my ID before they'll tell me what it means. I don't want to get in trouble. Forget it."

"Well, what can I do to help my friends?" she asked.

"Gee," said the sysop. "It's a tough one. The way you were doing it, they'd catch you for sure, just like I did. It looks like a little kid got at it."

I *am* a little kid, thought Elizabeth, but she didn't say anything.

I need help, she thought. But who could she go to? She turned to the sysop. "I want to talk to my brother Bobby, in milintel. Can you put me through to him?"

"I don't know," said the sysop, "but I'll ask the mailer demon." He irised shut for a second, then opened again. "The mailer demon says it's no skin off his nose, but he doesn't think you ought to."

"How come?" asked Elizabeth.

"He says it's not your brother anymore. He says you'll be sorry."

"I want to talk to him anyway," said Elizabeth.

The sysop nodded, and his window winked shut just as another irised open. An older boy who looked kind of like Elizabeth herself stared out. His tongue darted rapidly out between his lips, keeping them slightly wet. His pale eyes, unblinking, stared into hers.

"Begin," said the boy. "You have sixty seconds."

"Bobby?" said Elizabeth.

"True. Begin," said the boy.

"Bobby, um, I'm your sister Elizabeth."

The boy just looked at her, the tip of his tongue moving rapidly. She wanted to hide from him, but she couldn't pull her eyes from his. She didn't want to tell him her story, but she could feel words filling her throat. She moved new words forward, before the others could burst out.

"Log off!" she yelled. "Log off!"

She was in her bedroom, drenched in sweat, the sound of her own voice ringing in her ears. Had she actually yelled? The house was quiet, her father still snoring. She probably hadn't made any noise.

She was very scared, but she knew she had to go back in there. She hoped that her brother was gone. She waited a couple of minutes, then logged on.

Whew. Just her animals. She called the sysop, who irised on, looking nervous.

"If you want to do that again, Elizabeth, don't go through me, huh?" He shuddered.

"I'm sorry," she said. "But I can't do this by myself. Do you know anybody that can help?"

"Maybe we ought to ask Norton," said the sysop after a minute.

"Who's Norton?"

"He's this old utility I found that nobody uses much anymore," said the sysop. "He's kind of grotty, but he helps me out." He took a breath. "Hey, Norton!" he yelled, real loud. Of course, it wasn't really yelling, but that's what it seemed like to Elizabeth.

Instantly, another window irised open, and a skinny middle-aged man leaned out of the window so far that Elizabeth thought he was going to fall out, and yelled back, just as loud, "Don't bust your bellows. I can hear you."

He was wearing a striped vest over a dirty undershirt and had a squashed old porkpie hat on his head. This wasn't anyone that Elizabeth had ever seen in the system before.

The man looked at Elizabeth and jerked his head in her direction. "Who's the dwarf?"

The sysop introduced Elizabeth and explained her problem to Norton. Norton didn't look impressed. "What d'ya want me to do about it, kid?"

"Come on, Norton," said the sysop. "You can figure it out. Give us a hand."

"Jeez, kid, it's practically four o'clock in the morning. I gotta get my beauty rest, y'know. Plus, now you've got milintel involved, it's a real mess. They'll be back, sure as houses."

The sysop just looked at him. Elizabeth looked at Norton, too. She tried to look patient and helpless, because that always helped with her dad, but she really didn't know if that would work on this weird old program.

"Y'know, there ain't much that you or me can do in the system that they won't find out about, kids," said Norton.

"Isn't there somebody who can help?" asked Elizabeth.

"Well, there's the Chickenheart. There's not much that it can't do, when it wants to. We could go see the Chickenheart."

"Who's the Chickenheart?" asked Elizabeth.

"The Chickenheart's where the system began." Of course Elizabeth knew *that* story—about the networks of nerve fibers organically woven into great convoluted mats, a mammoth supercortex that had stored the original programs, before processing was distributed to satellite brains. Her own system told her the tale sometimes before her nap.

"You mean the original core is still there?" said the sysop, surprised. "You never told me that, Norton."

"Lot of things I ain't told you, kid." Norton scratched his chest under his shirt. "Listen. If we go see the Chickenheart, and *if* it wants to help, it can figure out what to do for your friends. But you gotta know that this is a big fucking deal. The Chickenheart's a busy guy, and this ain't one-hunnert-percent safe."

"Are you sure you want to do it, Elizabeth?" asked the sysop. "I wouldn't."

"How come it's not safe?" asked Elizabeth. "Is he mean?"

"Nah," said Norton. "A little strange, maybe, not mean. But didn't I tell you the Chickenheart's been around for a while? You know what that means? It means you got yer intermittents, you got yer problems with feedback, runaway processes, what have you. It means the Chickenheart's got a lot of frayed connections, if you get what I mean. Sometimes the old CH just goes chaotic on you." Norton smiled, showing yellow teeth. "Plus you got the chance there's someone listening in. The netexec, for instance. Now there's someone I wouldn't want to catch me up to no mischief. Nossir. Not if I was you."

"Why not?" asked Elizabeth.

"Because that's sure curtains for you, kid. The netexec don't ask no questions, he don't check to see if you maybe could be repaired. You go bye-bye and you don't come back."

Like Sheena, thought Elizabeth. "Does he listen in often?" she asked.

"Never has," said Norton. "Not yet. Don't even know the Chickenheart's there, far as I can tell. Always a first time, though."

"I want to talk to the Chickenheart," said Elizabeth, although she wasn't sure she wanted anything of the kind, after her last experience.

"You got it," said Norton. "This'll just take a second."

Suddenly all the friendly animals disappeared, and Elizabeth felt herself falling very hard and fast along a slippery blue line in the dark. The line glowed neon blue at first, then changed to fuchsia, then sulfur yellow. She knew that Norton was falling with her, but she couldn't see him. Against the dark background, his shadow moved with hers, black, and opalescent as an oilslick.

They arrived somewhere moist and warm. The Chickenheart pulsated next to them, nutrients swishing through its external tubing. It was huge, and wetly organic. Elizabeth felt slightly sick.

"Oh, turn it off, for Chrissake," said Norton, with exasperation. "It's just me and a kid."

The monstrous creature vanished, and a cartoon rabbit with impossibly tall ears and big dewy brown eyes appeared in its place. It looked at Norton, raised an eyebrow, cocked an ear in his direction, and took a huge, noisy bite out of the carrot it was holding.

"Gimme a break," said Norton.

The bunny was replaced by a tall, overweight man in his sixties wearing a rumpled white linen suit. He held a small, paddle-shaped fan, which he slowly moved back and forth. "Ah, Mr. Norton," he said. "Hot enough for you, sir?"

"We got us a problem here, Chick," said Norton. He looked over at Elizabeth and nodded. "You tell him about it, kid."

First she told him about her brother. "Non-trivial, young lady," said the Chickenheart. "Non-trivial, but easy enough to fix. Let me take care of it right now." He went rigid and quiet for a few seconds, as though frozen in time. Then he was back. "Now, then, young lady," he said. "We'll talk if you like."

So Elizabeth told the Chickenheart about Sheena and Oginga, about the testing center and the wet sweater and the monitor telling her to clean up the spit. Even though she didn't have to say a word, she told him everything, and she was sure that if he wanted to come up with a solution, he could do it.

The Chickenheart seemed surprised to hear about the euthanasia center, and especially surprised that Sheena was going to be sent there. He addressed Norton. "I know I've been out of touch, but I find this hard to believe. Mr. Norton, have you any conception of how difficult it can be to obtain components like this? Let me investigate the situation." His face went quiet for a second, then came back. "By gad, sir, it's true," he said to Norton. "They say they're optimizing for predictability. It's a mistake, sir, let me tell you. Things are too predictable here already. Same old ideas churning around and around. A few more components like that Sheena, things might get interesting again.

"I want to look at their records." He paused for a moment, then continued talking.

"Ah, yes, yes, I want that Sheena right away, sir," he said to Norton. "An amazing character. Oginga, too—not as gonzo as the girl, but he has a brand of aggressive curiosity we can put to use, sir. And there are forty-six others with similar personality profiles scheduled for euthanasia today at two." His face went quiet again.

"What is he doing?" Elizabeth asked Norton.

"Old Chickenheart's got his hooks into everythin'," Norton replied. "He just reaches along those pathways, faster'n you can think, and does what he wants. The altered data will look like it's been there all along, and ain't nobody can prove anythin' different."

"Done and done, Mr. Norton." The Chickenheart was back.

"Thank you, Mr. Chickenheart," said Elizabeth, remembering her manners. "What's going to happen to Sheena and Oginga now?"

"Well, young lady, we're going to bring your friends right into the system, sort of like the sysop, but without, shall we say, official recognition. We'll have Mr. Norton here keep an eye on them. They'll be our little surprises, eh? Timebombs that we've planted. They can explore the system, learn what's what, what they can get away with and what they can't. Rather like I do."

"What will they do?" asked Elizabeth.

"That's a good question, my dear," said the Chickenheart. "They'll have to figure it out for themselves. Maybe they'll put together a few new solutions to some old problems, or create a few new problems to keep us on our toes. One way or the other, I'm sure they'll liven up the old homestead."

"But what about me?" asked Elizabeth.

"Well, Miss Elizabeth, what about you? Doesn't look to me as though you have any cause to worry. You passed your tests yesterday with flying colors. You can just go right on being a little girl, and some day you'll have a nice, safe job as an executive. Maybe you'll even become netexec, who knows? I wiped just a tiny bit of your brother's brain and removed all records of your call. I'll wipe your memory of this, and you'll do just fine, yes indeed."

"But my friends are in here," said Elizabeth, and she started to feel sorry for herself. "My dog, too."

"Well, then, what do you want me to do?"

"Can't you fix *my* tests?"

The Chickenheart looked at Elizabeth with surprise.

"What's this, my dear? Do you think you're a timebomb, too?"

"I can *learn* to be a timebomb," said Elizabeth with conviction. And she knew she could, whatever a timebomb was.

"I don't know," said the Chickenheart, "that anyone can learn that sort of thing. You've either got it or you don't, Miss Elizabeth."

"Call me Lizardbreath. That's my *real* name. And I can get what I want. I got away from my brother, didn't I? And I got here."

The Chickenheart raised his thin, black eyebrows. "You have a point there, my dear. Perhaps you could be a timebomb, after all."

"But not today," said Lizardbreath. "Today I'm gonna learn to spit."

JOHN KESSEL
Invaders

{1990}

John Kessel (1950–), who writes both sf and fantasy, was the first director of the Creative Writing MFA Program at North Carolina State University. In 1985 he co-founded the Sycamore Hill Conference, an ongoing workshop for professional writers of the fantastic. At the peak of cyberpunk's popularity in the mid to late 1980s, Kessel was one of a group of important writers, including Connie Willis and Kim Stanley Robinson, sometimes identified with an alternative stream of "humanist" sf.

Kessel is especially well known for his award-winning short stories, including "Another Orphan" (1982), a fantasy based on Herman Melville's *Moby Dick*; "Buffalo" (1991), which imagines a meeting between Kessel's father and H. G. Wells; and "Stories for Men" (2002), winner of a Tiptree Award for speculative fiction that explores and expands our understanding of gender. Kessel's novels, often colored by his taste for 1930s screwball comedy, include the apocalyptic *Good News from Outer Space* (1989) and *Corrupting Dr. Nice* (1997), a time-travel satire set in a first-century Jerusalem where twenty-first-century commercialism has encouraged a thriving tourist industry, complete with junkets to the Crucifixion. In 1996 Kessel co-edited *Intersections: The Sycamore Hill Anthology*. With James Patrick Kelly, he has also co-edited several notable short-story anthologies, including *Rewired: The Post-Cyberpunk Anthology* (2007) and *The Secret History of Science Fiction* (2009).

"Invaders" is a variation on the classic time-travel story, introduced very early in the history of the genre by H. G. Wells in his first novel, *The Time Machine* (1895). Like many time-travel stories, Kessel's is structured around a series of juxtaposed temporal sites: in 1532, Pizarro and his priests and soldiers have invaded Peru and will soon complete the destruction of the Incan empire; in 2001, apparently friendly and funny aliens, the Krel—a name lifted from the classic film *Forbidden Planet* (1956)—arrive in the middle of a Washington Redskins football game demanding cocaine; and in a third time-stream, "Today," a science-fiction writer, whose description matches that of John Kessel, sits at his desk writing the story we are reading: "Like any drug addict, the SF reader finds desperate justifications for his habit. SF teaches him science. SF helps him avoid 'future shock.' SF changes the world for the better. Right. So does cocaine."

A generic self-consciousness that is both playful and thoughtful is one of the most appealing features of Kessel's writing. Stories such as "Herman Melville: Space Opera Virtuoso" (1980) are as interested in thinking about genre as they are about developing plots and characters. Like other instances of self-aware metafiction including Frederik Pohl's "Day Million" (1966) and Pamela Zoline's "The Heat Death of the Universe" (1967), "Invaders" makes use of a variety of strategies associated with postmodernist fiction, including irony and parody, intertextual appropriations of both earlier sf and mainstream literature, and impossible interactions among an array of fictional worlds, including the world of the fictional author. Kessel's story explores what it means to read and to write science fiction, not least through the challenge to genre conventions that it invokes in its final words: "and everyone lived happily ever after."

15 November 1532: that night no one slept. On the hills outside Cajamarca, the campfires of the Inca's army shone like so many stars in the sky. De Soto had reported that Atahualpa had perhaps forty thousand troops under arms, but looking at the myriad lights spread across those hills, de Candia realized that estimate was, if anything, low.

Against them, Pizarro could throw one hundred foot soldiers, sixty horses, eight muskets, and four harquebuses. Pizarro, his brother Hernando, de Soto, and Benalcázar laid out plans for an ambush. They would invite the Inca to a parley. De Candia and his artillery would be hidden in the building along one side of the square, the cavalry and infantry along the others. De Candia watched Pizarro prowl through the camp that night, checking the men's armor, joking with them, reminding them of the treasure they would have, and the women. The men laughed nervously and whetted their swords.

They might sharpen them until their hands fell off; when morning dawned, they would be slaughtered. De Candia breathed deeply of the thin air and turned from the wall.

Ruiz de Arce, an infantryman with a face like a clenched fist, hailed him as he passed. "Are those guns of yours ready for some work tomorrow?"

"We need prayers more than guns."

"I'm not afraid of these brownies," de Arce said.

"Then you're a half-wit."

"Soto says they have no swords."

The man was probably just trying to reassure himself, but de Candia couldn't abide it. "Will you shut your stinking fool's trap! They don't need swords! If they only spit all at once, we'll be drowned."

Pizarro overheard him. He stormed over, grabbed de Candia's arm, and shook him. "Have they ever seen a horse, Candia? Have they ever felt steel? When you fired the harquebus on the seashore, didn't the town chief pour beer down its barrel as if it were a thirsty god? Pull up your balls and show me you're a man!"

His face was inches away. "Mark me! Tomorrow, Saint James sits on your shoulder, and we win a victory that will cover us in glory for five hundred years."

2 December 2001

"DEE-fense! DEE-fense!" the crowd screamed. During the two-minute warning, Norwood Delacroix limped over to the Redskins' special conditioning coach.

"My knee's about gone," said Delacroix, an outside linebacker with eyebrows that ran together and all the musculature that modern pharmacology could load onto his six-foot-five frame. "I need something."

"You need the power of prayer, my friend. Stoner's eating your lunch."

"Just do it."

The coach selected a popgun from his rack, pressed the muzzle against Delacroix's knee, and pulled the trigger. A flood of well-being rushed up Delacroix's leg. He flexed it tentatively. It felt better than the other one now. Delacroix jogged back onto the field. "DEE-fense!" the fans roared. The overcast sky began to spit frozen rain. The ref blew the whistle, and the Bills broke huddle.

Delacroix looked across at Stoner, the Bills' tight end. The air throbbed with electricity. The quarterback called the signals; the ball was snapped; Stoner surged forward. As Delacroix backpedaled furiously, sudden sunlight flooded the field. His ears buzzed. Stoner jerked left and went right, twisting Delacroix around like a cork in a bottle. His knee popped. Stoner had two steps on him. TD for sure. Delacroix pulled his head down and charged after him.

But instead of continuing downfield, Stoner slowed. He looked straight up into the air. Delacroix hit him at the knees, and they both went down. He'd caught him! The crowd screamed louder, a scream edged with hysteria.

Then Delacroix realized the buzzing wasn't just in his ears. Elation fading, he lifted his head and looked toward the sidelines. The coaches and players were running for the tunnels. The crowd boiled toward the exits, shedding thermoses and beer cups and radios. The sunlight was harshly bright. Delacroix looked up. A huge disk hovered no more than fifty feet above, pinning them in its spotlight. Stoner untangled himself from Delacroix, stumbled to his feet, and ran off the field.

Holy Jesus and the Virgin Mary on toast, Delacroix thought.

He scrambled toward the end zone. The stadium was emptying fast, except for the ones who were getting trampled. The throbbing in the air increased in volume, lowered in pitch, and the flying saucer settled onto the NFL logo on the forty-yard line. The sound stopped as abruptly as if it had been sucked into a sponge.

Out of the corner of his eye, Delacroix saw an NBC cameraman come up next to him, focusing on the ship. Its side divided, and a ramp extended itself to the ground. The cameraman fell back a few steps, but Delacroix held his ground. The inside glowed with the bluish light of a UV lamp.

A shape moved there. It lurched forward to the top of the ramp. A large manlike thing, it advanced with a rolling stagger, like a college freshman at a beer blast. It wore a body-tight red stretchsuit, a white circle on its chest with a lightning bolt through it, some sort of flexible mask over its face. Blond hair covered its head in a kind of brush cut, and two cup-shaped ears poked comically out of the sides of its head. The creature stepped off onto the field, nudging aside the football that lay there.

Delacroix, who had majored in public relations at Michigan State, went forward to greet it. This could be the beginning of an entirely new career. His knee felt great.

He extended his hand. "Welcome," he said. "I greet you in the name of humanity and the United States of America."

"Cocaine," the alien said. "We need cocaine."

Today

I sit at my desk writing a science-fiction story, a tall, thin man wearing jeans, a white T-shirt with the abstract face of a man printed on it, white high-top basketball shoes, and gold-plated wire-rimmed glasses.

In the morning I drink coffee to get me up for the day, and at night I have a gin and tonic to help me relax.

16 November 1532

"What are they waiting for, the shitting dogs!" the man next to de Arce said. "Are they trying to make us suffer?"

“Shut up, will you?” De Arce shifted his armor. Wedged into the stone building on the side of the square, sweating, they had been waiting since dawn, in silence for the most part except for the creak of leather, the uneasy jingle of cascabels on the horses’ trappings. The men stank worse than the restless horses. Some had pissed themselves. A common foot soldier like de Arce was lucky to get a space near enough to the door to see out.

As noon came and went with still no sign of Atahualpa and his retinue, the mood of the men went from impatience to near panic. Then, late in the day, word came that the Indians again were moving toward the town.

An hour later, six thousand brilliantly costumed attendants entered the plaza. They were unarmed. Atahualpa, borne on a golden litter by eight men in cloaks of green feathers that glistened like emeralds in the sunset, rose above them. De Arce heard a slight rattling, looked down, and found that his hand, gripping the sword so tightly the knuckles stood out white, was shaking uncontrollably. He unknotted his fist from the hilt, rubbed the cramped fingers, and crossed himself.

“Quiet now, my brave ones,” Pizarro said.

Father Valverde and Felipillo strode out to the center of the plaza, right through the sea of attendants. The priest had guts. He stopped before the litter of the Inca, short and steady as a fence post. “Greetings, my lord, in the name of Pope Clement VII, His Majesty the Emperor Charles V, and Our Lord and Savior Jesus Christ.”

Atahualpa spoke and Felipillo translated: “Where is this new god?”

Valverde held up the crucifix. “Our God died on the cross many years ago and rose again to Heaven. He appointed the Pope as His viceroy on earth, and the Pope has commanded King Charles to subdue the peoples of the world and convert them to the true faith. The king sent us here to command your obedience and to teach you and your people in this faith.”

“By what authority does this pope give away lands that aren’t his?”

Valverde held up his Bible. “By the authority of the word of God.”

The Inca took the Bible. When Valverde reached out to help him get the cover unclasped, Atahualpa cuffed his arm away. He opened the book and leafed through the pages. After a moment he threw it to the ground. “I hear no words,” he said.

Valverde snatched up the book and stalked back toward Pizarro’s hiding place. “What are you waiting for?” he shouted. “The saints and the Blessed Virgin, the bleeding wounds of Christ himself, cry vengeance! Attack, and I’ll absolve you!”

Pizarro had already stridden into the plaza. He waved his kerchief. “Santiago, and at them!”

On the far side, the harquebuses exploded in an enfilade. The lines of Indians jerked like startled cats. Bells jingling, de Soto's and Hernando's cavalry burst from the lines of doorways on the adjoining side. De Arce clutched his sword and rushed out with the others from the third side.

He felt the power of God in his arm. "Santiago!" he roared at the top of his lungs, and hacked halfway through the neck of his first Indian. Bright blood spurted. He put his boot to the brown man's shoulder and yanked free, lunged for the belly of another wearing a kilt of bright red-and-white checks. The man turned, and the sword caught between his ribs. The hilt was almost twisted from de Arce's grasp as the Indian went down. He pulled free, shrugged another man off his back, and daggered him in the side.

After the first flush of glory, it turned to filthy, hard work, an hour's wade through an ocean of butchery in the twilight, bodies heaped waist-high, boots skidding on the bloody stones. De Arce alone must have killed forty. Only after they'd slaughtered them all and captured the Sapa Inca did it end. A silence settled, broken only by the moans of dying Indians and distant shouts of the cavalry chasing the ones who had managed to break through the plaza wall to escape.

Saint James had indeed sat on their shoulders. Six thousand dead Indians, and not one Spaniard nicked. It was a pure demonstration of the power of prayer.

31 January 2002

It was Colonel Zipp's third session interrogating the alien. So far the thing had kept a consistent story, but not a credible one. The only consideration that kept Zipp from panic at the thought of how his career would suffer if this continued was the rumor that his fellow case officers weren't doing any better with any of the others. That, and the fact that the Krel possessed technology that would reestablish American superiority for another two hundred years. He took a drag on his cigarette, the first of his third pack of the day.

"Your name?" Zipp asked.

"You may call me Flash."

Zipp studied the red union suit, the lightning bolt. With the flat chest, the rounded shoulders, pointed upper lip, and pronounced under-bite, the alien looked like a cross between Wally Cleaver and the Mock Turtle. "Is this some kind of joke?"

"What is a joke?"

"Never mind." Zipp consulted his notes. "Where are you from?"

"God has ceded us an empire extending over sixteen solar systems in the Orion arm of the galaxy, including the systems around the stars you know as Tau Ceti, Epsilon Eridani, Alpha Centauri, and the red dwarf Barnard's star."

"God gave you an empire?"

"Yes. We were hoping He'd give us your world, but all He kept talking about was your cocaine."

The alien's translating device had to be malfunctioning. "You're telling me that God sent you for cocaine?"

"No. He just told us about it. We collect chemical compounds for their aesthetic interest. These alkaloids do not exist on our world. Like the music you humans value so highly, they combine familiar elements—carbon, hydrogen, nitrogen, oxygen—in pleasing new ways."

The colonel leaned back, exhaled a cloud of smoke. "You consider cocaine like—like a symphony?"

"Yes. Understand, Colonel, no material commodity alone could justify the difficulties of interstellar travel. We come here for aesthetic reasons."

"You seem to know what cocaine is already. Why don't you just synthesize it yourself?"

"If you valued a unique work of aboriginal art, would you be satisfied with a mass-produced duplicate manufactured in your hometown? Of course not. And we are prepared to pay you well, in a coin you can use."

"We don't need any coins. If you want cocaine, tell us how your ships work."

"That is one of the coins we had in mind. Our ships operate according to a principle of basic physics. Certain fundamental physical reactions are subject to the belief system of the beings promoting them. If I believe that X is true, then X is more probably true than if I did not believe so."

The colonel leaned forward again. "We know that already. We call it the 'observer effect.' Our great physicist Werner Heisenberg—"

"Yes. I'm afraid we carry this principle a little further than that."

"What do you mean?"

Flash smirked. "I mean that our ships move through interstellar space by the power of prayer."

13 May 1533

Atahualpa offered to fill a room twenty-two feet long and seventeen feet wide with gold up to a line as high as a man could reach, if the Spaniards would let him go. They were skeptical. How long would this take? Pizarro asked. Two months, Atahualpa said.

Pizarro allowed the word to be sent out, and over the next several months, bearers, chewing the coca leaf in order to negotiate the mountain roads under such burdens, brought in tons of gold artifacts. They brought plates and vessels, life-sized statues of women and men, gold lobsters and spiders and alpacas, intricately fashioned ears of maize, every kernel reproduced, with leaves of gold and tassels of spun silver.

Martin Bueno was one of the advance scouts sent with the Indians to Cuzco, the capital of the empire. They found it to be the legendary city of gold. The Incas, having no money, valued precious metals only as ornament. In Cuzco the very walls of the Sun Temple, Coricancha, were plated with gold. Adjoining the temple was a ritual garden where gold maize plants supported gold butterflies, gold bees pollinated gold flowers.

"Enough loot that you'll shit in a different gold pot every day for the rest of your life," Bueno told his friend Diego Leguizano upon his return to Cajamarca.

They ripped the plating off the temple walls and had it carried to Cajamarca. There they melted it down into ingots.

The huge influx of gold into Europe was to cause an economic catastrophe. In Peru, at the height of the conquest, a pair of shoes cost $850, and a bottle of wine $1,700. When their old horseshoes wore out, iron being unavailable, the cavalry shod their horses with silver.

21 April 2003

In the executive washroom of Bellingham, Winston, and McNeese, Jason Prescott snorted a couple of lines and was ready for the afternoon. He returned to the brokerage to find the place in a whispering uproar. In his office sat one of the Krel. Prescott's secretary was about to piss himself. "It asked specifically for you," he said.

What would Attila the Hun do in this situation? Prescott thought. He went into the office. "Jason Prescott," he said. "What can I do for you, Mr. . . .?"

The alien's bloodshot eyes surveyed him. "Flash. I wish to make an investment."

"Investments are our business." Rumors had flown around the New York Merc for a month that the Krel were interested in investing. They had earned vast sums selling information to various computer, environmental, and biotech firms. Several of the aliens had come to observe trading in the currencies pit last week, and only yesterday Jason had heard from a reliable source that they were considering opening an account with Merrill Lynch. "What brings you to our brokerage?"

"Not the brokerage. You. We heard that you are the most ruthless currencies trader in this city. We worship efficiency. You are efficient."

Right. Maybe there was a hallucinogen in the toot. "I'll call in some of our foreign-exchange experts. We can work up an investment plan for your consideration in a week."

"We already have an investment plan. We are, as you say in the markets, 'long' in dollars. We want you to sell dollars and buy francs for us.

"The franc is pretty strong right now. It's likely to hold for the next six months. We'd suggest—"

"We wish to buy $50 billion worth of francs."

Prescott stared. "That's not a very good investment." Flash said nothing. The silence grew uncomfortable. "I suppose if we stretch it out over a few months, and hit the exchanges in Hong Kong and London at the same time—"

"We want these francs bought in the next week. For the week after that, a second $50 billion. Fifty billion a week until we tell you to stop."

Hallucinogens for sure. "That doesn't make any sense."

"We can take our business elsewhere."

Prescott thought about it. It would take every trick he knew—and he'd have to invent some new ones—to carry this off. The dollar was going to drop through the floor, while the franc would punch through the sell-stops of every trader on ten world markets. The exchanges would scream bloody murder. The repercussions would auger holes in every economy north of Antarctica. Governments would intervene. It would make the historic Hunt silver squeeze look like a game of Monopoly.

Besides, it made no sense. Not only was it criminally irresponsible, it was stupid. The Krel would squander every dime they'd earned.

Then he thought about the commission on $50 billion a week.

Prescott looked across at the alien. From the right point of view, Flash resembled a barrel-chested college undergraduate from Special Effects U. He felt an urge to giggle, a euphoric feeling of power. "When do we start?"

19 May 1533

In the fields the *purics*, singing praise to Atahualpa, son of the sun, harvested the maize. At night they celebrated by getting drunk on *chicha*. It was, they said, the most festive month of the year.

Pedro Sancho did his drinking in the dark of the treasure room, in the smoke of the smelters' fire. For months he had been troubled by nightmares of the heaped bodies lying in the plaza. He tried to ignore the abuse of the Indian women, the brutality toward the men. He worked hard. As Pizarro's squire, it was his job to record daily the tally of Atahualpa's ransom. When he ran low on ink, he taught the *purics* to make it for him from soot and the juice of berries. They learned readily.

Atahualpa heard about the ink and one day came to him. "What are you doing with those marks?" he said, pointing to the scribe's tally book.

"I'm writing the list of gold objects to be melted down."

"What is this 'writing'?"

Sancho was nonplussed. Over the months of Atahualpa's captivity, Sancho had become impressed by the sophistication of the Incas. Yet they were also queerly backward. They had no money. It was not beyond belief that they should not know how to read and write.

"By means of these marks, I can record the words that people speak. That's writing. Later other men can look at these marks and see what was said. That's reading."

"Then this is a kind of quipu?" Atahualpa's servants had demonstrated for Sancho the quipu, a system of knotted strings by which the Incas kept tallies. "Show me how it works," Atahualpa said.

Sancho wrote on the page: *God have mercy on us.* He pointed. "This, my lord, is a representation of the word 'God.'"

Atahualpa looked skeptical. "Mark it here." He held out his hand, thumbnail extended.

Sancho wrote "God" on the Inca's thumbnail.

"Say nothing now." Atahualpa advanced to one of the guards, held out his thumbnail. "What does this mean?" he asked.

"God," the man replied.

Sancho could tell the Inca was impressed, but he barely showed it. That the Sapa Inca had maintained such dignity throughout his captivity tore at Sancho's heart.

"This writing is truly a magical accomplishment," Atahualpa told him. "You must teach my *amautas* this art."

Later, when the viceroy Estete, Father Valverde, and Pizarro came to chide him for the slow pace of the gold shipments, Atahualpa tested each of them separately. Estete and Valverde each said the word "God." Atahualpa held his thumbnail out to the conquistador.

Estete chuckled. For the first time in his experience, Sancho saw Pizarro flush. He turned away. "I don't waste my time on the games of children," Pizarro said.

Atahualpa stared at him. "But your common soldiers have this art."

"Well, I don't."

"Why not?"

"I was a swineherd. Swineherds don't need to read."

"You are not a swineherd now."

Pizarro glared at the Inca. "I don't need to read to order you put to death." He marched out of the room.

After the others had left, Sancho told Atahualpa, "You ought not to humiliate the governor in front of his men."

"He humiliates himself," Atahualpa said. "There is no skill in which a leader ought to let himself stand behind his followers."

Today

The part of this story about the Incas is as historically accurate as I could make it, but this Krel business is science fiction. I even stole the name "Krel" from a 1950s SF flick. I've been addicted to SF for years. In the evening my wife and I wash the bad taste of the news out of our mouths by watching old movies on videotape.

A scientist, asked why he read SF, replied, "Because in science fiction the experiments always work." Things in SF stories work out more neatly than in reality. Nothing is impossible. Spaceships move faster than light. Atomic weapons are neutralized. Disease is abolished. People travel in time. Why, Isaac Asimov even wrote a story once that ended with the reversal of entropy!

The descendants of the Incas, living in grinding poverty, find their most lucrative crop in coca, which they refine into cocaine and sell in vast quantities to North Americans.

23 August 2008

"Catalog number 208," said John Bostock. "Georges Seurat, *Bathers*."

FRENCH GOVERNMENT FALLS, the morning *Times* had announced.

JAPAN BANS U.S. IMPORTS. FOOD RIOTS IN MADRID. But Bostock had barely glanced at the newspaper over his coffee; he was buzzed on caffeine and adrenaline, and it was too late to stop the auction, the biggest day of his career. The lot list would make an art historian faint. *Guernica. The Potato Eaters. The Scream.* Miró, Rembrandt, Vermeer, Gauguin, Matisse, Constable, Magritte, Pollock, Mondrian. Six desperate governments had contributed to the sale. And rumor had it the Krel would be among the bidders.

The rumor proved true. In the front row, beside the solicitor Patrick McClannahan, sat one of the unlikely aliens, wearing red tights and a lightning-bolt insignia. The famous Flash. The creature leaned back lazily while McClannahan did the bidding with a discreetly raised forefinger.

Bidding on the Seurat started at ten million and went orbital. It soon became clear that the main bidders were Flash and the U.S. government.

The American campaign against cultural imperialism was getting a lot of press, ironic since the Yanks could afford to challenge the Krel only because of the technology the Krel had lavished on them. The probability suppressor that prevented the detonation of atomic weapons. The autodidactic antivirus that cured most diseases. There was talk of an immortality drug. Of a time machine. So what if the European Community was in the sixth month of an economic crisis that threatened to dissolve the unifying efforts of the past twenty years? So what if Krel meddling destroyed humans' capacity to run the world? The Americans were making money, and the Krel were richer than Croesus.

The bidding reached $1.2 billion, at which point the American ambassador gave up. Bostock tapped his gavel. "Sold," he said in his most cultured voice, nodding toward the alien.

The crowd murmured. The American stood. "If you can't see what they're doing to us, then you don't deserve our help!"

For a minute Bostock thought the auction was going to turn into a riot. Then the new owner of the pointillist masterpiece stood, smiled. Ingenuous, clumsy. "We know that there has been considerable disquiet over our purchase of these historic works of art," Flash said. "Let me promise you, they will be displayed where all humans—not just those who can afford to visit the great museums—can see them."

The crowd's murmur turned into applause. Bostock put down his gavel and joined in. The American ambassador and his aides stalked out. Thank God, Bostock thought. The attendants brought out the next item.

"Catalog number 209," Bostock said. "Leonardo da Vinci, *Mona Lisa*."

26 July 1533

The soldiers, seeing the heaps of gold grow, became anxious. They consumed stores of coca meant for the Inca messengers. They fought over women. They grumbled over the airs of Atahualpa. "Who does he think he is? The governor treats him like a hidalgo."

Father Valverde cursed Pizarro's inaction. That morning, after matins, he spoke with Estete. "The governor has agreed to meet and decide what to do," Estete said.

"It's about time. What about Soto?" De Soto was against harming Atahualpa. He maintained that, since the Inca had paid the ransom, he should be set free, no matter what danger this would present. Pizarro had stalled. Last week he had sent de Soto away to check out rumors that the Tahuantinsuyans were massing for an attack to free the Sapa Inca.

Estete smiled. "Soto's not back yet."

They went to the building Pizarro had claimed as his, and found the others already gathered. The Incas had no tables or proper chairs, so the Spaniards were forced to sit in a circle on mats as the Indians did. Pizarro, only a few years short of threescore, sat on a low stool of the sort that Atahualpa used when he held court. His left leg, whose old battle wound still pained him at times, was stretched out before him. His loose white shirt had been cleaned by some *puric*'s wife. Valverde sat beside him. Gathered were Estete, Benalcázar, Almagro, de Candia, Riquelme, Pizarro's young cousin Pedro, the scribe Pedro Sancho, Valverde, and the governor himself.

As Valverde and Estete had agreed, the viceroy went first. "The men are jumpy, Governor," Estete said. "The longer we stay cooped up here, the longer we give these savages the chance to plot against us."

"We should wait until Soto returns," de Candia said, already looking guilty as a dog. "We've got nothing but rumors so far. I won't kill a man on a rumor."

Silence. Trust de Candia to speak aloud what they were all thinking but were not ready to say. The man had no political judgment—but maybe it was just as well to face it directly. Valverde seized the opportunity. "Atahualpa plots against us even as we speak," he told Pizarro. "As governor, you are responsible for our safety. Any court would convict him of treason, and execute him."

"He's a king," de Candia said. Face flushed, he spat out a cud of leaves. "We don't have authority to try him. We should ship him back to Spain and let the emperor decide what to do."

"This is not a king," Valverde said. "It isn't even a man. It is a creature that worships demons, that weaves spells about half-wits like Candia. You saw him discard the Bible. Even after my months of teaching, after the extraordinary mercies we've shown him, he doesn't acknowledge the primacy of Christ! He cares only for his wives and his pagan gods. Yet he's satanically clever. Don't think we can let him go. If we do, the day will come when he'll have our hearts for dinner."

"We can take him with us to Cuzco," Benalcázar said. "We don't know the country. His presence would guarantee our safe conduct."

"We'll be traveling over rough terrain, carrying tons of gold, with not enough horses," Almagro said. "If we take him with us, we'll be ripe for ambush at every pass."

"They won't attack if we have him."

"He could escape. We can't trust the rebel Indians to stay loyal to us. If they turned to our side, they can just as easily turn back to his."

"And remember, he escaped before, during the civil war," Valverde said. "Huascar, his brother, lived to regret that. If Atahualpa didn't hesitate to murder his own brother, do you think he'll stop for us?"

"He's given us his word," Candia said.

"What good is the word of a pagan?"

Pizarro, silent until now, spoke. "He has no reason to think the word of a Christian much better."

Valverde felt his blood rise. Pizarro knew as well as any of them what was necessary. What was he waiting for? "He keeps a hundred wives! He betrayed his brother! He worships the sun!" The priest grabbed Pizarro's hand, held it up between them so they could both see the scar there, where Pizarro had gotten cut preventing one of his own men from killing Atahualpa. "He isn't worth an ounce of the blood you spilled to save him."

"He's proved worth twenty-four tons of gold." Pizarro's eyes were hard and calm.

"There is no alternative!" Valverde insisted. "He serves the Antichrist! God demands his death."

At last Pizarro seemed to have gotten what he wanted. He smiled. "Far be it from me to ignore the command of God," he said. "Since God forces us to it, let's discuss how He wants it done."

5 October 2009

"What a lovely country Chile is from the air. You should be proud of it."

"I'm from Los Angeles," Leon Sepulveda said. "And as soon as we close this deal, I'm going back."

"The mountains are impressive."

"Nothing but earthquakes and slag. You can have Chile."

"Is it for sale?"

Sepulveda stared at the Krel. "I was just kidding."

They sat at midnight in the arbor, away from the main buildings of Iguassu Microelectronics of Santiago. The night was cold and the arbor was overgrown and the bench needed a paint job—but then, a lot of things had been getting neglected in the past couple of years. All the more reason to put yourself in a financial situation where you didn't have to worry. Though Sepulveda had to admit that, since the advent of the Krel, such positions were harder to come by, and less secure once you had them.

Flash's earnestness aroused a kind of horror in him. It had something to do with Sepulveda's suspicion that this thing next to him was as superior to him as he was to a guinea pig, plus the alien's aura of drunken adolescence, plus his own willingness, despite the feeling that the situation was out of control, to make a deal with it. He took another Valium and tried to calm down.

"What assurance do I have that this time-travel method will work?"

"It will work. If you don't like it in Chile, or back in Los Angeles, you can use it to go into the past."

Sepulveda swallowed. "Okay. You need to read and sign these papers."

"We don't read."

"You don't read Spanish? How about English?"

"We don't read at all. We used to, but we gave it up. Once you start reading, it gets out of control. You tell yourself you're just going to stick to nonfiction—but pretty soon you graduate to fiction. After that, you can't kick the habit. And then there's the oppression."

"Oppression?"

"Sure. I mean, I like a story as much as the next Krel, but any pharmacologist can show that arbitrary cultural, sexual, and economic assumptions determine every significant aspect of a story. Literature is a political tool used by ruling elites to ensure their hegemony. Anyone who denies that is a fish who can't see the water it swims in. Or the fascist who tells you, as he beats you, that those blows you feel are your own delusion."

"Right. Look, can we settle this? I've got things to do."

"This is, of course, the key to temporal translation. The past is another arbitrary construct. Language creates reality. Reality is smoke."

"Well, this time machine better not be smoke. We're going to find out the truth about the past. Then we'll change it."

"By all means. Find the truth." Flash turned to the last page of the contract, pricked his thumb, and marked a thumbprint on the signature line.

After they sealed the agreement, Sepulveda walked the alien back to the courtyard. A Krel flying pod with Vermeer's *The Letter* varnished onto its door sat at the focus of three spotlights. The painting was scorched almost into unrecognizability by atmospheric friction. The door peeled downward from the top, became a canvas-surfaced ramp.

"I saw some interesting lines inscribed on the coastal desert on the way here," Flash said. "A bird, a tree, a big spider. In the sunset, it looked beautiful. I didn't think you humans were capable of such art. Is it for sale?"

"I don't think so. That was done by some old Indians a long time ago. If you're really interested, though, I can look into it."

"Not necessary." Flash waggled his ears, wiped his feet on Mark Rothko's *Earth and Green*, and staggered into the pod.

26 July 1533

Atahualpa looked out of the window of the stone room in which he was kept, across the plaza where the priest Valverde stood outside his chapel after his morning prayers. Valverde's chapel had been the house of the virgins; the women of the house had long since been raped by the Spanish soldiers, as the house had been by the Spanish god. Valverde spoke with Estete. They were getting ready to kill him, Atahualpa knew. He had known ever since the ransom had been paid.

He looked beyond the thatched roofs of the town to the crest of the mountains, where the sun was about to break in his tireless circuit of Tahuantinsuyu. The cold morning air raised dew on the metal of the chains that bound him hand and foot. The metal was queer, different from the bronze the *purics* worked or the gold and silver Atahualpa was used to wearing. If gold was the sweat of the sun, and silver the tears of the moon, what was this metal, dull and hard like the men who held him captive, yet strong, too—stronger, he had come to realize, than the Inca. It, like the men who brought it, was beyond his experience. It gave evidence that Tahuantinsuyu, the Four Quarters of the World, was not all the world after all. Atahualpa had thought none but savages lived beyond their lands. He'd imagined no man readier to face ruthless necessity than himself. He had ordered the death of Huascar, his own brother. But he was learning that these men were capable of enormities against which the Inca civil war would seem a minor discomfort.

That evening they took him out of the building to the plaza. In the plaza's center, the soldiers had piled a great heap of wood on flagstones, some of which were still stained with the blood of the six thousand slaughtered attendants. They bound him to a stake amid the heaped fagots, and Valverde appealed one last time for the Inca to renounce Satan and be baptized. He promised that if Atahualpa would do so, he would earn God's mercy: they would strangle him rather than burn him to death.

The rough wood pressed against his spine. Atahualpa looked at the priest, and the men gathered around, and the women weeping beyond the circle of soldiers. The moon, his mother, rode high above. Firelight flickered on the breastplates of the Spaniards, and from the waiting torches drifted the smell of pitch. The men shifted nervously. Creak of leather, clink of metal. Men on horses shod with silver. Sweat shining on Valverde's forehead. Valverde stared at Atahualpa as if he desired something, but was prepared to destroy him without getting it if need be. The priest thought he was showing Atahualpa resolve, but Atahualpa saw that beneath Valverde's face he was a dead man. Pizarro stood aside, with the Spanish viceroy Estete and the scribe. Pizarro was an old man. He ought to be sitting quietly in some village, outside the violence of life, giving advice and teaching the children. What kind of world did he come from, that sent men into old age still charged with the lusts and bitterness of the young?

Pizarro, too, looked as if he wanted this to end.

Atahualpa knew that it would not end. This was only the beginning. These men would suffer for this moment as they had already suffered for it all their lives, seeking the pain blindly over oceans, jungles, deserts, probing it like a sore tooth until they'd found and grasped it in this plaza of Cajamarca, thinking they sought gold. They'd come all this way to create a moment that would reveal to them their own incurable disease. Now they had it. In a few minutes, they thought, it would at last be over, that once he was gone, they would be free—but Atahualpa knew it would be with them ever after, and with their children and grandchildren and the million others of their race in times to come, whether they knew of this hour in the plaza or not, because they were sick and would pass the sickness on with their breath and semen. They could not burn out the sickness so easily as they could burn the Son of God to ash. This was a great tragedy, but it contained a huge jest. They were caught in a wheel of the sky and could not get out. They must destroy themselves.

"Have your way, priest," Atahualpa said. "Then strangle me, and bear my body to Cuzco, to be laid with my ancestors." He knew they would not do it, and so would add an additional curse to their faithlessness.

He had one final curse. He turned to Pizarro. "You will have responsibility for my children."

Pizarro looked at the pavement. They put up the torch and took Atahualpa from the pyre. Valverde poured water on his head and spoke words in the tongue of his god. Then they sat him upon a stool, bound him to another stake, set the loop of cord around his neck, slid the rod through the cord, and turned it. His women knelt at his side and wept. Valverde spoke more words. Atahualpa felt the cord, woven by the hands of some faithful *puric* of Cajamarca, tighten. The cord was well made. It cut his access to the night air; Atahualpa's lungs fought, he felt his body spasm, and then the plaza became cloudy and he heard the voice of the moon.

12 January 2011

Israel Lamont was holding big-time when a Krel monitor zipped over the alley. A minute later one of the aliens lurched around the corner and approached him. Lamont was ready.

"I need to achieve an altered state of consciousness," the alien said. It wore a red suit, a lightning bolt on its chest.

"I'm your man," Lamont said. "You just try this. Best stuff on the street." He held the vial out in the palm of his hand. "Go ahead, try it." The Krel took it.

"How much?"

"One million."

The Krel gave him a couple hundred thousand. "Down payment," it said. "How does one administer this?"

"What, you don't know? I thought you guys were hip."

"I have been working hard, and am unacquainted."

This was ripe. "You burn it," Lamont said.

The Krel started toward the trash-barrel fire. Before he could empty the vial into it, Lamont stopped him. "Wait up, homes! You use a pipe. Here, I'll show you."

Lamont pulled a pipe from his pocket, torched up, and inhaled. The Krel watched him. Brown eyes like a dog's. Goofy honkie face. The rush took him, and Lamont saw in the alien's face a peculiar need. The thing was hungry. Desperate.

"I may try?" The alien reached out. Its hand trembled.

Lamont handed over the pipe. Clumsily, the creature shook a block of crack into the bowl. Its beaklike upper lip, however, prevented it from getting its mouth tight against the stem. It fumbled with the pipe, from somewhere producing a book of matches. "Shit, I'll light it," Lamont said.

The Krel waited while Lamont held his Bic over the bowl. Nothing happened. "Inhale, man."

The creature inhaled. The blue flame played over the crack; smoke boiled through the bowl. The creature drew in steadily for what seemed to be minutes. Serious capacity. The crack burned totally through. Finally the Krel exhaled.

It looked at Lamont. Its eyes were bright.

"Good shit?" Lamont said.

"A remarkable stimulant effect."

"Right." Lamont looked over his shoulder toward the alley's entrance. It was getting dark. Yet he hesitated to ask for the rest of the money.

"Will you talk with me?" the Krel asked, swaying slightly.

Surprised, Lamont said, "Okay. Come with me."

Lamont led the Krel back to a deserted store that abutted the alley. They went inside and sat down on some crates against the wall.

"Something I been wondering about you," Lamont said. "You guys are coming to own the world. You fly across the planets, Mars and that shit. What you want with crack?"

"We seek to broaden our minds."

Lamont snorted. "Right. You might as well hit yourself in the head with a hammer."

"We seek escape," the alien said.

"I don't buy that, neither. What you got to escape from?"

The Krel looked at him. "Nothing."

They smoked another pipe. The Krel leaned back against the wall, arms at its sides like a limp doll. It started a queer coughing sound, chest spasming. Lamont thought it was choking and tried to slap it on the back. "Don't do that," it said. "I'm laughing."

"Laughing? What's so funny?"

"I lied to Colonel Zipp," it said. "We want cocaine for kicks."

Lamont relaxed a little. "I hear you now."

"We do everything for kicks."

"Makes for hard living."

"Better than maintaining consciousness continuously without interruption."

"You said it."

"Human beings cannot stand too much reality," the Krel said. "We don't blame you. Human beings! Disgust, horror, shame. Nothing personal."

"You bet."

"Nonbeing penetrates that in which there is no space."

"Uh-huh."

The alien laughed again. "I lied to Sepulveda, too. Our time machines take people to the past they believe in. There is no other past. You can't change it."

"Who the fuck's Sepulveda?"

"Let's do some more," it said.

They smoked one more. "Good shit," it said. "Just what I wanted." The Krel slid off the crate. Its head lolled. "Here is the rest of your payment," it whispered, and died.

Lamont's heart raced. He looked at the Krel's hand, lying open on the floor. In it was a full-sized ear of corn, fashioned of gold, with tassels of finely spun silver wire.

Today

It's not just physical laws that science-fiction readers want to escape. Just as commonly, they want to escape human nature. In pursuit of this, SF offers comforting alternatives to the real world. For instance, if you start reading an SF story about some abused wimp, you can be pretty sure that by chapter two he's going to discover he has secret powers unavailable to those tormenting him, and by the end of the book, he's going to save the universe. SF is full of this sort of thing, from the power fantasy of the alienated child to the alternate history where Hitler is strangled in his cradle and the Library of Alexandria is saved from the torch.

Science fiction may in this way be considered as much an evasion of reality as any mind-distorting drug. I know that sounds a little harsh, but think about it. An alkaloid like cocaine or morphine invades the central nervous system. It reduces pain, produces euphoria, enhances our perceptions. Under its influence we imagine we have supernormal abilities. Limits dissolve. Soon, hardly aware of what's happened to us, we're addicted.

Science fiction has many of the same qualities. The typical reader comes to SF at a time of suffering. He seizes on it as a way to deal with his pain. It's bigger than his life. It's astounding. Amazing. Fantastic. Some grow out of it; many don't. Anyone who's been around SF for a while can cite examples of longtime readers as hooked and deluded as crack addicts.

Like any drug addict, the SF reader finds desperate justifications for his habit. SF teaches him science. SF helps him avoid "future shock." SF changes the world for the better. Right. So does cocaine.

Having been an SF user myself, however, I have to say that, living in a world of cruelty, immersed in a culture that grinds people into fish meal like some brutal machine, with histories of destruction stretching behind us back to the Pleistocene, I find it hard to sneer at the desire to escape. Even if escape is delusion.

18 October 1527

Timu drove the foot plow into the ground, leaned back to break the crust, drew out the pointed pole, and backed up a step to let his wife, Collyur, turn the earth with her hoe. To his left was his brother, Okya; and to his right, his cousin, Tupa; before them, their wives planting the seed. Most of the *purics* of Cajamarca were there, strung out in a line across the terrace, the men wielding the foot plows, and the women or children carrying the sacks of seed potatoes.

As he looked up past Collyur's shoulders to the edge of the terrace, he saw a strange man approach from the post road. The man stumbled into the next terrace up from them, climbed down steps to their level. He was plainly excited.

Collyur was waiting for Timu to break the next row; she looked up at him questioningly.

"Who is that?" Timu said, pointing past her at the man.

She stood up straight and looked over her shoulder. The other men had noticed, too, and stopped their work.

"A *chasqui* come from the next town," said Okya.

"A *chasqui* would go to the *curaca*," said Tupa.

"He's not dressed like a *chasqui*," Timu said.

The man came up to them. Instead of a cape, loincloth, and flowing *onka*, the man wore uncouth clothing: cylinders of fabric that bound his legs tightly, a white short-sleeved shirt that bore on its front the face of a man, and flexible white sandals that covered all his foot to the ankle. He shivered in the spring cold.

He was extraordinarily tall. His face, paler than a normal man's, was long, his nose too straight, mouth too small, and lips too thin. Upon his face he wore a device of gold wire that, hooking over his ears, held disks of crystal before his eyes. The man's hands were large, his limbs long and spiderlike. He moved suddenly, awkwardly.

Gasping for air, the stranger spoke rapidly the most abominable Quechua Timu had ever heard.

"Slow down," Timu said. "I don't understand."

"What year is this?" the man asked.

"What do you mean?"

"I mean, what is the year?"

"It is the thirty-fourth year of the reign of the Sapa Inca Huayna Capac."

The man spoke some foreign word. "Goddamn," he said in a language foreign to Timu, but which you or I would recognize as English. "I made it."

Timu went to the *curaca*, and the *curaca* told Timu to take the stranger in. The stranger told them that his name was "Chuan." But Timu's three-year-old daughter, Curi, reacting to the man's sudden gestures, unearthly thinness, and piping speech, laughed and called him "the Bird." So he was ever after to be known in that town.

There he lived a long and happy life, earned trust and respect, and brought great good fortune. He repaid them well for their kindness, alerting the people of Tahuantinsuyu to the coming of the invaders. When the first Spaniards landed on their shores a few years later, they were slaughtered to the last man, and everyone lived happily ever after.

GENE WOLFE

Useful Phrases

{1992}

Gene Wolfe (1931–) was raised in Texas, served in the Korean War, earned a degree in engineering, and settled in a suburb of Chicago. Although he spent a number of years working as an engineer and editing the magazine *Plant Engineering*, his science fiction does not emphasize technological expertise: it focuses on historical, philosophical, and spiritual themes, illustrated quite soundly by scientific speculation. He describes himself as a devout Catholic. He is best known for the multivolume series *The Book of the New Sun* (1980–83), *The Book of the Long Sun* (1993–96), *The Book of the Short Sun* (1999–2001), and *Wizard Knight* (2004), but he has also written magisterial novellas, including the three-novella cycle *The Fifth Head of Cerberus* (collected 1972), "Seven American Nights" (1978), and three stories with variations on the title of the first one, "The Island of Dr. Death and Other Stories" (collected as *The Wolfe Archipelago*, 1983). He has also written a number of stand-alone novels, as well as many short stories. In addition to science fiction, many of his works, including "Useful Phrases," might be thought of as ghost stories.

Wolfe's science fiction often has the trappings of fantasy, as in *The Book of the New Sun*, and his fantasy is as rigorously extrapolated and schematized as his science fiction, exemplified by the levels of existence outlined in *Wizard Knight*. Wolfe, in short, writes fiction that is difficult to categorize, and this is not the only difficulty that his fiction poses. His highly allusive work uses references ranging from Greek and Roman classics to Gnosticism, from comic books to Dickens. His fiction is also ambiguous, with multiple meanings blossoming from any action, utterance, figure of speech, or symbol. It is always beautifully crafted: every word, cadence, sentence, and clue is meticulously chosen. Thus, his stories are rewarding in direct proportion to the reader's efforts.

"Useful Phrases" is testimony to that last statement. Upon first reading, it is a story of alien contact with parallels to the movie *E.T.*, complete with government spies trying to capture the gentle alien. Because the story is somewhat familiar, is written so gracefully, and has echoes of a parable or a fairy tale, it has immediate rewards. The story is open-ended, however, its ambiguities providing the revelations of dream rather than chronicle. Like Ursula K. Le Guin's "Nine Lives" (1969), it evokes loneliness and the desire to make connections with others, as well as the responsibilities we have to one another. Another fruitful set of meanings might arise from considering how this story reminds one of the Christian journey from this life to the next, and yet another from a consideration of the various meanings of alienation. "Useful Phrases," like all Wolfe's stories, exemplifies in a very complex way sf's potential for literalizing metaphors while demanding that the reader be willing to arrive at multiple interpretations rather than authoritatively singular meanings.

I.

Show Me Something Better

I found the phrase book in my pocket. That itself seems to me extraordinary and significant, for I have a great many books, both at home—to confess the truth, my small apartment is furnished with little else—and in my bookshop. I need not, I hope, describe my shop to you, who have been in it so often. There are a great many used books there, as you know, a few new ones, and a small rack with magazines. There is a cat asleep in the window; her name is Lafiondalinda. There is the aspidistra, the cash register, and me. Mine is the last bookshop in the city, and has been for many years, to wrap purchases in brown paper and tie the package with string. I have some customers who give me their trade for that reason alone.

I frequently buy entire grocery boxes of books, when they can be bought cheaply enough, without examining their contents very thoroughly. After all, if I can get the whole boxful for three dollars, and I've seen two books that should bring five or more each, why shouldn't I? When I have more time, I go through the box with care, put the junk into the twenty-five-cent bin I set out on the sidewalk on fine days and (alas!) take home a book or three that I imagine I may someday wish to read myself.

No doubt the phrase book reached my pocket by that route, though I have no memory of having put it there. On a day in late winter or early spring, I must have purchased such a box (I wonder what else was in it?) from somebody who was moving. (I think I can guess, now, where he was going.) It must have intrigued me, even then, though not so much that I remembered it when I reached home. At the tail end of October, when the first ice storm swept in from the plains, I wore my winter coat again and discovered it.

It is small, and by no means thick, with a handsome blue cover I take to be simulated leather. The odd script on this cover means (as I now know) no more than "Useful Phrases"—*Tohish Ablar*. The full title, from the title page, is *Tohish Ablar Sens-Orriyya Ert*, that is to say, "Useful Phrases for Piteous Visitors to Earth." (I am guessing at the final word, which does not occur elsewhere; but this identification seems to me very probable.)

At first I could not make heads nor tails of the writing, of course. But opposite each phrase in the script of Tcôvé, the book supplies both a phonetic translation (likewise in the fifty-three characters of the diloveta, naturally) and a plain, written version in the terrestrial language involved: *Tem um melhor?* for example, which is "Show me something better" in Portuguese.

I concentrated on the English and French at first, for obvious reasons, and they provided me with the pronunciation of the characters of the diloveta, six of which are pronounced alike (as *P*) but one of which is pronounced in five different ways (*K, Q, CH, CH* in German *ich, X,* and *VK*) depending upon its position in the word and the word's in the sentence. As was only to be expected, I supposed then that the language was a merely terrestrial one with which I was unfamiliar.

Even so, many of the phrases thus translated struck me as peculiar. Who would wish to say, "You no longer recognize her," "Mine is a similar address," or "I will tell the trees to be quiet"? I studied all these phrases diligently, however—so much so that I sometimes found myself murmuring in my bath, *Pava pacch, tîsh ùtra. Neéve sort dufiji.* "How like a ghost are the fountain's waters! The flood carries away my riches." The paper is marvelously thin, and yet completely opaque; the print sharp-edged even when viewed through my best magnifying glass.

All this time, I should explain, I was fairly itching to put my bookplate in the book and index it as a permanent part of my library, neither of which I felt that I could properly do until I learned the location of Tcôvé, the linguistic group or groups to which its tongue belonged, and something of its history. I consulted atlases and encyclopedias, and found all equally unhelpful. Tcôvé, I decided, was surely one of those nations (like Deutschland and Hellas) which we call by quite different names. Still, I persisted in my determination. *A pêpennes tilyat scémpterrissomatya oto dommrosmoreii*, as has been so finely said: "I shall know the names of the angels on the peaks of my homeland."

II.

The Three Visitors

A year or more passed while I studied and planned (though only for my own amusement at first) the advertisement I eventually ran. Should I offer a reward? It could not be a large one—a hundred dollars, perhaps, or five free books. Should I include no more than my telephone number? And if so, should it be the number of the store or that of my apartment? What about a coded box at the newspaper, such as one sees in the Personals? In the end, I settled for the wording I give here:

HESITANT SPEAKER OF TCOVESE
WOULD WELCOME ACQUAINTANCE
OF NATIVE SPEAKERS
& DISCUSSION OF LANGUAGE AND CULTURE
PREVIOUS PAGES BOOKSHOP
444½ N. WASHINGTON

I was greatly tempted to write the ad itself in Tcôvese, as you may imagine; but it would have lost half its force (or so I felt) in the Roman alphabet, and would almost certainly have been disfigured by the printer.

My first visitor arrived on the first day my ad ran. He showed me a badge, and asked to speak with me in private. I took him into the little back room I call my office. He asked how I had found out about Tcôvese, and I asked whether he spoke it.

"Just a little," he said. "A few words."

I confessed that it was the same with me. *Naja pouvrei.*

"You could be useful to the Department," he told me. "We could pay you a little something. Not much."

The fixed stare of his narrowed eyes told me he was lying; I wished that I'd had a better look at the badge he showed me.

He pursed his lips, "Let's say twenty-five a head, fifty if we need you to ask them questions."

I indicated that additional income was always welcome, and asked what he wished me to do.

He gave me a business card. (I have it still; it identifies him as Detective Lieutenant James J. Ropinski. The address is that of the Eighteenth Precinct, but the telephone number is not theirs.) "First off, I want you to call me anytime somebody comes in about that ad. Give me a name and a description, and tell me everything he said. Try to get an address and so on.

Any hard information that you can. The Mob's been bringing in hit men from Tcôvé. We need to know about every one of those guys."

I nodded, although I had already decided that I would not cooperate.

"Am I the first one?"

I asked what he meant.

"The first one that's answered your ad."

I assured him he was, and asked what Tcôvese looked like, in order that I might recognize them. I had visualized small Orientals.

"Pretty much like you," he said, "or like me. Regular people."

I addressed him in Tcôvese, employing one of the phrases from the book: *Retop embrasôneia minmias costenti sus?* "Are you familiar with these lovely caverns?"

He stared at me and shook his head.

When he left, I looked up the number of the Eighteenth Precinct in the telephone directory, called, and asked for him. I was told, as I expected to be, that there was no one of that name.

My second visitor arrived almost a year to the day after my advertisement had appeared, long after I had surrendered hope of any further response. He was a very tall black man, exceedingly well dressed.

"I come for what you have say here." He extracted my advertisement, much folded and refolded and soiled, from an elegant ostrich-hide wallet. "I am consul Tcôvee. You hear? Not here this city, 'nother city. For me a long trip. You hear?" His hand shook as he held out the torn scrap of paper.

I addressed to him the phrase I had so often rehearsed: *Semphonississima techsodeliphindera lafiondalindu tuk yiscav kriishhalôné!* "How delightful to discover in the shrinking sea a crystal blossom of home!"

He dropped my advertisement and ran from the shop.

My third visitor arrived only last night; it is due to that visitation (if I may employ so pretentious a word) that I am writing this account for you.

The day had been dark, as winter days here so often are. At six, when I inspected the cat's food and water bowls and locked the front door of the shop, and pulled down the blind, the street lights were on. The thought of my cold, empty apartment, with its waiting stacks and boxes of books, held no attractions. I lit the gas ring in my office instead, and filled the kettle.

Then, settling into my old, wooden swivel chair, I mused upon the possibility of night hours. What if I were to close each day at two, nap, and reopen at night, remaining open till midnight? Might I not soon discover that I had acquired a new clientelé? Or however it's pronounced. Might I not increase my income sufficiently to afford a vacation? I wanted very badly to go somewhere, though I did not know where.

After a moment or two, I rebuked myself for wasting my time when I might, if I had gone to my apartment, be studying *Tohish Ablar*, then remembered that it was in the pocket of my overcoat and got it out.

Ensueshh nemblar sissert va? "Where may strangers erect their pavilions?"

Nemit mirrya orriy sus. "You will be my wife while I am here."

Arbitorri Tcôvesessit tanyat sklora. "Le paradis perdu n'est pas celui qu'on pense."

A ffuwtelle togong bluté. "I hunger for taller trees."

I dozed, and it seemed to me that I was walking beside a little rippling stream whose water was so pure as to be almost invisible, and so cold that flecks of ice tumbled in its current, flashing in the sunshine. Minute fish with wide wings of polychrome gauze that were in fact their pectoral fins leaped from the freezing water to catch flying seeds that seemed to know and fear them, darting this way and that like tiny green helicopters, then plunged back into the stream to breathe. The trees to either side of the stream (no doubt they were inspired by the last phrase I had read) were fifteen feet or more through the trunk, and seemed almost to touch the sky. Springs gushed from about their roots, bordered by flowers that turned their blossoms toward me as I walked as though eager to be seen; each was like the beautiful face of a young woman—I do not mean that they had eyes, noses, and so forth, but that they evoked the same response in me. I knelt, discovered that I was holding a small knife with a crooked blade . . .

And woke.

The shop was dark, and silent except for the hissing of my gas ring and the bubbling of the kettle; and yet I knew that I was not alone, that someone had entered while I slept, turned off the lights, and remained, waiting.

I got up and went out into the public part of the shop.

"Trifor nemell?"

Remember me?

A soft voice, vibrant and haunting. "No, no," I said, "I don't even know who you are!"

"A temmenti nogivé sus."

I forgive you.

"*Who are you?*" I shouted. "Where are you!"

"Qibbeia susentifeda sus shoonlend? Nebor?"

Why can't you forgive yourself? Please?

By that time I had reached the light switch. I shouted something more (I do not remember what I said) and turned on the lights.

I was alone, still old, still dressed in my old tweed jacket, which badly needed cleaning. (As do I, I suppose.) Nothing had changed. My cat, Crystal-flowermaiden, trotted busily about the shop, peering behind each freestanding bookcase, obviously looking for someone who was no longer present. When I returned to my little office to take the kettle off the gas ring, I found that someone had already brewed a cup of tea for me, and that there floated in it, briefly, a tiny pink-and-white blossom like those in my dream. As I watched it melted, filling that dusty little room with an indescribable fragrance. Which vanished too in half a minute or less.

III.

The Hidden Page

It was very late before I could bring myself to leave the shop and walk the five blocks that separated me from my apartment. Perhaps I should not include this here, but I was mugged, knocked down from behind by someone I never saw who took my money and my watch and searched me frantically, while I lay sprawled on the sidewalk, for something that he never found; I remember that he searched my left coat pocket twice, tearing it away to make certain it was empty.

Dazed and bleeding, I reached my building at last, locked and bolted the door of my second-floor apartment (for I was very much afraid my assailant had followed me, though I know how irrational that sounds), stripped and showered, contrived a clumsy bandage for the wound at the back of my head, which was still oozing blood, poured myself four fingers of Scotch, and took the phrase book from my ruined coat's remaining pocket.

I cannot explain how it came to be, but I felt now that I could paste my bookplate in it, and index it, too, acts that I had longed to perform ever since I (re)discovered it. I had advertised for speakers, but found no speaker more fluent than myself. I had walked through a forest of Tcôvé, if only in dream. Why not?

Bookplates are, as you are doubtless aware, properly attached to the inner surface of the front board, at or slightly below its center. Mine I designed myself, and had printed at a little shop not far from my own; thus they are not gummed as the commercial products are, and I am compelled to spread the back of each with thin mucilage before I attach it. I then close the book in question and put it under several others, usually until morning.

On this final occasion I did not wait so long. As I was preparing for bed, I realized that I had forgotten—though I had once known—the Tcôvese word for *love*, and a few minutes ago, unable to sleep, I surrendered to the impulse and got the *Tohish Ablar* from beneath its little stack of odd volumes.

A half drop of mucilage had escaped from beneath my bookplate and so gummed what I had believed to be the back of the front board to the flyleaf. When I opened the book, the false back was thus pulled away, revealing a black endpaper upon which someone has written, in silver ink, a name that is *not* mine, in the characters of the diloveta.

Thus I write to you now as I do, for I feel that I will not be with you much longer. Twice the telephone has rung. On the first occasion I answered it with "*Hello?*" as I usually do, and the caller hung up. On the second—but I will not tell you that.

Again and again I find myself drawn to the window; clouds gravid with snow hang low over the city, hiding every star but one.

I will finish this before morning, take it to my shop, and place it in an old book, or a new one, or perhaps in one of the magazines upon my little rack. There you have found it.

(That pinpoint of golden light!)

And I, I hope, have gone. May your torment, too, soon be ended.

(At noon! She said at noon!)

I will leave the book behind for you as well, my unknown reader and customer. You may know it by my bookplate.

Dejahheerna!

Greg Egan

Closer

• • • •

{1992}

Australian writer Greg Egan (1961–) has played a leading role in the contemporary renewal of hard science fiction—sometimes referred to as "radical hard sf" to distinguish it from the work of earlier writers such as Isaac Asimov and Arthur C. Clarke. His fiction is notable for its sophisticated engagement with some of the more daunting theories of contemporary mathematics, physics, and cosmology—for example, loop quantum gravity and string theory—and for its powerful philosophical explorations of human subjectivity and identity. Egan has a BSC in mathematics and has worked as a computer programmer. He is, as one reviewer has noted, "one of the genre's great ideas men."

Egan has published eight novels to date, the most recent of which is *Incandescence* (2008), and several short-story collections, including most recently *Dark Integers and Other Stories* (2008). His novel *Permutation City* (1995) won the John W. Campbell Memorial Award and his short story "Oceanic" (1998) won both the Hugo Award and the Locus Award. He is one of a group of contemporary writers—including Cory Doctorow, Charles Stross, and Damien Broderick—whose work has been referred to as "post-Singularity sf." As proposed by mathematician and sf writer Vernor Vinge, the Singularity will be a radically transformative techno-scientific event that will in all likelihood take place within the next thirty years or so, probably as the consequence of developments in artificial intelligence, communications technologies, and/or nanotechnology. Vinge's technological Singularity threatens to alter the course of human history to the extent that logical extrapolation into the future becomes virtually impossible. In contrast to the well-worn near-futures of cyberpunk sf, most post-Singularity fiction looks to the far future in its attempts to imagine the unimaginable.

Egan's stories are inhabited by some of the genre's most rigorously constructed versions of posthumanity. The evolution of the posthuman in his fiction can be traced through the sequence of novels that includes *Permutation City* (1994); *Diaspora* (1997); *Schild's Ladder* (2002), in which humanity has been extinct for thousands of years; and *Incandescence*, set a full million years in the future. These novels construct a speculative trajectory of increasingly complex virtual subjects and their environments, and they appeal powerfully to the reader's sense of wonder at the sheer scope and complexity of the physical universe.

"Closer" is set in the same fictional world as "Learning to Be Me" (1990), in which Egan first introduced the "Ndoli Device." Commonly referred to as "the jewel," the Device is a neural-net computer that can gradually take the place of the human brain, "down to the level of neurons," so that everyone has become virtually immortal. In other words, Egan's characters—like those in Stross's "Rogue Farm" (2003)—are posthumans who live on the far side of a technological Singularity. While the world of "Closer" is filled with extraordinary biotechnological wonders, its plot is, however, very familiar, following as it does the course of a love affair (reminiscent of Frederik Pohl's far-future "Day Million" [1966], whose narrator ironically promises "a boy, a girl, and a love story"). And the narrator's obsession is a very old philosophical conundrum: "assuming that other people existed, how did they apprehend that existence?" Can we ever know the other? What might be the consequences of such knowledge?

Nobody wants to spend eternity alone.

("Intimacy," I once told Sian, after we'd made love, "is the only cure for solipsism."

She laughed and said, "Don't get too ambitious, Michael. So far, it hasn't even cured me of masturbation.")

True solipsism, though, was never my problem. From the very first time I considered the question, I accepted that there could be no way of proving the reality of an external world, let alone the existence of other minds—but I also accepted that taking both on faith was the only practical way of dealing with everyday life.

The question which obsessed me was this: Assuming that other people existed, how did they apprehend that existence? How did they experience *being?* Could I ever truly understand what consciousness was like for another person—any more than I could for an ape, or a cat, or an insect?

If not, I was alone.

I desperately wanted to believe that other people were somehow *knowable*, but it wasn't something I could bring myself to take for granted. I knew there could be no absolute proof, but I wanted to be persuaded, I needed to be compelled.

No literature, no poetry, no drama, however personally resonant I found it, could ever quite convince me that I'd glimpsed the author's soul. Language had evolved to facilitate cooperation in the conquest of the physical world, not to describe subjective reality. Love, anger, jealousy, resentment, grief—all were defined, ultimately, in terms of external circumstances and observable actions. When an image or metaphor rang true for me, it proved only that I shared with the author a set of definitions, a culturally sanctioned list of word associations. After all, many publishers used computer programs—highly specialized, but unsophisticated algorithms, without the remotest possibility of self-awareness—to routinely produce both literature, and literary criticism, indistinguishable from the human product. Not just formularized garbage, either; on several occasions, I'd been deeply affected by works which I'd later discovered had been cranked out by unthinking software. This didn't prove that human literature communicated nothing of the author's inner life, but it certainly made clear how much room there was for doubt.

Unlike many of my friends, I had no qualms whatsoever when, at the age of eighteen, the time came for me to "switch." My organic brain was removed and discarded, and control of my body handed over to my "jewel"—the Ndoli Device, a neural-net computer implanted shortly after birth, which had since learnt to imitate my brain, down to the level of individual neurons. I had no qualms, not because I was at all convinced that the jewel and the brain experienced consciousness identically, but because, from an early age, I'd identified myself solely with the jewel. My brain was a kind of bootstrap device, nothing more, and to mourn its loss would have been as absurd as mourning my emergence from some primitive stage of embryological neural development. Switching was simply what humans *did* now, an established part of the life cycle, even if it was mediated by our culture, and not by our genes.

Seeing each other die, and observing the gradual failure of their own bodies, may have helped convince pre-Ndoli humans of their common humanity; certainly, there were countless references in their literature to the equalizing power of death. Perhaps concluding that the universe would go on without them produced a shared sense of hopelessness, or insignificance, which they viewed as their defining attribute.

Now that it's become an article of faith that, sometime in the next few billion years, physicists will find a way for *us* to go on without *the universe*, rather than vice-versa, that route to spiritual equality has lost whatever dubious logic it might ever have possessed.

•

Sian was a communications engineer. I was a holovision news editor. We met during a live broadcast of the seeding of Venus with terraforming nanomachines—a matter of great public interest, since most of the planet's as-yet-uninhabitable surface had already been sold. There were several technical glitches with the broadcast which might have been disastrous, but together we managed to work around them, and even to hide the seams. It was nothing special, we were simply doing our jobs, but afterwards I was elated out of all proportion. It took me twenty-four hours to realize (or decide) that I'd fallen in love.

However, when I approached her the next day, she made it clear that she felt nothing for me; the chemistry I'd imagined "between us" had all been in my head. I was dismayed, but not surprised. Work didn't bring us together again, but I called her occasionally, and six weeks later my persistence was rewarded. I took her to a performance of *Waiting for Godot* by augmented parrots, and *I* enjoyed myself immensely, but I didn't see her again for more than a month.

I'd almost given up hope, when she appeared at my door without warning one night and dragged me along to a "concert" of interactive computerized improvisation. The "audience" was assembled in what looked like a mock-up of a Berlin nightclub of the 2050s. A computer program, originally designed for creating movie scores, was fed with the image from a hovercamera which wandered about the set. People danced and sang, screamed and brawled, and engaged in all kinds of histrionics in the hope of attracting the camera and shaping the music. At first, I felt cowed and inhibited, but Sian gave me no choice but to join in.

It was chaotic, insane, at times even terrifying. One woman stabbed another to "death" at the table beside us, which struck me as a sickening (and expensive) indulgence, but when a riot broke out at the end, and people started smashing the deliberately flimsy furniture, I followed Sian into the mêlée, cheering.

The music—the excuse for the whole event—was garbage, but I didn't really care. When we limped out into the night, bruised and aching and laughing, I knew that at least we'd shared something that had made us feel closer. She took me home and we went to bed together, too sore and tired to do more than sleep, but when we made love in the morning, I already felt so at ease with her that I could hardly believe it was our first time.

Soon we were inseparable. My tastes in entertainment were very different from hers, but I survived most of her favorite "artforms," more or less intact. She moved into my apartment, at my suggestion, and casually destroyed the orderly rhythms of my carefully arranged domestic life.

I had to piece together details of her past from throwaway lines; she found it far too boring to sit down and give me a coherent account. Her life had been as unremarkable as mine: she'd grown up in a suburban, middle-class family, studied her profession, found a job. Like almost everyone, she'd switched at eighteen. She had no strong political convictions. She was good at her work, but put ten times more energy into her social life. She was intelligent, but hated anything overtly intellectual. She was impatient, aggressive, roughly affectionate.

And I could not, for one second, imagine what it was like inside her head.

For a start, I rarely had any idea what she was thinking—in the sense of knowing how she would have replied if asked, out of the blue, to describe her thoughts at the moment before they were interrupted by the question. On a longer time-scale, I had no feeling for her motivation, her image of herself, her concept of who she was and what she did and why. Even in the laughably crude sense that a novelist pretends to "explain" a character, I could not have explained Sian.

And if she'd provided me with a running commentary on her mental state, and a weekly assessment of the reasons for her actions in the latest psychodynamic jargon, it would all have come to nothing but a heap of useless words. If I could have pictured myself in her circumstances, imagined myself with her beliefs and obsessions, empathised until I could anticipate her every word, her every decision, then I still would not have understood so much as a single moment when she closed her eyes, forgot her past, wanted nothing, and simply *was*.

Of course, most of the time, nothing could have mattered less. We were happy enough together, whether or not we were strangers—and whether or not my "happiness" and Sian's "happiness" were in any real sense the same.

Over the years, she became less self-contained, more open. She had no great dark secrets to share, no traumatic childhood ordeals to recount, but she let me in on her petty fears and her mundane neuroses. I did the same, and even, clumsily, explained my peculiar obsession. She wasn't at all offended. Just puzzled.

"What could it actually mean, though? To know what it's like to be someone else? You'd have to have their memories, their personality, their body—everything. And then you'd just *be* them, not yourself, and *you* wouldn't know anything. It's nonsense."

I shrugged. "Not necessarily. Of course, perfect knowledge would be impossible, but you can always get *closer*. Don't you think that the more things we do together, the more experiences we share, the closer we become?"

She scowled. "Yes, but that's not what you were talking about five seconds ago. Two years, or two thousand years, of 'shared experiences' *seen through different eyes* means nothing. However much time two people spent together, how could you know that there was even the briefest instant when they both experienced what they were going through 'together' in the same way?"

"I know, but . . ."

"If you admit that what you want is impossible, maybe you'll stop fretting about it."

I laughed. "Whatever makes you think I'm as rational as that?"

When the technology became available, it was Sian's idea, not mine, for us to try out all the fashionable somatic permutations. Sian was always impatient to experience something new. "If we really are going to live for ever," she said, "we'd better stay curious if we want to stay sane."

I was reluctant, but any resistance I put up seemed hypocritical. Clearly, this game wouldn't lead to the perfect knowledge I longed for (and knew I would never achieve), but I couldn't deny the possibility that it might be one crude step in the right direction. First, we exchanged bodies. I discovered what it was like to have breasts and a vagina—what it was like for me, that is, not what it had been like for Sian. True, we stayed swapped long enough for the shock, and even the novelty, to wear off, but I never felt that I'd gained much insight into *her* experience of the body she'd been born with. My jewel was modified only as much as was necessary to allow me to control this unfamiliar machine, which was scarcely more than would have been required to work another male body. The menstrual cycle had been abandoned decades before, and although I could have taken the necessary hormones to allow myself to have periods, and even to become pregnant (although the financial disincentives for reproduction had been drastically increased in recent years), that would have told me absolutely nothing about Sian, who had done neither.

As for sex, the pleasure of intercourse still felt very much the same—which was hardly surprising, since nerves from the vagina and clitoris were simply wired into my jewel as if they'd come from my penis. Even being penetrated made less difference than I'd expected; unless I made a special effort to remain aware of our respective geometries, I found it hard to care who was doing what to whom. Orgasms were better, though, I had to admit.

At work, no one raised an eyebrow when I turned up as Sian, since many of my colleagues had already been through exactly the same thing. The legal definition of identity had recently been shifted from the DNA fingerprint of the body, according to a standard set of markers, to the serial number of the jewel. When even *the law* can keep up with you, you know you can't be doing anything very radical or profound.

After three months, Sian had had enough. "I never realized how clumsy you were," she said. "Or that ejaculation was so *dull*."

Next, she had a clone of herself made, so we could both be women. Brain-damaged replacement bodies—Extras—had once been incredibly expensive, when they'd needed to be grown at virtually the normal rate, and kept constantly active so they'd be healthy enough to use. However, the physiological effects of the passage of time, and of exercise, don't happen by magic; at a deep enough level, there's always a biochemical signal produced, which can ultimately be faked. Mature Extras, with sturdy bones and perfect muscle-tone, could now be produced from scratch in a year—four months' gestation and eight months' coma—which also allowed them to be more thoroughly brain-dead than before, soothing the ethical qualms of those who'd always wondered just how much was going on inside the heads of the old, active versions.

In our first experiment, the hardest part for me had always been, not looking in the mirror and seeing Sian, but looking at Sian and seeing myself. I'd missed her, far more than I'd missed being myself. Now, I was almost happy for my body to be absent (in storage, kept alive by a jewel based on the minimal brain of an Extra). The symmetry of being her twin appealed to me; surely now we were closer than ever. Before, we'd merely swapped our physical differences. Now, we'd abolished them.

The symmetry was an illusion. I'd changed gender, and she hadn't. I was with the woman I loved; she lived with a walking parody of herself.

One morning she woke me, pummeling my breasts so hard that she left bruises. When I opened my eyes and shielded myself, she peered at me suspiciously. "Are you in there? Michael? I'm going crazy. *I want you back*."

For the sake of getting the whole bizarre episode over and done with for good—and perhaps also to discover for myself what Sian had just been through—I agreed to the third permutation. There was no need to wait a year; my Extra had been grown at the same time as hers.

Somehow, it was far more disorienting to be confronted by "myself" without the camouflage of Sian's body. I found my own face unreadable; when we'd both been in disguise, that hadn't bothered me, but now it made me feel edgy, and at times almost paranoid, for no rational reason at all.

Sex took some getting used to. Eventually, I found it pleasurable, in a confusing and vaguely narcissistic way. The compelling sense of equality I'd felt, when we'd made love as women, never quite returned to me as we sucked each other's cocks—but then, when we'd both been women, Sian had never claimed to feel any such thing. It had all been my own invention.

The day after we returned to the way we'd begun (well, almost—in fact, we put our decrepit, twenty-six-year-old bodies in storage, and took up residence in our healthier Extras), I saw a story from Europe on an option we hadn't yet tried, tipped to become all the rage: hermaphroditic identical twins. Our new bodies could be our biological children (give or take the genetic tinkering required to ensure hemaphroditism), with an equal share of characteristics from both of us. We would *both* have changed gender, *both* have lost partners. We'd be equal in every way.

I took a copy of the file home to Sian. She watched it thoughtfully, then said, "Slugs are hermaphrodites, aren't they? They hang in mid-air together on a thread of slime. I'm sure there's even something in Shakespeare, remarking on the glorious spectacle of copulating slugs. Imagine it: you and me, making slug love."

I fell on the floor, laughing.

I stopped, suddenly. "*Where*, in Shakespeare? I didn't think you'd even *read* Shakespeare."

Eventually, I came to believe that with each passing year, I knew Sian a little better—in the traditional sense, the sense that most couples seemed to find sufficient. I knew what she expected from me, I knew how not to hurt her. We had arguments, we had fights, but there must have been some kind of underlying stability, because in the end we always chose to stay together. Her happiness mattered to me, very much, and at times I could hardly believe that I'd ever thought it possible that all of her subjective experience might be fundamentally *alien* to me. It was true that every brain, and hence every jewel, was unique—but there was something extravagant in supposing that the nature of consciousness could be radically different between individuals, when the same basic hardware, and the same basic principles of neural topology, were involved.

Still. Sometimes, if I woke in the night, I'd turn to her and whisper, inaudibly, compulsively, "I don't know you. I have no idea who, or what, you are." I'd lie there, and think about packing and leaving. I was *alone*, and it was farcical to go through the charade of pretending otherwise.

Then again, sometimes I woke in the night, absolutely convinced that I was *dying*, or something else equally absurd. In the sway of some half-forgotten dream, all manner of confusion is possible. It never meant a thing, and by morning, I was always myself again.

·

When I saw the story on Craig Bentley's service—he called it "research," but his "volunteers" paid for the privilege of taking part in his experiments—I almost couldn't bring myself to include it in the bulletin, although all my professional judgment told me it was everything our viewers wanted in a thirty-second techno-shock piece: bizarre, even mildly disconcerting, but not too hard to grasp.

Bentley was a cyberneurologist; he studied the Ndoli Device, in the way that neurologists had once studied the brain. Mimicking the brain with a neural-net computer had not required a profound understanding of its higher-level structures; research into these structures continued, in their new incarnation. The jewel, compared to the brain, was of course both easier to observe, and easier to manipulate.

In his latest project, Bentley was offering couples something slightly more up-market than an insight into the sex lives of slugs. He was offering them eight hours with identical minds.

I made a copy of the original, ten-minute piece that had come through on the fibre, then let my editing console select the most titillating thirty seconds possible, for broadcast. It did a good job; it had learnt from me.

I couldn't lie to Sian. I couldn't hide the story, I couldn't pretend to be disinterested. The only honest thing to do was to show her the file, tell her exactly how I felt, and ask her what *she* wanted.

I did just that. When the HV image faded out, she turned to me, shrugged, and said mildly, "OK. It sounds like fun. Let's try it."

Bentley wore a T-shirt with nine computer-drawn portraits on it, in a three-by-three grid. Top left was Elvis Presley. Bottom right was Marilyn Monroe. The rest were various stages in between.

"This is how it will work. The transition will take twenty minutes, during which time you'll be disembodied. Over the first ten minutes, you'll gain equal access to each other's memories. Over the second ten minutes, you'll both be moved, gradually, towards the compromise personality.

"Once that's done, your Ndoli Devices will be identical—in the sense that both will have all the same neural connections with all the same weighting factors—but they'll almost certainly be in different states. I'll have to black you out, to correct that. Then you'll wake—"

Who'll wake?

"—in identical electromechanical bodies. Clones can't be made sufficiently alike.

"You'll spend the eight hours alone, in perfectly matched rooms. Rather like hotel suites, really. You'll have HV to keep you amused if you need it—

without the videophone module, of course. You might think you'd both get an engaged signal, if you tried to call the same number simultaneously—but in fact, in such cases the switching equipment arbitrarily lets one call through, which would make your environments different."

Sian asked, "Why can't we phone each other? Or better still, meet each other? If we're exactly the same, we'd say the same things, do the same things—we'd be one more identical part of each other's environment."

Bentley pursed his lips and shook his head. "Perhaps I'll allow something of the kind in a future experiment, but for now I believe it would be too . . . potentially traumatic."

Sian gave me a sideways glance, which meant: *This man is a killjoy.*

"The end will be like the beginning, in reverse. First, your personalities will be restored. Then, you'll lose access to each other's memories. Of course, your memories of *the experience itself* will be left untouched. Untouched by me, that is; I can't predict how your separate personalities, once restored, will act—filtering, suppressing, reinterpreting those memories. Within minutes, you may end up with very different ideas about what you've been through. All I can guarantee is this: for the eight hours in question, the two of you *will* be identical."

We talked it over. Sian was enthusiastic, as always. She didn't much care what it would be *like*; all that really mattered to her was collecting one more novel experience.

"Whatever happens, we'll be ourselves again at the end of it," she said. "What's there to be afraid of? You know the old Ndoli joke."

"What old Ndoli joke?"

"Anything's bearable—so long as it's finite."

I couldn't decide how I felt. The sharing of memories notwithstanding, we'd both end up *knowing*, not each other, but merely a transient, artificial third person. Still, for the first time in our lives, we would have been through exactly the same experience, from exactly the same point of view—even if the experience was only spending eight hours locked in separate rooms, and the point of view was that of a genderless robot with an identity crisis.

It was a compromise—but I could think of no realistic way in which it could have been improved.

I called Bentley, and made a reservation.

In perfect sensory deprivation, my thoughts seemed to dissipate into the blackness around me before they were even half-formed. This isolation didn't last long, though; as our short-term memories merged, we achieved a kind of telepathy: one of us would think a message, and the other would "remember" thinking it, and reply in the same way.

—I really can't wait to uncover all your grubby little secrets.

—I think you're going to be disappointed. Anything I haven't already told you, I've probably repressed.

—Ah, but *repressed* is not *erased*. Who knows what will turn up?

—*We'll* know, soon enough.

I tried to think of all the minor sins I must have committed over the years, all the shameful, selfish, unworthy thoughts, but nothing came into my head but a vague white noise of guilt. I tried again, and achieved, of all things, an image of Sian as a child. A young boy slipping his hand between her legs, then squealing with fright and pulling away. But she'd described that incident to me, long ago. Was it her memory, or my reconstruction?

—My memory. I think. Or perhaps *my* reconstruction. You know, half the time when I've told you something that happened before we met, the memory of the telling has become far clearer to me than the memory itself. Almost replacing it.

—It's the same for me.

—Then in a way, our memories have already been moving towards a kind of symmetry, for years. We both remember what was *said*, as if we'd both heard it from someone else.

Agreement. Silence. A moment of confusion. Then:

—This neat division of "memory" and "personality" Bentley uses; is it really so clear? Jewels are neural-net computers, you can't talk about "data" and "program" in any absolute sense.

—Not in general, no. His classification must be arbitrary, to some extent. But who cares?

—It matters. If he restores "personality," but allows "memories" to persist, a misclassification could leave us . . .

What?

—It depends, doesn't it? At one extreme, so thoroughly "restored," so completely unaffected, that the whole experience might as well not have happened. And at the other extreme . . .

—Permanently . . .

— . . . closer.

—Isn't that the point?

—I don't know any more.

Silence. Hesitation.

Then I realized that I had no idea whether or not it was my turn to reply.

I woke, lying on a bed, mildly bemused, as if waiting for a mental hiatus to pass. My body felt slightly awkward, but less so than when I'd woken in someone else's Extra. I glanced down at the pale, smooth plastic of my torso and legs, then waved a hand in front of my face. I looked like a unisex shop-window dummy—but Bentley had shown us the bodies beforehand, it was no great shock. I sat up slowly, then stood and took a few steps. I felt a little numb and hollow, but my kinesthetic sense, my proprioception, was fine; I felt *located* between my eyes, and I felt that this body was *mine*. As with any modern transplant, my jewel had been manipulated directly to accommodate the change, avoiding the need for months of physiotherapy.

I glanced around the room. It was sparsely furnished: one bed, one table, one chair, one clock, one HV set. On the wall, a framed reproduction of an Escher lithograph: *Bond of Union*, a portrait of the artist and, presumably, his wife, faces peeled like lemons into helices of rind, joined into a single, linked band. I traced the outer surface from start to finish, and was disappointed to find that it lacked the Möbius twist I was expecting.

No windows, one door without a handle. Set into the wall beside the bed, a full-length mirror. I stood a while and stared at my ridiculous form. It suddenly occurred to me that, if Bentley had a real love of symmetry games, he might have built one room as the mirror image of the other, modified the HV set accordingly, and altered one jewel, one copy of me, to exchange right for left. What looked like a mirror could then be nothing but a window between the rooms. I grinned awkwardly with my plastic face; my reflection looked appropriately embarrassed by the sight. The idea appealed to me, however unlikely it was. Nothing short of an experiment in nuclear physics could reveal the difference. No, not true; a pendulum free to precess, like Foucault's, would twist the same way in both rooms, giving the game away. I walked up to the mirror and thumped it. It didn't seem to yield at all, but then, either a brick wall, or an equal and opposite thump from behind, could have been the explanation.

I shrugged and turned away. Bentley *might* have done anything—for all I knew, the whole set-up could have been a computer simulation. My body was irrelevant. The room was irrelevant. The point was . . .

I sat on the bed. I recalled someone—Michael, probably, wondering if I'd panic when I dwelt upon my nature, but I found no reason to do so. If I'd woken in this room with no recent memories, and tried to sort out who I was from my past(s), I'd no doubt have gone mad, but I knew *exactly* who

I was, I had two long trails of anticipation leading to my present state. The prospect of being changed back into Sian or Michael didn't bother me at all; the wishes of both to regain their separate identities endured in me, strongly, and the desire for personal integrity manifested itself as relief at the thought of their re-emergence, not as fear of my own demise. In any case, my memories would not be expunged, and I had no sense of having goals which one or the other of them would not pursue. I felt more like their lowest common denominator than any kind of synergistic hypermind; I was less, not more, than the sum of my parts. My purpose was strictly limited: I was here to enjoy the strangeness for Sian, and to answer a question for Michael, and when the time came I'd be happy to bifurcate, and resume the two lives I remembered and valued.

So, how did I experience consciousness? The same way as Michael? The same way as Sian? So far as I could tell, I'd undergone no fundamental change—but even as I reached that conclusion, I began to wonder if I was in any position to judge. Did *memories* of being Michael, and *memories* of being Sian, contain so much more than the two of them could have put into words and exchanged verbally? Did I really *know* anything about the nature of their existence, or was my head just full of second-hand description—intimate, and detailed, but ultimately as opaque as language? If my mind *were* radically different, would that difference be something I could even perceive—or would all my memories, in the act of remembering, simply be recast into terms that seemed familiar?

The past, after all, was no more knowable than the external world. Its very existence also had to be taken on faith—and, granted existence, it too could be misleading.

I buried my head in my hands, dejected. I was the closest they could get, and what had come of me? Michael's hope remained precisely as reasonable—and as unproven—as ever.

After a while, my mood began to lighten. At least Michael's search was over, even if it had ended in failure. Now he'd have no choice but to accept that, and move on.

I paced around the room for a while, flicking the HV on and off. I was actually starting to get *bored*, but I wasn't going to waste eight hours and several thousand dollars by sitting down and watching soap operas.

I mused about possible ways of undermining the synchronization of my two copies. It was inconceivable that Bentley could have matched the rooms and bodies to such a fine tolerance that an engineer worthy of the name couldn't find some way of breaking the symmetry. Even a coin toss might have done it, but I didn't have a coin. Throwing a paper plane? That sounded promising—highly sensitive to air currents—but the only paper in the room was the Escher, and I couldn't bring myself to vandalize it. I might have smashed the mirror, and observed the shapes and sizes of the fragments, which would have had the added bonus of proving or disproving my earlier speculations, but as I raised the chair over my head, I suddenly changed my mind. Two conflicting sets of short-term memories had been confusing enough during a few minutes of sensory deprivation; for several hours interacting with a physical environment, it could be completely disabling. Better to hold off until I was desperate for amusement.

So I lay down on the bed and did what most of Bentley's clients probably ended up doing.

As they coalesced, Sian and Michael had both had fears for their privacy—and both had issued compensatory, not to say defensive, mental declarations of frankness, not wanting the other to think that they had something to hide. Their curiosity, too, had been ambivalent; they'd wanted to *understand* each other, but, of course, not to *pry*.

All of these contradictions continued in me, but—staring at the ceiling, trying not to look at the clock again for at least another thirty seconds—I didn't really have to make a decision. It was the most natural thing in the world to let my mind wander back over the course of their relationship, from both points of view.

It was a very peculiar reminiscence. Almost everything seemed at once vaguely surprising and utterly familiar—like an extended attack of *déjà vu*. It's not that they'd often set out deliberately to deceive each other about anything substantial, but all the tiny white lies, all the concealed trivial resentments, all the necessary, laudable, essential, loving deceptions, that had kept them together in spite of their differences, filled my head with a strange haze of confusion and disillusionment.

It wasn't in any sense a conversation; I was no multiple personality. Sian and Michael simply weren't there—to justify, to explain, to deceive each other all over again, with the best intentions. Perhaps I should have attempted to do all this on their behalf, but I was constantly unsure of my role, unable to decide on a position. So I lay there, paralyzed by symmetry, and let their memories flow.

After that, the time passed so quickly that I never had a chance to break the mirror.

We tried to stay together.

We lasted a week.

Bentley had made—as the law required—snapshots of our jewels prior to the experiment. We could have gone back to them—and then had him explain to us *why*—but self-deception is only an easy choice if you make it in time.

We couldn't forgive each other, because there was nothing to forgive. Neither of us had done a single thing that the other could fail to understand, and sympathize with, completely.

We knew each other too well, that's all. Detail after tiny fucking microscopic detail. It wasn't that the truth hurt; it didn't, any longer. It numbed us. It smothered us. We didn't know each other as we knew ourselves; it was worse than that. In the self, the details blur in the very processes of thought; mental self-dissection is possible, but it takes great effort to sustain. Our mutual dissection took no effort at all; it was the natural state into which we fell in each other's presence. Our surfaces *had* been stripped away, but not to reveal a glimpse of the soul. All we could see beneath the skin were the cogs, spinning.

And I knew, now, that what Sian had always wanted most in a lover was the alien, the unknowable, the mysterious, the opaque. The whole point, for her, of being with someone else was the sense of confronting *otherness*. Without it, she believed, you might as well be talking to yourself.

I found that I now shared this view (a change whose precise origins I didn't much want to think about . . . but then, I'd always known she had the stronger personality, I should have guessed that *something* would rub off).

Together, we might as well have been alone, so we had no choice but to part.

Nobody wants to spend eternity alone.

JAMES PATRICK KELLY

Think Like a Dinosaur

{1995}

Although his first story, "Dea Ex Machina," was published in 1975, it was not until the mid-1980s that the science fiction and fantasy stories of James Patrick Kelly (1951–) began to appear regularly. Kelly has published several novels, most notably *Wild Life* (1994), an expansion of his Nebula Award–nominated novella "Mr. Boy" (1990), but he is best known for his prolific body of short fiction. Among his notable collections are *Think Like a Dinosaur and Other Stories* (1997), *Strange but Not a Stranger* (2002), and *The Wreck of the Godspeed and Other Stories* (2008). During the 1980s, he was one of a number of writers—including John Kessel, Kim Stanley Robinson, and Connie Willis—whose work was identified as "humanist" in contrast to that of "cyberpunks" such as Lewis Shiner and Bruce Sterling. Kelly's interests are wide-ranging, however, and in the 1980s he published several cyberpunk-accented stories, including "Solstice" (1985), which was reprinted in the classic *Mirrorshades* (1986) anthology of cyberpunk stories edited by Sterling. Kelly has co-edited several important short-story anthologies with John Kessel, the most recent of which is *The Secret History of Science Fiction* (2009). His short novel *Burn* won a 2007 Nebula Award.

Kelly frequently teaches and participates in sf writing workshops, including Clarion and Sycamore Hill (which was co-founded by Kessel). He has served on the New Hampshire State Council on the Arts since 1998, is a member of the Popular Fiction faculty for the Stonecoast MFA Program in Creative Writing at the University of Southern Maine, and contributes a regular nonfiction column, "On the Net," to *Asimov's Science Fiction*.

Kelly's stories, especially those written in the 1990s, often focus on cutting-edge developments in genetic engineering and artificial intelligence, resulting, for example, in the extreme body modifications of the characters in "Mr. Boy," in which the title character's mother is a three-quarter-scale copy of the Statue of Liberty. At the same time, he is skilled in handling the psychological and emotional elements conventionally associated with narrative realism, such as the troubled parent-child relationship that anchors the technological posthumanism in "Itsy Bitsy Spider" (1997).

"Think Like a Dinosaur" won a Hugo Award in 1995. Its most striking feature is its self-consciously intertextual engagement with one of the field's most famous examples of hard sf, Tom Godwin's "The Cold Equations" (1954). In Godwin's story, an innocent young woman must die in order to balance the "cold equations" of the laws of physics. In Kelly's story, another innocent young woman must die in order to "balance the equation." Kelly's story raises complex questions about identity and ethics. Is information the essence of an individual? Is the body an add-on that can be disposed of without moral consequences? Does science fiction encourage us to "think like dinosaurs"?

Kamala Shastri came back to this world as she had left it—naked. She tottered out of the assembler, trying to balance in Tuulen Station's delicate gravity. I caught her and bundled her into a robe with one motion, then eased her onto the float. Three years on another planet had transformed Kamala. She was leaner, more muscular. Her fingernails were now a couple of centimeters long and there were four parallel scars incised on her left cheek, perhaps some Gendian's idea of beautification. But what struck me most was the darting strangeness in her eyes. This place, so familiar to me, seemed almost to shock her. It was as if she doubted the walls and was skeptical of air. She had learned to think like an alien.

"Welcome back." The float's whisper rose to a *whoosh* as I walked it down the hallway.

She swallowed hard and I thought she might cry. Three years ago, she would have. Lots of migrators are devastated when they come out of the assembler; it's because there is no transition. A few seconds ago Kamala was on Gend, fourth planet of the star we call Epsilon Leo, and now she was here in lunar orbit. She was almost home; her life's great adventure was over.

"Matthew?" she said.

"Michael." I couldn't help but be pleased that she remembered me. After all, she had changed my life.

I've guided maybe three hundred migrations—comings *and* goings—since I first came to Tuulen to study the dinos. Kamala Shastri's is the only quantum scan I've ever pirated. I doubt that the dinos care; I suspect this is a trespass they occasionally allow themselves. I know more about her—at least, as she was three years ago—than I know about myself. When the dinos sent her to Gend, she massed 50,391.72 grams and her red cell count was 4.81 million per mm^3. She could play the *nagasvaram*, a kind of bamboo flute. Her father came from Thana, near Bombay, and her favorite flavor of chewyfrute was watermelon and she'd had five lovers and when she was eleven she had wanted to be a gymnast but instead she had become a biomaterials engineer who at age twenty-nine had volunteered to go to the stars to learn how to grow artificial eyes. It took her two years to go through migrator training; she knew she could have backed out at any time, right up until the moment Silloin translated her into a superluminal signal. She understood what it meant to balance the equation.

I first met her on June 22, 2069. She shuttled over from Lunex's L1 port and came through our airlock at promptly 10:15, a small, roundish woman with black hair parted in the middle and drawn tight against her skull. They had darkened her skin against Epsilon Leo's UV; it was the deep blue-black of twilight. She was wearing a striped clingy and velcro slippers to help her get around for the short time she'd be navigating our .2 micrograv.

"Welcome to Tuulen Station." I smiled and offered my hand. "My name is Michael." We shook. "I'm supposed to be a sapientologist but I also moonlight as the local guide."

"Guide?" She nodded distractedly. "Okay." She peered past me, as if expecting someone else.

"Oh, don't worry," I said, "the dinos are in their cages."

Her eyes got wide as she let her hand slip from mine. "You call the Hanen dinos?"

"Why not?" I laughed. "They call us babies. The weeps, among other things."

She shook her head in amazement. People who've never met a dino tended to romanticize them: the wise and noble reptiles who had mastered superluminal physics and introduced Earth to the wonders of galactic civilization. I doubt Kamala had ever seen a dino play poker or gobble down a screaming rabbit. And she had never argued with Linna, who still wasn't convinced that humans were psychologically ready to go to the stars.

"Have you eaten?" I gestured down the corridor toward the reception rooms.

"Yes . . . I mean, no." She didn't move. "I am not hungry."

"Let me guess. You're too nervous to eat. You're too nervous to talk, even. You wish I'd just shut up, pop you into the marble, and beam you out. Let's just get this part the hell over with, eh?"

"I don't mind the conversation, actually."

"There you go. Well, Kamala, it is my solemn duty to advise you that there are no peanut butter and jelly sandwiches on Gend. And no chicken vindaloo. What's my name again?"

"Michael?"

"See, you're not *that* nervous. Not one taco, or a single slice of eggplant pizza. This is your last chance to eat like a human."

"Okay." She did not actually smile—she was too busy being brave—but a corner of her mouth twitched. "Actually, I would not mind a cup of tea."

"Now, tea they've got." She let me guide her toward Reception D; her slippers *snicked* at the velcro carpet. "Of course, they brew it from lawn clippings."

"The Gendians don't keep lawns. They live underground."

"Refresh my memory." I kept my hand on her shoulder; beneath the clingy, her muscles were rigid. "Are they the ferrets or the things with the orange bumps?"

"They look nothing like ferrets."

We popped through the door bubble into Reception D, a compact rectangular space with a scatter of low, unthreatening furniture. There was a kitchen station at one end, a closet with a vacuum toilet at the other. The ceiling was blue sky; the long wall showed a live view of the Charles River and the Boston skyline, baking in the late June sun. Kamala had just finished her doctorate at M.I.T.

I opaqued the door. She perched on the edge of a couch like a wren, ready to flit away.

While I was making her tea, my fingernail screen flashed. I answered it and a tiny Silloin came up in discreet mode. She didn't look at me; she was too busy watching arrays in the control room. =A problem,= her voice buzzed in my earstone, =most negligible, really. But we will have to void the last two from today's schedule. Save them at Lunex until first shift tomorrow. Can this one be kept for an hour?=

"Sure," I said. "Kamala, would you like to meet a Hanen?" I transferred Silloin to a dino-sized window on the wall. "Silloin, this is Kamala Shastri. Silloin is the one who actually runs things. I'm just the doorman."

Silloin looked through the window with her near eye, then swung around and peered at Kamala with her other. She was short for a dino, just over a meter tall, but she had an enormous head that teetered on her neck like a watermelon balancing on a grapefruit. She must have just oiled herself because her silver scales shone. =Kamala, you will accept my happiest intentions for you?= She raised her left hand, spreading the skinny digits to expose dark crescents of vestigial webbing.

"Of course, I . . ."

=And you will permit us to render you this translation?=

She straightened. "Yes."

=Have you questions?=

I'm sure she had several hundred, but at this point was probably too scared to ask. While she hesitated, I broke in. "Which came first, the lizard or the egg?"

Silloin ignored me. =It will be excellent for you to begin when?=

"She's just having a little tea," I said, handing her the cup. "I'll bring her along when she's done. Say an hour?"

Kamala squirmed on the couch. "No, really, it will not take me. . . ."

Silloin showed us her teeth, several of which were as long as piano keys. =That would be most appropriate, Michael.= She closed; a gull flew through the space where her window had been.

"Why did you do that?" Kamala's voice was sharp.

"Because it says here that you have to wait your turn. You're not the only migrator we're sending this morning." This was a lie, of course; we had had to cut the schedule because Jodi Latchaw, the other sapientologist assigned to Tuulen, was at the University of Hipparchus presenting our paper on the Hanen concept of identity. "Don't worry, I'll make the time fly."

For a moment, we looked at each other. I could have laid down an hour's worth of patter; I'd done that often enough. Or I could have drawn her out on why she was going: no doubt she had a blind grandma or second cousin just waiting for her to bring home those artificial eyes, not to mention potential spin-offs that could well end tuberculosis, famine, and premature ejaculation, *blah, blah, blah*. Or I could have just left her alone in the room to read the wall. The trick was guessing how spooked she really was.

"Tell me a secret," I said.

"What?"

"A secret, you know, something no one else knows."

She stared as if I'd just fallen off Mars.

"Look, in a little while you're going some place that's what . . . three hundred and ten light-years away? You're scheduled to stay for three years. By the time you come back, I could easily be rich, famous, and elsewhere; we'll probably never see each other again. So what have you got to lose? I promise not to tell."

She leaned back on the couch, and settled the cup in her lap. "This is another test, right? After everything they have put me through, they still have not decided whether to send me."

"Oh no, in a couple of hours you'll be cracking nuts with ferrets in some dark Gendian burrow. This is just me, talking."

"You are crazy."

"Actually, I believe the technical term is logomaniac. It's from the Greek: *logos* meaning word, *mania* meaning two bits short of a byte. I just love to chat is all. Tell you what, I'll go first. If my secret isn't juicy enough, you don't have to tell me anything."

Her eyes were slits as she sipped her tea. I was fairly sure that whatever she was worrying about at the moment, it wasn't being swallowed by the big blue marble.

"I was brought up Catholic," I said, settling onto a chair in front of her. "I'm not anymore, but that's not the secret. My parents sent me to Mary, Mother of God High School; we called it Moogoo. It was run by a couple of old priests, Father Thomas and his wife, Mother Jennifer. Father Tom taught physics, which I got a D in, mostly because he talked like he had walnuts in his mouth. Mother Jennifer taught theology and had all the warmth of a marble pew; her nickname was Mama Moogoo.

"One night, just two weeks before my graduation, Father Tom and Mama Moogoo went out in their Chevy Minimus for ice cream. On the way home, Mama Moogoo pushed a yellow light and got broadsided by an ambulance. Like I said, she was old, a hundred and twenty something; they should've lifted her license back in the fifties. She was killed instantly. Father Tom died in the hospital.

"Of course, we were all supposed to feel sorry for them and I guess I did a little, but I never really liked either of them and I resented the way their deaths had screwed things up for my class. So I was more annoyed than sorry, but then I also had this edge of guilt for being so uncharitable. Maybe you'd have to grow up Catholic to understand that. Anyway, the day after it happened they called an assembly in the gym and we were all there squirming on the bleachers and the cardinal himself telepresented a sermon. He kept trying to comfort us, like it had been our *parents* that had died. When I made a joke about it to the kid next to me, I got caught and spent the last week of my senior year with an in-school suspension."

Kamala had finished her tea. She slid the empty cup into one of the holders built into the table.

"Want some more?" I said.

She stirred restlessly. "Why are you telling me this?"

"It's part of the secret." I leaned forward in my chair. "See, my family lived down the street from Holy Spirit Cemetery and in order to get to the carryvan line on McKinley Ave., I had to cut through. Now this happened a couple of days after I got in trouble at the assembly. It was around midnight and I was coming home from a graduation party where I had taken a couple of pokes of insight, so I was feeling sly as a philosopher-king. As I walked through the cemetery, I stumbled across two dirt mounds right next to each other. At first I thought they were flower beds, then I saw the wooden crosses. Fresh graves: here lies Father Tom and Mama Moogoo. There wasn't much to the crosses: they were basically just stakes with crosspieces, painted white and hammered into the ground. The names were hand printed on them. The way I figure it, they were there to mark the graves until the stones got delivered. I didn't need any insight to recognize a once-in-a-lifetime opportunity. If I switched them, what were the chances anyone was going to notice? It was no problem sliding them out of their holes. I smoothed the dirt with my hands and then ran like hell."

Until that moment, she'd seemed bemused by my story and slightly condescending toward me. Now there was a glint of alarm in her eyes. "That was a terrible thing to do," she said.

"Absolutely," I said, "although the dinos think that the whole idea of planting bodies in graveyards and marking them with carved rocks is weepy. They say there is no identity in dead meat, so why get so sentimental about it? Linna keeps asking how come we don't put markers over our shit. But that's not the secret. See, it'd been a warmish night in the middle of June, only as I ran, the air turned cold. Freezing, I could see my breath. And my shoes got heavier and heavier, like they had turned to stone. As I got closer to the back gate, it felt like I was fighting a strong wind, except my clothes weren't flapping. I slowed to a walk. I know I could have pushed through, but my heart was thumping and then I heard this whispery seashell noise and I panicked. So the secret is I'm a coward. I switched the crosses back and I never went near that cemetery again. As a matter of fact," I nodded at the walls of Reception D on Tuulen Station, "when I grew up, I got about as far away from it as I could."

She stared as I settled back in my chair. "True story," I said and raised my right hand. She seemed so astonished that I started laughing. A smile bloomed on her dark face and suddenly she was giggling too. It was a soft liquid sound, like a brook bubbling over smooth stones; it made me laugh even harder. Her lips were full and her teeth were very white.

"Your turn," I said, finally.

"Oh no, I could not." She waved me off. "I don't have anything so good. . . ." She paused, then frowned. "You have told that before?"

"Once," I said. "To the Hanen, during the psych screening for this job.

Only I didn't tell them the last part. I know how dinos think, so I ended it when I switched the crosses. The rest is baby stuff." I waggled a finger at her. "Don't forget, you promised to keep my secret."

"Did I?"

"Tell me about when you were young. Where did you grow up?"

"Toronto." She glanced at me, appraisingly. "There *was* something, but not funny. Sad."

I nodded encouragement and changed the wall to Toronto's skyline dominated by the CN Tower, Toronto-Dominion Centre, Commerce Court, and the King's Needle.

She twisted to take in the view and spoke over her shoulder. "When I was ten we moved to an apartment, right downtown on Bloor Street so my mother could be close to work." She pointed at the wall and turned back to face me. "She is an accountant, my father wrote wallpaper for Imagineering. It was a huge building; it seemed as if we were always getting into the elevator with ten neighbors we never knew we had. I was coming home from school one day when an old woman stopped me in the lobby. 'Little girl,' she said, 'how would you like to earn ten dollars?' My parents had warned me not to talk to strangers but she obviously was a resident. Besides, she had an ancient pair of exolegs strapped on, so I knew I could outrun her if I needed to. She asked me to go to the store for her, handed me a grocery list and a cash card, and said I should bring everything up to her apartment, 10W. I should have been more suspicious because all the downtown groceries deliver but, as I soon found out, all she really wanted was someone to talk to her. And she was willing to pay for it, usually five or ten dollars, depending on how long I stayed. Soon I was stopping by almost every day after school. I think my parents would have made me stop if they had known; they were very strict. They would not have liked me taking her money. But neither of them got home until after six, so it was my secret to keep."

"Who was she?" I said. "What did you talk about?"

"Her name was Margaret Ase. She was ninety-seven years old and I think she had been some kind of counselor. Her husband and her daughter had both died and she was alone. I didn't find out much about her; she made me do most of the talking. She asked me about my friends and what I was learning in school and my family. Things like that. . . ."

Her voice trailed off as my fingernail started to flash. I answered it.

=Michael, I am pleased to call you to here.= Silloin buzzed in my ear. She was almost twenty minutes ahead of schedule.

"See, I told you we'd make the time fly." I stood; Kamala's eyes got very wide. "I'm ready if you are."

I offered her my hand. She took it and let me help her up. She wavered for a moment and I sensed just how fragile her resolve was. I put my hand around her waist and steered her into the corridor. In the micrograv of Tuulen Station, she already felt as insubstantial as a memory. "So tell me, what happened that was so sad?"

At first I thought she hadn't heard. She shuffled along, said nothing.

"Hey, don't keep me in suspense here, Kamala," I said. "You have to finish the story."

"No," she said. "I don't think I do."

I didn't take this personally. My only real interest in the conversation had been to distract her. If she refused to be distracted, that was her choice. Some migrators kept talking right up to the moment they slid into the big blue marble, but lots of them went quiet just before. They turned inward. Maybe in her mind she was already on Gend, blinking in the hard white light.

We arrived at the scan center, the largest space on Tuulen Station. Immediately in front of us was the marble, containment for the quantum nondemolition sensor array—QNSA for the acronymically inclined. It was the milky blue of glacial ice and big as two elephants. The upper hemisphere was raised and the scanning table protruded like a shiny gray tongue. Kamala approached the marble and touched her reflection, which writhed across its polished surface. To the right was a padded bench, the fogger, and a toilet. I looked left, through the control room window. Silloin stood watching us, her impossible head cocked to one side.

=She is docile?= She buzzed in my earstone.

I held up crossed fingers.

=Welcome, Kamala Shastri.= Silloin's voice came over the speakers with a soothing hush. =You are ready to open your translation?=

Kamala bowed to the window. "This is where I take my clothes off?"

=If you would be so convenient.=

She brushed past me to the bench. Apparently I had ceased to exist; this was between her and the dino now. She undressed quickly, folding her clingy into a neat bundle, tucking her slippers beneath the bench. Out of the corner of my eye, I could see tiny feet, heavy thighs, and the beautiful, dark smooth skin of her back. She stepped into the fogger and closed the door.

"Ready," she called.

From the control room, Silloin closed circuits which filled the fogger with a dense cloud of nanolenses. The nano stuck to Kamala and deployed, coating the surface of her body. As she breathed them, they passed from her lungs into her bloodstream. She only coughed twice; she had been well trained. When the eight minutes were up, Silloin cleared the air in the fogger and she emerged. Still ignoring me, she again faced the control room.

=Now you must arrange yourself on the scanning table,= said Silloin, =and enable Michael to fix you.=

She crossed to the marble without hesitation, climbed the gantry beside it, eased onto the table and lay back.

I followed her up. "Sure you won't tell me the rest of the secret?"

She stared at the ceiling, unblinking.

"Okay then." I took the canister and a sparker out of my hip pouch. "This is going to happen just like you've practiced it." I used the canister to respray the bottoms of her feet with nano. I watched her belly rise and fall, rise and fall. She was deep into her breathing exercise. "Remember, no skipping rope or whistling while you're in the scanner."

She did not answer. "Deep breath now," I said and touched a sparker to her big toe. There was a brief crackle as the nano on her skin wove into a net and stiffened, locking her in place. "Bark at the ferrets for me." I picked up my equipment, climbed down the gantry, and wheeled it back to the wall.

With a low whine, the big blue marble retracted its tongue. I watched the upper hemisphere close, swallowing Kamala Shastri, then joined Silloin in the control room.

I'm not of the school who thinks the dinos stink, another reason I got assigned to study them up close. Parikkal, for example, has no smell at all that I can tell. Normally Silloin had the faint but not unpleasant smell of stale wine. When she was under stress, however, her scent became vinegary and biting. It must have been a wild morning for her. Breathing through my mouth, I settled onto the stool at my station.

She was working quickly, now that the marble was sealed. Even with all their training, migrators tend to get claustrophobic fast. After all, they're lying in the dark, in nanobondage, waiting to be translated. Waiting. The simulator at the Singapore training center makes a noise while it's emulating a scan. Most compare it to a light rain pattering against the marble; for some, it's low volume radio static. As long as they hear the patter, the migrators think they're safe. We reproduce it for them while they're in our marble, even through scanning takes about three seconds and is utterly silent. From my vantage I could see that the sagittal, axial, and coronal windows had stopped blinking, indicating full data capture. Silloin was skirring busily to herself; her comm didn't bother to interpret. Wasn't saying anything baby Michael needed to know, obviously. Her head bobbed as she monitored the enormous spread of readouts; her claws clicked against touch screens that glowed orange and yellow.

At my station, there was only a migration status screen—and a white button.

I wasn't lying when I said I was just the doorman. My field is sapientology, not quantum physics. Whatever went wrong with Kamala's migration that morning, there was nothing *I* could have done. The dinos tell me that the quantum nondemolition sensor array is able to circumvent Heisenberg's Uncertainty Principle by measuring spacetime's most crogglingly small quantities without collapsing the wave/particle duality. How small? They say that no one can ever "see" anything that's only 1.62×10^{-33} centimeters long, because at that size, space and time come apart. Time ceases to exist and space becomes a random probablistic foam, sort of like quantum spit. We humans call this the Planck-Wheeler length. There's a Planck-Wheeler time, too: 10^{-45} of a second. If something happens and something else happens and the two events are separated by an interval of a mere 10^{-45} of a second, it is impossible to say which came first. It was all dino to me—and that's just the scanning. The Hanen use different tech to create artificial wormholes, hold them open with electromagnetic vacuum fluctuations, pass the superluminal signal through and then assemble the migrator from elementary particles at the destination.

On my status screen I could see that the signal which mapped Kamala Shastri had already been compressed and burst through the wormhole. All that we had to wait for was for Gend to confirm acquisition. Once they officially told us that they had her, it would be my job to balance the equation.

Pitter-patter, pitter-pat.

Some Hanen technologies are so powerful that they can alter reality itself. Wormholes could be used by some time-traveling fanatic to corrupt history; the scanner/assembler could be used to create a billion Silloins—or Michael Burrs. Pristine reality, unpolluted by such anomalies, has what the dinos call harmony. Before any sapients get to join the galactic club, they must prove total commitment to preserving harmony.

Since I had come to Tuulen to study the dinos, I had pressed the white button over two hundred times. It was what I had to do in order to keep my assignment. Pressing it sent a killing pulse of ionizing radiation through the cerebral cortex of the migrator's duplicated, and therefore unnecessary, body.

No brain, no pain; death followed within seconds. Yes, the first few times I'd balanced the equation had been traumatic. It was still . . . unpleasant. But this was the price of a ticket to the stars. If certain unusual people like Kamala Shastri had decided that price was reasonable, it was their choice, not mine.

=This is not a happy result, Michael.= Silloin spoke to me for the first time since I'd entered the control room. =Discrepancies are unfolding.= On my status screen I watched as the error-checking routines started turning up hits.

"Is the problem here?" I felt a knot twist suddenly inside me. "Or there?" If our original scan checked out, then all Silloin would have to do is send it to Gend again.

There was a long, infuriating silence. Silloin concentrated on part of her board as if it showed her firstborn hatchling chipping out of its egg. The respirator between her shoulders had ballooned to twice its normal size. My screen showed that Kamala had been in the marble for four minutes plus.

=It may be fortunate to recalibrate the scanner and begin over.=

"*Shit.*" I slammed my hand against the wall, felt the pain tingle to my elbow. "I thought you had it fixed." When error-checking turned up problems, the solution was almost always to retransmit. "You're sure, Silloin? Because this one was right on the edge when I tucked her in."

Silloin gave me a dismissive sneeze and slapped at the error readouts with her bony little hand, as if to knock them back to normal. Like Linna and the other dinos, she had little patience with what she regarded as our weepy fears of migration. However, unlike Linna, she was convinced that someday, after we had used Hanen technologies long enough, we would learn to think like dinos. Maybe she's right. Maybe when we've been squirting through wormholes for hundreds of years, we'll cheerfully discard our redundant bodies. When the dinos and other sapients migrate, the redundants zap themselves—very harmonious. They tried it with humans, but it didn't always work. That's why I'm here. =The need is most clear. It will prolong about thirty minutes,= she said.

Kamala had been alone in the dark for almost six minutes, longer than any migrator I'd ever guided. "Let me hear what's going on in the marble."

The control room filled with the sound of Kamala screaming. It didn't sound human to me—more like the shriek of tires skidding toward a crash.

"We've got to get her out of there," I said.

=That is baby thinking, Michael.=

"So she's a baby, damn it." I knew that bringing migrators out of the marble was big trouble. I could have asked Silloin to turn the speakers off and sat there while Kamala suffered. It was my decision.

"Don't open the marble until I get the gantry in place." I ran for the door. "And keep the sound effects going."

At the first crack of light, she howled. The upper hemisphere seemed to lift in slow motion; inside the marble she bucked against the nano. Just when I was sure it was impossible that she could scream any louder, she did. We had accomplished something extraordinary, Silloin and I; we had stripped the brave biomaterials engineer away completely, leaving in her place a terrified animal.

"Kamala, it's me. Michael."

Her frantic screams cohered into words. "Stop . . . *don't* . . . oh my god, someone *help*!" If I could have, I would've jumped into the marble to release her, but the sensor array is fragile and I wasn't going to risk causing any more problems with it. We both had to wait until the upper hemisphere swung fully open and the scanning table offered poor Kamala to me.

"It's okay. Nothing's going to happen, all right? We're bringing you out, that's all. Everything's all right."

When I released her with the sparker, she flew at me. We pitched back and almost toppled down the steps. Her grip was so tight I couldn't breathe.

"Don't *kill* me, don't, *please*, don't."

I rolled on top of her. "Kamala!" I wriggled one arm free and used it to pry myself from her. I scrabbled sideways to the top step. She lurched clumsily in the microgravity and swung at me; her fingernails raked across the back of my hand, leaving bloody welts. "Kamala, stop!" It was all I could do not to strike back at her. I retreated down the steps.

"You bastard. What are you assholes trying to do to me?" She drew several shuddering breaths and began to sob.

"The scan got corrupted somehow. Silloin is working on it."

=The difficulty is obscure,= said Silloin from the control room.

"But that's not your problem." I backed toward the bench.

"They lied," she mumbled and seemed to fold in upon herself as if she were just skin, no flesh or bones. "They said I wouldn't feel anything and here . . . do you know what it's like . . . it's. . . ."

I fumbled for her clingy. "Look, here are your clothes. Why don't you get dressed? We'll get you out of here."

"You bastard," she repeated, but her voice was empty.

She let me coax her down off the gantry. I counted nubs on the wall while she fumbled back into her clingy. They were the size of the old dimes my grandfather used to hoard and they glowed with a soft golden bioluminescence. I was up to forty-seven before she was dressed and ready to return to Reception D.

Where before she had perched expectantly at the edge of the couch, now she slumped back against it. "So what now?" she said.

"I don't know." I went to the kitchen station and took the carafe from the distiller. "What now, Silloin?" I poured water over the back of my hand to wash the blood off. It stung. My earstone was silent. "I guess we wait," I said finally.

"For what?"

"For her to fix . . ."

"I'm not going back in there."

I decided to let that pass. It was probably too soon to argue with her about it, although once Silloin recalibrated the scanner, she'd have very little time to change her mind. "You want something from the kitchen? Another cup of tea, maybe?"

"How about a gin and tonic—hold the tonic?" She rubbed beneath her eyes. "Or a couple of hundred milliliters of Serentol?"

I tried to pretend she'd made a joke. "You know the dinos won't let us open the bar for migrators. The scanner might misread your brain chemistry and your visit to Gend would be nothing but a three-year drunk."

"Don't you understand?" She was right back at the edge of hysteria. "I am not *going*!" I didn't really blame her for the way she was acting but, at that moment, all I wanted was to get rid of Kamala Shastri. I didn't care if she went on to Gend or back to Lunex or over the rainbow to Oz, just as long as I didn't have to be in the same room with this miserable creature who was trying to make me feel guilty about an accident I had nothing to do with.

"I thought I could do it." She clamped hands to her ears as if to keep from hearing her own despair. "I wasted the last two years convincing myself that I could just lie there and not think and then suddenly I'd be far away. I was going someplace wonderful and strange." She made a strangled sound and let her hands drop into her lap. "I was going to help people see."

"You did it, Kamala. You did everything we asked."

She shook her head. "I couldn't *not* think. That was the problem. And then there she was, trying to touch me. In the dark. I had not thought of her since. . . ." She shivered. "It's your fault for reminding me."

"Your secret friend," I said.

"Friend?" Kamala seemed puzzled by the word. "No, I wouldn't say she was a friend. I was always a little bit scared of her, because I was never quite sure what she wanted from me." She paused. "One day I went up to 10W after school. She was in her chair, staring down at Bloor Street. Her back was to me. I said, 'Hi, Ms. Ase.' I was going to show her a genie I had written, only she didn't say anything. I came around. Her skin was the color of ashes. I took her hand. It was like picking up something plastic. She was stiff, hard—not a person anymore. She had become a thing, like a feather or a bone. I ran; I had to get out of there. I went up to our apartment and I hid from her."

She squinted, as if observing—judging—her younger self through the lens of time. "I think I understand now what she wanted. I think she knew she was dying; she probably wanted me there with her at the end, or at least to find her body afterward and report it. Only I could *not.* If I told anyone she was dead, my parents would find out about us. Maybe people would suspect me of doing something to her—I don't know. I could have called security but I was only ten; I was afraid somehow they might trace me. A couple of weeks went by and still nobody had found her. By then it was too late to say anything. Everyone would have blamed me for keeping quiet for so long. At night I imagined her turning black and rotting into her chair like a banana. It made me sick; I couldn't sleep or eat. They had to put me in the hospital, because I had touched her. Touched *death.*"

=Michael,= Silloin whispered, without any warning flash. =An impossibility has formed.=

"As soon as I was out of that building, I started to get better. Then they found her. After I came home, I worked hard to forget Ms. Ase. And I did, almost." Kamala wrapped her arms around herself. "But just now she was with me again, inside the marble . . . I couldn't see her but somehow I knew she was reaching for me."

=Michael, Parikkal is here with Linna.=

"Don't you see?" She gave a bitter laugh. "How can I go to Gend? I'm *hallucinating.*"

=It has broken the harmony. Join us alone.=

I was tempted to swat at the annoying buzz in my ear.

"You know, I've never told anyone about her before."

"Well, maybe some good has come of this after all." I patted her on the knee. "Excuse me for a minute?" She seemed surprised that I would leave. I slipped into the hall and hardened the door bubble, sealing her in.

"What impossibility?" I said, heading for the control room.

=She is pleased to reopen the scanner?=

"Not pleased at all. More like scared shitless."

=This is Parikkal.= My earstone translated his skirring with a sizzling edge, like bacon frying. =The confusion was made elsewhere. No mishap can be connected to our station.=

I pushed through the bubble into the scan center. I could see the three dinos through the control window. Their heads were bobbing furiously. "Tell me," I said.

=Our communications with Gend were marred by a transient falsehood,= said Silloin. =Kamala Shastri has been received there and reconstructed.=

“She migrated?” I felt the deck shifting beneath my feet. “What about the one we’ve got here?”

=The simplicity is to load the redundant into the scanner and finalize. . . .=

“I’ve got news for you. She’s not going anywhere near that marble.”

=Her equation is not in balance.= This was Linna, speaking for the first time. Linna was not exactly in charge of Tuulen Station; she was more like a senior partner. Parikkal and Silloin had overruled her before—at least I thought they had.

“What do you expect me to do? Wring her neck?”

There was a moment’s silence—which was not as unnerving as watching them eye me through the window, their heads now perfectly still.

“No,” I said.

The dinos were skirring at each other; their heads wove and dipped. At first they cut me cold and the comm was silent, but suddenly their debate crackled through my earstone.

=This is just as I have been telling,= said Linna. =These beings have no realization of harmony. It is wrongful to further unleash them on the many worlds.=

=You may have reason,= said Parikkal. =But that is a later discussion. The need is for the equation to be balanced.=

=There is no time. We will have to discard the redundant ourselves.= Silloin bared her long brown teeth. It would take her maybe five seconds to rip Kamala’s throat out. And even though Silloin was the dino most sympathetic to us, I had no doubt she would enjoy the kill.

=I will argue that we adjourn human migration until this world has been rethought,= said Linna.

This was typical dino condescension. Even though they appeared to be arguing with each other, they were actually speaking to me, laying the situation out so that even the baby sapient would understand. They were informing me that I was jeopardizing the future of humanity in space. That the Kamala in Reception D was dead whether I quit or not. That the equation had to be balanced and it had to be now.

“Wait,” I said. “Maybe I can coax her back into the scanner.” I had to get away from them. I pulled my earstone out and slid it into my pocket. I was in such a hurry to escape that I stumbled as I left the scan center and had to catch myself in the hallway. I stood there for a second, staring at the hand pressed against the bulkhead. I seemed to see the splayed fingers through the wrong end of a telescope. I was far away from myself.

She had curled into herself on the couch, arms clutching knees to her chest, as if trying to shrink so that nobody would notice her.

"We're all set," I said briskly. "You'll be in the marble for less than a minute, guaranteed."

"*No*, Michael."

I could actually feel myself receding from Tuulen Station. "Kamala, you're throwing away a huge part of your life."

"It is my right." Her eyes were shiny.

No, it wasn't. She was redundant; she had no rights. What had she said about the dead old lady? She had become a thing, like a bone.

"Okay, then." I jabbed at her shoulder with a stiff forefinger. "Let's go."

She recoiled. "Go where?"

"Back to Lunex. I'm holding the shuttle for you. It just dropped off my afternoon list; I should be helping them settle in, instead of having to deal with you."

She unfolded herself slowly.

"Come on." I jerked her roughly to her feet. "The dinos want you off Tuulen as soon as possible and so do I." I was so distant, I couldn't see Kamala Shastri anymore.

She nodded and let me march her to the bubble door.

"And if we meet anyone in the hall, keep your mouth shut."

"You're being so mean." Her whisper was thick.

"You're being such a baby."

When the inner door glided open, she realized immediately that there was no umbilical to the shuttle. She tried to twist out of my grip but I put my shoulder into her, hard. She flew across the airlock, slammed against the outer door and caromed onto her back. As I punched the switch to close the door, I came back to myself. *I* was doing this terrible thing—me, Michael Burr. I couldn't help myself: I giggled. When I last saw her, Kamala was scrabbling across the deck toward me but she was too late. I was surprised that she wasn't screaming again; all I heard was her ferocious breathing.

As soon as the inner door sealed, I opened the outer door. After all, how many ways are there to kill someone on a space station? There were no guns. Maybe someone else could have stabbed or strangled her, but not me. Poison how? Besides, I wasn't thinking, I had been trying desperately not to think of what I was doing. I was a sapientologist, not a doctor. I always thought that exposure to space meant instantaneous death. Explosive decompression or something like. I didn't want her to suffer. I was trying to make it quick. Painless.

I heard the whoosh of escaping air and thought that was it; the body had been ejected into space. I had actually turned away when thumping started, frantic, like the beat of a racing heart. She must have found something to hold onto. *Thump, thump, thump!* It was too much. I sagged against the inner door—*thump, thump*—slid down it, laughing. Turns out that if you empty the lungs, it is possible to survive exposure to space for at least a minute, maybe two. I thought it was funny. *Thump!* Hilarious, actually. I had tried my best for her—risked my career—and this was how she repaid me? As I laid my cheek against the door, the *thumps* started to weaken. There were just a few centimeters between us, the difference between life and death. Now she knew all about balancing the equation. I was laughing so hard I could scarcely breathe. Just like the meat behind the door. Die already, you weepy bitch!

I don't know how long it took. The *thumping* slowed. Stopped. And then I was a hero. I had preserved harmony, kept our link to the stars open. I chuckled with pride; I could think like a dinosaur.

I popped through the bubble door into Reception D. "It's time to board the shuttle."

Kamala had changed into a clingy and velcro slippers. There were at least ten windows open on the wall; the room filled with the murmur of talking heads. Friends and relatives had to be notified; their hero had returned, safe and sound. "I have to go," she said to the wall. "I will call you when I land."

She gave me a smile that seemed stiff from disuse. "I want to thank you again, Michael." I wondered how long it took migrators to get used to being human. "You were such a help and I was such a . . . I was not myself." She glanced around the room one last time and then shivered. "I was really scared."

"You were."

She shook her head. "Was it that bad?"

I shrugged and led her out into the hall.

"I feel so silly now. I mean, I was in the marble for less than a minute and then"—she snapped her fingers—"there I was on Gend, just like you said." She brushed up against me as we walked; her body was hard under the clingy. "Anyway, I am glad we got this chance to talk. I really *was* going to look you up when I got back. I certainly did not expect to see you here."

"I decided to stay on." The inner door to the airlock glided open. "It's a job that grows on you." The umbilical shivered as the pressure between Tuulen Station and the shuttle equalized.

"You have got migrators waiting," she said.

"Two."

"I envy them." She turned to me. "Have *you* ever thought about going to the stars?"

"No," I said.

Kamala put her hand to my face. "It changes everything." I could feel the prick of her long nails—claws, really. For a moment I thought she meant to scar my cheek the way she had been scarred.

"I know," I said.

GEOFF RYMAN
Everywhere

{1999}

Geoff Ryman (1951–) was born in Canada and moved to the United States when he was eleven. He majored in history and English at UCLA, and has lived in England since 1973, although he has spent extended periods in Brazil and traveled frequently in Cambodia; throughout his travels he continues to identify himself as Canadian. He has been closely associated with the British sf magazine *Interzone* since 1984, with much of his short fiction published there, including "The Unconquered Country" (1984), winner of the British Science Fiction Award, and "Everywhere." His thoughtful and beautifully crafted writing sets a standard for the literary aims of the magazine. His sf novels are equally strong, notably *The Child Garden* (1989), winner of both the Arthur C. Clarke and the Campbell Awards, and *Air* (2004), which won the Clarke and the James Tiptree Jr. Awards. Ryman writes powerful mainstream fiction as well, including *Was* (1992), a fiction about AIDS and the writing and filming of *The Wizard of Oz*; *253* (1997 online, 1998 in print), an interactive novel from the viewpoints of passengers on the London Underground; and *The King's Last Song* (2006), which like "The Unconquered Country," is about Cambodia. In 2004, he and several other writers proposed the idea of Mundane Science Fiction, focusing on stories set within the solar system and reflecting plausible uses of science and technology, as a way to avoid wish-fulfillment fantasies of escape from terrestrial problems. While the movement has taken on a life of its own, Ryman's attachment to it is loose. His fiction commonly explores the nature of time and personal identity, showing people struggling to encompass both synchronous and linear time, individual and group identity. Often his fiction offers glimpses of utopia and transcendence, especially in operatic conclusions. Ryman, who is gay, makes a point of exploring gender in a flexible and sympathetic way: see, for instance, *Was*, *The Child Garden*, and "Birth Days" (2003).

"Everywhere" incorporates a number of Ryman's characteristic themes, as well as remarkable emotional power, into a few pages written in the voice of an ordinary boy. As the boy tells an interviewer about the death of his grandfather, the reader learns about the economics and technology of a utopian future Newcastle, England. No one is rich or poor and all, including children, work to earn luxuries such as mechanical wings, shoe-cars, and the narrator's interactive watch. The child's perspective and the modesty of the vision make this a mundane speculative future. The story's striking central image, the Angel of the North, part of what gives the story its transcendent tone, is an actual sculpture that looms over present-day Newcastle, but Ryman transforms it into a storage house for the saved memories and recorded activities of the city's future residents. These records form the "soul" of the community. Just as the soul of the community is contained in its memories, its utopian nature is contained in the telling of the story about it, so the boy's narration brings utopia into being as he keeps finding answers to the question, "What do I do next?" This is a rare example of an explicitly utopian story in a century marked by disillusion and exhaustion. Forster's and Ellison's dystopian stories are more typical.

When we knew Granddad was going to die, we took him to see the Angel of the North.

When he got there, he said: It's all different. There were none of these oaks all around it then, he said, Look at the size of them! The last time I saw this, he says to me, I was no older than you are now, and it was brand new, and we couldn't make out if we liked it or not.

We took him, the whole lot of us, on the tram from Blaydon. We made a day of it. All of Dad's exes and their exes and some of their kids and me Aunties and their exes and their kids. It wasn't that happy a group to tell you the truth. But Granddad loved seeing us all in one place.

He was going a bit soft by then. He couldn't tell what the time was anymore and his words came out wrong. The Mums made us sit on his lap. He kept calling me by my dad's name. His breath smelt funny but I didn't mind, not too much. He told me about how things used to be in Blaydon.

They used to have a gang in the Dene called Pedro's Gang. They drank something called Woodpecker and broke people's windows and they left empty tins of pop in the woods. If you were little you weren't allowed out cos everyone's Mum was so fearful and all. Granddad once saw twelve young lads go over and hit an old woman and take her things. One night his brother got drunk and put his fist through a window, and he went to the hospital, and he had to wait hours before they saw him and that was terrible.

I thought it sounded exciting meself. But I didn't say so because Granddad wanted me to know how much better things are now.

He says to me, like: the trouble was, Landlubber, we were just kids, but we all thought the future would be terrible. We all thought the world was going to burn up, and that everyone would get poorer and poorer, and the crime worse.

He told me that lots of people had no work. I don't really understand how anyone could have nothing to do. But then I've never got me head around what money used to be either.

Or why they built that Angel. It's not even that big, and it was old and covered in rust. It didn't look like an Angel to me at all, the wings were so big and square. Granddad said, no, it looks like an airplane, that's what airplanes looked like back then. It's meant to go rusty, it's the Industrial Spirit of the North.

I didn't know what he was on about. I asked Dad why the Angel was so important and he kept explaining it had a soul, but couldn't say how. The church choir showed up and started singing hymns. Then it started to rain. It was a wonderful day out.

I went back into the tram and asked me watch about the Angel.

This is my watch, here, see? It's dead good isn't it, it's got all sorts on it. It takes photographs and all. Here, look, this is the picture it took of Granddad by the Angel. It's the last picture I got of him. You can talk to people on it. And it keeps thinking of fun things for you to do.

> Why not explain to the interviewer why the Angel of the North is important?

Duh. Usually they're fun.

> Take the train to Newcastle and walk along the river until you see on the hill where people keep their homing pigeons. Muck out the cages for readies.

It's useful when you're a bit short, it comes up with ideas to make some dosh. It's really clever. It takes all the stuff that goes on around here and stirs it around and comes up with something new. Here, listen:

> The laws of evolution have been applied to fun. New generations of ideas are generated and eliminated at such a speed that evolution works in real time. It's survival of the funnest and you decide.

They evolve machines too. Have you seen our new little airplanes? They've run the designs through thousands of generations, and they got better and faster and smarter.

The vicar bought the whole church choir airplanes they can wear. The wings are really good, they look just like bird's wings with pinions sticking out like this. Oh! I really want one of them. You can turn somersaults in them. People build them in their sheds for spare readies, I could get one now if I had the dosh.

Every Sunday as long as it isn't raining, you can see the church choir take off in formation. Little old ladies in leotards and blue jeans and these big embroidered Mexican hats. They rev up and take off and start to sing the Muslim call to prayer. They echo all over the show. Then they cut their engines and spiral up on the updraft. That's when they start up on Nearer My God to Thee.

Every Sunday, Granddad and I used to walk up Shibbon Road to the Dene. It's so high up there that we could look down on top of them. He never got over it. Once he laughed so hard he fell down, and just lay there on the grass. We just lay on our backs and looked up at the choir, they just kept going up like they were kites.

When the Travellers come to Blaydon, they join in. Their wagons are pulled by horses and have calliopes built into the front, so on Sundays, when the choir goes up, the calliopes start up, so you got organ music all over the show as well. Me Dad calls Blaydon a sound sandwich. He says it's all the hills.

The Travellers like our acoustics, so they come here a lot. They got all sorts to trade. They got these bacteria that eat rubbish, and they hatch new machines, like smart door keys that only work for the right people. They make their own beer, but you got to be a bit careful how much you drink.

Granddad and I used to take some sarnies and our sleeping bags and kip with them. The Travellers go everywhere, so they sit around the fire and tell about all sorts going on, not just in England but France and Italia. One girl, her Mum let her go with them for a whole summer. She went to Prague and saw all these Buddhist monks from Thailand. They were Travellers and all.

Granddad used to tell the Travellers his stories too. When he was young he went to Mexico. India. The lot. You could in them days. He even went to Egypt, my Granddad. He used to tell the Travellers the same stories, over and over, but they never seemed to notice. Like, when he was in Egypt he tried to rent this boat to take him onto the Delta, and he couldn't figure why it was so expensive, and when he got on it, he found he'd rented a car ferry all to himself by mistake. He had the whole thing to himself. The noise of the engines scared off the birds which was the only reason he'd wanted the boat.

So, Granddad was something of a Traveller himself. He went everywhere.

There's all sorts to do around Blaydon. We got dolphins in the municipal swimming pool.

We dug it ourselves, in the Haughs just down there by the river. It's tidal, our river. Did you know? It had dolphins anyway, but our pool lured them in. They like the people and the facilities, like the video conferencing. They like video conferencing, do dolphins. They like being fed and all.

My Dad and I help make the food. We grind up fish heads on a Saturday at Safeways. It smells rotten to me, but then I'm not an aquatic mammal, am I? That's how we earned the readies to buy me my watch. You get everyone along grinding fish heads, everybody takes turns. Then you get to go to the swimming.

Sick people get first crack at swimming with the dolphins. When Granddad was sick, he'd take me with him. There'd be all this steam coming off the water like in a vampire movie. The dolphins always knew who wasn't right, what was wrong with them. Mrs. Grathby had trouble with her joints, they always used to be gentle with her, just nudge her along with their noses like. But Granddad, there was one he called Liam. Liam always used to jump up and land real hard right next to him, splash him all over and Granddad would push him away, laughing like, you know? He loved Liam. They were pals.

Have a major water-fight on all floors of the Grand Hotel in Newcastle.

Hear that? It just keeps doing that until something takes your fancy.

Hire Dad the giant bunny rabbit costume again and make him wear it.

We did that once before. It was dead fun. I think it knows Dad's a bit down since Granddad.

Call your friend Heidi and ask her to swap clothes with you and pretend to be each other for a day.

Aw Jeez! Me sister's been wearing me watch again! It's not fair! mucks it up, it's supposed to know what I like, not her and that flipping Heidi. And she's got her own computer, it's loads better than mine, it looks like a shirt and has earphones, so no one else can hear it. It's not fair! People just come clod-hopping through. You don't get to keep nothing.

Look this is all I had to do to get this watch!

Grind fishfood on 3.11, 16.11, 20.12 and every Sunday until 3.3
Clean pavements three Sundays
Deliver four sweaters for Step Mum

Help Dad with joinery for telecoms outstation
Wire up Mrs Grathby for video immersion
Attend school from April 10th to 31 July inclusive

I did even more than that. At least I got some over. I'm saving up for a pair of cars.

Me and me mates love using the cars. I borrow me Dad's pair. You wear them like shoes and they're smart. It's great fun on a Sunday. We all go whizzin down Lucy Street together, which is this great big hill, but the shoes won't let you go too fast or crash into anything. We all meet up, whizz around in the mall in great big serpent. You can preprogram all the cars together, so you all break up and then all at once come back together, to make shapes and all.

Granddad loved those cars. He hated his stick, so he'd go shooting off in my Dad's pair, ducking and weaving, and shouting back to me, Come on, Landlubber, keep up! I was a bit scared in them days, but he kept up at me til I joined in. He'd get into those long lines, and we'd shoot off the end of them, both of us. He'd hold me up.

He helped me make me lantern and all. Have you seen our lanterns, all along the mall? They look good when the phosphors go on at night. All the faces on them are real people, you know. You know the ink on them's made of these tiny chips with legs? Dad's seen them through a microscope, he says they look like synchronized swimmers.

I got one with my face on it. I was bit younger then so I have this really naff crew cut. Granddad helped me make it. It tells jokes. I'm not very good at making jokes up, but Granddad had this old joke book. At least I made the effort.

Let's see, what else. There's loads around here. We got the sandbox in front of the old mall. Everybody has a go at that, making things. When King William died all his fans in wheelchairs patted together a picture of him in sand. Then it rained. But it was a good picture.

Our sandbox is a bit different. It's got mostly real sand. There's only one corner of it computer dust. It's all right for kids and that or people who don't want to do things themselves. I mean when we were little we had the dust make this great big 3D sign Happy Birthday Granddad Piper. He thought it was wonderful because if you were his age and grew up with PCs and that, it must be wonderful, just to think of something and have it made.

I don't like pictures, they're too easy. Me, I like to get stuck in. If I go to the sandbox to make something, I want to come back with sand under me fingernails. Me Dad's the same. When Newcastle won the cup, me and me mates made this big Newcastle crest out of real sand. Then we had a sand-fight. It took me a week to get the sand out of me hair. I got loads of mates now, but I didn't used to.

Granddad was me mate for a while. I guess I was his pet project. I always was a bit quiet, and a little bit left out, and also I got into a bit of trouble from time to time. He got me out of myself.

You know I was telling you about the Angel? When I went back into that tram I sat and listened to the rain on the roof. It was dead quiet and there was nobody around, so I could be meself. So I asked me watch. OK then. What is this Angel? And it told me the story of how the Angel of the North got a soul.

There was this prisoner in Hull jail for thieving cos he run out of readies cos he never did nothing. It was all his fault really, he says so himself. He drank and cheated his friends and all that and did nothing with all his education.

He just sat alone in his cell. First off, he was angry at the police for catching him, and then he was angry with himself for getting caught and doing it and all of that. Sounds lovely, doesn't he? Depressing isn't the word.

Then he got this idea, to give the Angel a soul.

It goes like this. There are 11 dimensions, but we only see three of them and time, and the others are what was left over after the Big Bang. They're too small to see but they're everywhere at the same time, and we live in them too, but we don't know it. There's no time there, so once something happens, it's like a photograph, you can't change it.

So what the prisoner of Hull said that means is that everything we do gets laid down in the other dimensions like train tracks. It's like a story, and it doesn't end until we die, and that does the job for us. That's our soul, that story.

So what the prisoner in Hull does, is work in the prison, get some readies and pay to have a client put inside the Angel's head.

And all the other computers that keep track of everyone's jobs or the questions they asked, or just what they're doing, that all gets uploaded to the Angel.

Blaydon's there. It's got all of us, grinding fish heads. Every time someone makes tea or gets married from Carlisle to Ulverton from Newcastle to Derby, that gets run through the Angel. And that Angel is laying down the story of the North.

My watch told me that, sitting in that tram.

Then everyone else starts coming back in, but not Dad and Granddad, so I go out to fetch them.

The clouds were all pulled down in shreds. It looked like the cotton candy that Dad makes at fetes. The sky was full of the church choir in their little airplanes. For just a second, it looked like a Mother Angel, with all her little ones.

I found Dad standing alone with Granddad. I thought it was rain on my Dad's face, but it wasn't. He was looking at Granddad, all bent and twisted, facing into the wind.

We got to go Dad, I said.

And he said, In a minute son. Granddad was looking up at the planes and smiling.

And I said it's raining Dad. But they weren't going to come in. So I looked at the Angel and all this rust running off it in red streaks onto the concrete. So I asked, if it's an Angel of the North, then why is it facing south?

And Granddad says, Because it's holding out its arms in welcome.

He didn't want to go.

We got him back into the tram, and back home, and he started to wheeze a bit, so me Step Mum put him to bed and about eight o'clock she goes in to swab his teeth with vanilla, and she comes out and says to Dad, I think he's stopped breathing.

So I go in, and I can see, no he's still breathing. I can hear it. And his tongue flicks, like he's trying to say something. But Dad comes in, and they all start to cry and carry on. And the neighbors all come in, yah, yah, yah, and I keep saying, it's not true, look, he's still breathing. What do they have to come into it for, it's not their Granddad, is it?

No one was paying any attention to the likes of me, were they? So I just take off. There's this old bridge you're not allowed on. It's got trees growing out of it. The floor's gone, and you have to walk along the top of the barricades. You fall off, you go straight into the river, but it's a good dodge into Newcastle.

So I just went and stood there for a bit, looking down on the river. Me Granddad used to take me sailing. We'd push off from the Haughs, and shoot out under this bridge, I could see where we were practically. And we'd go all the way down the Tyne and out to sea. He used to take me out to where the dolphins were. You'd see Liam come up. He was still wearing his computer, Liam, like a crown.

So I'm standing on the bridge, and me watch says: go down to the swimming pool, and go and tell Liam that Granddad's dead.

It's a bit like a dog I guess. You got to show one dog the dead body of the other or it will pine.

So I went down to the pool, but it's late and raining and there's nobody there, and I start to call him, like: Liam! Li-am! But he wasn't there.

So me watch says: he's wearing his computer: give him a call on his mobile.

So me watch goes bleep bleep bleep, and there's a crackle and suddenly I hear a whoosh and crickle, and there's all these cold green waves on the face of my watch, and I say Liam? Liam, this is me, remember me, Liam? My Granddad's dead Liam. I thought you might need to know.

But what is he, just a dolphin right, I don't know what it meant. How's he supposed to know who I am. You all right then, Liam? Catching lots of fish are you? So I hung up.

And I stand there, and the rain's really bucketing down, and I don't want to go home. Talking to yourself. It's the first sign, you know.

And suddenly me watch starts up again, and it's talking to me with Granddad's voice. You wanna hear what it said? Here. Hear.

Hello there, Landlubber. How are ya? This is your old Granddad. It's a dead clever world we live in, isn't it? They've rigged this thing up here, so that I can put this in your watch for when you need it.

Listen, me old son. You mustn't grieve, you know. Things are different now. They know how it works. We used to think we had a little man in our heads who watched everything on a screen and when you died he went to heaven not you. Now, they know, there's no little man, there's no screen. There's just a brain putting everything together. And what we do is ask ourselves: what do we think about next? What do we do next?

You know all about those dimension things, don't you? Well I got a name for them. I call them Everywhere. Cos they are. And I want you to know, that I'm Everywhere now.

That's how we live forever in heaven these days. And it's true, me old son. You think of me still traveling around Mexico before I met your Mamby. Think of me in India. Think of me learning all about readies to keep up with you lot. Think of me on me boat, sailing out to sea. Remember that day I took you sailing out beyond the Tyne mouth? It's still there, Landlubber.

You know, all the evil in the world, all the sadness comes from not having a good answer to that question: what do I do next? You just keep thinking of good things to do, lad. You'll be all right. We'll all be all right. I wanted you to know that.

I got me footie on Saturdays, Granddad. Then I'm thinking I'll start up school again. They got a sailing club now. I thought I'd join it, Granddad, thought I'd take them out to where you showed me the dolphins. I'll tell them about Everywhere.

Did you know, Granddad?

They're making a new kind of watch. It's going to show us Everywhere, too.

CHARLES STROSS
Rogue Farm

{2003}

Charles Stross (1964–) is a British writer currently based in Edinburgh, Scotland. He has academic degrees in pharmacy and in computer science and has worked as a technical writer, programmer, pharmacist, and freelance journalist specializing in Linux and free software. With Canadian sf writer Cory Doctorow, with whom his work is often associated, Stross has been active in the Creative Commons licensing and copyright movement. Although he published his first story in 1987, the majority of his fiction has appeared only since 2001. By his own reckoning, by June 2008 he had sold sixteen novels and two short-story collections. His first two novels, *Singularity Sky* (2003) and its sequel *Iron Sunrise* (2005), were nominated for Hugo Awards. *Accelerando* (2005), a "fix-up" novel comprised of previously published stories, was short-listed for the 2006 Arthur C. Clarke Award. *Glasshouse* (2006), a loose sequel to *Accelerando*, was nominated for both a Hugo Award and a Tiptree Award, and won the 2007 Prometheus Award of the Libertarian Futurist Society. Stross has also published several novels in a projected six-part fantasy series, *The Merchant Princes* (2004–).

Largely because of novels such as *Singularity Sky* and *Accelerando* and short stories such as "Rogue Farm," Stross's sf has come to be associated with that of post-Singularity writers such as Doctorow and Australian Greg Egan. Egan's story "Closer," for example, also explores some of the features of possible posthuman subjects in fictional worlds imaginatively transformed by radical new technologies. The idea of the Singularity poses an intriguing challenge to contemporary sf writers because it places an impermeable conceptual wall between present and future, so that the future becomes radically unknowable. At its most extreme, the Singularity spells the end of traditional sf extrapolation.

Not surprisingly, some sf writers such as Stross have responded to the challenge of the Singularity by telling stories that delight in imagining the many and varied weirdnesses of the post-Singularity future. *Singularity Sky* and *Accelerando* propel their readers into fast-moving technologically shaped futures populated by cyborgs and posthumans of all kinds, intelligences both artificial and alien, and bleeding-edge technologies both material and virtual—all defined by the sheer pace of transformation. The manic entrepreneur Manfred Macx in *Accelerando*, who makes a good living by giving away cutting-edge ideas, is emblematic of Stross's fiction at its best. In fact, Manfred is a good stand-in for Stross himself, a writer whose fiction is sometimes overwhelmed by the sheer proliferation of its ideas. The post-Singularity future in "Rogue Farm" is at once absurd and oddly gripping, colored by Maddi's tragic ennui, by Bob the dog's taste for drugs, by the rogue farm's efforts to reach Jupiter "on a mission for love," and by the near-infinite potential of technologies such as cloning tanks and matter replicators. A twenty-four-minute animated version of "Rogue Farm" was produced for Scottish Television in 2004.

It was a bright, cool March morning: mare's tails trailed across the south-eastern sky toward the rising sun. Joe shivered slightly in the driver's seat as he twisted the starter handle on the old front loader he used to muck out the barn. Like its owner, the ancient Massey Ferguson had seen better days; but it had survived worse abuse than Joe routinely handed out. The diesel clattered, spat out a gobbet of thick blue smoke, and chattered to itself dyspeptically. His mind as blank as the sky above, Joe slid the tractor into gear, raised the front scoop, and began turning it toward the open doors of the barn—just in time to see an itinerant farm coming down the road.

"Bugger," swore Joe. The tractor engine made a hideous grinding noise and died. He took a second glance, eyes wide, then climbed down from the tractor and trotted over to the kitchen door at the side of the farmhouse. "Maddie!" he called, forgetting the two-way radio clipped to his sweater hem. "Maddie! There's a farm coming!"

"Joe? Is that you? Where are you?" Her voice wafted vaguely from the bowels of the house.

"Where are you?" he yelled back.

"I'm in the bathroom."

"Bugger," he said again. "If it's the one we had round the end last month . . ."

The sound of a toilet sluiced through his worry. It was followed by a drumming of feet on the staircase; then Maddie erupted into the kitchen. "Where is it?" she demanded.

"Out front, about a quarter mile up the lane."

"Right." Hair wild and eyes angry about having her morning ablutions cut short, Maddie yanked a heavy green coat on over her shirt. "Opened the cupboard yet?"

"I was thinking you'd want to talk to it first."

"Too right I want to talk to it. If it's that one that's been lurking in the copse near Edgar's pond, I got some *issues* to discuss with it." Joe shook his head at her anger and went to unlock the cupboard in the back room. "You take the shotgun and keep it off our property," she called after him. "I'll be out in a minute."

Joe nodded to himself, then carefully picked out the twelve-gauge and preloaded magazine. The gun's power-on self-test lights flickered erratically but it seemed to have a full charge. Slinging it, he locked the cupboard carefully and went back out into the farmyard to warn off their unwelcome visitor.

The farm squatted, buzzing and clicking to itself, in the road outside Armitage End. Joe eyed it warily from behind the wooden gate, shotgun under his arm. It was a medium-size one, probably with half a dozen human components subsumed into it—a formidable collective. Already it was deep into farm-fugue, no longer relating very clearly to people outside its own communion of mind. Beneath its leathery black skin he could see hints of internal structure, cytocellular macroassemblies flexing and glooping in disturbing motions. Even though it was only a young adolescent, it was already the size of an antique heavy tank, and it blocked the road just as efficiently as an Apatosaurus would have. It smelled of yeast and gasoline.

Joe had an uneasy feeling that it was watching him. "Buggerit, I don't have time for this," he muttered. The stable waiting for the small herd of cloned spidercows cluttering up the north paddock was still knee-deep in manure, and the tractor seat wasn't getting any warmer while he shivered out here, waiting for Maddie to come and sort this thing out. It wasn't a big herd, but it was as big as his land and his labor could manage—the big biofabricator in the shed could assemble mammalian livestock faster than he could feed them up and sell them with an honest HAND-RAISED NOT VAT-GROWN label. "What do you want with us?" he yelled up at the gently buzzing farm.

"Brains, fresh brains for Baby Jesus," crooned the farm in a warm contralto, startling Joe half out of his skin. "Buy my brains!" Half a dozen disturbing cauliflower shapes poked suggestively out of the farm's back and then retracted again, coyly.

"Don't want no brains around here," Joe said stubbornly, his fingers whitening on the stock of the shotgun. "Don't want your kind round here, neither. Go away."

"I'm a nine-legged semiautomatic groove machine!" crooned the farm. "I'm on my way to Jupiter on a mission for love! Won't you buy my brains?" Three curious eyes on stalks extruded from its upper glacis.

"Uh—" Joe was saved from having to dream up any more ways of saying "fuck off" by Maddie's arrival. She'd managed to sneak her old battle dress home after a stint keeping the peace in Mesopotamia twenty years ago, and she'd managed to keep herself in shape enough to squeeze inside. Its left knee squealed ominously when she walked it about, which wasn't often, but it still worked well enough to manage its main task—intimidating trespassers.

"You." She raised one translucent arm, pointed at the farm. "Get off my land. *Now*."

Taking his cue, Joe raised his shotgun and thumbed the selector to full auto. It wasn't a patch on the hardware riding Maddie's shoulders, but it underlined the point.

The farm hooted: "Why don't you love me?" it asked plaintively.

"*Get off my land*," Maddie amplified, volume cranked up so high that Joe winced. "*Ten seconds! Nine! Eight*—" Thin rings sprang out from the sides of her arms, whining with the stress of long disuse as the Gauss gun powered up.

"I'm going! I'm going!" The farm lifted itself slightly, shuffling backwards. "Don't understand. I only wanted to set you free to explore the universe. Nobody wants to buy my fresh fruit and brains. What's wrong with the world?"

They waited until the farm had retreated round the bend at the top of the hill. Maddie was the first to relax, the rings retracting back into the arms of her battle dress, which solidified from ethereal translucency to neutral olive drab as it powered down. Joe safed his shotgun. "Bastard," he said.

"Fucking-A." Maddie looked haggard. "That was a bold one." Her face was white and pinched-looking, Joe noted. Her fists were clenched. She had the shakes, he realized without surprise. Tonight was going to be another major nightmare night, and no mistake.

"The fence." On again and off again for the past year they'd discussed wiring up an outer wire to the CHP baseload from their little methane plant.

"Maybe this time. Maybe." Maddie wasn't keen on the idea of frying passers-by without warning, but if anything might bring her around, it would be the prospect of being overrun by a bunch of rogue farms. "Help me out of this, and I'll cook breakfast," she said.

"Got to muck out the barn," Joe protested.

"It can wait on breakfast," Maddie said shakily. "I need you."

"Okay." Joe nodded. She was looking bad; it had been a few years since her last fatal breakdown, but when Maddie said "I need you," it was a bad idea to ignore her. That way led to backbreaking labor on the biofab and loading her backup tapes into the new body; always a messy business. He took her arm and steered her toward the back porch. They were nearly there when he paused.

"What is it?" asked Maddie.

"Haven't seen Bob for a while," he said slowly. "Sent him to let the cows into the north paddock after milking. Do you think—?"

"We can check from the control room," she said tiredly. "Are you really worried?"

"With that thing blundering around? What do you think?"

"He's a good working dog," Maddie said uncertainly. "It won't hurt him. He'll be all right; just you page him."

After Joe helped her out of her battle dress, and after Maddie spent a good long while calming down, they breakfasted on eggs from their own hens, homemade cheese, and toasted bread made with rye from the hippie commune on the other side of the valley. The stone-floored kitchen in the dilapidated house they'd squatted and rebuilt together over the past twenty years was warm and homely. The only purchase from outside the valley was the coffee, beans from a hardy GM strain that grew like a straggling teenager's beard all along the Cumbrian hilltops. They didn't say much: Joe, because he never did, and Maddie, because there wasn't anything that she wanted to discuss. Silence kept her personal demons down. They'd known each other for many years, and even when there wasn't anything to discuss, they could cope with each other's silence. The voice radio on the windowsill opposite the cast-iron stove stayed off, along with the TV set hanging on the wall next to the fridge. Breakfast was a quiet time of day.

"Dog's not answering," Joe commented over the dregs of his coffee.

"He's a good dog." Maddie glanced at the yard gate uncertainly. "You afraid he's going to run away to Jupiter?"

"He was with me in the shed." Joe picked up his plate and carried it to the sink, began running hot water onto the dishes. "After I cleaned the lines I told him to go take the herd up the paddock while I did the barn." He glanced up, looking out the window with a worried expression. The Massey Ferguson was parked right in front of the open barn doors as if holding at bay the mountain of dung, straw, and silage that mounded up inside like an invading odorous enemy, relic of a frosty winter past.

Maddie shoved him aside gently and picked up one of the walkie-talkies from the charge point on the windowsill. It bleeped and chuckled at her. "Bob, come in. Over." She frowned. "He's probably lost his headset again."

Joe racked the wet plates to dry. "I'll move the midden. You want to go find him?"

"I'll do that." Maddie's frown promised a talking-to in store for the dog when she caught up with him. Not that Bob would mind: words ran off him like water off a duck's back. "Cameras first." She prodded the battered TV set to life, and grainy bisected views flickered across the screen, garden, yard, Dutch barn, north paddock, east paddock, main field, copse. "Hmm."

She was still fiddling with the smallholding surveillance system when Joe clambered back into the driver's seat of the tractor and fired it up once more. This time there was no cough of black smoke, and as he hauled the mess of manure out of the barn and piled it into a three-meter-high midden, a quarter of a ton at a time, he almost managed to forget about the morning's unwelcome visitor. Almost.

By late morning, the midden was humming with flies and producing a remarkable stench, but the barn was clean enough to flush out with a hose and broom. Joe was about to begin hauling the midden over to the fermentation tanks buried round the far side of the house when he saw Maddie coming back up the path, shaking her head. He knew at once what was wrong.

"Bob," he said, expectantly.

"Bob's fine. I left him riding shotgun on the goats." Her expression was peculiar. "But that *farm*—"

"Where?" he asked, hurrying after her.

"Squatting in the woods down by the stream," she said tersely. "Just over our fence."

"It's not trespassing, then."

"It's put down feeder roots! Do you have any idea what that means?"

"I don't—" Joe's face wrinkled in puzzlement. "Oh."

"Yes. *Oh.*" She stared back at the outbuildings between their home and the woods at the bottom of their smallholding, and if looks could kill, the intruder would be dead a thousand times over. "It's going to estivate, Joe, then it's going to grow to maturity on our patch. And do you know where it said it was going to go when it finishes growing? Jupiter!"

"Bugger," Joe said faintly, as the true gravity of their situation began to sink in. "We'll have to deal with it first."

"That wasn't what I meant," Maddie finished. But Joe was already on his way out the door. She watched him crossing the yard, then shook her head. "Why am I stuck here?" she asked, but the cooker wasn't answering.

The hamlet of Outer Cheswick lay four kilometers down the road from Armitage End, four kilometers past mostly derelict houses and broken-down barns, fields given over to weeds and walls damaged by trees. The first half of the twenty-first century had been cruel years for the British agrobusiness sector; even harsher if taken in combination with the decline in population and the consequent housing surplus. As a result, the dropouts of the forties and fifties were able to take their pick from among the gutted shells of once fine farmhouses. They chose the best and moved in, squatted in the derelict outbuildings, planted their seeds and tended their flocks and practiced their DIY skills, until a generation later a mansion fit for a squire stood in lonely isolation alongside a decaying road where no more cars drove. Or rather, it would have taken a generation had there been any children against whose lives it could be measured; these were the latter decades of the population crash, and what a previous century would have labeled downshifter DINK couples were now in the majority, far outnumbering any breeder colonies. In this aspect of their life, Joe and Maddie were boringly conventional. In other respects they weren't: Maddie's nightmares, her aversion to alcohol, and her withdrawal from society were all relics of her time in Peaceforce. As for Joe, he liked it here. Hated cities, hated the Net, hated the burn of the new. Anything for a quiet life . . .

The Pig and Pizzle, on the outskirts of Outer Cheswick, was the only pub within about ten kilometers—certainly the only one within staggering distance for Joe when he'd had a skinful of mild—and it was naturally a seething den of local gossip, not least because Ole Brenda refused to allow electricity, much less bandwidth, into the premises. (This was not out of any sense of misplaced technophobia, but a side effect of Brenda's previous life as an attack hacker with the European Defense Forces.)

Joe paused at the bar. "Pint of bitter?" he asked tentatively. Brenda glanced at him and nodded, then went back to loading the antique washing machine. Presently she pulled a clean glass down from the shelf and held it under the tap.

"Hear you've got farm trouble," she said noncommitally as she worked the hand pump on the beer engine.

"Uh-huh." Joe focused on the glass. "Where'd you hear that?"

"Never you mind." She put the glass down to give the head time to settle. "You want to talk to Arthur and Wendy-the-Rat about farms. They had one the other year."

"Happens." Joe took his pint. "Thanks, Brenda. The usual?"

"Yeah." She turned back to the washer. Joe headed over to the far corner where a pair of huge leather sofas, their arms and backs ripped and scarred by generations of Brenda's semiferal cats, sat facing each other on either side of a cold hearth. "Art, Rats. What's up?"

"Fine, thanks." Wendy-the-Rat was well over seventy, one of those older folks who had taken the p53 chromosome hack and seemed to wither into timelessness: white dreadlocks, nose and ear studs dangling loosely from leathery holes, skin like a desert wind. Art had been her boy-toy once, back before middle age set its teeth into him. He hadn't had the hack, and looked older than she did. Together they ran a smallholding, mostly pharming vaccine chicks but also doing a brisk trade in high-nitrate fertilizer that came in on the nod and went out in sacks by moonlight.

"Heard you had a spot of bother?"

"'S true." Joe took a cautious mouthful. "Mm, good. You ever had farm trouble?"

"Maybe." Wendy looked at him askance, slitty-eyed. "What kinda trouble you got in mind?"

"Got a farm collective. Says it's going to Jupiter or something. Bastard's homesteading the woods down by Old Jack's stream. Listen . . . Jupiter?"

"Aye, well, that's one of the destinations, sure enough." Art nodded wisely, as if he knew anything.

"Naah, that's bad." Wendy-the-Rat frowned. "Is it growing trees, do you know?"

"Trees?" Joe shook his head. "Haven't gone and looked, tell the truth. What the fuck makes people do that to themselves, anyway?"

"Who the fuck cares?" Wendy's face split in a broad grin. "Such as don't think they're human anymore, meself."

"It tried to sweet-talk us," Joe said.

"Aye, they do that," said Arthur, nodding emphatically. "Read somewhere they're the ones as think we aren't fully human. Tools an' clothes and farmyard machines, like? Sustaining a pre-post-industrial lifestyle instead of updating our genome and living off the land like God intended?"

"'Ow the hell can something with nine legs and eye stalks call itself human?" Joe demanded, chugging back half his pint in one angry swallow.

"It used to be, once. Maybe used to be a bunch of people." Wendy got a weird and witchy look in her eye. "'Ad a boyfriend back thirty, forty years ago, joined a Lamarckian clade. Swapping genes an' all, the way you or me'd swap us underwear. Used to be a 'viromentalist back when antiglobalization was about big corporations pissing on us all for profits. Got into gene hackery and self-sufficiency big time. I slung his fucking ass when he turned green and started photosynthesizing."

"Bastards," Joe muttered. It was deep green folk like that who'd killed off the agricultural-industrial complex in the early years of the century, turning large portions of the countryside into ecologically devastated wilderness gone to rack and ruin. Bad enough that they'd set millions of countryfolk out of work—but that they'd gone on to turn green, grow extra limbs and emigrate to Jupiter orbit was adding insult to injury. And having a good time in the process, by all accounts. "Din't you 'ave a farm problem, coupla years back?"

"Aye, did that," said Art. He clutched his pint mug protectively.

"It went away," Joe mused aloud.

"Yeah, well." Wendy stared at him cautiously.

"No fireworks, like." Joe caught her eye. "And no body. Huh."

"Metabolism," said Wendy, apparently coming to some kind of decision. "That's where it's at."

"Meat—" Joe, no biogeek, rolled the unfamiliar word around his mouth irritably. "I used to be a software dude before I burned, Rats. You'll have to 'splain the jargon 'fore using it."

"You ever wondered how those farms *get* to Jupiter?" Wendy probed.

"Well." Joe shook his head. "They, like, grow stage trees? Rocket logs? An' then they est-ee-vate and you are fucked if they do it next door 'cause when those trees go up they toast about a hundred hectares?"

"Very good," Wendy said heavily. She picked up her mug in both hands and gnawed on the rim, edgily glancing around as if hunting for police gnats. "Let's you and me take a hike."

Pausing at the bar for Ole Brenda to refill her mug, Wendy led Joe out past Spiffy Buerke—throwback in green wellingtons and Barbour jacket—and her latest femme, out into what had once been a car park and was now a tattered wasteground out back behind the pub. It was dark, and no residual light pollution stained the sky: the Milky Way was visible overhead, along with the pea-size red cloud of orbitals that had gradually swallowed Jupiter over the past few years. "You wired?" asked Wendy.

"No, why?"

She pulled out a fist-size box and pushed a button on the side of it, waited for a light on its side to blink green, and nodded. "Fuckin' polis bugs."

"Isn't that a—?"

"Ask me no questions, an' I'll tell you no fibs." Wendy grinned.

"Uh-huh." Joe took a deep breath: he'd guessed Wendy had some dodgy connections, and this—a portable local jammer—was proof: any police bugs within two or three meters would be blind and dumb, unable to relay their chat to the keyword-trawling subsentient coppers whose job it was to prevent conspiracy-to-commit offenses before they happened. It was a relic of the Internet Age, when enthusiastic legislators had accidentally demolished the right of free speech in public by demanding keyword monitoring of everything within range of a network terminal—not realizing that in another few decades "network terminals" would be self-replicating 'bots the size of fleas and about as common as dirt. (The Net itself had collapsed shortly thereafter, under the weight of self-replicating viral libel lawsuits, but the legacy of public surveillance remained.) "Okay. Tell me about metal, meta—"

"Metabolism." Wendy began walking toward the field behind the pub. "And stage trees. Stage trees started out as science fiction, like? Some guy called Niven—anyway. What you do is, you take a pine tree and you hack it. The xylem vessels running up the heartwood, usually they just lignify and die, in a normal tree. Stage trees go one better, and before the cells die, they *nitrate* the cellulose in their walls. Takes one fuckin' crazy bunch of hacked 'zymes to do it, right? And lots of energy, more energy than trees'd normally have to waste. Anyways, by the time the tree's dead, it's like ninety percent nitrocellulose, plus built-in stiffeners and baffles and microstructures. It's not, like, straight explosive—it detonates cell by cell, and *some* of the xylem tubes are, eh, well, the farm grows custom-hacked fungal hyphae with a depolarizing membrane nicked from human axons down them to trigger the reaction. It's about efficient as 'at old-time Ariane or Atlas rocket. Not very, but enough."

"Uh." Joe blinked. "That meant to mean something to me?"

"Oh 'eck, Joe." Wendy shook her head. "Think I'd bend your ear if it wasn't?"

"Okay." He nodded, seriously. "What can I do?"

"Well." Wendy stopped and stared at the sky. High above them, a belt of faint light sparkled with a multitude of tiny pinpricks; a deep green wagon train making its orbital transfer window, self-sufficient posthuman Lamarckian colonists, space-adapted, embarking on the long, slow transfer to Jupiter.

"Well?" He waited expectantly.

"You're wondering where all that fertilizer's from," Wendy said elliptically.

"Fertilizer." His mind blanked for a moment.

"Nitrates."

He glanced down, saw her grinning at him. Her perfect fifth set of teeth glowed alarmingly in the greenish overspill from the light on her jammer box.

"Tha' knows it make sense," she added, then cut the jammer.

When Joe finally staggered home in the small hours, a thin plume of smoke was rising from Bob's kennel. Joe paused in front of the kitchen door and sniffed anxiously, then relaxed. Letting go of the door handle, he walked over to the kennel and sat down outside. Bob was most particular about his den—even his own humans didn't go in there without an invitation. So Joe waited.

A moment later there was an interrogative cough from inside. A dark, pointed snout came out, dribbling smoke from its nostrils like a particularly vulpine dragon. "Rrrrrrr?"

"'S'me."

"Uuurgh." A metallic click. "Smoke good smoke joke cough tickle funny arf arf?"

"Yeah, don't mind if I do."

The snout pulled back into the kennel; a moment later it reappeared, teeth clutching a length of hose with a mouthpiece on one end. Joe accepted it graciously, wiped off the mouthpiece, leaned against the side of the kennel, and inhaled. The weed was potent and smooth: within a few seconds the uneasy dialogue in his head was still.

"Wow, tha's a good turnup."

"Arf-arf-ayup."

Joe felt himself relaxing. Maddie would be upstairs, snoring quietly in their decrepit bed: waiting for him, maybe. But sometimes a man just had to be alone with his dog and a good joint, doing man-and-dog stuff. Maddie understood this and left him his space. Still . . .

"'At farm been buggering around the pond?"

"Growl exclaim fuck-fuck yup! Sheep-shagger."

"If it's been at our lambs—"

"Nawwwwrr. Buggrit."

"So whassup?"

"Grrrr, Maddie yap-yap farmtalk! Sheep-shagger."

"Maddie's been *talking* to it?"

"Grrr yes-yes!"

"Oh, shit. Do you remember when she did her last backup?"

The dog coughed fragrant blue smoke. "Tank thump-thump full cow moo beef clone."

"Yeah, I think so, too. Better muck it out tomorrow. Just in case."

"Yurrrrrp." But while Joe was wondering whether this was agreement or just a canine eructation, a lean paw stole out of the kennel mouth and yanked the hookah back inside. The resulting slobbering noises and clouds of aromatic blue smoke left Joe feeling a little queasy: so he went inside.

The next morning, over breakfast, Maddie was even quieter than usual. Almost meditative.

"Bob said you'd been talking to that farm," Joe commented over his eggs.

"Bob—" Maddie's expression was unreadable. "Bloody dog." She lifted the Rayburn's hot plate lid and peered at the toast browning underneath. "Talks too much."

"Did you?"

"Ayup." She turned the toast and put the lid back down on it.

"Said much?"

"It's a farm." She looked out the window. "Not a fuckin' worry in the world 'cept making its launch window for Jupiter."

"It—"

"Him. Her. They." Maddie sat down heavily in the other kitchen chair. "It's a collective. Usedta be six people. Old, young, whatever, they's decided ter go to Jupiter. One of 'em was telling me how it happened. How she'd been living like an accountant in Bradford, had a nervous breakdown. Wanted *out*. Self-sufficiency." For a moment her expression turned bleak. "Felt herself growing older but not bigger, if you follow."

"So how's turning into a bioborg an improvement?" Joe grunted, forking up the last of his scrambled eggs.

"They're still separate people: bodies are overrated, anyway. Think of the advantages: not growing older, being able to go places and survive anything, never being on your own, not bein' trapped—" Maddie sniffed. "Fuckin' toast's on fire!"

Smoke began to trickle out from under the hot plate lid. Maddie yanked the wire toasting rack out from under it and dunked it into the sink, waited for waterlogged black crumbs to float to the surface before taking it out, opening it, and loading it with fresh bread.

"Bugger," she remarked.

"You feel trapped?" Joe asked. *Again*? He wondered.

Maddie grunted evasively. "Not your fault, love. Just life."

"Life." Joe sniffed, then sneezed violently as the acrid smoke tickled his nose. "Life!"

"Horizon's closing in," she said quietly. "Need a change of horizons."

"Ayup, well, rust never sleeps, right? Got to clean out the winter stables, haven't I?" said Joe. He grinned uncertainly at her as he turned away. "Got a shipment of fertilizer coming in."

In between milking the herd, feeding the sheep, mucking out the winter stables, and surreptitiously EMPing every police 'bot on the farm into the silicon afterlife, it took Joe a couple of days to get round to running up his toy on the household fabricator. It clicked and whirred to itself like a demented knitting machine as it ran up the gadgets he'd ordered—a modified crop sprayer with double-walled tanks and hoses, an air rifle with a dart loaded with a potent cocktail of tubocurarine and etorphine, and a breathing mask with its own oxygen supply.

Maddie made herself scarce, puttering around the control room but mostly disappearing during the daytime, coming back to the house after dark to crawl, exhausted, into bed. She didn't seem to be having nightmares, which was a good sign. Joe kept his questions to himself.

It took another five days for the smallholding's power field to concentrate enough juice to begin fueling up his murder weapons. During this time, Joe took the house off-Net in the most deniable and surreptitiously plausible way, a bastard coincidence of squirrel-induced cable fade and a badly shielded alternator on the backhoe to do for the wireless chitchat. He'd half expected Maddie to complain, but she didn't say anything—just spent more time away in Outer Cheswick or Lower Gruntlingthorpe or wherever she'd taken to holing up.

Finally, the tank was filled. So Joe girded his loins, donned his armor, picked up his weapons, and went to do battle with the dragon by the pond.

The woods around the pond had once been enclosed by a wooden fence, a charming copse of old-growth deciduous trees, elm and oak and beech growing uphill, smaller shrubs nestling at their ankles in a green skirt that reached all the way to the almost-stagnant waters. A little stream fed into it during rainy months, under the feet of a weeping willow; children had played here, pretending to explore the wilderness beneath the benevolent gaze of their parental control cameras.

That had been long ago. Today the woods really *were* wild. No kids, no picnicking city folks, no cars. Badgers and wild coypu and small, frightened wallabies roamed the parching English countryside during the summer dry season. The water drew back to expose an apron of cracked mud, planted with abandoned tin cans and a supermarket trolley of Precambrian vintage, its GPS tracker long since shorted out. The bones of the technological epoch, poking from the treacherous surface of a fossil mud bath. And around the edge of the mimsy puddle, the stage trees grew.

Joe switched on his jammer and walked in among the spear-shaped conifers. Their needles were matte black and fuzzy at the edges, fractally divided, the better to soak up all the available light: a network of taproots and fuzzy black grasslike stuff covered the ground densely around them. Joe's breath wheezed noisily in his ears, and he sweated into the airtight suit as he worked, pumping a stream of colorless smoking liquid at the roots of each ballistic trunk. The liquid fizzed and evaporated on contact: it seemed to bleach the wood where it touched. Joe carefully avoided the stream: this stuff made him uneasy. As did the trees, but liquid nitrogen was about the one thing he'd been able to think of that was guaranteed to kill the trees stone dead without igniting them. After all, they had cores that were basically made of gun cotton—highly explosive, liable to go off if you subjected them to a sudden sharp impact or the friction of a chainsaw. The tree he'd hit on creaked ominously, threatening to fall sideways, and Joe stepped round it, efficiently squirting at the remaining roots. Right into the path of a distraught farm.

"My holy garden of earthly delights! My forest of the imaginative future! My delight, my trees, my trees!" Eye stalks shot out and over, blinking down at him in horror as the farm reared up on six or seven legs and pawed the air in front of him. "Destroyer of saplings! Earth mother rapist! Bunny-strangling vivisectionist!"

"Back off," said Joe, dropping his cryogenic squirter and fumbling for his air gun.

The farm came down with a ground-shaking thump in front of him and stretched eyes out to glare at him from both sides. They blinked, long black eyelashes fluttering across angry blue irises. "How *dare* you?" demanded the farm. "My treasured seedlings!"

"Shut the fuck up," Joe grunted, shouldering his gun. "Think I'd let you burn my holding when tha' rocket launched? Stay the *fuck* away," he added as a tentacle began to extend from the farm's back.

"My crop," it moaned quietly. "My exile! Six more years around the sun chained to this well of sorrowful gravity before next the window opens! No brains for Baby Jesus! Defenestrator! We could have been so happy together if you hadn't fucked up! Who set you up to this? Rat Lady?" It began to gather itself, muscles rippling under the leathery mantle atop its leg cluster.

So Joe shot it.

Tubocurarine is a muscle relaxant: it paralyzes skeletal muscles, the kind over which human nervous systems typically exert conscious control. Etorphine is an insanely strong opiate—twelve hundred times as potent as heroin. Given time, a farm, with its alien adaptive metabolism and consciously controlled proteome might engineer a defense against the etorphine—but Joe dosed his dart with enough to stun a blue whale, and he had no intention of giving the farm enough time.

It shuddered and went down on one knee as he closed in on it, a Syrette raised. "Why?" it asked plaintively in a voice that almost made him wish he hadn't pulled the trigger. "We could have gone together!"

"Together?" he asked. Already the eye stalks were drooping; the great lungs wheezed effortfully as it struggled to frame a reply.

"I was going to ask you," said the farm, and half its legs collapsed under it, with a thud like a baby earthquake. "Oh, Joe, if only—"

"Joe? *Maddie*?" he demanded, nerveless fingers dropping the tranquilizer gun.

A mouth appeared in the farm's front, slurred words at him from familiar seeming lips, words about Jupiter and promises. Appalled, Joe backed away from the farm. Passing the first dead tree, he dropped the nitrogen tank: then an impulse he couldn't articulate made him turn and run, back to the house, eyes almost blinded by sweat or tears. But he was too slow, and when he dropped to his knees next to the farm, pharmacopoeia clicking and whirring to itself in his arms, he found it was already dead.

"Bugger," said Joe, and he stood up, shaking his head. "*Bugger.*" He keyed his walkie-talkie: "Bob, come in, Bob!"

"Rrrrowl?"

"Momma's had another break-down. Is the tank clean, like I asked?"

"Yap!"

"Okay. I got 'er backup tapes in t'office safe. Let's get t' tank warmed up for 'er an' then shift t' tractor down 'ere to muck out this mess."

That autumn, the weeds grew unnaturally rich and green down in the north paddock of Armitage End.

TED CHIANG
Exhalation

• • • •

{ 2008 }

We conclude this collection with a recent story by one of sf's most intriguing writers of short fiction. Ted Chiang (1967–) was born in Port Jefferson, New York. He has a degree in computer science and is a graduate of the Clarion Science Fiction and Fantasy Writers Workshop. Although he has published only eleven stories to date, Chiang has won many prestigious awards for his beautifully crafted fiction, including a Nebula Award for "Tower of Babylon" (1990), the John W. Campbell Award for Best New Writer in 1992, and the Theodore Sturgeon Memorial Award for "Story of Your Life" (1998). His one collection, *Stories of Your Life and Others* (2002), includes "Seventy-Two Letters" (2000), for which he won a Sidewise Award, and "Hell Is the Absence of God" (2002), for which he won a second Nebula Award, a Locus Award, and a Hugo Award. In keeping with this impressive record, "Exhalation" won a British Science Fiction Association Award, a Locus Award, and the Hugo Award for Best Short Story in 2009. In the words of influential sf and fantasy editor Ellen Datlow, "Ted Chiang is one of the rare contemporary science-fiction writers who has made his considerable reputation without producing one novel. His stories brim with originality and seduce with their complexity."

Chiang's fiction is always meticulously constructed and full of surprising perspectives. There is no typical Chiang story, but he often emphasizes the pleasures of scientific discovery, even if that discovery is made by a mechanical creature who inhabits a world enclosed in chromium, as in "Exhalation." Chiang's first story, "The Tower of Babylon," is told from the point of view of a laborer working on the monumental title structure and, like "Exhalation," it concludes with a kind of epistemological epiphany. "Seventy-two Letters," a golem story, literalizes the idea that the use of language is a creative act. "Story of Your Life" examines memory and loss in the context of a xenolinguist's efforts to communicate with mysterious alien visitors to earth.

In "Exhalation," which is written as the memoir of an argon-breathing metal anatomist, scientific experimentation leads to apocalyptic revelation for a race of mechanical beings—Asimov's pulp-era robots updated for the twenty-first century—who inhabit a world bounded by an infinitely high wall of solid chromium. The characters and setting in Chiang's story are radically different from our own world. At the same time, "Exhalation" tells a familiar sf story, about sentience's urge to understand the complexities of the world that it inhabits, its unceasing curiosity about the origins and ends of life and about its own nature, and about the sense of wonder such explorations can evoke. Chiang's mechanical narrator concludes with advice to the reader: "Contemplate the marvel that is existence . . . [A]s I am inscribing these words, I am doing the same."

It has long been said that air (which others call argon) is the source of life. This is not in fact the case, and I engrave these words to describe how I came to understand the true source of life and, as a corollary, the means by which life will one day end.

For most of history, the proposition that we drew life from air was so obvious that there was no need to assert it. Every day we consume two lungs heavy with air; every day we remove the empty ones from our chest and replace them with full ones. If a person is careless and lets his air level run too low, he feels the heaviness of his limbs and the growing need for replenishment. It is exceedingly rare that a person is unable to get at least one replacement lung before his installed pair runs empty; on those unfortunate occasions where this has happened—when a person is trapped and unable to move, with no one nearby to assist him—he dies within seconds of his air running out.

But in the normal course of life, our need for air is far from our thoughts, and indeed many would say that satisfying that need is the least important part of going to the filling stations. For the filling stations are the primary venue for social conversation, the places from which we draw emotional sustenance as well as physical. We all keep spare sets of full lungs in our homes, but when one is alone, the act of opening one's chest and replacing one's lungs can seem little better than a chore. In the company of others, however, it becomes a communal activity, a shared pleasure.

If one is exceedingly busy, or feeling unsociable, one might simply pick up a pair of full lungs, install them, and leave one's emptied lungs on the other side of the room. If one has a few minutes to spare, it's simple courtesy to connect the empty lungs to an air dispenser and refill them for the next person. But by far the most common practice is to linger and enjoy the company of others, to discuss the news of the day with friends or acquaintances and, in passing, offer newly filled lungs to one's interlocutor. While this perhaps does not constitute air sharing in the strictest sense, there is camaraderie derived from the awareness that all our air comes from the same source, for the dispensers are but the exposed terminals of pipes extending from the reservoir of air deep underground, the great lung of the world, the source of all our nourishment.

Many lungs are returned to the same filling station the next day, but just as many circulate to other stations when people visit neighboring districts; the lungs are all identical in appearance, smooth cylinders of aluminum, so one cannot tell whether a given lung has always stayed close to home or whether it has traveled long distances. And just as lungs are passed between persons and districts, so are news and gossip. In this way one can receive news from remote districts, even those at the very edge of the world, without needing to leave home, although I myself enjoy traveling. I have journeyed all the way to the edge of the world, and seen the solid chromium wall that extends from the ground up into the infinite sky.

It was at one of the filling stations that I first heard the rumors that prompted my investigation and led to my eventual enlightenment. It began innocently enough, with a remark from our district's public crier. At noon of the first day of every year, it is traditional for the crier to recite a passage of verse, an ode composed long ago for this annual celebration, which takes exactly one hour to deliver. The crier mentioned that on his most recent performance, the turret clock struck the hour before he had finished, something that had never happened before. Another person remarked that this was a coincidence, because he had just returned from a nearby district where the public crier had complained of the same incongruity.

No one gave the matter much thought beyond the simple acknowledgement that seemed warranted. It was only some days later, when there arrived word of a similar deviation between the crier and the clock of a third district, that the suggestion was made that these discrepancies might be evidence of a defect in the mechanism common to all the turret clocks, albeit a curious one to cause the clocks to run faster rather than slower. Horologists investigated the turret clocks in question, but on inspection they could discern no imperfection. In fact, when compared against the timepieces normally employed for such calibration purposes, the turret clocks were all found to have resumed keeping perfect time.

I myself found the question somewhat intriguing, but I was too focused on my own studies to devote much thought to other matters. I was and am a student of anatomy, and to provide context for my subsequent actions, I now offer a brief account of my relationship with the field.

Death is uncommon, fortunately, because we are durable and fatal mishaps are rare, but it makes difficult the study of anatomy, especially since many of the accidents serious enough to cause death leave the deceased's remains too damaged for study. If lungs are ruptured when full, the explosive force can tear a body asunder, ripping the titanium as easily as if it were tin. In the past, anatomists focused their attention on the limbs, which were the most likely to survive intact. During the very first anatomy lecture I attended a century ago, the lecturer showed us a severed arm, the casing removed to reveal the dense column of rods and pistons within. I can vividly recall the way, after he had connected its arterial hoses to a wall-mounted lung he kept in the laboratory, he was able to manipulate the actuating rods that protruded from the arm's ragged base, and in response the hand would open and close fitfully.

In the intervening years, our field has advanced to the point where anatomists are able to repair damaged limbs and, on occasion, attach a severed limb. At the same time we have become capable of studying the physiology of the living; I have given a version of that first lecture I saw, during which I opened the casing of my own arm and directed my students' attention to the rods that contracted and extended when I wiggled my fingers.

Despite these advances, the field of anatomy still had a great unsolved mystery at its core: the question of memory. While we knew a little about the structure of the brain, its physiology is notoriously hard to study because of the brain's extreme delicacy. It is typically the case in fatal accidents that, when the skull is breached, the brain erupts in a cloud of gold, leaving little besides shredded filament and leaf from which nothing useful can be discerned. For decades the prevailing theory of memory was that all of a person's experiences were engraved on sheets of gold foil; it was these sheets, torn apart by the force of the blast, that was the source of the tiny flakes found after accidents. Anatomists would collect the bits of gold leaf—so thin that light passes greenly through them—and spend years trying to reconstruct the original sheets, with the hope of eventually deciphering the symbols in which the deceased's recent experiences were inscribed.

I did not subscribe to this theory, known as the inscription hypothesis, for the simple reason that if all our experiences are in fact recorded, why is it that our memories are incomplete? Advocates of the inscription hypothesis offered an explanation for forgetfulness—suggesting that over time the foil sheets become misaligned from the stylus which reads the memories, until the oldest sheets shift out of contact with it altogether—but I never found it convincing. The appeal of the theory was easy for me to appreciate, though; I too had devoted many an hour to examining flakes of gold through a microscope, and can imagine how gratifying it would be to turn the fine adjustment knob and see legible symbols come into focus.

More than that, how wonderful would it be to decipher the very oldest of a deceased person's memories, ones that he himself had forgotten? None of us can remember much more than a hundred years in the past, and written records—accounts that we ourselves inscribed but have scant memory of doing so—extend only a few hundred years before that. How many years did we live before the beginning of written history? Where did we come from? It is the promise of finding the answers within our own brains that makes the inscription hypothesis so seductive.

I was a proponent of the competing school of thought, which held that our memories were stored in some medium in which the process of erasure was no more difficult than recording: perhaps in the rotation of gears, or the positions of a series of switches. This theory implied that everything we had forgotten was indeed lost, and our brains contained no histories older than those found in our libraries. One advantage of this theory was that it better explained why, when lungs are installed in those who have died from lack of air, the revived have no memories and are all but mindless: somehow the shock of death had reset all the gears or switches. The inscriptionists claimed the shock had merely misaligned the foil sheets, but no one was willing to kill a living person, even an imbecile, in order to resolve the debate. I had envisioned an experiment which might allow me to determine the truth conclusively, but it was a risky one, and deserved careful consideration before it was undertaken. I remained undecided for the longest time, until I heard more news about the clock anomaly.

Word arrived from a more distant district that its public crier had likewise observed the turret clock striking the hour before he had finished his new year's recital. What made this notable was that his district's clock employed a different mechanism, one in which the hours were marked by the flow of mercury into a bowl. Here the discrepancy could not be explained by a common mechanical fault. Most people suspected fraud, a practical joke perpetrated by mischief makers. I had a different suspicion, a darker one that I dared not voice, but it decided my course of action; I would proceed with my experiment.

The first tool I constructed was the simplest: in my laboratory I fixed four prisms on mounting brackets and carefully aligned them so that their apexes formed the corners of a rectangle. When arranged thus, a beam of light directed at one of the lower prisms was reflected up, then backward, then down, and then forward again in a quadrilateral loop. Accordingly, when I sat with my eyes at the level of the first prism, I obtained a clear view of the back of my own head. This solipsistic periscope formed the basis of all that was to come.

A similarly rectangular arrangement of actuating rods allowed a displacement of action to accompany the displacement of vision afforded by the prisms. The bank of actuating rods was much larger than the periscope, but still relatively straightforward in design; by contrast, what was attached to the end of these respective mechanisms was far more intricate. To the periscope I added a binocular microscope mounted on an armature capable of swiveling side to side or up and down. To the actuating rods I added an array of precision manipulators, although that description hardly does justice to those pinnacles of the mechanician's art. Combining the ingenuity of anatomists and the inspiration provided by the bodily structures they studied, the manipulators enabled their operator to accomplish any task he might normally perform with his own hands, but on a much smaller scale.

Assembling all of this equipment took months, but I could not afford to be anything less than meticulous. Once the preparations were complete, I was able to place each of my hands on a nest of knobs and levers and control a pair of manipulators situated behind my head, and use the periscope to see what they worked on. I would then be able to dissect my own brain.

The very idea must sound like pure madness, I know, and had I told any of my colleagues, they would surely have tried to stop me. But I could not ask anyone else to risk themselves for the sake of anatomical inquiry, and because I wished to conduct the dissection myself, I would not be satisfied by merely being the passive subject of such an operation. Auto-dissection was the only option.

I brought in a dozen full lungs and connected them with a manifold. I mounted this assembly beneath the worktable that I would sit at, and positioned a dispenser to connect directly to the bronchial inlets within my chest. This would supply me with six days' worth of air. To provide for the possibility that I might not have completed my experiment within that period, I had scheduled a visit from a colleague at the end of that time. My presumption, however, was that the only way I would not have finished the operation in that period would be if I had caused my own death.

I began by removing the deeply curved plate that formed the back and top of my head; then the two, more shallowly curved plates that formed the sides. Only my faceplate remained, but it was locked into a restraining bracket, and I could not see its inner surface from the vantage point of my periscope; what I saw exposed was my own brain. It consisted of a dozen or more subassemblies, whose exteriors were covered by intricately molded shells; by positioning the periscope near the fissures that separated them,

I gained a tantalizing glimpse at the fabulous mechanisms within their interiors. Even with what little I could see, I could tell it was the most beautifully complex engine I had ever beheld, so far beyond any device man had constructed that it was incontrovertibly of divine origin. The sight was both exhilarating and dizzying, and I savored it on a strictly aesthetic basis for several minutes before proceeding with my explorations.

It was generally hypothesized that the brain was divided into an engine located in the center of the head which performed the actual cognition, surrounded by an array of components in which memories were stored. What I observed was consistent with this theory, since the peripheral subassemblies seemed to resemble one another, while the subassembly in the center appeared to be different, more heterogeneous and with more moving parts. However the components were packed too closely for me to see much of their operation; if I intended to learn anything more, I would require a more intimate vantage point.

Each subassembly had a local reservoir of air, fed by a hose extending from the regulator at the base of my brain. I focused my periscope on the rearmost subassembly and, using the remote manipulators, I quickly disconnected the outlet hose and installed a longer one in its place. I had practiced this maneuver countless times so that I could perform it in a matter of moments; even so, I was not certain I could complete the connection before the subassembly had depleted its local reservoir. Only after I was satisfied that the component's operation had not been interrupted did I continue; I rearranged the longer hose to gain a better view of what lay in the fissure behind it: other hoses that connected it to its neighboring components. Using the most slender pair of manipulators to reach into the narrow crevice, I replaced the hoses one by one with longer substitutes. Eventually, I had worked my way around the entire subassembly and replaced every connection it had to the rest of my brain. I was now able to unmount this subassembly from the frame that supported it, and pull the entire section outside of what was once the back of my head.

I knew it was possible I had impaired my capacity to think and was unable to recognize it, but performing some basic arithmetic tests suggested that I was uninjured. With one subassembly hanging from a scaffold above, I now had a better view of the cognition engine at the center of my brain, but there was not enough room to bring the microscope attachment itself in for a close inspection. In order for me to really examine the workings of my brain, I would have to displace at least half a dozen subassemblies.

Laboriously, painstakingly, I repeated the procedure of substituting hoses for other subassemblies, repositioning another one farther back, two more higher up, and two others out to the sides, suspending all six from the scaffold above my head. When I was done, my brain looked like an explosion frozen an infinitesimal fraction of a second after the detonation, and again I felt dizzy when I thought about it. But at last the cognition engine itself was exposed, supported on a pillar of hoses and actuating rods leading down into my torso. I now also had room to rotate my microscope around a full three hundred and sixty degrees, and pass my gaze across the inner faces of the subassemblies I had moved. What I saw was a microcosm of auric machinery, a landscape of tiny spinning rotors and miniature reciprocating cylinders.

As I contemplated this vista, I wondered, where was my body? The conduits which displaced my vision and action around the room were in principle no different from those which connected my original eyes and hands to my brain. For the duration of this experiment, were these manipulators not essentially my hands? Were the magnifying lenses at the end of my periscope not essentially my eyes? I was an everted person, with my tiny, fragmented body situated at the center of my own distended brain. It was in this unlikely configuration that I began to explore myself.

I turned my microscope to one of the memory subassemblies, and began examining its design. I had no expectation that I would be able to decipher my memories, only that I might divine the means by which they were recorded. As I had predicted, there were no reams of foil pages visible, but to my surprise neither did I see banks of gearwheels or switches. Instead, the subassembly seemed to consist almost entirely of a bank of air tubules. Through the interstices between the tubules I was able to glimpse ripples passing through the bank's interior.

With careful inspection and increasing magnification, I discerned that the tubules ramified into tiny air capillaries, which were interwoven with a dense latticework of wires on which gold leaves were hinged. Under the influence of air escaping from the capillaries, the leaves were held in a variety of positions. These were not switches in the conventional sense, for they did not retain their position without a current of air to support them, but I hypothesized that these were the switches I had sought, the medium in which my memories were recorded. The ripples I saw must have been acts of recall, as an arrangement of leaves was read and sent back to the cognition engine.

Armed with this new understanding, I then turned my microscope to the cognition engine. Here too I observed a latticework of wires, but they did not bear leaves suspended in position; instead the leaves flipped back and forth almost too rapidly to see. Indeed, almost the entire engine appeared to be in motion, consisting more of lattice than of air capillaries, and I wondered how air could reach all the gold leaves in a coherent manner. For many hours I scrutinized the leaves, until I realized that they themselves were playing the role of capillaries; the leaves formed temporary conduits and valves that existed just long enough to redirect air at other leaves in turn, and then disappeared as a result. This was an engine undergoing continuous transformation, indeed modifying itself as part of its operation. The lattice was not so much a machine as it was a page on which the machine was written, and on which the machine itself ceaselessly wrote.

My consciousness could be said to be encoded in the position of these tiny leaves, but it would be more accurate to say that it was encoded in the ever-shifting pattern of air driving these leaves. Watching the oscillations of these flakes of gold, I saw that air does not, as we had always assumed, simply provide power to the engine that realizes our thoughts. Air is in fact the very medium of our thoughts. All that we are is a pattern of air flow. My memories were inscribed, not as grooves on foil or even the position of switches, but as persistent currents of argon.

In the moments after I grasped the nature of this lattice mechanism, a cascade of insights penetrated my consciousness in rapid succession. The first and most trivial was understanding why gold, the most malleable and ductile of metals, was the only material out of which our brains could be made. Only the thinnest of foil leaves could move rapidly enough for such a mechanism, and only the most delicate of filaments could act as hinges for them. By comparison, the copper burr raised by my stylus as I engrave these words and brushed from the sheet when I finish each page is as coarse and heavy as scrap. This truly was a medium where erasing and recording could be performed rapidly, far more so than any arrangement of switches or gears.

What next became clear was why installing full lungs into a person who has died from lack of air does not bring him back to life. These leaves within the lattice remain balanced between continuous cushions of air. This arrangement lets them flit back and forth swiftly, but it also means that if the flow of air ever ceases, everything is lost; the leaves all collapse into identical pendent states, erasing the patterns and the consciousness they represent. Restoring the air supply cannot recreate what has evanesced. This was the price of speed; a more stable medium for storing patterns would mean that our consciousnesses would operate far more slowly.

It was then that I perceived the solution to the clock anomaly. I saw that the speed of these leaves' movements depended on their being supported by air; with sufficient air flow, the leaves could move nearly frictionlessly. If they were moving more slowly, it was because they were being subjected to more friction, which could occur only if the cushions of air that supported them were thinner, and the air flowing through the lattice was moving with less force.

It is not that the turret clocks are running faster. What is happening is that our brains are running slower. The turret clocks are driven by pendulums, whose tempo never varies, or by the flow of mercury through a pipe, which does not change. But our brains rely on the passage of air, and when that air flows more slowly, our thoughts slow down, making the clocks seem to us to run faster.

I had feared that our brains might be growing slower, and it was this prospect that had spurred me to pursue my auto-dissection. But I had assumed that our cognition engines—while powered by air—were ultimately mechanical in nature, and some aspect of the mechanism was gradually becoming deformed through fatigue, and thus responsible for the slowing. That would have been dire, but there was at least the hope that we might be able to repair the mechanism, and restore our brains to their original speed of operation.

But if our thoughts were purely patterns of air rather than the movement of toothed gears, the problem was much more serious, for what could cause the air flowing through every person's brain to move less rapidly? It could not be a decrease in the pressure from our filling stations' dispensers; the air pressure in our lungs is so high that it must be stepped down by a series of regulators before reaching our brains. The diminution in force, I saw, must arise from the opposite direction: the pressure of our surrounding atmosphere was increasing.

How could this be? As soon as the question formed, the only possible answer became apparent: our sky must not be infinite in height. Somewhere above the limits of our vision, the chromium walls surrounding our world must curve inward to form a dome; our universe is a sealed chamber rather than an open well. And air is gradually accumulating within that chamber, until it equals the pressure in the reservoir below.

This is why, at the beginning of this engraving, I said that air is not the source of life. Air can neither be created nor destroyed; the total amount of air in the universe remains constant, and if air were all that we needed to live, we would never die. But in truth the source of life is a difference in air pressure, the flow of air from spaces where it is thick to those where it is thin. The activity of our brains, the motion of our bodies, the action of every machine we have ever built is driven by the movement of air, the force exerted as differing pressures seek to balance each other out. When the pressure everywhere in the universe is the same, all air will be motionless, and useless; one day we will be surrounded by motionless air and unable to derive any benefit from it.

We are not really consuming air at all. The amount of air that I draw from each day's new pair of lungs is exactly as much as seeps out through the joints of my limbs and the seams of my casing, exactly as much as I am adding to the atmosphere around me; all I am doing is converting air at high pressure to air at low. With every movement of my body, I contribute to the equalization of pressure in our universe. With every thought that I have, I hasten the arrival of that fatal equilibrium.

Had I come to this realization under any other circumstance, I would have leapt up from my chair and ran into the streets, but in my current situation—body locked in a restraining bracket, brain suspended across my laboratory—doing so was impossible. I could see the leaves of my brain flitting faster from the tumult of my thoughts, which in turn increased my agitation at being so restrained and immobile. Panic at that moment might have led to my death, a nightmarish paroxysm of simultaneously being trapped and spiraling out of control, struggling against my restraints until my air ran out. It was by chance as much as by intention that my hands adjusted the controls to avert my periscopic gaze from the latticework, so all I could see was the plain surface of my worktable. Thus freed from having to see and magnify my own apprehensions, I was able to calm down. When I had regained sufficient composure, I began the lengthy process of reassembling myself. Eventually I restored my brain to its original compact configuration, reattached the plates of my head, and released myself from the restraining bracket.

At first the other anatomists did not believe me when I told them what I had discovered, but in the months that followed my initial auto-dissection, more and more of them became convinced. More examinations of people's brains were performed, more measurements of atmospheric pressure were taken, and the results were all found to confirm my claims. The background air pressure of our universe was indeed increasing, and slowing our thoughts as a result.

There was widespread panic in the days after the truth first became widely known, as people contemplated for the first time the idea that death was inevitable. Many called for the strict curtailment of activities in order to minimize the thickening of our atmosphere; accusations of wasted air escalated into furious brawls and, in some districts, deaths. It was the shame of having caused these deaths, together with the reminder that it would be many centuries yet before our atmosphere's pressure became equal to that of the reservoir underground, that caused the panic to subside. We are not sure precisely how many centuries it will take; additional measurements and calculations are being performed and debated. In the meantime, there is much discussion over how we should spend the time that remains to us.

One sect has dedicated itself to the goal of reversing the equalization of pressure, and found many adherents. The mechanicians among them constructed an engine that takes air from our atmosphere and forces it into a smaller volume, a process they called "compression." Their engine restores air to the pressure it originally had in the reservoir, and these Reversalists excitedly announced that it would form the basis of a new kind of filling station, one that would—with each lung it refilled—revitalize not only individuals but the universe itself. Alas, closer examination of the engine revealed its fatal flaw. The engine itself is powered by air from the reservoir, and for every lungful of air that it produces, the engine consumes not just a lungful, but slightly more. It does not reverse the process of equalization, but like everything else in the world, exacerbates it.

Although some of their adherents left in disillusionment after this setback, the Reversalists as a group were undeterred, and began drawing up alternate designs in which the compressor was powered instead by the uncoiling of springs or the descent of weights. These mechanisms fared no better. Every spring that is wound tight represents air released by the person who did the winding; every weight that rests higher than ground level represents air released by the person who did the lifting. There is no source of power in the universe that does not ultimately derive from a difference in air pressure, and there can be no engine whose operation will not, on balance, reduce that difference.

The Reversalists continue their labors, confident that they will one day construct an engine that generates more compression than it uses, a perpetual power source that will restore to the universe its lost vigor. I do not share their optimism; I believe that the process of equalization is inexorable. Eventually, all the air in our universe will be evenly distributed, no denser or more rarefied in one spot than in any other, unable to drive a piston, turn a rotor, or flip a leaf of gold foil. It will be the end of pressure, the end of motive power, the end of thought. The universe will have reached perfect equilibrium.

Some find irony in the fact that a study of our brains revealed to us not the secrets of the past, but what ultimately awaits us in the future. However, I maintain that we have indeed learned something important about the past. The universe began as an enormous breath being held. Who knows why, but whatever the reason, I am glad that it did, because I owe my existence to that fact. All my desires and ruminations are no more and no less than eddy currents generated by the gradual exhalation of our universe. And until this great exhalation is finished, my thoughts live on.

So that our thoughts may continue as long as possible, anatomists and mechanicians are designing replacements for our cerebral regulators, capable of gradually increasing the air pressure within our brains and keeping it just higher than the surrounding atmospheric pressure. Once these are installed, our thoughts will continue at roughly the same speed even as the air thickens around us. But this does not mean that life will continue unchanged. Eventually the pressure differential will fall to such a level that our limbs will weaken and our movements will grow sluggish. We may then try to slow our thoughts so that our physical torpor is less conspicuous to us, but that will also cause external processes to appear to accelerate. The ticking of clocks will rise to a chatter as their pendulums wave frantically; falling objects will slam to the ground as if propelled by springs; undulations will race down cables like the crack of a whip.

At some point our limbs will cease moving altogether. I cannot be certain of the precise sequence of events near the end, but I imagine a scenario in which our thoughts will continue to operate, so that we remain conscious but frozen, immobile as statues. Perhaps we'll be able to speak for a while longer, because our voice boxes operate on a smaller pressure differential than our limbs, but without the ability to visit a filling station, every utterance will reduce the amount of air left for thought, and bring us closer to the moment that our thoughts cease altogether. Will it be preferable to remain mute to prolong our ability to think, or to talk until the very end? I don't know.

Perhaps a few of us, in the days before we cease moving, will be able to connect our cerebral regulators directly to the dispensers in the filling stations, in effect replacing our lungs with the mighty lung of the world. If so, those few will be able to remain conscious right up to the final moments before all pressure is equalized. The last bit of air pressure left in our universe will be expended driving a person's conscious thought.

And then, our universe will be in a state of absolute equilibrium. All life and thought will cease, and with them, time itself.

But I maintain a slender hope.

Even though our universe is enclosed, perhaps it is not the only air chamber in the infinite expanse of solid chromium. I speculate that there could be another pocket of air elsewhere, another universe besides our own that is even larger in volume. It is possible that this hypothetical universe has the same or higher air pressure as ours, but suppose that it had a much lower air pressure than ours, perhaps even a true vacuum?

The chromium that separates us from this supposed universe is too thick and too hard for us to drill through, so there is no way we could reach it ourselves, no way to bleed off the excess atmosphere from our universe and regain motive power that way. But I fantasize that this neighboring universe has its own inhabitants, ones with capabilities beyond our own. What if they were able to create a conduit between the two universes, and install valves to release air from ours? They might use our universe as a reservoir, running dispensers with which they could fill their own lungs, and use our air as a way to drive their own civilization.

It cheers me to imagine that the air that once powered me could power others, to believe that the breath that enables me to engrave these words could one day flow through someone else's body. I do not delude myself into thinking that this would be a way for me to live again, because I am not that air, I am the pattern that it assumed, temporarily. The pattern that is me, the patterns that are the entire world in which I live, would be gone.

But I have an even fainter hope: that those inhabitants not only use our universe as a reservoir, but that once they have emptied it of its air, they might one day be able to open a passage and actually enter our universe as explorers. They might wander our streets, see our frozen bodies, look through our possessions, and wonder about the lives we led.

Which is why I have written this account. You, I hope, are one of those explorers. You, I hope, found these sheets of copper and deciphered the words engraved on their surfaces. And whether or not your brain is impelled by the air that once impelled mine, through the act of reading my words, the patterns that form your thoughts become an imitation of the patterns that once formed mine. And in that way I live again, through you.

Your fellow explorers will have found and read the other books that we left behind, and through the collaborative action of your imaginations, my entire civilization lives again. As you walk through our silent districts, imagine them as they were; with the turret clocks striking the hours, the filling stations crowded with gossiping neighbors, criers reciting verse in the public squares and anatomists giving lectures in the classrooms. Visualize all of these the next time you look at the frozen world around you, and it will become, in your minds, animated and vital again.

I wish you well, explorer, but I wonder: Does the same fate that befell me await you? I can only imagine that it must, that the tendency toward equilibrium is not a trait peculiar to our universe but inherent in all universes.

Perhaps that is just a limitation of my thinking, and your people have discovered a source of pressure that is truly eternal. But my speculations are fanciful enough already. I will assume that one day your thoughts too will cease, although I cannot fathom how far in the future that might be. Your lives will end just as ours did, just as everyone's must. No matter how long it takes, eventually equilibrium will be reached.

I hope you are not saddened by that awareness. I hope that your expedition was more than a search for other universes to use as reservoirs. I hope that you were motivated by a desire for knowledge, a yearning to see what can arise from a universe's exhalation. Because even if a universe's lifespan is calculable, the variety of life that is generated within it is not. The buildings we have erected, the art and music and verse we have composed, the very lives we've led: none of them could have been predicted, because none of them were inevitable. Our universe might have slid into equilibrium emitting nothing more than a quiet hiss. The fact that it spawned such plenitude is a miracle, one that is matched only by your universe giving rise to you.

Though I am long dead as you read this, explorer, I offer to you a valediction. Contemplate the marvel that is existence, and rejoice that you are able to do so. I feel I have the right to tell you this because, as I am inscribing these words, I am doing the same.

acknowledgments

The editors wish to acknowledge the generous support of DePauw University, Trent University, and the University of Iowa.

"Rappaccini's Daughter" by Nathaniel Hawthorne (*United States Magazine and Democratic Review*, Dec. 1844).

The excerpt from *Journey to the Center of the Earth* by Jules Verne (Hetzel, 1864) was translated from the French by Arthur B. Evans.

"The Star" by H. G. Wells (*The Graphic*, Christmas 1897).

"The Machine Stops" by E. M. Forster (*Oxford and Cambridge Review*, Nov. 1909).

"The Man Who Evolved" by Edmond Hamilton (*Wonder Stories*, April 1931). Copyright © 1931, 1959 by Edmond Hamilton. Reprinted by permission of the Edmond Hamilton Estate.

"The Conquest of Gola" by Leslie F. Stone (*Wonder Stories*, April 1931). Copyright © 1931 by Gernsback Publications. Reprinted by permission of Forrest J. Ackerman.

"Shambleau" by C. L. Moore (*Weird Tales*, Nov. 1933). Copyright © 1933 by Popular Fiction Publishing Company; renewed 1961 by C. L. Moore. Reprinted by permission of Don Congdon Associates, Inc.

"A Martian Odyssey" by Stanley G. Weinbaum (*Wonder Stories*, July 1934). Copyright © 1934 by Gernsback Publications. Reprinted by permission of Forrest J. Ackerman.

"Reason" by Isaac Asimov (*Astounding*, April 1941). Copyright © 1941 by Street and Smith Publications, Inc., from *I, Robot* by Isaac Asimov. Used by permission of Bantam Books, a division of Random House, Inc.

"Desertion" by Clifford D. Simak. Copyright © 1944. First published in *Astounding Science Fiction*, November 1944. Reproduced by permission of Pollinger Limited and the estate of Clifford Simak.

"Thunder and Roses" by Theodore Sturgeon (*Astounding*, Nov. 1947). Copyright © 1947. Reprinted by permission of The Estate of Theodore Sturgeon c/o Ralph M. Vicinanza, Ltd.

"That Only a Mother" by Judith Merril (*Astounding*, June 1948). Copyright © 1948. Reprinted by permission.

"Coming Attraction" by Fritz Leiber (*Galaxy*, Nov. 1950). Copyright © 1950. Reprinted by permission of Richard Curtis Associates, Inc.

"There Will Come Soft Rains" by Ray Bradbury (*Collier's*, May 1950). Copyright © 1950 by the Crowell Collier Publishing Company; renewed 1977 by Ray Bradbury. Reprinted by permission of Don Congdon Associates, Inc.

"The Sentinel" by Arthur C. Clarke (*Ten Story Fantasy*, Spring 1951). Copyright © 1951. Reprinted by permission of the author and the author's agents, Scovil Chichak Galen Literary Agency, Inc.

"Specialist" by Robert Sheckley (*Galaxy*, May 1953). Copyright © 1953. Reprinted by permission of the author's estate.

"The Liberation of Earth" by William Tenn (*Future*, May 1953). Copyright © 1953. Reprinted by permission of the author, Philip Klass.

"Fondly Fahrenheit" by Alfred Bester (*F&SF*, Aug. 1954). Copyright © 1954 and 1976 by the Bester Trust. Reprinted by permission of The Pimlico Agency, agents for the Estate.

"The Golem" by Avram Davidson (*F&SF*, March 1955). Copyright © 1955. Reprinted by permission of Grania Davis, proprietor, Avram Davidson Estate.

"The Game of Rat and Dragon" by Cordwainer Smith (*Galaxy*, Oct. 1955). Copyright © 1955, by Galaxy Publications, Inc.; copyright 1983 by the Estate of Paul Linebarger. Reprinted by permission.

"'All You Zombies—'" by Robert A. Heinlein (*F&SF*, March 1959). Copyright © 1959, 1987 by Robert A. Heinlein; © 2003 by the Robert A. and Virginia Heinlein Prize Trust. Reprinted by permission of Spectrum Literary Agency.

"The Cage of Sand" by J. G. Ballard (*New Worlds*, June 1962). Copyright © 1962, 1991 by J. G. Ballard. Reprinted by permission of the author and his agent, Robin Straus Agency, Inc.

"Slow Tuesday Night" by R. A. Lafferty. Copyright © 1965, 1993 by the Estate of R. A. Lafferty; first appeared in *Galaxy*, April 1965; from *Nine Hundred Grandmothers*; reprinted by permission of the author's estate and the estate's agent, the Virginia Kidd Agency, Inc.

"'Repent, Harlequin!' Said the Ticktockman" by Harlan Ellison (*Galaxy*, Dec. 1965). Copyright © 1965 by Harlan Ellison; renewed 1993 by The Kilimanjaro Corporation. Reprinted by arrangement with, and permission of, the author and the author's agent, Richard Curtis Associates, Inc., New York. All rights reserved. Harlan Ellison is a registered trademark of The Kilimanjaro Corporation.

"Day Million" by Frederik Pohl (*Rogue*, Feb/March 1966). Copyright © 1966. Reprinted by permission of the author.

"We Can Remember It for You Wholesale" by Philip K. Dick (*F&SF*, April 1966).

Copyright © 1966. Reprinted by permission of the author and the author's agents, Scovil Chichak Galen Literary Agency, Inc.

"Aye, and Gomorrah . . ." by Samuel R. Delany (*Dangerous Visions*, ed. H. Ellison, 1967). Copyright © 1967, 1995 by Samuel R. Delany. Reprinted by permission of the author and his agents, Henry Morrison, Inc.

"The Heat Death of the Universe" by Pamela Zoline. Copyright © 1967. First published in *New Worlds*, July 1967. Reprinted by permission of the author.

"Passengers" by Robert Silverberg (*Orbit* 4, ed. D. Knight, 1967). Copyright © 1968 by Agberg, Ltd. Reprinted by permission of the author and Agberg, Ltd.

"Super-Toys Last All Summer Long" by Brian Aldiss (*Harper's Bazaar*, Dec. 1969). Copyright © 1969. Reprinted by permission of the author.

"Nine Lives" by Ursula K. Le Guin. Copyright © 1969, 1997 by Ursula K. Le Guin; first appeared in *Playboy*, Nov. 1969; from *The Wind's Twelve Quarters*. Reprinted by permission of the author and the author's agents, the Virginia Kidd Agency, Inc.

"Seed Stock" by Frank Herbert (*Analog*, April 1970). Copyright © 1970. Reprinted by permission of the author's estate.

"The Seventh Voyage" from *The Star Diaries* by Stanislaw Lem (1971). Copyright © 1976 by The Seabury Press, Inc. Reprinted by permission of Houghton Mifflin Harcourt Publishing Company.

"When It Changed" by Joanna Russ (*Again, Dangerous Visions*, ed. H. Ellison, 1972). Copyright © 1972. Reprinted by permission of the author's agents, the Diana Finch Literary Agency.

"And I Awoke and Found Me Here on the Cold Hill's Side" by James Tiptree Jr. Copyright © 1972, 2000 by James Tiptree Jr. First appeared in *The Magazine of Fantasy and Science Fiction*, March 1972; from *Her Smoke Rose Up Forever*. Reprinted by permission of Jeffrey D. Smith and the Virginia Kidd Agency, Inc.

"Air Raid" by John Varley (*Asimov's Science Fiction*, Spring 1977). Copyright © 1977 by John Varley. Reprinted by permission of The Pimlico Agency Inc., agents for John Varley.

"Abominable" by Carol Emshwiller (*Orbit* 21, ed. Damon Knight, 1980). Copyright © 1980. Reprinted by permission of the author.

"Burning Chrome" by William Gibson (*Omni*, July 1982). Copyright © 1982. Reprinted by permission of the author's agent, Martha Millard Literary Agency.

"Speech Sounds" by Octavia E. Butler. Copyright © 1983 by Octavia E. Butler. Originally published in *Asimov's Science Fiction*, December 1983. Reprinted by permission of the Estate of Octavia E. Butler.

"Out of All Them Bright Stars" by Nancy Kress. Copyright © 1985 by Nancy Kress.

First appeared in *The Magazine of Fantasy and Science Fiction*, March 1985. Reprinted by permission of the author.

"Pretty Boy Crossover" by Pat Cadigan (*Asimov's Science Fiction*, Jan. 1986). Copyright © 1986. Reprinted by permission of the author.

"Forever Yours, Anna" by Kate Wilhelm (*Omni*, July 1987). Copyright © 1987. Reprinted by permission of the author.

"We See Things Differently" by Bruce Sterling. Copyright © 1989 by Bruce Sterling. Originally published in *Semiotext(e) SF*. Reprinted by permission of the author and the author's agents, Writers House.

"Chippoke Na Gomi" by Misha Nogha. Copyright © 1989 by Misha Nogha. First published in the *Witness Anthology of Experimental Fiction* (1989). Reprinted by permission of the author.

"Computer Friendly" by Eileen Gunn. Copyright © 1989. First published in *Asimov's Science Fiction*, June 1989. Reprinted by permission of the author.

"Invaders" by John Kessel. Copyright © 1990 by Mercury Press, Inc. First published in *The Magazine of Fantasy and Science Fiction*, October 1990. Reprinted by permission of the author.

"Useful Phrases" by Gene Wolfe. Copyright © 1992 by Gene Wolfe. First appeared in *tomorrow*, Jan. 1993; from *Strange Travelers*. Reprinted by permission of the author and the author's agents, the Virginia Kidd Agency, Inc.

"Closer" by Greg Egan (*Eidolon*, Winter 1992). Copyright © 1992. Reprinted by permission of the author and the author's agents, Scovil Chichak Galen Literary Agency, Inc.

"Think Like a Dinosaur" by James Patrick Kelly. Copyright © 1995 by Bantam Doubleday Dell Magazines for *Asimov's Science Fiction*, June 1995. Reprinted by permission of the author.

"Everywhere" by Geoff Ryman. Copyright © 1999 by Geoff Ryman. The author was specially commissioned to write this story by the Artists Agency as part of its Visions of Utopia project. First published in *Interzone*, February 1999. Reproduced by permission of the author.

"Rogue Farm" by Charles Stross (*Live Without a Net*, ed. Lou Anders, 2003). Copyright © 2003 by Charles Stross. Reprinted by permission of the author.

"Exhalation" by Ted Chiang (*Eclipse Two: New Science Fiction and Fantasy*, ed. Jonathan Strahan, 2008). Copyright © 2008 by Ted Chiang. Reprinted by permission of the author.

Further Reading

• • • •

General References

Science Fiction Studies, "Chronological Bibliography of Science Fiction History, Theory, and Criticism," http://www.depauw.edu/sfs/biblio.htm

Professional and Academic Journals

Extrapolation
Foundation: International Review of Science Fiction
Journal of Science Fiction Film and Television
Journal of the Fantastic in the Arts
The New York Review of Science Fiction
Science Fiction Studies
Utopian Studies

Encyclopedias and General Reference

Barron, Neil, ed. *Anatomy of Wonder: A Critical Guide to Science Fiction.* 5th ed. Westport, CT: Libraries Unlimited, 2004.

Bleiler, Everett. *Science-Fiction: The Early Years.* Kent, OH: Kent State University Press, 1990.

Bleiler, Everett, and Richard Bleiler. *Science-Fiction: The Gernsback Years.* Kent, OH: Kent State University Press, 1998.

Bleiler, Richard J., ed. *Science Fiction Writers: Critical Studies of the Major Authors from the Early Nineteenth Century to the Present Day.* 2nd ed. New York: Scribner's, 1999.

Bould, Mark, Andrew M. Butler, Adam Roberts, and Sherryl Vint, eds. *Fifty Key Figures in Science Fiction.* London: Routledge, 2010.

Bould, Mark, Andrew M. Butler, Adam Roberts, and Sherryl Vint, eds. *The Routledge Companion to Science Fiction.* London: Routledge, 2009.

Clute, John, and Peter Nicholls, eds. *The Encyclopedia of Science Fiction.* 2nd ed. New York: St. Martin's, 1993.

James, Edward, and Farah Mendlesohn, eds. *The Cambridge Companion to Science Fiction.* Cambridge: Cambridge University Press, 2003.

Prucher, Jeff, ed. *Brave New Words: The Oxford Dictionary of Science Fiction.* Oxford: Oxford University Press, 2007.

Seed, David, ed. *A Companion to Science Fiction*. Oxford: Blackwell, 2005.
Stableford, Brian. *Science Fiction and Science Fact: An Encyclopedia*. New York: Routledge, 2006.

HISTORIES

Aldiss, Brian, with David Wingrove. *Trillion Year Spree: The History of Science Fiction*. London: Gollancz, 1986.
Alkon, Paul K. *Origins of Futuristic Fiction*. Athens, GA: University of Georgia Press, 1987.
Alkon, Paul K. *Science Fiction before 1900: Imagination Discovers Technology*. 1994. New York: Routledge, 2002.
Ashley, Mike. *The Story of the Science-Fiction Magazines*. In 3 vols. Liverpool: Liverpool University Press, 2000–2007.
Disch, Thomas M. *The Dreams Our Stuff Is Made Of: How Science Fiction Conquered the World*. New York: Free Press, 1998.
James, Edward. *Science Fiction in the Twentieth Century*. Oxford: Oxford University Press, 1994.
Landon, Brooks. *Science Fiction after 1900: From the Steam Man to the Stars*. 1997. New York: Routledge, 2002.
Luckhurst, Roger. *Science Fiction*. Cambridge: Polity, 2005.
Nicolson, Marjorie Hope. *Voyages to the Moon*. New York: Macmillan, 1960.
Roberts, Adam. *The History of Science Fiction*. New York: Palgrave Macmillan, 2005.
Seed, David, ed. *Anticipations: Essays on Early Science Fiction and its Precursors*. Liverpool: Liverpool University Press, 1995.

NATIONAL STUDIES AND HISTORIES

Blackford, Russell, Van Ikin, and Sean McMullen, eds. *Strange Constellations: A History of Australian Science Fiction*. Westport, CT: Greenwood, 1999.
Bolton, Christopher, Istvan Csicsery-Ronay, Jr., and Takayuki Tatsumi, eds. *Robot Ghosts and Wired Dreams: Japanese Science Fiction from Origins to Anime*. Minneapolis: University of Minnesota Press, 2008.
Clareson, Thomas D. *Some Kind of Paradise: The Emergence of American Science Fiction*. Westport, CT: Greenwood, 1985.
Ginway, Elizabeth M. *Brazilian Science Fiction: Cultural Myths and Nationhood in the Land of the Future*. Lewisburg, PA: Bucknell University Press, 2004.
Greenland, Colin. *The Entropy Exhibition: Michael Moorcock and the British 'New Wave' in Science Fiction*. London: Routledge, 1983.
Ketterer, David. *Canadian Science Fiction and Fantasy*. Bloomington: Indiana University Press, 1992.

Lofficier, Jean-Marc, and Randy Lofficier. *French Science Fiction, Fantasy, Horror and Pulp Fiction: A Guide to Cinema, Television, Radio, Animation, Comic Books and Literature*. Jefferson, NC: McFarland, 2000.

Ruddick, Nicholas. *Ultimate Island: On the Nature of British Science Fiction*. Westport, CT: Greenwood, 1993.

Stableford, Brian. *Scientific Romance in Britain, 1890–1950*. New York: St. Martin's, 1985.

GENRE STUDIES

Baccolini, Raffaella, and Tom Moylan, eds. *Dark Horizons: Science Fiction and the Dystopian Imagination*. New York: Routledge, 2003.

Berman, Judith. "Science Fiction Without the Future." *The New York Review of Science Fiction* 13.9 (May 2001): 1, 6–8.

Csicsery-Ronay Jr., Istvan. *The Seven Beauties of Science Fiction*. Middletown, CT: Wesleyan University Press, 2008.

Csicsery-Ronay Jr., Istvan. "The SF of Theory: Baudrillard and Haraway." *Science Fiction Studies* 18.3 (Nov. 1991): 387–404.

Delany, Samuel R. *The Jewel-hinged Jaw: Notes on the Language of Science Fiction*. 1977. Middletown, CT: Wesleyan University Press, 2009.

Freedman, Carl. *Critical Theory and Science Fiction*. Middletown, CT: Wesleyan University Press, 2000.

Huntington, John. *The Logic of Fantasy: H.G. Wells and Science Fiction*. New York: Columbia University Press, 1982.

Huntington, John. *Rationalizing Genius: Ideological Strategies in the Classic American Science Fiction Short Story*. New Brunswick, NJ: Rutgers University Press, 1989.

Ketterer, David. *New Worlds for Old: The Apocalyptic Imagination, Science Fiction, and American Literature*. Bloomington: Indiana University Press, 1974.

Levitas, Ruth. *The Concept of Utopia*. Syracuse, NY: Syracuse University Press, 1990.

Le Guin, Ursula K. *The Language of the Night: Essays on Fantasy and Science Fiction*. Ed. Susan Wood. New York: Perigee, 1979.

Luckhurst, Roger. "The Many Deaths of Science Fiction: A Polemic." *Science Fiction Studies* 21.1 (Mar. 1994): 35–50.

Malmgren, Carl. *Worlds Apart: Narratology of Science Fiction*. Bloomington, IN: Indiana University Press, 1991.

Moylan, Tom. *Demand the Impossible: Science Fiction and the Utopian Imagination*. New York: Methuen, 1986.

Parrinder, Patrick, ed. *Learning from Other Worlds: Estrangement, Cognition*

and the Politics of Science Fiction and Utopia. Liverpool: Liverpool University Press, 2000.
Rose, Mark. *Alien Encounters: Anatomy of Science Fiction*. Cambridge, MA: Harvard University Press, 1981.
Sterling, Bruce. "Slipstream." *Science-Fiction Eye* 1.5 (July 1989): 77–80.
Sterling, Bruce. "Preface." *Mirrorshades: The Cyberpunk Anthology*. Ed. Sterling. New York: Arbor, 1986. vii–xiv.
Suvin, Darko. *Metamorphoses of Science Fiction: On the History and Poetics of a Literary Genre*. New Haven, CT: Yale University Press, 1979.
Wagar, W. Warren. *Terminal Visions: The Literature of Last Things*. Bloomington, IN: Indiana University Press, 1982.
Wells, H.G. "Fiction about the Future." 1938. *H.G. Wells's Literary Criticism*. Ed. Patrick Parrinder and Robert Philmus. Totawa, NJ: Barnes and Noble, 1980. 246–51.
Wolfe, Gary K. *The Known and the Unknown: The Iconography of Science Fiction*. Kent, OH: Kent State University Press, 1979.

CRITICAL AND CULTURAL STUDIES

Abbott, Carl. *Frontiers Past and Future: Science Fiction and the American West*. Lawrence: University Press of Kansas, 2006.
Bartter, Martha. *The Way to Ground Zero: The Atomic Bomb in American Science Fiction*. Westport, CT: Greenwood, 1988.
Bukatman, Scott. *Terminal Identity: The Virtual Subject in Postmodern Science Fiction*. Durham, NC: Duke University Press, 1993.
Foster, Thomas. *The Souls of Cyberfolk: Posthumanism as Vernacular Theory*. Minneapolis: University of Minnesota Press, 2005.
Graham, Elaine L. *Representations of the Post/Human: Monsters, Aliens and Others in Popular Culture*. New Brunswick, NJ: Rutgers University Press, 2002.
Hollinger, Veronica, and Joan Gordon, ed. *Edging into the Future: Science Fiction and Contemporary Cultural Transformation*. Philadelphia: University of Pennsylvania Press, 2002.
Jameson, Fredric. *Archaeologies of the Future: The Desire Called Utopia and Other Science Fictions*. London: Verso, 2005.
Jones, Gwyneth. *Deconstructing the Starships: Science, Fiction, and Reality*. Liverpool: Liverpool University Press, 1998.
Kilgore, De Witt Douglas. *Astrofuturism: Science, Race, and Visions of Utopia in Space*. Philadelphia: University of Pennsylvania Press, 2003.
Latham, Rob. *Consuming Youth: Vampires, Cyborgs, and the Culture of Consumption*. Chicago: University of Chicago Press, 2002.

McCaffery, Larry, ed. *Storming the Reality Studio: A Casebook of Cyberpunk and Postmodern Science Fiction*. Durham, NC: Duke University Press, 1991.

Rieder, John. *Colonialism and the Emergence of Science Fiction*. Middletown, CT: Wesleyan University Press, 2008.

Slusser, George, and Tom Shippey, eds. *Fiction 2000: Cyberpunk and the Future of Narrative*. Athens: University of Georgia Press, 1991.

Vint, Sherryl. *Bodies of Tomorrow: Technology, Subjectivity, Science Fiction*. Toronto: University of Toronto Press, 2007.

Wong Kin Yuen, Gary Westfahl, and Amy Kit-sze Chan, eds. *World Weavers: Globalization, Science Fiction, and the Cybernetic Imagination*. Hong Kong: Hong Kong University Press, 2005.

FEMINISM, GENDER, SEXUALITY STUDIES

Attebery, Brian. *Decoding Gender in Science Fiction*. New York: Routledge, 2002.

Barr, Marleen S., ed. *Future Females: A Critical Anthology*. Bowling Green, OH: Bowling Green State University Popular Press, 1981.

Donawerth, Jane. *Frankenstein's Daughters: Women Writing Science Fiction*. Syracuse, NY: Syracuse University Press, 1997.

Donawerth, Jane L., and Carol A. Kolmerten, eds. *Utopian and Science Fiction by Women: Worlds of Difference*. Syracuse, NY: Syracuse University Press, 1994.

Garber, Eric, and Lyn Paleo, eds. *Uranian Worlds: A Guide to Alternative Sexuality in Science Fiction, Fantasy, and Horror*. Rev. 2nd ed. Boston: G.K. Hall, 1990.

Larbalestier, Justine. *The Battle of the Sexes in Science Fiction*. Middletown, CT: Wesleyan University Press, 2002.

Larbalestier, Justine, ed. *Daughters of Earth: Feminist Science Fiction in the Twentieth Century*. Middletown, CT: Wesleyan University Press, 2006.

Lefanu, Sarah. *In the Chinks of the World Machine: Feminism and Science Fiction*. London: The Women's Press, 1988.

Melzer, Patricia. *Alien Constructions: Science Fiction and Feminist Thought*. Austin: University of Texas Press, 2006.

Pearson, Wendy, Veronica Hollinger, and Joan Gordon, ed. *Queer Universes: Sexualities in Science Fiction*. Liverpool: Liverpool University Press, 2008.

Russ, Joanna. *To Write Like a Woman: Essays in Feminism and Science Fiction*. Bloomington: Indiana University Press, 1995.

Wolmark, Jenny. *Aliens and Others: Science Fiction, Feminism and Postmodernism*. Iowa City: University of Iowa Press, 1994.

Yaszek, Lisa. *Galactic Suburbia: Recovering Women's Science Fiction*. Columbus: Ohio State University Press, 2007.

SCIENCE FICTION FILM AND TELEVISION

Booker, M. Keith. *Science Fiction Television.* Westport, CT: Praeger, 2004.

Hunter, I.Q. *British Science Fiction Cinema.* London: Routledge, 1999.

Jenkins, Henry. *Textual Poachers: Television Fans and Participatory Culture.* New York: Routledge, 1992.

Kuhn, Annette, ed. *Alien Zone: Cultural Theory and Contemporary Science Fiction Cinema.* New York: Verso, 1990.

Kuhn, Annette, ed. *Alien Zone II: The Spaces of Science Fiction Cinema.* New York: Verso, 1999.

Landon, Brooks. *The Aesthetics of Ambivalence: Rethinking Science Fiction Film in the Age of Electronic (Re)Production.* Westport, CT: Greenwood, 1992.

Nama, Adilifu. *Black Space: Imagining Race in Science Fiction Film.* Austin: University of Texas Press, 2008.

Penley, Constance, Elizabeth Lyon, and Lynn Spiegel. *Close Encounters: Film, Feminism and Science Fiction.* Minneapolis: University of Minnesota Press, 1991.

Redmond, Sean. *Liquid Metal: The Science Fiction Film Reader.* London: Wallflower, 2004.

Sardar, Ziauddin, and Sean Cubitt, eds. *Aliens R Us: The Other in SF Cinema.* London: Pluto, 2002.

Slusser, George, and Eric Rabkin, eds. *Shadows of the Magic Lamp: Fantasy and Science Fiction in Film.* Carbondale, IL: Southern Illinois University Press, 1985.

Sobchack, Vivian. *Screening Space: The American Science Fiction Film.* 2nd ed. New York: Ungar, 1987.

Telotte, J. P. *A Distant Technology: Science Fiction Film and the Machine Age.* Middletown, CT: Wesleyan University Press, 1999.

Telotte, J. P., ed. *The Essential Science Fiction Television Reader.* Lexington: University Press of Kentucky, 2008.

Tulloch, John, and Henry Jenkins. *Science Fiction Audiences: Watching* Doctor Who *and* Star Trek. New York: Routledge, 1995.

about the editors

Arthur B. Evans is a professor of French at DePauw University and managing editor of *Science Fiction Studies*. He has published extensively on Jules Verne and French science fiction and is general editor of Wesleyan University Press's "Early Classics of Science Fiction" book series.

Istvan Csicsery-Ronay Jr. is a professor of English at DePauw University and a coeditor of *Science Fiction Studies*. He has published numerous articles on science fiction and techno-culture and is the author of *The Seven Beauties of Science Fiction* (Wesleyan, 2008). He is also coeditor of *Robot Ghosts and Wired Dreams: Japanese Science Fiction from Origins to Anime* (Minnesota, 2007) and managing editor of *Humanimalia: A Journal of Human/Animal Interface Studies*.

Joan Gordon is a professor of English at Nassau Community College; a coeditor of *Science Fiction Studies*; a Fulbright Distinguished Chair at Marie Curie University in Lublin, Poland; a former president of the Science Fiction Research Association and recipient of its Clareson Award; and coeditor of several volumes of scholarly essays on science fiction.

Veronica Hollinger is a professor of Cultural Studies at Trent University in Peterborough, Ontario. She is a coeditor of *Science Fiction Studies* and a member of the editorial board of Liverpool University Press's "Science Fiction Texts and Studies" series. Her publications include articles on feminist and queer sf, cyberpunk, postmodernism, and posthumanism. Her most recent coedited collection is *Queer Universes: Sexualities in Science Fiction* (Liverpool, 2008).

Rob Latham is an associate professor of English at the University of California, Riverside. A coeditor of the journal *Science Fiction Studies* since 1997, he is the author of *Consuming Youth: Vampires, Cyborgs, and the Culture of Consumption* (Chicago, 2002). He is currently completing a book on 1960s New Wave science fiction.

Carol McGuirk, a professor of English at Florida Atlantic University, has been a coeditor of *Science Fiction Studies* since 1997. She teaches sf classes in FAU's MA English track in science fiction and fantasy. Her interests center on theorizing sf and on rediscovering sf writers of the cold war era. She is also widely published in eighteenth-century studies and Romanticism, with a focus on Robert Burns, poetry and history, and Scottish popular song.